Lone Soldier

Leo Rozmaryn

2

To all the lone soldiers serving in the Israel Defense Forces

Preface

This is a work of historical fiction. The protagonists in this story are hybrids of people I have known in my life. There has been no attempt to depict historical events exactly as they occurred. There may be people reading this who will say: "I was there and that's not the way it really happened." While I understand that concern, I do hope that I've been able to capture the spirit of the time between the summers of 1969-1974 as the characters move through those years. It was a period of great social and political ferment both for the United States and Israel. Many suppositions and assumptions about life and society were examined and discarded. Dreams and illusions were shattered.

I had much to learn when I wrote this book and owe a great debt of gratitude to those "specialists" who assisted me in thrashing out the technical aspects of the plot. I have never been a basketball player or coach, a martial artist or a sailor of any worth. I've never served in the Israeli army nor do I have any first-hand knowledge of the inner workings of the Israeli government or special forces training. So, I enlisted the aid of people who know about these things who graciously shared their time and experience with me.

Finally, I want to dedicate this book to all the lone soldiers who have left behind lands of peace, security, comfort and affluence to come to a dusty strip of land on the eastern shore of the Meditteranean to serve in the Israeli Defense Force. Most come without family or friends in Israel. Many decide to stay to realize a 2,000-year old dream of rebuilding Jewish life in their ancestral homeland and to live freely as Jews without explanation or apology. Others return home. Some have made the ultimate sacrifice in battle or as victims of terror. We are forever in their debt.

Book 1

Chapter 1

The camp buses finally pulled into the dirt-covered parking lot, raising a huge cloud of dust and grime that reeked of diesel fuel. A big, blue and white, hand-painted sign with giant letters in Hebrew read BRUCHIM HABAIM LE MACHANEH MOSHAVA and underneath in English: WELCOME TO CAMP MOSHAVA.

The three-hour trip from lower Manhattan had seemed interminable. It had been bad enough that the air conditioner on the bus had failed and all that had come into the open windows were blasts of hot, dry, dusty air. The bus reeked of stale tuna fish sandwiches and body odor. To make matters worse, Pinkie Mermelstein, a lanky, pimply sort who had gotten overcome by the fumes, had puked his guts out into the aisle of the bus, further increasing the general misery.

It was clear to Arik that most of the kids on the bus knew each other from having gone to "Mosh" together for many years, many of them since the fifth grade. The social stratification of the kids on the bus was typical: The cool kids, those who were athletic and popular, sat in the last six rows of the bus, while the nerdy, bookish ones sat in the front.

The popular kids traded barbs incessantly, yelling and boasting.

"Hey! Is Pinnie still going out with Ilana Friedman?"

"I heard they broke up over winter break."

"I heard he got to second base with her!"

There were giggles all around.

"Any new prospects for this summer?"

"I hear that Ronit is desperate for me to ask her out on a Friday night walk."

"Yeah, right. In your dreams!"

"A Flatbush knockout like that wouldn't even look in your direction."

"Oh, yeah? I bet you ten dollars I get her into the bushes on the first Friday night."

"You're on, big shot!"

"Ronit's nothing compared to Dahlia Gilad. Dahlia's the hottest momma on the planet. She could be a Playboy centerfold."

"That's the only way you'll ever get close to her. In the bathroom."

"Shut up, Lenny. That's disgusting."

"That Dahlia snob wouldn't look at any of us. She's so stuck up. She always thinks she's better than everybody else."

"Maybe because she is!"

"I don't even know why she keeps coming back here to be with us lowlifes. Most of the rich and snobby kids go to Camp Raleigh."

"I hear she's still dating that tennis counselor guy, Effie."

"I wonder if he got anything off her. What a piece of ass she is!"

"Who's going to be playing on the camp's basketball team? Coach told me we're going to be playing Morasha, as early as in two weeks. They have absolute legends playing for them: Larry Pollack and Stuie Fishman? This year, as juniors at Yeshiva University High School, they already played for Yeshiva

College. And they're averaging twenty points a game each. If we play those guys, they're going to wipe the floor with us."

"The Morasha guys were already making fun of us the last week of school."

"Hey, does anybody know if we're all going to be in Bunk Aleph? Or are they going to mix us in with all the nerds and faggots, like they tried to do last year?"

"I know, right? All that talk about achdut, unity, is so lame. If they want us to have a good time this summer, they should just put us with our friends and be done with it."

Arik sat quietly, next to the window in the middle of the bus. He passed his time keeping his nose out the window whenever possible and otherwise reading his Sports Illustrated special edition devoted to Lew Alcindor and the UCLA basketball team. Arik had tried to doze off, if only to avoid the gregarious kid who had sat next to him and was incessantly trying to make conversation. Richard Green seemed nice enough, but Arik was absolutely wiped out after the long overnight flight from LA, the interminable traffic jam getting into the city from Kennedy Airport, and now this hot, dusty three-hour ride up into the Pocono Mountains. Arik leaned back and closed his eyes, still trying to get some rest, and Richard buried his nose in some book with the phrase "Boolean Logic" in the title.

Arik began to wonder whether he had wandered too far out of his comfort zone, coming east to a whole new world of people who had an entirely different mind-set than his own. He felt a twinge of insecurity in the pit of his stomach. He had been in school with Orthodox kids back in LA, but these seemed much more provincial and clannish. They all seemed to know one another and share the same New York dialect. Even the nature of their banter was completely out of his frame of reference. Arik couldn't imagine having anything in common with any of these guys, let alone making friends with them. Nonetheless, here he was, and so he would have to make the best of it. This was the center of Zionist Jewish life in America, after all, so he told himself he would focus on that: experiencing as much of it as he could, firsthand.

As the bus slowed to a halt, everybody jumped up, all at once, pushed into the aisle to retrieve their gear from the overhead rack, and then cheered, pushed, and jostled toward the front of the bus.

Uri Shalev, a big burly Israeli counselor with a large handlebar mustache, climbed into the front of the bus, stood there and bellowed, in heavily accented English, into the PA system,

"If you don't all get back to your seats and get up when you are called, you are going to be staying here on de bus all afternoon."

Welcome to Camp Moshava, Arik thought. Now, to be treated like a seven-year-old.

The bus slowed to a halt alongside several dozen others already crowding the fumes-filled parking lot. The scene outside the buses was one of barely organized mayhem. Hundreds of campers, aged ten to seventeen years, were running about looking for their heavier baggage, which consisted of large camp trunks and green duffel bags. All of these were piled into dozens of stacks, some twenty feet tall, in no particular order. It was a gigantic scavenger hunt. Around the perimeter of the lot, bunk counselors holding clipboards were standing next to hand-painted white signs that directed campers to their appropriate age groups. Whoops of recognition went up when campers spotted friends that they hadn't seen in a year. The whoops were followed by hugs, giggles, and backslaps all around.

Beneath the overt noise, there was considerable haggling and secret deal making going on, especially among the high schoolers as soon as they learned who would be in each bunk. So, despite a general attempt by the camp to socially homogenize the campers, the cool crowd ended up together, leaving the rest to fend for themselves. The athletic bunk counselors assisted in this effort, because the nonathletic campers had a greater tendency to whine. It was much easier to be counselor for a bunk full of jocks.

Eventually, all luggage and campers were reunited, and the campers circled around their respective bunk banners: boys on one side of the parking lot and girls on the other.

Mixing of the genders in Orthodox Jewish coed camps was a highly regulated affair. The Ultra-Orthodox solved the gender issue by having separate camps for girls and boys. Modern Orthodox Zionist camps were coed, but they went to great lengths to supervise contact between boys and girls. This meant a strict official neghia (no touch) policy, which meant that even holding hands was prohibited. Sports and Israeli dancing usually were separate. Campfires, hikes, educational activities, and meals, on the other hand, were coed, as were major sporting events, such as tournaments and color war. Although Davening (prayer) was mixed, boys and girls sat separately, separated by a partition called a mechitza. Even with all of these efforts, however, many couples paired off. For them, summer love was in the air.

Arik quickly found his duffel bag and slung it over his shoulder. He wondered why everyone needed both a trunk and a duffel bag. What all do they have in there? They'll only be here for four or, at most, eight weeks!

Arik felt a bit incongruous standing with his bunkmates. He appraised the situation and realized that he was definitely with the nerds. Nearly six feet four inches tall, he towered over them. They definitely had not had the benefit of the California climate that he was so used to. They were pale and either too skinny or too chubby. Even the jocks appeared to be only marginally more fit than the others. Don't Jewish kids on the East Coast get any sun or exercise? This summer is definitely going to be interesting. Arik chuckled to himself.

"Okay, Mach Hach, let's go!" Uri's voice blared from the bullhorn. "You all know where the campus is. You're assigned to Bunk Aleph, Bet, or Gimel. You have ninety minutes to get unpacked and get ready for evening camp assembly, Mifkad."

Everyone began following the counselors along the dirt road that led to the boys' campus, dragging their trunks behind them.

When Arik spied the crowd of Mach Hach girls on the other side of the parking lot, he noted that most of the New York "princesses" were much the out-of-shape female equivalent of their male counterparts. They were a loud, gregarious, giggling lot that all gathered in small cliques. They appeared to be catching up on all the events of the previous school year. I guess the girls don't get much exercise either.

The girls were dressed in loose trousers or duty-length—down to at least the knees, according to camp rules—skirts or shorts. They wore long T-shirts, most with some school logo, on top.

As he watched the girls start to head to their campus with their counselors, Arik noticed one who was lagging behind the group and didn't quite fit the mold. She was taller than the others, and she had an athletic build. Her long, straight, brown hair was parted in the middle, revealing a perfectly suntanned olive complexion and dark-brown eyes. She sported a pair of fashionable sunglasses, which were perched firmly above her forehead.

She was struggling to keep up with the crowd, having to drag an oversized wooden-and-leather steamer trunk like one that might have been used by a first-class traveler on an ocean liner in the 1930s.

"You're going to tear that expensive trunk to shreds on that pavement!" Arik said.

"Unfortunately, they don't provide valet service at this resort." The girl struggled to get out her words between hasty inhalations.

"Here, let me take it for you," Arik offered.

In one quick, sweeping motion, the trunk flew out of her hands—as if of its own accord—and onto Arik's head, supported on either side by his arms.

"Wow, you are strong! How in the world did you do that?" A dozen girls turned around to spy on them and smirk at the newcomer. No doubt, many of them noticed the pair of powerful arms that were exposed by his sleeveless UCLA sweatshirt.

"Oh, years of practice," Arik said, kidding. "I'm Arik. What's your name?"

They began to follow the other girls.

"I am Penny. Penny Moreno. Here, I am supposed to be Peninah, though."

Arik couldn't help but notice her Spanish accent. "You're not from New York. You sound like you're from Mexico, but Penny doesn't sound like such a Spanish name."

Penny smiled. "And how would you know that, may I ask?"

"Where I come from, I'm in contact with loads of Mexicanos."

"Where is that?" Penny asked.

Arik pointed to his shirt. "Los Angeles, born and bred."

"An Angeleño! What in the world are you doing here, of all places?"

"It's a long story. What about you? Where are you from?"

"My parents call me Penelope. I live in Mexico City, which has a very large Jewish community, but most are either entirely secular or Haredi—you know, Ultra-Orthodox. There is only a small religious Zionist community there."

"So, you're from even further away from home than I am!"

"True. While I would much rather have spent my summer sailing and sunning in Cabo, at my parent's beach house, they insisted that I go to a religious Zionist summer camp so I would appreciate Israel and Judaism more.

So I said to them, 'Why don't you just send me to Israel itself then?' 'No supervision there for you,' they said. 'Who knows what you'll get up to in Tel Aviv? We want you to have a quality Israel experience.' So, I've been coming here for two summers already. I guess it's okay."

Arik laughed. "I guess this is where you get off. Last stop: Eidah Gimel, girls' bunk."

He dropped the trunk onto the rotting wooden slats that made up the floor of the bunk's porch and stuck out his hand to shake Penny's.

"Nice meeting you, Penny."

Many heads turned to look and then shyly turned away, giggling. The other girls went into their bunk.

"You cannot shake my hand here! It's neghia!" Penny whispered.

"Whoops! Sorry, I forgot! See you later then," he said as he waved at her and left.

Penny dragged the trunk past the flimsy screen door that served as protection from the outside elements.

The bunk was nothing more than a musty, uninsulated bungalow divided into two sections, each with sleeping accommodations for ten campers and a counselor. The simple beds—metal-spring frames with thin, narrow, lumpy mattresses—were laid out in a row around the perimeter of the room. The bathroom, which was a sparse affair with bare wooden walls covered in graffiti some decades old, was shared by both sections and was relatively clean . . . so far.

Penny found a bed in the corner and saved the bottom of the adjacent bunk bed for her best buddy.

"Who was that guy?" Gila Feinman asked. "Oh, my god. He's gorgeous! Did you see the muscles on him? Where do you know him from?"

"I don't know him from Adam. He just appeared out of nowhere. One second, I was struggling with my trunk, and the next second, he popped up next to me and put my trunk on his head. He seems nice enough. He's from LA."

Shirah Epstein, a busybody with large glasses and a long, wavy ponytail, asked, "Don't you think it's odd that someone would come all the way from LA to Moshava, when they already have a Camp Moshava in Malibu, California?"

"How do you know that?" Penny asked, a little defensively.

"Because my cousin Bracha lives in LA, and she goes there. Okay?"

"You are such a yenta, Shira!" Penny shot back. "You have not changed a bit since last summer. You always need to know the inside scoop. Not everything is worth knowing."

"Oh, Penny! I think you like him. You never considered any of the boys here good enough for you, proof being you never had a boyfriend at camp."

"Why would I want a boyfriend at camp when I live in Mexico City? You all go back to New York, so if—in the unlikely event, Shira—you ever landed a boyfriend, you could continue during the year." Penny smirked.

At that moment, before anyone's feelings could be seriously hurt, the girls' counselor, Suzie Schiff, came in and announced the cleaning and organization assignments.

There was a mad rush to see who would get the cubbies farthest away from the toilet. Trunks flew open, and girls and clothing flew in a mad flurry and chattering noise.

Above the din, someone called through the screen door and into the bunk.

"The Baltimore/Washington bus has just arrived!"

Penny smiled at the thought of seeing Dahlia again.

Although she made it her business to be active in all camp activities, tried to be friendly to everyone, and even bought into most of the Zionist ideology that they were spoon-fed, she never felt deep down that she had a whole lot in common with the New York crowd. She found them, as a whole, too narrow-minded, too clannish, and too self-absorbed, maybe because few of them had ever been out of the New York area, except, that is, to Israel.

One girl was different. The daughter of Israel's ambassador to the United States, Dahlia Gilad had traveled almost all of the known world, spoke four languages fluently (Spanish was one, so that the two girls could share secrets with each other while at camp), was a model of refinement, and was an outstanding athlete. She was Israel's junior-division tennis champion. For the two summers that she had been coming to Camp Moshava, she had been widely regarded by the boys as the prettiest girl at camp and had been the object of affection of several potential suitors—including, as rumored, the director of the tennis program, Effie. Dahlia was tall, with long, straight, blonde hair, blue-gray eyes, and a sweet, friendly smile.

Suddenly, the screen door swung open, and there was the girl who Penny knew that she could always hang out with and confide in.

"Penny!"

Dahlia leapt through the door and gave Penny a big hug.

"Dahlia! How was your trip? It's so good to see you!"

"Long and exhausting." Dahlia then announced to the girls in general, "You people from New York have no idea how lucky you are. It took us nearly seven hours to get here in traffic!"

After the customary half embraces with all of her bunkmates, Dahlia dumped her trunk and oversized, blue-and-white gym bag, which bore the logo of the Israeli Olympic team, on the bunk bed next to Penny's.

"How are your mom and dad doing, Dahlita?

"My parents are doing fine. My dad is incredibly busy at work. We hardly get a chance to speak lately. I've been sailing all springtime out of Annapolis, like we did over Pesach in Cabo. Such great fun! Several of the security guys at the embassy are really good sailors, and I have been going with them. Perhaps if you come visit us for Sukkot we'll get a chance to go out. How's your Papi doing? Is he feeling better?"

"He's out of the hospital. He's recovering slowly under my Mami's watchful eye."

Mauricio Moreno was one of Mexico's richest men, but he had arrived there a young, penniless teenager from Europe, the only child of a family who had perished in the Holocaust. His parents, descended from aristocratic, ancient Sephardic Moroccan families, had been turned over to the Gestapo by the Vichy French. All of their property had been confiscated. Mauricio had been put into the care of Jesuit nuns in a monastery in France. By the end of World War II, Mauricio had been the only member of his family left alive. He had been baptized and would have remained a Catholic had he not been discovered by the American Va'ad Hatzalah rabbis who, after the war, had combed all the convents of Western Europe, looking for Jewish children who had been placed in the care of the Catholic Church.

As a young teen, Mauricio ended up in Mexico, in a youth hostel run by The Jewish Agency. Armed with a sharp mind and keen fighter's wits, he clawed his way into the construction trade. By successfully winding his way through Mexico's byzantine government bureaucracy—learning who to bribe and when—while avoiding organized crime syndicates, he had built much of Mexico City's skyline and national network of highways. In the process, he became one of Mexico's wealthiest men. But the years of stressful wheeling and dealing, as well as his incessant chain-smoking of Cuban cigars, had taken their toll. Shortly after the Passover holiday, he had suffered a major heart attack.

Unpacking her bags, Dahlia asked Penny, in Spanish, "¿Cuál es la situación chico como en el campamento? ¿Lo de siempre? Ni siquiera sé por qué hice esa pregunta o tiene alguna pensamiento sobre los chicos de aquí. Hay tantas otras zonas donde conocer chicos distintos de este cultivo de regordetes, prepotentes y arrogantes neoyorquinos." ("What's the boy situation like in camp? The usual? I don't even know why I asked that question or have any thoughts about the guys here. There are so many other places to meet guys other than this crop of pudgy, pushy, arrogant New Yorkers.")

"Too early to tell," Penny replied in English. "I did meet a strange new guy, though, who helped me with my trunk on the way here from the parking lot. He's from LA, and he's pretty cute. Strong as an ox, too. I'll point him out to you."

"Always looking for valet service and flirting with the help!" Dahlia laughed.

***

After carrying Penny's steamer trunk to her bunk, Arik returned to the parking lot to retrieve his own bag. His khaki duffel bag had gotten covered in dirt. He brushed it off and set out to find Bunk Bet, in the Mach Hach.

The Mach Hach program had its own campus separate from the rest of the camp. Because that age group was made up of sixteen- and seventeen-year-olds going into their senior year of high school, the program differed from that of the younger campers. In the Mach Hach, the Zionist indoctrination intensified somewhat, and there was the expectation that the graduates of the Bnei Akiva (Orthodox Zionist youth movement) camp system would spend a gap year, called Hachshara, before college on a kibbutz in Israel. The hope was that after college these people would form a Garin, a unified, cohesive group that would emigrate to Israel together and settle on a kibbutz.

Entering the musty bunk, which Arik thought looked pretty much the same as the girls except that it was in an even worse state of repair, he said hello to his bunkmates and tried to memorize their names: Moishie, Nathan, Sol, Joey, Eitan, Ilan, Richard, the guy who sat next to him on the bus ride to camp and so could not be forgotten, and Pinkie Mermelstein, the one who had vomited on the bus. Arik noted that none of the guys who had sat in the back of the bus were in his bunk.

"Hey, Arik! You come all the way from LA?" Eitan asked. Eitan was a skinny kid with a few crooked front teeth and a broad smile. "Wow! That is sooo coool!"

Richard walked out of the bathroom and extended his hand toward Arik.

"Hi, Arik. Looks like we're going to be neighbors!" Richard pointed to the empty bunk, which was next to where he had set up his own. "High five!"

Not wanting to be to be impolite, Arik obliged.

The bunk that Arik was left with was the one nearest the toilets. Judging by the smell, one already had backed up. Arik dumped his army-surplus duffel bag onto the narrow, worn mattress. The only cubby left was across from his bed, even nearer the toilets, and missing a hinge so that the door hung limply from the top hinge. When he looked inside the cubby, Arik noticed that the cubby had been put together sloppily, with protruding, rusty nails lining the inside.

I'm going to have to fix that, he thought.

The bunk counselor strode in. "Hi, guys, I'm Shmuel Berman. I'll be your madrich for the next four weeks. Looks and smells like you've already trashed the bunk. That's unacceptable; there's a closet, next to the toilets, that has a broom and a mop. I expect them to be used. You all know the drill. Most of you have been coming here for years."

Shmuel took Arik aside. "You must be Arik. I've heard a good deal about you in conversations with Rav Shaul Rabinovich. I understand he was your rabbi this past year, at Rambam Academy in LA. Rav Shaul was in the advanced kollel at Yeshivat Kerem B'Yavneh when I did my year in Israel there, and I took Talmud classes with him. He's a great guy and a big Torah scholar. He told me what it's taken for you to get here. There's a lot that you're going to have to get used to, but I'm sure you'll do just fine."

"It's been a real education already." Arik smiled.

Shmuel raised his voice to get everyone's attention again. "Okay. Everyone out! Mifkad in ten minutes!"

Mifkad, loosely translated, meant camp assembly, but it was so much more than that. Everyone in the entire camp lined up in a large, U-shaped formation with its opening facing two flagpoles, one each for the American and Israeli flags. Girls on one side, boys on the other. In front of the flags stood the camp director, the head counselor, and assorted shlichim from Israel. Shlichim were "messengers" sent to Camp Moshava by The Jewish Agency and Bnei Akiva's central office in Tel Aviv. Their mission was to inject a genuine Israeli atmosphere into the camp. They gave classes on Israeli geography, Israel's roots in the Bible, the philosophy of religious Zionism, and modern Jewish and Israeli history. They taught new and old Israeli songs and dances, and they were generally in charge of ruach (spirit) at the camp. They spoke Hebrew to the campers and encouraged them to answer in kind. When they weren't busy doing all of that, they erected zip lines, rope courses, and obstacle courses in order to demonstrate how the American Jewish kids were hopelessly out of shape compared to Israelis their age.

The campers stood in a formation based on age, with each bunk counselor standing in front of his or her charges. In front of the counselors stood the division heads, who were barking out, "Amod dom!" (Atten hut!).

As soon as they had the campers' attention, they barked,

"Amod noach!" (At ease!)

There was a definite military feel to the Mifkad, and that was on purpose. Many of the division heads and shlichim wore traditional kibbutz-style khaki pants and shirts or old Israeli army shirts that they either kept after finishing active army service or bought in an open-air market in Jerusalem.

Mach Hach usually had its own Mifkad, but on the first day there was this combined Mifkad so that everyone was welcomed together. The mission of the summer was discussed and rules were set down, with some thinly veiled threats made about misbehavior. Basic housekeeping items and activity schedules were doled out to the division heads to be passed down to the counselors and campers.

Mifkad ended with the singing of "Yad Achim," Bnei Akiva's anthem, and then "Hatikvah," Israel's national anthem.

In an orderly fashion, by bunk, everyone found their way to Bet Knesset, the synagogue, for Minchah (afternoon prayer) then off to the chadar ochel (dining hall) for dinner, which was usually a "sumptuous" feast of meatloaf, rice, and gravy with pound cake for dessert.

The first night of camp was a major get-together around a large bonfire. Most of the campers sat in a large, multilayered circle, singing either religious Jewish songs or Israeli songs, while some accompanied the group by playing guitars or accordions. In the periphery of the circle, a smaller number of campers simply milled about and socialized, catching up on a whole year of life.

Arik took in the scene with a measure of fascination. He had nobody to catch up with. A few people came over to introduce themselves, but the others were content to walk by him on their way to speak with their old friends. He watched as people assembled themselves into cliques, happily chatting away in tight circles.

After wandering around for a bit, meeting nobody in particular, he decided to scout out the grounds. He walked down one of the dirt paths that snaked around the camp and passed the baseball fields, which were lit up in the darkness. They appeared a bit run-down compared to the playing fields he was used to in LA. The night air was humid and thick with the deafening sounds of crickets chirping. He passed the tennis center, which he had heard was a new addition to the camp, with its hard-court surfaces lit up. Next to the tennis courts was a small clubhouse that housed equipment and the tennis director's office.

Arik passed the outdoor basketball courts, with their cracked asphalt surfaces. The baskets had no nets. That meant something to him. To the side of the tennis center stood a very large, old, wooden building that housed a gym. When he looked inside, he saw that the equipment was a bit better in there. There were two baskets, with nets, one at each end of the wooden floor. There were also baskets without nets on the sides of the gym, for half-court play. In the corner, there were piles of rubber gymnastics floor mats and, to one side, an old pommel horse. In the corner, rings were suspended from the ceiling. They appeared a bit old, and the ropes seemed worn. *Will they hold my weight?* In the other corner was an old set of parallel bars.

Arik climbed up on the parallel bars and then, testing their strength, he began to swing between them, gripping each bar with alternating hands. This was followed by several handstands. Finally, with a backward flip, Arik dismounted.

He walked up to the hanging rings, grabbed them, gently lifted himself up into an iron cross position, flexed his legs into a ninety-degree angle, and swung himself on the rings like a pinwheel before dismounting. *These will do.* Then he curled his legs into the rings and did fifty hanging sit-ups.

When he heard voices coming down the road, he slipped his heels out of the rings and quietly joined the procession back to the bunks.

He was dog-tired from the whole day, and he still was wondering whether he had made the right decision coming to Camp Moshava. To say that he felt like a fish out of water was an understatement. He felt like a fish in the middle of the Sahara Desert.

The bunk was a beehive of activity as everyone finished unpacking and made preparations for bed. *A quick shower would be great,* Arik thought, but then he found that the shower stall was a rusty metal, mildewed affair with a torn shower curtain and a rush of cold water from even the hot tap. That certainly woke him up. After the shower, he wrapped a towel around his waist and reentered the main bunk room. They had visitors.

"Well, well. It looks like we just stumbled into the nerds' bunk! How are all you faggots doing? Welcome to camp!" The intruders roared with laughter.

It looks like some of the jocks from Bunk Aleph have decided to pay us a visit.

One of the guys held a large water balloon in his hand. "I heard that your bunk needed a bit of cleaning. Well, well, well. If it isn't Richie the Bitchie! I can't believe you've come back for another summer of punishment. I think your bed needs the most cleaning of all!"

The bully, a brawny sort named Rubin Goldsmith, began to wind up to throw the balloon at Richard's pillow. All the guys in the bunk stared blankly at Rubin.

Arik emerged from the bathroom, bare chested with a towel around his waist.

"I wouldn't do that if I were you," he said, in a low, even, matter-of-fact voice as he stared Rubin down.

"Look who's here to save the day. Tarzan! Well, Tarz—"

"The name's Arik. Arik Meir. You'll call me Arik," he said with a hint of a smile, but his cool gaze told Rubin that he meant business.

"What the hell's going on here?" Shmuel had walked in. "What are you guys doing in here? Get back to your bunk on the double or there'll be trouble on the very first day."

The Bunk Aleph crowd filed out. In the doorway, Rubin turned around and shot a look of hatred at Arik. But Arik just stood there, arms folded, towel still around his waist, smiling.

"That's enough for one day. Lights out!"

When they had all gotten into their beds, Arik said into the darkness, to no one in particular, "What's the story with that jerk? It seems like he's done this before."

"Rubin Goldsmith's dad, Myron, is a huge Wall Street wheeler-dealer and a major donor to Mizrachi and Bnei Akiva. When they moved Camp Moshava from the tents in Gelatt to the new campus, here in Beach Lake, he cosigned on the property, so Rubin walks around like he owns the place, which he probably does."

***

Arik awoke at 4:30 a.m. and headed back to the gym. He had noted the night before that the building was situated far enough from the bunks that he likely wouldn't disturb anyone. He turned on the light, closed the door, and quickly assembled the rubber mats and spread them across the floor. He already was dressed in a tank top and gym pants, so he threw off his sneakers and began by doing a floor exercise: forward and backward flips and somersaults, one-handed, two-legged swivels first clockwise and then counterclockwise, backward to a handstand, once around the mat, and then he finished with two backward vaults.

He spent ten minutes on the pommel horse and then fifteen on the rings. After that, he put his sneakers back on and wheeled the rack of basketballs to the top of the key. He sank eight consecutive jump shots in thirty seconds. He dribbled a basketball in front of himself and behind himself, and then he took off running down the court, bouncing the ball through his legs. At the top of the key, he launched himself into the air, legs spread, and dunked the ball into the basket from about a foot above the rim.

Ten or twelve quick layups followed, punctuated by forward dunks, backward dunks, alley-oops, and turnaround dunks. Arik stared at the clock on the wall: 6:00 a.m. Crap! Reveille would be at 6:30 a.m., so he had no time that morning for Jeet Kune Do. Instead, he finished with 100 push-ups and 30 hanging sit-ups and then ran back to the bunk for a quick shower. He snuck back into bed just as the bugle sounded over the camp loudspeaker and everyone roused.

Everyone in Mach Hach went outside, into the middle of the square, for hitamlut (calisthenics). Most were wearing pajamas, yawning, and rubbing their eyes, but a few had taken the time to slip on sneakers and gym shorts. The campers sprawled on the grass and waited for something to happen.

Uri Shalev, bullhorn in hand, stood in the middle of the lawn.

"Let's go! Get up, you fat, lazy campers! Jumping jacks. Thirty of them."

The campers lined up into neat rows.

"Achat, shtayim, shalosh," Uri counted off the jumping jacks.

The jumping jacks were followed by running in place, twenty sit-ups, and ten push-ups. Arik stood in the back and watched the others while he quietly did as he was told. Barely any of them could do more than fifteen sit-ups or five push-ups.

Richard sidled up to Arik. "That Israeli is going to kill us with these exercises!" he managed to say as he gasped for breath.

"Probably." Arik smiled.

From the front, Uri had seen Arik smiling. He stared angrily at him and called out, "Hey, big shot. You think this is some kind of joke? Why don't you come up here and show everyone how you do twenty push-ups!"

Arik quietly went forward, did the twenty push-ups, and then stood up.

"Another twenty!"

Arik knelt again and did twenty more.

He stared at Uri politely but intently.

"Okay, everyone," Uri said, still staring at Arik. "Morning prayers are in thirty minutes. Don't be late!"

After prayers, breakfast, and study session, the Mach Hach boys assembled at the outdoor basketball court at 10 a.m. The air was already hot and sticky, and the sun was beating down.

"Okay, guys. Settle down!"

Coach Gary Schoenfeld was standing at half-court, wearing a T-shirt and warm-up pants and with a whistle in his mouth. "Let's start with ten laps around the court."

The boys began jogging around. Arik fell in line with the front runners, in an easy trot. The rest of Bunk Bet lagged behind, huffing and puffing. Arik pulled up next to Rubin and ran alongside him without saying a word. Rubin, feeling a bit unnerved, sped up without looking at him. Arik easily kept pace.

"What do you want?" Rubin's voice was quiet but harsh.

"Just trying to make friends." Arik smiled. That little interchange, though subtle, was noticed by everyone else.

"All right. Good," Coach said. "I want to see some layups!"

Everyone stood in line, with Coach standing on one side and feeding the ball to each player in turn. It was fairly clear who the ballplayers were and weren't. It also had become clear to Arik that basketball had greater significance than as just a sport in this camp. How good you were at sports had a great deal to do with where you stood in the social pecking order. It had been like that at Rambam, the Jewish high school in LA that Arik had attended the previous year, but not to this extent. The kids out west were a bit more laid back in that regard. Status there had more to do with the number and quality of your possessions, such as cars and clothes. Back in LA, either you were an athlete or you weren't, and that was that.

So, this intensity was new for Arik. What made it somewhat amusing was that only one or two of the guys were any good.

The other thing that had become clear to Arik was the lack of sportsmanship and camaraderie—even among the Bunk Aleph crew.

"Yossie, you suck! You call that a layup?"

"I can kick your butt on the court" was the retort.

This went on and on. It was as if the guys were playing for social acceptance and not for the love of the sport.

Arik stepped up, the coach passed the ball to him, and he casually strode up to the basket and easily laid the ball into the basket.

"I want to see more commitment, Arik!" Coach bellowed. "You look like you ought to have some talent. Let's see some more hustle."

Cackles came from the Bunk Aleph crowd.

After some more shooting drills and some passing drills, coach divided the group up into squads and made sure to homogenize the squads.

"Hey, Coach! Why'd you put me with these faggots?"

"Shut up, Steven, or I won't let you play at all!" Coach answered. "You haven't grown up one bit since last year!"

The format of the scrimmage was a round-robin with five points to win a game, and the squad with the most wins got one less kitchen clean-up duty. The games were certainly spirited, with lots of running about, some dribbling and passing, but mostly shooting. It was fairly well understood that Coach was watching these games and making mental notes about who to play in the camp's upcoming game against Camp Morasha. As such, there seemed to be more emphasis on trying to impress the coach with individual skill than on playing as a team.

"Squad 4 versus squad 2," Coach announced through the bullhorn.

Arik would be playing center against Heshie Steinhardt, the camp's basketball legend for years.

Jump ball!

The format was five-on-five with sloppy full-court, man-to-man coverage. Arik detected no group cohesion or any formal plan of attack on offense or defense. There were no guards, forwards, or centers. It was just a free-for-all. The ball handling was sloppy, and passes were frequently missed. More often than not, players shot the ball even when a teammate had a better look. Arik took a deep breath and struggled to simply blend in to the melee.

What's the point of getting upset or disgusted? This isn't my world, and it's not why I came east.

Arik continued to play at a casual pace, sometimes missing an outside shot or layup on purpose. He was careful not to jump too high under the boards for a rebound, and he passed the ball whenever he saw an opportunity. There was no point in standing out.

Coach whispered to his assistant, "Do you notice something about Arik? He looks talented and he's built like a beast, but he always seems to be a step behind and half a foot short in the jump. It's like he's not trying for some reason."

His assistant, Mendy, replied, "Another thing, Gary. He's the only one on the court who hasn't even broken a sweat. Everyone else is drenched from running around in the hot sun. Don't you find that odd?"

"Now that you mention it, I do!"

Arik's squad was beaten soundly, 5-2.

As everyone was packing up, Coach took Arik aside.

"What's up, buddy?"

"What do you mean, Coach?"

"I've been coaching basketball for many years now, after four years of playing for YU, and I can spot talent when I see it. Now, it's obvious you have the raw talent to play, but it's like you're holding something back.

"I think you're good enough to make the camp's squad for the Morasha game next Sunday, but I'm not seeing the fire—the hustle—that I ought to be seeing from you.

"I'm thinking of putting you on the alternate list, but we'll have a final scrimmage on Thursday night. I'll make my final decision then."

"I'll certainly try harder. Thanks, Coach," Arik replied.

Chapter 2

Dahlia and Penny wasted no time getting into the swing of things. Both were known as excellent athletes, and since they were pretty evenly matched they were never assigned to the same team. Dahlia was clearly the better tennis player, but Penny always captained the winning volleyball squad, playing the setter position. There was always friendly banter between them, and both of them realized that they were far more sophisticated than their companions. Nonetheless, they worked hard to fit in and not seem elitist, trying to enjoy the company of their bunkmates with good humor and fair play. Although their attempt was not entirely successful—they were thought of as snobs by some of the jealous girls—the girls in the Eidah Gimel bunk generally got along together very well. There was less intrigue than in the boys' bunks, with only the occasional meltdown about hair dryer malfunctions, boy trouble, secrets kept and then exposed, or eating too much or too little.

One thing that Penny and Dahlia did together, just for themselves, was an early morning run long before everyone else woke up. They had done it during the previous two summers at camp and had continued it whenever they saw each other during the year. In Cabo during Pesach, they had run for miles along the beach and had seemed never to tire.

They preferred to run in the very early morning, getting up at 4:30 a.m. The dress code in camp mandated that during any sport the girls had to wear dresses or loose-fitting shorts, down to the knees, and long T-shirts. At 4:30 a.m., however, with everyone else asleep, they put their hair in ponytails and donned bandanas, tank tops, and running shorts. The camp had a perimeter trail, and they were able to pump out five miles at an easy pace, shower, and get back in bed before anyone else was awake.

Just as their run on the third morning of camp was winding down, at about 5:30 a.m., they passed behind the indoor gym building. Surprised that the lights were on, they stopped short and stared at each other.

"What's that sound coming out of there?" Dahlia asked. "Those loud, pounding noises sound like someone playing jungle drums badly!"

"Who could possibly be in there at this time of the morning?" Penny said.

Creeping up to a side window, one at each corner, they stared at the scene in amazement.

All the rubber gym mats were laid out on one side of the gym, and Arik was in the middle of a roll-up back handspring. He was sporting navy-blue gym shorts and a UCLA tank top. He was barefoot and was sweating from head to toe.

He broke into a run, and then did a power hurdle, front handspring, and handstand. That led into a forward roll and then a pike down back extension roll into a push-up position. He fell to the mat, did a split, went into a pancake position, and then stood up. He ran, hurdled into a back handspring rebound and stuck a perfect landing. He finished the floor exercise with a double front flip and landed on his feet.

"This guy is at least a level 5 gymnast," Dahlia whispered to Penny. "I've seen these routines at the Wingate Sports Institute in Netanya. He's really good!"

Arik mounted the pommel horse. For what seemed like several minutes, he swung his legs around the supports, alternating his grips. He scissored his legs, progressed into a handstand between the supports, and then did a forward flip and landed flush on his feet with only a slight knee bend and his arms raised high.

Next, he jumped up to the rings, went into a standing iron cross and then a prone iron cross, did a double flip off the rings, and landed on his feet.

In his final gymnastics moves, he did fifty hanging sit-ups on the parallel bars and then sat motionless on the bars, erect in a lotus position with his arms out to the side, his palms forward, and his back toward them, for what seemed like an eternity.

But his workout was not finished yet. He went through fifteen Jeet Kune Do forms and movements, ending with a side kick to the sand bag, in midair, that sent the sandbag flying.

Dahlia gasped. "Penny! Do you have any idea how heavy that bag is? I tried some of my kickboxing routine on that bag. I couldn't budge it, and I nearly broke my foot against it when I kicked it full force!"

"That's the guy I was telling you about. The one from LA," Penny said. "I told you he was strong!"

Dahlia said, "He looks like the typical California surfer dude you see in the movies. He's got the dirty-blonde, shaggy hair thing going, the washboard abs, big chest and arm muscles. At the same time, his fluid movements have a poetic quality to them when he incorporates gymnastics into his martial arts."

Arik couldn't see out the window, because it was still pretty dark outside, but he stared in their direction as he put on his sneakers. The two girls darted down from their perches in unison, trying to muffle their giggles like silly schoolgirls.

When they heard the sound of basketballs bouncing, they delicately raised their heads above the sill again. They saw Arik wheel the ball cart around the top of the key and sink ten shots in rapid succession. Next, he performed several flying dunks from the foul line and then some forward, backward, and twisting layup dunks. He did a ball handling drill with such speed and agility that they couldn't always tell whether he was going to bounce the ball in front of himself, behind himself, or through his legs. And he did all of this at full sprint.

"My god, this guy has a four-foot vertical leap!" Dahlia said. "I'm know the guys on Israel's national basketball team, and none of them come near this level of skill. This guy could play in the NBA."

"Do you know what is weird?" Penny asked. "I bumped into Heshie yesterday, and he told me he had played with Arik in scrimmage and he seemed slow and clumsy. What is going on?"

"He was probably talking about someone else."

"No! He referred to him by name."

Arik looked at the wall clock, quickly rearranged the mats, put away the basketballs, and sprinted out the door at the other end of the gym.

Dahlia said, "I can't wait to tell everyone what we've seen. But will they believe us?"

"I think telling would be a bad idea. I think that for some reason Arik doesn't want anyone to know. Let's think about it first," Penny said.

They got up and ran back to their bunk.

***

Arik sat riveted in the morning's first study session. An Israeli, David Fischer, and detailed the 1948 Battle for Jerusalem, the heroic last stand in the Old City, the siege of the city, the blockade runners, and the final victory at Kastel, in Jerusalem's western suburbs, which opened the road to Tel Aviv and the coast.

Arik drank it all in. Finally, these events had some explanation, some context, which opened up even more disturbing questions. Arik wanted to know about that desperate struggle to secure Jerusalem as Israel's capital. The United Nations (UN) already had decided that the city was to be "an international open city," even though it had passively ceded East Jerusalem to the Jordanians. Not until 1967, two years ago, would the rest of the city be liberated by the Israelis. The whole thing was terribly exciting but confusing and painful to him, all at the same time, for reasons that rung only a distant bell.

The second activity of the day was a softball game. Arik played left field, dutifully catching the balls that were hit toward him. He struck out once, hit a fly ball, and got one base hit, a single. He felt as if he were simply going through the motions, and he was struck suddenly with a sense of loneliness. He had been in camp for nearly a week and met and made small talk with many people, but he did not feel a connection developing with anyone. He had really stuck his neck out by coming here, and for what? He felt a bit foolish having come so far from home, both geographically and culturally.

As the day wore on, anticipation for the night's basketball scrimmage grew. Coach had personally chosen each of the players who would participate. There were twenty in all—two squads of ten—from the top two divisions. These blue and white teams would play and then, based on their performance, Coach would pick a roster of ten players—five starters and five bench warmers—for the game against Camp Morasha.

Arik really tried to psych himself up for the scrimmage. When he walked down to the court at 8 p.m., he saw it all lit up and the bleachers filled with campers and staff members. Big cheers erupted from the stands as the two lines of gladiators made ready for battle.

A quick "Hatikvah," Israel's national anthem, and the ball was in play. Just as in college basketball, there would be two twenty-minute halves. This was a considerably better game than the earlier one, with better running, ball handling, shooting, and passing. Arik threw himself into it and tried to enjoy himself. They were playing man-to-man coverage and, again, he was playing opposite Heshie. About the same height, they were locked in combat under the boards. After the initial excitement wore off, Arik's again felt that for all the smoke there was no fire. There was no real sense of team and no strategy to speak of. The passing and shooting seemed to go on without any pattern, as if it were every man for himself. Everything seemed to blur around him.

Penny and Dahlia were sitting in the stands with their flock of girlfriends, taking in the whole spectacle and enjoying every moment. They both reveled in the feeling of competition.

Dahlia said, "This is fun to watch, even though we really don't stand a chance against Morasha. Not with the twin towers they have. They're going to absolutely kick our ass, as they've done for the past two years."

Penny said, "What's up with that Arik? He seems to be playing in a daze. He's scored eight points, I think, but this is nowhere near the performance we saw this morning. Look closely, Dahlia. Heshie's sweating like a hog, while Arik's been matching his jumps and runs and hasn't even broken a sweat."

"We've already seen that he can sweat." Dahlia giggled.

"It's almost as if he is adjusting his play to match the others, in some desperate attempt not to stand out. All this while, everyone else is playing their hearts out to impress the coach and, of course, us. But this guy is just the opposite. He is not making any jump shots. His layups are ordinary. What is going on?"

"I don't know, but I don't think this genie is going to stay bottled up forever. Just my intuition."

The game ended with Arik's side losing 42-40 and Arik being chosen for the camp's team as an alternate, a bench warmer.

***

The usually frenetic pace of camp activities suddenly slowed on Friday afternoon, as final preparations for Shabbat, the Sabbath, were made but at an unhurried pace. Activities were truncated and the afternoon was mostly free time, with campers indulging in water fights and hanging out, playing music loudly on portable phonographs connected to improvised speakers. Arik got to spend more time with the Bunk Aleph crowd and get to know them over a pickup game of basketball. He enjoyed the friendly banter a bit more than he had thought he would.

Afterward, Arik sat on his bed and chatted with his closest neighbor, Richard, the kid who had sat next time him on the bus. As it turned out, he was a nice kid and a real Brainiac. This guy amused himself by reading books about calculus and differential equations. He particularly loved talking about Boolean logic and algorithms, telling Arik that they would be the basis of a whole new generation of Universal Automatic Computer (UNIVAC) machines. Arik could follow along with some of what Richard described. He himself was interested in the brand-new science of semiconductors, which recently had been declassified from U.S. military labs and now was being used in the Apollo space program. Like Richard, Arik had strong interest in math and science and hoped to get an engineering degree one day.

"You know," Arik said, "I think one day there will be a computer in every home in America, just like TVs are now."

Richard smiled and agreed. "The first thing we need to do, though, is make them smaller."

"How small are you talking about?"

"Eventually, there will be devices you can hold in the palm of your hand that will have more computing power than those that are about to send the Apollo astronauts to the moon next week. "I believe that will happen in our lifetime."

"You've been watching too many episodes of Star Trek, Richard." Arik snorted. "That's not going to happen for another two hundred years."

"I'm telling you, Arik, this is all going to happen—within the next fifty years. I've already seen pieces of it. The technology is coming together in the space program."

"That would be amazing!" Arik winked at him. "Hey, if nothing else, Richard, you're a good daydreamer."

After showering and getting ready for Shabbat, Arik settled down for some quiet time, during which he wrote a letter home to his parents. It had been an interesting week, to say the least.

He was feeling a bit more comfortable, but even so the camp's transition to Shabbat was a unique experience for him. The entire camp settled down even further into a slow, relaxed rhythm when sunset descended, and lines of campers—boys in white shirts and girls in navy blue skirts—converged on Bet Knesset, the synagogue. Together, they sang songs, some joyous and some pensive, and then listened to a short Torah address given by one of the shlichim.

It was dark by the time services ended, and a small mob assembled outside the synagogue and made its way, slowly, to the dining hall for a sumptuous feast—at least by camp standards. The food was traditional: gefilte fish, chicken soup, roast chicken, and potato kugel. For some reason, food always tasted better on Shabbat.

At the meal, there was a great deal of spirited singing, which seemed to go on for an hour. All was laughter and good cheer until after benching (the blessing after the meal), when the serious work of picking up a member of the opposite gender for a Friday night walk began. Although most activities at camp were either separated by gender or done in groups of both genders, Friday night was the time for informal courting and socializing. For several days now, the boys had been discussing their prowess at picking up girls and who would be their next quarry.

Now the time had come. Groups of guys gathered near groups of girls, in circles, and little by little couples paired off. These walks were usually innocent affairs, but afterward in the bunk there would be boasting about who had done what with whom and what base they had gotten to in the bushes.

Arik wandered out of the dining hall and mingled casually with the other unattached guys. Several girls from the Mach Hach program and the Eidah Gimel girls' bunk shyly approached him to introduce themselves and find out a bit more about the "handsome stranger." He thought they were nice enough. They were Rivkie, Miriam, Tzippie and, Devorah. Arik tried to keep their names straight.

Shirah wandered over and asked Arik whether he knew her cousin, Bracha Epstein, from LA. He did know her, from Rambam Academy. In fact, they were good friends and confidants. Shirah and Arik compared notes for a while and laughed. Others drifted by and introduced themselves. Arik was friendly enough, but he didn't really notice any of the nonverbal cues that were being thrown at him by the young ladies who wanted a shot at the tall, cool-looking, blond guy from California. Eventually, the girls drifted off and Arik was left standing alone.

Scanning the crowd, he saw a boy his age sitting in a wheelchair at the perimeter, smiling, and similarly surveying the scene. Arik surmised from his hand and arm movements that he had a rather severe form of cerebral palsy. He seemed to be rather social, with many people going over to him to wish him "Shabbat Shalom."

Arik wandered over to him and held out his hand as he introduced himself.

"Shabbat Shalom. I'm Arik Meir."

"Shabbat Shalom to you! I'm Eliezer Moskowitz. My dad is the camp director. Nice to meet you."

Arik saw that Eliezer's speech was labored and somewhat slurred but clear enough. Arik asked him what activities he enjoyed doing at camp.

"Running and basketball aren't my strong suits." Eliezer laughed. "I do enjoy wheeling about and talking to people and getting to know them. I also love the arts, especially painting and music. I paint in the modern style."

"I'd really like to see your work sometime," Arik said.

"But the thing I enjoy most," Eliezer said, leaning his head forward a little, "is to study Gemara" (the second part of the Talmud). "It keeps the mind sharp."

Arik said, "You know, I've done a good deal of Talmud study myself this year. I was hoping to find a study partner at camp, but I really haven't found anyone interested. Would you like to study with me?"

Eliezer smiled broadly. "I don't see why not. Friday night is a great time to learn, so there's no time like the present!"

"Why don't we head up to the Bet Knesset and study there? It's quiet, and we'll find the books we need to get started."

"I've been studying the laws of Passover in the Talmud. It's really interesting—"

"Sounds great," Arik replied.

Eliezer wheeled himself toward the entrance of the Bet Knesset.

"I need to go around the other side of the building, to the ramp, to get inside. There are ten steps here."

"No need for that! You strapped in? Hang on!" In an instant, Arik picked up Eliezer, in his wheelchair, and bounded up the stairs while Eliezer let out a whoop of delight.

Several heads turned and stared.

"Did you see that?" one girl standing nearby said. "That Arik guy is so strong!"

Arik and Eliezer were oblivious to the others as they made their way inside. They sat opposite each other at a table, and Arik quickly realized that Eliezer had a brilliant mind to go along with his quick wit. Arik was still learning how to study the Talmud, and Eliezer proved an able, patient teacher. They quickly lost themselves in the text they were studying, trying to decipher the Rashi and Tosaphot commentary beside the main text. Before they knew it, ninety minutes had passed. Eliezer announced that he was tired and needed to go to bed.

Arik offered to wheel him back. "How do you take care of yourself in terms of dressing and undressing yourself? I can help you, if you like."

"That's not necessary. I have Sam. He waits for me to come back to my room in my parents' bungalow, and then he helps me."

Arik accompanied Eliezer home. Afterward, as he walked back from the camp director's house, he passed the dining hall. It was after 10:30 p.m., and curfew on Friday night was extended to midnight.

A few stragglers in small groups still were milling about and socializing. He noticed that on the grass about fifty feet from the dining hall, twenty campers were sitting in a circle, singing slow, inspirational Shabbat songs.

A kumsitz without a fire, Arik thought.

He sat on a wooden railing and watched the group.

The head of one of the participants turned toward him.

"Hey, Arik! Why don't you come over and join us?"

Penny was waving him over and smiling exuberantly.

Arik did as she had suggested. Others made room for him, and he sat next to her, cross-legged. Penny introduced Arik to everyone else, and faces in the dark peppered him with friendly questions. There were more new names and faces to remember. These were the Eidah Gimel boys and girls, a shevet (grade) younger than his.

There was more singing, clapping, and good-natured talk. Arik stared up at the completely clear sky covered with stars and let the singing wash over him. His Hebrew was fluent, but he had never heard any of these songs. They spoke to his soul. The group sang until almost midnight, and then Arik walked Penny back to her bunk and wished her "Shabbat Shalom."

I guess I got in my Friday night walk, after all, Arik mused.

Penny entered the bunk in the dark and made her way into the corner.

"How are you feeling, Dahlia?"

"A bit better. My migraine started during Tefillah, and by the time it ended I felt so sick I couldn't stand. I took some Anacin and slept for about two hours. I think I'm better now. So, how was tonight? Have you met the love of your life yet?"

"Don't be silly. But you'll never guess who I walked home with from the kumsitz."

"Really? Don't keep me in suspense!"

"Arik."

"Arik? Do you think he likes you?"

"I didn't get that vibe. He's friendly, though. Anyway, it's hard to tell if there's any attraction. He appears to have a shy streak that's rather sweet. With everything that he has going for him, if he were a New Yorker, he would strut around like he owned the world. But . . . I don't know, he has this faraway look."

"Do you think he's creepy?" Dahlia asked.

"No, I didn't mean it like that. It just seems like he thinks he doesn't really belong here."

"Well, it's his first week in camp, and everything is new to him. That's probably all it is."

Chapter 3

Sunday finally arrived, and everyone at camp boarded the buses for the forty-mile trip to visit Camp Morasha, another coed Orthodox Jewish camp, in Lake Como. A whole day of intercamp competitions had been planned. Camp Morasha, which emphasized sports, had excellent athletic facilities. The day would include meets and matches in track and field, baseball, tennis, volleyball, and swimming. In addition, there would be other Jewish and Israeli-themed events. The buses arrived to a carnival-like atmosphere. A huge outdoor barbecue had been planned for later, and already there was a pervasive, delicious aroma in the air.

The Camp Moshava crowd felt a bit intimidated by the mint condition of the fields and courts. That intimidation was a not-so-subtle home-field advantage.

The younger groups were fairly evenly matched and competition swung both ways. There was a great deal of cheering.

Penny had wasted no time, from the first day of camp, in training her volleyball squad, and they beat their opponents handily by playing as a smart, disciplined team.

Dahlia had no trouble beating her tennis opponents in straight sets and then winning medals in the 100-meter and 200-meter freestyle swims.

The track and field events were fairly balanced between the two camps, but Camp Moshava's senior boys got hammered in the afternoon softball game.

As the afternoon drew on, the anticipation for the evening began to mount. The crown-jewel event, the one that everyone was waiting for, was the senior boys' basketball game. A friendly rivalry had existed between the two camps for a decade, with Camp Moshava usually getting the short end of the stick. Through its affiliation with Yeshiva University, Camp Morasha was able to cull the best athletic talent from the college and its feeder high schools, MTA and BTA, meaning that its team typically played varsity athletes against Camp Moshava's "amateur" athletes . . . with predictable results.

This year, Camp Morasha still had its twin towers, those legends of the New York Jewish high school basketball scene, Pollack and Fishman. For the past three years, those two young men had led MTA. to consecutive titles in the Yeshiva league. They even had taken on and demolished first-rate teams from private Catholic schools. They were feared and respected. The outcome of today's game was in no doubt.

Camp Morasha had a giant modern indoor basketball arena with room for several hundred spectators. After the Minchah prayer service and the barbecue, campers and staff from both camps began to file into the arena.

There was a perceptible change in the sportsmanlike attitude that had pervaded the competition during the day. As the arena began to fill, the Camp Morasha kids began to poke fun at their guests.

"Prepare to die!" they catcalled.

"I don't even know why you're putting yourself through the torture of playing us tonight. You guys suck so bad!"

"We might not let you score at all!"

"Does anyone on your team even know how to play?"

On several occasions, the Camp Morasha rabbis had to chide the Camp Morasha fans for being bad hosts and try to silence them.

The two basketball teams began to warm up. Arik felt calm and relaxed. He hadn't had much to do all day except be a spectator. He took jump shots and casual layups with the other players.

The energy in the room rose to a fever pitch when both teams faced each other at half-court. The Camp Moshava players wore blue-and-white uniforms, while the Camp Morasha players wore green-and-gold uniforms. After the playing of the "Star-Spangled Banner" and "Hatikvah," the teams retired to their benches.

Coach Gary called the players around him.

"We'll stick to our plan and play our game. I've coached these guys from YU. They'll try to lure you in. If you play their game, we'll be playing catch up all night long. They're smart, and they stick to the game plan they've developed in varsity play: a two-on-two offense and a zone defense. Heshie, Yoni, Pinkie, Yossie, and Rubin will start. You guys play with so much heart there's a real chance you can pull out the upset."

"These guys are so big they can almost dunk!" Yoni complained.

"Never mind," Coach said. "Just do your best."

The buzzer sounded. Stuie Fishman and Heshie positioned themselves for the jump ball. The moment the ball left the referee's hands, the two guys were up in the air. Camp Morasha gained possession of the ball. Benji Schulman, the point guard, brought the ball up the court, and after two passes, Larry Pollack scored on an easy layup.

As the game progressed, it became clear to Arik that the Camp Morasha squad had played together in the past. Although they were pretty talented, they also played selfishly. Their passing was sloppy, and so was their zone defense. The Camp Moshava squad, however, wasn't talented enough to take advantage of Camp Morasha's weaknesses.

Camp Morasha played a very physical game, and many fouls were called. The other players on the Camp Morasha team seemed content to bring the ball up the court and then let Stuie and Larry score all the points. For Camp Moshava, Heshie and Yossie played together well and scored most of the team's points. At halftime, the score was 30-18. Camp Morasha had a deep bench, so the coach was able to rotate players in and out, keeping the team fresh. Coach Gary, somewhat flustered by the deafening noise and the catcalls, decided to stick with his starters and only put in a bench warmer when a starter was completely out of breath. It was clear from the beginning that Stuie was gunning for Heshie, and by halftime the wear was showing. By halftime, the twin towers were still relaxed and confident but Heshie and Yossie were fatigued.

Arik sat on the bench, with his hands folded in his lap, and began fidgeting. It appeared that he was going to be a spectator for the rest of the game. He wasn't sure why Coach wasn't letting the bench warmers play. The Laker's Coach Mullaney always stressed the importance of creating a dynamic relationship between the starters and the first three guys on the bench, in essence creating an eight-man squad. But Arik wasn't going to debase himself by asking Coach to put him in. Besides, Coach had much more on his mind at the moment.

During the first three minutes of the second half, Camp Moshava went on a 7-0 run, pulling within 5 points of Camp Morasha. The next seven minutes were a furious exchange between the teams, with multiple turnovers and fouls. Emotions bubbled over when Benji elbowed Rubin in the eye. A small shoving match erupted in the stands when the Camp Morasha fans laughed and cheered the assault. Counselors from both camps had to break it up, and the referees threatened to call off the game if things didn't settle down. Arik chuckled to himself, because he had somewhat mixed feelings about that foul.

Without much else to do, Arik let his eyes wander into the stands on the other side of the court. He saw Penny. Beside her sat a stunningly beautiful blonde girl with the sweetest smile. The two of them were chattering away but intently watching the game. Whenever the Camp Moshava side turned over the ball or missed a basket, they shook their heads in disgust. Not only were they into the game, but they also knew the rules.

Turning to the player next to him on the bench, Arik asked, "Bobby, who's that girl sitting next to Penny?"

"Which side?"

"Um, the Miss America side?" Arik laughed.

"Oh! You mean Dahlia Gilad." Bobby shook his head. "Don't even think about it. She's out of your league. She's out of everyone in this camp's league. She's the high-flying daughter of Israel's ambassador to the U.S., the Israeli tennis champ, she's supermodel gorgeous, has a stunning sexy body, and has never, ever considered, going on a Friday night walk with anyone in camp. Effie, the tennis director, had a crush on her last year, and he ran all over camp like a fool, telling everyone she was his girlfriend. Until she publicly told him where to get off. She's stuck with him a bit though this summer, because she has to. The camp administration has asked her to run the girls' tennis program. I think she really hates him."

"Easy, tiger!" Arik said. "I didn't say I wanted to date her. I just wanted to know who she was, that's all."

With ten minutes left in the game, Camp Moshava was down 52-40. The catcalls and jeering from the Camp Morasha side of the stands were growing louder, and the Camp Moshava fans were groaning in response to another year of failure. Yoni brought the ball down the court and drove it into the corner, where he was smothered by a sea of hands. He managed to pass the ball to the top of the key, to Heshie, who instead of shooting found Pinkie inside. But when Pinkie jumped for the layup, he was swept off his feet by Benji's leg. Pinkie came crashing down to the hardwood. His knee twisted into a sickening position, making a loud 'pop' sound. The ball went out of bounds.

The referee blew his whistle.

"Morasha ball!" he called out, pointing toward the other end of the court.

The Camp Moshava fans erupted in anger.

"He was tripped on purpose!"

"Are you blind, ref?"

"Flagrant foul! Flagrant foul!"

There was considerable pushing and shoving in the stands, and things threatened to get out of hand. The two coaches met and decided to take a ten-minute time-out. Two paramedics from the Camp Morasha health center splinted Pinkie's knee and called for an ambulance from the regional hospital in Scranton.

Gary approached Arik. "Do you think you can play guard?"

"I'll try, Coach."

"Then go out there, and give 'em hell!"

"I will, Coach,"

Arik took Heshie and Yossie aside and told them, flatly, "When it's our possession, one of you take the ball out and just pass it to me."

"I don't understand. What for?" Heshie asked.

"You'll find out in less than thirty seconds. Morasha is not going to be scoring any more tonight."

"What do you mean?" Yossie gave Arik a quizzical look.

Arik said, "It's show time!"

Camp Morasha inbounded the ball and brought the ball down to midcourt. Benji passed the ball to Larry, but it never got to him. In a blue-and-white flash, Arik whizzed by, grabbed the ball and, in a dazzling display of ball handling, broke away in a gallop. When he reached the foul line, he launched himself into the air and executed a two-handed dunk with his hands six inches above the rim. The rim reverberated with a loud twang as Arik hit the floor like a cat. There was stunned silence from the Camp Morasha fans.

Arik turned around, looked at Heshie, and said, "And that's why I wanted you to give me the ball. Got it?"

Stuie and Larry looked at each other in bewilderment and passed the ball back and forth. Arik was all over Larry, making it impossible for him to dribble. Arik motioned to Heshie to remain down court, and Heshie complied. Arik's hands found the ball as it came down between Larry's legs. Arik palmed the ball and tossed it, like a baseball, all the way down court and directly into the hands of Heshie, who laid it up and in.

Arik had spent the whole game closely observing Camp Morasha's offense. He had identified three distinct patterns. The team was so well coached that each play was executed in sequence with little improvisation. Arik easily read the plays and knew where to position himself. With him covering Larry and Heshie and Yossie double-teaming Stuie, there was little the Camp Morasha team could do.

When Stuie went up for a layup, Heshie stripped the ball and passed it to Arik, who was standing at the top of the key. Arik took the ball back down court in a full sprint, and just past midcourt he threw the ball at the backboard with such force that the impact sounded like a shotgun blast. As the ball reverberated back at him, Arik jumped, caught the ball with one hand on his way up, and gently laid the ball into the basket, where it sailed through the rim without a sound.

There was astonished silence as the fans looked on in disbelief.

Penny and Dahlia gave each other knowing looks.

Dahlia said, "I knew this genie wouldn't stay in the bottle for long. This is the Arik we saw."

Penny said, "He really picked his moment. His timing could not have been better."

"These Morasha fans are really going to get a taste of their own medicine."

There were five minutes left in the game, and the score was 52-46, still in favor of Camp Morasha.

Benji brought the ball up the court and passed it to Larry, who passed it back to Benji who passed it back to Stuie, who attempted a shot. But Arik jumped a full foot higher than Stuie and easily blocked the shot. He then tapped the ball to Yossie, who brought it down court and then sent an alley-oop pass back to Arik. Arik, who already had jumped two feet in the air to come at the basket from the side, hooked his right arm in midair, passed the ball to his left hand, and gently laid the ball in backward.

Camp Morasha took possession and brought the ball back down court. The Camp Morasha offense spread out.

"Zone defense!" Arik called out to his teammates.

On Arik's cue, Yossie, Heshie, and Arik converged, from three directions, on Larry as he stood at the top of the key. With nowhere to go, he took a wild shot. Arik again jumped a full foot higher than Stuie. He grabbed the ball and passed it to Yossie, who brought the ball down court. Yossie went right and passed it to Arik when he got to the top of the key. Arik stood there, dribbling the ball through his legs so fast that Larry was unable to locate the ball let alone try to steal it. One second it was in front of him, and the next it was behind him. All the while, Arik stood face-to-face with Larry, grinning at him.

"Say goodnight, Larry!" he said.

With Heshie standing behind Larry and with a clear path to the basket, Arik made eye contact with Heshie for an instant and then, in a flash, the ball went through Larry's legs and into Heshie's waiting arms. Heshie laid it up and in.

Two minutes left in the game, 52-50.

What happened next must have seemed, to onlookers, to be in slow motion. Arik intercepted Benji's inbound pass, ran toward the basket, and executed a 180-degree midair turn followed by a backward dunk. The score was 52-52.

Pandemonium broke out in the Camp Moshava stands. The fans' deafening roars grew louder. The campers were shrieking, crying, and bellowing. Their rhythmic cheers crescendoed.

"Arik! Arik! Arik! Arik!"

With a minute left in the game, Morasha inbounded the ball, but it was intercepted by Yoni, who passed it to Yossie in the corner. Yoni tossed it a foot over Larry's head, to Arik. Arik caught the ball above the rim and guided it gently down into the basket. Frustrated, Larry elbowed Arik in the side as he was coming down.

Arik looked at him. "If you want to have a normal life-span, don't ever do that again. Capiche?"

Larry saw by the look of the devil in Arik's eyes that he meant business. At that moment, the whistle blew! Foul! One free throw!

Arik went to the foul line and, with a casual toss, sunk the ball into the basket without touching the rim. 55-52.

On the next play, Yitz inbounded the ball and passed it to Stuie, while Larry ran crosscourt with Arik hard on his heels. Larry passed the ball to Benji who, in a panic, threw a sloppy set shot at the basket. It went in, making the score 55-54 with thirty seconds left in the game. The Camp Morasha coach called a twenty-second time-out.

Out of the time-out, Yoni inbounded the ball to Arik, who lazily bounced the ball down court as the Camp Morasha defense stood at the ready, waiting for his next move. With ten seconds left, he stopped at the midcourt line, looked around, smiled and, with the lightness of a feather, let loose a tall, arcing shot that went straight into the basket. Swish! The scoreboard showed 57-54.

The Camp Morasha players had the final inbound, but they were so dazed that their attempt to get the ball down court was unfocused. When their outside shot missed wildly, the final buzzer sounded.

There was stunned silence. Everyone in the stands was in disbelief of what they had just witnessed.

Everyone, including the coaches and players, was staring at Arik.

Arik looked around and shrugged as if to say, "What?"

A moment later, he was surrounded by his teammates, who jumped all over him and one another and fell into a sweaty, joyous heap.

When the players had picked themselves up off the gym floor, Coach Gary walked up to Arik. His face showed his astonishment.

"Where in the world did you learn how to play basketball like that? And why have you kept it a secret until now?"

Arik replied, "It's really a very long story, and it speaks to why I came east instead of staying in LA for the summer."

"All right, but we're talking about this tomorrow."

"Okay."

The medal ceremony at half-court was such a delirious blur for Arik that he couldn't remember the exact moment the MVP medal had been placed around his neck.

He packed up his gear into his gym bag and left the locker room. Pollack and Fishman were waiting in the corridor.

"You played a great game. It's been a long time since someone made chumps out of us," Larry Pollack said. "And sorry about that elbow."

Stuie Fishman said, "Do you have plans for college yet? If you're even considering going to YU, please call me. It would be great for the three of us to be on the same team. We'd beat all the Division I teams in the state."

He handed Arik a slip of paper with his phone number on it.

"I really haven't made up my mind yet about college, but I'll be sure to give you a call." Arik smiled broadly. "It's nice to finally meet you guys. I'd heard so much about you."

He headed outside, into the cool night air. There was a crowd of people waiting to congratulate him. He greeted all of the well-wishers and shook dozens of hands.

"You played a great game!"

"That was historic!"

"I've never seen anybody play like that in my life!"

"Can we have your autograph?"

Arik looked down at two bucktoothed, freckle-faced ten-year-old boys from Eidah Aleph, who were gazing admiringly up at him. One was Yudi Steinhardt, Heshie's younger brother. He knelt down to them and smiled broadly.

"And why, pray tell, would you want that?"

"Because you're Superman!"

"Hardly. Anybody with a little bit of talent can learn to play basketball if they're taught correctly and have the right attitude."

"Could you teach us?" they asked in unison.

"If the sports counselors let me, I'd be happy to give you guys a clinic or two."

"All right!" They cheered. "Thanks, Superman!"

Arik was still   on one knee, looking down and signing their caps, when he heard a familiar voice call down to him,

"Well, if isn't the hero of the hour!"

Arik looked up to find Penny staring down at him.

"Hey, sweet cheeks. What's shakin'?" Arik smiled at her.

"Tell me something, big shot. Why is it that for the past ten days you have been a complete klutz on and off the court and now, all of a sudden, this? The little guys are right. You had this Clark Kent thing going on. And now, poof!" Penny threw her hands up into the air.

"The reasons are actually very complicated and not really for now, but I'm sure we could talk about this some other time," Arik answered.

"Oh! I'm sorry. I've been rude."

Arik stood up.

"Have you met my best buddy, Dahlia?" Penny asked.

Dahlia had been standing there, next to her but off to the side, and Arik hadn't noticed her while he was on his knees.

"Nice to meet you, Dahlia. I'm Arik."

He reached out to shake her hand and grasped hers. Her steel gray-blue eyes shot through him, and he felt as if he had received an electric shock. Her gaze was serene but firm, which revealed a sophistication that betrayed her perfect white smile. She was even more beautiful up close.

"Very nice to meet you, too, Arik," Dahlia said with the hint of an Israeli accent. "That was some great play tonight. I think you're good enough to play for Maccabi Tel Aviv or even Israel's national team. So, tell us: Why have you been playing like a shpaas since you come to camp and all of a sudden you explode onto the scene like that?"

"I see you really want to know." Arik smiled.

"We're all ears." Dahlia laughed.

"Well, I didn't come to camp to play basketball. I do enough of that at home with guys who will, in all likelihood, end up in the NBA. As far as talent goes, I'm completely outclassed by the guys I play with there."

"Who do you play with?" Penny asked.

"First, if you want to learn how to play basketball, you don't play with Jews. You play with blacks. I play street basketball in an urban park in Watts, a neighborhood that nice Jewish girls would be afraid to venture into. There are parts of LA that are rough and segregated, but these poor neighborhoods are a hotbed of basketball talent. Many people who live there feel that playing ball is their ticket out of poverty and the ghetto. So, there's a real desperation in the way they play. For them, it's a matter of survival. It's not just about social acceptance, as it is here. Basketball is also used to keep young black kids out of trouble. I play in a community basketball league twice a week when I'm not playing in the park. I'm the only white kid there."

"How did you come to do this?" asked Penny.

"Long story. Hey, the Mach Hach bus is leaving. I've got to go, but we'll talk later. Nice to meet you, Dahlia."

"Nice to meet you, too," Dahlia said.

Arik sprinted off.

"He's certainly not run of the mill," Dahlia said.

"You're right about that! There's something about him. I just can't put my finger on it. . ."

Arik got on the bus and was instantly greeted with cheers:

"A-rik!" Clap, clap. "A-rik!" Clap, clap.

Arik turned bright red with embarrassment, but he managed to thank everyone. Heshie had saved a seat for him, in the back of the bus this time.

The ride home was a raucous event filled with silly camp songs and cheers, like this one:

They say in Moshava the food is mighty fine.

You eat it up at seven and throw it up at nine.

Oh! I don't want to go to Moshava.

Gee, ma. I want to go back to Ontario.

Gee, ma. I want to go home.

They say in Moshava the girls are mighty fine.

How the heck do they know?

They never slept with mine.

Oh! I don't want to go to Moshava.

Gee, ma. I want to go back to Ontario.

Gee, ma. I want to go home.

Chapter 4

The next day, after lunch, Arik headed to Coach Gary's office. Located in the back of the gym, his office was completely cluttered with old and new sporting equipment, basketballs, volleyballs, soccer balls, baseball bats, balls, and gloves, and piles of field hockey sticks and nets. Against the wall was a small desk with stacks of clipboards, schedules, and rosters.

"Come on in, Arik. Have a seat."

"Thanks, Coach."

"That was a quite a performance yesterday. We haven't beaten Morasha in eight years. Your play wasn't just your own personal thunderbolt. It energized the entire team. This is all that folks have been talking about all morning. But in all the excitement, I'm left with more questions than answers. Questions like 'Where did you learn how to play like that?' I've only seen play like that in the NBA. What was the point of all the secrecy? Like, have you been undercover or something? You seem pretty straight, so level with me. Won't you?"

Arik said, "Permission to speak freely and confidentially, sir?"

Coach laughed. "Of course. You're among friends."

"Well, I didn't come here to play ball at all. If that's all I wanted to do, I could have stayed home and played a much better brand of basketball. I came to experience what Judaism and Zionism felt like. I grew up with neither, which is a long story."

"But where did you learn to play like that?"

"I play street basketball in Watts in LA and in a community league in the neighborhood YMCA. I played in an NBA youth league in Anaheim last summer. I'm looking at several schools, but right now I'm considering my options—including whether I want to go to college at all."

"Where would you go if not to college?"

"I've been considering enlisting in the army."

"But you'll end up in Vietnam. Is that what you want?"

"The Israeli Army, sir."

"I see. Well, at least they know how to win wars! So, why all the mystery?"

"Well, sir, from the moment I stepped foot on the bus in New York, I saw this unfair social stratification among the campers. Real meanness and bullying of some of the more vulnerable by an arrogant class of jocks who walk around like they own the place. It's everywhere, in big ways and small ways. The defining line between the two groups is prowess in sports. If you're good, you're in. If you're not, you're invisible at best and subject to ridicule at worst.

"Look at the difference between how I've been treated the past week and today. All week, I was this awkward, brawny sort, a blond-haired curiosity from California. And today? Today, I'm a rock-and-roll star. And because of what? Because I can bounce and shoot a basketball better than anyone else they've seen in person? I'm still the same person I was yesterday.

"Also, everyone should be coming here to play and have fun and grow spiritually and emotionally as well as physically. Basketball is a big part of that, for whatever reason. If I had showed up the first day and played like I did yesterday, every time I got on the court I'd dominate play easily. The novelty of the acrobatics would wear off pretty quickly, and the other campers would suddenly realize that their games were being ruined by me. I really just want to get along and fit in. I'm not interested in being thrust into that role."

"Well," Coach said, "I think you may have done just that. You may have opened a door you can't go back through. If you wanted to keep it a secret, why did you expose everything yesterday?"

"It was the catcalls and the jeering by the Morasha fans. If you don't mind my saying so, you played your starters way too much and didn't utilize your bench well enough. The other side did, to their credit. The bench shouldn't be second-rate players that only enter the game if we're losing or winning by a lot or if one of the starters has a heart attack and dies on the court. They should be used as an asset.

"I've watched Joe Mullaney, the coach of the Lakers, when I played in the NBA youth league. And I've seen up close how he strategically moves his players in and out, reading the needs of the team on the court at the moment and using the talent he has. I'm afraid you panicked. And since you thought your starters were your best players, you kept them on the court more than you should have. Please, don't get mad at me for saying that."

"I'm not mad at you at all. Go on."

"The whole process just feeds on itself. The good players get chosen to start. They have the high self-esteem and social status, which makes them more likely to get chosen in the future. And so it goes. Everyone else gets left out. Kids at this age are vulnerable and impressionable. Stuff that authority figures do to them now can have a lifelong effect on them. Sports is about so much more than just running around. It's supposed to build a sense of teamwork, accomplishment, fair play, and sportsmanship. Above all, it's supposed to make kids feel like they're worth something. There should be a way of accomplishing that with every kid whether they're an athlete or not."

"Are you saying we should let everyone play on the senior team regardless of their talent?"

"No, Coach. I'm not saying that at all. What I'm saying is there's much more talent out there than you think. There are guys out there who could be rather good and even better than some of the guys who are starting if they were only taught better and really given a chance. Some of the guys get so intimidated by other players and insecure on the court, because they've never had a chance to develop their skills. Instead, they're fed a steady diet of intimidation and expectation of failure."

"Can you give me an example?"

"Okay. Take Richard Green, for instance, I've had a chance to shoot the ball around with him. He's quite athletic and has some real moves, but he's so intimidated by the jocks who verbally abuse him that he has absolutely no self-confidence. I bet if I spent one week training him he'd be good enough to be on the team."

"You really think so?"

"I do! The other thing is that, for all their bluster and arrogance, when these guys get on the court there's no playmaking, no strategy—despite all the drawings you give them to learn and despite all the drills. All I see is a bunch of guys trying to imitate what they see on TV. They bring the ball down the court, and then there's just random passing until someone decides to shoot. More often than not, they shoot without looking to see if someone else has a better shot. Everyone just seems to be concerned with how many points they've scored and how many rebounds they've gotten."

"So, what do you propose, Arik?"

"Well, it appears that kids come back here year after year, so you can start young and grow talent. I'd break down the game and hammer into them the fundamentals of the game and what it means to function as a team before letting them play a game. I'd teach team situational awareness and slide the fundamentals of ball handling, passing, and shooting into that framework. The most important thing is to teach the kids what it means to be a team—and that includes all the kids, not just the jocks. It means being good to each other and watching out for each other."

"This is all well said and well taken. You're a very impressive guy and mature beyond your years. I'm going to think on this and come up with some plans for the program, but I warn you, Arik, you will be part of those plans. And I expect you to put your actions where your mouth is."

"I'll do all I can. This is a good project." Arik smiled.

"We'll talk more later," Coach said.

***

When Arik walked out of the coach's office, he found Dahlia sitting in a lotus position on top of a desk, slowly clapping her hands.

"Bravo! Well spoken! I couldn't have said it better myself." She beamed.

Arik smiled. "Do you usually listen in on people's private conversations?"

"What do you mean? First of all, the door was partly open. And second of all, you guys were taking so loud they could probably hear you in Scranton. Besides, I was interested. The stuff you were talking about has been a sore point with me as long as I've been coming here. There's an intensity about sports here, sure, but nobody has a clue what real competition means. My mom's been involved with the Israeli Olympic team and the Maccabia games, for years, so I've been around the real deal my whole life. For all the bluster and arrogance I see at camp, I could pick out less half a dozen kids here that would ever stand a chance of competing at that level."

Arik smiled at Dahlia's answer. "So, what brings you here to speak to Coach?"

"Well, he's the athletic director, and I'm trying to organize a tennis day, here at camp, that I've been working on since May. Through my contacts, I've asked Billie Jean King to come to camp to put on an exhibition and run some clinics for the kids. You know—promote the game for a few hours. It'll be the perfect time for her. She will have just finished Wimbledon, and she won't be playing any major tournaments until the U.S. Open, in Forest Hills, at the end of August. I'm trying to get this going for next week, but there are so many unfinished details and the tennis facilities are in such poor shape. It's an embarrassment, really."

"What's wrong with the courts? I haven't paid much attention to them."

"For one thing, the courts need grooming. There's fencing that needs to go up. And we even don't have any bleachers for people to sit on. It feels like we're starting at square one."

"Why aren't you talking to Effie about this. It's his tennis program."

"The less I interact with that jerk, the happier I am. When he's not trying to flirt with me he's just obstructionist. If I relied on him, nothing would ever get done so I decided to go over his head. I really don't give a crap what Effie says or thinks."

Arik understood. "Well, let me know what Coach says and how I can help."

"Will do. Thanks!"

Dahlia went inside to speak to Coach.

"So, Dahlia, what sort of progress have you made? I understand that Billie Jean said yes?"

"Yes! The plan is for her to come here a week from Tuesday, so nine days from now. I have a program set up that will include a small ceremony welcoming her and then a tennis tournament involving Eidah Gimel, Mach Hach, and staff. Billie Jean can walk around the different courts and join in the fray and teach at times. We'll set up a portable microphone for her to carry so everyone can hear her."

Dahlia was visibly excited. "We'll play short sets so that everyone gets a chance to play. The winners of the tournaments will play a final on the main court, and then she'll award the trophy to the champ. Then she'll give a talk about her experiences on tour and a pep talk about getting out there and playing. And, finally, she'll have a chance to sign autographs and take pictures!"

"Well, Dahlia, I'm impressed. But I have a question: Which is the main court? We have five courts, and they're all the same."

"Well, that's my concern, too. Usually, finals are played on center court, with spectators, and we don't even have any room for spectators. Court number one could serve as center court, maybe—"

"What are you suggesting?"

"I'm suggesting that the courts need serious reconditioning, first of all. The basic surfaces are okay, but they need a coat of paint and new stripes and nets. The fencing on both ends of the court needs repair and green sheeting along them. All that should be pretty easy. The issue will be the bleachers. How do we make seating for about 250 people in a week?"

"This is starting to look impossible—"

"Maybe not," Dahlia said. "Camp has always been big on construction projects, especially for Mach Hach and Machane Avoda. What better thing for them to do than build these bleachers? I think we could do it in a week if we got organized and had enough people."

"But who do we have who knows how to build such a thing?"

"Actually, Itai Lapid—you know him, the director of the woodworking shop—was an officer in the Chel Handasa, Israel's Army Corp of Engineers. When I spoke to him about it, he told me that one time on his base there was going to be a tekes, a graduation ceremony for officers with top brass in attendance, and he organized and built bleachers for several hundred people in just three days, starting from scratch."

"Maybe . . . But this thing is still liable to cost upwards of five hundred dollars."

"Probably, but I've been planning this with Penny. When she called home and mentioned it to her parents, they said they'd be glad to donate the bleachers to the camp. They said it was for a good cause."

"Okay . . . do you think we have enough people capable of executing this project?"

"I do," Dahlia said triumphantly. "I've compiled a list of big, strong men and even some of the girls who are interested in helping."

"Have you discussed any of this with Effie?"

"No, and I have no intention of doing so. He'll want to do this his way, which is usually the wrong way, and he'll end up just being in the way. I can't stand the sight of him. So, what do you think, Coach?"

"Crazy as it is, this sounds like it could work. Let me run it by the Rosh Mosh and Rabbi Moskowitz, and I'll get back to you later today. Okay?"

"Okay!"

***

Later that afternoon, Dahlia went to the woodworking shop. Itai Lapid was busy at a makeshift drafting table, with T square and compass in hand, drawing out the basic specs of the bleachers when she walked in.

"Ahalan, Itai. Ma'nishma?" ("How's it going?") Dahlia said. "I see you've heard the project is a go!"

Itai wasted no time rattling off the specs and process for the project. "We are going to need about two hundred fifty 16-foot 2×12s and five hundred joists. We will pour concrete footers and put in 6×6 posts, which will vary in height. The frame will be bolted together, but the benches will have to be nailed on. We can do all the cutting and drilling here in the woodshop and then carry the stuff to the site. I want to get this done in four days, because it has to be painted green before Shabbat, but . . ."—Itai pointed his finger in warning—"we will have to work all day, every day. We are going to need about twenty volunteers. I will do most of the power cutting and the crew will do the rest, but we will need an overseer who has a good grasp of mechanics and design."

***

After Mifkad that evening, Dahlia approached Arik.

"I have a proposal for you, if you're still interested," Dahlia said.

"Shoot," Arik said.

"We're going to do that crash project to revitalize the tennis center. We're going to announce Billie Jean's visit to the camp tomorrow night and really hype it up. The problem, of course, is not only everything we have to build but also that we need to have it done by Shabbat.

"Itai has designed the bleachers and has all the specs," Dahlia said. "I have his drawings. But now I need fifteen guys who are big and strong and have some basic intelligence, which may be a limited commodity in Eidah Gimel and Mach Hach. I also need a brainy guy with some engineering and design sense who can oversee all of this."

"Which category do I fall into?" Arik smiled.

"Hmm . . . I haven't decided yet." Dahlia smirked.

Arik went back to the boys' bunks and pulled aside a bunch of the guys. He gave them an outline of what needed to be done and the backbreaking work that would be in store for the volunteers. After rallying some troops, he took the freehand drawings that Dahlia had given him to Richard for him to look at.

"So, Richard, what do you think?" Arik asked.

"You're going to need much more concrete and more 6×6 uprights, because the number of supports you've got isn't going to hold the weight for the long haul. You might get away with it for this summer, but as the years go by stress fatigue will set in here, here, here, and here. You need to have the perpendicular supports no more than 4 feet apart, especially for the upper rows."

"I knew I picked the right guy to be foreman!" Arik said, slapping Richard on the back.

Heshie and Yossie agreed to help with the construction project, and so did Steve and Yoni.

Arik next went looking for some big, muscled guys from Eidah Gimel. He bumped into Rubin.

Arik pulled him over to the side and, in a conspiratorial tone, said, "Hey, Rubin. Don't suppose you can take a week off from being an asshole to work on a worthwhile project? It's going to be hard work, for you particularly, because it involves actually thinking about someone else but yourself."

"Very funny, schmuck!"

Good-naturedly, Arik wrapped a meaty arm around Rubin's neck and gave him a noogie.

"Okay, big shot. What's the project?" Rubin even smiled.

Arik outlined the whole thing to him but left out the part about Billie Jean King. Rubin had a big mouth.

"When do we get started?" Rubin asked.

"Oh! By the way, you'll be working directly under Richard. You know, Richie the Bitchie? He's the site foreman, so you're all going to have to get along."

Rubin rolled his eyes.

Half an hour later, Arik found Dahlia in the administration office.

"Okay!" he announced. "I've got your crew. I know you said you needed twenty people. Well, I got you fifteen, plus a smart guy to be foreman. Will that do?"

"Perfect! Because… I got the other five." Dahlia smiled.

"Girls? How are they going to help? This will be very physical work."

"Oh! So, you think girls can't do a man's job?" Dahlia's smile became sly.

"No, I wasn't—"

"Oh, yes, you were. Us girls are going to kick your ass!" Dahlia smiled even more broadly.

***

At 8:30 p.m., the entire crew assembled in the dining hall.

Itai called the meeting to order and gave everyone a rundown of the plans as well as the need for discipline, safety, and teamwork on the job.

"I know that not everyone gets along, but for the duration of this project you will," he commanded.

Richard shot Rubin a pointed look.

Feeling the need to emphasize his point, Itai continued. "Richard is the site foreman for this project, and you will all obey his orders. I will have eyes and ears everywhere, so if there is any crap you will be off the project instantly."

Richard stood and gave everyone a rundown of the structure of the bleachers, going through all of the schematics and the order in which they would have to be assembled and why. Then he answered questions and adjourned the meeting.

Arik, Dahlia, and Penny were standing outside, chatting, when Richard bounded down the stairs.

"Good job in there, Richard!" Arik said. "I think we're going to do just great. You know Dahlia and Penny?"

"Sort of," Richard said. He shook their hands.

"Arik has told me that you're some kind of math and computer genius," Penny said.

"I don't know about all that, but I'm hoping to study computers at MIT one day." Richard smiled.

"Well, we'd all better get some sleep," Dahlia said. "Tomorrow is going to be a very busy day."

The next morning, the camp awoke to a torrential thunderstorm. Arik stood on the bunk's porch, surveying the scene. There was an incessant pounding of rain on the roof that sounded like so many tiny hammers. The dirt roads had turned into rivers of mud, and there were deep pools of water in the ruts and potholes. As the campers walked to the synagogue, their ponchos got completely soaked and their hiking boots were soon ankle deep in mud.

The construction crew met after breakfast.

"The weather forecast says rain for the next two days without stopping," Itai said. "In the interest of safety, we must delay the project until Thursday."

There were groans from the campers assembled, and Dahlia, for one, wasn't taking no for an answer.

"The event is set for Tuesday," she said. "There isn't going to be time to finish it if we start on Thursday. Billie Jean's schedule is incredibly tight. We're lucky to have her, and I'm not going to cancel after she's done me this amazing favor and rearranged her schedule to come here. Is there anything we can do to get this started today?"

Richard spoke up. "Itai, I think there's plenty we can do even in the rain. One group can go to Honesdale, to Frederick's Building Supply, with the school bus, to pick up the wood and the hardware. And the other group can stay back here to dig the holes for the footers."

Heshie was the next to speak up. "Richie, you're forgetting something. You're going to have to load all that lumber in through the emergency back door of the bus. The back door is alarmed, and it sounds like ten fire engines when you open it. We're going to have to drive all the way back from Honesdale, in the pouring rain, with the alarm going off, because the wood beams are two feet too long to allow the door to close. We're also going to have to make several trips. Can't we get them to deliver the wood in a large flatbed truck?"

"Not in the pouring rain," Richard said. "I already called them to ask. It's some insurance–union thing."

"This is going to be hilarious," Rubin said.

Arik said, "It's already 10 a.m. I'll stay back here and start digging. I need ten people to stay back to dig. Richard, do you have a complete list of all the supplies? That way you can give it the bus crowd. I need you here to show me where the footers go."

"I've already given it to Penny," Richard said. "She'll organize the foray into Honesdale. Dahlia, are going or staying?"

"I'm staying. I'm doing some digging today!" She pumped her fists into the air. She looked as if she meant business, in rolled-up, baggy khaki shorts, hiking boots, an old, green U.S. Army surplus T-shirt, and a beaten-up Washington Redskins cap.

Arik chuckled.

"What are you laughing at, big shot?"

"I just can't wait to see you with a shovel in the mud." Arik smiled.

"You just wait!"

The groups split up and the diggers chuckled as they watched the old, beaten-up, yellow school bus, with Itai at the wheel, bumping down the rutted road in the pouring rain.

For the diggers, there was no point in trying to stay dry. They trudged off into the deluge of rain coming down in buckets. The howling wind served only to increase their misery. Arik reviewed the soggy schematic drawing and, with Richard's help, marked the footer sites with orange flags. Yoni and Dahlia fetched the shovels.

Arik called out, "Three feet deep, ten inches in diameter. And we need thirty holes."

Arik sunk his shovel into the ground and found semiliquid mud. The shovel went in about a foot, but no sooner had he withdrawn the shovel than the hole filled with mud and water.

"Crap!"

Yoni and Yossie fared no better. Dahlia's shovel slipped, and she fell face-first into the mud.

"Had enough, Dahlia?" Arik laughed.

"Oh, shut up, Arik!" But she laughed as she flung a clump of brown mud at him, hitting him in the face.

"That's going to cost you." Arik laughed and then grabbed a large clump of mud. He starting to chase her down the muddy path.

"Will you two morons stop clowning around so we can figure out what to do?" Richard yelled above the din of the downpour.

Everyone gathered around.

"Okay. Listen up!" Richard said. "We're going to need to get pincer shovels—special shovels for this purpose—and dig out the mud in a narrow hole down to the three-foot depth. The holes will still fill up with water and collapse, but not so much."

Arik stared at the tarpaulin that was protecting the hard-court surface from the rain.

"I have an idea. Once we dig, say, about ten holes, we cover the holes with the tarp. We'll keep sliding it over as we dig, to keep them from filling up with water."

"That's such a bad idea," Dahlia said. "I'm sure Effie got up at midnight, when the rain started, and, by himself, pulled out all the tarps from the shed to protect his precious hard courts. They're like his baby. He'll have a stroke when he sees what we've done."

"I don't give a crap what Effie thinks. The courts will dry," Arik said.

"It's not that simple. Effie is a control freak with a nasty temper. And he can be a real troublemaker."

"Wow! I'm shaking in my boots!" Arik cried out in mock alarm.

The digging began in earnest, with everyone using the tarp as they went along.

***

Meanwhile, the school bus had arrived at the loading dock of Frederick's Building Supply for the camp's first load of supplies.

"Who's in charge here?" bellowed a fiftyish man in torn coveralls. He was wearing a heavily stained Budweiser T-shirt, and he spoke through a lit cigar that looked more chewed than smoked.

"I am," Penny said. "I think that you are the one who I spoke to over the phone."

"Look, girlie. This ain't gonna work. Ya can't be pilin' lumber into the back of a school bus and drivin' these dirt country roads in this rain. First of all, those boards are too long to fit in the bus. Ya gonna have to drive with the back door wide open, and that damn alarm is gonna make quite a racket. And if that ain't enough, ya gonna have to make a buncha trips. Ya can't fit much in there. Can't you wait 'til Thursday, and I'll bring the whole thing in ma' truck with fellas to help ya unload?"

"We don't have enough time, with the pressure we're under," Penny said.

"So, lemme get this straight. You folks are building bleachers in the rain. Am I gettin' this?"

Penny and Itai nodded.

"I hope you have your footers in already. And covered," he said.

"They're digging them right now," Penny said.

"Have ya lost your minds? Ya can't be diggin' footers in the mud. Oh, well. Ya problem, not mine."

He looked at the list, shook his head, and said, "Get your crew, and let's get started."

***

By lunchtime, the ten diggers had completed twelve holes and gotten them covered. They marched into the dining hall, completely covered in mud and looking like zombies from the brown lagoon. Three hundred heads turned around and burst out laughing.

Rosh Moshava, the head counselor, approached Dahlia.

"How are you guys doing? Have you heard from the others?"

"We're okay," Dahlia said. "Definitely getting wet. Nothing yet from Honesdale."

While they were talking, the others showed up, soaking wet.

"You won't believe it!" Penny announced. "We got stopped by the police on the way back here. We were bouncing on the road, with thirty pilings sticking out the back of the bus and the alarm screeching the whole way. As we passed through town, we made such a racket that the police stopped us. But I talked our way of it."

Itai smiled and shrugged.

After lunch, the rain let up a bit, which allowed the diggers to dig the rest of the holes while the others unloaded the bus. Then they poured fast-setting concrete into the holes and set the pilings in them. A small crowd gathered to watch. Richard and Itai strode around making sure that the uprights were actually upright. The tarp covered the remaining holes.

"What the hell is going on here? What are you guys doing?" It was Effie.

He was not happy that the bleachers were being built without his knowledge or consent. He was even more upset that his beloved tarp and tennis court one were completely covered in mud.

"This is my tennis center, and I make the decisions!" Effie scowled.

Arik said, "This is the camp's tennis center, not yours. Long after you're gone, the tennis center and these bleachers will still be here. Besides, we're doing this for you. I don't know if it's occurred to you, but you can't have Billie Jean King here without bleachers. Anyway, I'm sure that when we're all done you'll take all the credit for this. But you should have come forward and spearheaded this yourself, big shot."

Dahlia smirked her approval.

"Oh, eat shit, Arik!" Effie snapped. He glanced in Dahlia's direction and then stomped off.

"Nobody's ever spoken to him like that," Dahlia said to Arik. "He's a spoiled rich kid, from Scarsdale, used to getting his own way. He grew up playing tennis and golf at the Briarwood Country Club. He's a pretty good tennis player but arrogant as hell. I play tennis with him because there is really nobody else for me to play. But last summer he got the wrong idea and started running around camp, telling everyone that we're an item."

"Are you?"

"Are you kidding? I wouldn't be caught dead with that putz. You should give me more credit than that." Dahlia sneered.

"I'm sorry, but I really don't know you well enough." Arik smiled.

"Touché."

Arik turned around, to the pilings, and went back to work. Dahlia stared after him.

***

Richard turned out to be a very good foreman, and he assigned the work intelligently. He and Itai stayed up well into Tuesday night, revising the schematic drawings so that they were to scale. Luckily, Wednesday and Thursday were sunny and hot. The bleachers began to take shape. On Wednesday afternoon, the flatbed truck from Frederick's Building Supply, with the rest of the wood and hardware, arrived, and the delivery men unloaded it. The construction crew bolted the crossbeams and supports in place and installed the planks for the seating and walkways. The work was the talk of the camp, and everyone walked by to catch a glimpse.

Effie wandered by, wearing his tennis whites and carrying his tennis bag with racquets protruding, on his way to a lesson at tennis court two.

He announced, "Nice job, you guys! Keep it up! Keep it up! And, oh, by the way, don't forget to clean the tarp and the mess you've made on court one by Shabbat. The tarp needs to be folded neatly and placed in the tennis office storage shed."

Penny whispered to Dahlia, in Spanish, "Would you mind terribly if I smashed in his brains with my hammer?"

Dahlia chuckled. "I'm sorry, Paapi, but you're going to have to get in line, and I'm ahead of you."

Arik had been assigned the task of carrying up and then fastening into place the upper seat planks. Barechested and covered in sweat in the hot sun, he pounded away on the top levels of the bleachers with a sledgehammer.

Dahlia worked on the support beams on the other end of the bleachers. She stole a lustful glance at Arik, who was wearing torn jean shorts, construction boots, and a backward baseball cap. She allowed herself a moment to admire his physique. Something she had not noticed before caught her eye: He had a six-inch scar across the top of his left pectoral muscle and a small indentation on his powerful left upper arm.

He must be accident prone, she mused.

***

By Thursday evening, the bleachers were complete. By noon on Friday, two coats of pine-green paint had been applied. The courts were then hosed down and bright-white lines were painted on them. Green netting was wrapped around the fences on both sides of the courts.

The members of the construction crew stood by, admiring their work and congratulating one another.

Penny walked over to Richard.

"You were a spectacular manager. I do not think that we could have done any of this without you. The camp really owes you a debt of gratitude."

Richard blushed. "Thanks, Penny. Thank you very much. I really appreciate that."

***

Shabbat started, with the same peace descending as it had the previous Friday afternoon. The construction crew was so relieved that the week was done and proud of what they had accomplished. Dinner was a spirited affair. Afterward, people trickled out of the dining hall, to the courtyard, to socialize in small groups.

Arik sat on one of the fence railings. He was in good spirits, chatting with the passersby.

Dahlia snuck up on him. "Hey, sailor. What's a girl got to do around here to get a Friday night walk?"

"Hey, Dahlia! What's up with you?" Arik smiled.

"Want to take a stroll?" Dahlia asked.

"Wait a minute. Aren't the boys supposed to ask the girls for a walk? Besides, I already have a date."

"Oh! I'm sorry. I didn't realize."

"And here he is!" Arik pointed to Eliezer Moskowitz, who was wheeling himself over.

"Shabbat Shalom, Arik. Are you ready to study?" Eliezer asked. When he noticed Dahlia standing there, he added,

"Shabbat Shalom, Dahlia!"

"Shabbat Shalom, Eliezer," Dahlia said with a broad smile.

"Can you give us a minute, Eliezer?" Arik asked.

"Sure!" Eliezer wheeled himself off to the side.

"How long do you study with him?"

"About an hour and a quarter. Then I take him back home."

"Well, how about I pick you both up from the Bet Knesset at 9:30?"

"That works." Arik smiled.

***

Dahlia and Penny wandered about, taking in the night air.

"Do you like him?" Penny asked.

"I think so. At least enough to want to find out more about him. He's sweet and unassuming . . . but I still get the feeling that there's more to him than meets the eye. I find that a major turn-on, if you must know. . . Underneath the smile and friendliness, I sense something else. I can't put my finger on it, but it's like there's more that he's not telling. Like, why would he come all the way here from LA, by himself, without any friends? Maybe he doesn't have many friends. Maybe that's why he has that faraway look sometimes."

***

An hour later, Dahlia walked into the Bet Knesset and sat at a short distance from the Arik and Eliezer, who were totally immersed in an animated discussion of a point of Talmudic law.

Eliezer looked up at the clock. "9:30 already? Wow! The time just flew by."

Arik looked up and saw Dahlia standing there smiling, looking absolutely radiant in her Shabbat finery and with her long, flowing blonde hair. His breath caught in his throat.

Once outside, Arik picked up Eliezer in his wheelchair, lifted him overhead, and ran down the stairs.

"Wheee!"

When he had put down the wheelchair, Arik looked at Dahlia and said, "He loves that."

"Apparently!" Dahlia laughed. "Damn, you're strong!"

After they left Eliezer at his home, the two were finally alone. A fresh, cool breeze was blowing down the dark dirt road, and Dahlia fastened her sweater.

Arik gazed at her. "So, what's a nice girl like you doing in a place like this?"

"Well, to tell you the truth, I'd rather be back in Israel, where most of my friends are. But my dad has been stationed here since the Six-Day War. Before that, he was ambassador to France. Our family commuted back and forth from Israel to Paris. My mother insisted, though, that we stay in Israel during the school year. She felt that it would be a better place to grow up than in France. Once he became ambassador here, we all came over, but we fly back and forth all the time anyway.

"There are perks to his job, though. In Washington, I get to socialize with my Israeli friends. They're so much more physical and cooler than teenagers here.

Washington is an okay place to live. They have a very nice Jewish community and a pretty sophisticated crowd at Adas Israel, the shul my family goes to. We have lots of parties at the residence and the embassy, and it's pretty exciting to meet all those senators, congressmen, philanthropists, and diplomats from all over the world. I even got to shake hands with President Johnson once when the Prime Minister, Mr. Eshkol, came over to negotiate the deal for Phantom jets for Israel. Eshkol picked my dad to be ambassador to the U.S., and after he passed away in February Golda Meir kept him on here."

"Very cool," Arik said. "Where do you go to school?"

"The Jewish Academy of Greater Washington. At home, we're what they call Masorti in Israel. It's not really conservative, so we keep Shabbat, holidays, kosher, and all that. My coming here to camp is my parent's idea, not mine. I'd rather go to Europe or back to Israel for the summer, but my dad insists that I have better Zionist exposure here than in Tel Aviv, believe it or not. Anyway, I don't agree. To me, Camp Moshava is fantasy Zionism. It's like they're in some kind of time warp and think that every summer it's 1948. Modern Israel is so much more than a bunch of gun-toting kibbutzniks wearing khaki shorts, sandals, and army shirts, dancing horas in the fields. Israel is now a very complicated society, with people from a hundred different countries each with their own culture. Plus, everyone is trying to imitate Americans, and they're crazy about Elvis. The place is crawling with discotheques.

"But how about you? What are you doing here in Pennsylvania when you could have just as easily gone to Moshava in LA?"

"Long story," Arik said. "I've been in LA my whole life. I mean, I've done some traveling—but just to Hawaii and Mexico and stuff. This may sound corny, but I think I needed to get away from LA to discover my Judaism and possibly my Zionism, to see if there really is a place for me in it. The Jewish kids in LA are fairly provincial and laid-back. They're friendly enough to me, but since they all live together in the same area—either in Beverly Hills or the Valley—they pretty much live in their own cliques. I live in a non-Jewish neighborhood, and I don't socialize with them outside of school, on the weekends, mainly Shabbat, which is when most of the socializing happens. The bottom line is I don't feel at home in LA, not really. And I don't see myself living there in the future."

"Where do you want to live?" Dahlia asked.

"I've considered living in Israel, but since I've never been there it's probably a bit premature to decide."

"I've noticed you speak fluent Hebrew to the Israeli counselors. For someone who's never been to Israel, how do you speak like an Israeli? Jewish kids who go to day school in the States speak Hebrew poorly and with a thick American accent."

"Well, to make a long story short, my parents are Israeli and they moved here in 1952, when I was six months old. My dad lost a leg in 1948 in the fighting around Jerusalem. . . Not able to make a living in Israel and get good care for his stump, he joined my uncle in business. Both my dad and uncle are Buchenwald Concentration Camp survivors. Before the War, my dad's name was Wolf Myerowitz, and he was a well-known middleweight boxer. Other family members have told me he was as strong as an ox in his youth, and in 1938 he became a boxing champion in his weight class in Poland. My dad survived the camps because one of the SS officers was a boxing fan and recognized him. The Germans staged boxing matches among the inmates several times a week. The fighting was like gladiators in ancient Rome. The loser of the match went to the gas chambers. My dad simply never lost.

"He snuck out of the Bergen-Belsen DP camp in 1946 and got to Israel by illegal immigration, Aliyah Bet, by hiding in the hold of a fishing boat, up to his neck in rotting fish, to get through the British blockade. He jumped off the boat, at night, at Atlit on the Northern coast of Palestine and immediately joined the Palmach shock troops. I never saw him as a strong man, though. A broken shell of an amputee is all I've ever seen. He's been helping my uncle in the building supply business ever since, sort of."

"I guess that explains your athleticism. You're quite the gymnast and kung fu practitioner, if that's what that is," Dahlia said.

"How do you know that?" Arik smiled shyly.

Dahlia looked embarrassed at having been caught spying. "Penny and I go running at 4:30 every morning. We do about eight kilometers before everyone else wakes up; otherwise, we'd atrophy with the exercise program here. Well, the gym is on our path, so occasionally we take a break and watch you work out." She giggled.

"Why, you little sneaks!" Arik laughed. "Why didn't you come in and say hello?"

"We didn't want to disturb your workout. You look so intense."

"What about your parents?" Arik asked.

"Well, before the War, my mom lived in Vienna. She was from a well-to-do family, and she was a track and field star in high school. She might have competed nationally, but the Nazis came in during the Anschluss, in 1938, and she wasn't allowed to compete anymore. After the War started, she was sent to the Theresienstadt camp. She was there for three years.

"Then the oddest thing happened. The Germans had developed a program called Lebensborn, which was based on the concept that blonde Jewish girls could be integrated into the Third Reich, because of their Aryan features, and so be 'rehabilitated.' My mom is blue-eyed and blonde, so she was removed from the camp and was placed with a German family in Munich until the end of the War.

"She was one of the lucky ones. After the War, she was taken to Palestine, where she lived with her uncle and aunt, who had moved to Palestine in the 1920s, since none of her family had survived. My Omah Liesel and Opah Alfred moved to Antwerp to pursue the diamond trade after Israel became independent. In 1947, my mom joined the Haganah, where she met my dad. My dad's family came to Palestine in the Second Aliyah, at the turn of the century, and he was born in Kibbutz Hagoshrim in the Galil."

"I guess that's where you got your blonde hair," Arik said. "You don't look like a typical Israeli."

"What does a typical Israeli look like?"

"I don't know, but not blonde like you."

"Now you're being silly," Dahlia said.

They talked for hours, and they lost track of the time. By the time they checked their watches, it was 1:30 a.m.

"Oh, crap!" Arik said. "We'd better get back. We've missed curfew!"

Arik walked Dahlia back to her bunk in silence. Her hand brushed his very lightly, and he took it.

"I've had a great time tonight," Dahlia said. In the glow of the bunk lights, she looked straight into Arik's eyes and smiled.

"Me too!" Arik said, feeling an electric shock surge through him. "Good night, Dahlia. See you tomorrow."

"Shabbat Shalom!" Dahlia smiled and walked into her bunk.

When she entered the dark recesses of the room, everyone seemed asleep. She tiptoed to her bed and got ready to go to sleep.

"Dahlita," Penny whispered, "¿Como estuvo?" (How was it?)

Dahlia whispered back, "Él es tan increíblemente dulce y considerado. Nunca he conocido a nadie como él. Se puede ver que él es muy inteligente y de mente abierta. Él puede ser gracioso y muy serio al mismo tiempo. Él tiene esta seriedad que es rara en alguien de nuestra edad, como si fuera mucho mayor que nosotros. Da la sensacion de que esa madurez nace de una gran tristeza interior. Él parece vulnerable y solo." (He is so incredibly sweet and considerate. I've never met anyone like him. You can see that he is very smart and open-minded. He can be silly and serious at the same time. He has this seriousness that is rare for someone our age, as if he were much older than us. I get the sense that his maturity comes from a great inner sadness. He seems vulnerable and lonely.)

"¿Cómo lo sabes?" (How do you figure?)

"Él es el hijo único de un héroe de guerra Israelí amputado. Su familia no tiene un centavo a su nombre, por lo que necesitan dádivas de su tío. Creo que incluso están apoyados en la seguridad social. Él no parece tener amigos judíos en Los Ángeles tampoco. Él ni siquiera vive en un barrio judío." (He is the only son of an Israeli war hero amputee. His family doesn't have a penny to its name, so they need handouts from his uncle. I think they're on welfare. He doesn't seem to have Jewish friends in LA either. He doesn't even live in a Jewish neighborhood.)

"Eso es tan raro! Los veteranos Israelíes no reciben apoyo a la discapacidad de por vida? ¿Por qué iba a tener que vivir así? En segundo lugar, cómo en el mundo llegó hasta aquí? Este lugar bien podría ser en la luna para él.

Tantas preguntas sin respuesta ... ¿Seguro que quieres mezclarte con este chico? Creo que puedes estar recibiendo demasiado involucrado con él." (That is so weird! Do not Israeli veterans receive lifelong disability support? Why would he have to live like that? Second, how in the world did he get here? This place might as well be on the moon for him. So many unanswered questions ... Are you sure that you want to get mixed up with this guy? I think that you may be getting in over your head.)

"Tienes razón, por supuesto. Eso es lo que mi cabeza me está diciendo. Estoy un poco asustada, pero él me tocó la mano caminando a casa esta noche, y mi corazón se salto un latido. Me sentí momentáneamente mareada. Sólo quiero estar con él—" (You're right, of course. That's what my head is telling me. I'm a little scared, but he touched my hand walking home tonight, and my heart skipped a beat. I felt momentarily dizzy. I just want to be with him—)

"¡Oh, mi!" (Oh, my!) Penny teased. "Creo que mi novia se está cayendo por alguien. Bueno, todo lo que se puedes hacer ahora es dejar que esta cosa jugar fuera. El campamento es un lugar muy seguro para hacer esto. Nunca has tenido ojos para nadie más por aquí. Muchas cosas pueden pasar en seis semanas." (I think that my friend is falling for somebody. Well, all that you can do now is let this thing play out. Camp is a very safe place to do this. You have never had eyes for anyone else around here. A lot can happen in six weeks.)

"Gracias. Buenas noches, Paapi!" (Goodnight, Paapi!)

"Buenas noches, Penita!" (Goodnight, Penita!)

Dahlia lay wide awake for another hour, her mind racing.

As Arik walked back to his bunk in the dark, his head was filled with thoughts of Dahlia. First, she was Israeli. But beyond that, she came from such a different world than he did. She was a child of privilege, with her parents providing not only every creature comfort but also a high-flying jet-setting social life. It was odd that she should land here. She was clearly spoiled, but she didn't appear arrogant or snobbish. Most of the guys thought her aloof and distant, but that was because none of them appeared to have attracted her interest; to them, she seemed friendly enough but also always seemed to have something better to do. But she laughed easily and had a zany sense of humor. Arik sensed, underneath it all, an inner strength of will and determination that could drive her parents mad if they ever crossed her. So, there she was: sexy, smart, good-natured, and beautiful. The complete package. Then again, he had felt the same way about Christine.

He felt a sudden shudder go through him. Dahlia was the first girl he had been with since Christine. How would he feel if things with Dahlia didn't pan out? He resolved to keep his powder dry and protect his feelings. But part of him already knew that he would be unable to do so.

***

The next several days were the happiest that Arik could remember. He had always been cynical of love songs, but now they seemed to be whispering in his ear, just for him to hear. Is love visiting as an ephemeral ghost to tease me? Will I ever be able to stretch out my arms to capture and embrace the love ghost? This lovely ghost, or angel, had suddenly descended upon him, and all perception seemed different—brighter and more hopeful.

He and Dahlia spent a blissful, sunny afternoon walking along the wooded running trail.

"I've never seen this place during full daylight," Dahlia said. "It's really beautiful and quiet here. Nothing but the distant call of birds in flight."

Arik stared at her. The light between the trees flickered through her golden hair, and the warm, gentle breeze animated it, giving it a life of its own. He gazed into her eyes. They were steel gray with just a hint of blue. They radiated sophistication and warmth.

The pair held hands.

"What are you looking at, young man?" Dahlia asked.

"Don't know." Arik leaned over and gave her a gentle kiss on the cheek. She had the faintest fragrance of lavender.

Dahlia smiled and looked at him.

"Who are you, Arik? And how did you parachute into my life like this? I swore that I would never get involved with anyone in camp, and here you come sneaking around and stealing my heart!"

They found a grassy clearing in the woods and sat down.

"So, Dahlia," Arik said, "you're Israel's tennis champ at just sixteen?"

"Not such a big deal,'" Dahlia said. "It's in the junior division. My family has always been involved in sports. After the state of Israel came into being, my mom was demobilized from the Haganah. She was one of the founders of the Orde Wingate Institute, named after one of the few sympathetic British officers who helped us before the War of Independence and helped set up the Palmach.

"She was an excellent example to the young athletes, because she brought with her the no-nonsense attitude from Vienna. She eventually headed up the Institute and developed the Israeli Olympic team, along with several other diehards. She's now on the board, because we spend so much time out of Israel that she can't be involved in the day-to-day operations anymore."

"I never realized tennis was even played in Israel. You never hear about it," Arik said.

"Tennis has been in Israel for a long time. It was brought by the British in the 1920s, but it didn't gain popularity among Israelis until the late 50s. Herzliya, where I live, is the center of competitive tennis in Israel. I was introduced to it at a very young age, and I never stopped. Many international tennis celebrities visit Israel over Arab objections. It may be a Christian interest, but while they are there they seek out the local tennis community and play exhibition matches with the locals."

"So, is that how you met Billie Jean King?"

"I was their golden girl when Billie Jean King came to town last February. I got to play with her, and we really hit it off. There were many photo ops and receptions, and I got to go to all of them. She's always trying to promote the game, so when I asked her whether she'd be interested in coming here to camp, she said yes, depending on her schedule. Even knowing her interest, I was still so surprised! Then she called me in early June and told me that it was a go, so here we are."

"That's great," Arik said. "Perhaps I should get someone from the LA Lakers to do an exhibition clinic here at camp?"

"Ha ha! Very funny, Arik." Dahlia laughed.

"Tell me something, Dahlia. Do beautiful girls know how beautiful they are?"

"Well, I think that every girl should always try to look her best with whatever gifts she was born with."

"Bravo, Gloria Steinem. But, seriously, do you have any clue what effect you have on people around you, especially guys?"

"Stop it. Really?"

"You turn guys' heads wherever you go. They're mostly staring at your butt, though." Arik smirked.

Dahlia blushed deeply. "That's disgusting, Arik. Is that what you do, too?"

"I'm sorry I embarrassed you."

"No, don't be silly. But you don't seem like a flatterer."

"I'm not trying to flatter you, Dahlia, but you are extremely attractive. And that's a fact, not flattery."

Dahlia leaned over, caressed Arik's chin, and kissed his nose.

"So, Arik, now it's your turn. Tell me about kung fu."

"Well, kung fu is a Chinese martial art. Its recorded history dates back to around 525 AD, but it wasn't popularized in the United States until about eight years ago, by Bruce Lee, when it became known as Jeet Kune Do. It's sort of a hybrid system, and its philosophy centers on combat realism without a set or fixed movement. It has some classic elements like kicking, punching, trapping, and grappling, but the movements flow smoothly between them. The concept is to not telegraph your moves so that your opponent doesn't realize where your attack is coming from. It also involves intercepting your opponent's attack at the same time you launch your own so that your opponent is still busy trying to attack you and isn't thinking defense. That's when you get them. The decisions are made on the spot during live combat, and the approach allows you to react with lightning speed.

"Training includes weight training, running, yoga-style stretching, and fencing and boxing techniques . . . which explains my interest in gymnastics. Bruce Lee trained his disciples primarily in Oakland, but his main student, Dan Inosanto, moved to the LA area about three years ago. I've studied traditional karate since I was eight, and since then I've studied with Inosanto at his academy in Marina Del Ray. I had to unlearn a bit of what I had mastered to begin training with him.

"I'm probably going on too long, but I want you to understand that there's so much more to kung fu than the fighting and acrobatic movements you see in Bruce Lee movies. Kung fu—and Jeet Kune Do, for that matter—are grounded in the philosophy of Taoism. Taoists seek to live in harmony with the Tao, the natural forces that govern the world. Kung fu aims to keep us in harmony and balance. Meditation and deep introspection is a big part of kung fu practice.

"Does kung fu have belts, like judo and karate?" Dahlia asked.

"Originally, it didn't, but recently the powers that be felt it was necessary to allow disciples to know how far they've come in the art, both physically and spiritually, so a belt system was instituted, similar to karate."

"So, are you a black belt?" Dahlia asked.

"I'm a first-level master, which is sort of like a third-degree black belt in karate," Arik said in an almost whisper as he stared at the ground, playing with a blade of grass.

Dahlia stared at him for a moment, admiring his unassuming humility.

"Okay. . . . That explains some things but not everything. Like, how did you learn to play basketball like that? And how did you get involved with the Negros? They certainly know how to play better than the white guys. The whole game of basketball has changed over the past ten years, because of them."

"It's a good thing none of them are here to hear you call them that," Arik said. "They're very sensitive about things like that these days. They literally came from nothing and have had a belly full of people calling them Negros, Niggers, Boy, and other terrible names. They just want to be called black people or Afro-Americans.

"Most of the black people in California came from the South, after World War II, in search of a better life. Where they came from, not only were they dirt poor but they had to drink from separate water fountains, use segregated toilets, and couldn't eat out in a restaurant or even sit on a park bench that was for 'whites only.' Their churches got burned to the ground while white people could commit any crime against them—even rape or murder—and get away with it. It's really not much different from what our parents and grandparents went through in Poland and Austria.

"Many black people left the South in search of a new life. Some went up north, while others went out west, to California, which was considered the land of opportunity and riches. Hollywood played a role in creating that myth. But it didn't matter where they started. They always had to work as domestics, janitors, and manual laborers. Even in California, they became segregated into the poorest neighborhoods, like Watts and Compton where my friends live. In fact, just a few years ago, because the black community has so little political power, the jerks in the state government in Sacramento decided to lay down the San Diego Freeway right through the neighborhood, tearing it in half.

"So, how about you, Dahlia? Do you have any contact with black people in Washington? There are some black slums only a few blocks from the White House."

"I must say I have had very little to do with them," Dahlia said. "We have a black cook, Thelma, at the residence, and our house cleaners are black."

"That's my point exactly. Have you ever actually sat down and spoken to any of them, apart from asking 'What's for dinner?' or 'Where are my shoes?'"

Dahlia blushed.

"I don't want to sound mean. I'm just trying to make a point. I didn't expect you would have, because most white people don't, even though it's already 1969, years after all the civil rights marches. Blacks just aren't seen as people like you and me, with hopes, dreams, fears, and needs. They're looked upon as objects to either fear, order around, deride, or—worst—ignore. Though I came to it entirely by accident, I feel more at home with my black 'family' than with other Jews."

"You're right, Arik, but I'm in a unique situation. I live here and act like an American, but all that is going to change very soon. When I'm done with high school here, I'm going back home to the Israeli Army. And, after that, who knows where I'll be."

"But don't you see? Discrimination isn't just about the white-black thing here. You have it in Israel, too. You have the Sephardim hating the Ashkenazim. The secular Israelis hate the religious crowd. And Israelis, in general, treat the Arabs like crap, too."

"It's not so simple in Israel, Arik. You've never been there. There are many historical reasons for the animosity among Jews, and we'd get along a lot better with the Arabs if they weren't constantly trying to kill us. They would have destroyed us and pushed us into the sea in '67 if they'd had the chance."

"Well, how would you feel if some outsider came in and took away your land? Wasn't Herzliya built on top of the ruins of some Arab village?"

"You've been reading Arab propaganda. Israel would have been very tiny indeed if the Arabs had accepted the UN resolution in 1947, and we could have lived side by side, with them, in peace. How can we help it that they constantly try to attack us and we beat them and each time we end up with more land? I'm surprised you speak this way, with what your family has been through."

"I'm just wondering if it was all worth it. That's all," Arik murmured.

They spoke for another hour and then made it back to camp just in time for dinner.

That night, the camp had a massive game of capture the flag, followed by a bonfire and singing with guitars. Arik sat close to Dahlia and watched the light from the flames dancing on her face and hair.

"It all feels different somehow, with you near," Arik whispered.

Dahlia nodded and smiled.

Back at the bunk, Arik got some ribbing from his bunkmates.

"Hey, Arik! I heard you're going out with Dahlia Gilad! How'd you ever land that fine piece of ass nobody has ever been able to get to?" Rubin asked.

"I guess she just adores my outstanding wit and personality," Arik kidded.

"More likely, she's fallen for 'the basketball hero,'" Yossie said.

"Possibly," Arik said, "but that will get you only so far. It's an intro, but if you're no good for each other it won't last. Look at all these pro athletes who get married to hot women. They get divorced after a year, when their wives discover they've been screwing around with somebody else."

"Lights out," their counselor bellowed.

Arik snuck in one more comment: "We'll see how this summer ends. That's what's important!"

The next morning, at breakfast, Coach walked over to Arik. "You know, Arik, I've given a lot of thought to what you said, and I do think it would be a good idea for you to teach the younger boys how to play basketball. You can be my unofficial assistant. Eidah Aleph has basketball at 10 a.m. in the gym. I've already spoken to the head of Mach Hach, and he's okay with you being there. Are you in?"

"Definitely! Can I get Yossie and Heshie to help?"

Coach nodded.

"You should come watch!" Arik continued excitedly. "I've spent some time at Lakers' practices while I was in the NBA summer league, and I picked up a few tips."

***

When the campers arrived at the gym, they found that the baskets had been lowered by one third. Arik looked like a towering giant next to the ten-year-olds. Dressed in a T-shirt and navy-blue warm-up pants, with his massive, suntanned biceps coming out of his sleeves, and wearing a whistle around his neck, he looked every bit the gym teacher.

Arik stood in the middle of the gym and blew his whistle.

"Okay, everybody, gather 'round at half-court," Arik called out.

The ten-year-olds gathered around him in a circle, like so many little goslings, none standing higher than Arik's waist.

"How many of you want to learn how to play basketball like I did?"

Eighteen little hands went up.

"Okay, then. In that case, you have to open your eyes and ears and minds to what we're going to teach you. And that means paying attention to what we're doing, what I'm saying—and no complaining!

"First of all, you have to start with a different mind-set than what you see the older guys do around here. Everybody tries to show the world that they're a basketball superstar. That's not the way they play in college or the pros. Basketball is a team sport, and the team that plays like a team is the one that wins. A big part of that is to play unselfishly and see what your teammates are doing on the court. You set up plays for them instead of just going up for the 'chuck' so you can impress everyone with your scoring stats. Now, I'm going to teach you the basics, because without those foundations you can't go any farther. Who knows what I mean when I say, 'the basics'?"

Hands went up and a few of the boys shouted out answers.

"Dribbling!"

"Passing!"

"Shooting!"

"Setting a pick!"

"Very good," Arik said, "but there two things even more basic. Anyone?"

After a moment of silence, Arik said simply, "Fitness and sportsmanship!"

He got some quizzical looks from the boys.

"A big part of playing the game is running back and forth on the court, especially when you're playing full-court. I've seen many games where a team's game falls apart in the second half simply because they're running out of steam. So, we're going to start every practice session like we're training for the playoffs. We'll run five times around the court at a preset pace, not faster or slower. There will be guys who are more fit and some who are less fit. We'll start with a slower pace and then pick it up.

"Remember: We're all on the same team, and I'll bench anybody who makes fun of the way someone else plays. For example, I never want to hear anyone say to someone else, 'You suck.'

"Now, everyone gather 'round. Put your hands inside the circle, and yell out, 'Go, team!'"

"Go, team!" the boys yelled.

With that, the boys started running around the perimeter of the gym. Arik blew the whistle in a cadence.

"Everybody at the same speed!" Arik called out.

Some fell back, and he allowed them to rest a lap before joining the rest.

At the conclusion of the sprints, everyone collapsed in a heap.

"Now, everybody to half-court! There are three offensive skills that Yossie, Heshie, and I want to teach you. You mentioned these earlier: passing, dribbling, and shooting. We're going to divide you up into three squads of six. Every skill has several components, and you'll have fifteen minutes to learn the skill before you rotate through to the next skill station. After the three skill stations, you'll get a break. Then we'll do it all again. Constant motion for two 45-minute segments. Got it?"

The teenagers divided the boys into squads. They already had set up stations with small orange cones that simulated passing lanes, shooting positions, and dribbling zones. The boys were taught the shooter's mind-set, the correct way to stand and position their hands for shooting, and visualizing the ball going into the hoop. The other squads were taken through ball handling skills and stationary and on-the-run passing. They were drilled on how to play as a team and how to develop court awareness. They did lay-up drills and learned the basics of man-to-man and zone defense. By the break, all the boys were out of breath and gulping down mouthfuls of water.

Sometime during the 45-minute segment, Coach had come out of his office to observe the practice. He was smiling broadly at the scene of completely organized chaos. Arik, Yossie, and Heshie were in total control of the boys.

Dahlia and Penny stopped by the gym's door and peered in.

"Okay, guys! Time to do it all again! Anyone want to quit?" Arik asked. Nobody raised a hand.

"Let's go, then!"

And off they went.

Arik was so good with the little kids. He was strict and disciplined, but he was so patient and had such a gentle manner about him that he had the boys eating out of his hand. And what was more was they appeared totally absorbed in what he was teaching them. Dahlia shivered with delight.

"Look, Dahlia," Penny said, "the kids just love him!"

"I see that! He's like the pied piper. He gets his point across in such a calm manner that he teaches without any disciplinary problems."

"I think you got yourself a keeper," Penny said.

"I think so. Speaking of which, how did it go Friday night with Richard? I forgot to ask you."

"He was so sweet. He suffers from a lack of confidence, because of all the bullying he has suffered over the years from those two-dimensional, knuckleheaded, arrogant jocks. He came up to me after dinner and practically stammered out an invitation to walk. When I said yes, he seemed genuinely startled! But his nervousness faded quickly when we started to talk. I think I put him at ease. And then I found out that he is absolutely brilliant! He is both worldly and well-read. He functions at a postgraduate level in math and physics, and he has a very deep knowledge of computer science. He talked about a future when computers will be in every home and even small enough to hold in the palm of our hands eventually. Did you know that the military and NASA have computers that can talk to each other? I told him that is like science fiction, but he called it computer networking and said that one day millions of computers will be part of a global network that will share information and fundamentally change the way people live. He said it will be the biggest change in human history, since the invention of the printing press. It was so fascinating listening to him that I did not notice the time passing. So, to make a long story short, yes, I like him."

Dahlia smiled.

***

Tuesday came, and all was ready for the tennis day. The camp had a bright, festive atmosphere. The weather was perfect: There wasn't a cloud in the sky, and the air was crisp and clean at 80 degrees. When Billie Jean King's limo pulled into the front parking lot, a crowd of campers and staff was there to greet her. A huge hand-painted sign read, WELCOME TO CAMP MOSHAVA, BILLIE JEAN!

Dahlia, Effie, and the senior camp staff members greeted Billie Jean, shaking hands, and then escorted her and her entourage to the newly renovated and groomed tennis center. The new green fencing and painted lines shone to perfection.

The bleachers filled, and the crowd came to order with the singing of the "Star-Spangled Banner" and "Hatikvah." Arik sat next to Dahlia, who had taken the opportunity to wear her usual tennis whites rather than the standard below-knee-length skirt, much to the delight of the male campers. A judge's tower stood at the side of the net opposite the bleachers.

Effie stood at the podium and officially welcomed Billie Jean to Camp Moshava. "I and my staff have worked tirelessly toward the realization of this day . . ."

Arik whispered to Dahlia, "Wow! He's either living in a dream world or thinks that we are. What a piece of work!"

Then Billie Jean went to the podium to say a few words. "Today's event is the product of several months of planning between my staff and your Dahlia Gilad. You may or may not know that Dahlia is the Israeli junior tennis champion. Tennis in Israel is relatively new, but it is growing in popularity. Visiting Israel was a deeply impressive time for me. I was greatly moved by their great sense of moxie and drive. I look forward to seeing Israeli women reach a high level of competitiveness in the international tennis scene. I love reaching out to young people to promote this great game, and I sincerely hope that the wonderful program we have planned for you today will leave a lasting impression on you, especially on you younger campers, and encourage you to play the type of tennis that will provide you with a lifetime of pleasure. Who knows? Perhaps a future Wimbledon champion is sitting here among you." She smiled and returned to her seat.

Effie returned to the podium. "We're going to start with what should be an exciting exhibition set featuring Billie Jean and Dahlia. Let's give them both a round of applause."

There were applause and cheers, which Effie quickly quieted down. "After that, we'll have a round-robin clinic and tournament. We have four courts, and we'll have doubles sets on each court. Each Eidah, boys and girls will get a court, and each foursome will play sets to the best of five games. Billie Jean will give pointers on swing technique, course presence, and strategy. The two winners from each Eidah will play each other in a best-of-five-games final set. We'll conclude with a men's singles set, followed by an awards ceremony."

Dahlia whispered to Arik, "Here we go!"

"Break a leg, sweet cheeks."

When Dahlia went up to play, the crowd cheered—too loudly for Effie to quiet. She played with style and aggressiveness and matched Billie Jean stroke for stroke. Although the outcome was never in doubt, they put on a good-natured performance that delighted the crowd. At the end of the set, they hugged and posed for photographs.

The round-robin was equally entertaining. Billie Jean, Effie, and Dahlia spread out and supervised all the sets. Dahlia was impressed at Billie Jean's patience with the kids and her sense of fun. Her enthusiasm was absolutely infectious. The finals were played on court one, in front of the packed bleachers. Billie Jean, with a microphone in her hand, sat in the judge's chair at midcourt. Trophies were awarded to the winning players.

Finally, Billie Jean announced, "We'll conclude our program with the men's singles set. Effie will pick an opponent to play a full set against. Effie?"

Effie stood up and announced, "I will play our superstar athlete, Arik Meir. Come on down, Arik!"

The crowd cheered for Arik even as he remained seated, uneasily, in the stands.

Dahlia whispered, "Arik, do you even know how to play tennis? Did you know about this in advance?"

"I play some tennis, but this is a total surprise. I think he's trying to humiliate me, in public, on his terms."

"Do you think it's because of the way you spoke to him the other day when we were working on the courts?" Dahlia asked.

"I think it has nothing to do with me and everything to do with you!" Arik gave Dahlia a knowing look.

Dahlia shook her head and glared in Effie's direction.

Arik went down to the court, and play began.

Arik played with an easy, relaxed manner. His movements were smooth and fluid, and he appeared to be in no rush. Effie played with real intensity, and he was technically overpowering. Arik matched him, but he appeared to be a step slow and his ground strokes lacked speed. Although he had good control, his shots made him easy prey for Effie's onslaught. In the end, Effie won 6-3.

Effie went up to the podium. He thanked Billie Jean for coming to camp and gave her a sterling silver menorah with a Star of David on top as a token of thanks. He declared the program at an end.

Billie Jean went up to Dahlia and thanked her for having hosted the event. "I had a marvelous time. I hope everyone else did, too, and got something out of it." Billie Jean said.

"The event was outstanding. I so appreciate your coming," Dahlia said.

Billie Jean added, "Did you notice anything odd about the men's set?"

"How so?"

"That fellow who played the tennis pro looked like he had a great deal of talent but either wasn't interested in the game or was deliberately letting the pro win. Why would he do that in front of the whole crowd at the marquee event of the day? He should have played his heart out."

"I noticed the same thing," Dahlia said. "He tends to do that, with annoying regularity. He can be hard to understand sometimes."

After the ceremony and good-byes, Dahlia found Arik.

"Congratulations on a fantastic event. You were amazing today!" Arik beamed at her.

"What was the meaning of your performance today?" Dahlia asked. "You made a complete fool of yourself in front of everyone."

"Why do you say that?"

"Because you and I both know you threw that game. You let that asshole beat you in front of the whole camp! Why did you do that? Even Billie Jean noticed and thought it was odd."

"Okay, well, if you want to talk about that, hear me out. First of all, I already told you I didn't come to camp to play sports. It's just being thrust on me, all the time, for reasons that aren't clear to me. I have nothing to prove to anyone, so I don't give a damn if Effie beats me or not. But the real reason is this: How would it look if I beat the tennis pro? He's supposed to be the best tennis player in the camp. That's why they hired him. Now, if I went and made him look like a chump, he'd have to pack up and go home. Wouldn't he? Then I'd have to be the tennis pro, something I have absolutely no interest in. Me? I'm still good." Arik smiled like a Cheshire cat.

"So, Rod Laver, how good a tennis player are you really?" Dahlia smirked slyly.

"Let's just say I'm good enough to beat you." Arik yawned.

"In your dreams, big shot. I can kick your sorry ass!" Dahlia smiled.

"Only one way to find out."

"Let's go! Right now, under the lights!"

"Not now," Arik said. "Tomorrow at 4:30 a.m. We're both up, anyway. Penny can watch if she's wants to."

***

Early the next morning, Arik was already waiting on the bleachers when Dahlia arrived. She looked so fetching in her tennis whites and short skirt that he didn't know whether to play against her or take her in his arms.

Dahlia served first. Arik answered her stroke for stroke but maintained a slow, even stride.

"Damn it, Arik! You're so frustrating! Will you please just play without screwing around?"

"You're not beating me, so what difference does it make?"

"I can't play, because you're not. You're distracting me."

"Oh, nice. I'm glad," Arik teased.

"Play!" Dahlia commanded.

"Okay. Here goes."

Arik stood at the service line, with Dahlia at the opposite end of the court. Arik tossed the ball into the air and then brought the racquet down on it with such force that a loud twang reverberated through the cold, moist morning air. The ball rocketed directly toward Dahlia and, before she could react, hit her directly in the forehead. She recoiled, and Arik immediately bounded over the net.

"I'm so sorry, Dahlia! Are you okay?"

Dahlia looked at him with dark determination. "Game on! I'll make you regret that. Now, play!"

Arik served again. This time Dahlia was ready. She returned the ball with full force and deadly accuracy. For the next ninety minutes, they played each other into exhaustion, clearly evenly matched. Furious ground strokes and overhead lobs, backhands, and forehands were exchanged in devastatingly long volleys, with each unable to break the other's serve.

At 6-6, they decided to play a tiebreaker until 9. Dahlia finally prevailed, at 9-8, after an excruciatingly long final volley. Afterward, she and Arik met at the net. They both were red-faced, out of breath, and covered in sweat.

"I told you I'd kick your ass." Dahlia puffed.

"Yeah, you really whooped me. Wow! I never stood a chance," Arik answered sarcastically. "But, my sweet, there's always tomorrow."

"Yes, there will be. Arik Meir, I like you." Dahlia's gray eyes sparkled.

"What's not to like?" Arik replied. He gripped his chin. "Look at this cute face."

Dahlia shook her head, and they both laughed.

They played every morning for several days, alternating so that Dahlia could still get in her runs with Penny. She didn't want to simply drop her best friend. They tried kept their budding relationship low-key so that it wouldn't distract them from camp activities, but they still took every opportunity to meet.

Arik was happier than he had ever been.

***

By this time, Arik was studying with Eliezer twice a week. With their additional time, they varied the works of Jewish philosophy that they studied. It seemed to Arik that no matter which text they chose, Eliezer had total command of it.

Arik read the works of Rav Kook and began to understand more about the attraction to Israel. He also found himself connecting on a deeper level with the evening camp songs. In fact, he enjoyed all of the night activities, but that may have been because they were always coed, which meant he didn't have to steal away to speak to Dahlia.

The next Friday night, after they had returned Eliezer to his home, Arik and Dahlia walked for hours. They finally settled on the new tennis bleachers—the ones they had worked so hard to construct.

Arik saw her face in the moonlight and suddenly blurted out, "Dahlia, I love you."

Dahlia gently caressed his face. "I love you, too! I don't know why, but I feel so at ease with you, and I find myself missing you when you aren't around. I know I light up when I do see you. It's like an involuntary reaction. I almost feel like I can't help myself!

"I never met a Jewish girl like you before."

"What's that supposed to mean?"

"Well, I mean . . . isn't it obvious you and Penny are completely different than the others."

"Is that why you like me? Because I'm different?"

"No. I feel like you fill a void in my soul. Like a key that fits a lock perfectly, you open a door to so many possibilities. For the longest time, I've felt lonely even when I'm in a crowd. It's a deep ache that never seems to go away. My life has been so complicated. Being with you makes my life seem hopeful somehow."

"And I want to hear about all of that. I want to know you and love you," Dahlia said.

Arik leaned over and kissed her.

Soon, it was time for Arik to walk Dahlia back to her bunk. They held hands in an easy, free manner.

"I'll see you tomorrow. Sleep tight," Arik whispered.

"You too!" Dahlia smiled.

***

Dahlia walked into her bunk. It was late, and she expected everyone to be asleep, but instead she found Shirah sitting on the edge of her bed.

"Dahlia, I have to talk to you," Shirah said.

"Can't this wait until tomorrow?"

"No!" Shirah whispered intensely.

"Why not? What is it?"

"It's about Arik, things you ought to know. Let's go outside."

Penny perked up. "I am not asleep," she said, "and I am coming with you."

"I'm not sure that's such a great idea," Shirah said.

Dahlia said, "Anything that I know, Penny should know, too."

"Okay. You asked for it."

They left the bunk and walked down the gravel path until they were out of earshot.

"Now, what can't wait until tomorrow, Shirah?" Dahlia asked impatiently.

"How much do you know about Arik?"

"I think I know a lot," Dahlia said.

"I mean, about his past, his life in LA, why he's really here."

"What in the world are you talking about?"

"I got a letter from my cousin Bracha after I called her and told her Arik was here at camp. She lives in LA. She included this newspaper clipping. Read the letter and the clipping. I'm doing this for your own good, Dahlia."

Dahlia and Penny read the letter and the clipping. Dahlia nearly fell backward, stunned and not knowing what to say.

Penny asked Shirah, "Have you shown this to anyone or told anyone about this?"

"No, not yet. I wanted to show it to—"

"If you even breathe a word of this to anyone, I will beat you into a coma and dump your body in the woods for the bears to eat. Do I make myself perfectly clear?" Penny asked.

"Y-y-yes," Shirah stammered.

"Now, leave us alone, Shirah. Give me the letter and the clipping, and go back to the bunk," Penny spoke in an even, quiet tone that indicated that she meant business.

Shirah did as she was told.

Penny and Dahlia sat by the edge of the path. It was 1 a.m.

"I am sure that there is a reasonable explanation for this, Dahlia. We will get to the bottom of it."

Dahlia was sitting cross-legged, with her face in her hands, crying softly. Penny sat next to her and held her. Time passed, and the night grew even colder. Dahlia began shivering.

"Please, don't stay up for me anymore, Penny. I think I need to be alone right now, anyway. I've made a total fool of myself, and I'm the one who has to figure out a way out of this. How could I have fallen for this guy? Arik told me that he had a painful past, but I never imagined. . ." Dahlia dissolved into tears again.

Penny stood up and rested her hand on Dahlia's shoulder. "Okay, but go to bed soon. And know that I am always here for you."

Dahlia shook her head and then covered her face and resumed her quiet sobbing.

Chapter 7

Arik woke up in fine spirits. After shul and lunch, he milled around in the courtyard in front of the dining hall, waiting for Dahlia as they had arranged. He waited about an hour and a half, chatting with passersby amiably all the while— but still no Dahlia! He didn't want to venture to the girls' campus, because they sunbathed on the grass and took a dim view of boys visiting at that time.

Finally, Arik went back to his bunk and hung out with Richard. He believed that Richard had much more basketball talent than he showed, due to his lack of confidence. He just needed some instruction in techniques, and he would be all right. They talked about that, and then Richard tried—albeit with limited success—to teach Arik the fundamentals of set theory. Afterward, Richard took a nap and Arik joined the Bunk Aleph crowd in a raucous game of volleyball.

Saturday night was roller hockey in the gym for all of the campers in the upper-class bunks. By then, Arik was truly worried about Dahlia. He scanned the loud and merry crowd, but she was nowhere to be found. He played in one of the roller hockey games and then, after unlacing his boots, he spotted Penny. He walked hurriedly toward her.

"Hi, Penny. Where's Dahlia? I haven't seen her all day. Is she okay? I know she sometimes gets these terrible migraines—"

Penny was looking at him darkly.

"Come outside. We can take a short walk and talk about it," Penny said.

They left the gym.

"Look, Arik, it is over between the two of you. Dahlia does not want to speak to you or even see your face again. So, please, I am asking you nicely—just stay away from her. Okay?"

Arik felt a sudden, heavy, sickening feeling in his stomach, as if he had been punched in the gut.

"What? What's going on? What did I say? What did I do to cause this? I saw her last night, and everything was great." He was fighting back tears.

"Arik, it is not what you have done. It is who and what you are."

"I don't understand."

"Arik, it is clear that you have a lot of personal problems. You need some serious help before you drag a sweet girl like Dahlia into your life."

"Penny, I have no idea what you're talking about."

"No?" Penny glared at him. "That is the way it is going to be? Well, I have said enough. You know well what I am talking about—so, stay away from her!"

Penny walked off.

Arik stood there, thunderstruck. He wracked his brains trying to figure out what could have caused Dahlia to break up with him, if that was what this was.

He walked back to his bunk, alone. Why did I come here? Here I am opening my heart to someone, only to get it callously stepped on. And for what?

I'll never understand girls. I thought Jewish girls would somehow be different. Dahlia is the first one I've fallen for since Christine. I thought I'd begun to heal my emotional wounds . . . and now this. . .

These questions played repeatedly in Arik's mind. He couldn't sleep at all that night. All the pain that had been churning around in his subconscious during the previous eighteen months sudden shot up into his awareness like a volcano erupting. He vacillated between panic and nausea and felt himself falling into a vortex of misery. He woke up early and did his usual early morning workout in the gym, but then he wandered through the day like a zombie, just going through the motions. For a moment after breakfast, he caught a glimpse of Dahlia walking with her friends, but she didn't acknowledge his gaze. Does she even realize I'm looking at her? Is she trying to ignore me? He felt foolish as he fought off the sharp pain of loss that he felt deep in his gut.

That night was the start of Tisha B'Av, the saddest day of the Jewish calendar because it commemorates the destruction of the Jewish temple in Jerusalem. At Camp Moshava, the day was marked with fasting, the reading of Lamentations (the most mournful book in the Hebrew Bible), and the singing of dirges. The entire day was spent in soul searching and introspection.

The service was conducted in the field under a sallow half-moon in the sticky, hot and humid darkness illuminated by candlelight. At the conclusion of the service, everyone sang "Ani Maamin," a song about the belief in the eventual coming of the messiah, which was sung by Jews in the cattle cars on the way to Auschwitz and the gas chambers. There was much emotion in the air. Arik sat cross-legged, rested his face in his hands, and cried. He cried for all of it—for his family and what they had gone through in the concentration camps, for what had happened to his father, for his family's poverty, for all of it. Everyone except Arik stood to sing "Hatikvah" and, all at once in the distance at the other end of the open field, a wooden model of the Jerusalem temple went up in a gigantic ball of flame, the dark wood silhouetted against the fire until it was consumed.

Arik sat in a daze and stared into the darkness. At the end of the program, he wandered around the crowd and started to slowly make his way back to the bunk. On the road, he practically bumped into Dahlia.

They stood there staring at each other.

"Why, Dahlia? Why? What have I done to you?" Arik asked, holding back tears.

"You're a fraud, a sleaze, a slick con man, and I'm sickened at the thought that I almost fell for you, you creep!" Dahlia hissed.

"My God! What in the world are you talking about?"

"The charade is over. Okay? I know all about the orgies, the drugs, and this." She reached into her jeans pocket and pulled out a newspaper clipping from the LA Times dated February 8, 1968, a little more than a year and a half earlier.

"I'm sure that you have a reasonable explanation!" Dahlia was burning with rage.

The headline was "Jewish Youth 'Crucifies' Son of Anglican Bishop of Los Angeles." The article described "an unprovoked assault at Redondo Beach by a 15-year-old named Arik Meir on Derrick Smyth, the son of Bishop Archibald Smyth. Mr. Meir is being held without bond in LA County Jail pending a grand jury indictment for aggravated assault and attempted murder. He will be charged as adult. . ."

The article included a grainy black-and-white photo of Arik in handcuffs, being led away from the scene by the sheriffs.

"And to think I almost entered into a relationship with a criminal! Maybe you should go home, back to your pathetic life, before I go public with this here at camp!" Dahlia scowled. "All the phony wholesomeness, Mr. Nice Guy, considerate, religious, all that studying with Eliezer, Mr. Fair Play. You're disgusting. You're nothing but a fraud!"

Arik suddenly erupted. "How dare you stand there and judge me regarding things you have no clue about? Sweetheart, you're way out of your depth. While you were gallivanting around Paris or sunning yourself on the beach in Cabo, my life has been a constant fight for survival! From the time I was eight years old, I've had to drag my one-legged father around the house, up and down the stairs. I bathed him, cleaned his butt, and dressed his infected stump. My father is an angry and bitter man, and in return for my nursing him he beat me silly when I disobeyed him. And do you have any idea why I had to do all this? Because we were too poor to hire any private help for him. LA County Social Services gave us six hours of help a day and told us we didn't qualify for more.

"My father was a bona fide hero, but he was royally screwed by the Israeli Defense Ministry. He lost his leg rescuing five friends out of a burning armored bus that was hit by an artillery shell on the second day of the Battle for Kastel to help reopen the road to Jerusalem. He was behind them in an open Jeep, and after the bus was hit he heard their screams. The door mechanism had melted from the heat. But he managed to wrench the door open and pull out the burning men one by one. After he got them out, he walked around to get the driver, who was probably already dead, and just as he approached the bus for a sixth time it blew up, taking his leg and burning him over 40 percent of his body.

"He lay in the hospital for a year. When he was finally discharged, he was denied any services or compensation given to wounded soldiers. Every door was shut to him, and he eventually became homeless when his savings gave out. He was reduced to begging for change on a street corner in the Tachana Merkazit, the central bus station in Tel Aviv. My mom found him in the street and recognized him. She'd been his nurse in the hospital, so she knew of his sacrifice. She took him in and eventually married him. They tried to make do with her salary, but his medical needs were too complex and he began to weaken. We eventually came to the United States, with my uncle paying our way and taking him into his business and getting him care at the UCLA Medical Center as a charity case. He's always in and out of the hospital. So much for Zionism and your wonderful Israeli government. Hatikvah Hallelujah!

Dahlia just stood there, open-mouthed and unable to speak.

"I grew up speaking Hebrew at home, because my mother insisted on it. My father would have rather we didn't even do that. He hates Jews—and

Israelis, for that matter. He made it a point to eat pork at home and doesn't even keep Yom Kippur. I was never Bar Mitzvah'ed. He completely disapproves of my coming here, so his rage still burns.

"The only Jewish experience I ever had as a kid was Yom Kippur when I was eight years old. My dad took me to shul. In the middle of Kol Nidre, he got up and started screaming at the Holy Ark, 'God, you want me to come here today to ask for forgiveness from you! It's you who needs forgiveness from me! Two years in Buchenwald, the War for Independence, and the living hell you have put me through since.' Waving a crutch at the Ark, he screamed, 'Go to hell!'

They threw him out of the synagogue, with me in tow. How humiliating for an eight-year-old to be part of that. Word got around the community about my father's outburst, and we became more isolated than ever."

Dahlia recoiled in horror.

"After that, I began to spend more and more time out of the house. I took up gymnastics at the YMCA and martial arts with Dan Inosanto. I played basketball, basketball, and more basketball. I did it to escape from my father, because he treated me like his whole crappy life was my fault.

"I entered Lynwood High School and played junior varsity football and basketball and continued training in gymnastics and martial arts. None of my friends were Jewish. In my freshman year, I started dating Christine Spellman, an Irish Catholic cheerleader who was a year older than me. We partied, we drank, we experimented with pot and hashish. I wasn't unusual. Everyone did it. I know that's out of your overly sheltered frame of reference, but so be it!"

"Arik, I—"

"One night, we got really high. Christine, me, and a few of her cheerleader friends. We were sitting in her basement while her parents were away for the weekend. Someone had the idea for all of us to get naked and have group sex, so we did. Not something I'm likely to repeat, but it doesn't keep me up at night either. These are the '60s, after all, Dahlia.

"And speaking of the '60s, those were the early days of racial integration and school busing. The blacks lived in Watts and rarely ventured west of the Harbor Freeway, but now we had black kids being bused to our school. It was only a matter of time before trouble erupted. One day, as I was walking out of school at the end of my freshman year, a group of white guys were beating up on a small, vulnerable black kid in an alley. They punched him and kicked him to within an inch of his life. Then they took out their dicks and pissed on him. They were laughing and yelling, 'This is what we'll do to all the fucking niggers who dare come to our school.' There were four of them, and I was alone. I stepped in and told them to leave him alone.

"'Oh, what have we here?' one of them said. 'Arik, the little Christ-killing nigger-loving kike, here to save the day?' In about thirty seconds, I rendered three of them unconscious. That left the ringleader, Derrick Smyth, a nasty, arrogant, white-supremacist prick with a massive shock of white-blond hair that made him look like a Hitler Youth member. 'I'm going to kick your circumcised Jew ass so you look just like little nigger boy here!' he shouted at me. We fought for about half an hour. He'd had martial arts training, in kenpo karate, and he was a black belt, too. He was as wiry as a jackal. In the end, I dropped him unconscious with a roundhouse kick to the face.

"I picked up the black boy and carried him—all bloodied and urine-soaked—back to his house. When I reached his street in Watts, a crowd of people gathered around. His dad came out of the house and cried out, 'Look what they did to my boy!' His brothers went berserk, running toward me to beat me up, like I was the one who'd done that to their little brother. 'Look what those honkies did to Junior, Dad,' one of them said. 'Let's kick the crap out of this one!' His father, who turned out to be Reverend Dr. J.J. Clarence Perkins, bellowed out, 'You will do no such thing, Tyrone. You sit your butt down, and you do what you are told. And you, too, Antwan. This is not our way. This is not what Dr. King has taught us. Haven't you learned anything?'

"I carried the boy into the house and laid him on a bed. I asked the reverend, 'Shouldn't we take him to the hospital? He could be seriously injured. Shouldn't we call the police?'

"Dr. Perkins said, 'We won't do any of that. Let's see how Kevin does. I'll have Dr. Jackson come in to see him, and we'll see what he says. And no police either. I don't want any trouble. No use riling up the whole neighborhood. Remember the riots here two years ago?'

"'What's your name, cracker?' the boy named Tyrone asked me.

"Dr. Perkins told him to mind his manners, that I was a guest in their house. So, Tyrone asked me again, without the 'cracker' bit.

"When I told him my name, he asked me if I was a Jew. I said I guessed I was. And then I explained as much as I could about what had happened to his little brother.

"Mrs. Perkins came running in from the store, where she'd heard. She wailed about 'Where's my baby' and 'What have they done to my baby?' for about ten minutes before Dr. Perkins could calm her down.

"He introduced me as something like 'the fine young man that saved Junior. And, even though he knew I was Jewish, he told me I'd always be welcome in their house and community. It turns out that Dr. Perkins is a community organizer and pastor of the Mount Zion Baptist Church.

"I stayed for dinner. I'd never had collard greens with pork before, but it was so good!

"Over dinner, Tyrone asked if I played basketball. I told him yes but that he'd probably laugh at me, that I played like a white guy. He and his brother Antwan invited me to join them in a game at the local park after dinner.

"That game was so much fun. After that, I was in. I played with them after school, two days a week, for months, and they really taught me how to play basketball. I played midnight basketball with them, too, and I joined their community playground league. I made some very close friends. I must have looked odd being the only white guy for miles. Dr. Perkins got me a tryout at the NBA summer youth league in Anaheim, and I was accepted.

"I was still dating Christine, and we were pretty serious. We had sleepovers every chance we could. I thought we were really in love. We used to surf every Saturday morning at Venice, Malibu, or Redondo Beach, depending on where the surf was the best.

"My life was like a Beach Boys song. Well, except for my father. Until one Saturday morning, warm for February, when we went surfing at Redondo Beach. We were heading back to Christine's Mustang convertible. I was carrying my surfboard, barefoot and wearing just my T-shirt and wetsuit. Three guys in leather jackets and caps appeared out of nowhere, each with a hunting knife in one hand and a club in the other. At first, I didn't recognize the leader, because he'd shaved his head, but sure enough it was my old buddy Derrick Smyth. He was out for blood, for revenge for what I'd done to him. This time, he made sure he had the advantage. His buddies at the beach were more experienced gang members than the pals he'd had with him in the alley.

"It was three against one. I turned to Christine and pleaded with her to call the police. But she just stood there frozen. She even seemed fascinated by the spectacle. Derrick called me a 'nigger-lovin' kike' that 'killed our lord and savior Jesus Christ.' He said I was all alone and he was going to seriously fuck me up. "They all lunged at me, all at once. One guy aiming for my chest got me here in the arm."

Arik lifted up the sleeve of his T-shirt, tearing it in his haste, revealing a deep scar on the side of his shoulder.

"I landed a flying side kick on one guy. That broke his nose and threw him against Derrick's knife so that it pierced his kidney. He went down. I picked up a wooden fence post that was lying in front of me, and when another guy came at me I hit him in the jaw. It broke instantly, with a sickening crunch. He even spat out some teeth. I hit him again, and a rusty nail sticking out of the fence post caught him in the neck. It bled like crazy. That was two down, and Derrick was the only one left.

"I turned around to Christine and asked her again to call the police. But she was still frozen.

"When I turned back, Derrick was coming at me full force, aiming his knife for my heart. I felt the knife go in, but I turned to the left at the last second and it slashed down my rib cage. My shirt was soaked with blood."

Arik lifted his T-shirt to show Dahlia the scar above his left nipple. Her face went white with horror.

"He told me he was going to cut my throat, and then he grabbed me from behind and leaned against the fence. I tried to wrench his grip on the knife loose, but my hands were slippery with my blood. Just as his left hand was coming down toward my neck, I managed to grab the knife out of his hand and fling it away. It went into the center of his palm and pinned it against the wooden fence. He screamed like a hyena, but he grabbed my throat with his other hand. I felt myself losing consciousness. When my hand went down, I found the other knife he had, on his belt. With one last effort, I grabbed that knife and flung it. It pinned his other hand to the fence, too. He was screaming obscenities at me. My nose was gushing with blood, and I'd had enough. I told him good-bye. And then I knocked him out, just as he stood, pinned against the fence, with his arms outstretched, with a final kick to the face. He just stayed there, limp but upright.

"I could hear the sirens finally coming down the road to the beach. Christine hadn't called them, but someone must have. She looked at me, crossed herself on her chest, and yelled that I'd crucified him just I did to Jesus. I couldn't believe what she was saying. She'd seen the whole thing. They'd attacked me, and I was unarmed. I'd just defended myself.

"When the police got there, they freed Derrick. And they told me that I 'had a right to remain silent.' They took me to St. Joseph's Hospital. I spent hours getting sutured under local anesthesia while my hands were cuffed to the bed rail, and then the doctors declared me fit enough to go off with the police.

"Meanwhile, Derrick was rushed to the operating room at the Joseph Boyes Hand Center at Orthopaedic Hospital in Inglewood. Apparently, I'd cut the median nerves on both sides and a major artery and three tendons in his palm. He was discharged from the hospital the next day. The other guys were taken to the trauma unit at LA County Hospital. They were both in intensive care after hours of surgery. None of them was charged with assault.

"It turned out that Derrick's dad was a bishop of the Anglican Church and was a golfing buddy of the LA police chief and the district attorney. He even had some political connections. Christine was taken to the police station. In her statement, she told the police that I attacked Derrick, that his friends came to his aid, and that I was a kung fu master armed with knives. I think she was afraid for her own life, that that's what made her do it. To this day, I still don't know.

"By the time I got discharged from the hospital, the media had been alerted and there I was on the front page of the LA Times Metro section, in my bloody T-shirt and handcuffs." Arik pointed at the newspaper clipping. "It was a media circus. Reporters and local TV cameras swarmed around the jail. His eminence, the bishop, expressed his shock and outrage that his son had been crucified. It was bad enough that his little bubbele had been assaulted, but there was the perceived sacrilege of how it happened—especially when it became public knowledge that I was Jewish. I kept hearing 'Jewish, Jewish' all the time, but I had no idea what people were talking about. Other church leaders weighed in and voiced their support for the Smyth family, wishing Derrick well.

"But I had nobody. Nobody! My father was brought into the holding cell I was caged up in, but all he did was let loose a torrent of abuse at me. He complained that he was having to go through this abuse after everything else he'd gone through in his life with the Holocaust and all. He said he'd put faith in me as the future of our family and I'd turned out to be a criminal. When bail was posted, he refused to pay it. I sat in jail with murderers and rapists for six weeks.

"The elites of the Jewish community distanced themselves from me, too. They said I was an 'aberration' from an isolated, dysfunctional family. They publicly apologized to the church elders for the 'despicable act perpetrated by a member of the Jewish race.' The Anti-Defamation League was nowhere to be found. Besides, the Six-Day War had just been won less than a year before, and the Jewish community was still in a festive mood. They didn't want anything to spoil their fun.

"Media trucks were camped out in front of the jail. There wasn't a day I wasn't in the newspaper. One afternoon right before the grand jury hearing when I was supposed to be charged with attempted murder, I heard the roar of a crowd. I looked out of the barred window of my cell, and I couldn't believe my eyes. The entire black community from Watts and the rest of the city were marching up Wilshire Boulevard, arms locked, singing 'We Shall Overcome.'

"There must have been over 5,000 people out there, carrying signs that said, FREE ARIK and END RACISM. They were shouting in unison, 'Free Arik now! Free Arik now! We shall overcome!' They crowded in front of the courthouse across the street from the jail. And in front of the whole mob stood the Reverend, Dr. Perkins, arm in arm with Reverend Ralph Abernathy, Dr. Martin Luther King's second in command, who had flown in from Atlanta for the occasion. They hastily set up a podium, and the local TV station covered the event live. Newspaper and TV reporters were everywhere.

"Reverend Perkins stood nose to nose with Bishop Smyth, in silence but refusing to back down. The TV crews were eating it up. Dr. Abernathy yelled into a bullhorn, saying he had a special message to read. What he read was so amazing that I think I have it memorized.

"'To all men and woman of goodwill, a greeting.

"'Today, we are here to right an injustice. The great city of Los Angeles, the city of angels, has been beset by the scourge of racism. There are those who don't cherish that basic right by which our great republic was founded—that all men are created equal. There are those who undermine that right and attempt to do so by means of violence. We must stand firm against such violence. One brave teenager has done this at great peril to himself. He has resisted the forces of darkness and has paid a terrible price. Arik Meir, a youth of the Hebrew faith, a youth who understands the meaning of bigotry and persecution, stands shoulder to shoulder with all freedom-loving people, whether they be white, black, Jew, or Gentile. He is now a prisoner of conscience, incarcerated because of his principles and beliefs. We demand his release and the prosecution of those who use hatred and terror to further their nefarious aims.

"'Let us all look forward to the day when all men and women are brothers and sisters living in peace and harmony.

"'With Best Wishes, Dr. Martin Luther King Jr.'

"Dr. Perkins came in to see me, and he was shocked by the way I looked. I was still wearing the bloody, torn T-shirt. He said they'd really worked me over. I smiled at him. He told me they were going to get me out of there and get the bastards who were responsible.

"For weeks, there were nightly candlelight vigils in front of the courthouse. Hundreds of people from the black community showed up. They walked in slow circles, singing spirituals and attracting reporters and crowds who stood and watched the singing and speeches.

"The LA district attorney tried to stonewall, but in the end the NAACP got in a big civil rights attorney from Atlanta who filed a complaint in federal court under the Civil Rights Act of 1964. The U.S. attorney from the Justice department got involved. He got a court order to search Derrick Smyth's home, and they found a closet in his basement full of World War II era Nazi regalia: bloody weapons, Aryan Nations hate literature and, most incriminating, photographs that the arrogant prick took of twelve of his victims after he'd beaten them up. Of course, they were all black. He was taken into custody. And when Christine was interrogated again—this time by the FBI—she changed her story. She agreed to cooperate with the authorities in return for immunity from prosecution for perjury.

"Unluckily for Derrick, two of his victims died of their injuries. He's now serving two consecutive thirty-year terms in a federal prison on two counts of premeditated first-degree murder. I was released from jail after six weeks, all charges were dropped, and I got a hero's welcome when I got back to Dr. Perkins's house. Even my dad apologized and admitted I was a hero. He said he was 'proud' of what I'd done.

"When I testified at Derrick's trial, I saw him for the pathetic creature he was: in a green jumpsuit, shackles, and the last remaining fragment of his arrogance, his bald head tattooed with a swastika. Underneath the swastika it said 'Kill all Jews,' on one side, and on the other side it had the emblem of the White Knights of the Aryan Nations and the words 'Kill All Niggers.'

"I began to wonder about everyone calling me a Jew. I didn't get it. I didn't practice Judaism. I didn't even know much about it. I didn't even look like a Jew. Yet Jewishness was pinned on me.

"I decided to find out what it meant to be Jewish. My uncle Itzik suggested that I speak to a neighbor of his in Beverly Hills—Rabbi Shaul Rabinovich, an Israeli teacher at the Jewish Rambam Academy. I went to talk to him, and he recognized me at once from the news. He suggested that I consider enrolling in the Jewish day school.

"There was the matter of the tuition, though. It was over a thousand dollars a year. After the scandal broke and the public support I had from the black community became clear, though, the Jewish community sort of woke up to the whole affair, especially when they realized Derrick wasn't just a racist but a neo-Nazi, too. A philanthropist stepped forward and made a big public display of awarding me a scholarship to Rambam Academy for the rest of my high school career. The United Jewish Appeal, the UJA, even paid for my coming here to camp. I appreciated the kindness and money, but I wish they'd done the whole thing in private. What is it about Jews? When they give charity, they have to let the whole world know about it. That's fine when you give the money to an institution. They put up a nice plaque in front, and everybody's happy. But when they dragged me into the UJA office and made a whole ceremony about my 'heroism' and then presented me with a check for the money in front of the Jewish Times of LA, with photographers and reporters, well, all they did was tell the world I was a charity case. That's social suicide in a Jewish school in LA, where a person's worth is judged by how much money their parents make.

"Anyway, Rabbi Rabinowitz took me under his wing last summer, while I played basketball in the youth league. I studied with him for three hours a day to prepare to go to the Academy in the fall. Then I worked my ass off all year. But despite my best efforts to make friends with the kids there, I was always known in school as the schvartze, because of my continued close affiliation with the black community.

"I'd get asked by religious kids from good families, 'How can you go into dangerous neighborhoods with those schvartzes? Aren't you afraid of getting mugged?'

"I tried to shrug them off, saying, 'It's not the blacks I'm afraid of. It's the whites.'

"I found many of the kids at school to be petty, arrogant, materialistic, and self-absorbed.

"Dahlia, I know where you got that clipping. It was Bracha Epstein, someone I considered my confidante and friend. In the end, she's turned on me just like Christine did and just like you're doing now.

"You know, Dahlia, you stand there so smug, judging me, calling me disgusting. You're the disgusting one, for not giving me the benefit of the doubt and confronting me with questions that I would've gladly answered, like I am now. Besides, it all would have come out in time. Just not all at once like this. I wasn't trying to hide anything from you.

"Please, excuse me for not being one of those immature, two-dimensional, sheltered yeshiva boychicks around here that drool over you every time you pass by. I came here to get away from LA and all that baggage for the summer and to continue my studying and spiritual growth. Instead, I got all the old crap thrown back in my face. I've tried so hard to get over the past and live a good Jewish life, to achieve some sort of spiritual redemption, but all I see is Jews being judgmental of each other. There really isn't repentance and return. Is there? While Jews constantly ask God for forgiveness, they're completely unwilling to forgive each other. It's you and your kind that are frauds and phonies. Not me. I've always been true to myself and what I believe in.

"Go on, Dahlia. Go live your pretty little, sheltered, charmed life, and find yourself a nice, rich Jewish boy who'll provide for you in the manner you're accustomed to. Go back to your little yentas. For a while, I thought you were somehow better than them, but you aren't.

"Tisha B'Av is about the Temple's destruction because of baseless hatred among Jews. But Jews haven't learned a damned thing in 2,000 years. I shouldn't have told you all of this. You don't deserve it. You're a waste of oxygen.

"I'm going back to LA! Happy Tisha B'Av." Arik turned around.

Dahlia realized that Arik had finished. With tears of sorrow streaming down her face, she said, "I'm so sorry, Arik! I'm so very sorry for what I've said, for the way I've treated you. I've acted like an idiot and stirred up a hornet's nest. I beg you, please forgive me!" She reached out to him.

"Don't come near me, Dahlia. And don't ever speak to me again. I can't stand the sight of you, and I don't need your pity." He threw his torn T-shirt at her feet and walked away, leaving her stunned and silent.

***

Dahlia ran back to her bunk at breakneck speed, turning heads in the process. All she wanted to do was to crawl into a hole and die. Penny was waiting for her on the porch when Dahlia arrived breathless and in tears. Penny had seen Dahlia and Arik's "talk" from a distance.

"Penny!" Dahlia wailed, "I've done something bad. Very, very bad! I'll never forgive myself!" She threw herself at Penny and sobbed onto her shoulder.

They took a long walk, and Dahlia related everything that Arik had said.

"It may be a bad time to bring this up, but I think that you need to independently verify what Arik said," Penny said. "And I think you also need to try to get some sleep. We will figure something out tomorrow. You have done nothing but cry for the last two days."

The next day, after the morning prayer, Rabbi Moskowitz approached Dahlia and indicated that he needed to talk to her. Dahlia followed him to his office.

"Please, have a seat," he said.

Dahlia sat quietly in front of his desk.

"You have something in common with my son, Eliezer. You both have become very close to Arik. Your relationship with Arik is what we call an open secret here at camp. Ever since you met him, you have become a very different person—more open, perhaps. I am not the only one who sees the change in you compared with the way you have been here for the past two years. People talk. I have heard it said that you have an extra bounce in your step. You are so much more exuberant, less reserved. You have an inner glow that has not gone unnoticed."

"What is this all about?" Dahlia asked.

The rabbi pulled a folder out of a desk drawer.

"There is something you need to see."

He handed Dahlia a scrapbook. When she opened it, she realized that it contained a collection of all the local newspaper clippings about the Derrick Smyth case. It formed a chronological account, in detail, of what had happened, from the time of the attack until Smyth's conviction. All in all, there were about thirty articles over two months and from several newspapers, with pictures. The article that Shirah had shown her was included. She looked at Smyth's evil face and imagined him trying to cut Arik's throat. Dahlia closed the scrapbook and looked up at the rabbi.

"I got this scrapbook from Arik's rabbi in LA, Rav Shaul Rabinowitz, who has been instrumental in bringing Arik into Jewish life," Rabbi Moskowitz said. "Arik comes from a very troubled past, through no fault of his own, yet he has been haunted by the ghosts of what he and his family have had to endure. He has a kind, gentle, generous soul and a keen sense of what is right and wrong. And he nearly paid for that with his life.

"I went to the same yeshiva in Israel as Rabinowitz, and I know him well. I met him at a family wedding I attended in LA last Chanukah. He told me all about Arik and what he has been through. He suggested that Arik come here to camp to get away from LA and explore something new.

"He sent me this, to look at, before Arik came, so I would know more about what he had been through. Eliezer told me about the blowup you and Arik had. I made some discreet inquires and discovered Shirah Epstein's involvement in all of this. That is the problem with getting only part of the story. One does not get the benefit of the context, and it brings one to rash conclusions that may lead to great harm and hurt."

Dahlia began to cry. "I've done just that. When I confronted Arik with the newspaper clipping, I was so nasty to him. His side of the story came out in a furious torrent. When I tried to apologize, he told me to leave him alone and that he was going to catch the next flight back to LA. I feel so awful."

"It is not really your fault, Dahlia. How could you know how complicated Arik is? Anyone would have reacted the way you did to seeing that newspaper clipping. I will venture a guess that you have never met anyone quite like Arik before."

"So, it's all true? All of it?"

"I am afraid so. I have already talked with Shirah. She understands everything now, and she is sworn to secrecy. You do not need to worry about her. She too feels awful about the whole affair."

"But what are we going to do now?" Dahlia asked. "He wants to go home, and he's probably already making arrangements to do so. I've screwed this up so badly. How are we going to keep him here? I don't want him to leave."

"Leave that to me." Rabbi Moskowitz smiled. "Besides, it would break Eliezer's heart to see him go. They have become very close."

For the first time in three days, Dahlia smiled.

***

Later that afternoon, Rabbi Moskowitz went looking for Arik. He found him at the ropes course, with the other Mach Hach boys, swinging back and forth from a knotted rope about twenty-five feet in the air, using only one arm.

"Hey, Arik, are you some kind of monkey? Get down from there!"

"Sorry, Rabbi, I was just hanging around," Arik quipped.

"Very funny," the rabbi said.

Arik climbed down the rope in less than five seconds.

"Seriously, though, Rabbi, there is something I need to talk to you about. I think I want to—"

"Do you know Elgin Baylor?"

"Yeah, he plays for the Lakers."

"I did not ask you if you knew who he is. I asked if you knew him."

"I do," Arik said quietly.

"I would like you to arrange a basketball day like the tennis day we had with Billie Jean. I thought that it was a great success. And the kids all loved it."

"Yes, it was," Arik said. In retrospect, however, he had mixed feelings about everything that had to do with that day.

"Do you think you can you get him to come here for a clinic and demonstration?" Rabbi Moskowitz asked.

"Well, I don't know . . . Possibly? He comes from Washington, D.C., and during the summer he's at home with his family when he's not traveling around, doing good works. I can get his agent's info from the Lakers' front office and give him a call."

"Frankly, Arik, I think that the tennis day was a bigger hit with the girls. The guys will absolutely love this. Keep it under wraps, though. If you can pull it off, it will make a nice surprise!"

***

In an effort to distract himself, over the next few days Arik spent a good deal of time wearing a whistle around his neck while teaching basketball to the younger boys. He lowered the basket to four feet above the head of the tallest boy. That way, the boys could work on developing basic skills before combining all of the elements. There was a noticeable improvement in the quality of play.

Arik also made Richard Green his project. He convinced him that there was more to life than differential equations and that he had the potential to improve his physical skills. Arik and Richard played one-on-one in the gym, and Arik patiently put Richard through a long series of ball handling and shooting drills. Slowly, Richard's self-confidence improved. He even found that he could hold his own in a pickup basketball game with the Bunk Aleph crowd. The guys seeing another side of him opened up new possibilities for friendships. Richard's relationship with Penny also was progressing. Well, at least that makes one of us, Arik thought. He steered clear of the tennis courts. In the camp library, Arik read voraciously about the history of modern Israel and Zionism. He felt that his study brought things into sharper focus and that he was gaining a deeper perspective of the forces that had shaped his life.

Several days later, Arik met with Rabbi Moskowitz and delivered the good news: Elgin Baylor had agreed to come to Camp Moshava to run a clinic the following week!

The campers were mystified when, at Mifkad on Sunday evening, the Rosh Moshava announced that all of the following afternoon's activities for the upper two divisions would be canceled. Rumors abounded, and Arik became excited about introducing to the camp, in person, a level of basketball that none of them had ever seen.

After lunch the next day, all the older campers—boys and girls—were instructed to go to the gym. They packed into the stands. Dahlia and Penny found seats in the upper back row, in the corner.

Arik stood at midcourt, holding a microphone and wearing a Camp Moshava T-shirt, UCLA warm-up pants, sneakers, and a whistle on a lanyard around his neck. He blew the whistle and then began the announcement.

"You're probably all wondering what's going on. Rumors have been flying around for the past day or so—everything from color war to nuclear war."

The crowd laughed.

"Well, you're all in for a treat. How many of you follow the NBA?"

Most of the campers raised their hands.

"How many of you have heard of the Los Angeles Lakers?"

There were some jeers, but the hands stayed up.

"Okay, two for two. Now, how many have heard of that legendary NBA All Star Elgin Baylor?"

The hands remained in the air.

"Okay, then," Arik yelled, "Let's give a huge welcome and a round of applause to Mr. Elgin Baylor!"

Startled disbelief and excitement led to a huge cheer as the six-foot-five-inch LA Lakers forward bounded into the gym, from a side entrance, bouncing a basketball. He jumped up toward the basket and executed a 180-degree backward dunk. He then approached Coach, smiled, and shook hands with him. When he saw Arik, he ran to him and gave him a hug.

"How are you doin', man?" Elgin asked.

"Never better! So good to see you. And thanks for coming!" Arik said.

Elgin was an old hand at running youth basketball clinics, so he rapidly divided the boys into squads and put them through ball handling, passing, and shooting drills. He was a great instructor, demonstrating each skill and giving constructive criticism. Arik stood off to the side and watched. Heshie went up to him.

"You know this guy?" Heshie asked Arik.

"Yes," Arik said quietly.

"It's not every day you get Elgin Baylor to give you a basketball clinic," Heshie said.

"He's a great player but an even nicer person," Arik said.

The squads began to scrimmage, and Elgin ran alongside the older players, giving them a sense of strategy and court presence. He drew up some basic offensive and defensive plays on a large chalkboard on the sideline and showed the players how to set a pick and roll, the basics of no-look passing, and the art of a long-distance jump shot in which you let the ball float off your fingertips without taking your eyes off the rim.

Coach walked over to where Heshie and Arik were standing.

He said, "It's good for the players to see this stuff from a real legend."

Arik said, "I wish I could take credit for this, but it was all Rabbi Moskowitz's idea."

Heshie asked, "So, Arik, how do you know him?"

Arik turned away and smiled cryptically.

Suddenly, a messenger from the administration office came up to Arik discreetly and whispered into his ear, "Arik, you need to come to the admin office right away. You have a long-distance call from LA."

Arik frowned. "Do you know who it is?"

"I think it's your mom."

Arik said to Coach, "Gary, you know the program. Do me a favor and hold the fort? I'll be back in a couple minutes."

Arik slowly walked out of the gym. At soon as he was outside, he started a sprint to the office.

He picked the phone and spoke in Hebrew. "Hello. Imma, are you okay?"

Miriam, Arik's mom, answered. "Shalom, Arik. Abba's stump has developed a large abscess. It's all swollen and red. He's been admitted to USC Medical Center for emergency surgery and antibiotics on an IV. They'll see how he responds, but if he's not any better by Thursday they'll have to do surgery to remove more of the leg."

"That's terrible. How are you doing?" Arik asked.

"I'm okay."

"I'll come home. You shouldn't be alone. I'll get on the next flight out of New York. I'll call in a couple hours to give you my flight information."

"No, Arik. I don't want you to do that. You need to be where you are right now, and I won't let you leave. You're having a good time, and you're making new friends. I love your letters. I just called to let you know what's going on. Please don't worry about me. Uncle Itzik and Aunt Chana are helping me, and I'm staying with them so I don't have to be alone. I'll be very upset if you come home."

"Are you absolutely sure, Imma?"

"Absolutely!"

"You're such a Yiddish Mama, Imma. I love you so much."

"I love you too, chaboob!" Miriam said.

Meanwhile, back in the gym, the last scrimmage had ended. Elgin addressed the crowd about the importance of fair play, being a good sport, and avoiding drugs. He took questions from the spellbound audience about what it was like to be a professional basketball player. One highly knowledgeable camper asked him about the last playoff game and whether, with hindsight, he would have played Bill Russell differently in the final two minutes of the game.

He was asked what he ate, what his daily practice regimen was like, and how he got along with Jerry West and Wilt Chamberlain. Elgin was engaging and funny.

Finally, someone asked, "So, Mr. Baylor, how do you know Arik?"

Dahlia's ears perked up, and she broke off her conversation with Shirah and Penny.

"That's a long story." Elgin smiled. "I don't know how much you know about him, because he don't like to talk much about himself, but he's a very special guy. You know he's from LA."

Dahlia felt her heart fall into her stomach. "Crap, he's going to expose Arik. Oh, no!" she whispered to Shirah.

Elgin continued, "Arik has made quite a name for himself in LA. He's risked his life for civil rights and racial equality and was nearly killed for it. He's a hero in the black community, and he was all over the news last year. He was even given an award by Dr. Martin Luther King. He's also an incredible ballplayer. He played in the NBA summer youth league last year, and he's been a regular player on the street basketball circuit in Watts and Compton for several years now. In LA, outside the college and professional circles there's a whole culture of street basketball, where players are out there day and night. And there's an unspoken hierarchy of teams and players judged purely on talent. Many colleges and professional teams look for hot prospects from this talent pool. Guys like Walt Hazzard and Lew Alcindor came out of that system. Interestingly, NBA players, college players, and even Harlem Globetrotters play in the parks during their time off. To hone their skills and tricks, they're happy to play with the street guys.

"Arik has earned the respect of all the players in the league for his incredible speed, ball handling skills, and dangerous shooting ability. Out in Watts, all the top ballplayers are called by nicknames. Arik is called White Lightning. He's also earned respect from the guys because of his religious convictions. Over the past year or so, he's become religious, and he won't play on Friday night or Saturday even if he gets pressure to. This coming year, he'll probably get courted by Division I scouts, and he's good enough be offered a full-ride basketball scholarship to Michigan, Indiana, or even UCLA."

There was a hushed silence in the gym as Elgin's words sank in.

Dahlia buried her face in her hands, which were resting on her knees, and pulled her hat down low over her head. She had never felt so ashamed in her entire life. Penny understood and hugged her tightly.

"It is going to be okay, Paapi," Penny whispered.

Elgin continued to field questions from the floor.

Arik snuck in through a side door.

"Is everything okay?" Coach whispered to him.

"It's my dad. He's back in the hospital for the 300th time. What did I miss?"

"He's been answering questions, but I think he's wrapping it up."

"Well, you've all been great, but I've got to go," Elgin told the campers. "I'll take one more question."

A young camper from the junior division, Eidah Aleph, raised his hand and asked, "Can you play one-on-one with Arik?"

A loud roar and a cheer went up from the crowd.

Arik turned bright red and made a hand gesture as if to shoo away the idea.

Arik walked up to Elgin, took the microphone from him, and smiled. "Mr. Baylor has a very busy schedule, and we're so grateful he was able to spend so much time with us. He has a plane to catch, back to D.C."

Elgin took back the microphone, smiled broadly, and said, "I don't see why we can't play a little. I'm not in that much of a hurry."

The crowd cheered, "A-rik! A-rik! A-rik!"

Elgin laughed as he took off his warm-up pants and jacket, exposing his LA Lakers practice jersey. He smiled, winked at Arik, and said, "C'mon, you chicken or something?"

Arik laughed and called out, "I've never backed away from a challenge, and nobody calls me chicken." When Arik took off his own warm-up pants, the cheers were deafening.

Elgin said, "We'll play to eleven."

Arik leaned over to Elgin and whispered: "Let's give 'em a show!"

Elgin smiled. "You got it!"

Although the winner of the contest was never in doubt (Elgin won 11-6), the dazzling display of artistry, athleticism, and basketball skill was something that no one in that gym would ever forget. It was twenty minutes of lightning-fast ball handling, shooting, blocking, and aerial acrobatics, complete with midair twists, turns, and dunks. When Elgin scored the last point, the crowd was on their feet. They gave both exhausted, sweaty men a prolonged standing ovation. Elgin and Arik hugged each other and smiled. Elgin stayed for another thirty minutes, posing for photographs and signing autographs on any surface offered: notepads, hats, shirts, basketballs . . . Someone even presented his forearm!

When they walked out of the gym in a sea of campers, Arik asked Elgin, "Do you want to stay for dinner?"

Elgin smiled. "I'd love to, man, but I've got to catch a plane from Scranton in two hours. When are you going to be home, Arik? They're wondering about you in South Central."

"I'll be home the last week of August. I'll give you a call when I get back there. Please, send my love to the reverend."

"He asked about you, bro," Elgin said.

"Tell him I'm doing good things!"

"Of that I have no doubt!" Elgin smiled as he bent and got into his limousine.

Arik was mobbed by well-wishers who thanked him for organizing such a wonderful program.

"Don't thank me! It was Rabbi Moskowitz's idea."

Eliezer, who had had a convenient perch at the front of the bleachers during the game, wheeled himself over to Arik as his father followed behind. "You're the man!" he said. He gave Arik a high five.

"And you are my best friend in camp!" Arik winked at him.

Eliezer beamed.

"And to think you wanted to leave camp and go home!" Rabbi Moskowitz said.

"How did you know that?" Arik asked.

"I am not just a pretty face, you know."

"So, that's what this was all about." Arik smiled broadly.

As the whole mob made their way down the dusty road to the dining hall, in the twilight, Dahlia walked over to Arik.

"You were spectacular tonight," she said. "Your one-on-one with Elgin was breathtaking."

"Thanks," Arik said in an emotionless tone. He said nothing further but simply walked slowly and stared straight ahead blankly.

Dahlia searched for something to say, but she could find nothing to break the ice. It was as if a black hole had opened up between them, sucking out all of their connection and speech.

The intense pain that Arik had experienced had begun to fade over the past few days, but now it had come back in all its fury. He thought, Why should I open myself again to this shallow, judgmental blonde who, on a dime, could cut me so deeply? He was so fed up with the struggle, with his inner need to feel a measure of the dignity that had been denied him for so long. He had thought that with Dahlia he could feel that warmth, affection and, more than anything, acceptance. But then, on a whim, she had shown another side of her, one that frightened him. So what if she knows the truth now and feels bad about it? I'm the hero of the hour again, so being with me would suit her just fine. Arik knew that he needed so much more, and he wondered whether any woman, let alone Dahlia, would ever be capable of filling that gaping hole in his soul.

Dahlia, for her part, finally understood that this perfect specimen of a man had a very tortured, insecure soul born of years of physical and emotional deprivation. She recognized that he was so different from her. Now she knew that he had endured a great deal of pain in his life and that all he wanted was comfort and acceptance. Instead, all he had gotten from her, in the end, had been venom. She felt guilty, but she wondered how he could have expected her to, based on the newspaper clipping, draw any conclusion other than the one that she had. She believed that anyone would have thought what she had.

Dahlia felt an urge to nurture Arik. She understood that urge was a poor reason to carry on a relationship with a man who had never asked for her help. He was too proud to have done that. She had hurt him deeply and, in so doing, had destroyed his trust in her. She had a sense that, once hurt, he would find it difficult to forgive. And yet, at the same time, she couldn't walk away from this beautiful man.

"Arik, take care of yourself,"

"You, too!" Arik smiled weakly, but his eyes shone with sadness.

"So . . . what did you say to him?" Penny asked eagerly when Dahlia had found her.

"Nothing. Absolutely nothing! I couldn't find a word to say to him."

"Did he say anything to you?"

"No! He was as cold as ice, with no emotion whatsoever. I would have settled for anger, verbal abuse, anything. But all I got was a sense of distance, like I wasn't there. I saw terrible pain in his eyes, though.

"I had this jewel in my hands, and I let him slip through my fingers. I was such a bitch in the way I spoke to him about that article. Penny, have you ever met anyone like him before? I've thought of nothing else for the past week. I'll tell you what. I think I've fallen in love with him, and I won't go down without a fight!"

"You're a very clever girl, Dahlia. You'll figure out a way."

Another Shabbat arrived at camp.

By then, Arik had learned the routines and found comfort in them. The good cheer, new songs, and friendly conversation made him feel at home. There were some customs that Arik didn't understand, but he took them in stride. As he got to know the other campers a bit better, he began to really enjoy their company. He even found most of them to be genuinely decent and even idealistic people. Many of them planned to eventually move to Israel. If for nothing else, attending camp had been useful. Arik already would have friends when he moved to Israel, too.

Now that his past was out in the open and his fear of discovery was gone, he was able to relax. In truth, he was quite surprised at how naturally and favorably everyone reacted to the revelations. He felt that their reactions said a lot about them. He still played ball with his friends, but he intentionally toned down his game so that he could play with everyone else. The others appreciated that. Even Rubin turned out to be okay when someone showed interest in him. When Arik discovered that Rubin's bullying was just a cover for his low self-esteem, he made a point to approach him naturally. Arik saw that much of the clannishness that had been rampant in Mach Hach at the beginning of the summer was slowly disappearing.

No one had blossomed as much as Richard, who had gained every guy's respect by having landed a hot girlfriend, Penny. Their relationship matured as they spent more time together.

After dinner, Arik went upstairs, to the shul, where he found Eliezer already waiting for him with a pile of books.

"Tonight, I want to study something different," Eliezer said. "This is a time of deep introspection in preparation for the days of awe, Rosh Hashanah and Yom Kippur. It's a time to think about what we've done over the past year and ask the Almighty for forgiveness while we pray for health and happiness for the coming year. The precondition for getting forgiveness from Above is forgiving each other so that we can all start with a clean slate. We can't change the past, but we can change how we interpret it and how we react emotionally to it. Past events generally motivate us to act in a certain way. The sages have taught us that we aren't rats running on a wheel, that we can mature and move beyond our past. That is the Jewish way."

Arik listened to him intently and then said, "I'd like to study Maimonides's guidelines for the achievement of teshuva, which means more than repentance. It means to return to a state of innocence before sin and the mechanisms for achieving that—"

Eliezer looked up from the text. "Arik, a big part of that is letting go of feelings of anger and hurt. Keeping them inside will just eat away at you from the inside. People aren't perfect. Except for me, of course."

They smiled at each other.

Eliezer said, "People say things and do things, at times, that they regret and later feel terribly sorry about. When they said it they honestly felt like they were doing the right thing, but when cooler heads prevail they realize how much hurt they caused."

Arik sighed and ran his fingers through his hair. "You're right, of course. How'd you get so smart?"

Arik suddenly felt that they weren't alone. He turned around and saw Dahlia standing behind him. She was beautiful but also pale and apprehensive.

"Hey, Dahlia, why don't you come in and join us," Eliezer said.

"I don't want to disturb you if you're studying."

"Not at all. Come on in!" Eliezer said.

"Is it okay?" Dahlia asked Arik.

"Yeah, it's okay," Arik said quietly. He noticed how nervous and tentative she seemed as she sat down across the table from him. When she laid her hands on the table, he saw that they were trembling. Now what? he thought.

Eliezer continued with his exposition of Maimonides, and Arik suddenly realized that this was all a set-up by Eliezer to get him and Dahlia to talk to each other. Well, so be it. Arik decided that if Dahlia was contrite enough to confide in Eliezer to try to reconcile, then he at least would behave civilly to her.

After another hour, Eliezer suddenly announced that he was tired and ready to go back to his room.

They walked him there, making small talk along the way. When they dropped Eliezer off, Arik and Dahlia were left alone.

"You're a persistent bugger. I'll grant you that," Arik said.

Dahlia sighed. "In our time apart, I've learned so much about you."

Arik shook his head. "You and the rest of the camp."

"I've already told you how sorry I am, so I just want to say how deeply you've touched me. I have a lot to learn, but I guess that's part of growing up. I've always thought of myself as the smartest person in the room. I've spent my life flitting around and being a social butterfly. Apart from Penny, all of my relationships and friendships have been superficial. I never believed for a moment that someone would come along and blow me out of the water.

"But you've done that, Arik. I've had a great deal of time to think and reflect about the past ten days, about my life, about you, about us."

"Dahlia, I—"

"Please, let me finish. I've searched my soul, and I've come to the conclusion that I've completely fallen for you. I'm in love with you, Arik. There, I've said it."

As Dahlia waited for a response, she looked at Arik apprehensively.

"Dahlia—"

She rushed at him and kissed him, holding his cheeks in her hands. Arik embraced her and felt a warm rush of relief flood his senses. He knew then that there was no point in remaining angry. He let go of his anger. They held each other for a long time, and she buried her face in his shoulder.

"I will never, ever let you go again!" Dahlia whispered. "I'm so desperately sorry for what I said to you. I'm so good at prejudging people. This time it exploded in my face." She clutched Arik in a tight bear hug around his waist.

Arik finally allowed himself to smile. He wrapped his arms around her shoulders.

"Dahlia, I forgive you. Some of this is my fault for not coming out with everything sooner. There was so much to explain, and it's all so painful for me to talk about. I guess I was hoping to do it slowly, in my own time, and maybe even let the whole summer pass without having to deal with it. That's why I came east for the summer rather than going to Camp Moshava in LA. I really didn't expect it to come out all at once."

They walked hand in hand in the darkness. When they got to the bleachers, they sat down.

"I think we did a good job with these." Dahlia smiled, looking down at the bleachers.

"My favorite part was chasing you down in the pouring rain with a pile of mud in my hands." Arik laughed.

Dahlia thought for a moment. "You know, so often these summer-love relationships peter out when the summer ends and everyone goes back to their lives. Camp is a special, magical time, though. Can't relationships formed here be long lasting, with enough work and commitment? I'm ready for that commitment. But, as if that wasn't hard enough, how are we going to do this long distance?"

Arik said, "I think that spending a week together in the fall, say, over Sukkot, and in the spring, during Pesach, would be perfect. Why don't we figure out a way I can come to you for one of those weeks, so I can enter your world, and you can come to LA, to see mine, for the other week? That would go a long way for us to see what we're getting ourselves into, you know, if we're going to be long-term. Maybe in the winter we could plan a ski trip, say, in Colorado, on neutral ground."

"I'd like that, Arik. I love you! I want nothing more than to be with you."

They held each other for a long while in the darkness.

Chapter 10

Visiting day at Camp Moshava resembled a barely organized circus. Starting in the early morning, a line of cars formed at the gate and ushers directed literally hundreds of cars into the makeshift parking lots that were set aside for the visitors. These parking lots were little more than muddy fields that hundreds of sneakers and sandals twisted about in, adding to the misery of what always seems to take place on the hottest, most humid day of the summer. Most of the parents made the three-hour drive from the New York City area, but some came from as far away as Philadelphia, Baltimore, Washington, D.C., and even the South.

Parents brought huge cartons of candies and snacks for their children. One would have thought that either their children had been gone for a year or that no food was served at camp. Younger and older siblings accompanied the parents, which added to the crowd. With so many people, finding a patch of grass on which to sit, let alone shade from the hot sun, was difficult. But the crowd was friendly and good-natured and the atmosphere festive.

The campers put on performances for their visitors. The most notable were a choral concert and the yearly synchronized flag dance in which Israeli flags are waved about furiously in a well-orchestrated routine. The visitors toured the grounds and the bunks. Sometimes they even tipped the counselors.

Those campers who had no visitors had two choices: be taken into town to forage through the Woolworths store or stay and help the counselors set up the camp for the visitors.

Arik chose to stay and help set up. There were rows of folding tables and chairs to set up and crates of fruits, vegetables, soggy tuna and egg salad sandwiches, bottled soda, and lemonade to carry. Arik was happy to not be an organizer; he preferred to be a workhorse. It was hot, sweaty, dirty work, and Arik loved the mindless repetition of it. After all, he had nothing else to do and nowhere to hide from the throngs of people wandering about. Besides, he needed the exercise, because he hadn't had a chance to work out that morning.

At about 10 a.m., a navy-blue Mercedes Benz pulled into the parking lot where the driver had been directed. Benny and Leah Gilad already were exhausted from their six-hour drive from Washington, D.C. They had dispensed with their chauffeur, because Benny wanted to drive himself so that he would appear more a "man of the people," a decision that he already regretted. During the drive, Leah had chided Benny for not wanting to start the journey the previous evening and stay overnight at a cheap motel in Frackville, the halfway point. Little six-year-old Doron was tired and cranky from the long trip, and his whining added to the general malaise.

Finally among the crowds in the main square, they lost no time finding their girls.

"Shalom, Abba." Dahlia kissed her dad and then turned to her mom. "Imma, how are you? How was the trip? You guys look absolutely beat."

Leah shook her head. "Don't ask!"

Benny looked down at the smiling, freckle-faced, strawberry-blonde eleven-year-old in pigtails. "Shalom, Nurit. How's Abba's big girl? I see you've grown, and it's only been a month!"

"Great, Abba. Camp is so much fun!"

"Dahlia, you look a bit tired. Are you okay?" Benny asked.

"I'm fine, Abba. There are just too many night activities here. You know, capture the flag, campfires and marshmallows, lots to do." Dahlia smiled.

The family's cook, Thelma, had prepared a small feast for them, which they had brought, along with cold drinks, in a cooler. They found a tiny patch of grass under a tree out of the blistering heat and away from the swirling crowds.

"I can't wait to see the bleachers that you built," Leah said to Dahlia.

After about an hour of lunch and small talk, Benny asked Dahlia, "So, with so many nice bachurim I see running around here, did my princess snag a boyfriend for the summer?"

Dahlia blushed.

"Benny, you don't ask such embarrassing questions of a sixteen-year-old girl! What's the matter with you?" Leah scolded.

"I was just curious. There are so many nice boys and girls here, it feels like Israel. I think that's why I like it so much."

"Abba, I've been too involved in sports this summer, mostly tennis. I've been the girls' tennis instructor, which is so much fun. There's also a lot of Zionist brainwashing—I mean, instruction—going on, but I've learned some stuff." Dahlia laughed.

"How's Penny doing?" Leah asked.

"She's great! We've had a blast together all summer. She's helping to set up lunch, because her parents couldn't be here. You know, her dad is recovering—Wait, there she is!"

Dahlia waved Penny over.

"Hi, guys! I hope that you had a good trip up." Penny said.

"Very tiring," Benny said. "How's your father feeling?"

"He is getting better slowly. My mami has him on a tight leash." Penny smiled.

"Abba, Imma, there's someone I'd like you to meet," Dahlia said.

She scanned the crowd and spotted Arik carrying three wooden crates of overripe fruit from the kitchen to the designated concessions spot, in one go while everyone else was carrying one crate at a time.

She turned toward her parents and said, "I'll be right back."

She ran to Arik, who was unpacking the fruit. "Hey, buubs, how are you holding up?" She smiled up at him.

"Never better. I'm definitely getting in my exercise for the day." He laughed.

"My parents would like to meet you. Can you tear yourself away for a minute?"

"Do you think that's a good idea? Look at me! I'm in a torn T-shirt and jeans and covered in sweat, mud, and probably rotten fruit. You never get a second chance to make a first impression."

"Oh, don't worry so much. As parents go, they're pretty cool."

Arik followed Dahlia. Penny was smiling, glad to see the two of them back together.

"Abba, Imma, this is Arik."

"Shalom, Arik. It's very nice to meet you. I'm Benny Gilad."

As he and Dahlia had approached her parents, Arik had gotten a look at them. Benny was in good shape, about six feet tall, with wavy brown hair and a creased, weathered face that gave way to an easy, distinguished smile. Leah was tall and slender with a long, blonde ponytail rolled up in a bun. She was casually dressed, but her clothing and discreet jewelry betrayed her impeccable taste.

Arik stiffened a bit, but he accepted a meaty handshake before he remembered that his hands were dirty. "Very nice to meet you, Mr. Ambassador. I'm honored. It's very nice to meet you, too, Mrs. Gilad."

"Please, call me Benny. That's what my friends call me."

"That will be a bit hard for me, sir."

Arik seemed intimidated, but Dahlia beamed at him.

"You look like they're really putting you to work." Benny chuckled.

"I love the hard work." Arik said.

"One could never tell that Arik has lived here his whole life," Dahlia said. "He speaks Hebrew like a Sabra. He was born in Israel, but he came here as a baby."

"Oh! Yafeh meod! Kol hakavod. That's terrific," Leah said.

Dahlia beamed. "Arik's father fought and was wounded during the '48 war."

"You should be very proud of him," Benny said.

"I am," Arik said.

"Arik's going to enlist in the Israeli Army." Dahlia was trying to keep the conversation going.

"Oh, very nice. When?" Leah asked.

"Next summer, probably," Arik said.

"Do you want to be a pilot, a tank operator, a paratrooper. . .?" Benny asked.

"I want to fight with my feet on the ground, so probably infantry. Maybe paratroops."

"Very good," Benny said. "You know, I feel that every Jewish boy and girl should serve in the Israeli Army. We don't just fight for Israel. We fight for every Jew around the world."

"I'm not planning on serving and going home. I want to make Aliyah and live my life there. You might say I want to finish what my father couldn't," Arik said.

Dahlia gazed at Arik with a gleam in her eye, something that was not unnoticed by her mother.

"That is very admirable, Arik," Benny said. "Why don't you sit down with us and have something to eat? It looks like you've been running around all day. And Leah brought a wonderful lunch with us."

"I'd love to, but I really must go back to work. It's very nice to meet you, Mr. Ambassador—Benny. . . And you, too, Mrs. Gilad." Arik smiled, shook hands again, and trotted back to the dining hall.

"He seems to be a fine young man," Leah said. "Where is he from again, Dahlia?"

"He's from Los Angeles."

Benny said, "He seems to be a long way from home. If memory serves, there's a Bnei Akiva camp in California. I wonder why he would come all the way out here."

"It's a long story, Abba," Dahlia said, aware that she was growing somewhat defensive.

"Anyway, Arik is very respectful and appears to be quite physically strong as well!" Leah said.

"If he has the intelligence and mental toughness to match, he'll be a great asset to Tzahal," Benny said.

And make a great husband for me, Dahlia added in her mind.

Benny walked over to the backpack and pulled out some moist towelettes. "One would think that someone would wipe their hands before greeting someone, though."

"I pulled him away suddenly from his work. He didn't have time to clean his hands," Dahlia said. She didn't like the disapproval from her dad.

"Oh, Benny, you're such a dandy," Leah said.

"I'm just saying, that's all. Do you think that he's a convert?"

Dahlia was taken aback. "Why would you even think such a thing? Is it because he's tall and has blond hair and a California suntan? I don't know if you noticed, but Imma and I are also blond."

"No, it's not that, booba. It's just that he appears to be a bit rough around the edges, if you know what I mean, like he wasn't born Jewish."

"I already told you that his father fought and was wounded in '48!"

"So, what does that mean? There were many Americans who loved Israel and came over to fight then. Don't you remember David Marcus?"

"David Marcus was Jewish."

"Still, it's just an intuition. What do you really know about him?"

"I know enough!" Dahlia was really getting annoyed. She didn't like the way the conversation was going. She was chafing at how overprotective her dad was of her. At times like those, she greatly looked forward to the time, soon, when she would be out on her own.

"What difference does it make, Benny?" Leah said. "The main thing is that he's Jewish now. Conversation over."

***

By 4:00 p.m., the crowd had thinned. The heat let up, and camp began to return to normal.

The Gilads bid their daughters good-bye and began the long trek home, dreading how little Doron would fare for all those long hours.

"Next time, Benny, we're staying in a hotel!" Leah said as they drove away.

On the way home, as they were driving down Interstate 95, Leah looked out the side window and mused aloud, "You know, Benny, Dahlia is in love with that Arik."

"Don't be silly. How could you know this?"

"You men don't see anything. Didn't you notice the way she was looking at him? She's crazy for him! A mother knows these things."

"Leah, that prospect doesn't excite me, to be frank. He seems a bit of a boor. I still think that he's a convert. Dahlia loves to feel independent, even if it involves getting under my skin. Why can't she be attracted to a nice Jewish boy?"

"You mean the chubby, effeminate, spoiled American Jewish boys we see everywhere?"

"There are plenty of Israeli boys—even in the diplomatic corps—that she can pick from."

"I don't know if you've noticed, Benny, but she's growing into a woman who will very shortly be making her own decisions—without any advice from you!"

"That's what worries me. I hope she'll be making the right decisions."

"This isn't the final shidduch, Benny. She'll go through many boys before she settles down. Don't worry."

***

The rest of summer was fairly uneventful for Arik and Dahlia. In the color war, they were deliberately put on opposing teams. They spent those days at odds with each other, but even though they were highly competitive it was all in good fun. They spent three days in the traditional Machane Chutz, affectionately known as Machane Schmutz, which was supposed to be a backpacking, hiking, and camping trip in the woods but turned out to be three days of wallowing in dirt and mud.

In mid-August, the campers got word of a mammoth music festival only forty miles north of Camp Moshava, near White Lake, New York. More than 100,000 people were expected to attend. Rubin smuggled in an issue of the Village Voice newspaper that described the upcoming festivities. The performers were a complete who's who of rock and roll: Janis Joplin, Jimi Hendrix, Crosby, Stills & Nash, Jefferson Airplane, Richie Havens, and many others. Arik, Richard, Dahlia, and Penny formulated a meticulous plan to escape from camp and hitch a ride to Woodstock, but they were caught near the bus station in Honesdale and nearly thrown out of camp for their efforts.

Finally, the summer ended, and with that end came tearful farewells, hugs, and promises to write. Dahlia was about to board her bus to Washington, D.C. and Arik his bus to New York, where he would catch a plane to Los Angeles that night. The pair stood apart from the other campers, arms locked, holding each other's hands and staring into each other's eyes.

"This was the best summer of my life," Dahlia said.

"Mine too," Arik said. "I'll write you every week and try to arrange to come visit you for Sukkot."

"That would be wonderful. I miss you already." Dahlia became teary-eyed.

"I'll miss you terribly. I can't wait to tell Reverend Perkins about you."

"I look forward to meeting him."

Penny and Richard walked by.

"Hey, Penny, let me help you with your trunk," Arik teased.

"Thanks, Arik, but Richard already put it in the bus."

Richard smiled and said, "Strong like bull!"

"I'm so jealous," Dahlia said. "You guys get to spend the bus ride home together." She hugged Penny tightly. "Let's plan a ski trip for winter break, the four of us."

"That would be amazing," Arik said. "We could meet halfway. How about Colorado?"

"Sounds great!" Richard said.

Everyone boarded the buses, which drove off. And the camp fell silent for another year.

Chapter 11

Dahlia's bus ride home to Washington, D.C., in Labor Day traffic, felt impossibly long. Her head leaned against the bus window as she dozed and daydreamed. She thought about arriving home to a clean bed, real showers, and all of the great food that the embassy staff would prepare for her. All of her school friends and other kids from the diplomatic corps would be in Washington; autumn meant that everyone was back and the receptions and parties would start up again in earnest.

The Washington Redskins season would start in ten days, and she loved going to RFK Stadium to watch the team play. She loved tailgating almost as much as she loved screaming her guts out when the Skins scored a touchdown. The acoustics made the entire stadium shake when the fans got riled up, which made playing there a nightmare for the visiting team. Through the embassy, she had fifth-row seats at the forty-yard line, so close to the field that she almost could smell the players.

The High Holidays were coming up, too, and her whole family, including her uncles, aunts, and cousins in Israel, would be in town to celebrate. So, Dahlia had a lot to look forward to even as she mused about her summer and how emotional and unexpected it had been. It had been a real coming of age for her. Her previous summers at Camp Moshava had included sports, good times, and flirtations, but something profound had happened to her during the past two months, and she knew it. A mysterious stranger with a checkered past had come out of nowhere and into her life, and now nothing could or would ever be the same. Just thinking about Arik made her heart race.

What do I see in him? she asked herself. He was certainly an amazing athlete who loved sports and played them at a high level, just as she did. But, more importantly, he really understood the spirit of competition and fair play. That was a rare trait these days. Also, he was, of course, very physically attractive to her. But he came from such a different upbringing than she did.

Through her relationship with Arik, Dahlia had begun to appreciate that her entire life had been handed to her and that she lived from one day to the next with very little care. Just as Arik had said, she was admired wherever she went, but for what? She hadn't done much to deserve the admiration. Was it really all about her appearance? Or her family name? Those things were just an accident of birth. She just have easily could have been born into Arik's family and Arik into hers. Her father just as easily could have lost his leg or worse.

Arik has had to fight and claw for everything he has. He had few material possessions to speak of, and he lived by his wits and his God-given physical and intellectual talents. It was amazing what he had accomplished already, and she had a feeling that he would accomplish so much more in the future. She didn't feel sorry for him—that would be silly, because he never showed a trace of feeling sorry for himself—and, besides, feeling sorry for someone is no reason to be in love with him. No, she simply felt that he had such a mature goodness about him, more than anyone she had ever met. He was self-confident in a quiet way, and he never showed arrogance; he was kind and self-deprecating; he spoke his mind, but he also knew when to shut up. If Arik didn't know something, he didn't feel embarrassed in the slightest about saying so; he was always eager to learn something new.

She could go on and on about his qualities, but what Dahlia didn't know was whether their relationship would be a simple summer fling or something more. Only time would tell. *I hope that Arik will visit me for Sukkot. It's so lovely in Washington then,* she thought as she fell asleep.

***

Arik took a cab from Los Angeles International Airport to his home in Lynwood, in southern Los Angeles County. As he walked up the stairs to the three-bedroom, stucco bungalow with the small but tidy front lawn ringed by two date palms, he felt a strange sense that the house was smaller than he remembered it being only two months earlier. So much had happened to him over the summer. He had met many new people, and he had been welcomed into a new society that he had not known existed. He could barely wait to see Rabbi Rabinovich and tell him about all that he had learned.

Arik was looking forward to trekking out to Watts, after he had settled in, to see Reverend Perkins. Reverend Perkins had followed Arik's journey into Judaism with great interest. He had told Arik that he was gratified that Arik was serving as a good role model for his two older sons, Tyrone and Antwan, by engaging them in long conversations about God and trying to find meaning in life. Tyrone and Antwan attended church much more regularly than they had before, and they were talking about getting good grades and going to college. Mostly, though, Arik wanted to tell the reverend about a beautiful young woman he had met at camp. He wasn't sure what would happen between him and Dahlia. After all, he was in LA, and she was in Washington, D.C. He knew that long-distance relationships take a great deal of work. Long-distance phone calls were so expensive, but how could they carry on a long-term relationship simply by letter writing?

When he walked into the house, the first thing that hit him was the odor. There was a distinct smell of Lysol that was attempting to cover an underlying stench. *What is that smell?* It seemed like a combination of rotting flesh and bedpans. When Arik thought about it honestly, he realized that he had been brought up in a nursing home. It was as if he were smelling and seeing the house for the first time. The rooms were tiny. The house was filled with secondhand furniture. There was a six-foot-tall plastic palm tree in the corner of the living room. The couch was forever encased in a plastic cover that made it look hideous. He had always been told that the cover was to protect the cloth of the couch. But from what? And why? Almost no one ever visited. What was the sense of worrying about dirtying the cloth when the couch spent its whole existence buried in yellowed, torn plastic dust covers that looked more and more disgusting over time? It was one of those mysteries of life that Arik would never understand.

"Imma! Abba! Is anybody home?" Arik called out in Hebrew.

Miriam Meir came out of the kitchen, wiping her wet hands on her apron. She was heavyset, and her face was creased from long years of toil about which she never uttered a complaint. Despite it all, her eyes still sparkled and she had a broad, ready smile, especially for her baby, Arik. She ran up to him and grabbed him around the waist. He leaned down to allow her to kiss his cheek.

"How was the rest of your summer, chaboob?" Miriam asked.

"It was wonderful, Imma. I made many new friends. I also met someone special—"

"Ooh! Arik! You must tell me all about it." Miriam beamed at him.

"Where's Abba?" Arik asked.

"He's upstairs, in bed watching TV. The doctors had to take off another three inches of bone and give him several weeks of antibiotics. He just got home three days ago, and he's still in considerable pain, but the wound looks like it's finally healing."

Arik had heard that about a dozen times before.

"Go see him, motek. I'm making dinner."

Over the past year, Arik had prevailed on his mother to make the kitchen kosher, which she had done dutifully. She had been raised Orthodox before the War, so keeping kosher was not new to her. But she did it discreetly and quietly so that Arik's father, Ze'ev, never really noticed. He just ate whatever Miriam gave him. He was usually too sick, miserable, or pained to see that anything had changed.

Arik entered his father's bedroom. When he did, the noticed the much more intense smell.

"Shalom, Abba. How are you feeling?"

Ze'ev smiled weakly. His face was ashen, and he looked tired. Clearly, this most recent stint in the hospital had worn him out. He always showed a brave face to the world, regardless of the situation, and he was always intensely proud, refusing help from family and friends unless there was absolutely no choice. He always expected help from Arik, however, making demands on his time and energy whenever he wanted. While growing up, Arik had made conscious efforts to avoid his Abba, for fear that he would be given a new task or chore no matter how inconvenient it was for him at the time. Arik never openly turned his father down, though. He always dropped whatever he was doing and did what was expected of him.

Arik's father began a monologue that Arik did not attempt to interrupt. "Oh Arik, you're here. Help me get onto the bedpan. Careful, easy . . . the leg! Ahh! That's much better. You know, since you've been gone, nobody has seen to the yard in the back. The grass is nearly a foot high. You know, Arik, we're not millionaires. We can't afford a gardener. Now that you're back, you'll need to take some responsibility around here. Uncle Itzik is supporting us by paying me even though I can't go to work. We're not charity cases, though. You spend so much of your time playing sports and doing your judo. You give no thought to getting a job to help support the family. You're big and strong, and you could easily work while you're in school. I've already spoken to Uncle Itzik about your working with him after school for a few hours. It's the least we can do. You'll be working with his men at the warehouse. You'll learn some good skills, like driving a forklift. He might even let you drive the delivery truck."

Arik slowed his breathing and maintained his composure. When he was younger, he lashed out and yelled at his father when he used him as a prop. Ze'ev never seemed to care about anyone but himself. He lived his life believing that the world owed him something. Even if this was true, it was still unfair for him to project those emotions and attitudes on those around him, his family and his few friends. Nonetheless, the people who had wronged him were nowhere to be found, so he lashed out with his irascible temper and sarcastic wit at anyone he could. He rarely inquired about someone else's welfare. Were it not for Imma's generous, open nature, the couple probably would have had no friends at all.

"Abba, I believe I asked you how you were feeling, but you never asked me how camp was," Arik said evenly.

"How should I feel? They took off more of my leg. I was sick as a dog. The pain is getting a bit better. At least when I'm better it will be easier to get around."

"How do you figure?"

"They took ten pounds off my leg." Ze'ev laughed. "I think I'm on to something—a brand-new weight-loss program. Absolutely foolproof!"

"That's just great, Abba!" Arik smirked. "Have you been outside at all? Let me take you out. The weather is warm and dry. The air will do you some good."

"Not today, Arik. Maybe tomorrow. I'm very tired. So, how was your summer? Did you get the taste of Israel you wanted? Have you had enough, or have you become a religious fanatic? I hope you've given up the crazy idea of going into the Israeli Army. Do you want to end up like me?"

Ari opened his mouth to speak, but his father cut him off before he was able to say even one word.

"Don't be naive, Arik. You don't know what war really is. You think it's like the movies, like John Wayne. Reality, my boy, is much different. Everyone goes into the army, thinking 'Hakol yihiyeh b'seder,' that everything will be okay! Nobody thinks that anything bad will happen to them. After the war, everyone focuses on the victory but not the cost. If you survive the war untouched, you forget those who didn't. Even the best of them forget."

Arik had heard this speech a hundred times. Any thought of telling his Abba about Dahlia vanished. What would be the point? He won't pay attention to things that are important to me, anyway.

"When do you start school?"

"Next Tuesday, after Labor Day. I'm going out now."

Arik left his father's bedroom and went downstairs.

"Imma!" Ari called, "please don't wait for me for dinner!"

"Where are you going, motek?" she asked.

"To see the reverend."

"Send him my best."

"I will."

***

Somehow, Arik got the beat-up 1962 Chevy Chevelle to start. He pulled out of the driveway and onto the Harbor Freeway. In twenty minutes, he was knocking on the Perkins family's door.

"Well, Jesus have mercy on me! If it isn't my favorite adopted son, back from the dead!" Maimie called out so loudly that everyone in the house came running. She grabbed Arik and gave him a bear hug and an affectionate kiss on the cheek. "I want to hear all about your summer, Arik."

"How was your summer, Maimie? I missed you all so much. There's a lot to tell. Is the reverend home?"

"Well, lookie here!" the reverend entered with a big grin. "How was your summer, son?"

Arik gave him a meaty handshake and a hug.

"Did you find what you were looking for back east? You left here a man on a mission," the reverend asked.

"I think I did. And some things I wasn't looking for. I also found out some things about myself from seeing how the outside looks in, if that makes any sense."

"Well, isn't that always the way?" The reverend looked at Arik reflectively, with his big brown eyes that always shone with deep wisdom. "A man's journey is dotted with people, places, and events that shape and mold you but also send you opportunities. So, Arik, what have you learned?"

Arik told him about his growing ties to Judaism and Israel, how he had made real friends for the first time with other Jews his own age, and how he felt that he understood for the first time what it meant to be part of the Zionist movement or any movement.

"So, it looks like you might be going to go into the Israeli Army after all," the reverend said.

"I think I may. The emissaries from Israel that were in camp are very active in trying to recruit people to immigrate. I spoke to one at length, and he told me he'd work with his contacts at The Jewish Agency to help set it up. . . I also met a girl."

Antwan, who had been in the other room, bolted in. "Hey, bro! Wassup?" He jumped at Arik and gave him a warm hug. "What you sayin', Arik? You got youself a squeeze?"

Arik blushed. "I think so."

"I bet you really dig this chick," Antwan said. "Look at you, blushin' like a girl!"

"Hey, Antwan! Let the man speak." The reverend laughed.

Arik told them all about Dahlia and his feelings for her but also about how the whole thing had blown up when she heard about the Derrick Smyth affair. Arik showed them a Polaroid photo of Dahlia and him, taken just before Shabbat.

"She's as fine as Georgia pine. You did good, bro." Antwan winked at Arik.

The reverend shook his head. "Sweet Jesus, bad news does travel fast. There's no telling the far-reaching effect an evil tongue can have. Ah, Arik, tell us more about this girl."

Arik gave them a more complete account of their relationship.

"An ambassador's daughter!" the reverend said. "Wow, Arik, you really hit the jackpot. Not too shabby. The main thing though: Is she a good person? Growing up with that privilege, she might be arrogant and spoiled."

"She's really very sweet . . . though she can be a bit judgmental at times. She needs to grow up a bit, I think, but she will."

Antwan cut to the chase. "How you gonna carry on this relationship, you bein' here and her back east?"

"We'll see. I'm going to Washington for a week after the High Holidays to spend time with her and her family. So, we'll see how that goes."

"That ought to be interesting." Antwan smiled. "Say, Arik, you gonna play ball this year? I heard Baylor came to camp to teach all the little white kids how the game supposed to be played."

The reverend shot him a look.

"You know what I'm talking 'bout, Arik. I meant it in a good way." Antwan laughed.

"It was actually amazing. Those kids didn't know what hit them. Elgin and I put on a show for them. It was the only time I got to really play during the whole summer. The rest of the time, I was running clinics for the kids. Even that was good, though."

Arik told them about the basketball game against Camp Morasha. His account of taking over at the end of the game sent the three of them into paroxysms of laughter.

"It was definitely a Kodak moment." Arik chuckled. "The best part about that night was that I noticed the most beautiful girl in the room sitting in the bleachers across the court. I guess I wanted to give her a show." Arik suddenly turned serious. "I don't know about this year, though. I want to spend as much time as I can playing with the guys in the Cage . . . but my dad's sickness, you know, makes him unable to work at all. My uncle's supporting my family fully, and now my dad feels that I should work part-time in my uncle's shop as payback. But if I stop playing, I'll get rusty . . . and I haven't played any real basketball all summer. But that means cutting down on the martial arts. And I still have the dual curriculum of religious and secular studies."

The reverend said, "Regardless of how you spend your free time or whether you go to the army or college, you'll need to really focus on your studies this year. Whatever challenges life throws at you, you always have your education to fall back on. Nobody can take that away from you. When do you start school?"

"Next Tuesday. But I'm going to have to start working tomorrow for my uncle, all week before I go back."

"Maimie will cook up something you can eat, Arik. Please, stay for dinner," the reverend said.

"Then we can head to the park, see what the Jewish kids taught you 'bout shootin' hoops." Antwan smirked.

"Sounds like a plan, but I'll still kick your butt. I'm rusty but not that rusty!" Arik laughed and wrapped an arm around Antwan's shoulders. "I'm starved. Let's eat!"

***

Watts is a 2.12-square-mile neighborhood in South Central Los Angeles that originally was settled by Mexican rail workers. The next major population influx came in the 1940s, during World War II, when tens of thousands of African American migrants left segregated southern states in search of a better life in California. At that time, the city built several large housing projects for the thousands of war-industry workers. By the early 1960s, these projects were populated entirely by African Americans. As local factories shut down, poverty rates in the area soared. In August 1965, longstanding resentment about police brutality and inadequate public services exploded in what became known as the Watts riots: large sections of the neighborhood were burned down by mobs until the insurrection was finally put down by the California National Guard. The late 1960s saw the rise of street gangs vying for control of the increasingly lucrative trade in illegal drugs. This forced the remaining whites and middle-class blacks out of the area. The advent of the freeway system further isolated Watts from the rest of Los Angeles, hemming the black community into ever-denser living conditions as the population continued to grow.

At night, the street corners and alleys were dotted with drug dealers busily plying their trade and the sounds of sirens and gunfire kept pace with the darkening sky. Kids found their way into gangs, ended up in prison, or hung out on street corners, looking for something to do. Yet, even in Watts, there was a use to which a young man's talent, ambition, and desire to stay out of harm's way could be put: basketball.

Hidden behind the Nickerson Gardens housing project were a dozen basketball courts. They were filled every night with restless teenagers who played there for hours until exhaustion took them over. High school dropouts and aging players who had never made it to college also showed up there to show off their waning skills.

These players followed an established routine. They got into shape by playing half-court one-on-one games while their compatriots cheered them on.

Playground basketball did not have coaches, official referees, or timekeepers. Without these authority figures, the city game was defined by creativity, improvisation, and freedom. It valued tempo control, individual performance, and intimidation through improvisation.

Although the squads were generally pickup, there were unwritten rules and hierarchies determined by talent and seniority. Each player had to prove himself to be promoted to the next level of play.

At the center of the array of courts stood a single court that was surrounded by cobbled-together bleachers and a large chain-link fence that controlled the flow of people who could watch the games up close. On any given night, an NBA player, NCAA player, or even, on occasion, a Division I scout might grace the bleachers. This particular court, which was played on by only the most elite squads, was lovingly referred to in the neighborhood as the Cage. Entry was strictly enforced by neighborhood toughs who carried handguns tucked under their belts. The Cage served to keep gamblers, hustlers, drug dealers, and other assorted petty hoodlums out of the court, forcing them to watch the elite games from behind the chain-link fence. This protection was important, because it was not uncommon for drug dealers to swagger about at neighborhood tournaments and try to do a bit of recruiting of their own or betting on the game.

In this neighborhood, which was ravaged by drugs and gang violence, the Cage offered a cherished sanctuary. It also provided the only opportunity for ghetto kids to see basketball played at a high level, because tickets to see the pro and college teams play were expensive or at least expensive enough that they were way out of those kids' league.

Even the drug dealers and other hoodlums refrained from vandalizing the Cage, because in Watts the possibility of transcendence through basketball—namely, a scholarship to a Division I college—was the holy grail cherished by everyone. The main goal was to get out of Watts and reach for the American dream, which was denied to most of the young people at the playground. Even if an NBA contract was not in the cards for a player, his talent and tenacity on the basketball court could reward him with a college education, a decent job, and a one-way ticket out of Watts.

On this night, soon after the orange court lights at the Cage had come on, displacing the encroaching darkness, two players at either end of the court climbed the fence, sat atop the backboards, and hung the nets. This was the sign that serious play was about to begin.

Darkness brought only a cool, vaporous breeze—nothing to distract the players from the game. The five-on-five contest brought out the best two teams in the neighborhood. When they practiced, they seemed to move as if the spontaneous, magical geometry of the game had been rehearsed in advance. "Tiny" Nate Archibald did tricks with the ball that made it seem as if it was dangling on a string, and then he gunned it to his teammates, in a series of behind-the-back passes, sidearm passes, and shovel passes.

The game between the two evenly matched, ferociously physical, aggressive teams turned into a furious stalemate, and a large crowd formed around the Cage's inner sanctum. The other courts and even the parking lot emptied as people streamed in to watch the death match taking place in the Cage. Stripe-shirted "officials" struggled to keep pace with the sweaty, gleaming, shirtless players, who were streaking back and forth on the court.

With only seven seconds left in the game and his team down by one point, Arik—completely incongruous among the sea of black players—sprinted down the court, illuminated by the orange lights, called out to Antwan, "Homeboy! Homeboy!" Standing under the basket at the other end of the court, having just pulled down a rebound, Antwan let fly a long, improbable pass that Arik caught at the foul line. Arik launched himself into the air and dunked the ball in one ballet-like leap. The rim let out a loud twang. Pandemonium ensued, with spectators jumping up and down, screaming, and climbing the fences around the Cage in their attempts to get to the court as time ran out.

"Yo, bro!" Antwan yelled, "Make it bleed, Arik! Make it bleed!" Arik raised his arms jubilantly and danced a jig, having been rendered momentarily insane by the sheer giddy pleasure of playing basketball to perfection. He felt home at last.

After six grueling hours, the Camp Moshava bus finally pulled into the parking lot of the Ohev Shalom: The National Synagogue, on Sixteenth Street in the Shepherd Park neighborhood of northwest Washington, D.C., a lovely tree-lined neighborhood with large, Old world homes, cul de sacs, and winding streets that evoked the Hampstead Garden Suburb northwest of London. The area's residents were members of Congress, members of the diplomatic corps, and well-to-do lobbyists and businesspeople with significant interest in the federal government.

The Gilads lived on Chesapeake Street, a quiet, dead-end street in the Forest Hills section of northwest Washington, D.C., on the west side of Rock Creek Park. Their home was a Tudor mansion that backed up to the park and was outwardly modest in appearance, The front stone wall and circular driveway belied the inner grandeur of the large hallways, winding staircases, receiving and dining halls, and 25-foot floor-to-ceiling glass windows that overlooked the patio and the wooded park beyond.

The location was ideal, because it was both walking distance from Adas Israel Synagogue and on a sufficiently quiet street to facilitate security for an Israeli ambassador and his family. Furthermore, it was only a fifteen-minute drive from the Israeli embassy on Van Ness Street. The ambassador's security detail consisted of former commandos from Israel's elite combat units. They were responsible for protecting not only the ambassador but also his family. Because the deployments were for several years, the bodyguards became like members of the family. They never relaxed enough, however, to let down their guard. Tucked discreetly under their blazers were loaded 9mm automatic machine pistols that were always at the ready. The bodyguards were no more than boys, really, with the oldest barely twenty-five years of age, but their youthful appearance belied the fact that they were highly trained killers.

Leah Gilad supervised the kitchen staff and frequently took in her own hands the matter of cooking. There was an endless schedule of receptions, dinners, cocktail parties, and visits of ministers from Israel. On occasion, Golda Meir, the Israeli prime minister, dropped in for a "chat" with President Nixon. At those times, the prime minister stayed at the residence. It was Leah's job to ensure that everything went off without a hitch.

When Dahlia got off the Camp Moshava bus, she was greeted by Tomer, the chief of the security detail. He had closely cropped dark hair and a deep tan, and he seemed always to wear his sunglasses and earpiece.

"Shalom, Dahlia. Ma Nishma? How was camp? Did you have a good time?"

"I did! Tremendous fun. But all good things must come to an end. Junior year here is very hard, and I'll have to take my SATs too!"

Tomer laughed. "You are so lucky that you are here, Dahlia. In Israel, you would be starting to study for your Bagrut exams, which are a hundred times more difficult than that silly American SAT."

"You're probably right. What's new at home?"

"Not too much. Rabin was here last week to meet with Nixon about the Phantom sale. Coordinating security with the U.S. Secret Service can be a challenge. They are so arrogant. They are constantly trying to teach us about security methods. What a joke! If they are so good, then why was Kennedy killed? We've never lost a prime minister—or any cabinet member, for that matter."

He kneeled down in front of Dahlia's sister and asked, "And how about you, Nurit? Did you have a good time?"

"Yes, it was amazing. The sports were great, but the boys smelled."

Dahlia and Tomer both laughed.

"I think that one day she will change her mind." Dahlia said.

The trunks were loaded into the back of the limousine. Within fifteen minutes, they were home.

When Dahlia walked through the door, her Mom greeted and kissed her. "How was the rest of camp, booba sheli?"

"It was great. I had a great summer. I almost got thrown out of camp, though, when we tried to sneak out to go to Woodstock. We got caught in town, trying to hitch a ride to White Lake." Dahlia laughed.

"Woodstock? With all those drug-crazed hippies? I saw images of all the mud, pot, and open sex that went on there. I would've been very upset at you if you had gone. I'm glad you didn't."

"I'm not. I think it would've been the experience of a lifetime. There were nearly half a million people there, and there was no violence or crime—just peace and love. Imagine that . . ."

"Oy! What a miracle that people got together and they didn't even try to kill each other! Mazel tov!"

"Besides, Imma, I wasn't alone. Four of us went, and Arik was there to protect me—"

Whoops, Dahlia thought.

"Tell me, Dahlia. Are you and Arik . . .?"

"We've become very close friends, let's just say." Dahlia smiled slightly.

"Dahlia?"

"Please don't tell Abba. I'd rather he not know just now."

Dahlia saw that her Mom needed more convincing. "You know what he's like! Besides, the whole thing just happened by accident. Summertime is magical in camp. Things just happen. I know you're going to think that I'm being silly and childish, but I think I love him. I feel it inside the pit of my stomach. Whenever I see him, my heart starts to race. And I can't control it. I find myself falling asleep at night thinking of him, and he's the first thing I think about when I wake up."

"Sweetheart, you're very young, and this is the first boy you've ever really looked at, though God knows how many boys have looked at you. It's nice to have a summer crush. It's part of being a teenager. But now summer is over, and you have a hard year in school ahead of you, which you need to focus on."

"Oh, you know I won't let anything interfere with that. But my feelings for him are very strong. I want him to come visit us for Sukkot."

"Do you think that's a good idea, Dahlia? Where will he stay?"

"I thought he could stay here, with us. We have plenty of room."

"Well, we won't, because Doda Ruti and the whole family are coming from Israel to stay with us for the chagim, which also means that you'll have to spend time entertaining your cousins and playing tour guide. It's their first time in Washington. I need to think about this. I don't think that Abba will agree to have him come—"

"Why not?" Dahlia could not hold back her emotions. "Abba didn't like him from the beginning, did he?"

"It's just your imagination, Dahlia."

"It is not! I could tell by the way he spoke about him that Arik made a bad first impression on him."

"We got the sense that Arik has been brought up very differently than you. That's all. He seemed a bit coarse . . . uncultured."

"Just because he grew up in poverty? He's had to fight for everything he has. His father was a war hero in Israel and was severely wounded. He was denied compensation by our government after the war and was left to fend for himself. It's no wonder they had no money coming in. What do you expect? Shame on us, not him."

"There must have been some reason he didn't get compensation, Dahlia."

"Who knows? Couldn't Abba help him? Will you speak to him about it? Or should I?"

"Abba has been very busy. The defense minister came in last week, and I didn't see him at all. He's been putting in eighteen-hour days. And the negotiations with the Americans about getting fighter jets to help with the War of Attrition, on the Suez Canal, have gone into a very delicate stage. Nixon has an advisor, a German Jew called Kissinger, who thinks that because he's Jewish he can boss us around like we're children and Nixon can say and do what he wants without worry of being called an anti-Semite. Abba hasn't had time for anything else lately. Now, get unpacked, and wash up for dinner. What do they do to you at camp? You both look happy and healthy, but the filth in your trunk is not to be believed."

Ambassador Gilad ambled into the kitchen, snuck up behind Dahlia, grabbed her by the waist, and picked her up off the floor, sending her into giggling squeals of delight.

"Metuka! How was the rest of your summer?" Benny hugged her and kissed her cheek. "How we've missed you! It's been so quiet around here without you and your sister creating chaos. Although there has been enough chaos at work, I suppose. Golda and Rabin are coming in this week to seal the deal with Nixon, and not a moment too soon. The Egyptians have received massive aid from the Soviets. There are thousands of Russian troops in Egypt, posing as advisors. They have more than replaced Egypt's tanks and artillery that Egypt lost in the war, and to make matters worse they've completely restocked their air force with brand-new MiG-21s and the latest missile air-defense systems. They've just shot down several of our Super Mystères over the canal. Our intelligence tells us that Russian pilots are themselves flying their planes and operating their radar. We need those American planes and weapon systems to keep our edge. Our positions on the canal are being shelled on almost a daily basis, causing casualties. But enough business talk. Leah, is dinner ready?"

"In a few minutes," Leah said.

"Dahlia, you've come back from camp looking like a grown woman. It's amazing what summer camp can do. All that fresh air, which reminds me. . . Tomorrow night there's going to be a big reception for Golda and Yitzhak at the Mayflower Hotel. Why don't you join Imma and me? It'll be a big thrill for you to meet them."

"That sounds great! I'd love to come. But will there be anyone else my age, or will I have to stand around all evening being bored and acting polite?"

"Let me see who I can come up with," Benny said. "All of our diplomatic attachés will be there, and some have teenagers in your class. Don't you go to school with Sar-el and Irit?"

"That would work," Dahlia said. She looked at her mother. "But what in the world would I wear?"

"You have several evening cocktail dresses to choose from in your closet. We'll go have a look after dinner. Worst comes to worst, we'll head over to Chevy Chase tomorrow and see what we can find at Bloomingdale's. You don't start school until next Monday, so we can spend the next few days shopping and getting organized anyway."

Juan, the chief steward, who was wearing his uniform of a smart dinner jacket, nodded discreetly to Leah, indicating that dinner was ready.

Dahlia sauntered into the kitchen and saw Thelma hard at work putting the finishing touches on the roast beef. She felt a pang in her stomach. She saw Thelma in a new light after the conversations that she and Arik had had.

"Hi, Thelma! How was your summer?" she asked.

"Just fine, Miss Dahlia, just fine," Thelma said. "Had my sister and aunt come up from South Carolina, and we had a good visit on my days off. I hope you had a good time in camp?"

"I did." Dahlia smiled. "It's good to be back home, though."

"It's good to have you back, Miss Dahlia."

***

Early the next morning, Arik got his rusty light-blue 1963 Chevelle and tooled down Topanga Canyon and into the San Fernando Valley. When it entered the industrial zone, the road became little more than a dirt track. The dump truck in front of him kicked up a cloud of dust and sand. When Arik's view cleared, he saw that he had arrived at a large factory–warehouse compound. A large sign hung over building 6: IKE MYER CONSTRUCTION SUPPLY, INC.

Arik parked and then entered a grimy, hot waiting room. Large advertisements for construction machinery were plastered to the walls;

incongruously, each had managed to sneak a scantily clad, buxom woman into the frame. Arik sat on one of a row of attached orange molded-polymer chairs.

"You Arik?" Gladys, the gum-chewing receptionist, had a large orange bouffant hairdo and was wearing a low-cut sweater and tight jeans that looked as if they had been painted onto her.

He nodded.

"I'll tell Mr. Ike you're here." She gave Arik a lascivious look.

In a moment, Uncle Itzik came out of his office, smiling broadly. Itzik was a big, sweaty bear of a man. He was over six feet tall, and he weighed nearly three hundred pounds. His years of self-indulgence showed in his potbelly, and a sweaty shirt was barely holding back his massive, hairy chest. He had a wry sense of humor, but he could unleash a fierce temper if anyone dared to cross him.

"Shalom, Arik! How was your summer? I heard you went back east to summer camp."

"It was good to try something new," Arik said.

"Ze'ev tells me that you're looking for a way to make some extra money."

"One can always use a bit of extra money."

"How many hours do you want to work?"

"I'm not sure yet. I'm in the Rambam Academy this year, and they have a double curriculum, so I'm busy most of the day. I don't work anymore on Shabbat, so that leaves Sunday and some evenings during the week."

"Well, that's not very much. . . Your father told me your schedule outside school was pretty much wide open. He told me you could give me twenty hours a week."

"I've got martial arts . . . and basketball . . . and with Jewish studies, my days are full."

Itzik scratched his head.

"I'll do the best I can," Arik added.

"Well, we'll get started and see how it goes. What sort of skills do you have?"

"I did some construction in camp, and I'm fairly handy with power tools."

"Can you drive a truck?"

"Not officially. I just got my driver's license. I can drive a car and motorcycle, and I've driven some small trucks, but I don't have a trucker's license."

"Do you have any office skills like bookkeeping or inventory management and the like?"

"Not really."

"Well, boychick, what am I going to do with you?" Itzik sighed. He surveyed Arik's powerful arms through his worn, cutoff sweatshirt. "We'll start you out in the loading yard. You'll work with Marcelo, my overseer. Gladys, have Marcelo come up front."

Marcelo arrived in a moment. He was Mexican, short—about five feet eight—but very stocky with thick, meaty arms. He appeared to have no neck, just a thick jaw that jutted directly out of his chest. Arik mused that he bore a faint resemblance to Fred Flintstone.

"Marcelo, I need you put Arik to work," Itzik said.

Marcelo surveyed Arik up and down as if he were a horse he had just bought. "So, you're the boss's nephew! You think you're a real tough guy, huh? Well, we'll see. Follow me."

As Arik followed Marcelo, Itzik smiled and called out, "Good luck, Arik!"

Marcelo led Arik to the loading dock behind the building. The dock area was filled with dust, smoke, and diesel exhaust fumes from the seemingly endless train of eighteen-wheel tractor trailers coming in. There were several teams of men moving 75-pound sacks of sand and cement from a forklift pallet to an open flatbed truck. Marcelo pointed to the team that was smaller than the others. "You'll work with this crew."

He introduced Arik to the other members of the crew. Soon Arik was loading sacks, grateful for the workout.

"Welcome to the chain gang, whitey! How'd you get stuck doing nigga work with us?" asked a barrel-chested, middle-aged black man with gleaming white teeth. He reached out a huge, powerful hand to shake Arik's. "I'm Darnell Gibson."

"I'm Arik Meir."

"You from Israel?"

"No, not yet." Arik smiled. "But my dad is."

"Mr. Bossman Myer ain't, though. Ain't they brothers?"

"It's complicated. They both survived the war, but then they got separated. Uncle Itzik—I mean, Ike—came directly to the States from Europe. My dad went to Israel to fight in the War of Independence in '48. Then he came here."

"So, whatcha doing here, man?"

"Just trying to make some extra pocket money."

"I figure that. But I mean, why'd your uncle put you with out here, with us? This work'll break you in two, no matter how tough you think you is. You gotta get used to it, and if you're anythin' like your pansy-ass cousin, Ethan, the boss's son, you won't last a day here. Speakin' of . . ."

A bright-red Ford Mustang convertible pulled up. Arik's cousin Ethan jumped out of the driver's seat.

"Hey, you lazy pieces of shit! My dad doesn't pay you to stand around and socialize like a bunch of girls. Oh, look! I should have known. Arik, are you directing this yapfest?"

"Oh, hi, Ethan." Arik smiled thinly. This was the only thing Arik truly dreaded about working for his uncle: Ethan. Ethan was a spoiled, arrogant punk who had gotten everything in his life handed to him. He was always ready with a smug, self-satisfied, rude comment, knowing that Arik couldn't confront him because of Arik's dad's dependence on Ethan's dad. It took every bit of Arik's self-control for him to hold his tongue in situations like these.

Ethan was the oldest child of Itzik and Chana Myerowitz. The couple had met in the Bergen-Belsen Displaced Person's Camp after the War. They both had survived the Buchenwald concentration camp. When presented with the opportunity to emigrate to Palestine after the War, they instead had chosen to go to the United States—the goldene medineh, or golden country. Having survived four years of horror, they had wanted no part of the crazy experiment in Palestine. They hadn't wanted to witness 80 million Arabs finishing Hitler's work by exterminating Palestine's 600,000 Jews. They had felt that they were entitled to the good life and that America offered it to them. They had gone aboard the refugee ship the USS Langfitt and bypassed the East Coast, preferring the warm weather and easy living of Southern California. When they had arrived, Los Angeles was a sleepy town in the sun, but things had begun to heat up in the late '50s, when the Brooklyn Dodgers came to town. Along with several other Jewish Holocaust survivors, they had bought up large tracts of land in the San Fernando Valley just as the building boom was starting. As far as the eye could see in the broad Valley there sprang up residential homes, shopping centers, and business parks. Instead of remaining in real estate, however, Itzik had elected to go into the construction supply business. His company had become the primary source of building material for the Valley. Itzik Myerowitz quickly had become a multimillionaire, changed his name to Ike Myer, and entered the ranks of the Jewish nouveau riche in LA.

While in the Bergen-Belsen DP camp after the liberation, Itzik had implored his older brother, Wolf, to go to the States with him rather than tempting fate. They had been the only survivors of their extended family. In the camps, there had been several times that Itzik was chosen for the gas chambers only to be saved at the last second by Wolf who, because of his prewar boxing fame, had some fans among the SS. They had been inseparable in the DP camp after the war, but they had argued constantly about what do and where to go. Going back to Poland had been out of the question. Some Jews, having made it through the whole Holocaust, had tried to do that and been killed by the locals. Wolf had been hell-bent on going to Palestine, but Ike had had none of it. Ike had been devastated when he had woken up one morning and Wolf was gone. He had gone to Palestine with Aliyah Bet, the illegal Jewish immigration organization, and he had been snuck in right under the noses of the British. Upon his arrival in Palestine, Wolf had changed his name to Ze'ev, which means Wolf in Hebrew. Ike had lost touch with Ze'ev for five years, until he had been contacted by Miriam Meir, Ze'ev's wife. By that time, Ze'ev had been transformed into a penniless invalid.

Itzik had secured passage and a visa to the United States for Ze'ev, Miriam, and their newborn son, Arik, and found a place for Ze'ev in his business. Although Ze'ev spent more time in the hospital and convalescent homes than at work, Itzik was happy to care for the only flesh and blood that he had in the whole world. Itzik well understood that he was still alive only because of Ze'ev. He felt enormously protective of his now-crippled older brother, and he had committed himself to the care of his brother for the rest of his life. Ze'ev, for his part, was an intensely proud man. Although Ze'ev had no choice but to accept Itzik's charity, the exchange had never been a smooth one.

"Hey, Arik! I want you to meet my girlfriend, Shelly."

Ethan and Shelly stepped out of the car.

"Hi, Shelly," Arik said. "Nice to meet you." He smiled.

Shelly wore tight cutoff jeans shorts that barely concealed her buttocks, lace-up boots to the knee, and a short halter top that barely covered her large breasts, which Arik judged as mostly manufactured. It seemed to Arik as if Ethan had picked her up on a street corner like Hollywood and Vine.

"Arik's working for my dad to earn some extra money for himself." Ethan smirked.

Arik kept smiling and stared intently at Shelly. She seemed not to react to Ethan's patronizing tone.

"You know, Ethan, some people have to do that," Shelly said. "Aren't you guys cousins?"

Ethan sneered. "Yeah, we are." He added, in an undertone, "Lucky me," but then he raised his voice again. "Okay, enough socializing. You need to go back to work, Arik. We've got to go. We're off to the Crosby, Stills & Nash concert at the Hollywood Bowl."

Ethan and Shelly jumped back into the Mustang. Ethan gave Shelly a lengthy smooch and then laughed. He drove away, screeching the Mustang's tires on the dirt and covering Arik and the other men in dust.

"Real nice guy, that Ethan." The voice belonged to Leroy Johnston, a gregarious younger black man who was missing two front teeth. "He really your cousin?"

"I'm ashamed to admit it," Arik said.

"Hey, ain't you that guy from the papers, who beat up that Nazi?" A voice called out. "You know, the one who was killin' black kids in Watts?"

"Yeah. That's me."

"You're in tight with Reverend Perkins, right? I'm Shawntay Wilkins." A tall lanky fellow no more than eighteen years old reached out and shook Arik's hand.

"Hey, man, good meeting you," Arik said. "Wait a minute, I think I know you from somewhere. Don't you play basketball at the Rosecrans Community Center in Gardena?"

"Yeah, man! I play there Monday and Thursday nights." Shawntay looked at Arik again, more closely. "Now I remember. You got some pretty good game for a white dude."

Everyone laughed.

"You gonna be working here full-time?" Shawntay asked Arik.

"No, just a few hours during the week and then on Sundays. I still have another year of school."

"You see, fellas, Arik's a smart Jew boy. He's stayin' in school so he don't end up like us," Leroy said. "I suppose you'll be goin' to college after that."

"I don't know yet. I may be going to the army."

"Gonna be shootin' up gooks and babies in 'Nam with all the other brothers? You take care you don't come home in a body bag like everybody else," Leroy said. "You know, you don't hear much about Jews goin' to 'Nam. They mostly in college, studyin' to be rabbis and such. That leaves us niggas to do the fightin'. Then we comes home and gets treated like shit back here. Ain't that somethin'? The white man sendin' the black man to fight the yellow man to protect the country he stole from the red man."

"Well, you know, Leroy, my grandparents weren't white slave owners either," Arik said. "While you guys were down south, my ancestors were getting the crap kicked out of them by the Cossacks and the Polish peasants, until some German dude named Hitler decided we were all better off barbecued, so I can sympathize with you."

Shawntay gave Arik a high five. "You ain't as white as you look. That's why they dig you in Watts."

Darnell adopted a more serious tone. "You seem like a good man. I thought all Jews were like Ethan. You know, bein' all about the money and such and always actin' like such an asshole."

"C'mon, guys, you all know about stereotypes," Arik said.

"I s'pose so." Darnell smiled. "I s'pose so."

They all went back to work, loading the cement bags and sand bags until the truck was piled five feet high. Arik felt completely at home with his new crew, and he loved the banter. As long as that prick Ethan wasn't around, this job might not be so bad after all.

By this time, the sun was scorching hot and all the men were covered in sweat and dirt.

Marcelo walked out of the warehouse. "I need three volunteers: you, you, and you." He pointed at Arik and two others.

"How come he calls them volunteers, when he just picks us?" Shawntay said under his breath.

Arik snickered.

Marcelo continued as if he hadn't heard. "We got an order for 12 tons of mulch fertilizer from Garden Gate Landscapers. We keep it away from the main plant, for obvious reasons. You guys are gonna come up with me to the Topanga Canyon annex and fill two hundred and fifty bags of it then load it onto the trucks that are already waiting there."

"Two hundred and fifty bags of shit," Shawntay whispered to Arik.

Arik laughed again. "You heard the man," he said.

The so-called volunteers jumped into the back of the pickup truck, and Marcelo drove them through the dust and into the canyon. They could smell the huge pile of manure from two miles away. Finally, they stopped at the base of a 20-foot mountain of bovine excrement.

Marcelo gave the work orders: "See those bags on the side?" He pointed to a pile of burlap sacks. "Bring them over here, fill them to 80 pounds, and make sure you weigh them. Place them onto the stitching machine, then load them on the trucks. We got three days to finish. This all got to go out by Wednesday. No time like the present, boys! Start shoveling."

The smell of rotting excrement in the burning-hot sun was indescribable. The trio set to work with hand shovels. Arik returned home hours later, totally exhausted and covered in fertilizer.

When he entered the kitchen, Miriam turned around.

"How was your first d—Oh, my God in heaven, what is that terrible smell?"

"I was in Ethan's presence, and you know how 'full of it' he is." Arik laughed, but his mother did not join him.

"Please, Arik, stop saying things like that. One day, someone will hear you. You know how good Itzik is to us."

"You know how much I hate Ethan, Imma."

"Keep your thoughts to yourself, then."

"One day, Imma, you won't be dependent on them. I'll take care of you in the manner you deserve, so we won't have to live like this anymore," Arik promised.

"From your mouth to God's ears! Amen!"

"Miriam!" a voice bellowed from upstairs. "I need clean sheets. I've soiled myself."

Arik felt as if he had gotten heat stroke from doing all that filthy, degrading work in the hot sun. Maybe it had impaired his judgment. He felt that he needed to connect with something beautiful, something human, after a day like he'd had. And he knew that today was just the beginning. He jumped in the shower and, as the cool water splashed over him, he allowed his mind to wander 3,000 miles to the east, to a loving soul with long, blonde hair that flowed and shimmered in the sunlight. Her eyes and smile beckoned to him in his daydreams and again at night before he drifted off to sleep with her face burned into his consciousness.

Arik spent the whole week before school started working at the warehouse shoveling manure and hauling lumber and galvanized steel pipe. In the evenings, he was back at the Cage. On Wednesday evening, the pros showed up to play. Among them were Elgin Baylor and Lew Alcindor. After an aggressive five-on-five scrimmage that lasted half an hour, Arik's team lost and were left on the sidelines, watching the winning team play on. Evenings at the Cage were survival of the fittest at its simplest, and Arik loved the raw honesty of the system. There was no prejudice, no preconceived notions, and no rank pulling. There was only the love of the game, which applied to the pros, the college guys, and the locals alike.

"Hey, Arik! You got a bit rusty over the summer. You're a half second too slow."

Arik turned around to face a giant man with a goatee and a broad smile.

"Hey, Wilt! Go easy on the boy!" Elgin Baylor popped out of nowhere. "I visited that Jewish camp he was at over the summer. He really didn't have anyone to play with."

"That's okay!" Wilt Chamberlain said. "A few weeks back with us, he'll be as right as rain. I'll take you under my wing." Wilt winked at Arik.

***

When he got home from the loading yard on Friday afternoon, Arik looked and smelled like a Pennsylvania coal miner. He stumbled into the kitchen, where Miriam was hard at work putting the finishing touches on chicken soup and gefilte fish.

"Imma, I'm starved!" Arik said as he reached into the soup pot, with his grimy fingers, to steal one of Miriam's famous matzo balls.

"Hey, schmendrick, get out of there with those filthy hands!" Miriam feigned anger.

Arik wrapped his arms around her waist and gave her a bear hug.

"Oy, Arik! You smell like a wild animal! Go take a shower before Shabbat."

"I will, Imma." Arik grabbed a box of matzo crackers and inhaled a mouthful.

"Oh, Arik! I almost forgot. You got a very nice-smelling letter from Washington, D.C. Maybe it's from Mrs. Nixon?" Miriam winked at him.

"Thanks, Imma!"

Arik took the letter. He felt the faint lavender scent send a shockwave through his body. His pulse quickened at the mere thought of opening the envelope. No! He decided that he would not open it until he had showered, until he had cleansed himself of the life he was being forced to endure.

My Dearest Arik,

I feel like it's been a month since I've seen you, touched you. Coming home from camp this year, everything around me seemed transformed. So much changed over the summer. My life feels so different now—in large part because of you. Being with you has made me understand myself better. I truly have been living in this privileged bubble my whole life without realizing how other people have to get by. I always understood there were haves and have nots, but it never occurred to me before that the "haves" have BECAUSE the "have nots" have not. (I hope I got that right.)

I'm not the smartest person in the room, after all, but I'm starting to realize that one can reach great heights with humility. You've taught me that. I've also watched you achieve greatness through sustained effort and struggle. And I know that greatness will only continue. I spent the last three weeks of camp just staring into your eyes and I can already sense what awaits you. I want to be part of that.

The most important thing I learned this summer is that I can love someone with all my heart and soul. You've brought out feelings in me that I never knew existed. Being with you makes me feel important and worthy as a human being, and not because I'm anybody's daughter. You have this amazing gift of making people around you feel good about themselves, like they are important and they belong. I'll always strive to make myself worthy of your love and trust, as I love and trust you with my soul.

How are you doing? How are your parents doing? Is your dad getting a bit better now that he's home?

I'm sure you went back to Watts the day you came home and that you're back playing street basketball with your "homies" down at the Cage. I'm certain that after this summer you must look upon that in a totally different light, too.

School here starts next week. I've spent the whole time since I've been home shopping for clothes, shoes, and school gear and hanging out with my school friends. Junior year here is tough and everyone has to take the SATs. I'm not sure why I have to take those. I'll be going back to Israel when I'm done with high school here, to do my Tzahal service, so they just seem irrelevant.

I can't wait to see you here for Sukkot. It will be a week of bliss for me just to be with you, hold you, and sneak an occasional kiss or two. Have you figured out yet how you're going to pay for the plane tickets? Please keep me posted! Perhaps I can help you pay for those, as a loan of course. I would pay anything just to see you.

Please write soon!

Love you with all my being,
Faithfully yours,
Dahlia

Arik reread the letter three times. He felt a quiver of joy course through him, although it was tinged with just a twinge of resentment over Dahlia's offer to pay his way. There was no way he would let Dahlia pay for anything for him ever. When he tucked the letter in his desk, the lavender scent wafted up one more time before he shut the drawer and felt a strange sense of peace come over him.

***

Arik started school the following Tuesday morning, after Labor Day. After a grueling junior year, senior year was a time to take stock, to think about college applications and the future. Returning to school after a summer at Camp Moshava, Arik felt much more at home in the Jewish environment than he had during the previous school year. That an increased sense of ease helped him to get back into the swing of things.

He made his way into the school with the massive throng of students who were all greeting one another.

"Hey, Arik! What did you do this summer?"

Arik turned around to greet Murray Bodner, one of the most popular kids in the class. Arik and he had shared a few laughs and practical jokes together.

"I went to Camp Moshava in Pennsylvania," Arik said, smiling.

"Why the hell did you do that? We have one right here in Malibu. We're not good enough for you? We were all wondering about that." Murray joked.

"Apparently not! Seriously though, I needed to get out of Dodge for the summer. Family reasons, you know."

"Did you pick up any hot chicks there? There was some significant action in camp this year. You missed out!"

"I guess it was my loss." Arik laughed. He would not be discussing his romantic interest from camp with anyone who had as big a mouth as Murray, of that he was sure.

Ira, Pinnie, and Yitz sauntered by and joined in the reunion.

"Hey, Arik! What's up, dude? We missed you over the summer!" Pinnie said.

"Rabinovich told us you went back east," Ira said. "What were you looking for there? New York girls are such dogs!"

"They were okay, but they definitely need to work on their tans. And they definitely don't get enough exercise," Arik said.

Yitz laughed. "Speaking of tans, I bet the schvartzes you hang out with missed you, too!"

"Come on, Yitz. You're better than that," Arik said. "You definitely don't want to know what they call us."

Rabbi Hirsch walked over. "Come on, boys. I know you're still in summer mode, but playtime is over. Classes start in five minutes."

The students dispersed.

Arik spent the morning studying the Talmud. While most of his classmates had shunned any kind of study during the summer, Arik felt that his time with Eliezer had been extremely well spent. Eliezer was a master Talmudist who had taught him not only the material but how to study the texts, how to look for the hidden voice of the analysis. He could now anticipate difficulties in the flow of the material and questions that would naturally arise. He found himself asking the same questions that medieval commentators had asked. The morning flew by, and on his way to lunch he heard a familiar voice behind him.

"Shalom, Arik! How was your summer?" Rabbi Rabinovich was smiling broadly.

"Shalom, Rabbi Rabinovich. Good to see you. I was going to try to touch base with you last week, but all my plans were hijacked by my dad. I figured I'd see you today."

"And what were you going to tell me?" the rabbi asked with a smile.

"Well, the summer was really transformational for me. I had a chavruta, a study partner, all summer—the camp director's son—who was really outstanding. And it was great to be in a different environment. I got to do Jewish 24-7, which was really interesting."

"I'm so glad to hear it, Arik. The only news I had, came when I spoke to Rabbi Moskowitz after your little incident. He called to ask if I had any more information about your case—"

"I didn't realize there still was a 'case,'" Arik said, a little defensively.

"You know what I mean, Arik."

"Maybe one day I'll just be Arik. Not Ze'ev's son or 'the guy in the papers.' That's why I went east to begin with. You know that! The whole thing nearly blew up in my face, and I thought about leaving on the spot. It was so tough to explain what had happened, to people who had absolutely no idea what I was talking about, even with the scrapbook you sent. I just wanted to be Arik, have some fun and fit in. No more, no less. But now it turns out I'm walking around with a permanent shadow. I'm so fed up." He sighed. "I feel like so many people consider me a work in progress, in one way or another. What's wrong with how I am now? Why can't people just accept me for who I am?"

"Did you ever figure out how it got back there?" Rabbi Rabinovich asked.

"Yes, but I can't share that. It would be just be more lashon hara, more slander."

"Okay. I know you need to hurry to lunch. Come to my office Thursday, after your last period, and we'll talk some more. Do you want to keep studying this year?"

"Definitely!"

Arik ate lunch and then headed to his fourth-period class. He hoped to be an engineer one day, so he was taking advanced classes in both math and physics.

He bumped into Bracha Epstein outside his calculus class.

"Hi, Arik!" she said cheerfully. "How was your summer at Mosh?"

"It was a brand-new experience for me," Arik said evenly. "With my past and all."

"I know. Did you hang out with my cousin Shirah?"

"I did, some. Our relationship took a rather cold turn after the third week of camp, when she received a poison letter from you about me. How could you do that, Bracha? I thought we were friends. Last year, you knew everything about me. We spoke constantly. That letter nearly destroyed everything I'd been trying to do!"

"I didn't mean anything bad by it! I just wanted Shirah to know that a celebrity was coming to camp. You know I collected those clippings because of my involvement in the civil rights movement. In fact, I want to write a paper about you for my senior thesis about breaking the whole 'Black-Jewish'-enmity stereotype. You're an excellent case study. We talked about it, and you said it was fine." Bracha regained her wits after having been momentarily set on her heels by Arik's attack. "We're both on the same team, Arik!"

"I'm not on any team, Bracha. I said it was okay to write the paper—not to go blabbing about it casually, out of context, all over the country. I'm no civil rights campaigner. I don't go to sit-ins, teach-ins, love-ins, or even Holiday Inns for that matter. I'm just a guy who tried to do the right thing. And this crap has been following me around for nearly eighteen months now. I don't play basketball with my friends or hang out in Watts with the reverend and his family to make some grand political statement about civil rights or human equality. I simply do it because I've found family there. I love them. They're the only people I associate with that don't prejudge me, try to lecture me, or try to change me in some way to fit some mold. They accept me as I am. For me, there is no white or black. You're either a mensch or you aren't, no matter what you look like. Speaking of which, what did you hope to gain by sending that newspaper clipping with the picture of me in handcuffs?"

"Oh, my God! Is that the one I sent? I meant to send the one in the Review section, with the commendation you got from the mayor. I was so proud of you."

"Why are you patronizing me? You're not my mother. You had no right to send anything about me without my knowledge and permission. I was nearly thrown out of camp because of it, and it was just dumb luck that kept it from getting into the wrong hands and being made public. I wasn't even upset at Shirah. She responded in the way she felt she had to. Anyone would try to expose a criminal if he were in a summer camp with children around and was trying to keep it a secret. Even the whole scrapbook that Rabinovich sent there ahead of my arrival wouldn't have stemmed the tide of derision. You know why I left town. All I wanted to do was to try to fit in."

"I'm so sorry, Arik! I really didn't mean to hurt you."

"It goes beyond that, Bracha. While I understand now that you didn't mean any harm, you violated my trust and friendship. I'm not really angry with you. I've gotten over that already. It's just that I don't want to be friends with you anymore. I've never said to anyone before, and I never thought I would. There. It's out there now. I've thought for the past month about what I'd say to you when we met, and this is the only thing I could come up with. Not very elegant, but then again nothing about me is. What did you call me last year? A diamond in the rough?"

Arik didn't wait for a response. He just shook his head and walked away.

After classes were finished for the day, Arik went to Rabbi Rabinovich's office.

"Come in, Arik! Have a seat."

When Arik had made himself comfortable, the rabbi said, "It was Bracha who sent the letter."

"It doesn't matter anymore. It's done."

"You had words with her this afternoon, and you left her extremely upset."

"Rabbi, you've always told me that evil gossip has consequences. She'll learn and move on. If she wants to be friends with me, she'll have to regain my trust. I'm not much for the easy apology. Don't worry about it. Let's move on. I've been betrayed so many times in my life that the whole idea of trust has become very precious to me. I try to be loyal and faithful to my friends and the people who rely on me, but I expect the same from others, too. Recently, though, I've had to set the bar lower and lower."

"I still get a sense that you're torn between two worlds. You still spend a great deal of time with goyim while you're trying to come closer to a Torah life. Living a Torah life is all-encompassing, as you discovered in camp. It's a full-time job. Spending so much time among people with a completely different set of morals and values can be detrimental to that process. If you love basketball so much, why don't you try out for the Yeshiva varsity team? I'm sure they would love to have you, and God knows they could use the help. You could even consider trying to get on the West Coast contingent that's going to the upcoming Maccabiah Games in Ramat Gan, near Tel Aviv. This way you could combine your Yiddishkeit and your obvious athleticism. Rabbi Moskowitz told me about the basketball storm you created in camp. This would also be a way for you to connect with Israel in a positive way and go there after high school, perhaps to spend a year there to study in a yeshiva."

"I must be honest with you, Rabbi, I spent a great deal of time studying about Israel, anti-Semitism, and the Torah at camp. I've read about modern Israeli history from the time of Herzl and tried to connect the dots regarding the Bible and Israel's geography. I read The War Against the Jews, by Lucy Davidowitz, and I understand why Jews rushed to Palestine in our century. But there's the rub: In Zionist camps and yeshivas, we're only taught one side of the story. When we went into Palestine, there was a whole population of Arabs that had been living there for centuries. So many of them were killed, too, in the conflicts, and most were uprooted from their homes. Is there any wonder that they hate us? Jewish kids are never asked to confront those uncomfortable questions. The Arabs didn't commit genocide on us. The Europeans did. And to allay their guilty consciences, they took land that belonged to the Arabs and gave it to us."

"These are difficult questions with no easy answers, Arik. Only God can ultimately judge who is right here. The Jewish people lived in Israel for fifteen hundred years before we were thrown out, longer than any European nation lived on their lands. The Muslims showed up four hundred years after we were gone. We never gave up our claims to that land, though—not for one day. We prayed for it every day for nineteen hundred years. There were many attempts to return to the land. Only now were we successful. When the Chalutzim, the pioneers, came to the land ninety years ago, they found a barren country and only settled on barren land or land bought from the Arabs. When the UN voted to partition Palestine in November 1947, the Jews were only going to get the land they were already on, mostly a thin coastal strip and some of the Negev. The Arabs were to get the entire heartland of the country. We were satisfied with the deal, and we accepted it without question. The Arabs rejected it outright, feeling that the whole thing belonged to them. There were even Arab moderates, like King Abdullah, who were willing to deal, but they were killed by a radical ruling fringe led by a terrible anti-Semite, the Grand Mufti of Jerusalem, who was Hitler's personal guest in Berlin during World War II.

"The Arabs chose war, and the day the State of Israel was declared seven countries—in a coordinated effort—invaded Palestine to kill the State before it could be born. It was just by the grace of Hashem and the tremendous heroism of our soldiers that we prevailed and even nearly doubled the size of the land we got. Only two years ago, we were attacked again, by three countries simultaneously, all of them screaming for our blood and for us to be pushed into the sea. Again, we prevailed. We've never sought a fight with them. We'd be happy to live with them in peace and security, but they feel nothing about attacking our innocent woman and children."

Arik said, "I think we have to answer for those crimes as well."

"How so?"

"Rabbi, what happened at Deir Yassin? Almost three hundred Arab civilians—mostly women and children—were killed in cold blood there, by Israelis in an unprovoked attack."

"You're quite right, Arik. It was a terrible episode perpetrated by Irgun criminals, many of whom were never brought to justice. They will be judged by God. But that was one incident. The Arabs perpetrated hundreds of incidents against us. We paid a very heavy price for that episode, in Kfar Etzion, where hundreds of settlers, isolated from the military reach of the Haganah, were slaughtered outright and their bodies mutilated. A convoy of Haddasah doctors and nurses were attacked in Jerusalem and brutally murdered just days after the incident, as well, in retaliation. There have been countless attacks by Arabs on our innocent civilians. War is never clean. It's a very messy business."

"I know, from personal experience," Arik said. "My dad was a war hero in 1948. He lost a leg trying to save five of his buddies, and he received no compensation after the war. That's how we got here. To this day, my dad has no idea why he was blackballed."

The rabbi sat in silence.

Arik's story was unlike the clean, beautiful narrative that Israelis want to teach their children in school and Zionist shlichim like to brainwash the kids with in camps such as Camp Moshava.

"Rabbi, there was really no reason for me to have grown up in poverty after what my dad sacrificed for the Jewish people. Do you have any idea how embarrassing it is for me to be on full scholarship at Rambam? Our family lives from week to week from financial support my uncle gives us. Without that support, we'd be thrown into the street. Who I hang out with pales as an issue in comparison with everything else that goes on in my life. If I accept or reject a religious lifestyle, it wouldn't be because Reverend Perkins or his family talked me out of it. The truth of the matter is that they're pure, decent, kind, God-fearing people that are quite supportive of what I'm doing. In fact, when I go over there for dinner, Mrs. Perkins bends over backward to make sure I have kosher food.

"All I ever hear around here are racial epithets and stereotypes—'niggers,' 'schvartzes.' It's pretty sickening, if you ask me, especially since so many of our students are children of Holocaust survivors who felt the lash of racial hatred. I wonder sometimes whether Jews are upset that the Holocaust happened or that it happened to us!

"Rabbi, these are the questions that are bouncing around in my head that will ultimately determine what type of Jew I become, not who I play basketball with. I'm sorry to be so direct. Besides, why should I play and help the team out? I still feel like an outsider here. Here people are judged by how much money their parents have, what kind of car they drive, what kind of house they live in, what neighborhood they live in, or how religious they are. I have none of those things going for me. Do you realize I've been coming to this school for a year and in that whole time nobody has ever even thought to invite me for Shabbat? I thought religion was somehow supposed to make you a better person all around, or at least that's what's taught around here. But people seem to relate more to commandments between man and God and not between fellow people—Jews or non-Jews. I've already felt the lash of evil slander."

"Let's continue this conversation next time," Rabbi Rabinovich said. "In the meantime, I'd like to make sure that you get invited for Shabbat regularly. Otherwise, you'll never get to shul, as there is no Jewish community within walking distance from your house. You're quite right. It's embarrassing that you've never been invited. I'll speak to some of your friends here—"

"It's okay, Rabbi, if you invite me, but I don't want you to force the issue with anyone else, even if it means I spend Shabbat at home by myself. I'm not an especially proud person, but I won't be made to feel like I'm some kind of charity case. I have a right to some dignity."

"Fair enough, Arik. Then let's start with Rosh Hashanah and Yom Kippur at my house."

Arik got up to leave and extended his hand. "Thank you very much, Rabbi. And good talk."

That night, Arik sat down and wrote a long letter to Dahlia, outlining everything that had happened since he had gotten home plus his travel plans to D.C. Because Sukkot was in the first week of October, Arik had more than enough time to earn the money for a round-trip ticket. He decided that he would spend every spare minute he could working at the loading yard, even if it meant putting up with Ethan. Arik's mom had told him that every penny he earned at the loading yard would be his and his alone.

"We'll manage just fine without your money," she had told him. "That money is for you to build your life with." This small fact was never shared with his dad.

***

When school started, Dahlia went back to her gaggle of friends, mostly Israeli Foreign Service "brats." She threw herself into her studies and spent her free time captaining the school tennis team. Through her connections, she was even able to get her classmates time on the practice court and team instruction at the Rock Creek Park Tennis Center on Sixteenth Street.

She missed Arik terribly and wrote to him every week. To her amazement, Arik was so good at answering on the schedule they had agreed upon. So un-guylike, she thought. Equally impressive was his clear, beautiful handwriting. She once had been told that people's souls could be revealed through their handwriting. She had wondered what Arik's writing would reveal. She concluded that Arik had a clear, beautiful soul.

It was two days before Yom Kippur, and Dahlia had not yet talked to her parents about Arik's visit. Arik had already bought his plane tickets, but Dahlia had no idea how to broach the subject with her parents. She decided to confide in Tomer, the household's chief of security. Ever since he had taken her and Nurit sailing over a year ago, they had been buddies, and Dahlia had told him almost everything that had happened to her during the summer.

"So, you have a chaver, Dahlia? I was wondering when someone would be lucky enough to catch you," Tomer teased. Turning serious, he said, "I think you need to get it out in the open and be done with it."

"Do you think that Abba will approve?"

"Probably not, knowing him. Besides, you already told me that his first impression of him was just so-so. But it all starts from within. If you are sure this is a good idea, you can convince your parents of anything. Are you certain you want to do this? Why haven't you told them yet? Now, Arik has bought a ticket with every penny he has. What are you going to do if your Abba puts his foot down and says no? I think you may have waited too long."

"Crap! You're right, of course. If he says no, I'll have to go through Imma. I might have better luck with her. . . I've taken Arik for granted. Tomer, am I a bad person?

"No, Dahlia, you are not. You just have a bit of growing up to do. You will."

Chapter 13

"What do you mean Arik is coming for Sukkot?" Benny asked at dinner, not realizing that he was shouting. "Is that a request or a statement of fact?"

Dahlia stared quietly down at her dinner plate. "I've invited him to come for Sukkot."

"What do you mean you invited him? What exactly do you mean?" Benny roared. "Where did you get the idea that you can invite someone to stay in my home, for a week, without permission?"

"Our home," Dahlia said quietly.

"You will call him on the phone and tell him that you didn't realize our whole family is coming in from Israel and that we simply don't have room for him."

"That's so nasty, Abba! Besides, you know full well it isn't true. We have plenty of room. We live in a mansion for goodness sakes! You didn't give me trouble went I invited Penny to come last year without asking you first. Why not?"

"Inviting a boy is very different from a girl!"

"What do you think is going to happen?"

"Dahlia, you are not to continue this line of conversation! There are young children at the table."

"So, it's okay for you to act mean in front of them?"

"You will call him to cancel. I won't have him in my house."

"Why, Abba? What did he ever do or say to you to make you hate him so much? He was nothing but polite and respectful to you when you met him. You yourself said that he was a fine fellow. Besides that meeting, you know absolutely nothing about him."

"I'm a very good judge of character. My job depends on it. I deal with hundreds of people all day long!"

"You aren't a good judge of his character, Abba." Dahlia glared at her father, with fire in her eyes.

The two of them were locked in a staring contest.

Benny turned. "Leah, do you know anything about this?"

Leah looked at her husband impassively. "Dahlia did bring it up when she came back from camp."

"And you said yes?"

"I didn't say yes. I told her that we'd discuss it when the time came."

"And now is the time!" Dahlia said.

"After you've gone ahead and invited him?" Benny returned his gaze to Dahlia.

"If he isn't allowed to come, I won't be here for the whole chag either," Dahlia said in a low, calm voice.

"You will go nowhere without my consent," Benny practically growled.

"I'm not a child anymore, and I won't be led around like one any longer! You always told me to assert my independence and be assertive, and so I am! I'm nearly seventeen. You're depending on me to be the entertainment director for a whole flock of bratty cousins coming in, and I agreed to do it without complaint. I even set up a whole schedule of events. How about you take them around instead? I think you'll find that dealing with them will be a lot harder than dealing with Kissinger. I know you expect me to run off crying and slam doors and then beg and plead until Imma forces you to give your permission, but I'm done with all that. I'm simply informing you that he's coming and that's that!" Dahlia stood up from the table.

Benny reluctantly excused the children from the table. Afterward, he and Leah spoke in the library.

"Leah, do you think that this is a good idea?"

"What do you mean? His coming for the chag or the fact that Dahlia has fallen in love with him?"

"That's total nonsense. What do you mean 'fallen in love'? She's just a child."

"Benny, I was just a year or so older than Dahlia when we met, and you told me that you loved me only a month after that."

"Leah, those were different times. We were much more grown up then. We were in the underground. You had survived a war! We were adults. These are pampered, silly children with no maturity or life experience. There's no telling what they'll get up to!"

"These are the children we raised, Benny. The experiences they grew up with are the ones we gave them. They're extremely fortunate. Would you rather that they had the lives we had? Our generation fought and died so that our children could grow up to be . . . not pampered but carefree. So, how can you deride who she has become? Dahlia spoke to me a bit about Arik last week. He's quite a remarkable young man. He has grown up in an extremely poor and depressing home, and his life has been a continuous struggle. Even with all of that, he has grown up to be an extremely bright, kind, sensitive young man. He has already achieved remarkable things in his life, but he remains modest and unassuming. I, for one, would be happy if Dahlia ends up with a boy like that."

"What could a seventeen-year-old boy possibly have achieved?"

"You know what? I'm not going to tell you. You can either take an interest in your daughter's life and talk to her about it or you can turn loose some of your Mossad boys to spy on him if you want to know. Besides, you've hardly said a word to her since she's been home."

"You know very well how crazy busy we've been with the White House negotiations and the opening of the U.N. General Assembly next week. Again, they're trying to throw Resolution 242 in our face. Secretary Rogers is trying to broker a deal between us and the Egyptians where we give up everything in return for vague guarantees."

"Well, then, Benny, if you're so busy, you'll hardly notice Arik being here. Let him come. And at least try to be civil to the boy while he's here. There's no way you'll ever be able to tame Dahlia's thoughts and feelings. She has a keen intellect and sharp wits. At this age, all you can do is offer fatherly advice. I'm certain that this Arik infatuation will simply burn itself out if you just let it. Confronting her will simply fan the flames of her emotions for the boy. You're quite right, Benny: These are different times. The whole world is changing."

***

Ari passed the flight from Los Angeles to D.C. in a whir of emotions. Being at home for the past five weeks, having to deal with his abusive dad and even more abusive cousin and working in the blistering heat, shoveling and hauling sacks of cement and manure for fifteen hours a week, was such a different world than he had been in the previous month at camp. Through it all, his mind had never drifted far from the sweet, beautiful angel that was waiting for him; he lived from letter to letter. And now he would see her at last.

His mom had seen to it that he would have white shirts and clean slacks for the holiday. "You can't go to visit a stranger's family for Sukkot looking like a boor," she had told him.

Dahlia had written about all the children who would be running around the house and her 'job' as entertainment coordinator. She had asked whether he would mind. He thought that it would be fun to be like a counselor, sort of like he'd been with the younger boys in his basketball clinics at Camp Moshava. The fact was that he wouldn't mind shoveling more manure if it would mean being with Dahlia.

When the plane landed, he gathered his worn suitcases, which his mom had tied up with belts and tape. "One can't be too careful!" she had told him. He headed out to the arrivals area of Washington National Airport.

Dahlia stood at the end of the ramp. She was a vision of loveliness. Her voluminous blonde hair was tied up in a ponytail and tucked behind a burgundy-and-gold Washington Redskins cap, with her sunglasses perched high above the rim. She was wearing a loosely fitting T-shirt, tight designer jeans, and high heels. She was shining one of her million-dollar smiles and carrying a sign in front of her, like a limo driver, that read, in Hebrew, BOOBA SHELLI (My Doll).

In an instant, Arik bounded up the ramp and Dahlia threw herself into his arms. They kissed for a long while.

Tomer stood a respectful distance away to give the young couple their privacy. He marveled at how that pretty little girl he'd been watching over for the past two years had grown into such a wonderful young woman. He had hoped all along that Dahlia wouldn't end up with some dimwitted American Jewish boy. They lacked the balls to stand toe to toe with an Israeli counterpart. They probably would run about like frightened mice if they had to go into the Israeli Army and face combat. He realized quickly that he need not have worried. When Dahlia introduced him to Arik, he saw a tall, blonde, suntanned, powerfully built young man with piercing blue eyes and a bright smile. His handshake was not only strong but showed that he worked very hard physically. Tomer was professionally trained to make a quick, accurate assessment of a person, and he very much liked what he saw in Arik.

"Good to meet you, Tomer," Arik said in Hebrew. "Dahlia has written much about you. I hear you're an excellent sailor, but can you surf?"

Tomer laughed. "You teach me to surf, and I will teach you to sail."

"Deal!" Arik smiled.

"Where did you learn to speak Hebrew like an Israeli?" Tomer asked.

"I'm an Israeli by birth . . . long story."

Dahlia had deliberately left out a few details about Arik's life when she had confided in Tomer. Perhaps more than a few.

When Tomer brought the car around, Arik was a little taken aback at the black stretch Lincoln Continental.

"Welcome to my world, Arik." Dahlia took his hand.

Before Arik could reach for his suitcases to place them in the trunk, Tomer grabbed them.

Smiling, Tomer said, "Here, you are our guest, and I am happy to do this for you."

"It's just that nobody has ever done that for me before." Arik shrugged.

Dahlia wrapped her arms around Arik's waist and gently kissed him on the ear. "I love you, Arik!" she whispered.

As the limousine pulled past the security gate and up to the house, Arik looked out at the manicured lawn, the circular driveway, and Rock Creek Park, which all were silhouetted against a bright, cloudless sky. Gazing at the Tudor mansion, he mused aloud, "I've got to get me one of these!"

"Well, it doesn't really belong to us," Dahlia said. "But being ambassador does have its perks. When our stint here is done, we go back to Israel and reality."

When they entered the residence, Arik stared up, in some amazement, at the marble floors, cathedral ceilings, and winding staircase. A curly-haired blonde dog ran up to them, barking and excitedly wagging his tail. He jumped up onto Arik's leg and began licking his hand. Arik went down on one knee and stroked his neck and back. The dog jumped up and licked his face.

"That's Kordy. He's a labradoodle. He's so clever and affectionate that he seems more human than dog. He can read my mind and knows when I'm happy or sad. Most days, he's the only one happy to see me when I get home."

There was a wonderful smell of dinner coming out the kitchen. Suddenly, the shrieks of four children under the age of ten rose up from a blur that galloped past the kitchen.

"Doda Ruti and her family arrived last night." Dahlia laughed. "Welcome to Romper Room. Don't say you weren't warned."

The oldest, Gila, and Nurit trailed behind the others. "That's Dahlia's boyfriend!" Nurit said, giggling, and they both ran off.

Leah came out of the dining area, with a broad smile and open arms.

"Shalom, Arik! Welcome! How was your trip? You must be exhausted. You've come just in time for dinner. They don't feed you much on the plane."

"Thank you for having me, Mrs. Gilad. My trip was fine." Arik reached into his green canvas backpack and pulled out a box of Barton's chocolate that his mom had stuffed in, as he was leaving, to give to Dahlia's mom as a hostess gift.

Arik insisted on helping to set the table. He was duly introduced to Thelma and the kitchen staff. Arik gave Dahlia a knowing glance and smiled.

"Abba is working late at the embassy tonight. We'll eat without him," Leah said.

After dinner, Dahlia and Arik took a long walk, hand in hand, through Rock Creek Park. There was a definite chill in the crisp autumn air. The leaves on all the trees were turning shades of bright yellow, gold, orange, and red. The rays of sunset reflected off Dahlia's golden hair.

"I've never seen this before—all the colors on the trees," Arik said. "This doesn't happen in Southern California."

He kissed Dahlia on her cheek.

"How did you spend Yom Kippur?" she asked.

"I was with Rabbi Rabinovich. My parents don't keep Yom Kippur at home. You know, it never mattered to me before whether we kept Yom Kippur or not. This year, it really got to me. I felt so drawn to shul. I was really touched by the brutal honesty of the prayers, you know. You sit there all day, telling God what kind of sucky person you are, in great detail, and ask him to forgive you anyway. It was my first Yom Kippur since that time when I was eight. And fasting definitely adds to the experience and makes you feel more spiritual. After a while, I felt like I was really talking to God.

"Now, imagine that exactly when you're feeling most spiritual you're told in the Torah reading that you shouldn't have sex with your mother, sisters, dogs, and cats. Imagine talking about stuff like that on Yom Kippur!"

Dahlia drew closer to him.

"How about sex with girlfriends?" Dahlia looked at him intently as she waited for a response.

Arik kissed her.

"The thought had definitely crossed my mind," Arik whispered, smiling. "It's funny how we never really broached the subject. Have you ever . . .?"

"No, I'm still a virgin." Dahlia blushed. "But I want you to be my first . . ."

Arik held her close for a long while without saying a word.

***

The next day was organized chaos, as is the case on any day before a major Jewish holiday. Leah took breakfast orders from children and adults alike, while the rest of the kitchen staff had awoken extra early to prepare food for the many festive meals that would follow during the Sukkot holiday.

The air was filled with the aromas of cooking gefilte fish, chicken soup, broiled chicken, duck, roast beef, and a whole host of foods that Arik had never smelled before. Arik and Dahlia had been up for hours and had taken a five-mile jog through Rock Creek Park in the falling multicolored leaves and the early-morning autumn chill.

After showering and dressing, Arik plowed through the morning prayer in his room. Afterward, when he went into the sunlit dining room, he found the table set with crystal, silver, china, and linen. In the center of the table were arrayed fresh fruit, hot and cold cereal, freshly squeezed orange juice, pancakes, waffles, smoked salmon, cheese platters, whitefish, fresh, hot bagels, and freshly ground and brewed coffee served in bone china pitchers. The air was filled with the squealing and cackling of small children. He quietly found a seat next to Dahlia.

"I have a whole day's activities scheduled for us today," Dahlia said. "I want to take you on a whirlwind tour of the monuments, and maybe we'll get a chance to visit the White House and the place where they make the money."

"Definitely!" Arik laughed. "As long as they give out free samples."

Benny Gilad sat at the head of the table, chatting amiably with his brother-in-law Srulick, who was sitting beside him.

"Good morning, Arik. I trust that you had a good rest after your long flight over," Benny said over the din.

"I did. Thank you, sir."

"Have you been to Washington before?" Benny asked.

"No, sir, this is my first time. I'm really looking forward to—"

"Oy! Look at him—so polite, always saying, 'sir.'" Doda Ruti was gushing. "I wish that Israeli young men would be so polite. They are always so crude. Don't you think, Srulick?"

Arik blushed.

"Arik is Israeli!" Dahlia said.

"Oh, I didn't know. Where are you from?"

"Los Angeles."

"Your parents are emigrants, then, yordim. I wish that more Israelis would appreciate what they have in Israel and not go looking for their fortunes in America. We have everything you need in Israel. It is not like it was in the early years. Sometimes I feel like the country is emptying out. There is a joke going around in Israel that there is a sign over the airport departure gate: 'Will the last Israeli out of the country please turn out the lights?'" Ruti laughed heartily at her own joke.

Arik politely tried to smile.

Dahlia sensed Arik's discomfort and explained, "Arik's parents didn't come here because they wanted to. They came because they had to."

Juan broke the tension by entering the room and speaking discreetly to Benny. All eyes turned toward them.

"It would appear that the construction crew that was supposed to come today to build our Sukkah was called away on another job," Benny announced.

"What are we going to do?" Leah asked with some alarm. "Sukkot is tonight, and we were depending on them. We have over a dozen guests invited for the holiday meals, including the foreign minister and several members of Congress."

Arik looked at Dahlia and smiled slightly. She immediately knew what he was thinking.

"But we were supposed to go out," Dahlia whispered to him.

"We can do our tours during Chol HaMoed."

"What about the kids?"

"We'll find something for them to do. We can have them make Sukkah decorations. Nurit can supervise that. I have full confidence in her. I take it that all the materials we need are already here? That you won't make me drive all the way to Honesdale to get the building supplies? You know I would do that for you." Arik winked at her.

Dahlia giggled. "I know you would, you lunatic!"

"But I'm your lunatic."

"Yes, you are, buubs!" Dahlia whispered.

Dahlia announced to the rest of the family, "Arik and I will assemble the Sukkah, starting right after breakfast."

"You were supposed to take all the children out for the day, Dahlia," Leah reminded her daughter.

"We have it all figured out. We'll put the children to work making decorations, and Nurit will supervise." Dahlia smiled at her little sister, who looked pleased to be put in a junior leadership role.

"I will believe that when I see it," Dahlia's Uncle Srulick said. "You would be a miracle worker to get these wild animals to do anything except run around. Besides, are you two up to the task by yourselves? I could lend a hand."

"I didn't bring you all the way here to put you to work. That's embarrassing!" Leah said.

"Nonsense," Srulick answered good-naturedly. "Besides, it's a mitzvah!"

"We'll have the Sukkah up in no time," Arik assured everyone. "Dahlia and I became construction experts while we were at camp."

"I must admit—you guys did an excellent job in camp with those bleachers," Benny said. "Well, there's no time like the present. Let's get to work. I'll lend a hand as well!"

"That's something I want to see. His excellency, the ambassador, with a hammer in his hands!" Leah laughed.

"What do you mean, Leah? I was very good with my hands. I was a kibbutznik."

"Not recently. Just be careful. I'd have to answer to the foreign ministry if anything happened to you."

The impromptu crew wasted no time in getting to work. The Sukkah was an array of interlocking fiberglass panels that assembled to form four 16' × 24' walls covered by thatched matting. Arik assigned himself the task of carrying the 4' × 8' panels from the shed at the back of the garden to the flagstone patio adjacent to the dining area, where Dahlia, Benny, and Srulick assembled them. Tomer, who had just finished his guard shift, joined in the fun. Dahlia set up the portable speaker system on the patio and played cassettes of music from the Israel Song Festival.

Nurit wasted no time in organizing the other kids to create yards of colored-paper chains from strips of construction paper and paste. As soon as she sensed that her brawn was no longer needed, Dahlia took half of the kids off Nurit's hands and set her group to drawing colored posters with New Year's and Sukkot motifs. When Dahlia's group began making figures of fruits from papier-mâché, Nurit's group revolted. They all wanted to get their hands dirty with the wet cardboard and glue. Dahlia left the now-united group of children to search out strings of colored lights that she and her mom had bought the previous year at the after-Christmas sale at the McCrory's store down the road.

Arik brought out a dozen 16 foot × 2 foot × 4 foot joists to support the vast mats of thatch that would serve as the roof of the edifice and then strung out a 24-foot string of 60-watt lightbulbs to illuminate the Sukkah. Folding tables and chairs followed, and the whole project really began to take shape.

After three hours, Leah and Ruti walked out to the patio. They were astonished to find the Sukkah nearly complete.

"Where are the children?" Ruti asked. "I have not heard from them in over two hours. They must be up to no good."

She walked to the family room and quietly looked in. She was just as surprised to find them engrossed in their task, supervised by Dahlia.

"I have never seen them so quiet in my life!" Ruti whispered to Leah. "Dahlia certainly has the magic touch with them."

"Ever since Dahlia came back from camp, she's become so much more focused and settled," Leah said. "It's like she really grew up, and I think that Arik has something to do with it. I've never seen her so enamored with a boy before. Believe me, Ruti, he seems very big and strong, but he is really so gentle and polite. He's done nothing but try to help around the house since he's come here, and he's gotten Dahlia to be more helpful as well."

"Well, sure, Leah, he seems to have good character. But what about his family? Do you know anything about them?"

"That's a bit of a mystery, I admit. I know that they lived in Israel for a time and that his father was wounded during the '48 war. Apart from that, though, I don't know much. I mean, obviously, Dahlia is way too young to consider a serious relationship. . . She has to finish high school, and then she has two years in the army. But I do like the fact that she's starting to get some experience in such things, especially since he seems to be such a fine fellow."

Ruti pushed the matter a little more firmly. "Yes, Leah, but don't you find it odd that he would come here for the chag when he should be home with his family?"

"Oy, Ruti, you're such a yenta! Why do you feel the need to find out everything! The fact is that I don't know the answer to that question, but I see no reason to delve any further at this point. All I see is that he wants to be with Dahlia as much as she wants him to be here. . . And I'm okay with that. Besides, he appears to be a perfect gentleman, if you know what I mean." Leah winked at Ruti.

"What does Benny think about this?"

"He was very hesitant at first, but I think he's coming around."

As the sun tilted into the west, the Sukkah fell into shadows. The sparkling colored lights in the thatch looked like so many stars in the firmament. The walls were covered in rich, multicolored oriental drapery and tapestries, giving the Sukkah the appearance of Aladdin's palace. Long tables, lit by spotlights, were covered in starched white tablecloths and expertly set with colored linens, china, and crystal.

Dahlia and Arik stood hand in hand, alone, in the doorway, gazing into the interior of the Sukkah.

"This is so beautiful in the evening. I've never seen anything like it before," Arik whispered.

"This could have never been done without you," Dahlia whispered. "Everyone here loves to talk, but you got it done. You have this way of positively motivating everyone around you. It's a gift."

She drew close to him.

"I love you, Dahlia," Arik whispered.

"I love you so much, Arik."

The holiday was a whirlwind of guests, including many dignitaries, festive meals, and services at Adas Israel synagogue. Arik liked the services, particularly because he got to sit next to Dahlia, something that he never could have done at Camp Moshava, which was Orthodox and therefore required the separation of the genders with a partition in between them.

The following week, Dahlia and Arik took the gaggle of children to the Glen Echo Amusement Park and the National Zoo. They trekked through the many monuments and the halls of the National Museum of Natural History, where they gaped at the dinosaurs. Arik always had one of the children on his shoulders, and they continually fought about who would be the lucky one to be chosen; as soon as one kid was hoisted up, the rest began to clamor that that kid's turn was over. Ari also carried a backpack full of mammoth quantities of food and supplies for every conceivable contingency—even if all they ended up needing were the bandages for minor scrapes.

"The kids love you." Dahlia said.

They walked past the White House. Arik commented about how much smaller it looked than he had imagined it. They heard a great racket coming out of Lafayette Park, across the street from the White House, and they wandered over to see what it was all about. About a thousand people were standing and sitting, holding signs:

END THE WAR!

GET OUR TROOPS HOME!

HEY, NIXON! PULL OUT, LIKE YOUR FATHER SHOULD HAVE!

STOP THE BABY KILLING!

There were chants such as "One, two, three, four. We don't want your fucking war!"

Arik and Dahlia stood and looked at the unwashed masses with their long hair, bandanas, beards, torn jeans, psychedelic T-shirts adorned with peace symbols, and army-surplus jackets. There were women breast-feeding in public and folks playing guitars. Dahlia backed the children away from the crowd.

Around the mob were D.C. mounted police in a long line. They were watching and waiting.

A woman walked up to Arik and said, "Hey, dude! Why don't you come join us? We're gonna take down the establishment and their pigs! We're gonna have a teach-in at six at the Lincoln Memorial, about the goddamn war, in preparation for the Vietnam Moratorium next month."

"Actually, we're just passing through . . . and we've got kids here," Arik said. "We do support what you're doing, though. Keep it up!"

Little Dudi looked up. "Dahlia, what's that funny smell?"

Arik looked at Dahlia, inhaled deeply, and chuckled.

"Motek, people are smoking cigarettes. You know how bad they are for you. They can cause cancer!" Dahlia said, barely suppressing laughter herself.

Dudi said, "Abba smokes, and it doesn't smell like that, Dahlia."

Arik came to Dahlia's rescue. "I know! Why don't we go up that hill? You see that tall, pointy thing? It's very windy up there. We can go fly kites. I brought some!"

All the kids cried out, "Yeah!" almost in unison, and off they went. Dahlia smirked at Arik and breathed a sigh of relief.

They flew kites on the mall near the Washington Monument and then took a boat ride on the Potomac River.

One late afternoon, they took the older children to see the Washington Senators play the New York Yankees.

On Sunday, when they were given a day's reprieve from the kids, they went to see the Washington Redskins play the San Francisco 49ers at RFK Stadium. The stadium was packed for the game, and it rocked from the continuous roar of the fans. Arik was amazed at Dahlia's command of the game and the intensity of her interest, not to mention how cute she looked in a Redskins jersey and cap. Arik had never seen a girl swear like a longshoreman at a referee's bad call or go nearly delirious when her team scored a touchdown. She knew every word of the 'Skins fight song, "Hail to the Redskins." He also was surprised that his sweet girl could down several beers without flinching. "Please don't tell my parents!" she pleaded.

Arik was getting fairly smashed himself. Luckily for them, Tomer, who was waiting for them in the limo parked on East Capitol Street, outside the D.C. Armory, knew how to keep a secret, too.

In the early mornings, Arik and Dahlia went running down the C&O Canal Trail along the Potomac River to Point of Rocks, the chill stinging their faces until they were bright red. They stopped at Thompson Boat Center and sipped hot chocolate while watching the Georgetown University Hoyas' rowing shells silently gliding in long, dark rows silhouetted against the glistening water.

The weeklong holiday drew to a close. After the festive afternoon meal on the last day, the two lovers took a long, slow walk through Rock Creek Park, hand in hand. They found a bench under an elm tree that was in flaming red color.

Dahlia looked deeply into Arik's eyes. "What am I going to do with you, Arik?" Dahlia said at last, shaking her head.

"What do you mean?"

Dahlia gave a long sigh and looked down at her fingernails. "Arik, if we were out of college or out of the army and we were like this . . . you'd ask me to marry you, and I'd say yes, and we'd live happily ever after."

"So, what's the problem?"

"No, Arik, there is no problem with that—except that we aren't twenty-five. We're still in high school. You aren't supposed to meet the person you're going to marry when you're sixteen. You're supposed to fool around and play at relationships at our age—go steady, go out, make out, party, break up, and find someone else and start all over again. We've gotten so far, so deep, so fast."

"Does that scare you?"

"Not really, it's just that . . . how do we keep this going? The intensity, I mean. We live three thousand miles apart. The soonest we'll see each other again is winter break, three months from now."

"Are you afraid I'll have wandering eyes for other girls? I won't. You can trust me. I am and will always be faithful to you. I'm up to my ass in work at school, my uncle's loading yard, and I'm not spending nearly enough time playing basketball. I played against Wilt in the Cage a few weeks ago, and he made a total fool out of me."

"Wilt Chamberlain?" Dahlia gasped. "You're embarrassed because Wilt Chamberlain, one of the world's best basketball players, made a chump out of you? Seriously, Arik?"

"When you're in the Cage, Dahlia, it's not about rank or fame. It's just about the game. And these pros come down to play with us to hone their skills, and sometimes they get whooped. But let's get back to what we were saying.

"Look, Dahlia, I know that in you I've found my soulmate, the great love of my life. I don't care how old we are. If we're meant to be, we will be. Let's take this a day and a week at a time. We'll write each other every week. We'll see each other during winter break. I've already looked for airfare and hotel rooms for the four of us in Aspen."

"Will we make love then? I want to. . ."

Dahlia sat on Arik's lap and lay her head on his chest.

"Does your father like me?" Arik asked.

"Why do you ask that?"

"I just get the feeling he doesn't care much for me."

"Did he say anything to you?"

"No, but do you know how you get that feeling?"

"What do you mean?"

"He seemed friendly enough to me in the beginning, but I got the sense he was trying hard to be nice. And then, halfway through the week, it was like he just stopped trying. I'd try to make conversation with him, and he seemed like he had something better to do. I don't know—"

Dahlia kissed Arik lightly. "I think that you're reading too much into things. My Abba has a lot on his mind. Bad things are going on at the Suez Canal. We're losing soldiers every day. They are calling it a 'War of Attrition.' He's under tremendous pressure."

"I just hope I made a good impression. That's all. They're going have to get used to me."

Arik took Dahlia's head in both hands and kissed her deeply.

***

Early the following morning, it was time for Arik to go to the airport.

At the gate, Tomer stood a discreet distance away to allow the couple to part in private.

"I had a wonderful week, Dahlia. Thanks so much for letting me come."

"Don't be silly, Arik. This week was like paradise for me. I miss you so much already. About what we said yesterday, I'll always be faithful to you, too, always. I love you, Arik."

They shared one last kiss, and then Arik disappeared down the gangway. Dahlia felt a great warmth wash over her, tinged with sadness about how much she had looked forward to Arik's visit but now, in a flash, it was over. Tomer, sensing this, placed a fatherly arm around her shoulders.

"Arik is a wonderful fellow, such a chevreman, with such a good heart," Tomer said. "So polite to the staff, so good with the children. He spent hours playing with them. He taught them how to play basketball. He even played ball with the security crew when you were out with your mother, shopping. And what an athlete! He could easily play for Maccabi Tel Aviv."

"I know. The question is How do I keep him?" She smiled sadly.

When they returned to the house, Dahlia bounced into the main hall, in high spirits again. She found her father and mother sitting in the library.

"Come in, Dahlia. Have a seat," Benny said. "Join us."

"So, what did you think? Isn't Arik amazing! He was so much fun to be with, so popular with the kids. Did you see how fast he got the Sukkah up? He's such a great guy!" Dahlia gushed.

"Booba, how much do you know about Arik?" Benny asked, his hands folded.

"What do you mean?"

"About his past."

"I don't really like where this conversation is going."

"Dahlia, do you know that Arik has a criminal background? That he's been in jail?" Benny asked.

"I do know that, but it's much more complicated—"

"Then how could you bring him into our house?" Leah asked. "For a week! We had small children here! I had a bad feeling about this, from the beginning."

"Abba, how did you find out about Arik? Were you spying on him! Did you use your position as ambassador to send out an intelligence detail? How could you? How could you? What would drive you to even want to do that? I noticed, the whole week, while Arik bent over backward to be courteous, helpful, and friendly, you barely gave him the time of day. When he tried to engage you in conversation, you answered him as if you had something better to do. For God's sake, Abba, he was a guest in your house. Do you think he didn't notice that you don't like him?"

"A guest that you invited!"

Leah jumped in. "Look, Dahlia, we only want the best for you. He just seemed a bit rough, a bit too worldly for you. You're sixteen, and you should be seeing boys like you, with your upbringing. Arik is coming from another world. There are so many nice boys here in Washington or back home that you could date. We're not against you starting to explore those types of relationships. Dahlia, sweetheart, you can do so much better than him."

"Do you know why he was in jail, Abba? Did your goons get that information, too?"

"Dahlia!" Leah gasped.

"I'm serious, Imma. Do you know that Arik was falsely accused of assaulting a neo-Nazi who turned on him when he saved the life of a little Negro boy? Do you know that he was nearly killed because of his heroic act and that he was commended by not only Dr. Martin Luther King Jr. but the mayor of Los Angeles? Did your men find out that the neo-Nazi is serving three consecutive life sentences for multiple murders and would have hurt more people if Arik hadn't stepped in?"

"Still and all," Benny said, "Arik clearly has a violent streak in him. He's been involved in gang violence, for whatever reason, with knives and what have you. He's a tough guy from the streets of Los Angeles—that's the element that Arik is involved with. Do you know that Arik came back east to camp because he has virtually no Jewish friends at home and that he came to camp to start a new life?"

"So, what's wrong with that?"

"Do you know that he spends most of his time with shady Negro types in the worst sections of Los Angeles?"

"Shady in which way?"

"Well?"

"Are they shady because they're Negros?" Dahlia scowled.

"Lower your voice, Dahlia. Thelma can hear us."

Dahlia closed the door to the library.

"Arik has been virtually adopted by the family of a black reverend, a leader in their community. Arik's family was shunned by the Jewish community when he was very young. He grew up as a complete goy, was thrown into Judaism because of his traumatic experience, and has struggled to fit into the Jewish community ever since. He's still patronized by his 'friends' at school and only feels like he has family in the black community. They are the only people who accept him for who he is."

"And that is someone who is not suited for you. Your Imma and I feel that you should stop seeing him," Benny said.

"Dahlia, motek, you know that we only want the very best for you," Leah added. "Back in Vienna, we used to call it kinderschtube. It means 'coming from a proper upbringing.' The type of boy that we wish for you, a boy you deserve, should come from a proper home, a proper community, not a boy from a marginal family. What can a boy like that offer a girl like you, with your breeding?"

"We're not breeding dogs here! I won't stop seeing him. I won't let you run my life like this. I love him with all my heart. That's the type of boy who is suitable for me!"

"Dahlia, what are you saying?" Leah asked. "He's an American who lives 3,000 miles away from you. In a year, when you graduate high school and go back home and enlist in Tzahal, he will still be in America. What kind of future is there to this, this relationship?"

"Arik is also going to be in Israel. He plans to enlist in the army, and we'll be together."

"How can you be so sure?" Benny asked. "You've already told us that he's this big basketball star who's going to be offered a scholarship . . . at least, that's what he told you. You don't even know if that's the truth. Well, if it is, he won't be going anywhere. He comes from nothing. He'll never be able to resist all the money and inducements that will be thrown at him. Do you know what boosters are? I've read all about this."

"No."

"They're money men that work for the big universities to recruit the best talent for their teams. Under the table, these players are offered money, fancy clothes, travel, cars, and even sex with women to join their school. Do you think that a young man like Arik will be able to resist any of that to be loyal to a summer camp girlfriend that lives on the other side of the country? Besides, if he plays basketball, he'll be playing on Shabbat and traveling on Shabbat. Do you think that he will eat kosher? Explain to me how you anticipate any type of future with this boy."

"First of all, please stop calling him a boy. His name is Arik. And I'm not your little girl anymore. I'm convinced about my feelings for Arik. They're deep and strong. I won't break it off with him. You can either accept this or, if you try to prevent me from seeing him, I'll find a way anyway. As you both like to say, 'Conversation over!'"

Dahlia stormed out of the room.

Chapter 14

Saying good-bye to Dahlia at the airport had been so much harder for Arik than when he they had parted at the end of camp. Their relationship had deepened significantly during the holiday week together, yet Arik was seized with fear. *How can our relationship survive such a long separation? It will be almost three months before I can see her again.* Her letters might come, but from certain angles they just looked like slips of paper—too flimsy to bind them across distance and time.

All he really wanted was to be with her, but instead there lay ahead of him a mass of things he needed to do, places he needed to be, and people he needed to spend time with—even though he knew that they would play very little role in his future. The reverend had once told him, "Never be disturbed by an adversary or adversity that you know will have no bearing on your life in five years." But what if that adversity remained with you every day and hung over you like a piano suspended above your head and held by only a thin rope? You couldn't just walk away from that or laugh it off.

So, there he was in mid-October, with no clear plan for his future. His work and school schedules were so busy that he ended up submitting his applications to UCLA and USC too late. *If only he had been more careful.* If not for a chance meeting with Mr. Goldblum, the guidance counselor, in the hall, Arik may not have sent in the applications at all. Now, despite his good grades and high scores on the SAT, he had been put on the waiting list at both schools. If not for Mr. Goldblum's intervention, the schools might not have accepted his applications at all. *How could I be so careless to miss those deadlines?*

Maybe subconsciously he had been acting out of a different kind of fear. *Even if I got in, how would I pay for school?* He hadn't figured that out, and there was no point inquiring about work-study programs until he heard from the admissions office. The student body at Rambam Academy hailed mostly from affluent families who generally were not concerned about college scholarships. Arik called the admissions offices every week and even visited them in person several times, only to be told politely that he just needed to be patient and wait and if there was any news that he would be the first to know. In the meantime, he considered applying to one of the West LA community colleges and going there, mostly at night, for two years with the hope of transferring after that.

Of course, all of this hung on the assumption that he would go to college at all. Rabbi Rabinovich had connected him with Shlomo Yardeni at the Israeli consulate. Arik spent several hours one afternoon, talking to him about his prospects if he were to enlist in the Israeli Army. Arik wondered, *Can I make such a momentous decision without ever having been in Israel? Not that my life in the U.S. is such great shakes anyway.* On the one hand, he figured that enlisting was the only way that he could have a future with Dahlia, and Arik wanted nothing more than that. But *what if I get to Israel and hate it? I won't be a very good mate to Dahlia if I'm miserable there, will I?* Enlisting in the Israeli Army would mean that he would be stuck there for at least three years, because he had been born there—despite the fact that he had emigrated to the United

States when he was an infant. That accident of birth made him an Israeli citizen, and Israel's rules applied to him.

Dahlia also was conflicted about Arik's choice, and they had spoken about it many times. She understood the great leap of faith that Arik would have to make to leave his parents, who needed him at home. If he emigrated to Israel, he would have no family there, nobody to rely on—at least, until she got there.

Now that Arik had met with Yardeni and made his presence known, Yardeni took to calling him on a weekly basis, asking him whether he had made up his mind. Arik joked that they were they going to send Mossad agents to kidnap him and whisk him away to Israel one night if he refused to enlist. That's silly. Or is it?

Arik continued his dialogue with Yardeni as he pored over the brochures and reading material, about the Israeli Army, that had been provided to him. Arik read Leon Uris's Exodus and a new book just written by Abba Eban about the history of modern Israel. He also read books about the Six-Day War. Those soldiers were pretty badass, he thought as he leaned one way, toward enlisting, and then back as the pendulum swung.

He took things one day at a time. Between school, homework, Sunday work at Uncle Itzik's business, one or two nights a week of basketball and two nights of martial arts at Inosanto's, Arik had little time to fuss about long-term plans. It still irked him that he had gotten no Shabbat invitations from his classmates. They were friendly enough when he saw them in school or shul, but he could never break through their clannishness. In the end, he expected little from them, so it was really no shock when that was what he got.

Arik avoided the gym at school, and when forced to play in gym class he held himself back. He'd had lots of practice doing that. The basketball coach at Rambam Academy said that he had heard rumors about Arik's playing ability, but Arik assured him that they were just that. The last thing he wanted was to spend hours that he didn't have to spare going to varsity team practice and playing with guys who were no better than the 'talent' he had played with at camp, if that.

Rambam Academy's team regularly got trounced by the other parochial school teams in its league and was in last place. Arik thought, Why should I lift a finger to help them? Why should I carry the team and show off my skills to the cackling yeshiva girls in the bleachers who consider me a goy? He would much rather play in the Cage, with his homeboys, out of sight and out of mind from his classmates. Perhaps he had set up a self-fulfilling prophecy. Perhaps if he had reached out to his schoolmates more they would have reached back. But his fundamentally shy nature and the fact that he didn't have much in common with his classmates created a vicious circle.

Wednesday, October 22, 1969

My Dearest Dahlia,

To say that coming back home meant crashing back to reality is an understatement. After camp, I had Sukkot to look forward to, and that's what kept me going. But the week passed so quickly after such a long period of anticipation. I know you were afraid that having to spend so much time with the kids would interfere with our time together, but I think the opposite was true. I got such a kick out of us being with them. They were really well behaved, considering their ages. In my mind, I pretended that we were married and we were out with our children. I liked seeing you as a mom. You'll be such a great one, just like your mother is, with a patient and loving touch. I feel so lucky to have you. You're like a beam of bright light in the recesses of my soul. I've always felt a void in my soul that I couldn't explain. That void was dark, and it's dark again because you're not here. When I'm with you, you illuminate everything.

I hope that your parents didn't mind too much having me. I know it was a bit strange for them to have your new boyfriend stay with the family for a week. They seemed to be okay with it, or at least your mom was. But they need to get used to having me around, right? After all, I'm going to be their son-in-law. KISSES TO YOU!!!

School's okay. This week is tryouts for the varsity basketball team. No matter how hard I try, I can't build up any interest in it. So far, I'm flying under the radar in that regard. I think the witches of Epstein have kept their mouths shut after I tore Bracha a new one. She was very contrite and she's trying so hard to be nice to me. Unfortunately for her, she's blessed with Shirah's personality. The only other person who knows what happened at camp is Rabbi Rabinovich. I told you about that. He's still trying to get me to play for the team, but he's agreed to keep my "basketball prowess" secret for now. Rambam's team is totally outclassed by the other teams in their league who are either Catholic or WASPy private schools with players that are going to the NCAA. I refuse to pound my head against the wall trying to make something out of nothing. Besides, it will take away from my guys. I've been trying to get out to the Cage twice a week if possible, but mostly I've had to spend at least one afternoon during the week after school working for Uncle Itzik, in addition to Sundays. That leaves almost no time for schoolwork and martial arts. We have intramural pickup basketball games during PE, so I'm careful how I play. I'm glad you're not here to see that. I know how much that annoys you when I do that.

Have you heard from Penny about winter break yet? I heard that Aspen is better than Telluride and a lot easier to get to. Let me know when you hear from her.

Have to go.

Miss you, love you, need to hold you and kiss you.

Thinking already of our week alone together. Sorry this letter is so soppy.

Yours for always,
Arik

***

The two men sat at center court of the Cage, engaged in low, serious conversation while waiting for play to begin. To outsiders, Watts appeared a homogeneous hotbed of black poverty, crime, and discontent. To those who called Watts home, however, the community was divided along sharp territorial lines determined by the housing projects that had been built by the federal government after World War II. These sub communities had their own infrastructures, for good or bad. Cultural life and community activities were separate, but more sinister was the fact that each community had its own gangs and hoodlums. Continuous low-level internecine feuds were punctuated by more serious outbreaks of violence. The result of this territoriality was that members of one community feared walking into the others' neighborhoods.

During the Watts riots the year before, the entire community had coalesced for a brief period to battle outside forces, including law enforcement, which everyone saw as a common enemy, and eventually even the National Guard. When the riots had ended, Reverend Perkins had led a meeting of community leaders, both religious and secular, to organize a binding truce among rival neighborhoods. One benefit of this truce was the growth of a friendly rivalry among the very best basketball players in each community. Ever since, every year in early November, there was a championship clash between the teams. Tonight's contest, held at the Cage, was between the home team, Nickerson Gardens, and its chief rival, Jordan Downs. The excitement built to a crescendo as both teams entered the court through openings in the chain-link fence and began their pregame drills, falling into ruler-straight lines to practice layups, ball handling drills, and crosscourt passing ever faster. This was followed by an intense volley of outside shooting from every corner of the court and an aerial ballet of dunks and hook shots on both ends of the court.

Jump ball!

Play commenced with ferocity on both sides of the court.

The two men sat entirely entertained. Deeply ensconced in the rigors of organized athletics, they were, on the one hand, unaccustomed to the freewheeling, improvisational style of playground basketball. If NCAA and NBA basketball were a classical symphony, what they were witnessing was jazz. This game valued tempo control, individual performance, and intimidation through improvisation rather than set-piece playmaking and with an emphasis on teamwork.

To the uninitiated, this style of play was fun to watch, but because it was entirely undisciplined, it left too much to chance. The legendary Coach John Wooden of UCLA deliberately avoided the playground scene in his search for hidden talent. Instead, he narrowed his search to the most talented players from the best high school programs all over the country. He rarely looked in his own backyard.

Perhaps the reason lay in his stern, Midwestern Protestant upbringing. Wooden had risen through the organized athletics system as player, assistant coach, and finally coach of a basketball team that had won the national championship in five of the last six years, with only the University of Texas at El Paso (UTEP) breaking UCLA's streak, in 1966. The style of play at the Cage, on the other hand, which had been shaped by generations of playground pickup games, reflected an urban ethos that was selfish and undisciplined—the complete opposite of everything Wooden stood for. Although Walt Hazzard and Lew Alcindor had spent a good part of their precollege careers playing ball on this playground, they still had a firm grounding in organized basketball.

Coach Wooden did not know that the two men were sitting at center court this evening, and if he had he may not have approved. But the UCLA basketball team was at a crossroads. Lew Alcindor and three other seniors had gone on to the NBA, and the team was in serious need of a point guard who could play opposite John Vallely, the only remaining senior. The team needed someone who could play a high-post offense with a free but balanced run-and-shoot offense of screens, cuts, pick setting, and quick passing.

Denny Crum, a player at UCLA under Wooden in the late 1950s, had returned only last year as an assistant coach, replacing Jerry Norman. Crum was serious and thoughtful, but he kept an open mind when it came to looking for gems of undiscovered talent. For a coach, making such a discovery would prove his eye for talent, the ability to spot a diamond in the rough where others see a lump of coal. Scouts might see five hundred games a year and thousands of young players, so knowing how to pick out the few exceptional talents and pursue them was a marketable skill. Of course, the scouts also had to know enough about the players to be able to tell them what they wanted to hear.

This scouting mission was different than most, however. There was no high school coach to visit, no statistics, and no tournament performance records to review. Instead, the player they had come to see had played the summer before last in an NBA summer youth league and been noticed by some current Lakers. They had been sufficiently impressed with his performance that they had contacted Gail Goodrich, a former star of the UCLA team who was now a Laker, to stop by the Cage and evaluate the phenom. Goodrich himself had been discovered in a similar, although not identical, way.

During Goodrich's junior year of high school, Wooden had attended the LA city high school tournament, and something Goodrich did caught Wooden's attention. Goodrich showed incredible quickness and determination, caring little that bigger, taller players were standing between him and the basket. In addition, Goodrich was intensely driven and confident. Apparently, the player that Crum had come to see had a very similar playing style to Goodrich's.

Crum wondered whether the player that they had come to see would fill his team's needs. He admitted that a blond-haired, blue-eyed white guy playing regularly in the heart of one of the worst areas of LA was a curiosity. Crum pulled out his clipboard and, in his methodical style, jotted down some scouting notes:

- height: 6'4"
- estimated weight: 210 lbs.
- minimal body fat
- powerful build
- 6-foot arm span
- 40" vertical leap
- extreme quickness
- great court presence

Arik drove to the baseline, while two huge defenders converged on him. Because Arik had already left the ground when he saw the situation developing, there was nothing for him to do but twist between his outsized opponents, spin 180 degrees, and effortlessly roll the ball off his fingertips and into the basket.

Moving around the perimeter, without the ball, he ran a slalom course past crowded multiple picks to lose his man. Suddenly, he was in the clear. He snatched a crosscourt pass out of the air. The defender, having fought his way through a wall of picks, hurled himself at him, but Arik lifted in his own good time and, at the apex of his jump, pulled the trigger. Twenty feet away, the net danced on its strings.

Arik dribbled the ball through the legs of one opponent, bounced it over another defender, wiggled into the lane, drove to the basket, and double-pumped, reversing the ball from his right hand to his left hand before laying it in.

At half-court, Arik stood, calmly dribbling the ball as if he had all the time in the world. He stopped and stood facing the basket and cocked his arms to 90 degrees. He appeared to jump 36 inches in slow motion, and then he released the ball at the top of his jump, rotating the ball to such an extent that it seemed to float off his fingertips and through the center of the net, which barely stirred as the ball sailed through.

"He's a little fancier on the court than we like. That might be a problem. He might not fit in with our style of play," Crum said.

"Maybe we can mold him to our way of thinking," Goodrich replied. "You know, Denny, he plays black. You rarely see a white guy play like that. The dudes in the park call him White Lightning!"

"He does play with real intelligence," Crum conceded. "He doesn't just show off for the hell of it. His no-look pass is nearly perfect, and he's an expert at coming off the pick. Still, this isn't team play. It's too undisciplined. Wooden might agree to give him a look if he's ever played in a real team setting. Perhaps with experience?"

Before the game ended, the two men stood up and quietly made their way out of the Cage.

***

Two weeks later, Ruvie Kaplan and Shimie Tennenbaum floundered for over an hour, driving through the ghetto streets of South Central LA. They had never been in that part of town before, and they were scared out their wits by the brunt of angry, suspicious stares from groups of black men wearing tank-top shirts and baggy pants and walking on sidewalks or sitting on the front stoops of their ramshackle homes. They felt as if they were putting their lives in danger in a war zone. This place was so foreign to their world that they wondered how Arik could call it home. Avoiding the trash and automotive debris that lay scattered along the road, they continued to bump along, block after block, desperately trying to avoid potholes. Frightened to get out of the car to ask for directions, they finally gathered enough courage to open the window while they were stopped at a street corner.

"Excuse me. Can you direct us to the Cage?"

Their car was soon surrounded by a curious group of men who approached to eye the intruders.

"Who wants to know?" A tough-looking, heavily muscled black man wearing a large gold necklace spoke up first. He was wearing a sleeveless T-shirt with the image of Malcolm X emblazoned on it.

Ruvie and Shimie were not sure whether they should give their real names. They fidgeted.

"What I mean is what you lookin' for? This is the third time you driven up this block. I think you kiddies best run along."

"We're friends of Arik Meir. We've come to see him play," Ruvie said hopefully.

Shimie was prepared to gun the accelerator and shoot the car onto the freeway entrance ramp up the street before they got themselves shot.

"Malcolm X" looked at Ruvie appraisingly. Eventually, a smile crept onto his face, showing several gold front teeth.

"You guys friends of Arik? Well, that's somethin' else. You shouda said so before I capped your little white asses." He pointed to the revolver under his belt, in the front of his pants. "Yeah, Arik's playin' tonight at the Cage. Take a left at Third and Magnolia, go two blocks, and turn right where you see the sign that says Nickerson Gardens. Go down to the end of the road. You'll see the lights. Park close to the playground, and pray you still have tires on your car when you leave."

They did as they had been told and found a parking spot a short distance away from the basketball courts. The boys were wearing jeans and hooded sweatshirts, and they wasted no time pulling up their hoods to try to hide themselves. They figured it was best to fit in as much as possible, if possible. They quickly joined a large crowd of men and boys walking out of the projects. The basketball courts were laid out in long rows under the glare of high-powered spotlights that erased the blackness of night. Some had come to play; others had come to watch. The air was filled sounds of shouts, catcalls and, above all, the rhythmic din of basketballs pounding against asphalt, which sounded like hundreds of jungle drums played slightly off rhythm from one another.

Both boys stood in awe. They had never witnessed such basketball. They quietly strolled along the courts, where play was in progress, and admired the raw athleticism of the players. They slowly made their way to a brightly lit, fenced-in enclosure at the center of the playground area, where a large crowd was forming. Some were waiting in line to get inside, where the few bleachers were almost full. Most had already given up hope or been turned away by bouncer-looking characters who were guarding the entrance to the enclosure. Those who could not get in congregated around the enclosure, peering through the chain-link fence. Some lithe creatures climbed halfway up the fence and clung on for dear life to get a better view. The two boys found standing room with a corner view of the courts and prepared to stand for a long time.

A local teenager, Andre, sidled up next to them. "If you comin' ta see how da game is played, you come ta da right place. Deez dudes is da best of da best. A lotta dees guys is good 'nough ta play in da NBA, and sometimes dem dudes actually comes down here ta play, too. All doz playin' outside in da other courts would kill for a chance ta play in here. Most never gets ta be good 'nough. Where you guys from?"

"Santa Monica!" Shimie said. There was no way he was going to say Beverly Hills.

In a moment, the two teams shot out of a side entrance to the Cage.

"Tonight, it's da Cobras against da Black Panthers. If you dudes wanna lay down some cash, I can fix ya up wid some bookies takin' numbers. They is all aroun' the fence. The security guys don't let dem inside."

"We're only here to watch the game," Shimie said. "But thanks anyway."

They watched silently as the two teams warmed up, each with their team logos embossed on their sleeveless T-shirts. They stood mute, watching Arik in his Cobra jersey, warming up for the game by drilling 15-foot jumpers from the top of the key, one after another, firing no-look passes, in midstride, to darting teammates. He even took off from the foul line toward the basket and effortlessly dunked the ball with one hand.

Someone in the stands yelled, "Do a 360, Arik!"

Arik looked into the crowd and smiled.

"I'll kill myself if I do that. But okay."

Starting from the corner, he shot up to the basket and performed a gorgeous gyrating, twisting dunk. He then took off near the foul line and soared toward the basket while splitting his legs and extending one arm high above his head like a torch before throwing down a backboard-rattling jam.

"Cash! Count it, Lightning!" Rashid, one of Arik's teammates, called out to him. Arik sauntered over to him, smiled, and slapped Rashid a low five.

The eyes of many of the other spectators had been drawn to the center court bleachers, where three men who clearly did not belong had sat down quietly. The crowd wondered what they were doing there. The one in the center was a dour, lean, middle-aged man in a gray suit, white shirt, and thin, dark tie. His glasses seemed too large for his face. He seemed more likely to be sitting in a university library than in bleachers in the middle of the ghetto at night. He sat expressionless, staring out at the players while he arranged a stack of index cards on a clipboard. He occasionally looked from side to side to say a word or two to his companions.

"Shimie! Do you know who those guys are?" Ruvie asked.

Shimie shook his head. "Dunno, but they as sure as hell don't live here!"

"That's Coach John Wooden of UCLA, the Wizard of Westwood! That's his assistant, Denny Crum, and that's Gail Goodrich. What are they doing here?"

"Scouting some talent, I bet."

Ruvie slapped Shimie on the head. "Of course, they are, dunce! The question is who are they looking at?"

"That Arik is so full of shit, pretending to play ball like a dork during intramurals," Shimie said. "He's an absolute beast! Rumor has it he created a firestorm when he played Camp Moshava at Beach Lake last summer, and now I see why. Why the hell won't he play varsity ball for us at school? He'd be the best in the whole league."

"He probably has a good reason," was all Ruvie could say.

The game commenced.

The players from both teams ran up and down the court at lightning speed. Each of the players exhibited extraordinary acrobatic moves, grace, balance, soft touch, and thundering dunks. Showing incredible poise, they knocked down wide-open jump shots and launched deep, high-arching jump shots from the corners as if they were warming up or practicing.

Arik was standing at the top of the key when Rashid tore down a defensive rebound. Making eye contact with Rashid, Arik raced down court ahead of the pack and looked back just long enough to time the ball. He picked it up at the foul line, in midstride, and lofted it up near the top of the backboard. In one motion, he leaped toward the basket, caught the ball in his right hand, and violently stuffed it in.

The teams were evenly matched, which meant that the play became very physical, more combat than basketball. The "referees," either due to incompetence or fear for their lives, chose to ignore obvious fouls. Wooden shook his head at the lack of discipline and order. He was definitely old school.

Suddenly, something Arik did caught his attention. When he was bringing the ball down court into heavy traffic at the low post, he found that there was nobody for him to pass it to. He drove toward the hoop, took off at the foul line, and levitated into the air as three players converged into the paint. As he floated toward the basket, he contorted his body to avoid the defense, switched the ball from one hand to the other, double-pumped, and then gently dropped the ball into the hoop. Wooden had never seen that move before.

Shimie and Ruvie stood in mute shock at Arik's raw power. In school, he was always so shy and unassuming. There was a Talmud midterm exam the next day. When in the world did Arik have time in his double life to study for it? They stood quietly staring through the chain-link fence as the game ended. They had no idea who had won the game.

Goodrich approached Arik to congratulate him on a fine performance, and then he led him over to introduce him to Wooden, who smiled broadly as he shook Arik's hand and held Arik's forearm with his other hand. They stood and chatted amiably for about ten minutes. Wooden pulled out a business card and handed it to Arik.

Chapter 15

On Thursday morning, Arik drove to the Lakers training facility on the campus of Loyola Marymount University. He had been invited to watch practice because of his closeness with some of the players and because the Lakers coach, Joe Mullaney, had taken a liking to him when Arik had played in the NBA summer youth league.

When Arik stepped into the coach's office, he marveled at the huge wood paneling with floor-to-ceiling photos of basketball legends and political figures. There was a glass showcase filled with NBA championship trophies. The tops of the walls were festooned with banners and pennants dating back decades.

Joe came in through a side door. "Have a seat, Arik. Good to see you, my boy. How was your summer?"

"Very nice. It really was a brand-new experience. You heard Elgin came over for an afternoon to do a clinic with the kids? They loved him. Or, should I say, they were in absolute awe of him."

"Why shouldn't they be? The man's a living legend," Joe said.

"I think he had a good time, too."

"He told me he did." Joe took a deep breath. "Okay, so, it's no secret that UCLA scouts have gone to watch you play. And, because they know we're friends, I've also been getting calls from scouts from Michigan and Indiana asking about you. I guess the word is out. If you go through NCAA ball and you don't get hurt, you'll most likely play in the NBA. You could make upwards of thirty thousand to fifty thousand dollars a year. That's nice pocket change. Anyway, I got a call this week from John Wooden, wanting to learn more about you. That's nothing to sneeze at, with their fifth national title and all. He wants you to come out to Westwood to tour the facility, hang out at the practices, and meet the players when they get into full swing in mid-November. It's a brand-new team this year, now that Lew Alcindor's graduated. John's got a whole new bag of tricks for revitalizing his feared "fast break" for this year's squad to try to snag a sixth title. If you go there next year, you'd be practically coming in on the ground floor. You probably wouldn't get much court time the first year, as a freshman, but you could practice with the team and learn so much from Wooden. He's a living legend. Most guys would kill to be in your position."

"Coach Wooden came down to Watts the other night to watch me play. I didn't know until he introduced himself to me afterward. He did give me his card, and he told me to call him to set up a visit at UCLA. I'm going into this with mixed feelings, though. You know how much I love the game. Two years ago, I would have jumped at the chance, but my life has taken such a detour. I have to discover who and what I am, where I come from, before I decide where I'm going to. Over the summer, I really got in touch with this Judaism thing. It was the main reason why I went back east. I have to decide if I want to continue or not. I still feel a bit over my head with all this. If I go the NCAA route, I'd have to play on Friday night or on Saturday before nightfall. I'm torn between two worlds, and I don't know what to do. I definitely don't want to leave the LA area for college, because of my parents."

"Arik, you remind me of the time when Sandy Koufax refused to pitch on Yom Kippur despite it being the third game of the World Series. I respect your views. It's not often I see guys with good character and high moral standards like you. It's what would make you not just a good ballplayer but a great one! Can't you get your rabbi to bless the ball?"

"I don't think it works like that." Arik laughed.

"What am I going to do with you, knucklehead?" Joe smiled thoughtfully. "Just go to him with an open mind. Maybe you'll be able to come to some sort of arrangement. Wooden's a religious guy himself. He should understand."

***

UCLA's Westwood campus was situated on four hundred acres of gently rolling land off Sunset Boulevard between Santa Monica and Beverly Hills, a perfect setting for a Hollywood movie. On a clear, sunny day the vista revealed chaparral-covered hills leading to mountains in the far distance, with lush greenery, including oak and palm trees, in the immediate foreground. Walking through campus, one could detect the scents of eucalyptus, jasmine, and freshly cut grass while listening to the soothing sounds of chirping birds and bubbling water fountains.

Many Americans viewed UCLA as the classic Hollywood image of college: a sunny, spacious, serene environment replete with red brick buildings, year-round sunshine, and glamorous coeds. It had become a prized destination for top athletic recruits from all over the country, for all of the reasons above but mostly because its teams won. Going to UCLA and playing in any sport meant a shot at that sport's top prize. In basketball, it also meant a chance to play for legendary Coach Wooden in a brand-new arena, Pauley Pavilion.

When Arik walked through the wrought-iron gates and stepped onto the campus, he felt like a stranger in paradise. Although he lived only a forty-five-minute drive away, he felt as if he had entered a whole new world. In fact, he had never imagined that a place like it existed. He made his way toward Pauley Pavilion, the home of the NCAA basketball champions, the UCLA Bruins.

Passing through the great hall of the arena, he gazed through an open archway and reverentially stared up at the retired jerseys of Don Barksdale and Walt Hazzard and, behind them, five NCAA championship banners hanging from the rafters above the court. He had watched the championships on TV. The place had been packed with more than 12,000 screaming fans. Now the vast hall lay silent, empty, and cool, bathed in a gloomy half-light, thousands of seats stretched up into the darkness in all directions, and the scoreboard and basketball court were vacant.

Slowly walking down, the long hallway, Arik passed rows of glass showcases filled with banners, memorabilia, trophies, and dozens of black-and-white team photos and action shots of UCLA sports greats from years gone by. He recognized Lew Alcindor and Gail Goodrich hoisting up the championship trophy while surrounded by screaming fans.

The hallway was empty that early on Sunday morning, and Arik heard his own footfalls against the smooth granite floor. He saw that Coach Wooden's office stood at the end of the long hallway. He knocked on the half-open door.

"Door's open. Come in, Eric."

Arik slowly walked through the anteroom and into the open door to John Wooden's office.

"Good morning, Eric. Please, sit down."

Coach Wooden's wood-paneled walls were covered with banners and photographs dating back thirty-five years, throughout his high school, college, and professional basketball career. There were photos of the numerous teams that he had coached and of the senators and congressmen whose paths he had crossed over the decades. Behind his desk hung a signed photograph of Wooden with President Nixon. Numerous awards, diplomas, and commendations were scattered among the photographs. Wooden sat behind a large mahogany desk, which was adorned sparsely except for a leather-bound Bible. In the center of the wall, behind Wooden, hung a large poster of a pyramid: The Pyramid of Success. Arik stared, transfixed, at the poster.

"Eric, these are the words and structures that I live by. Words that have been my moral compass and guided me ever since I was a child. These are words that I have taught each and every student athlete I have had the privilege of leading and coaching throughout the years. We are proud of what we do here at UCLA. Has anyone shown you around campus yet?"

"No, sir." Arik said, feeling tentative and nervous. Arik was way too intimidated to correct the coach by telling him that his name wasn't Eric but rather Arik. There was no point. If anything came of the meeting, there would be plenty of time for that later.

Wooden smiled. "I have been doing some homework since I saw you play at—What was it you folks call it? The Cage? You have quite an impressive talent. Why haven't you applied to our school?"

"I have, sir. I've been a bit overwhelmed by my work schedule and somehow the deadline passed me by. I've recently sent in my application and was placed on the waiting list."

"Where else have you applied?"

"In the state university system, I applied to Irvine, Davis, San Diego, and some community colleges. Those are the only ones I may possibly be able to afford. Anywhere I'm accepted, I'll have to apply for a scholarship or some work-study program." Arik stared down at his fingernails.

"Have you considered any of the sports programs in any of the schools?"

"No, sir. I never thought I'd have a chance to get into those. I play ball just because I love doing it. I've never considered doing anything with it. I'm focused on my academic studies."

"What do you want to study?"

"Engineering and computer science, sir."

"Have you taken the SAT yet?"

"Yes, sir."

"How did you do?"

"I got a 1480, sir."

Wooden was taken aback. He leaned forward in his chair and stared hard at Arik.

"Good heavens, Eric! That's twice the score of the average NCAA basketball player. Did you know that?"

"No, sir."

"Have you ever played basketball in school?"

"I played JV ball at Lynwood High as a freshman, but that's it."

"Why did you stop?"

"Well . . ." Arik wasn't sure how to phrase what he wanted to say. "I went through some experiences in my life . . . and my life took some unexpected turns . . . so, it never worked out for me to play in an organized league, except for three weeks over the summer of '68, when I played in the NBA youth league." Arik hoped that his explanation would be good enough.

"We have looked into your background, Eric, and it appears that you have been through and accomplished some incredible things in your life. I was shown back issues of the Los Angeles Times, from two years ago. It also explains why you are the only white player ever to have played street basketball in Watts. You are revered in that community. It is so rare for a white player to become prominent in a black ghetto. Nowadays, all we hear about are blacks desperate to get out of there, and here you are going in. Very unusual."

Arik looked down without saying a word.

"More than your playing skills, I am impressed by your character. That, to me, is extremely important. I have seen students come through here with wonderful talent, but they squander it with reckless behavior—staying out late, drinking, gambling, chasing women and, in general, what I call adhering to a low moral standard. You appear to be very clean-cut, not like those long-haired, dirty hippies running around the campus. They claim to be antiwar, but in reality, they are nothing more than a bunch of anarchists. I am having a hard time keeping them off my team. Do you drink or smoke pot, Eric?"

"No, sir."

"Do you pray?"

"Yes, sir, three times a day. My life experiences have opened up a whole new understanding of who I am. I've been trying to live a religious Jewish life, which includes keeping the Sabbath, keeping kosher, and praying every day."

"I'm glad you have found your faith, Eric. That is very commendable. I have some good friends that are Jewish, although they do not appear to be very observant. The important thing is that you live by a moral code."

Wooden thumped the Bible that lay on his desk.

"This is the key to personal growth, Eric—not all those newfangled Spock books. When I watched you play, I had to separate out your playing skill from the chaos I witnessed. To the uninitiated, the playground game may look elegant, but nothing could be further from the truth. What you have is pandemonium, intuitive basketball with no rhyme or reason. I believe, Eric, that you are a diamond in the rough and you will need considerable polishing and shaping.

"A player's individual style, if not integrated, can make a team's play inconsistent. In group activity, there must be supervision and leadership and disciplined effort by all—or our united strength will be dissipated by pulling against ourselves. If you discipline yourself toward team effort under the supervision of the one in charge, even though you might not always agree with the decisions, much can be accomplished.

"The thing that excites me about you, Eric, is that you can lock people up on defense. I saw that the other night. Sure, you can bring the ball down and score, but defense and court intelligence are rare to find in a point guard. Plus, you can tear your way up to the basket in tight traffic. I believe you have the potential to manufacture points for the team when you need to. That is what I am looking for in this post-Alcindor era. But you have to learn discipline and how to take direction.

"Without those two things, your lot is certain failure. I am interested in each player as an individual, but I will always act in the best interest of the team. Do you think you can make the transition to organized basketball?"

"I'm not understanding what you mean, sir," Arik said nervously.

"What I am saying is that I am offering you the opportunity to try out for a basketball scholarship here at UCLA, the NCAA champions." Wooden smiled.

Arik sat there, open-mouthed and unable to speak.

"We are only interested in a select few. We can afford to be very choosy. But this invitation is contingent on two things. First, I want to see you practice with our team, to see if you will fit in and if you can take instruction. And second, I want you to sign up for your high school varsity team and be coached by a high school coach. I will have some of my staff watch you play in a high school setting."

"Sir, I go to a small Orthodox Jewish high school. There is very little bask—"

"Do they have a varsity team?"

"Yes, sir."

"Then I want you to sign up. I am sure you will have no trouble getting on the team." Wooden winked at Arik.

"Sir, the team is awful. They play in a parochial school league, and they come in last place every year!"

"Well, Eric, I think that they are about to advance in the rankings."

***

Arik woke up early in the morning, dog-tired from having played a game late the previous night and not getting home until 1 a.m. How am I going to pass my math midterm today?

When he sleepily opened the front door, to bring in the milk, he found a box that was addressed to him lying on the front stoop. He opened it and found a brand-new pair of blue-and-white striped Adidas sneakers in his size. He had never owned anything other than high-top Converse Chuck Taylor All Stars, which were accepted on the court and also had the benefit of being cheap. Who in the world would give me a new pair of sneakers—and Adidas no less? Arik wondered. Could it be Dahlia? The return address was local, so it could not. A small card was attached to the inner box. It read as follows:

To the boychick who's NBA bound:

We're having a team get-together next Sunday at my home:
2163 Queensborough Lane, Bel Air, 3 p.m.
You'll get a chance to meet the fellas.
Don't forget to bring your bathing suit.

Compliments,
"Papa" Sam Gilbert

Who's that? And what team is he talking about? Arik didn't know, and he had never met anyone who lived in Bel Air, a section of LA famous for its mansions and its swimming pools that probably had footprints twice the size of Arik's house. There must be some mistake. Arik inspected the outside of the box to make sure that his name was on it. Of course, his curiosity would ensure that he would be at Queensborough Lane on that Sunday afternoon even though he would have to let Uncle Itzik know that he wouldn't be at work that day.

***

Driving down the road on that bright, cloudless, Sunday afternoon, Arik passed a wrought-iron gate and saw an Italianate sprawling mansion in the distance. As he wound his way past formal gardens replete with fountains and Roman columns and statues, he began to feel that his Chevelle was looking the worse for wear. It's not that my car is too old. The cars that he saw parked in the driveway were, in fact, much older than his. They were from the 1920s and 1930s. But those gleaming Duesenbergs, Packards, and Bentleys were priceless classic cars worth hundreds of thousands of dollars. His Chevelle was a pile of rusted junk. Feeling terribly out of place and nervous, he pulled up under the tan-and-navy striped awning.

Arik handed his car key to the valet, who discreetly and quickly took the car off to be parked. So much the better.

A portly, balding, middle-aged man with a broad smile and wearing a tan leisure suit greeted him. "Eric! I've heard so much about you! Come in, come in. Welcome. I'm Sam Gilbert."

"Nice to meet you, sir, and thanks for the sneakers. It really wasn't necessary, though." Arik smiled tentatively.

"Nonsense, boychick! It's the least I can do for a member of the tribe, if you know what I mean," Gilbert said in an undertone as he winked.

"If you don't mind my asking . . . Well, I haven't really been able to figure out what's going on."

Gilbert laughed. "Of course! Nobody told you! I'm part of the UCLA welcoming committee."

"Papa" Sam Gilbert was a construction magnate, a team booster with deep pockets and a web of business connections. The son of Jewish Lithuanian immigrants, Gilbert had grown up in LA and attended UCLA in the 1930s. Afterward, he had had a short, unsuccessful career as a middleweight boxer and then as a technician in a Hollywood film processing lab. Later, he started his own construction company. He eventually made millions of dollars from successful patents, of which one of the best known is the Waterpik.

Gilbert knew the 'right kind' of people, meaning people who could be counted on to return personal favors. He acted as UCLA's basketball program's padrone, someone who kept the players happy with jobs, gifts, and whatever other "help" they required.

Arik and Gilbert walked into the grand, two-story marble foyer, which was festooned with large oil paintings. He noticed a particular emphasis on the American Southwest, including works by Georgia O'Keeffe, William Henry Jackson, and Marsden Hartley. At the end of the foyer, when they passed underneath large, ornate chandeliers, the art genre seemed to shift to Expressionism, with works by Mark Rothko and Andy Warhol leading through an immense family room. They emerged on a Romanesque patio that overlooked an impossibly expansive lagoon-shaped pool equipped with a swim-up bar. The entire valley spread out in the distance like a gleaming beige carpet.

Arik was met with loud shouts, laughter, and splashing water from the crowd of partygoers who were clearly having the time of their lives. He was struck by the number of tall, muscular black men and bathing beauties, of every race imaginable, in bikinis, who seemed hell-bent on entertaining the men. When he saw the beverages in everybody's hands, he realized that he still had in his hand a bottle of Johnnie Walker Red that he had brought for the host.

"I brought this for you, Mr. Gilbert."

"Please, call me Sam or Papa, and thanks very much for the gift." Gilbert seemed touched by the gesture. "I see you brought your bathing suit. There are cabanas over there, where you can change, and then I'll introduce you to the boys."

The next several hours were a whirlwind of polite introductions. Arik met guys he had only seen on TV, and he felt completely star struck. The big names included Curtis Rowe, Steve Patterson, Sidney Wicks, Henry Bibby, and John Vallely. These were the men who would lead UCLA basketball into the post-Alcindor era and hopefully bring more national championship banners home to Pauley Pavilion.

A uniformed waiter walked discreetly over to Gilbert and Arik.

"Have a shrimp cocktail, Eric. They're excellent," Gilbert offered, smiling.

"No thanks, sir. I'm a vegetarian," Arik said nervously.

Gilbert gave Arik that knowing look again. "I didn't realize you kept kosher, Eric. Sorry about that. You really are Jewish, aren't you? No matter, we'll find something you can have."

They made their way to a group of players who were standing next to the poolside bar.

Gail Goodrich wandered over with a luscious blonde on his arm.

"Hey, Cindy, why don't you go for a swim and I'll join you in a couple minutes?" He gave her a pat on the butt and off she went but not before feasting her eyes momentarily on Arik's physique.

"Hey, guys." Gail got the attention of the other players. "This is the fella I've been telling you about. His name is Eric Myer, the guy who's been tearin' up the playground circuit in Watts. Crum and I spotted him first. The man's got some serious game, and Wooden is about to make him an offer."

Thus, began Arik's banter with the UCLA Bruins.

"You a senior in high school?"

"Yes."

"What school do you go to?"

"Rambam Academy."

"Can't say I've heard of that one. Do you play varsity ball?"

"No, no yet."

"What are you waiting for? You're almost done!"

"Long story." Arik smiled.

"You got any other offers?"

"Nothing official. I never applied for a scholarship!"

"You're kidding me! You're just sittin' around, minding your own business, and you get an offer to play basketball for the national champions? That's nuts! A thousand guys would kill to be in your position!"

"Frankly, I'm as surprised as you are. I really don't know what to make of it myself," Arik said.

"Hey, aren't you that guy in the papers, who saved that little black kid a couple years back in Watts? You know, single-handedly fighting off the gang of crazy white Nazis like you was Bruce Lee? The kid who became like Dr. Perkins's adopted son?"

"Yeah, that's me," Arik said quietly.

"I heard you did some jail time."

"Yeah, I did," Arik replied quietly, not sure who else could overhear the conversation.

"But that's good jail time!"

"I never knew there was such a thing." Arik chuckled.

"You know what I mean. You were falsely accused and got out of there a hero."

"Yeah, but I was nearly killed by those assholes."

"I heard that Dr. King personally intervened on your behalf."

"He did. It really hit me hard when he passed."

"Maybe that's why Coach is interested in you."

At that point, Goodrich stepped in. He stated definitively, "Coach was interested in him before he knew the rest."

"You ought to come down to Pauley and watch some of our practices. Maybe we'll catch a glimpse of what the phenom's got."

"I think we better not invite him until Coach says so. He's pretty weird about stuff like that. He's liable to get pissed off—even though he'd never use that expression, of course. Plus, we need to make it seem like it was his idea. Coach doesn't even know we're here. He don't like us hanging out with Papa

Gilbert. He feels that it's unethical or something. I, personally, don't think there's anything wrong with it."

"What do you mean 'wrong'? Papa Gilbert is always there for us. We can always go to him when we need anything, even advice on life and girls. He gets us cars, stereos, airline tickets, threads, all kinds of entertainment . . . if you know what I mean." Goodrich winked, pointing his eyes at some of the bikinis.

Arik turned to look, too.

"Look around, Eric. When you're a ballplayer on campus, you're a celebrity. UCLA has, by far and away, the greatest quantity of high-quality pussy compared to any other school in the United States of America, possibly the world. The Beach Boys are absolutely right about California girls. And it's all yours for the sampling when you're a Bruin. Eric, my boy, you have hit the jackpot!"

Arik laughed. "I'll make a mental note of that. Thanks for the heads up."

But he thought about Dahlia.

"Hey, guys, it's hot as hell out here," one of the players said. "The last one in the pool sucks dick!"

In an instant, Arik was left standing alone at the side of the pool, all the others having disappeared in a large splash.

"Hey, Whitey! You gonna stand there burnin' your ass off, or you comin' in?"

Arik was already in the air and en route to the bottom of the pool.

The afternoon passed in the good cheer of acceptance. Arik had never been hit on by so many attractive women in his life. In his pants pocket, he held the phone numbers of at least five nice young ladies who were interested in getting to know him better.

Even better, he thought, is getting to know the guys I've only read about in Sports Illustrated. In person, they were really fun to be around. It suddenly hit him that he could soon be wearing a Bruins jersey and not just Bruins fan gear. He felt like pinching himself to make sure that he wasn't dreaming.

Later, when the sun started to dip in the west, the crowd began to thin out. Arik collected his things. The day had been quite the whirlwind.

"Hey, boychick, you in a hurry to go?" Gilbert asked him.

"No, sir."

"Then stay for a while. I'll have the staff rustle up something for you to eat. Let's take a walk."

They walked through the rose-lined paths of the garden as the sun went down.

"So, what's your story, Eric?"

"Well, let's see. The short version is I'm just a kid who grew up on the wrong side of the tracks . . . to an invalid dad who never could rub two nickels together. Although, I did inherit his athleticism."

"What sport did he play?"

"He was a championship boxer."

"What university did he go to?"

"Buchenwald University!"

"Oh, sorry, Eric. I didn't mean anything by it."

"It's okay. Sometimes I think I inherited his edge, too."

"Is that how he became an invalid?"

"No, no. He lost his leg in the Israeli War of Independence."

"A real war hero, huh?"

"I suppose," Arik answered thoughtfully.

"So, what did Wooden say to you?"

"He told me to come by UCLA practices and that I needed to play varsity ball at school. I'm happy to do the first thing but less enthusiastic about the second."

"Why's that?"

"There's nothing there for me. Have you ever seen yeshiva boys play basketball?"

Gilbert laughed. "But just think of all those nice Yiddish maidles that will be drooling all over you. They won't know what hit them when they watch you play."

Arik shook his head. "No thanks. I'm good."

"Let me tell you what's really going on here, Eric. The NCAA, in its drive to bring black players in, has suddenly discovered that they play so much better that white guys, and soon the NCAA and the NBA will be almost exclusively black, which is fine as far as it goes, but there always needs to be room made for white players if they can keep up, or it will become too obvious what's going on. It's sort of like being the token white guy. It's a real role reversal, but you still need to know how to play the game."

Gilbert adjusted his glasses and tried to lock eyes with Arik.

"What are the three things you look for in a college, Eric?"

"Academics, athletics, and social life," Arik said.

"You sound like you've been asked that question before. Have you been approached by any other recruiters?"

"No, not as of yet, sir."

"Eric, you're the perfect candidate for this program. The way you project yourself and exude your personality . . . you're the complete package. I know where you're coming from. You've had a rough time growing up, your father being an invalid and all. You're not that different from the black guys you play with. I don't know if you know this, but Jews dominated basketball until the Second World War, just like the blacks do today. I remember, as a kid, it wasn't so easy for Jews in this country. They were stuck in their ghettos and used basketball to escape from the conditions they were living in, just as the blacks do now. Only for you, personally, the struggle goes on.

"But now you're now being handed an opportunity to get out of all that forever. This is the second most important decision you'll ever make, after who you pick to be your wife. Your next four years will dictate your next forty. UCLA is a big family, and if you pick us we'll take care of you. We'll help guide you and mold you into the best person you can be. Wooden has made a lifelong career of molding young men into future leaders.

"We take a personal interest in our players, and I want you to remember that. We'll protect you from those charlatans, agents who want to associate with you only to make a fast buck. Other schools, like Houston, Michigan, or Indiana, are going to be trolling for you when they find out about you. You'll be offered money, cars, and even female students when you're being recruited. But your place is here, and I promise I'll watch over you."

"Well, thanks for all that and for having me here today. It was very cool," Arik said.

"It's only the beginning, Eric."

***

December 7, 1969

My Dearest Dahlia,

So much to tell you. I did something I swore I'd never do, for reasons you won't believe. Let me start by saying that I've joined Rambam's varsity basketball team. You should have seen the looks on the coaches' and players' faces when I came into the gym during team practice. All play stopped, and everyone turned around to stare at me. The coach asked me what the purpose of my visit was, and I told him I wanted to try out for the team. Every member of the team applauded me. What the hell! I think Rabinovich spilled the beans about what happened at camp. The others looked at me like I was some kind of superhero. It was so stupid. I hadn't even touched the ball yet. Coach just patted me on the shoulder and said, "Okay, you've tried out . . . and you've made it. Congratulations! You're our new shooting guard." It was actually kind of funny. I'm going to work with the team and try to make everyone better, kind of like what I did with Richard at camp, rather than be a basketball snob. Maybe now one of these guys might get the idea that it would be nice to invite me over to his house for Shabbat . . . which still hasn't happened. I just don't get it.

You're probably wondering why I had a change of heart. Well, I had an interesting visitor at the Cage. We were playing a team from Compton, and on the sideline sat none other than John Wooden, the head coach of UCLA, the NCAA champions. This guy is one of the busiest guys in the world, but he found time to come down to see me play. To say that he stuck out like a sore thumb is an understatement. He's this gray-haired dude in a gray suit, white shirt, and black tie. He's got huge professor's glasses and looks like a little bit of a mouse, to tell you the truth. He sat there with a rolled-up newspaper in his hand. Can you imagine him in the middle of the ghetto? Everyone was watching him more than the game!

He came over to me afterward and invited me to visit UCLA. He practically offered me a scholarship right then and there. He's a real straight shooter like some Protestant minister. He asked me if I pray. It's a good thing I went to Mosh! He did tell me that I needed to play basketball on a school team to learn how to play "organized basketball." So here I am.

Things got really crazy then. I got invited to some millionaire's mansion who's a big contributor to UCLA's basketball team. He had this huge pool party for all the basketball players to kick off the new season. It was like a Playboy mansion party in the movies, crawling with college "Playmates" who were throwing themselves at the players. It was hysterical to watch. And no, I didn't pick up anyone or run off with anyone! You have nothing to fear, my precious. The millionaire guy is Jewish, and he kept calling me boychick. Apparently, he has these parties all the time.

How are you doing? What's going on with Yaniv and the others? Did they get away with the prank they pulled? Tell me every detail. I can't believe your school is so disorganized and poorly run. If someone did something like that at Rambam, there'd be hell to pay. That is, unless the culprits were some of the kids of the super-rich donors to the school. That crowd could piss on the principal's shoes and convince him that it's raining. It's amazing how rabbis put down material possessions in their sermons and then turn around and kiss their donors' butts.

Anyway, have you been in touch with Penny about the trip? Has she made the hotel reservations? I've got my plane tickets already and I'm crazy with excitement to see you, my soul. I dream about you every night. I just want to kiss your lips.

My heart is yours for always,
Arik

December 14, 1969

My sweet boy,

You aren't the only one crazy with anticipation. I wake up in the middle of the night with my heart racing just at the thought of seeing you again very soon. In those moments between wakefulness and sleep, I lie in bed staring out into the darkness and I see you standing there with your sweet smile looking down on me. How I wish that you were lying here next to me. Who knows? You might get lucky!

I've had my skis sharpened and my bindings adjusted at Emilio's, and I bought some sexy ski outfits for your viewing pleasure. I also bought some other clothes, but I'm afraid I can't tell you what they are. You'll just have to find out for yourself.

School's fine. I have three final exams this week just before winter break, but I should have no problem with them. The whole carp thing was such a blast. Yaniv and two other guys snuck into Mrs. Feldstein's office. She's the assistant principal and such a bitch. Everyone hates her. She really had it coming. Anyway, Yaniv is an excellent lock picker. He got in there before morning Tefillah (prayers) and stuck this two foot long carp into the ceiling panel above her desk. Nothing happened for about three days, but as the fish started to decompose it began to drip drip drip brown goo on her desk and head and stink like you wouldn't believe.

I wish I was a fly on the wall so I could have seen the look on her face when the ceiling dripped goo. By the next day, she couldn't stand being in her office. The maintenance guys had to climb up into the ceiling to retrieve "Charlie the tuna's" dead carcass. A major shakedown ensued. Yaniv was the prime suspect, because he's done crap like this before. After a stern reprimand from Rabbi Loenbach, the principal, nothing else happened to him. His father is the chargé d'affaires at the embassy. Here in Washington big money isn't the most important thing. Your prestige is measured by political or power status and the people at the top of that food chain also think that they can get away with murder.

Anyway, I've been thumbing through Harper's Bazaar magazine and they have a whole section dedicated to Aspen—everything from restaurants, new ski runs and all the bands that are going to be playing at all the hot spots in town over Christmas. By the time we get there, I'll be a complete expert!

Are you sure you don't know how to ski? You've lied about stuff like that before. Well, we'll find out soon enough. Call me long distance with your flight information please. I want us all to meet at the arrivals lounge and head over to the Hotel Jerome together. It's beautiful and has just been renovated.

Missing you like crazy,
Loving you forever,
Dahlia

Chapter 16
Aspen, December 1969

The snow spread out before Arik like an endless carpet of white as the Rocky Mountain Airways flight made its final approach over a majestic mountain range into Aspen/Pitkin County Airport. Arik marveled over the snow. He had never seen snow before let alone touched it. That just happens if you're from Southern California and have never had the means to travel much. He knew snow would be cold, but he wondered whether it would feel wet, like sand or like ice. He felt a sudden chill when the plane rolled to a stop at the terminal and the flight attendant opened the door to a gust of frigid air that enveloped him. He found himself trembling slightly. Is it the icy wind that suddenly flooded into the plane, or is it the expectation of what is to come?

This was going to be a week of firsts, that much he was sure of: the first time for snow, for skiing, and for tobogganing and, perhaps most poignantly, the first time he would be away, unchaperoned, with the love of his life. It would be only moments before he would see her. Was that why his heart was involuntarily pounding like a drum in his chest? He reached up into the overhead compartment to take down his borrowed brown ski parka. Moish Laufer, a classmate who had lived back east, had found one for him in a trunk that he kept in his basement. Arik put it on, but it didn't feel very warm and it didn't stop his shaking. Perhaps if I wear two sweaters? His new army-surplus boots that he squeaked in as he walked toward the cabin door didn't feel particularly warm either. No matter. I'm a big boy. I'll adjust. The sky was a bright navy-blue illuminated by a golden sunset; the sunset reflected across the entire narrow valley and came to rest on the opposite mountain range. In between, everything in its path seemed to glow a golden yellow. Aspenglow.

The transfer bus pulled up to the terminal where he was supposed to meet the others. When he walked into the terminal, he felt a blast of hot air bombard his senses, affording him some relief. That moment gave way as he took in the scene in the terminal: a cacophony of hundreds of skiers milling about in ski suits, hats, and gloves, all in a riot of bright colors. Long, multicolored ski bags and shorter ones for boots were strewn everywhere. In the center of the arrivals lounge stood an enormous Christmas tree, with flashing brightly colored lights, which was surrounded by a forest of green and red poinsettias. People dressed up as Santa Claus were wandering through the terminal. In the corner stood a chorus of men and women, dressed up as if they had just walked out of a Charles Dickens novel, singing carols.

Arik felt his pulse quicken again. And then he knew why. Suddenly, he saw her, from behind. Dahlia: a vision of loveliness. She was wearing tight designer jeans, a gleaming white ski parka with matching fur-ruffled snow boots, and a white fur headband over her long, full, golden ponytail.

Penny was the first to spot him, but with a finger on his lips Arik warned her not to react. He snuck up behind Dahlia, put both arms around her waist, and kissed her behind the ear.

"Arik!" she squealed as she spun around and covered his face in kisses. "How was your flight? Oh, my God! It's so good to finally see your face!"

"Great, sweetcakes. How was yours? So, glad to see you, too. It feels like it's been years! I've been going nuts."

"My flight was awful."

"Really? Why? Did you hit turbulence?"

"No, silly!" She swatted at him playfully. "It was so long, because all I could do was count the minutes until I would see you. That's why I thought the flight would never end!"

"I can't believe we're finally here," he said in a low whisper.

"Me neither!" Dahlia kissed him.

"Hi, Penny! How was your flight?" Arik gave her a hug.

"You know how I feel about the cold," Penny said. "Mexico City is even hotter than LA, so the cold takes a little getting used to. I will be happy to get in front a large warm fireplace."

Arik wondered how Penny could feel the cold at all in the fur jacket she was wearing.

"Hey, where's Richard?" Arik asked.

At that moment, Richard emerged from the men's room, wearing a fluorescent-yellow ski parka with the name Salomon etched in black down one arm. Arik thought that he looked a little bit like a road sign.

"Hey, Richie, how're you doing? How was your flight? You look great, man!"

"It was fine. I'm just so glad I'm here. I couldn't wait for school to end. Finals were such a bitch. I heard you went to D.C. to see Dahlia for Sukkot. Lucky, you! This is the first time I've seen Penny since camp."

Richard put his arm around Penny's shoulder, and she kissed his cheek.

"So, Arik, how'd did it go down?" Richard asked. "I mean, with her parents and all?"

Arik smiled and looked at Dahlia. "I think it went fine. Don't you?"

"Absolutely. They loved you!"

"So, be honest. What did you girls tell your parents about this trip?" Richard asked.

Dahlia said, "We told them that we were going on a camp reunion . . . which is really no lie!"

Everyone laughed.

After they had picked up their bags, they piled into a red Volvo cab. Arik stared out the window in wonderment at the sparkling jewel box that was Aspen at night. He had expected a Swiss-style village, like he had seen in National Geographic. Instead, Aspen looked like a Western town right out of the movies but without the tumbleweeds. It was snowing, and the flakes reflected the brightly colored lights of the quaint shops, boutiques, and bars that lined the storybook avenues. Every doorway seemed to be filled with the raucous holiday crowd that was milling about dressed in either European-style skiwear or cowboy hats and jeans.

"An Aspen traffic jam." Dahlia laughed as she pointed at a line of horse-drawn sleighs that were jangling slowly up the street and blocking all access.

"I've never seen anything like this before," Arik whispered to her. "It's so beautiful here, like a fantasy."

She caressed his neck and kissed it softly. "I'm so glad we're here together."

Arik turned toward her and rubbed noses.

"Here we are, the Hotel Jerome," the cabbie announced. Penny paid the fare with a plastic card.

Arik bent down to touch the snow and ran a handful of it through his fingers.

"What are you doing?" Dahlia looked at him in some wonderment.

"This is a first for me. I've never touched snow before." Arik smiled.

"There will be many firsts this week, my love," she whispered in his ear.

The Hotel Jerome, a fixture in Aspen for a hundred years, had the look and feel of an old Western saloon without any of the actual aging. The immaculate lobby was appointed in fine leather and crystal. It presented an understated elegance that was echoed by the well-heeled men and women who lined the mahogany-and-brass lobby bar, listening to live piano music. Tiffany lamps shed subtle light over the richly carved old Western reception area.

Penny approached the front desk. "Two rooms for the Greens and the Meirs."

She pulled out the plastic card again and handed it the reception clerk.

"How are we going to take care of the finances?" Arik asked somewhat nervously.

"Do not worry about it." Penny smiled slyly. "My dad gave us this whole trip as my seventeenth birthday gift. Hence, the Diners Club card."

"I'm not sure I've ever seen one of those before," Arik said. "How does it work?"

Arik's question made Penny laugh gently. "Well, I hope it does work, first of all! The card is connected to my father's bank account. Every time I use it, they take the funds out of there. It is like writing a check only much more convenient."

"I probably won't be able to get one of those until I'm out of the army, although my Abba has one," Dahlia said.

"Still, I'd like to pay my share," Arik said.

"Yes, Penny, I thought we agreed," Richard said.

Penny laughed. "It will be a long week. There will be plenty of places and ways for you guys to spend money on Dahlia and me, and I will hold you to it." She wagged her finger at them.

"Deal!" Arik said.

The bellmen carried off everyone's ski equipment, leaving the four teenagers standing with their luggage in the middle of the entrance foyer.

Penny coyly held up four room keys. "So, boys and girls, how are going to split these up?"

The four stood there in a small circle, staring at each other and pondering for a brief, awkward moment.

Finally, Dahlia leaned her head on Arik's shoulder, reached out, and took two keys from Penny's hands. "Arik and I will take room 403," she said quietly.

"Well, Richie, it looks like we are stuck with 407." Penny grinned.

"Poor us!" Richard laughed.

"I don't think Rabbi Moskowitz would approve." Arik smirked.

Dahlia looked at Arik with sudden intensity. "I'm sure that even if he found out he would be tickled pink to dance at our wedding." She ran her hand down Arik's back. "Let's go!"

"I have made dinner reservations at the Prospect restaurant, downstairs, for 9 p.m.," Penny said. "That gives us about an hour and a half to freshen up."

A brass cage elevator took them up to the fourth floor.

Dahlia and Arik's room was richly appointed with a mahogany four-poster queen bed. The white ceramic bathroom was equipped with a four-legged bathtub and gleaming chrome fixtures that harkened back to the previous century.

Arik brought the suitcases into the room and placed them by the window. The room was dark, except for the light coming in from the street and the night-light in the bathroom. Dahlia turned, tackled him onto the bed, and pinned him down. She kissed him deeply. Locked in an embrace, they lay there for a long while.

"Arik, my soul, this is going to be the best week of our lives. Stay right where you are, and don't move a muscle. There's something I want to show you. I'll be out in a minute, chamud."

Dahlia disappeared into the bathroom for what seemed an eternity to Arik. He lay on the bed in the dim light, feeling his heart beating almost out of his chest.

The bathroom door opened, and Dahlia emerged, silhouetted against the night-light behind her.

"Hi," she purred.

Arik's heart stopped.

The four teenagers sat in a quiet corner booth away from the throngs of people that milled in and out of the bustling restaurant and the wait staff who seemed constantly on the run trying to keep up with the holiday crowd. One of the servers ran by and dropped off the menus. Another came by and put down four cold, foaming Coors beers in large, clear glass mugs.

"How's your room?" Richard asked.

"Amazing! This place is absolutely beautiful. Busy as hell, though," Arik said.

"Kudos to Penny for picking this place," Dahlia said.

"A toast to friendship!" Richard said.

All raised their glasses.

"We loved the room from the moment we walked in. Didn't we, Arik?" Dahlia said as she rubbed her toe against Arik's leg.

He smiled and blushed. Penny chuckled into her beer. Everyone perused the menu.

"Let's see: rotisserie chicken, French oxtail soup, veal cheeks, flatiron steak in blue cheese butter, seared scallops," Dahlia said. "Here's some stuff we can eat."

"I'll have the Gem lettuce with goat cheese," Arik told the waiter.

"Rainbow trout with hazelnuts for me," Penny said.

Richard ordered the tuna carpaccio, and Dahlia ordered the striped bass in tomato basil sauce.

"Arik, aren't you going to order anything more than a salad?" Penny asked. "You'll starve!"

"Can we eat the fish? I thought that if the fish was cooked in nonkosher pots and pans you couldn't eat it. What do I know? I'm just a goy. Maybe I got it wrong?"

Dahlia took on a protective tone. "Well, buubs, the way it works is there is a concept of batel beshishim, which means that if you have more than sixty to one kosher vs nonkosher mixture then it's okay. It's sort of like whatever you can't see can't hurt you. Many religious people follow that concept to eat fish out at restaurants. There's no need to worry about the fact that the food is made in nonkosher pots."

"Wow, I never realized that. Well, you learn something new every day. If that's the case. . ."

Arik called the waiter back over to their table. "I'll have the red snapper roasted in truffle oil with the goat cheese and arugula."

"Lots of firsts," Arik said, looking at Dahlia.

After a sumptuous meal topped off by French vanilla ice cream on crème brûlée along with cappuccinos, the two couples went for a walk through the glittering, snowy streets.

"This place looks like a Christmas card," Dahlia said. "Arik, you're shaking with cold. Are you okay?" She held him tighter. "Your hands are freezing. Did you bring gloves or a wool hat? Your ears are so red they look like they're going to fall off."

"I'm okay, really. I'll be fine. I brought an extra sweater."

"You won't be fine, booba. You'll be outside the whole day tomorrow. It gets very cold at the top of the lifts, and you could get frostbite. I'm serious. Let's go in here and take a look at the ski clothes. I can only keep you warm at night. Tomorrow, you're on your own." Dahlia turned to Penny and Richard. "You two go on off without us. Arik and I are going shopping. We'll meet you back at the hotel."

Penny and Richard walked away, saying something about looking at the art galleries on West Main Street.

Arik and Dahlia walked into Elli's, arguably the most exclusive skiwear and equipment shop in Aspen. The walls were festooned with large ski posters of Olympians slalom racing or powder skiing in Aspen, Vail, and Park City. Near the ceiling hung banners advertising the upcoming NASTAR ski racing competitions and their sponsors Rossignol, Salomon, Lange, K2, and Dynastar. Leaning against the back wall were hundreds of skis of every size, length, and color, all arranged according to type: racing, recreational, and novice. There was an entire wall of ski boots in a riot of colors, shapes, and sizes.

Arik looked for the clearance rack but saw none. Dahlia led him toward the racks of ski parkas and ski pants.

"Here, try this on." She handed him a bright orange and black parka with the word Atomic emblazoned across the shoulders.

"Perhaps something with smaller letters? I'll glow in the dark."

"Just for size, then."

Arik tried on several parkas and black insulated stretch pants. He finally compromised on a navy-blue parka and the pants. But when he looked at the price tag, he gulped. Together, the ensemble cost nearly one hundred fifty dollars, which would basically clean him out for the entire trip.

"Dahlia, I don't think this a great idea. I really think I can make do with what I have. I don't need some fancy threads from Austria with the logo Edelweiss on them."

"Nonsense, Arik. Your jacket is too thin, and you can't ski in jeans. They'll get wet, and you'll freeze your butt off."

Arik looked at her with some concern. He whispered, "But did you see the price of these? I'll have no spending money left for the rest of the week. I still intend to pay Penny for our room."

Dahlia smiled at him coyly. "Who said anything about you buying them? I never considered that for a minute. I'm buying these for you. What do you think of the jacket?"

"You can't do that. I won't allow it. Please!"

"Believe me, I know that you're sensitive about these things, but you've come here to ski, and ski you will. And I won't have you catching pneumonia."

"Perhaps another shop with a clearance—"

"Stop it, Arik. I'm buying this stuff for you, and that's that. You have no idea how much joy it gives me to get this for you. I love you so much. Please, let me do this. Please—"

Arik kissed her lightly. "Thanks. I do appreciate this, Dahlia. More than you know."

"Good. Now, let's get you a nice ski hat and gloves, too." She looked at his hands. "You need an extra-large. You know what they say about guys with big hands?"

"No. What do they say?" Arik smirked.

"Big feet!" Dahlia giggled and headed toward the cashier. On the way, she picked up a heavy Nordic sweater in Arik's size along with the hat and gloves.

When they went outside, Arik put on his new parka. "It really feels great," he said.

"Now you look like Jean-Claude Killy," Dahlia said. She put her hand in Arik's pocket and nudged closer to him. "Let's go to bed and really get warm. We need to get an early start in the morning. The lifts open at 7 a.m., and the lines will probably be horrible. You will need to rent skis, as well, even earlier than that."

Chapter 18

Arik awoke at 5:30 a.m., still not fully comprehending that the love of his life lay next to him in bed. Someone who had populated only his dreams and fantasies for so long was suddenly there, so real and so warm, next to him. He stared at her face as she remained fast asleep. Breathing softly, she was completely at peace, the calm after the storm. The night before had been a night like no other: a union of two souls, a fusion of hearts. For both of them, their senses had exploded into brilliant color in the darkness of night. They had reached a realization of lifelong yearning, a sense of coming home. He gently kissed her closed eyelids. She reached out to hold him. Half asleep, she murmured, "I love you, Arik."

"I love you more than my life, Dahlia."

"Never let me go, Arik. You're the one."

She blinked her eyes open then stared deeply into his eyes. "Do you believe that God decides on your mate forty days before you're conceived?"

"Not sure. I wasn't there." Arik smiled.

"No, I'm being serious."

"I believe that God has given people the ability to choose for themselves how to live their lives but with those choices come some consequences, whether for good or ill. I believe that choosing a mate is one of the most important choices a person can make in their lives. Why would God take that decision away from us?"

When Dahlia didn't reply, he added, "Just saying."

"Well, I'm glad you did. I never thought of it that way. Arik Meir? I choose you. You're my choice."

"I want nothing more than to be the way we are right now for the rest of our lives. How can we keep this flame burning as bright as it is now?" Arik asked.

"Are you worried about that?"

"I am, a bit. I want to run away with you now and build our home, but both of us know that's not possible yet. I can't bear the thought of being without you, but we live so far away. Regardless of what I end up doing next year, I may not see you for a whole year. The thought of that fills me with such dread. I lay awake at night thinking about that. Why does life have to throw so many curveballs? There's so much that has to happen before we can tie the knot. I know you're the one, but how can we survive until then? We've never even properly discussed the whole UCLA thing. How's that going to work out? Everyone is acting like my going there is a foregone conclusion."

"Don't think that I don't worry about that, too, sweetheart. But we still have a little bit of time to figure out what to do about UCLA. You haven't even been given a formal offer yet. It may be the greatest thing that's ever happened to you—outside of me, of course. But we have to take this one day at a time, one month at a time, one letter at a time. Long-term relationships are hard, but they can work by lots of little short terms turning into the long term. Even though we're apart, our letters hold us together."

"Wow! Smart and good looking, too!"

"I'm serious. I've never seen a guy who was so good about writing letters as you. Every time I get one from you, my heart skips a beat. I never told you this, but I showed a part of one of your letters to a handwriting specialist. Not one of the personal parts—don't worry. They say that you can tell a lot about a person from his handwriting, and I believe it."

"What did this specialist say?"

"Well, let's see: strong-willed, faithful, spiritual, principled, kind, organized, passionate, bright . . . It was rather disappointing, actually."

"Why is that?"

"Because she didn't tell me anything I didn't already know." Dahlia drew him close. "I'm the luckiest girl on earth. I must have done something right in life. But please, let's not think about the future anymore this week. Let's live in the present only. Let's build memories this week that will last a lifetime."

***

It was barely dawn, yet the streets were teaming with thousands of colorful-parka-clad skiers carrying skis over their shoulders and clomping and crunching about in half-open ski boots. The air was crisp and cold, and the cloudless sky had nearly concluded its journey from navy blue to bright sky blue. After loading their skis in the rack behind the red shuttle bus, the group of four climbed into the back of the bus.

"Where are you two going to start?" Dahlia asked Penny and Richard.

Richard rattled off their plans: "We want to get to the top of Ajax by lunchtime and take Spar Gulch down. While it's not terribly steep, it has roller-coaster turns with banks on both sides, like a bobsled track. As you go down, you have to swoop from side to side along the track. It goes on like that for miles! It gets technical when it gets icy, but they had at least a foot of new powder on it so it should be amazing fun."

Arik was impressed by Richard's knowledge of the slopes. He also thought it was cute when Penny squeezed Richard's hand gently and added, "I think it would be best to warm up on Buttermilk. It is our first time out this season, so best to get our legs tuned up. Then we can head out to Ajax."

"So, Richard, how long have you been skiing?" Arik asked.

"Ever since I was a kid. My dad insisted that we learn how to ski, from the time we could walk. Our family has season lift tickets at Hunter Mountain in Upstate New York, but during winter break he'd take us up to Killington, Vermont. Both spots have great skiing, for an eastern resort, with a good variety of terrain. There's no powder skiing there, though. This is my first time skiing out west, in powder, and I can't wait! . . . I'm not fancy like these girls. They trotted off to Chamonix in the French Alps last winter break, so Aspen is a big step down for them."

"That is not true, Richie," Penny protested. "Every ski area has its own charm and challenges. I have never skied in Colorado before, and I have really been looking forward to coming here. Especially with you guys."

"Where else have you skied, Dahlia?" Richard asked.

"When my dad was ambassador in Paris, we skied all over the French Alps. We also crossed over to Switzerland and skied at St. Moritz, Grindelwald, and Davos. Grindelwald was my favorite. The view of the Eiger coming down First Mountain is so breathtaking that I almost broke my neck staring across the valley. I was rounding a curve, going pretty fast, and didn't notice a mogul. I caught an edge, and off I went!"

"Were you hurt?" Arik asked.

"Only my ass and my pride. It was a good warning, though."

"Speaking of my ass, I plan on spending a lot of time on it today. I should have stuffed a pillow down the back of my pants," Arik said.

"Have you really never skied before, Arik? Or are you going to fake being a beginner, fall all over the place, and then to save a damsel in distress you'll burst into giant slalom mode and rocket down the slope at sixty miles an hour and save the day?" Penny laughed.

"I swear this is my first time. I'll be happy if I can stay erect." Arik laughed.

"You appeared to have no trouble last night," Dahlia whispered in his ear.

"I heard that," Penny howled.

"Heard what?" Richard asked.

"Nothing!" The other three said in unison.

The shuttle bus stopped at the base of Buttermilk Mountain, and the foursome piled out in front of the Aspen Mountain Ski School.

"You two go on," Dahlia said. "I'll stay here with Arik today. With his native athleticism, he should be skiing like a champion by lunchtime."

"I hate making you do that, Dahlia, standing around for nothing. Why don't you join them for the morning? I'll enroll myself in the ski school and take my lumps out of sight of the rest of you. I prefer to make a fool of myself in private anyway." Arik smiled. "Then come a fetch me at about 12:30, and we'll have lunch at Crepe Suzette before heading out. You came here to ski, not to babysit."

"I came here to be with you, buubs."

"I know, but let me just figure this out on my own. Please, sweetheart?"

"Okay. But let me get your rentals with you and make sure they give you the right-length skis and well-fitting boots. I also want to watch them fix your bindings. They're going to take one look at you and overtighten them. I don't need you breaking a leg on your first day. I need you in one piece."

Dahlia looked at Penny and said, "You two go. I'll catch up with you at the top."

***

"These skis seem rather short. They're barely bigger than ice skates," Arik said.

"They're called GLM skis—graduated length method. They start off short, and as your skills increase so will your ski lengths."

When Arik left the shop, he tightened his boots and dropped them into the skis with a click. He pointed himself toward the meeting point for the ski school. Dahlia popped on her skis effortlessly, flew down fifty yards, and turned around like an elf.

"Okay, boychick, push off and come toward me!" Dahlia called out.

Arik did as he she said but in a moment sailed out of control, arms flailing in the air, as he went hurtling past her and toward the orange plastic fence sheeting.

"Oh, shit!" Arik called out as he tried to stop. "Where are the brakes on these things?"

He tried to twist his body to stop and, in a moment, collapsed in a heap in a snow bank when his bindings released.

"Arik, until this very moment, I still harbored some slight delusion that this might not be your first time skiing . . . but what you did just now is impossible to fake, so I believe you." Dahlia giggled.

"Crap, these things are slippery!"

"They're supposed to be, genius."

"Okay, okay. Now, go off with the others and leave me here to stew in my own juices. They're probably still in the lift line. They'll let you push in. Go, booba, go!"

"I'll meet you at the front entrance of the restaurant, by the NASTAR sign, at 12:30. Okay? I love you!" She kissed him lightly.

"I love you too. Now, go!"

Dahlia flew off toward the lift line.

Arik enrolled in the beginner class, and he was placed with a group of eight other beginners. His classmates either were ten years old or weighed over two hundred pounds. I guess you have to start somewhere.

They were joined by a blonde cheerleader type who was wearing a tight red ski jumpsuit, a white headband, and matching white Atomic skis. The ski school's logo was embossed over her ample left bosom.

"Good morning everyone," she said. She had a big, bright smile and rosy cheeks from having spent so many days out in the sun. "I'm Suzie, and I'll be your GLM ski instructor this morning. I take it that nobody has skied before? Let's take this gentle slope slowly, going to the T-Bar. "

She led the group like a mother goose, snowplowing her way down, followed by all the goslings trying to do the same. Arik stayed in the back of the group. He quickly realized that he would never learn how to ski if he snowplowed. He resolved to try to keep the skis parallel as much as possible, even if it meant falling several times. He watched intently as other skiers nearby moved down the slope just off the vertical fall line and then turn back and forth, keeping their skis parallel until they initiated a turn. He watched them shift their bodies so that their skis shifted from one edge to another during their turns. He tried it and after several fits and starts found that he could do it.

Up and down the hill they went, the instructor stopping the class at intervals to explain how to initiate twists and turns with the waist while keeping the upper body still and urging them to try to keep the front tips of their skis from crossing each other. Arik remained reserved, allowing the others to do the whining and squirming for him; as usual, he preferred to listen and observe. He watched Suzie's body movements as she skied and intently absorbed every instruction she gave.

After about two hours, Arik found that he was able to navigate the runs with reasonable control. Nothing to it! he thought, just as he lost control, both of his legs went in different directions, and down he went. He felt a little foolish and self-conscious when Suzie skied by.

"Let me help you up, Arik," Suzie said, reaching out a hand. "You're doing really well—that is, up until a moment ago. Are you sure this is your first time?"

"Isn't it obvious?"

"Actually, it's not. If this is your first time, then you're a natural athlete. A couple more hours of instruction, and you'll be able to take a chair up to the blue trails. The group lesson is almost done. Stay, and I'll give you some private instruction. I'll have you up and running by lunch."

"I really can't afford a private lesson. I was just going to practice what you taught me already."

"Don't sweat it. I have no other lessons 'til one, so this one's on me."

"I really couldn't ask you to—"

"You're not asking. I'm offering." Suzie smiled. "You'll pick it up a lot quicker one on one."

"Okay. Thanks."

She dismissed the rest of the class and headed for the lifts. Arik skied gamely behind her.

"Let's head up to the novice slopes," she said. "They're signposted by green circles."

The chairlift took them halfway up the mountain.

"Are you sure I'm ready for all this?" Arik asked while they were riding up.

"I think you're going to do just fine. Buttermilk is the ideal teaching mountain. There are lots of novice and intermediate trails going down from the top, and the trails are wide, so just execute the turns the way I showed you and you'll do great." She patted Arik's knee. "Okay, now keep your tips up, and just stand up on the platform when the chair reaches it and let the chair push you off the snow mound."

For the next hour, they went up and down numerous trails of increasing complexity. Slowly, Arik's confidence grew and he began to enjoy himself.

The chairlift stopped in midslope when a skier fell off ahead of them and had to be retrieved.

"I can't believe how fast you've picked this up," Suzie said. "I've never seen anyone learn as fast you have. What other sports do you play?"

"I mostly play basketball, and I do martial arts and gymnastics. I've never even seen snow before last night."

Suzie burst out laughing. "You can't be serious. Really? You must be either from Southern California or Florida."

"Good guess. I'm from LA."

"That's pretty cool. Are you here with family?"

"No, friends."

They skied off the lift. Arik kept his tips up and let the chair push him away as Suzie had instructed him to do.

"Here we go! I'm going to take you down a mogul field. It's more technical, but you've got some pretty strong legs. Use all the turning skills I taught you. You can go around them or over them. We'll take it slowly at first. Prepare to get some air."

"What do you mean?" Arik called out in the wind, which had picked up.

"You'll find out!" Suzie yelled back.

The mogul field looked to Arik more like a mine field, with endless mounds sculpted out of the hill. The grade was fairly steep as well. Arik became very nervous and tentative.

"Just follow behind me, and turn when I turn," Suzie called out from about twenty feet in front of him.

Suzie sped ahead, and Arik struggled to keep up with her. They were picking up speed. Suzie flew ahead but turned around every so often to check on him.

"Arik, you're doing great! Keep going!"

Arik's abdominal and quadriceps muscles were burning as they were being asked to do something that they had never done before. Fatigue set in and he lost his focus momentarily. He came to the uphill side of a large mogul and, suddenly, he was launched into the air. He saw it all happen as if in slow motion. Suzie was waiting for him on the downhill side of the mogul. In an instant, he landed squarely on top of her.

They lay in the snow.

Arik, mortified, asked, "Are you, all right? I'm so sorry!"

Suzie laughed. "I'm fine, but you certainly know how to make an entrance!"

Arik lifted himself off her and helped her up. He was quite embarrassed and thought it odd that Suzie didn't appear shocked or perturbed in any way.

"I'm really sorry, Suzie. I was going too fast."

"I'll say!" She winked at him. "Now, let's see if we can find you some more moguls." She looked at her watch. "Oh, shit! It's nearly 1:00. We have to head back. I have a lesson to teach."

Arik felt a sudden pain in his gut. Dahlia, who was never late, had been waiting for him at the restaurant since 12:30. He could just see her in the distance, down at the bottom of the mountain. He had lost track of the time. He shook his head. They skied down to the bottom of the mountain, near the chairlift.

"Hey, Arik, what hotel are you staying at? I'm done at 6:00, and I can come get you. Maybe we can go out for drinks?"

"Suzie, I'm sorry if I gave you the wrong impression, but I'm here with my girlfriend. If I led you on, I really want to apologize. I didn't mean to."

"You didn't. It was all me. But I'll tell you what. If you were my boyfriend, I wouldn't let you out of my sight for a second. You're a bona fide cutie, and you never know who may come along and snatch you away." Suzie winked at him.

"I'm flattered. Thanks."

"You're very sweet! Thanks for a nice morning."

"Thank you for teaching me how to ski."

Suzie reached out, gave him a hug, and then skied off. "See you around, cutie!" she called back to him.

"Where have you been, cutie?" Dahlia, who had walked up to Arik, demanded. "I've been waiting here for half an hour."

"I was having a private lesson and lost track of the time," Arik mumbled. "I'm sorry."

"Obviously, you were. Very private! I thought you were going to have a group lesson?"

"I did, and then the instructor insisted on giving me a private one."

"Oh, really? So, how much did Suzie Chapstick charge you for your one-on-one session?"

"Nothing. I wanted to pay her, but she insisted on doing it for free."

"Wow, that's so charitable of her. She's a real Mother Teresa. She's probably a volunteer for Hadassah Women, too!"

"Dahlia, please, it's not like that. We got done with the lesson and I was going to ski off, and she offered to spend more time with me. I figured the time would be more productive spent with her than trying to just practice what I'd learned so far. I was so excited about surprising you with my newfound skills."

"Well, you certainly surprised me, cutie. Do I hug as well as she does? You know that Jewish girls can't compete with shiksas when it comes to that."

"Dahlia, stop it! That was the furthest thing from my mind. I just lost track of the time, that's all. You told me not to wear my watch. You said if I fell it could break my wrist. So, I didn't. I went up to the summit and couldn't see the clock tower from up there."

"Did she ask where you're staying? Well, did she?"

"As a matter of fact, she did, and I told her that I'm here with my girlfriend and that if I gave her the impression I was available I was sorry."

"And what did she say?"

Arik remained silent but blushed.

"I can read you like a book, Arik. What did she say then?"

"She said that if I was her boyfriend she wouldn't let me out of her sight for a second, and then she skied off."

"Arik, you're a shithead."

"Dahlia, please! Nothing happened. You're completely overreacting. I never led her on, ever! I swear. It's just that I felt so inadequate next to the three of you, never having skied before. I felt like I was holding everyone back, like I needed to be babysat, so I was determined to learn how to ski as fast as I could. That was it!"

"I wanted to teach you." Dahlia appeared to be softening.

"You still can, but we could at least have more fun doing it on an intermediate slope."

"You didn't approach her in any way? Promise?"

"Well, there was the time when we got stuck on the chairlift together when it stopped halfway up so we decided, 'What the heck, let's have sex up here,' so we did. Man, I nearly froze my ass off."

"I hope that you didn't freeze anything else off up there. You're going to need that thing tonight!"

"Dahlia, come on! You know how much I love you. I'd never do anything to hurt you. Never. Come here, booba."

He kissed her.

"Let's go have some nice blueberry crepes and hot chocolate, then we'll go up to the summit of Buttermilk and I'll show you what I've learned. She really was a great teacher. I mean . . . of skiing."

They skied back to the restaurant, past Suzie, who was gathering her afternoon class. Dahlia glared at her, thumped her index finger to her own chest, and skied off.

"What was that about?" Arik asked.

"I just let her know that you're mine and not hers. I was marking my territory."

Arik held her waist and whispered in her ear, "Forever, for the rest of our lives. But you really can be a jealous bugger."

"I know what I want, and when I get it I hold on for dear life," Dahlia said.

***

After lunch, they headed up to the summit of Buttermilk Mountain and spent the afternoon practicing on the green and blue trails at West Buttermilk. Dahlia was amazed at how much Arik had learned during the morning.

They skied in tandem, calling out to each other.

"Are you sure that this is your first time skiing?" Dahlia joked.

"I think you should go back down to Suzie and thank her for being such a good teacher!" Arik said.

"After she tried to nail my boyfriend?"

"She didn't even get close."

Arik turned to Dahlia as she sped by him.

"Arik, watch where you're going!"

"Oh, crap!"

The tips of Arik's skis got caught on the edge of a mogul, launching him into the air sideways. He recoiled into the woods.

Dahlia was already downhill. She took off her skis and started uphill, but Arik was nowhere in sight. How could he disappear into thin air in just a second?

"Arik! Arik, are you okay? Where are you? Answer me! . . . Arik, where are you?" A note of alarm suddenly rang in her voice. Is he hurt? Why isn't he answering? She began walking up and down where she thought she had last seen him. "Arik, please answer me!"

Dahlia could feel the panic welling up inside her. Stay calm. Where could he be? She scanned the woods. Perhaps he hit a tree and is unconscious? She looked around for somebody to go get help. There was nobody. She began to turn downhill, to ski for help, when she noticed a jagged line in the snow at the top of a mogul leading into the woods.

"Arik?"

She decided to follow the line. Suddenly, she saw a mound of snow with some navy-blue cloth peeping through.

"Arik! Are you—"

"Ahhh!" Arik jumped out of the mound and grabbed Dahlia, like a zombie from the black lagoon.

She let out a loud shriek when he dragged her down. He was laughing hysterically.

"Not funny, Arik! You had me scared half to death."

He pulled her down on top of him.

"Why did you do that dopey prank?"

"As I was skiing behind you, I was watching you wiggle about and I got the sudden urge to make out with you. I couldn't ask you politely to join me in the woods, so I figured I'd play dead and make you come find me. . . I've always wanted to make out in the deep snow in the woods."

"Yeah, right! Until yesterday, you didn't even know what snow was."

"Okay, you got me. So, how about a quick smooch, and then we'll go back out."

"But just for five—"

Arik rolled, and in a moment, he was on top.

Dahlia giggled. "What am I going to do with you, lunatic?"

***

Dahlia and Arik spent the rest of the afternoon quietly skiing down the intermediate trails Buckskin, Ptarmigan, and Sterner Gulch. By 3:00 p.m., they had negotiated the Racer's Edge and Javelin, both of which were black diamond trails.

"You're so amazing, Arik! I'm proud of what you did today."

Penny and Richard met them back at the Hotel Jerome bar. After ordering four Belgian wheat beers, bowls of assorted dips, tortilla chips, and a pile of unshelled hot roasted peanuts, the couples settled in two loveseats by the fireplace.

"Penny," Dahlia said, "I think that Arik was bullshitting us again."

"I knew it! Arik went down the black diamond trails?"

"He did, like an expert! We're going out with you guys tomorrow, after Arik gets some longer skis. It's official. He faked being a beginner so that he could get picked up by a cute ski instructor."

"That's right," Arik said. He raised his arms and indicated claws on his hands. "I lay in ambush until the cutest instructor skied by, and then I pounced!"

"Well, I am glad that you are a quick study!" Penny said. "You will need it tomorrow, when we go up to Big Burn at Snowmass."

"What's Big Burn?" Arik asked.

"Big Burn is this amazing bowl of snow that is set against a peak almost 12,000 feet tall. It is a sloped clearing about two miles long and two miles wide. Not only is it steep, but the powder is more than two feet deep, which makes skiing challenging. You have to keep your tips up the whole time by leaning backward. Otherwise, you bust your ass when you go down. . ." Penny became rhapsodic. "But it is not only the best powder skiing in the country. It is also the most beautiful snow, with this purple tinge to it. I think it is from the way the light comes off the Maroon Bells peaks—"

Richard interrupted her reverie. "She's making it sound a trifle harder than it is. It's not as hard as Ajax, for example. There, you get off the summit and 80 percent of the trails are double black diamond expert trails that are unforgiving. They have ridges, gullies, gulches, and catwalks. The skiing is very technical and the inclines are very steep—"

"Also, I almost forgot," Penny said, "there is a great restaurant called Sam's Smokehouse at 11,600 feet that is mostly barbecue but has a great selection of salads and sandwiches for lunch. It is not very crowded, because it is so high up, and the views of Snowmass and the Maroon Bells are unbelievable."

"Again, with the views," Richard teased.

"Well, it sounds great, Penny," Arik said. "I'm game!"

"As long as you don't get lost in the powder," Dahlia said.

"What do you mean, Dahlia?" Richard asked.

Dahlia related Arik's prank. Richard and Penny laughed.

"You are the man, Arik!" Penny giggled.

"If you do that tomorrow, boychick, I'll simply leave you up there to freeze your ass off." Dahlia smiled.

"Where would you guys like to eat tonight?" Arik asked the others. "I've looked up some spots. The Copper Kettle, on Bleeker Street, looks great. They have some good fish and vegetarian options. Then I thought we could go to The Little Nell, in Aspen center, for some hard rock and cold beer."

The Little Nell featured Three Dog Night that evening, and the place was crowded to capacity with screaming, drunk, holiday partygoers. There was no room to sit, so the four crowded next to the bar and drank and danced until nearly midnight.

They walked home, crunching on the fresh snow, as a new layer of snow fell from the sky.

Dahlia shivered and huddled close to Arik. He held her tightly.

"You aren't mad at me for today, I hope?" Arik asked.

"Don't be silly," Dahlia said. "I don't think I'd be interested in you if you couldn't make me a bit jealous now and then. My litmus test is 'Would I do the same to you if I had the chance?' My answer is 'Absolutely, yes!' Plus, I've been told that the secret to a happy marriage is never go to bed angry."

"Speaking of which . . . going to bed is not the same as going to sleep," Arik teased.

Dahlia whispered into his ear, "Yummy! I'm going to love being married to you."

Early the next morning found them at the summit of Big Burn. From that vantage point, they could look south toward a chain of 14,000 foot monsters, from Snowmass Mountain, to the Maroon Bells, and all the way across to Pyramid Peak. The mountaintops stood out like huge, black cathedral spires capped in white, in stark contrast to the blue-magenta sky of sunrise. Below them sat Hanging Valley, which was covered in deep snow. Arik and Dahlia stood at the edge of the ridge and looked into the howling wind.

"Look at this place, Dahlia! It feels like we're on top of the world. I never would have believed anything like this could even exist. It's really spiritual. It's cold as crap up here, though. The thermometer on top of the lift station read twenty below zero."

"Aren't you glad I got you the Edelweiss Nazi ski clothes? What would you do up here in jeans?"

"You know what they say? Behind every great man. . ."

"Is that what they say?" Dahlia lifted his jacket and pinched his butt. "I'm just checking what's behind there, if that is to be my place in the future."

Penny and Richard flew over the crest of Big Burn and headed down into the immense, deep bowl of powdered snow.

"Now you're going to get it, Dahlia Meir," Arik called out.

"You're going to have to catch me first!" Dahlia cried as she shot over the ridge of the bowl, with Arik in fast pursuit, howling like a coyote into the deep, powdery snow.

The rest of the week passed quickly, too quickly. The days that the teenagers didn't ski they went snowmobiling on Castle Creek Road and dogsledding in the Roaring Fork Valley. One evening, they huddled under a blanket in a horse-drawn sleigh as it wended its way through the storybook streets. They ice skated at the Brown Ice Palace and then treated themselves to massages, whirlpool baths, and saunas, a welcome break from the cold and courtesy of Mauricio Moreno and Penny's Diners Club card.

The evenings were spent listening to jazz at The Red Onion and improv comedy at The Crystal Palace. When they walked into a hippie folk singing club called Galena East, the smell of marijuana overcame them. Dahlia and Penny wanted to stay and try some of the merchandise, but Arik and Richard vetoed the idea.

"I hope you guys don't mind, but there are parts of my life I really don't want to revisit," Arik said.

"Of course, I understand," Dahlia said.

"There's a great place up the street, called the Leather Jug, where the music is supposed to be just as good and the crowd is a bit more upscale," Arik said. "Tonight, there's this local folk legend performing there who is really great. His name is John Denver."

"Don't know him," Richard said. "A bit corny for him to have a name like Denver, living here. Don't you think?"

"I think he changed it from Duchinoff," Arik said.

"Really? Maybe I should call myself Dahlia Tel Aviv."

"I much prefer Dahlia Meir," Arik said.

The hardest part of the week was saying good-bye at the airport. The two couples embraced and tears were shed, even by the young men. It was decided that Richard would to Mexico City for the Passover break while Dahlia would spend the holiday in LA with Arik.

"Arik, this was the best week of my life," Dahlia said. "I so don't want it to end."

"It won't end, my precious. I've tasted the ambrosia of what life with you will be like, and I'm ready to jump in head first."

"I'm glad I passed the interview," Dahlia teased.

"Yes, you'll do."

Arik held her face, and they kissed for a long time.

"I know you'll write often, Arik. I don't even need to ask. I miss you so much already."

Chapter 19

As Arik spent more on the basketball court, he found less time to work for his uncle. That really didn't disturb him, because his mom had always insisted that he keep his earnings. If he could get by with less, he could work less. His father would never know the difference anyway.

The lumberyard at Ike Myer Construction Supply was open on Sundays, because that was the perfect time to prepare the orders for the next day's shipments. When the contractors' trucks filed in early Monday morning, they were highly appreciative that the Myer's crew was primed and ready to load the trucks immediately.

On one such Sunday, Marcelo assembled the crew.

"You're all in luck! We're gonna have you working indoors today, in the warehouse. You're gonna load sacks of cement onto these pallets. Darnell will man the forklift, piling them on the shelves up front near the loading dock for the trucks. We got 20 tons of concrete to load today, so get your asses in gear! We don't got all day."

Arik was assigned to Darnell's team. He was working with Shawntay, Paco, and Leroy. He really liked his assignment. Over the previous few months, these guys had become like brothers to him. They even went down to the Cage to watch him play. At work, the four of them watched out for one another, especially when boss man Ike came around. Whenever they were not being monitored, they played practical jokes on one another. Arik took it as a point of honor that the crew let him join in the fun—once they realized that there was no way that Arik would turn them in to the powers that be. Arik had worked hard to earn that trust and show the guys that he was one of them.

They set off to work. In the back of the warehouse, dump trucks had dumped a small mountain of cement on Friday. The four men shoveled the cement into 100-pound sacks that were sewn shut with a large industrial machine. These were then placed in neat crisscross piles on each pallet. Darnell came by periodically, with the forklift, and transported each completed pallet to the shelves. The sacks and the pallets began piling up.

After two hours, Shawntay said, "Gotta go pee."

"Hey, Shawntay, why don't you go piss out the back door like the rest of us?" Leroy said. The others snickered. "Why you got to go all the way to the can just to take a leak. Even Jew boy does it here. I think maybe you're really a girl and gots to sit down to relieve yourself."

"I ain't no fuckin' animal, that's why, like the rest of you. I got class," Shawntay said good-naturedly.

Paco said, "I think, manno, that you tryin' to get out of workin'. Dat's what I thinks."

"Shut up, Mexican!" Shawntay trotted off.

Ten minutes passed. A bloodcurdling shriek suddenly filled the warehouse. Arik and the other two men dropped their shovels and ran toward the sound.

"Shit!" Darnell shouted. "Come quick! Shawntay's been hurt bad!"

The three men ran through the maze of shelves and found Shawntay hanging from the third shelf by his left hand, which was crushed under a wooden palette piled high with concrete sacks that had slid off the forklift and landed there.

Arik took control of the situation.

"What happened?" Arik asked as he ran toward Darnell and Shawntay.

Darnell was in shock, but he managed to say, "I was roundin' the corner at full speed, 'cause I saw Shawntay climbin' up onto the third shelf. I wanted to scare him, so I turns the forklift fast around the corner to put the pallet on that shelf, to make him jump off, and the pallet slipped and came down on top of him before he could jump off."

Arik and Leroy climbed up to the third shelf in about a second, and in under two minutes they had taken all the concrete palettes off Shawntay, who fell to the ground and into Darnell's waiting arms.

"Ma hand! Ma hand!" Shawntay cried out in excruciating pain.

"What was you doin' up there, little brother!" Darnell was frantic.

"I was comin' back from the can, and I saw the sacks fallin' off the pallet, and I climbed up to straighten them out so you could load the next one up there. I was climbin' down, and I didn't see you comin' around the corner."

Paco ran to the foreman's office to get a clean hand towel to wrap Shawntay's hand in.

The hand was mangled almost beyond recognition. All five of Shawntay's fingers were broken to pieces, with fragments of bone protruding from the bloody gray mass that had been a hand.

"I'm gonna get help. I'm calling an ambulance. You guys stay with him!" Arik said.

Arik ran at full speed back to the front office. It was deserted. He ran into Ike's office, to tell his uncle, and he found Ethan sitting in Ike's chair, his legs up on his father's desk while he was talking on the phone with one of his buddies.

". . . so, Debbie got up on the table, T-shirt all wet, without her bra on, and started dancing like crazy. She was so wasted. She was jiggling everywhere. You shoulda seen it—Hold on a second. . . What do want, Arik? You guys done already? I'll find something else for you to do."

"I need the phone now. Shawntay's been hurt. He got his hand badly crushed under a pallet, and I need to call an—"

"What the fuck, Arik? Can't you see I'm on the phone? You're just gonna have to wait 'til I'm done. You know what? Use the phone at Gladys's desk."

"I can't. Your dad rerouted all the phone lines to the phone you're using. Shawntay's bleeding bad! I have to use the phone now!"

"That dumb nigger is just gonna have to wait a couple of minutes until I get off the—"

"Give me the fucking phone, you worthless piece of shit!" Arik lunged at Ethan to wrestle the phone out of his hands, in the process knocking Ethan out of his chair and tearing the phone line out of the wall. Ethan was putting Arik in a choke hold when Itzik walked in.

"What the hell are you guys doing?"

"Arik attacked me while I was on an important phone call, and he tore the phone line out of the wall, probably trying to choke me with it."

"That isn't true! Shawntay's been hurt. He got his hand crushed under a pallet, and I was trying to call an ambulance, but Ethan here refused to get off the phone. I was trying to grab the phone when it came out of the wall."

Ethan sneered. "If you wanted the phone, you should have just walked in like a human being and asked for it, not bust in here like a lunatic and destroy my dad's property."

While they were talking, Darnell and Leroy walked in, carrying Shawntay, who was clutching his bloodied hand in a grease-stained hand towel.

"Mr. Myer, sir, Shawntay's been hurt real bad. He needs a doctor right away, sir." Darnell pleaded.

"Okay. Arik, load Shawntay into your car and take him to the hospital." Itzik could tell from his wartime experience that there was no time to wait for an ambulance.

Before they left, Itzik pulled Arik aside into another room. "One more thing. If they ask you at the hospital how he got injured, tell them he got hurt at home. I don't need the health inspector snooping around here. Understand?"

"Yes, sir."

"When you drop him off, have Darnell stay with him, and you and Leroy come back here. I want to have a word with you and Ethan."

"Okay, Uncle Itzik."

Several hours later, Arik walked back into Itzik's office.

"What took you so long, Arik?" Itzik asked.

"I couldn't leave. Darnell was so distraught he couldn't speak, which was much the better as far as you're concerned. I told them what you wanted me to say. They're not sure they can save the hand. They might have to amputate it at the wrist. I stayed until they took him into the operating room."

Ethan walked into the office.

"Sit down, son," Itzik said. "Now, what the hell is going on between the two of you? Why can't you just get along? You're like chalk and cheese."

Ethan began. "You mean me get along with this self-righteous jerk who's always in my shit about everything? How ungrateful can you get, Arik? We take care of your family, always have. Without us, you and your family would be in the street. You come here, we give you a job to help support yourselves, and all you do is come around and act like you're my boss. Who are you to tell me what to do and not do? Always lecturing me about how I treat the help around here. No, Dad, I can't get along with Mr. Goody Two Shoes here, always making social statements like some kind of civil rights activist, trying to make me feel like crap."

"Not calling them niggers might be a good start, Ethan," Arik said.

"The fact is, Arik," Ethan said, you're a big talker but you can't do anything for them. We give them jobs and a livelihood. Any one of these niggers can leave if they want, but they don't. And you know why? Because we pay them well for what they do and they like being here, working for us."

"Is that so? Have you ever taken the time to talk to any of them, to find out what they're really thinking? All you ever do is order them around like they were your slaves. Well, they're not. They're ordinary people just like you and me. They've just gotten the shaft from society, because of the color of their skin. They work here, because they can't get any other jobs.

"Jewish folks need to be more sensitive because of the crappy way we were treated just for being Jews. But I guess you wouldn't know much about that. There isn't much anti-Semitism in the valley."

"There you go lecturing again," Ethan said. "I'm gonna tell you what's what, Arik. My dad feels a debt of gratitude to your dad about the war, but I don't." Ethan looked at his father. "I'm telling you now, Dad, your retirement isn't that far off. When I take over this company, I'm cutting off these welfare payments." He looked back at Arik. "You and your family are a bunch of parasites, Arik. There, I've said it. Someone had to say it."

Itzik was completely taken aback by his son's tirade. "Ethan, when we came to this country, your mom and I had nothing. I built this company up with my bare hands. I knew nothing in Poland and during the war but pain and hardship. I swore that when I came here to America I was going to make damn sure that my children would never want for anything. I gave you everything you wanted and needed. What I raised instead was a spoiled punk." Itzik sighed in disgust.

"Dad, I was in the middle of an important phone call when Arik barged in."

"Ethan, have you ever in your life done anything important? If I know you, you were probably on the phone with your girlfriend or something. Go home."

Looking at Arik, Itzik said, "I'm sorry about how all this turned out. It would probably be a good idea, Arik, if you didn't come around here anymore. I've got enough to worry about in my life. I don't need this additional stress. But I promise you this: As long as I'm alive, I'll take care of your mom and dad. If you need me to recommend you for another—"

"That won't be necessary, Uncle Itzik. Thanks for giving me the opportunity to work for you." Arik walked out, feeling defeated and shaking his head.

When he got to his car, he saw a small crowd of his coworkers gathered around Darnell.

"Hey, Arik. Where you goin', bro?" Leroy asked.

"I got fired 'cause I jumped Ethan. How's Shawntay?"

Darnell walked over to Arik and gave him a hug, tears streaming down his face. "They had to take the hand off. Couldn't save it. It was all my fault. Shawntay's such a young kid. How's he ever gonna find work now?"

"It was just a freak accident, man. It was nobody's fault. Nobody saw this comin'," Arik said.

"Ethan had it comin', that gringo punk," Paco said. "He always hides behind his daddy's money. I tell you what, he wouldn't last two minutes in my neighborhood. My buddies would eat him for breakfast and fart him out."

Everyone had a much-needed laugh.

"So, what you gonna do, man?" Leroy asked Arik. "Where you gonna gets some bread from?"

"I don't know yet. But at least I'll have more time to play ball. So, come on by and watch me play at the Cage."

"Count on it, bro! You're the best honky I know."

Arik felt flattered but a bit inadequate walking into the immaculate, well-appointed practice hall at Pauley Pavilion to watch the Bruins run through their paces. The two-hour practices were held strictly out of the public eye. Planned to the exact minute, Wooden's practices reflected his faith in order and efficiency. Like the conductor of a symphony orchestra, Wooden, dressed in a zippered navy-blue woolen sweater and gray slacks, with his ever present whistle on a lanyard hanging from his neck, ran through the flock of tall black and white storks, who were clad in white silk jerseys, as they flitted up and down the highly polished parquet wooden floor.

Wooden worked from a rigid outline set forth in a stack of 3″ × 5″ index cards. He used these cards to organize drills that each ran for only five to ten minutes. The shorter the drill, the longer his players could sustain high intensity and focus. The coach kept his demonstrations and criticisms concise and punctuated; he never lectured. His coaching philosophy emphasized conditioning and drilling on the fundamentals rather than undermining self-confidence.

Arik had taught the kids at camp that basketball was a team sport, but he had never seen every minute accounted for like Wooden did. With the entire session choreographed, planned in advance by the coaching staff, which had met for two hours prior to the practice, the players never had to wait for the coaches to decide what to do next.

Wooden ran up and down the court, whistle in his mouth, calling out crisp, short commands:

"Pass from the chest."

"Move your feet, and don't reach."

"Keep your hands up when free throws are thrown."

"You're too slow! Hustle!"

"Be quick, but don't hurry!"

If a player made a mistake, Wooden quickly corrected him, pointing out specific details. His players had to understand what they were doing wrong and how to do it correctly. Arik could see that ego was never allowed to creep into the process, and that suited his outlook perfectly. This was just business, and the business was winning. It was all done Wooden's way. Five national championships had elevated his instruction to gospel truth.

Only once, when a player questioned an instruction, did Wooden lash out in the only strong language that his Protestant upbringing had exposed him to. "Goodness gracious, sakes alive, Steve. If you refuse to execute a pick and roll, I'll have Curtis do it."

When the practice ended, some of the players ambled over the bleachers, where Arik was sitting, to say hello. There were handshakes all around.

"Hey, Eric, whaddaya say? You should consider it a big honor to come to a practice. Nobody is allowed in to watch. It can only mean one thing. . ." Curtis Rowe winked at him.

"I haven't heard anything yet." Arik smiled. "Don't you guys stay on after practice to play?"

"Nope!" Curtis said. "By the time Wooden gets done with us, we're done. He doesn't want us to play unsupervised. He's a bit of a control freak, really. He doesn't want us to reinforce bad habits. We play plenty of full games in practice but under his supervision. We sometimes go out to the parks to play so we can spread our wings, if you know what I mean."

"Why don't you guys come on down to the Cage sometimes? We're pretty loose down there, and the neighborhood kids would get such a kick out of seeing you guys come and play. Some of the Lakers and ABA guys stop by sometimes and mix it up with the locals. It's great fun."

Sidney Wicks handed Arik an index card with his and Curtis's phone number on it. "Eric, give us a call when you've got a good game going on down there, and if we can tear ourselves away we will. We can't let Wooden find out, though. He'd go ape-shit."

They looked around and hurried to the locker room.

"Well, well, Eric, I am so glad you could come."

Arik had not heard Coach Wooden approach, but there he was in front of him.

"I hope you enjoyed seeing the practice," Wooden said. "You just observed the inner workings of what it takes to craft a national championship team. That is what you and I discussed: Consistent excellence is what it takes to win, not fancy flourishes."

Arik didn't know what to say, so he thought it best to remain silent.

Wooden continued, "As you know, Denny has been going over to watch you play at your high school. Your play is starting to calm down. I understand that your high school team has become number one in the parochial school league." Wooden smiled. "I could be wrong, Eric, but I guess it has something to do with you."

"As you've taught me, sir, it's all about the team and I'm just a member of the team."

Wooden laughed heartily.

"Well said, Eric. Well said! I don't know if you really believe that or you're just being sarcastic."

"Several months ago, I probably would have said it sarcastically, though I've preached it to younger players. I think that now I'm actually starting to believe it myself." Arik smiled.

"Very good, Eric. Come with me. There are several gentlemen from the admissions and scholarship committees waiting in my office. They are quite interested in speaking to you."

Dahlia sat at the dinner table, feeling apprehensive. It was an emotion that welled up from deep inside her. What was there for her to be so nervous about? She usually got her way, so what was the big deal? She knew that she was in for at least a minor dustup with her parents about Arik. What difference should it make? She had gone away for other holidays. Why should Pesach this year be any different? She tried to convince herself that things were going to be okay, but she had a hard time doing so. As she walked toward the library, her mouth and throat went dry and her hands seemed ice cold. She willed her hands to stop shaking.

Her parents already were sitting in the plush leather loveseat.

Dahlia collapsed into an armchair, folded her hands, and stared nervously at her parents.

"What is it, booba?" Leah asked. "What do you want to tell us?"

"It's not what I want to tell you. It's what I want to ask you."

"Okay?" Benny said.

"I want to go to Los Angeles for Pesach." Her own voice sounded, to Dahlia, as if it had come from outside her body, as if somebody else had spoken the words.

Benny furrowed his brow. "What in the world for? Who will you be spending the chag with?"

Dahlia felt at a loss for words. There was no way for her to tell a lie, even a white lie. There was no way of sugarcoating this.

"I want to spend Pesach with Arik and his family," she finally blurted out.

"I didn't realize that you still had anything to do with the boy," Benny said. "His name hasn't come up in this house since Sukkot. So, you've been in touch with him . . .?" Benny tried to keep his composure. He, too, was not in a mood for a fight, although he sensed that was where this conversation was headed.

"I keep in touch with him all the time, Abba. We write to each other every week, without fail. Our relationship is as strong as ever. Long-distance relationships can work. We both love writing and getting letters from each other."

"So, you're pen pals. You're going to leave your family for Pesach to spend it with strangers, with your pen pal? Have you lost your mind, Dahlia?" Benny looked at Leah. "What do you think about all of this, Leah?"

Leah jumped into the fray. "I have misgivings about this on many levels. I stood up for you when it came to bringing Arik here for Sukkot, but at least he was coming here, under our supervision. Now, you're going away to be alone with him?"

"We're not going to be alone, Imma. We'll be with his family."

"I thought you told me that his family didn't keep kosher and that they didn't keep Shabbat and the holidays. Where are you going to have a seder and have Pesach food?"

"We'll spend the actual chag at the Bnei Akiva rabbi's house, where we'll have the seder. We don't need to keep two days of the holiday, because we're both Israelis, so for the rest of the time we'll manage. It'll be just fine."

"Leah, do you think that it is even remotely acceptable for Dahlia to go off on her own to spend the chag with a strange man? You're her mother, for God's sake!" The volume of Benny's voice had risen, and his voice had become shriller.

"Benny, I'm very well aware of the fact that I'm her mother," Leah said testily. "But I want to keep this conversation civil and not let it degenerate into the type of shouting match that you and Dahlia have become so fond of having."

Leah turned toward Dahlia. "Booba, I think that you're too young to be running off on your own. We're planning a wonderful Pesach here. Yitzhak and Leah Rabin and their whole family are coming for the seder. We'll have a wonderful time, and I think you'll find it extremely interesting. I mean, how many people can say that they spent the seder with—"

"I'm not interested in spending time with the Rabins. I don't get along with their kids, and I'm really not that interested in what he has to say. Sorry that I can't play my role as the ambassador's daughter. I want to be with Arik. We haven't seen each other since winter break—"

"You saw each other over winter break?! You never told us! Why didn't you tell us?" Benny was dumbfounded.

"What was there to tell? You both knew that I went to a camp reunion. Why would you suppose that he wouldn't be there? Why would the camp single him out? Oh, yes! I'm going to ski with my friends at the Mosh Choref, the winter camp reunion, and, oh, by the way, Arik is going to be there. You see, the camp was not going to let him go initially, you know, him being from a rough background with those black people and all, but I intervened especially so that we could go off together to be alone for a whole week.

"I didn't tell you, because I didn't realize it was an issue, that you hated him so much. You know, this is real sinat chinam, hatred for no good reason. Arik is a wonderful person. You just don't know him. If we wanted to fool around, we had ample opportunity to do so at the reunion. That's not why I want to go to see him now! You need to give me more credit than that!" Dahlia was practically shouting. The conversation wasn't going well. Unfortunately, that wasn't unexpected.

"Dahlia, you're too young to become so serious with a boy." Leah tried to smooth her daughter's ruffled feathers. "You need to meet lots of boys and go on dates, break a few hearts or even get yours broken, too, on occasion. That's the normal way. You're an extremely attractive girl. You'll have absolutely no trouble getting anyone to ask you out. Why are you attaching yourself to this boy? This makes no sense!"

Dahlia mustered whatever inner strength she had left for the end of this fight.

"I'm letting you know that, either way, you won't see me for Pesach. If you won't let me go, I'll make myself scarce anyway, while you sit there satisfied that you got your way. All you will have accomplished is making me miserable. You can try as you might to keep us apart, and you might succeed in the short term, but you won't be able to keep us apart forever. You may as well get used to the fact that. . ." Dahlia's tone had risen to a defiant conclusion, but she was hesitant to say it out loud.

"What fact, Dahlia?" Benny said.

"That I'm going to marry Arik, Abba."

Dahlia was shocked that she had let those words slip out of her lips, and she regretted having said them as much as she loved hearing them. Why did I tip my hand so soon? Damn it to hell!

"I'm beyond words, Dahlia. I'm hearing things beyond my imagination." Benny shook his head and rubbed his brow.

"I'm not a little girl anymore. I'll be eighteen next December. You may as well let me go now, because a year from now I'll be in the army and forever out of the house and I'll do what I want anyway. I'm not twelve anymore. I know what I'm doing, and I know what I want. I want to be with Arik. I love him!"

Benny stood to leave. "Dahlia, you always know how to get under my skin. I'm so tired of arguing with you about everything. Why can't you be like all of your friends here? None of my colleagues get as much grief from their children as you give me. I won't stand in your way. Go, if you must, but know that I'm completely opposed to this liaison. So, is he going to be playing basketball with the goyim next year?"

"No, he's probably going to Israel to be inducted into Tzahal in August," Dahlia said smugly.

"Maybe they will make a mensch out of him."

"He's already a mensch, but you just can't see it!" Dahlia said to her father's back. Imma, let's call Tzippy so she can set up my flights."

"Okay," Leah finally whispered.

Chapter 22

Arik saw his vision of heaven standing at the curb outside the United Airlines domestic arrivals terminal at the Los Angeles International Airport. She was wearing skintight white silk slacks, a blue and white pullover, and white patent leather high-heeled shoes, and her long, thick, blonde hair flowed effortlessly past her shoulders. She was surrounded by hot-pink luggage of various sizes.

When he spied her from a distance, his heart-stopping excitement became tinged by shame that such a magnificent creature should be picked up curbside by a rusted, dented, 1962 Chevy with a nonfunctional muffler that made it sound as if it were better suited for the runway on the other side of the terminal than the arrivals bay.

That ashamed part of him wanted to drive past her at full speed without stopping. But, if Dahlia is going to be with me, he reasoned, she'd better see everything, no matter how awful it might make me feel.

Dahlia saw him when he slowed down, and she waved her arms wildly.

"You get out of that car immediately, young man, and give me an extremely significant kiss! You hear me?"

Arik needed no prompting. They were finally pried apart by a cop.

"Sorry to interrupt, Romeo and Juliet, but can you take this to wherever you're going? Half the city of Los Angeles is waiting to pull in here."

"Sorry, sir. We were just waiting for my chauffeur to load the bags into the trunk of the limo." Arik smiled.

Dahlia and the policeman burst into laughter. Arik decided that maybe if he could make light of the disparities between his poverty and Dahlia's wealth he might just make it through his discomfort.

"Very nice," the cop said. "Now, come on guys. Get going."

In less than five minutes, they were on 105 East, Century Freeway, headed toward Lynwood.

Arik turned to Dahlia. "How was your flight, my angel?"

Dahlia sidled over to him on the front bench seat and hugged him and kissed the side of his neck. "It's a good thing you don't have bucket seats in this thing. There's no telling what I might be up to while you're driving." She smiled slyly.

"I realized that, so I had these bench seats made special just for the occasion." He laughed.

"My flight was so long! I had a two-hour layover in Chicago, and we had to land there in the middle of a thunderstorm."

"All you have to worry about here is the smog. Take a deep breath. Living here is like smoking a pack of cigarettes a day."

"The air stinks."

"You'll get used to it, sort of. Our plans have gotten just slightly more complicated. My dad is back in the hospital, with yet another stump infection. They've been trying to fit him with a prosthesis, but he keeps on getting pressure sores. This latest one really broke down, and he has infected bone coming out of the skin. It's pretty gross. Sorry. I promise that it won't impact us much. In fact, it might be better for all concerned. You see, he's actually in a better mood when he's in the hospital. Everyone knows him there, and he loves the attention. When the nurses are cute, so much the better. When he's home, he just gets ornery and drives Imma crazy. He'll probably be there for about three weeks. Perfect timing, really."

Dahlia frowned. "If you say so, Arik. It really doesn't matter to me what we do here, as long as I get to do it with you. If you want me to go shovel manure with you at your uncle's, I'll do it."

"Not in that outfit, you won't. Besides, I got fired from there."

"You never told me."

"Not much to tell."

He related the whole tale of Shawntay's injury to her, who listened intently without saying a word until he was done.

"Arik, I love you so much. You always figure out a way to be a hero."

"Munchkinface, I don't look for this crap, but it always seems to find me. That asshole Ethan . . . on the phone talking about a wet T-shirt contest. . . I just kind of lost it." Arik shook his head.

Dahlia smirked. "Would you have me do the wet T-shirt contest?"

Arik laughed. "Oh, sure! At Rabbi Rabinovich's house during the seder!

Dahlia giggled.

"Here we are. Home sweet home."

When she heard the car pull into the driveway, Miriam ran out the open door, wiping her hands on her apron, to greet Arik's special guest. She took Dahlia's hand in both of her own.

"It's so nice to meet you, Dahlia. Arik has told me so much about you. Now I see that my son has very good taste! I'm sure that Arik has told you that his father has taken very ill over the past two weeks and will have to undergo another operation on his leg in the morning. I haven't even had a chance to tell him that you're coming, not that he'd remember anything anyway. He's in such terrible pain and doesn't have a head for anything. They have him on a morphine drip and he sleeps most of the day. Arik, I've prepared dinner for you both, and I want you to make your guest comfortable. I've called a cab to take me to the hospital."

"Imma, let us drive you there, please! Why do you have to be a martyr?"

"Absolutely not. I won't hear of it. You have a special guest. I'll find my way. It isn't far."

"We'll pick you up later, then?"

"Okay, fine. I'll call you when I'm ready. Meanwhile, I've prepared your room for Dahlia, and you know where to sleep."

Before going to the airport, Arik had taken out his army-surplus sleeping bag from camp and rolled it out onto the plastic-covered sofa under the shade of the plastic palm tree.

Miriam led the couple into her tiny kitchen. Arik was grateful that the wafting beef stew aroma of the feast that his mother had prepared was drowning out the foul odor that usually permeated the house. He had been dreading

Dahlia's reaction to entering his family's house and being hit by the smell that his father generated. He was sure that she would try to be polite and unfazed.

While Arik and Dahlia were setting the table in the dinette, a cab honked outside the house. Miriam donned her hat and left.

***

"I really want to meet your dad," Dahlia said.

"Are you sure? He's in pretty rough shape. You came here to have fun and spend time with me. You don't need to visit him, really. He doesn't look very well. He's developed gangrene in the stump again, and it smells like death. I'll take my mom and visit him in the early morning, and by the time you're up I'll be back."

"Why are you saying this? First of all, it's a mitzvah to visit the sick. Second, part of getting to know you and what I'm marrying into is getting to know your parents. And third, it bugs the crap out of me that he's had to endure his life which could have been made so much better and easier if he'd been rewarded for his heroism. I think that you want me to have a good first impression of him. I already have a good first impression of him. He's your dad, and that's enough for me. I don't care that he's not dolled up. We're going to see him, and that's that."

"Okay, if you really want to. We'll drive my mom to the hospital early tomorrow morning. She spends the whole day there, at his bedside. Everybody at the hospital knows her. He's admitted there so often. My car practically drives itself there. It's in East LA, just up the 710."

USC Medical Center was a large, gray, imposing structure just east of downtown LA. The massive granite edifice looked out of place among the terra-cotta jungle that surrounded it in every direction, it would have appeared more at home in New York City than in Southern California. Easily the busiest hospital in LA, it specialized in the care of trauma victims without regard to their ability to pay.

Miriam, Arik, and Dahlia made their way to the intensive care ward. They were immediately assaulted by the odor emanating from Ze'ev's room. When they quietly entered his room, they saw a gaunt, ashen-faced man sleeping fitfully to the beeping rhythm of the cardiac monitor overhead. Skin and muscles seemed to be hanging off a once-large frame, like an old, crumpled shirt on a hanger.

Miriam walked to the head of the bed and kissed Ze'ev softly on the cheek. A nurse adjusted the antibiotic-laden IV fluid coursing into his veins.

"Ze'ev, you have company," Miriam said softly, trying to rouse him.

"He's been sedated, as he's been restless and agitated all night," the nurse said.

Miriam nodded.

Ze'ev slowly opened his eyes. He stared at Dahlia, blinking slowly. She was taken aback by his dull, gray eyes in dark sockets. Arik noticed that she seemed a bit unnerved by Ze'ev's gaze.

"Abba, how are you feeling?" Arik asked.

"How should I be feeling? They're about to take off more of my leg. I'm starting to feel like a salami. What will they find to cut off when they get to my hip? Arik, have you called Uncle Itzik to apologize yet? They're still very upset at you over that whole incident. I can't have the whole family broken up over this."

"Ze'ev, now isn't the time or place," Miriam said. "Arik has a special guest who has come all the way from Washington, D.C. to spend Pesach with us. Her name is Dahlia."

Ze'ev again stared at Dahlia and blinked. "It's very nice to meet you, Dahlia. I'm afraid we don't have much Pesach around here to celebrate. I don't believe much in that nonsense, anyway. Why am I supposed to feel happy about something that happened four thousand years ago?"

"It's nice to meet you, Mr. Meir." Dahlia extended her hand in greeting.

"Is my Arik behaving himself?" Ze'ev managed a smile.

"Oh, yes! He's been a perfect gentleman." Dahlia smiled, sitting down on a chair near Ze'ev's head.

"You should tell him that he needs to do more to help to support the family. I'm an invalid. Arik's mother is getting on and isn't as strong as she used to be. Arik, on the other hand, is a horse! He should be more helpful in taking care of me. Perhaps you will have some good influence on him. I can't seem to have any. Always doing what he wants, without any regard. . ." And with that, Ze'ev drifted off to sleep.

Dahlia looked up at Arik.

Arik shook his head. "I bet you didn't realize I was such a bad person."

"Arik, don't pay him any mind," Miriam said. "You're a wonderful son, better than he deserves. He never appreciates anything you do for him, and it's never enough."

"Did you notice that he never asked anything about you?" Arik asked Dahlia. "Here you are, a special guest coming to see him. . . He's so consumed with himself. . ."

"Don't you think that if you were in the same position, God forbid, that you might act the same way?" Dahlia asked.

"I don't think so," Arik said. "Was it my imagination, or was he staring at you when you first walked into the room?"

"I did notice that. He looked at me like he knew me or something. It was weird."

"That's ridiculous, of course. How could he possibly know you?" Ari mused aloud.

"Enough, you two! Ze'ev isn't very good company, and your time together is so precious. Go out and have fun. It's a beautiful day. They say it may hit 85 degrees this afternoon. Go out and have some fun."

Arik hugged her mother and kissed her on the cheek. "Try to have a good day, Imma."

Arik and Dahlia made their way out of the hospital and out to the parking lot.

"I was thinking about going horseback riding in Griffith Park and then heading over to Santa Monica Beach," Arik said excitedly. "There are a bunch of people from Rambam going there this afternoon."

"You go to the beach in April?"

"Nobody surfs. The water's too cold. We play volleyball, though, and just hang out in the sun."

"I only brought string bikinis. Are you sure that you want me to go traipsing about in those in front of your horny little friends from school? I'm liable to give one of them a coronary."

"Well, then, why don't we go to Disneyland? I can't wait to see you go down the Matterhorn roller coaster. You'll scream your guts out!" Arik laughed.

***

In the late afternoon, Arik sat out on his front stoop, dressed in his Cobras jersey and worn jeans, for what seemed like an eternity while he waited for Dahlia to finish getting ready in his bedroom. What's taking her so long? We aren't going to the opera. It was a good thing that he had told her that dinner at the reverend's was at 5 p.m. rather than at 6 p.m., or they would have been late for sure.

Dahlia eventually walked out the front door, dressed in patent leather high heels, skintight white silk slacks, and a low-cut, hot-pink blouse, topped off with her flowing, unbound hair.

"I'm ready! I want to look like the superstar's girlfriend. How often do I get to meet NBA All Stars?"

Arik kissed her.

"Mamita, you look like a schoolboy's dream, but I'm afraid if you dress like that we'll never get out of there alive. As it is, you'll cause a major stir when we show up. Tomorrow night, I'll take you to the Chinese Theatre in Hollywood and you can dress like that. For tonight, I'll give you my UCLA sweatshirt to wear with a pair of jeans, sneakers, and your pony tail under a baseball cap. That'll cover your assets. Seriously, booba. When we get there, you'll understand."

"Okay." Dahlia smiled wryly. "I think I understand already. Do I really look like a schoolboy's dream?"

Arik smiled back. "More than you know."

Dahlia went back inside to change.

***

Dahlia sat wide-eyed in the car as Arik drove them north, along Compton Avenue, into Watts. She had never, in her wildest imagination, thought that she would ever venture into a place like this. Her first impulse was fear. As the cross-streets slipped by, she noticed the steady deterioration in the houses and front lawns, which became smaller and less well maintained. The roads became more uneven, with larger potholes. Some stores were closed, even boarded up, while those that were open had bars on their windows. Groups of older men were congregated in front of stores, sitting on milk crates and playing dice, cards, or checkers. Spent liquor bottles and beer bottles were strewn all over the sidewalk and in the gutter. The walls were covered in spray-painted graffiti murals.

On street corners, groups of young black men and teenagers wearing white tank tops, head stockings, thick, gold chains, and baggy pants congregated. They were talking and sometimes wrestling with one another. What are they doing there? she wondered. Buying drugs? Are these the gangs of South Central LA that I've heard about?

How can Arik call this home? What can he have in common with these people? Arik had said that he sometimes felt as if he were on Mars when he was at camp. She could see why. Here, she felt as if she were on Pluto. She was so glad that Arik had made her change her clothes. What would my parents say if they knew I was here? They probably would each have a stroke.

Her heart stopped when Arik slowed down at a street corner where a dozen rough-looking black men were gathered around a spray-painted, battered mailbox. They peered through the windshield.

Arik hopped out of the car. "Hey, Darnell! What's up? How's Shawntay doin'? I've been meaning to stop by to check him out." Arik gave each man the ghetto handshake.

Dahlia watched with wonder as she saw all the men's faces light up when they recognized Arik. She had found herself checking her door to make sure it was locked when they stopped, and now she felt a bit ashamed.

Arik and the men engaged in a lively conversation for about five minutes, although it felt to Dahlia like an hour. She wished that they would continue on to the reverend's house already. She nervously tried to remind herself that these were Arik's friends. Suddenly, Arik stuck his head in the window.

"Hey, Dahlia! Come on out. The guys want to meet you."

Dahlia slowly got out of the car and managed a nervous smile that she hoped would reflect shyness rather than fear.

Darnell stuck out his hand, and Dahlia shook it with extra emphasis.

"Nice to finally meet you, Dahlia! Arik told us all about you when he was workin' with us on the chain gang for his uncle. You is fine, fine, woman. You is everythin' he said you is."

Dahlia smiled broadly.

"Arik told me all about you guys as well. I'm so glad to finally meet all of you. So sorry about Shawntay. Arik told me the whole story. I'll have him in my prayers."

Her last remark sparked broad smiles all around. The guys jostled for an opportunity to shake Dahlia's hand or at least slap her a high five.

Ra'Shawn said, "I heard there's gonna be some serious excitement at the Cage tonight. You playin', Arik?"

"You're absolutely right, Ra'Shawn. If I were you fellas, I'd get over there early. The game starts at 9, and you definitely want to get a seat in the outer bleachers. You won't get inside the Cage, for sure. I don't know if you heard, but it's pro-am night. Our All Stars are goin' up against some of the

Lakers and UCLA guys, who are stoppin' by for some playtime. The gate managers are definitely collectin' money tonight. I got them to donate the gate money to the youth league, for jerseys and equipment. The official money, that is."

There was laughter all around.

"I don't suppose we can get some of the bookies to pony up some cash for a worthy cause?" Arik asked, smiling slyly.

Leroy said, "I'll talk to my brother. I'll sees what I can gets out of him."

"You headin' over to the reverend's?" Darnell asked.

"Yeah! Dahlia and I are having some dinner before we head out to the park. I think he'll even join us tonight. He wouldn't miss the pro-am for the world, especially once he heard money will be going to charity."

Arik said good-bye to each man individually. "Okay, see you guys later."

"Nice meetin' ya, Dahlia," they called out, practically in unison.

"Same here." Dahlia smiled, desperately trying to conceal her relief that she and Arik were leaving.

As they pulled away from the curb, with the car's windows open, Dahlia could hear the guys talking among themselves.

"Whatchoo say? That Arik has got hisself a fine little babe, a fiiine little babe! Ooo wee!"

Dahlia gave Arik a look.

"I've never in my life been happier to be told that I was dressed inappropriately." Dahlia sighed with relief.

"I bet you thought they were going to eat you," Arik said. "I know. I know this place has its gang violence, and there are tons of drugs, but I also know that most of the people who live here would rather be somewhere else, if given the choice. There's an unwritten rule here: If you want respect, you have to give respect. The vast majority of the people here are decent law-abiding, God-fearing folk who are trying to give their kids a better life than they have here. There are a few very bad apples, like anywhere else, and I steer clear of them. I'll point some out to you—in a subtle way, of course."

They drove up to a small but well-kept two-story house on the corner of East 105th and Hickory streets. This block was decidedly cleaner and better kept than the others, with a small stand of date palms running down an island in the center of the street.

In the front of the house, there was a small terrace with rocking chairs. As Arik and Dahlia climbed the stairs, a large man rose from his seat. His distinguished dark-brown eyes lit up when they saw Dahlia.

In a booming bass voice, the man said, "Well, well. Finally! I've heard so much about you, Dahlia. I feel like I've known you forever."

The reverend gave Dahlia a bear hug, which she warmly reciprocated.

"Same here! It's so good to finally meet you, too. Through Arik, I feel so at home here." Dahlia smiled.

Arik smiled, too.

Tyrone, Antwan, and Kevin bounded down the stairs to greet their new visitor.

"Guess who comin' to dinner?" Antwan called out with a smile, until the reverend shot him a look that caused him to recoil like a wounded snake.

"Hi, guys." Dahlia said with a broad smile that disarmed them. "Arik's told me so much about you all."

"I hope not everything!" Tyrone said, eliciting a chuckle from everyone.

Dahlia knelt down. "You must be Kevin," she said.

He nodded shyly and said, quietly, "Nice to meet you, Dahlia."

"You changed Arik's life," she said just as softly.

Her words hung in the air as everyone else processed what she had said.

Maimie came out of the kitchen. "Goodness gracious! Y'all must be starved. I know I am! I've made a feast for dinner. And I made it in special pots with only glatt kosha meat."

"It's so nice to meet you, Mrs. Perkins."

"Nice to meet you, too, honey child."

"Maimie has mastered the kosher laws, so we'll be treated to kosher Southern-style cooking. Smells so good!" Arik said. "You know, Maimie, Antwan and I won't be able to eat too much, or we won't be able to play tonight."

"Don't you worry none, Arik. You eat as much as you want. I'm not gonna force you. I'm no Jewish mama." Maimie smiled mischievously.

"I beg to differ, Maimie." Arik laughed.

Over the hearty dinner and good conversation, Dahlia felt her heart come home. It was validation of what Arik had been telling her all along. When she looked at Kevin, she flashed back to the newspaper photo of Arik that she had seen. She began to understand, on a visceral level, the sense of belonging that Arik had found with this wonderful family. She thought of Thelma, back in D.C. She marveled at the warm interaction over dinner. My parents could take a few lessons from the Perkins. She felt a deep sense of joy, and she was so pleased she was there. If my parents knew I was here, with these people, what would they say? She squeezed Arik's hand under the table.

After dinner, they all squished into the reverend's old Ford Country Squire station wagon and headed for the playground. There was a spot, right next to the courts, reserved for the reverend's car. They got out and joined the throngs of people converging on the Cage.

"Antwan and I are heading to the back. See you after the game!" Arik said.

"Don't worry, Arik. I'll take care of Dahlia here." The reverend smiled.

"Keep her away from the bookies. I don't want her betting on the game." Arik laughed.

"Oh, Arik, now you're spoiling all my fun!" Dahlia said.

Arik smiled at her, and then he was gone.

There was a momentary break in the loud jostling near the gate of the Cage when the reverend and his family approached. The crowd parted as they walked up to the guards.

"It's like the parting of the Red Sea," Dahlia whispered to Maimie. "They treat the reverend with such respect."

"They do, but I think the crowd is parting for you, not him." Maimie smiled.

The crowd went completely silent when the pros went on to the court to warm up.

Reverend Perkins turned to Dahlia. "These three guys are from UCLA: Henry Bibby, Curtis Rowe, and Sidney Wicks. The other fellows may be more familiar to you. There you have Wilt Chamberlain, Elgin Baylor, Happy Hairston, and Willie McCarter from the Lakers. This was all Arik's idea, to get these guys over here to raise money for the local youth sports league, my pet project. It's so nice to see such a great turnout and even more nice to see folks part with their money without feeling like they're being robbed. Arik's quite the fellow, you know. We all love him here."

"I know." Dahlia smiled. "I saw Elgin Baylor when he came to camp last summer. He was a big hit with the kids."

"Arik told me all about that." The reverend smiled.

When the neighborhood All Stars filed on to the court to warm up, they were met by deafening cheers.

The warm-ups were quite a curiosity. The pros warmed up in two crisp, straight lines, passing and making layups and jump shots in fluid choreography. On the other end of the court, the locals were everywhere, bouncing, spinning, and whipping their passes behind their backs and through their legs and gyrating and spinning their layups and dunks like whirling dervishes, in no particular pattern or order. The "referees" announced that the game would follow the no-dunk rule set forth by the NCAA after Lew Alcindor's freshman year.

Just like downtown, it was decided that the two teams would face each other at center court to hear the national anthem. The excitement reached a fevered pitch at the first tip-off. The game proceeded at a gentlemanly pace as the two teams took the measure of each other but then, midway through the first half, the pace quickened dramatically.

Chamberlain was dominant, dropping hook shots over defenders, slapping the ball to the basket with his right hand, and swinging his elbows to ward off defenders.

Arik loved playing against the UCLA guys. He felt that the Lakers were out of his reach but that he could stand toe to toe with the college guys. He fully realized that he was good enough to call the Bruins his teammates.

For their part, Bibby, Rowe, and Wicks enjoyed the game immensely. They were able to play as creatively as they dared, out of Wooden's overbearing presence. At the Cage, they could be themselves. They also enjoyed watching their new teammate play, and they knew that this would be their only chance until the fall. This Eric guy had some great moves and, more importantly, he was smart on his feet and had great court sense. He played unselfishly. They were certain that he could make the transition from the playground to Pauley Pavilion.

Wicks stymied the locals' defense. A fierce rebounder, on offense he planted himself under the boards, squeezed in between defenders, and anticipated where the ball would bounce off the rim. He played the same way on defense, severely limiting the other team's second-chance shots.

Rowe was stunned when, while attempting a 25-foot jump shot, he saw Arik launch himself like a rocket, timing his jump with the ball's arc and swatting it out of play. He smiled at Arik.

"Nice move, Eric."

Arik shrugged, smiled, and ran backward.

From Arik's perspective, the matchup was extremely instructive. He got to feel, at the ground level, the differences in playing style between improvisational basketball and structured basketball. His teammates attempted gamely to flick the ball loose on defense, dive for balls to scoop them off the floor, or dribble artfully to zigzag around defenders and then flip the ball to open teammates. But their performance was, ultimately, haphazard, because the elements of their play never assembled into a coherent whole. This lack allowed the pros to take control in the final five minutes of the game. Their structured, efficient play had allowed them to conserve energy while the locals tired. All things considered, the neighborhood players didn't embarrass themselves too badly, and that was reflected in the final score: 61-53. Arik scored 14 points, made 7 assists, and pulled down 5 rebounds.

The game ended as elegantly as it had begun, with high fives, slaps, and hugs all around. Both teams received a standing ovation for a wonderful evening's performance. The invited guests inside the Cage had a chance to mingle with the players. Arik, red-faced and covered with sweat from head to toe, went over to Dahlia and the Perkins. He took Dahlia by the hand.

"You were wonderful," Dahlia gushed.

Arik gave her a sweaty kiss. Dahlia giggled.

"Come, I want to introduce you," Arik said.

Elgin and Wilt were gathering their gear.

Wilt said to Arik, "Nice game, kiddo. Your rhythm is back. How've you been? I heard Wooden is looking at you. It's about time! Say, why don't you come by Marymount and hang out with us after practice sometime?"

"Definitely! After Passover, I'll get a chance. How's your knee holding up?"

"It has its good days and bad days," Wilt said. "And who is this fine young lady, if I may ask?"

"This is Dahlia, my girlfriend. She was in the stands at camp when Elgin came to visit over the summer."

"Ah! Very nice to meet you. Dahlia, is it?"

"Yes." Dahlia smiled.

Dahlia shook hands warmly with Wilt and Elgin. She was astonished at how tall they really were up close. She craned her neck straight up to look at them. Perhaps a telescope would work better, she thought.

"I'm pleased to meet you, too," she said to Elgin. "You were so great with the kids at camp. They talked about nothing else for the rest of the summer."

"Oh, I'm so glad. It's so important to reach kids when they're young and impressionable. I like going to those summer camps to interact with them." Elgin smiled.

The two men high-fived Arik and thanked him for having organized the game. They said their good-byes to Dahlia, and then they were off. Arik introduced Dahlia to his future teammates from the Bruins, who had wandered by to say hello.

"Hey, Eric! Nice game. I'm glad you'll be playing for our side. You've got a nasty jump shot," Wicks said.

"Thanks. Looking forward to it," Arik said.

They gave Arik a wink and a "fine catch" look when Dahlia turned her head. Arik chuckled.

Dahlia whispered to him, "Why do they keep calling you Eric?"

"I have absolutely no idea. I keep on introducing myself as Arik, and they keep calling me Eric. What the heck?" He shrugged.

"Thanks for tonight, Arik. I love you so much. I'm so glad we came here. When are we going to get you off the couch and back into your bedroom, where you belong?"

"Hmmm . . . that couch is really starting to get uncomfortable, come to think of it. We have to be really quiet, though. The walls are made of paper." He looked at her with a twinkle in his eye.

She kissed him again. "I can be as quiet as a little old mouse when I have to be."

The following day, they went to see the Angels play the Yankees at the baseball stadium in Anaheim. They sat in the upper deck bleachers, looking down at the tiny red and white dots as they darted around the khaki and green diamond.

"Why don't you follow the Dodgers?" Dahlia asked.

"They're too highbrow for my tastes. The Angels are much more folksy and down to earth. I feel more comfortable here," Arik said.

"Arik, I hope that the Rabinovichs are okay with me coming here to be with you for the week. I hope that they won't consider it odd or inappropriate. Rabbis tend to be a bit conservative in that way."

"I gave them advance notice weeks ago, and they seemed very pleased that you were coming. The fact that I have a Jewish girlfriend who is religious makes Rav Shaul feel like he did a good job with me. Remember what I was when he first met me. They're very warm and friendly, and you'll fit right in, especially because you're Israeli."

When they entered the stucco ranch house, Dahlia took a deep breath.

"As I walk in here, I feel like I'm back in Israel. I can't put my finger on it, but the sense is real. It's more than just the furniture. It's the way everything is set up. It's as though they transported a small bit of Israel here."

Ilana Rabinovich welcomed them with a warm smile. She was slightly shorter than Dahlia, her hair was covered in a snood, according to Orthodox custom, and one could tell exactly what was for dinner simply by looking at her apron. She gesticulated with her hands when she spoke, and she appeared genuinely happy and enthusiastic to meet Dahlia.

"Thank you for having Dahlia and me for Pesach and the seder," Arik said.

"It's our pleasure," Ilana said as she shook Dahlia's hand. "Arik has told us so much about you."

"I hope only good things!" Dahlia said.

"Of course!" Ilana said. "Welcome to our home. I trust that your accommodations at the Feldstein's are comfortable."

"They're great. Thanks."

Rav Shaul joined them. "Arik, I'm afraid you'll have to share a bedroom with Hillel. We have my family from Israel staying with us this year. Usually, we go there."

"No problem. I'll take my bags up." Arik bolted up the stairs.

The Rabinovichs' kitchen was abuzz with activity when Dahlia and Ilana walked in bearing bottles of sweet seder wine. The savory aromas of chicken soup, matzo balls, gefilte fish, and rib stew were overwhelming. The stovetops, ovens, and countertops were full of pots, pans, and serving dishes piled high in preparation for the mountains of food that they would soon contain.

Ilana had been busy in the kitchen, making final preparations for the seder: roasting the eggs and the shank bone and cutting up the bitter herbs and the walnuts needed for the charoset, the burgundy-colored, sticky goo that the bitter herbs were dipped into to make them minimally palatable. The countertops were covered in contact paper and the stovetops were entirely wrapped in aluminum foil to make them usable for Passover.

Shaul was in the dining room, setting up the table for the seder, so Arik went down to the basement and brought up the fifteen wooden folding chairs and the remainder of the pots, pans, and assorted appliances that the Rabinovichs would need for the holiday. There were going to be twenty around the table, and they would reenact the night that the Israelites had been redeemed from Egypt. The children were preparing the Hagaddah passages and costumes that they would use in their Passover play.

"I still have two cakes and several trays of almond and coconut macaroons to bake, and then some fruit compotes, and we'll be all done," Ilana told Dahlia.

"Let me help you. Where do you keep the aprons?"

"No, please. Just sit and relax. You're a guest."

"I insist." Dahlia smiled.

Ilana handed Dahlia an apron. "Thank you very much. Could you get down the boxes of sugar, matzo meal, and almond paste?"

In a few moments, Dahlia was rolling dough covered in matzo meal while Ilana was cutting up the fruit that would go into the compote.

"I went with Arik to buy a suit for the holiday. I couldn't believe that he doesn't own even one. He absolutely resisted the idea. I practically had to drag him to the store! He was such a baby about it, but he looks so good in a suit," Dahlia said that last bit to Ilana in an undertone, in Hebrew.

"I think you should have just let him go like an Israeli, with a white shirt and dark pants. After all, he'll be in Israel soon enough," Ilana said.

"Do you really think so? He appears determined to stay here to play basketball. It's driving me crazy. I know full well what this means to him, that it's the first real break he's ever had. Everything has been such a struggle for him up to now. And so, frankly, I'm torn about it myself. I don't know what to do or what to say to him."

"You two appear to be pretty serious."

"We are. But how can it work with him here and me there? I have to return home to enter the army next July." Dahlia frowned.

"I don't think that Arik fully grasps the religious implications of playing basketball for a team like UCLA," Ilana said. "What will he do about playing on Shabbat? How will he keep kosher? He's come such a long way over the past two years. He won't even play street basketball on Shabbat now. I don't think that he's thought the rest through, though. What will he do later on?"

"I've been afraid to broach the subject with him," Dahlia said. "It's just sitting there like an unspoken chasm between us. It's been very hard for me."

Ilana smiled. "We'll have some time to speak over the holiday, perhaps tomorrow afternoon. It's good that we're all together. All of the very important people in his life are here, and we'll speak with one voice."

***

Outside Beth Jacob synagogue, on Olympic Boulevard in Beverly Hills, a large crowd of high schoolers were standing around socializing in their holiday finery before services. All heads turned as Arik and Dahlia approached from farther down the street, together with Rav Shaul and his family.

"Who the heck is that with Arik?"

"Arik said his girlfriend from back east was coming to visit for Pesach."

"They met at Mosh in Pennsylvania last summer."

"So much for Eastern girls being dogs. Arik's hit the jackpot with that one."

"She's the Israeli ambassador's daughter," Bracha Epstein said.

"Holy crap! How do you know that?"

"My cousin Shirah was at camp with them."

"Bracha, isn't that the one you told me about. . . ?"

"Shut up, Rina. Don't say another word."

"Does she know how he lives? What he does in his spare time?"

"It's like beauty and the beast." Murray laughed.

"That's rude. You liked him well enough when he scored thirty points against Sacred Heart to win the title."

"I'm just saying."

"Why is everyone staring at us?" Dahlia whispered to Arik as they approached the synagogue.

"Not us." Arik smiled. "I've gotten used to the effect you have on people."

"Hi, guys! I want you meet Dahlia. Dahlia, these are my classmates."

They spent the next thirty minutes playing Jewish geography, trying to make connections with friends and cousins who Dahlia might know from the New York area and Camp Moshava. Arik felt invisible and uncomfortable, because the whole conversation was directed at Dahlia rather than him, but he remained impassive and even smiled slightly. He tried not to show even a tinge of jealousy when some of the wealthier, more popular guys approached Dahlia and chatted her up as if he were not standing right there. Suddenly, Arik felt at a loss for words. How can I compete with guys who live in Beverlywood mansions and drive Mustangs and Corvettes to school? Those cool guys were always so sure of themselves, and they always knew what to say. The world was truly their oyster, because they always had their families' money to back them up. Arik knew that if he had not saved them on the basketball court they probably would not address him at all. He so hated to feel disadvantaged. He wondered why Jewish kids were so cliquey and so good at making outsiders feel crappy about themselves.

Dahlia glanced up at Arik and immediately knew what he was feeling. She turned away from a pair of overeager teenaged boys in heat and smiled at Bracha.

"You must be Bracha," Dahlia said. "You resemble your cousin. Shirah and I were bunkmates and buddies at camp."

Bracha blushed but tried to maintain her cool.

"Shirah and I correspond regularly. She told me all about camp."

"I know," Dahlia said. She smiled knowingly.

"Do you see her at all?"

"No, I live in Washington. But I'm probably going back to camp next summer, for a month."

"Are you going back to camp, Arik? You said you might go to Israel? Would you work on a kibbutz? Attend a yeshiva?" Bracha asked.

"Everything's up in the air right now," Arik said. He had not shared his dilemma with his classmates, and he wasn't going to start now. They would have to initiate a real relationship with him first. Especially not Bracha.

"Why don't the two of you come out to Nate Lefkowitz's house in the Hollywood Hills the night after the chag. We're having a big get-together for the whole crowd."

"That would be great," Arik said, looking at Dahlia. "We'll definitely come."

Arik and Dahlia walked into shul on their own.

"I'm okay with it if you are," Arik said.

Dahlia had other things in mind to talk about. "You seemed at bit jealous out there."

"I wasn't, not really. It's just like I was telling you. You see what these kids are like. Folks here are judged by the quality and quantity of their possessions, and I lose big-time on that score. That's why I didn't want to play ball for my high school. They don't deserve to win. If it wasn't for Wooden—"

"My precious boy, if I wanted some rich dude, I could probably run out and get one by sundown. I want you! I choose you! You will never have to worry about me. My heart is yours forever."

***

The evening prayer service at Beth Jacob was a formal, solemn affair replete with an operatic rendition of the holiday service by Cantor Berkowitz and an inspiring sermon by Rabbi Dolgin, who not only laid out the meticulous rules by which the traditional seder was to be performed but also added an inspiring holiday address about the meaning of freedom as opposed to licentiousness. Freedom meant independence, freedom to choose how to chart one's path, freedom to worship and to hear the words spoken by the Almighty himself on Mount Sinai only seven weeks after the Jews' exodus from Egypt.

Arik couldn't wrap his head around what all that loftiness had to do with some of the peculiar practices he had studied and would soon see at the seder, such as having a Haggadah with a ruler on the back cover so that one can measure a seven-inch-square piece of rock-hard hand-baked matzo to fulfill the minimum requirement to eat an olive-sized portion. One had to stuff it into one's mouth before being allowed to utter a sound. Similarly, one had to eat an olive-sized portion of raw horseradish in one go, also without speaking. It was like swallowing the culinary equivalent of a hand grenade. He had attended the seder at Rav Shaul's the previous year, too, but he had been too ignorant to understand what was happening. He decided that he would just go with the flow. At least he was with Dahlia, and she seemed to be thoroughly enjoying herself.

They arrived back at the Rabinovichs' home to find a long, white table adorned in crystal, silver, and china. The seder table was contained rows of wine bottles and a large, fully appointed seder plate. At each place setting sat a Haggadah. After Kiddush, the blessing, a child stood up to ask the four questions, starting with "Why is this night different from all other nights?"

Arik sat and listened intently to the Haggadah, which told the story of the Jews' exodus from Egypt and all the miracles that had preceded it. In one hand, he held the Haggadah, and the other hand, he held Dahlia's under the table.

"You look so handsome in your suit," Dahlia whispered to him.

Arik chuckled. "You're not too bad yourself."

All the children had prepared a skit, in costume, reenacting the exodus. Arik hadn't forgotten how much wine one was required to drink during a seder. He had never tolerated alcohol very well, and he felt himself getting dizzy. My little Dahlia seems to have no trouble with the alcohol, Arik mused. Maybe it's all that wine that makes the whole matzo and horseradish thing tolerable.

He sat in the warm glow of the wine and caressed Dahlia's arm. She smiled at him.

"We'll have this in our home, Arik," she whispered to him.

After a sumptuous meal of Passover fare—boiled eggs in salt water, gefilte fish with more horseradish, chicken soup with matzo balls, beef stew with carrot tzimmes and potatoes, and fruit compote—the seder concluded with another two hours of grace and singing about hope for the coming of the Messiah. They even opened the door to let in the prophet Elijah.

"What would they all do if some old dude with a long, gray beard and robe, looking like Merlin, actually showed up and walked in on them? Everyone would run for their lives. Well, what can you do? Like Tevye said in Fiddler on the Roof, 'It's tradition!'" Arik whispered to Dahlia, who broke into giggles at the thought.

"It's sort of like Santa Claus." Dahlia said.

The following morning, after services, the "social club" met again outside the synagogue, to plan the afternoon's activity. To Arik's amazement, Dahlia and he were invited to join.

Over lunch, Rav Shaul asked Arik what his plans were for the week of Passover break.

"Dahlia and I are planning to drive up the coast, to Santa Barbara, ending in Carmel and Monterey. We're leaving tomorrow morning."

"You can't do it, Arik. It's still chag for you, and you can't travel," Ilana said.

"I don't understand," Arik said. "Aren't you all going to La Jolla tomorrow? Why can't I travel?"

"We can go, because we're Israeli. In fact, Dahlia could go, too, but you can't, because you're American," Ilana said.

"But we're all Jewish. And, in fact, you all are far more observant than me, so why am I stuck here all alone while the rest of you can run off?" Arik asked the question even as he knew that the answer he was about to receive would be far above his "pay grade."

Rav Shaul said, "It has to do with when there was a temple. The new moon was declared by witnesses who trekked up to Jerusalem to let the high court know that they had seen it. Based on that, everyone would know when the holidays were. The Jews in Babylonia, however, were left in the dark as to when the witnesses came, since there was no rapid communication from the Holy Land . . . so, they had to keep an extra day just in case."

"But now we have a calendar, and everyone on earth knows when the holidays are instantly."

"Once the diaspora started, to keep two days became a tradition, and nobody wants to change it."

"Or has the courage to change it," Arik said. "Well, all of you are sitting right next to me here in the diaspora, so you should keep two days, too, just like me . . . unless Israelis living here in LA have some inside info on when the new moon is in Jerusalem which Americans don't have. If you want to be consistent, everyone should do two days here and one day when they're in Israel. Am I getting this right?"

"Theoretically, yes, but the way it works out is that Israelis do it their way and Americans do it their way," Shaul said.

"And God is keeping track of all this? Wait a minute. I was born in Israel. Wouldn't that make me an Israeli, too?"

"But you haven't lived there since you were a baby," Shaul said.

"So, the law provides for a statute of limitations? How many weeks or years does one have to be there before you're magically transformed into an Israeli? What about Dahlia? She lives here, too."

"But she's with the Israeli embassy," Ilana said.

Arik furrowed his brow. "So, let me get this straight. Dahlia gets diplomatic immunity from the American Pesach law even though she's living here?"

"But she's going back!" Shaul said.

"Well, what if I go back there, too? You've been trying to talk me into doing that for months, Rav Shaul."

Arik turned to look at Dahlia, who smiled one of her million-dollar smiles, her eyes twinkling.

"So, you've made a decision about next year, Arik?" Dahlia asked.

A stony silence enveloped the room.

"Talk about being put on the spot," Arik said. "Dahlia and I need to talk it over this week. That was one of my goals for this long drive up the coast. The time alone would give us both time to think and talk."

"Then, go tomorrow, and have a wonderful trip," Shaul smiled at him. "You have my dispensation to go."

Arik took Dahlia's hand and kissed it. To heck with neghia!

The following morning, at the crack of dawn, Arik and Dahlia headed north on Highway 1 through Malibu and Ventura counties and toward Santa Barbara. Driving up the foggy coast along the winding, two-lane ribbon of highway outside Oxnard, they heard the roaring waves crashing against the rocks below, even over the din of the Chevelle's failing exhaust system. Wildflowers lined the road in two long rows, flanked by the cliffs to their left and rolling scrubland to their right and backed, in the distance, by the San Gabriel Mountains. Squawking seagulls circled overhead and dove for their breakfast. All along the beach below, for miles in both directions, they saw a huge number of barking, splashing seals lounging on the sand and scampering up and down the rocky outcroppings just offshore.

With all the windows open, both of them were bathed in a continuous blast of salty sea air. Arik turned to look at Dahlia, whose hair was being blown in all directions by the wind.

Dahlia nestled herself close to Arik and lay her head against his shoulder.

"Where do you want to stop for breakfast?" she asked.

"I figured we'd get to Santa Barbara and spend part of the morning there. It's a wonderful town, with tons to do. We're about forty minutes away. There's an excellent breakfast place called Mesa Verde—strictly vegetarian, and they have a whole range of amazing salads. Plus, they've got the best coffee in town. Afterwards, we could take in the sights. There are miles and miles of bike trails all over town, with bike rental places along the seashore. The weather there is nearly perfect most of the time."

"Sounds wonderful. I'm starved."

Santa Barbara shone brightly in the early morning sunshine. The downtown was reminiscent of southern Spain, with its Moorish architecture. Walls of whitewashed stucco with terra-cotta roofs were everywhere. Looking eastward, all the way up to the foothills of the Santa Ynez Mountains, lay a forest of white homes set in a subtropical botanical garden. To the west lay Santa Barbara Harbor, its glistening, blue water dotted by white sailboats.

Arik parked along the shoreline, and the couple rented a pair of ten-speed bicycles. They turned into Shoreline Drive and then found the restaurant several blocks inland. After breakfast, they rode their bicycles and took in the sights. They began with the Mission Santa Barbara, with its immaculate white stucco brick and twin bell towers. Off their bikes, they wandered through the Spanish courtyard garden with its arched stucco porticos and bubbling fountains surrounded by stands of roses, they spoke quietly to each other. Their voices dropped even lower when they entered the interior of the church, which lay hollow and majestic in its Romanesque splendor, with its long rows of plain wooden pews and an altar featuring a 30-foot Christ on the cross.

Afterward, they hiked in the Santa Ynez Mountains. They went through Mission Canyon, up the Jesusita Trail, and made their way through the rocks and scrubland up to Inspiration Point, where they had a panoramic view of the entire city of Santa Barbara, the harbor, and the ocean between there and the Channel Islands.

Looking out from on top of the world, in the bright sunshine, they stood in silence, hearing only the wind in their faces.

"This place reminds me of the view of Haifa from the top of Mount Carmel," Dahlia finally said. "It's so peaceful up here."

Arik sat in a lotus position, and Dahlia lay her head on his lap and looked up at his face.

"Arik, I've had a wonderful time. This week has been like a dream I won't soon forget. Our time together is so precious. I feel so fulfilled when I'm with you."

"I'm waiting for the other shoe to drop," Arik said.

Dahlia stared at him for a long while without saying a word.

"What are we going to do, Arik? More specifically, what are you going to do? Have you come to any decision?"

Arik found his words but in halting fashion. "I wish I had. I'm so torn. If I decide to stay here, we could continue the way we have, next year. I want to be with you so much, but even if I go to Israel we'd still be apart next year—and even more so than now. Also, if I stayed here, the amount of money I'd get for living expenses from UCLA alone could support my parents. I'd even have enough left over for a plane ticket to Israel! I'd probably live at home. After my run-in with Ethan, my uncle's generosity could run out any day, despite his assurances. Ethan is planning on taking over the company soon, and he's already told me that the support for my mom and dad will stop then. How can I leave them like that? Not to mention the fact that I'd be walking away from the opportunity of a lifetime. Did you know I'd the first person in history to turn down a basketball scholarship to UCLA? Ever?" Arik ended by shaking his head.

"Don't think for a second that what you're telling me hasn't gone through my mind a thousand times. I've agonized over this just like you have, but each time I think of it I only see one way forward for us. After I graduate high school next June, I'm going into the army for two years. If we think that our relationship will survive our being apart for that long, we're kidding ourselves. As it is now, we have to steal away for a week here and there to see each other. I can assure you that it'll be virtually impossible to match our times off to spend time together if I'm there and you're here with your game and practice schedule. In the army, days off come with very little notice, and on a whim a commander can cancel your leave. Then you'll have come all the way to Israel for nothing! There's a really good chance we wouldn't see each other for two whole years. No relationship can survive that—not even married ones, most of the time.

"And what about playing and traveling on Shabbat? What will you eat, especially when you're on the road? How will you keep kosher? You've come all this way on your spiritual journey, just to throw it all away and become a goy again? Is that what you want? Playing Division I basketball is a full-time job. Many of the guys can't keep up with their schoolwork let alone try to maintain a Jewish identity. You always hear about these athletes flunking out of school.

"You'll be mixing with a different crowd. Think of all the temptations that'll be thrown your way! You said it yourself. At the party at Gilbert's house, a half dozen half naked attractive women approached you with phone numbers. And that was just one party. You're a young man. You can't resist that forever. Nobody can."

"That didn't even occur to me," Arik said.

Dahlia shook her head and continued. "We talked about you going into the Israeli Army, so many times. You seemed so sure. I go to Israel often, with my dad, so I can see you often. After a year, I'll be there and we can be together. Many Israelis marry young, so we could get married as soon as you finish the army. Then, we'd have a life together in Israel."

"But what would I do after the army?" Arik asked. "I can't afford anything. I want to go to college and get an engineering degree. How will I do that? I have nothing. The odds of me getting into a place like the Technion are slim to none, even if I could afford it. They barely have places for all the Israelis that apply there. If I stay here, I could start studying engineering right now." Arik felt that he was on the verge of pleading.

"That wouldn't be a problem for you. My father knows so many people and could easily get you in—you know, the thing you hate." Dahlia smiled slightly. "Protectsia! Sorry to say, but that's what makes Israel go 'round. Another thing: You've dedicated your life to finding out what happened to your father, why he was shafted so badly. You'll never find that out from UCLA. That I can assure you. For God's sake, Arik, these UCLA guys can't even pronounce your name properly. Eric! Judaism teaches that there is much in a name. Names represent the essence of a person. These people don't understand your essence. They don't give a crap about you. For them, you're just a replacement for Lew Alcindor, whoever he is, another warm body so that they can win another national championship. You need to make the choice. Be alone with strangers who will lead you astray or be with your people, your destiny, with someone who wants to spend her life with you. We'll have a great life together in Israel, I can assure you. Choose me, Arik, or you'll end up with another Christine Spellman. Guaranteed. You'll be right back where you started."

Arik looked down and shuddered.

"Arik, I'm begging you. Choose me, choose me! I'll make you happy for the rest of your life. You'll never regret your decision. Your life will come full circle, and I so want to be a part of that. Your place isn't in Carmel, California, but Mount Carmel outside Haifa, Israel." Dahlia's eyes became moist, but she remained smiling. She rubbed noses with him and kissed him.

He took her into his arms and silently looked out at Santa Barbara Harbor. They remained like that for a long time.

After eating the lunch, they had brought with them, they hiked back down into town and to Arik's car. They got in and headed north, toward San Simeon and Hearst Castle. The following morning, they continued up the coast, to Carmel, where Arik taught Dahlia to surf.

***

May 1, 1970

To my reason for living,

I went in to see Coach Wooden yesterday and told him my decision. Of course, I didn't mention you. I put it in terms of going home, going back to my roots, trying to make sense of my father's life and further discovering who I am. I told him about my connection to Israel and fulfilling the two-thousand-year-old dream. I told him that I don't want to be yet another generation living in the diaspora, that I want to contribute to the Jewish people. I thanked him for the opportunity that he offered me and his confidence in me.

I expected him to yell at me, to call me an ingrate or something. Instead, he just looked down at his desk, tapping his fingers and stared at his Bible. He sighed and, very slowly and deliberately, told me how disappointed he was. He told me that I was the first person in the history of the program to turn down a full-ride basketball scholarship to go into the army. He told me dozens of high school phenoms would kill to be in my position.

And I knew all that. What I didn't know until he told me then was that he'd been planning to rebuild the team around me in the post-Alcindor era. He said that I had real leadership potential because of my "superior intelligence."

He called the head admissions officer of the whole college, Sam Riley, into his office to try to change my mind. Mr. Riley made a big deal that I have such an "excellent scholastic record," a rarity in top athletes. He also whispered to me that the college game had been completely taken over by black players over the past ten years and that it would be good to have a white guy with my level of talent on the team. Why did he have to whisper that? We were in a locked office. Was he afraid the office was bugged by the NAACP? Anyway, they offered me a free ride at UCLA for four years. They asked me what I wanted to study. I said electronics and computer science. They said that was "serious" and not some bullshit degree. That would make good copy for the article Sports Illustrated was already planning to publish about me. Division I Jewish college basketball stars are a rarity. They also offered me free housing on campus and living expenses. It's a chance of a lifetime, he told me, and I was walking away from it. They were pretty upset that I had waited so late in the year to break the news to them, but they gave me 24 hours to reconsider my decision. And then Wooden basically threw me out of his office.

That afternoon, I got a phone call from Sam Gilbert to go to his house. He asked me point blank if I was out of my "freakin" mind walking away from UCLA. He told me how much he'd already invested in me. How was I supposed to know that? I never asked him to do anything for me. He told me he was as Jewish as me and the proof was that he had bagels and lox every Sunday morning at his country club before heading out to the golf course. He said he admired "Moshdiane" (I guess he meant Moshe Dayan) as much as the next Jew but that the Israelis had won the Six-Day War without me and they wouldn't need me in the future either. I recalled what you said about names. Finally, Gilbert told me I was making the biggest mistake of my life and I'd soon regret it but there'd be no going back.

He has all this inside info about what's going on, but I don't understand how he knows everything. He told me Wooden is already making plans in case I don't accept. That was fast, but I guess he has a team to run. Gilbert said they were looking at some 6' 11" high school basketball wizard from La Mesa called Bill Walton. Apparently, he plays both center and forward. I had to give Wooden my final decision by the next day, which I did.

I called Yardeni, from the Israeli consulate, and told him about my decision, and he had me go down to talk to him in person. He had me meet with two other guys who didn't tell me what their positions were. Anyway, the following day they sent me a one-way ticket to Tel Aviv. When I told them, I don't have any family in Israel, they told me I'd be a "lone soldier." I guess you don't qualify as family, not yet anyway. Someone is supposed to meet me at the airport and take me to some place called the Bakkum at a hospital called Tel Hashomer or something in Ramat Gan. I guess that's the induction center.

I graduate on June 25th and have to report to the Bakkum by July 14th. I tried to get a stopover in Washington on the way over, but they insisted on a nonstop flight. I have no money to do anything different.

I've decided to make the leap into the unknown. All I know is that I'm desperately in love with you and I've decided to trust you with my life and future. I'm giving you all I have, my sweet love. I'm sacrificing everything for you. I pray that you will always feel the same intense affection for me.

With all my heart and soul,
Arik

Chapter 25

The hot mid-July sun baked down on the new batch of recruits that had converged on the large Quonset hut that served as their registration center in a huge enclosed area adjacent to Tel HaShomer Hospital. As they stood in the dusty desert wind, they saw that they were surrounded by vendors hawking their wares, whether ice cream, newspaper, soda, or falafel.

"Haalo, haalo! Artic, Artic!"

"Kaasata, kaasata, lux kaasata! Belirah, belirah!"

"Maariv, Yedioth! Haalo! Maariv, Maariv!"

Arik stood alone holding his duffel bag and canvas rucksack. He surveyed the scene around him. All around him stood tearful eighteen- and nineteen-year-olds hugging their families. It occurred to him that these kids were saying good-bye to not only to their relatives but also their childhoods.

The recruits came from every stratum and segment of Israeli society. They were European, Anglo Ashkenazim, Moroccan, and Yemenite Oriental. They were religious and nonreligious, kibbutzniks, and even some Hassidim. The Israeli Army was the great melting pot, the great leveler in which prospective soldiers were judged, for the most part, by individual skill.

Each recruit and his or her extended family waited for the recruit's name to be called. The recruit then approached the desk and was assigned to one of the long line of khaki buses parked next to the hut. Once filled, the buses made their way to the Bakkum, the main induction center, for the next step in the transition from civilian to soldier.

Arik's fear of the unknown was tinged by a profound sense of loneliness as he heard the hugs, tears, and kisses. He had nobody there to wish him good-bye and good luck, nobody's shoulder to cry on, nobody to share his thoughts and feelings with. He stared blankly at the registration desk, waiting for his name to be called and trying to keep his mind as blank as possible. He had decided that it was better not to think too much about what was happening.

Suddenly, he was grabbed from behind.

"Arik!"

"Dahlia? What are you doing here? I thought you said you were going to be at camp? Tennis—"

Dahlia planted a hard kiss on his lips.

"You didn't think that I would let you just disappear onto that army bus without saying good-bye and Godspeed, did you? Without planting as many kisses on your sweet face as I could manage until they called your name? I told you that going back and forth to Israel is easy for me and I'd visit you often. I've done nothing else for the past month but think and dream about you every night."

Arik was too stunned to reply, so Dahlia continued to fill his silence. "Don't ever think—not for a minute—that I don't appreciate what you've done for me, for us. I'll never disappoint you, Arik."

She was rambling. "Do your best to get off for at least forty-eight hours over the Sukkot holiday. It shouldn't be very hard. The bases nearly close down for the chag, unless there's some kind of security alert. You'll never be a 'lone soldier.' Okay? Never forget that for a second. I am your family now. Every second I'm awake, I think of our future life together. It's no longer theoretical. It's all finally coming together. I just can't wait to see you in your uniform. You'll look so handsome. I'm so proud of you, Arik!"

Arik finally recovered his voice. "I'll make you proud, Dahlia. I promise."

They hugged again, clutching at each other. Dahlia rested her head under his neck.

"Stay safe, Arik! Stay safe for me! Do you hear me?"

"Arik Meir!" a voice boomed from the registration desk. "Arik Meir!"

"Got to go!" Arik said. "I'll write to you as soon as I get a chance."

"I know you will, booba sheli! I know you will!"

***

August 1, 1970

My Soulmate,

Well, I'm officially an Israeli soldier now: Private Arik Meir, serial number 746488, at your service. I've enclosed my induction picture for your entertainment. So, how do I look?

As soon as I got off the bus at a place called Kelet Bakkum (or something like that), they made us line up in a long line stretching forever, hundreds and hundreds of guys. I felt like a Ford Model T on am assembly line. After I got measured, they gave me a slip of paper with all of my vital information. I then proceeded down a long hallway where I was given a large green kitbag. After that, there were stall after stall where people threw everything but the kitchen sink at me—uniforms, belts, canteens, blankets, boots, even a toothbrush and a mess kit. I was then put into a tent with ten other guys. The good thing was that nobody knew each other, so there were no cliques . . . yet. We all were on the same footing. When the guys heard I was an American, they assumed I couldn't speak Hebrew, so they talked about me to each other in front of me. Imagine their shock when they found out that my Hebrew is as good as theirs! The fact that I was born here went a long way with them.

After that, we had orientation—but, to my amazement, no sergeants came by to scream at me that I was nothing more than scum on a worm's ass, like they do in the movies with the U.S. Army. The corporals and sergeants are very matter of fact instead, all business. I like that.

For the next several days, I was separated from all of the others because I'm a foreigner. Since all Israelis are prescreened in their senior year of high school, by the time they come here the army already knows everything about them. I'm a complete mystery to them, on the other hand. For four days, from morning to night, they put me through a battery of physical, psychological, and intelligence tests they call the Kaba. After the complete medical exam, they gave me a 97 score, which I'm told is the highest you can have. I'm a beast!!! Your beast!!! I also scored a 9.5 on the Dapar intelligence test, which translates into an IQ of 150. I never knew I was a genius, but apparently, I am! Wahoo!!!

On the fifth day, I had an all-day interview with a bunch of psychologists and screening officers trying to determine where I would be best suited to serve. I was offered a chance to be a fighter pilot, but I don't have much interest in that. I want to fight with both feet on the ground. That's why I turned down the tank division and the navy, too. I don't want to sit in some death trap for three years. I want to be able to get away from danger on my own two feet if I have to. I told the interviewers that being a paratrooper would be perfect for me. They asked if I wanted to try out for an elite commando unit. I remembered what you said about being careful not to get my ass shot off or end up like my dad, so I told them that becoming a regular paratrooper was fine by me. They told me that they would be making the final decision. I won't even know where I've been placed until I get there. What's the big secret? Well, whatever.

They took me to a base in the northern Negev, just outside Arad. And that's where I am now. Anyway, I've got to go. I've got to do stuff of vital national importance—There are floors to clean, pots to wash, and tents to assemble and disassemble. And we need to run around the base, carrying our cots over our heads, in our underwear all night long. What a riot!!!

Here we go!

Your humble lover,
Arik

August 20, 1970

My Dearest Arik,

I'm so ecstatic and proud to hear how you're doing. I can't believe that they found out that you have an IQ of 150 and I thought that you were just some dumb jock. Just kidding! No shock about the perfect 97 physical score. I would have guessed that anyway. You know why you're just 97 and not 100? You lose three points for your circumcision. Why would they deduct for that? What does that have to do with being a soldier? Unless they're concerned about how you would "perform" as a soldier. I hear that they assign the prettiest girls in the army to be gunnery instructors. I hear that they're pretty aggressive toward the cute recruits, too. I'm not worried about you, though. And I miss your physical deficit.

It's ridiculous to think that making you run around the base, holding your cots over your heads, for hours in the middle of the night will make you a good soldier. This whole hazing thing is so ridiculous. Abba tells me that when Rabin was chief of staff he tried to do away with all of that but traditions die hard in the army. Sergeants feel like since they had to go through with it we should. I'm sure that this will all pass quickly and you will get down to the business of soldiering. I bet you're having no trouble with all the push-ups, running, and obstacle courses. I'm sure your instructors don't know what hit them.

Somebody from the embassy met Ted Williams, the manager of the Senators baseball team, and he was able to get me a summer job as an assistant in their locker room, working with the players. I get to assist the trainers and do all the heating pads, ice packs, and bandages on the players before and after the games. I have to help clean the locker room, but I guess you have to start somewhere if you want to work as a trainer with athletes. There's a whole new field called sports medicine, believe it or not. I think that's something I want to get involved with.

I like working so much better than being at camp. I've grown out of all that. I couldn't wait to leave Mosh, even though I'd been made the head of the tennis center. I left at the end of July, after the first session. That jerk Effie wasn't rehired. Did you know that? Ha ha! Joke's on him! The bleachers that we made still look great—even after the winter. Sitting there alone, I imagined myself waiting for you to show up so that we could play. That made me so lonely . . . thinking about last summer. I felt your spirit everywhere and everything reminded me of you. Everyone is asking about you. They're so proud of what you did. Just like I am. I miss you so much.

All I can think about is seeing you. I'm going crazy thinking about Sukkot, when I'll see your adorable face. I can't wait to take a picture with you in your uniform! Next year's picture will have us both in uniforms. That will be so amazing. We should take a picture of us every year as we grow old together. Our lives are finally coming together. I wonder what our kids will look like. One thing's for sure—they'll be good looking!

I know I'm just being silly, but writing to you is so much fun. I'll send you my flight information as soon as I know so you can somehow plan for your time off. I've already written to Aunt Ruti, the one you met last year, that you're coming. She's very excited that you're in Israel and even more excited that you're in the Army.

You should have no trouble hitching a tremp from the base. People just love to pick up soldier hitchhikers in Israel. You'll see.

Your letters give me such joy!

Smooches and tight hugs,
D

August 30, 1970

Dahlia, the love of my life,

I miss you more than I thought it was possible to miss another human being. It's only been six weeks since we saw each other, and there were certainly intervals longer than that last year. It must be the fact that I'm so far away that makes the pain of separation so much worse. I feel it in the pit of my stomach.

I'm never bored, though. When we have downtime—which isn't very often—I study my physics and electronics, but my mind is never far away from you. Every night before I fall asleep, my thoughts wander back to you. I see your angelic face lit by the setting sun with wind in your hair. I think about our nights together. And my soul is filled with joy. That joy, of course, is tinged with the pain of your absence. But then I leap ahead to the thought of seeing you on Sukkot, and it makes my head spin! I hope you'll be able to make it. I hope your parents are okay with you coming to Israel. Perhaps if they see me in an Israeli Army uniform they'll think more of me. I remember what you told me. I want to make them proud of me, too. More importantly, I want them to like me.

No matter, I'll just continue to be who I am. There's no reason to put on a show. I'm confident they'll grow to like me.

In other news, training has really started in earnest. We run and do push-ups day and night. They've started us on an obstacle course. For me, the whole thing is child's play. I can vault the wall that the others get stuck on. The ropes and rings are ridiculously easy, but I'm trying very hard not to show off. You know me. It's like the whole basketball thing at camp and then at school—best to keep a low profile. They have team building exercises where the squad that finishes first wins. The wall is the hardest, so I sit on top of it and pull my whole squad up. We keep winning, but that really pisses off my corporal. Ha ha!

They've issued me an Uzi . . . with real bullets and everything! They showed us how to assemble, disassemble, and clean it in under a minute. We have to oil it daily and keep it clean. Having even a small grain of sand on it is treated like a federal offense. We have to have it on us at all times—even in bed! They say it's my new girlfriend. I must say, though, it's nowhere near as cute as you are. Speaking of which, one of the firing range instructors tried to get familiar with me, but I pretended not to understand Hebrew.

When we're not doing all of that, they have us working—peeling thousands of potatoes, washing hundreds of pots, cleaning trash, and sweeping the dining room floors.

We've also started hiking. At first, we started off easy, going maybe 7 km, and then we started building up the mileage. They say that at the end of the course we'll walk 90 km with full packs. It's a really competitive race. The platoon that comes in first gets an extra day's leave that they tack on to the weekend. That's really important, because it's a day we can do stuff in town after probably having slept the rest of the time.

I help the guys out on marches by pulling them from the front when I see them falter. I don't expect anything in return, but I get the sense that it isn't always appreciated. Not that I care one way or another, but I can't just stand there and watch someone else fail. Once, on a night march, I had to carry a big fat guy on my shoulders for about 5 km. He was removed from the unit the next day. I felt bad about that, but he was lying flat on his back huffing and puffing on the road and refusing to move. We get timed and credit for coming in first if we all finish on time as a unit. What was I supposed to do? He would have made us lose.

I'm really trying to fit in with my tent mates, but I'm very different than them. I struggle to find things in common with them—despite my Hebrew. It's weird. I just come from a different world and I've been thrust into this one. Not that I'm complaining.

They've started a new form of torture for us now. It's called Masa Alunkot, forced stretcher march. We all have to carry some fat guy on a stretcher. I don't mind it so much. I don't find it that heavy, so I've been carrying both rungs from the front and allowing the other guys to share the load from the sides. When the sergeant saw that our stretcher went faster than all the others, they put me on top instead. I really feel bad about that, but the other guys aren't mad at me. I'm really starting to make friends here.

Many of the guys are walking around like the living dead with eyes half shut. Some fall asleep in class and get water thrown in their faces. I think the hardest part of all this is the perennial lack of sleep. They keep waking us up in the middle of the night to do the dumbest things. I thought Israeli kids would be tougher than their American Jewish counterparts. So far, frankly, I'm not seeing it. Sorry.

Oh, my God! I'm going to see you in less than a month! It looks like if I choose to stay on base for Rosh Hashanah and Yom Kippur I'll be given 72 hours off for the beginning of Sukkot. Be prepared to have a sore face from the number of kisses I'm going to place on it.

My soul is yours,
Arik

***

"I have grave concerns about Dahlia's trip to Israel for Sukkot," Benny said to Leah. He had shut off the TV in the family room, indicating that it was time for a "talk."

"Why, Benny? What's wrong with her going to spend the holiday with Ruti?"

"Don't you see that Dahlia's trip has nothing to do with Ruti and everything to do with that boy Arik? She's hell-bent on pursuing this liaison with him despite every effort of ours to dissuade her. This boy is simply not suitable for her. What sort of life could she have with him?"

Leah answered thoughtfully, "He seems to be a very nice fellow. Dahlia is a good judge of character, and she isn't prone to rash decisions. I, personally, don't see anything wrong with him. Why do you have so much against him? It gets tiring hearing you talk about him. I'm sorry, Benny, but I simply don't share your disdain for him."

"Well, for one thing, he's uneducated. He has very little knowledge of our way of life, and he prefers the company of kushim to other Jews. If he had his way, he'd live with them rather than people like us. We raised Dahlia to associate with royalty, not some low-class hoodlum. How do we know that he's not a member of a gang? We already know that he's been involved in street fighting, so, obviously, he has a penchant for violence. What guarantee do we have that he won't ever be physically abusive to Dahlia? Is that what you want for her?"

Benny was on a roll. "It's our job to protect her from that sort of thing. She can't make these decisions for herself. She's still a child. She needs a boy from a good family, someone with class and refinement. She'd have a life of struggle with him. And, after the whole infatuation wears off, then what is she left with?"

"He was very polite and helpful when he was here with us," Leah said meekly.

"It was just an act. How would you expect him to behave as a guest in our house?"

"So, you don't see any potential in him at all?"

"Frankly, Leah, I don't. Dahlia told me that he didn't even own a suit! She had to take him shopping for one when she was there during Pesach. Is this what you want for a daughter of an ambassador? Is this the type of boy you want to represent us at a ball, mingling with diplomats and heads of state? I don't. He'd be an embarrassment. He has no clue how we live. For all we know, he could be involved with drugs or alcohol. That curse is rampant in the Negro community. "

"Why can't you at least wait to see how this progresses, for a while?" Leah said. "Besides, Arik is in Israel now, so how could he end up living with Negroes in America?"

"Even if he stayed in Israel, he'd fare no better. I wouldn't be surprised if he ended up living with the frenkim from Morocco or Yemen in some godforsaken development town in middle of the Negev desert. Is that what you want for our eldest daughter? What if he joins the Black Panthers or any of the other troublemakers when he's in Israel? I know these types of people. I'm telling you now! You'll regret your decision to let her go see him on Sukkot," Benny practically hissed.

"Perhaps you're right. At the end of the day, we have to do what's right for our daughter," Leah said. "But let her go see the boy. Then she won't see him until the summer, anyway, and by then she'll be over him. Perhaps she'll meet another boy meanwhile, during the year. She's entitled to continue the life that she's grown accustomed to. We're the ones who had to struggle so that she'd have a better life. She shouldn't actively put herself into a position where she'd have to get a job to support a family because her husband can't. She should marry someone with good prospects."

Chapter 26

In the sixth week of basic training, formal hand-to-hand combat training began. It was a welcome break from the endless push-ups, sit-ups, and running drills. Arik's whole plugah, or company, was broken up into kitot, small squads for more individualized instruction from seasoned veterans of commando units. They sat in a wide circle on the dusty sand in the hot sun for more than two hours, waiting for the class to begin.

The instructor, Eldad, strutted in. He was wearing baggy fatigue pants, combat boots, and a worn T-shirt that exposed his hairy, bearlike arms. Eldad was stocky and had a scraggly face that was deeply lined and tanned from years spent in the desert. His thick head appeared to sprout directly from his shoulders. He feigned a smile that exposed a mouth of yellow, rotting teeth from smoking and poor dental care.

"All right, you pathetic creatures. It is my unfortunate task to teach you how to defend yourselves. It is a fact that more lives are lost in hand-to-hand combat than any other type of combat, and it is a particularly gruesome way to die! I am the only person standing in the way of your coming home in a body bag as opposed to the bus. By the looks of you"—Eldad surveyed the group and sneered—"you would all get home in body bags"

"In the next three weeks, I am going to teach you the techniques that you will use to get the better of your enemy. Now, who is my first victim? You! Skinny one with the pimply face. Get up here! Take your knife out, and come at me!"

The recruit did as he was told. In one moment, his knife was taken away and he was felled by a swift kick to the ribs. The guy lay writhing in pain on the sand.

"You are a little pussycat. An Arab soldier would make kabobs out of you. The Israeli Army used to have men. Is this the best that Israeli society has to send me? Do you think that you could cross the Sinai in six days? You couldn't cross the street in six days to run an errand for your mommies."

One by one, another six recruits were put down, with either punches to the abdomen or kicks to the chest. One was punched so hard that he lay in a fetal position, vomiting profusely. Some were thrown to the ground and had their faces pushed into the sandy dirt by Eldad's boot.

Arik sat there and shook his head. Is this the way self-defense is supposed to be taught? This guy isn't a teacher. He's just a bully. These guys won't be any more able to defend themselves after this class than they were before.

Arik must have had an odd expression on his face, because Eldad called him out next. "Hey, Mr. Big Shot! You think that this is just a big joke? Yeah, you. Mr. Fancy American Big Shot! Get up here now!"

Arik did.

"So, you think that because your father is a big, fancy American multimillionaire you are better than us? Well, I am going to teach you a little different. You Americans are big, fat, soft, and stupid. You are all tembelim, overfed cows. Walking all over the world with such arrogance!

"We won a war against five countries in six days, while your stupid, idiotic countrymen have been sitting in a land a hundred times smaller than America for seven years already. That's right. I am talking about Vietnam, where you are getting the shit kicked out of you. And do you know why?"

Arik said nothing.

"I am talking to you, boy! I asked if you know why!"

"No, sir, I don't."

"Because you're fat, worthless, and stupid. Did you just say something?"

"No, sir!"

"What did you say? Now you are lying. I do not tolerate liars."

Eldad assumed a boxer's stance and sent a meaty fist directly into Arik's gut. The impact was audible. But Arik remained impassive and didn't budge. Eldad was stymied that his punch, delivered at full force, had had no effect on the boy.

"I am going to make a man out of you! This will leave an impression!" Eldad bellowed.

He lunged at Arik with a loud grunt, his left foot headed straight for Arik's groin. Arik saw it coming and leaned back six inches so that Eldad's foot flew harmlessly to waist level. In an instant, Arik grabbed Eldad's foot in midair and spun it around, twisting him ninety degrees with such force that his other foot left the ground. Arik let loose a right hook that found Eldad's left temple and rendered him instantly unconscious.

When Eldad lay motionless in the sand, Arik turned to the others, who were startled speechless, and said, "Here's another survival rule: Never start a fight you can't finish."

In a moment, six military policeman swarmed Arik, their Uzis trained on him. Arik raised both hands, but they were thrown to his back and he was handcuffed.

Again! he thought.

Arik was thrown into the makeshift jail, a small, old, mud-and-stone house that probably had served as an Arab's house a century earlier. He was put in an 8' × 8' rat-infested cell with a six-inch barred window, a chamber pot in the corner, and a small pile of straw on the floor for him to sleep on. Twice daily, he was given a moldy pita, a small plate of hummus, and a canteen of water. The chamber pot was never emptied. Instead, he was expected to dump its contents into a corner of the cell. The cell quickly became infested with flies, and the stench in the midday heat was overpowering. He sat in that cell for a week without uttering a sound.

On the seventh night, at midnight, two military police officers (MPs) entered the cell, guns drawn, and ordered him to get up and follow them. They led him to the office of the base commander, Major Gavi Shiloni.

"Stand at attention, soldier!" Gavi shouted.

Arik straightened up and stood stiffly.

"Okay, Bruce Lee, where did you learn how to fight like that?"

"I'm a first-degree Jeet Kune Do master, and I've trained and competed for ten years with Dan Inosanto in Los Angeles."

"Well, is that so?" Gavi was holding Arik's file and thumbing through it slowly and methodically. "It does not say anything about that in here. The Mossad has already collected quite a dossier on you. Hmmm . . . it says here, for example, that you are a convicted criminal. You served nearly two months in the Los Angeles County Jail for aggravated assault. You nearly killed three people with your bare hands. Is that what your kung fu instructor taught you how to do? These techniques are supposed to make you into more of a gever, not a criminal. Now you are assaulting people here."

"I'm no criminal, sir,"

"Shut up, Private Meir. The Mossad says different. Now, who am I to believe? A Mossad intelligence report or a lying piece of crap like you? Huh? I do not understand why the defense ministry allows Jewish criminals into Israel. We do not need Jews like you here. Well, who am I to question?"

Gavi held up another, much older folder.

"It appears that the apple does not fall far from the tree. We did some more homework, and look what we found."

He threw the dossier on the table next to Arik. Arik saw the name Ze'ev Myerowitz on the front of the folder.

"Your father was a criminal, and you are a criminal too!"

Arik clenched both of his fists, at his sides. "My father was a war hero, not a criminal. In fact—"

Gavi slammed his fist onto the table.

"Really? Really? Do you call the unprovoked mass murder of 256 noncombatant, unarmed women and children 'being a hero'? Your father was one of the Irgun criminals that perpetrated the massacre at Deir Yassin. Now, I am no lover of Arabs, mind you, but this crime brought all sorts of hell down on us in revenge and may have caused us to lose the old city of Jerusalem for nineteen years! And for what? Nothing! There was no strategic value in the town. It was just mass murder. Your father was a mass murderer!"

"My father wasn't at Deir Yassin. He was in Kastel, and he lost a leg saving five comrades from a burning van!"

"Is that what your father told you? You stupid jerk. Do you think that your father would tell you that he was a criminal? It says here that after the war he was on the run from the authorities, posing as a beggar, and then skipped the country to evade capture. They looked for him for years. Well, apparently, he surfaced in Los Angeles and made you! The next generation of scum!

"Eldad is lying in Tel HaShomer Hospital, critically ill with a concussion. If he dies, you will go to prison for a long time, for murder. I could simply throw you out of the army and have you deported back to the United States, but that would be too easy. I am going to keep you right here and break you like a twig. All of your holiday leaves are cancelled. I am going to give you a Yom Kippur and Sukkot you will never forget for your whole life!"

"May I please make a phone call? There are people expecting me for Sukkot." Dahlia will have traveled to Israel for nothing, Arik thought as he trembled with a combination of fear and rage.

"No phone calls. Your basic training begins tomorrow at 4 a.m. Now, get the hell out of here!"

The MPs released him and sent him back to his tent.

***

Dahlia bounded into her aunt's house, carrying two suitcases: one full of her clothes and another full of 220-volt electric appliances that her mother had bought on a shopping expedition to New York's Lower East Side. This was a time-honored tradition, because the prices of appliances in Israel were three times the prices in the United States.

"Is Arik here yet, Aunt Ruti?" Dahlia asked euphorically.

"No, not yet, motek! I am sure that he will be here soon."

"I just can't wait to see him already. I'm going crazy!"

During the Sukkah dinner, Dahlia sat quietly at the table, an island of misery in the midst of the holiday celebration. The dinner was noisy and festive. Ruti had gathered all of Dahlia's first cousins who hadn't seen her in more than a year, and they were excitedly trying to engage her in conversation. Dahlia forced a smile with some difficulty and made an effort to engage in small talk. However, she stared down at her food and pushed it around on her plate without tasting a morsel. She was seized with painful nausea.

"Would you please excuse me?" she said.

Dahlia got up from the table and walked to her bedroom, where she fell face down on her pillow and began to sob. Her all too familiar migraines were back in earnest. Her head was pounding.

Aunt Ruti followed to make sure that Dahlia was all right.

"I am sure that there is a good reason for his not showing up. Perhaps he was delayed at the base? Arad is hours away. He can still come. Do not be so sad. It is the chag!" Ruti said.

"He would have called if there was a delay. He's always so punctual and considerate. Something's wrong. I can feel it. We always say that we're like two bodies and one mind. Something bad has happened. If he knew that he couldn't get here in time, he would've called. Can I call his base to see if he's left? There are so many car accidents on the road. I told him to take a tremp. Perhaps he should have just taken an Egged bus. I'm so worried! He could have been kidnapped by Arabs. I'm going to call the base."

"But you can't use the phone today. It's the holiday!"

"It's an emergency! We have to know where he is. If something terrible happened to him, they have no one to call. He has no family here, no next of kin. He could be in a hospital somewhere. I have to find him."

The duty officer who answered Dahlia's phone call was courteous but unhelpful. "I am sorry, ma'am, but we have thousands of recruits at the base and our sign-out procedures get overwhelmed before a holiday. Thousands of soldiers ran out of here, in every direction. It is impossible keep tabs on them. They are not children, you know."

Dahlia spent the rest of the holiday in her room, emerging for only a few minutes in the afternoon. She then went out for long walk, alone, in the tree-lined lanes of the Park Leumi, the national park.

By the time she returned, after dark, the holiday had ended.

"Any word?" she asked Ruti.

"No, nothing."

"I'm going to call around to every hospital and every Kupat Cholim clinic from here to Arad to see if he's there. Please, give me the phone book." Dahlia had fire in her eyes.

It took the rest of that night and the next day for her to navigate the Byzantine bureaucracy that was the Israeli health care system. She experienced hours of being put on hold, being told that this, that, or the other director, chairman, supervisor, and so forth was too busy to speak or on vacation for the holidays, and being spoken to rudely.

She barely ate or slept. Finally, at midnight on the following day, she reported, "He hasn't been injured. I've checked every hospital and clinic from here to Arad."

"You are an amazing, determined, dedicated mate. You will make your husband very happy one day," Ruti said, trying to console her.

"Aunt Ruti, I know my parents feel otherwise, but Arik will be my husband—whether they like it or not."

"It upsets me so to see you in pain. Come have something to eat, and we will find your intended."

Dahlia spent several more days trying to make arrangements to go to Arik's base, but she was met with a brick wall. Paratrooper training facilities were kept confidential for security reasons, and her calls to the Kiriya, Israel's military command center, were completely fruitless. All she was told was that Arik's base was somewhere in southern Israel. She could get no further clarification. The day before Simchat Torah, the last day of the Sukkot holiday, Dahlia phoned home.

When she knew that she had her mother on the other end of the line, Dahlia broke down, sobbing, and her words spilled out in a rush of emotion. "Imma, Arik never showed up. He didn't even call. I know that he hasn't been injured, but I have no idea where he is or what's happened to him. Why didn't he come? I've sat here alone, waiting for any sign of him—any sign of life—for an entire week. I've even called military headquarters. They won't even give me the time of day. I'm absolutely beside myself. I want Abba to call and find out where he is and why he never came. Please, Imma, please!"

Leah said softly, "Ruti called and told me that you've been impossible the whole week. This isn't like you. Your aunt has been very worried about you. She's never seen you like this. They had family come from all over just to see you and, I'm sorry to say, you've ruined their holiday with your behavior. You cast a pall on the whole house. They were nice enough to have invited Arik in the first place. I know that you're very upset, but the whole world doesn't revolve around you, motek. You've affected many other people. I'm sure that there's a logical explanation for his disappearance. People just don't vanish into thin air."

"Look, I'm sorry that I ruined their holiday. I didn't mean to, but how can I fake being calm and pleasant when my head's exploding? I want you to call Abba now and tell him to find Arik and let me know what's going on. I want to know! I need to know!"

"And I suppose that if Abba doesn't do this you'll make his life a misery until he does so. Correct?"

"Something like that." Dahlia managed a smile. "I want to stay on a few more days. Perhaps I'll—"

"I'm sorry, Dahlia. I can't allow that. You start school on Monday, and I don't want you missing any days. If you haven't accomplished anything yet, a few more days won't make any difference. I'll speak to Abba. Leave this to him. I'm sure that with his contacts it won't take long to find out what's going on. Come home, Dahlia."

"But he hates him, Imma. I'm sure he'd be happy to get rid of him once and for all, and this is his chance!" Dahlia was practically shouting.

"Dahlia, you're being a child. Regardless of how he feels about Arik, he loves you and can't bear to see you unhappy. He knows what Arik means to you. Have some faith in him, motek. Okay? Abba will make this right. Come home, Dahlia. Come home."

"Okay," Dahlia finally whispered.

***

October 23, 1970

My Dearest Dahlia,

Please don't be angry at me for not being able to get away for Sukkot. My base commander, Gavi Shiloni, has set up a continuous punishment program for me. He's making my life a living hell. This was entirely out of my control. I was so desperate to see you. I've been accused of assaulting an officer the day before Yom Kippur. I did no such thing! The guy attacked me, and I just defended myself. Things got out of hand, and I hit him harder than I meant to and knocked him out. I was told that I put him into a coma. I didn't mean to hit him that hard, I swear. The guy just kept coming and coming at me. He tried to kick me in the groin. What was I supposed to do? Worse yet, I was told by my sergeant that the guy I kicked the crap out of, Eldad, is Gavi's cousin. What a stroke of bad luck!

I've been kept in total isolation since the incident. First, I was thrown into the jail for a week with the rats and snakes. I had to crap in a pail next to a pile of straw that was my bed. When I was released, my leaves were canceled and Gavi wouldn't even allow me to make a phone call. I tried to sneak out, but I was caught and charged with insubordination. They then kept me awake for 48 hours, filling sandbags until I'd built a wall twenty feet high and fifty feet long. Then I was told to empty the bags, haul the sand to the other side of the base, and build the wall again. I spent the whole Sukkot holiday virtually alone at the base, because everyone else had gone. They made me dig a gigantic hole for the company's "new latrine" and had me transfer all of the crap from the old latrine to the new one with a wheelbarrow. I never in my life thought people could be this cruel and—as you know—my life hasn't been easy. But this is a whole new level. It seems like no matter how hard I try I always end up shoveling somebody's shit.

I think Gavi is out to break me. But I quietly do what I'm told no matter what. I hope that my time in this base comes to an end soon. One thing is for sure—I will NEVER let them see they're getting to me. I have nobody to fall back on or to support me in any way. I have nobody to complain to. But I'm strong. I can withstand anything they throw at me. I will prevail. Please don't be angry at me. I'm begging you. You're all I have. This hell will end and we'll be together again.

Please write to me and tell me you understand. You know I'd never do anything to hurt you.

I love you with all my heart.
Arik

October 23, 1970

My Dearest Arik,

I'm beside myself with misery and grief. My anger and worry at you not showing up for Sukkot has turned into a demon in my soul. It's ripping me apart. I'm not eating. I'm not sleeping. I can't stop thinking about you. I miss you so much that it hurts. I'm physically sick. Why won't you write to me? What have I done to deserve this? Are you upset at me for convincing you to go into the Army instead of doing what you really wanted to do? Are you trying to punish me? I did it for us! I did it with the best of intentions. I wasn't being selfish. I really believed that this would be a whole new life for us. A loving life. A life in Israel. I knew what you were giving up. I never made light of it. I really felt that going to UCLA would take you away from your destiny, something that you've worked so hard for over the past two years: your Jewish life. I dream every night about our married life together, about making love to you.

I know that you aren't dead or incapacitated. I asked my father to locate you, which he did. He even showed up at your base and spoke to your commanding officer, who told him that you're progressing very well. He told me that he saw you doing one of your drills and that you looked content.

Please don't be angry at me. I'm begging you. I will so make it up to you. I'm beyond worried sick over you. You're out of my reach. I feel that I've lost you. WHY ARE YOU DOING THIS TO US? Why are you shutting me out? For weeks, I haven't left my room except to go to school. I cry myself to sleep every night. You haunt my dreams. Arik, you're the love of my life. I'm begging you. Please come back to me. Please don't do this! I'm not angry at you anymore for not coming to see me on Sukkot. I forgive you. Please forgive me. Please, for God's sake, write to me, call me, anything! PLEASE! If only to tell me that you've found someone new. Your silence is tearing me apart. I miss you so much! I love you so much!

I live day by day waiting for a letter, anything, just to let me know that you're okay and that we're okay.

I know that this letter is soppy but my heart is tearing out of my chest.

Dahlia

October 31, 1970

Dahlia, my soul,

I'm broken. I'm beside myself. I've been so brutalized and sleep deprived that I can barely see straight. They had me in complete isolation and there was no way for me to get in touch with you. It's just now that I've had my first opportunity to write to you again. It kills me that you had to come all to way to Israel for nothing. Knowing you, your emotions are probably swinging from rage at me to worry for me. Just know that I've been desperate to get in touch with you but I was barred from doing so by my commanders. We have forced stretcher marches all night long. And when the others get to sleep, I get singled out for some imaginary offense and get more punishment detail. I sleep on average three hours a night. I ache all over. I walk around with a permanent splitting headache. I don't know how much longer I can go on like this. If I could just see your face, I'd be okay. But my soul is so tortured. Looking at your picture makes the longing worse.

I'm wearing cool camouflage fatigues—brown, green, and tan. They're made of pretty heavy fabric, so they offer some protection at night but they're hot as blazes during the day. I wouldn't mind marching around bare-chested, but we have to be in uniform all the time. We're spending most of our time out in the field sleeping in pup tents on the bare ground, so I have to choose between sleeping on the ground with my blanket on top of me so I don't freeze my ass off or sleeping on top of my blanket so I don't wake up with pressure blisters. Small wonder that there's so much stealing in the Army. Despite the fact that there are heavy fines and sometimes jail time for stealing even clothing, people still do it. It's so bad that if you lose a pair of socks you have to fill out an incident report. I haven't had anything stolen yet. I think people know I won't fill out a report if anything is missing, but that's not why they leave me alone. I think they don't want to mess with me because I'm a lot bigger than most of them.

My rifle is something else. I have to oil it and scrape it every night. Guys have gotten into serious trouble for letting even the slightest bit of rust get on their rifle. I'm dragging around a World War II era machine gun on my back. I take it everywhere—even to the toilet. I sleep hugging the stupid thing in front of me.

We're in the field pretty continuously now, which suits me just fine. We alternate our time between marching, say, 35-40 miles and getting to where we're going, where we have more field exercises. We've been in the field for three weeks so far.

In reality, these are war games. We train day and night. We storm up hills to take fortified objectives. We have target practice on the run. We practice ambushes and hiding out. My favorite is urban warfare. They've set up an entire city in the desert made up of plywood to simulate doorways, alleys, streets, plazas and what have you. Sometimes another squad plays the enemy. Judges stand by to decide when we're "killed." Some guys have gotten killed several times already. I've never been killed . . . so far. I'll send you a letter if I'm dead. Bad joke, sorry.

I just picked up my paycheck today. I get it monthly. I think it's the equivalent of $35. That's less than I made working for Uncle Itzik. At this rate, it would take me five months to afford the Nazi ski jacket.

Most days, they keep us so busy I don't have a chance to even crap, no less think. In the Army, there's no past or future. We're just living in the present from one minute to the next. I've taken to sleeping with my clothes and socks on. Number one, it's much warmer at night like that. Number two, when we're in the field we get woken up without warning and have less than two minutes to be ready for action. Some guys even sleep in their shoes. I don't. Good luck to them.

When we're not in the field, they have on the firing range, where we each shoot hundreds of rounds of ammo with Uzis, assault rifles, handguns, and MAG machine guns. Despite the headphones we get to wear, the racket is so loud that after an hour my ears are ringing and my head is pounding.

They have this thing called quick march. It's a 40-km march in full battle gear. It took us about 12 hours to do it. The pack isn't heavy for me, but it is for some of the other guys. I offered to carry them for a few of the little guys, but I got into trouble. I think they're trying to weed out the weaklings. When we do night marches, I still take the packs from the other guys. It's so dark that nobody can see me. When we have stretcher marches at night, I end up doing twice as much carrying as the rest of the guys, which suits me fine. I'm pretty miserable but not as much as most of the other guys.

The big problem are my feet. My socks are wearing out and I have blisters the size of golf balls on the soles of my feet. I used to be an athlete. Now I just have athlete's foot. My feet are chafed raw. I've got to get some powder or something.

Things are going to get crazier and crazier until the end of February or so when we have this 90-km march that will culminate in our graduation ceremony where we get our red berets.

Missing you terribly,
Arik

Chapter 27

Dahlia sat at the dinner table, staring down at her plate and not uttering a sound. Mechanically, she poked at her food and put the smallest nibbles into her mouth. For weeks, she had been irritable, lashing out at everyone with the slightest provocation and spending the rest of the time alone in her room.

It unnerved Leah to pass by Dahlia's door and hear her weeping. Having to hear from Dahlia's friends—and, worse, their parents—that she was a changed person, that she'd lost interest in social life and extracurricular activities, added to the corrosive atmosphere that had descended on the household. Dahlia's anger had turned into a silent melancholy. She had become quiet, almost noncommunicative. When she wasn't going through the motions of doing her homework, she sat and stared silently at Arik's picture on her desk.

Leah quietly walked into Dahlia's room.

"May I talk to you, booba?"

"Yes," Dahlia whispered. She looked down. "What about?"

"Have you heard anything from Arik?"

"Nothing, nothing at all. It's like he vanished off the face of the earth. It's impossible to understand. Why would he do this? I thought I knew him. It's one thing for him not to show up for Sukkot, without any explanation. That was bad enough. But then to not hear anything from him since then! I want to go to Israel to look for him. I want to go!" Dahlia wept softly. "I miss him so much. I feel like I've lost half of myself, like I can't go on without him. I want to go and find him. I want Abba to help me find him."

"Abba has already told you that he located Arik and that he was doing fine. I, too, don't understand this. The army is full of temptations for a young man, especially when he is under stress. The young women there can be quite aggressive, and Arik is a very handsome young man. I know that you don't want to hear this, but you need to consider the possibility that Arik may not be the person you thought he was. You can't force him to love you just because you love him. I know that I'm telling you terrible things, but sometimes a mother has to. You've given your heart away to a boy who has spent a good deal of his formative years in the street. He had no parents who could really guide him. You told us that yourself. So, why are you so surprised that he's acting the way he is? Maybe he simply lacks the social skills to know how to break things off with you, so he's picked the coward's way out by simply breaking off contact? You may not know him as well as you thought you did."

Dahlia sat, unbelieving, while Leah concluded her oration.

"You're too young to grieve for a boy the same way a wife grieves for a child or a husband. This was a summer romance followed by a long period of letter writing. I know you spent a week here and a week there with him, but that's not enough time to create a mature, long-lasting relationship. Most of your feelings about him are based on impressions you formed in his absence. You were so blinded by your infatuation that you didn't see him for what he is. You simply don't know him as well as you thought you did. Your Abba and I saw this in him immediately and tried to talk to you about it, but you wouldn't listen."

"But I love him, Imma! I love him so much! How can I talk myself out of my feelings for him?"

"What are you going to do? Try to chase him down all over Israel? And what if you find him and he's moved on? What if he has another girlfriend? You will have gone all that way to be made a fool. I just can't allow that. I won't expose you to that sort of thing. When you asked to go there for Sukkot, Abba was against it but I stuck up for you and defended Arik. But now Abba has proven himself to be right, and I'm coming around to his opinion."

"What can I do? This is eating me alive! I have to do something."

"You have no choice, Dahlia. You can't sit about like some sailor's widow waiting at the seashore for her man to reappear over the horizon. You're so young. You need to get on with your life. There are so many wonderful boys out there, boys from good families, boys of your social class. There's a whole world for you to explore. I refuse to believe that you won't find anyone else who will make you equally as happy and fulfilled—or even more so. Over the next several months, Abba and I will be attending many social events in town. There are many sophisticated, eligible, fine young men who attend these things. We see them all the time. You used to attend these social gatherings yourself, before you tied yourself to Arik. You're a beautiful young woman, Dahlia, so full of life. Give yourself a chance to be happy. Get back into the swing of things in school. This will be your last year of leisure for a while. Don't waste it in your room. And now, will you please come down to eat?"

Over dinner, Benny looked long and hard at Dahlia. Dahlia returned his gaze listlessly before her eyes dropped back down to her untouched food.

Benny began a discussion right in the middle, because everyone knew what the elephant in the room was. "I never cared for the boy, you know that, but I do care about you. I can't watch you sink into this type of depression. I agree with your Imma. I know that you will find it hard to agree with me when I say this, but the only cure for a boy is another boy. Next Saturday night will be the Ambassador's Ball at the Mayflower Hotel. We're honoring one of the most prominent Jewish families in the United States and one of the largest financial supporters of Israel in the world, the Ehrenreichs. I believe that they have a son about your age. The cream of American Jewry will be there, not to mention members of Congress and foreign dignitaries. It's the main event honoring Israel on the social calendar this year. Let this be your debutante 'coming out' party. Wear something elegant like the princess that you are, and you'll steal the show when you walk in! Take small steps like this at first, and before long you'll be back to yourself from before you met Arik. He was never good enough for you. As time goes by, you'll see that for yourself. I know that you're mourning for him, but time is a great healer."

Benny grinned at Leah, who nodded her approval.

"Abba, when you visited Arik at his base, did you speak to him?" Dahlia asked. "Did you find out when he has leave, so I can go see him?"

"My sweet girl, I certainly did not speak to him. I won't lower myself to approach an eighteen-year-old boy to find out why he's finished with my daughter. Can't you see how inappropriate that sounds? What father would do such a thing? I saw him from a distance, marching and drilling. He appeared to be content. That's what I saw. I spoke to his base commander, and he told me that he's doing very well. He certainly isn't sitting around in his tent, moping over a girl. He is in serious paratrooper training, and he spends nearly all of his time in the field, doing training exercises. He has virtually no time off. What are you going to do? Run around the Negev or the Sinai looking for him? This isn't like the movies that always have happy endings . . . where the man and woman find each other, at last, just before the credits appear. This is real life, and real life throws real disappointments at you. That's a given. You'll live with disappointments all of your life. The real test of maturity is how you live with them. As you know, I was severely burned during the war, and I still have times when I feel pain from the scars, but I don't let it stop me. I always look to the future and never dwell on the past. Nor should you. Imma will take you to Lord and Taylor and find you an evening gown to match your beauty."

Dahlia sighed. "All right, I'll go, but I really don't want to. I don't want anyone but Arik. I don't want to meet some random guy. I've already found what I want."

Dahlia went to her room.

"Benny, Dahlia is definitely her father's daughter," Leah said. "She's so determined and headstrong. When she sets her mind to something, she's rarely swayed. It's so difficult to point her in the right direction so that she makes good decisions. Was Arik really so bad for her? He was always very polite and respectful."

Benny said resolutely, "An act. Fellows will do anything, say anything in order to get a girl they want. The last thing this hoodlum thought was that he'd land a prize like Dahlia. Who wouldn't want her? If this were a passing fling, I'd let it slide, but Dahlia has already told us that she wants to marry him. What kind of life would she have with a boy like that? What does he have to offer her? What sort of home does he come from? Who are his parents? I'm going to do what I have to do to put an end to this liaison. I've had enough.

"The Ehrenreichs have a son Ze'evi who's a real gem. He sits on the national executive committee of Israel Bonds. He's a year out of college, and he works in his father's company, Ehrenreich Technologies International, where he's risen to the board. They say that he's brilliant and he's being groomed to take over the company when his father retires. After IBM, it's the largest multinational technology corporation. It even has subsidiaries in ten countries. Ze'evi's been listed as one of the ten most eligible bachelors in New York by Forbes magazine, not bad for a Jewish fellow. I've met him, and he's extremely charming, with a wonderful sense of humor. He's had a full Jewish education, and his family keeps kosher and is Shomer Shabbat. He's really the perfect boy for Dahlia. He'd be able to give her the lifestyle she's entitled to. We raised a princess, and a prince is what she should have, not a bum from the streets of Los Angeles. I'm going to introduce them at the dinner and let nature take its course."

"But is he a boy with good character?" Leah asked.

"You know that I'm a very good judge of people. I've interacted with him on several occasions, and I've been very impressed with him. His family has donated millions of dollars for civic projects in development towns all over the Galilee and Negev and, due to Ze'evi's good works, there are a dozen community centers and orphans' homes all over Israel named after the Ehrenreichs. He takes a personal interest in running the charitable activities of the Ehrenreich Foundation. The family just gave ten million dollars to the Jewish National Fund to plant trees in the Judean Hills and up on Mount Carmel. The next time you drive up to Jerusalem, you'll see a big sign just past the Latrun Junction that says the ZE'EVI EHRENREICH FOREST. Israel has no better friends than the Ehrenreichs. When the family's private jet touches down in Lod Airport, there's always someone from the prime minister's office on hand to greet it. Not bad for a twenty-three-year-old. He's the sort of a fellow that lights up a room when he enters it. I think that he'll charm you, too." Benny said.

"He sounds wonderful, like the perfect fellow for Dahlia. I suppose you're right. Time is a great healer. If Dahlia likes this boy, she'll forget all about her puppy love, summer camp romance. She deserves to be happy and have someone appropriate for her. I can't bear to see her so upset."

Chapter 28

Dahlia slowly came down the stairs, decked out in a shimmering formal evening dress of teal blue, a perfect match for her gray eyes. The dress was strapless with a contrasting white ribbon across the top of the bodice and the perfectly fitted waist, from which the wide, flared skirt fell to the floor. Her professionally styled, long, blonde hair flowed far past her bare shoulders and accented her pale arms, which ended in pure-white silk gloves. Benny and Leah, with broad smiles, watched her from the door.

"Dahlia, you look like a princess," Leah said. "You'll create a stir when you enter the ballroom. All you need now is a smile to go with your loveliness."

"I don't feel lovely," Dahlia said, looking down.

"Come, Cinderella," Benny said. "The Ambassador's Ball is the most glittering black-tie event on the Jewish social calendar in Washington. The cream of American Jewry comes from all over the country: wealthy philanthropists, UJA activists, as well as American politicians and diplomats from two dozen countries. We've brought in the top kosher caterer from New York and he's promised to shoot the moon. We've brought in top designers to decorate the grand ballroom of the Mayflower Hotel. The place will look like Buckingham Palace."

"I've been to these in years past. So, what's the big deal this year?" Dahlia asked.

"We have a surprise keynote speaker," Benny said excitedly. "Golda herself has decided to join us. We're going to be celebrating the end of the War of Attrition and the signing of the cease-fire with the Egyptians. The daily death toll on the Canal has finally stopped, and the mood in Israel has lightened remarkably. There's a feeling in the streets that we may one day sign a permanent peace treaty with the Egyptians. That, in itself, is cause for celebration. We're also going to be honoring a major philanthropist, Howard Ehrenreich, who has done more for the institutions of Israel than anyone else in recent memory. His donations are helping to build the new cancer center at the Hadassah Medical Center. He's the father of the fellow I was telling you about—"

"Is Arik going to be there?"

"Come, booba." Leah smiled sadly. "Tomer's brought the car around."

Even from a distance, one could see the facade of the Mayflower all lit up in blue and white light. The flagpoles on each side of the shimmering burgundy-and-gold grand entrance sported two large Israeli flags fluttering in the late October wind.

The Gilads entered the elegant lobby. Hundreds of people dressed in immaculate formal evening attire flitted to and fro, engaging in friendly conversation while being discreetly approached by wait staff offering fluted glasses of champagne and sumptuous hors d'oeuvres. Background music had been provided the David Wakely Orchestra, a twenty-piece ensemble that was widely regarded as the finest in the country. Dahlia stood quietly at her father's side and forced a polite smile when people approached to speak to her father, who made it his business to introduce her. Relax! she told herself. This really was a beautiful event. She decided that she would enjoy it and thus take a brief vacation from the grief and rage that had possessed her soul, even if just for tonight. She took a deep breath.

When she was introduced to Golda Meir, she winced briefly at the mention of the last name.

"So nice to meet you, Madame Prime Minister," Dahlia said as she shook her hand.

"It is good to see that Israel is being so well represented by such a lovely young lady. You are the belle of the ball! Are you still in high school?"

"Yes, but I'm finishing in June. Then I'll be coming home to start the army at the end of July."

Golda smiled. "Very nice! Good luck!"

"Thank you."

Golda engaged Benny and Leah in conversation, and soon they were joined by Abba Eban, the foreign minister, a heavyset man with a highbrow English accent.

Dahlia looked about for some of her friends, who had promised to meet her at the ball, but they obviously had not shown up yet. With nothing to do, she wandered around the room, taking in the sights. She still felt too distressed to eat anything that was offered to her by the waiters, but she did help herself to several glasses of the bubbly, enough to give her a warm, lightheaded feeling.

"So, what's the prettiest girl in the room doing standing alone with the saddest eyes I've ever seen?"

Dahlia slowly spun around.

"Hi, I'm Ze'evi Ehrenreich."

"Oh, so you're the famous Ze'evi Ehrenreich my parents have gone on and on about for the past week."

"Why have they been talking about me, for heaven's sake?"

"Well, for one thing, your parents are the guests of honor. And they were going on and on about your being this major mover and shaker in the Jewish world, all the stuff you've accomplished at such a young age. I think that they're trying to set me up with you."

"Did they tell you that I'm married?"

"Oh, well, that settles it then." Dahlia smiled.

"I'm just kidding." Ze'evi laughed.

Ze'evi was about three inches taller than Dahlia. His perfectly styled, wavy, dark-brown hair and piercing blue eyes accented his perfect tan. He was strikingly handsome, and he had the whitest teeth that Dahlia had ever seen on a homo sapiens. His cologne was. . . She couldn't quite place it, but it smelled very expensive. He looked dashing in his perfectly tailored tuxedo.

"So, is this is your debutante party?" he asked.

"I'm young but not that young."

"How old are you? I don't want to go to jail." Ze'evi smiled.

"I'll be eighteen in December."

"Okay, then, I'll walk away and come back in two months."

"I'm really good at lying about my age, though." Dahlia laughed.

"I can see why. Can I buy you a drink?"

"Sure! I'll have a vodka tonic."

"Whoa! Not bad for a seventeen-year-old."

"I can be full of surprises."

"Well, I must admit. You've got my attention. What are you doing after high school?"

"I'm sure you've figured out that I'm an Israeli. I'm going into the army in July."

"Man, you'll look cute in a uniform! If memory serves, you're going in for two years."

"Memory serves correctly. So, you're a big executive, huh?"

"I don't know about 'big.' I work with my dad, making satellites for weather forecasting and telecommunications. We subcontract for NASA, making guidance, telemetry, and communications systems for the Apollo project. Have you ever see on TV, when it says, 'Live via satellite'? Well, that's us!"

"Have you seen any lift-offs from Cape Canaveral?"

"Many of them! And not just from across the bay, like those rednecks with their coolers and beach chairs, up on the hill they always show on TV. I sit in the control center, with a ringside seat. My dad came into this early on, recruited by President Kennedy. I started worked at the company as an intern when I was in college, and after graduation I joined full-time. I was there for Armstrong's moon walk. "

"How old are you?" She was trying to piece things together in her head. "I mean, when did you graduate?"

"I'm twenty-three, and I graduated from NYU two years ago. I majored in computer science."

"Does everyone major in computer science these days?"

"Now, what does that mean?" he laughed.

"Oh, nothing! Nothing that I care to talk about . . . yet." She smiled cryptically.

"I'll have to get you out on the dance floor first. Do Israelis know how to dance? And not just the hora, I mean."

"Easy, tiger! No need to stereotype now. Yes, this girl knows how to dance."

They flew out onto the dance floor, and though Ze'evi was an excellent ballroom dancer, Dahlia easily kept pace with him. She let him lead, however, something that was not lost on him. He liked that.

Standing off to the side, Benny and Leah were approached by Howard and Michelle Ehrenreich.

"Good evening, Ambassador, Leah."

"Good evening to the guests of honor! I hope that you're both having a good time."

"Very nice, indeed. I've gotten a few words in with Golda. Or, should I say, she got in a few words with me." Howard laughed.

"I understand," Benny said. "Golda is a tough cookie. She says what she thinks, and she doesn't pull any punches."

"I've spoken to some of the fellas on the House Armed Services Committee last week, up on the hill, and it looks like the F-4 Phantoms are a go. We just have to get it through the Senate. I don't think it'll be a problem. We have the votes. We should have it on Nixon's desk for his signature by Christmas."

"Thanks for your help on this."

They all looked out at the dance floor.

"Well, it looks like my Ze'evi has taken a shine to your daughter. She is indeed lovely."

And not a moment too soon! Benny thought.

"Word's gotten around town about all of Ze'evi's philanthropic activities. He's quite a fine young man. There are countless people in Israel who owe him a debt of gratitude," Benny said.

"We tried to raise him with the right priorities. He's done a fine job at the company, and when I retire ETI will be in good hands." Howard was a very proud father indeed.

"Come, let's sit down." Leah motioned to the seating area. "I believe that we're sitting at the same table."

The music died down as the program began and everyone found their seats. The Gilads, Golda Meir, the Ebans, and the Ehrenreichs all were seated at the head table.

Dahlia and Ze'evi left the dance floor, both somewhat out of breath, and found that the only two empty seats at their families' table were next to each other.

"A not so subtle hint," Ze'evi said, laughing.

Dahlia giggled.

The seeming endless string of speeches and testimonials ended with the inevitable presentation by Golda Meir of a citation bearing the Ehrenreichs' names. Golda then gave an inspiring call to arms as the keynote address. There was a long, standing ovation at the conclusion of her speech.

For Dahlia, however, the climax of the evening was going back out onto the dance floor with Ze'evi. His touch was electric and sure. She shivered at it. He oozed confidence and grace. There seemed to be nothing he had not done, no place he had not been, and nothing he had not tried. Is he just boasting? She couldn't tell yet, but she knew that he turned her on. There was something about him that physically attracted her, even as she felt a twinge of guilt, as if she were cheating on Arik.

But I'm not cheating. Am I? Would I be better off, more faithful, if I sat alone in my room and cried? Arik had had ample opportunity to get in touch with her but had chosen not to, for reasons that she could not fathom. She had faithfully written to him. Besides, developing new friendships did not mean that she was being unfaithful. I'm sure that Arik is meeting new people—male and female—where he is. Why shouldn't I? Her heart was still with Arik, though. That she knew for certain, although she felt that if Arik suddenly "returned from the dead" she would demand an explanation and an apology.

When they were back on the dance floor, Ze'evi interrupted her thoughts. "So, what do you do for fun, Dahlia?"

"Let's see . . . I play tennis, I go to Redskins games, I ski, and I love to sail."

"I just think that female football fans wearing jerseys are so cute, such a turn-on."

"Well, I know all the rules, too—in case you were wondering."

"Somehow, I guessed that."

Ze'evi stroked her arm. Dahlia felt a jolt go up it, all the way to her eyes.

"I'll tell you what. I've got a sailing skiff at my family's marina on City Island in New York. I could call and have it brought down here. It'll just take three days along the Intracoastal Waterway. I'll moor it at the Annapolis Yacht Club, and we'll spend the day out on the bay. You'll be my first mate. What do you say?" he asked.

"What kind of boat is it?"

"What do you usually sail?"

"Thirty-foot, single-masted, one jib, one mainsail."

"My boat is considerably larger than that, but it handles very smoothly. You'll love it. How about this coming Sunday? I'll check the weather. November is the perfect time to sail the Chesapeake, if the weather's good. You need to dress warmly, though, with a good windbreaker. I don't want you catching a cold."

"Yes, Daddy!" Dahlia laughed. "I think that it sounds like a great idea. I'll make sure that we don't have anything else planned."

The evening ended too soon for Dahlia's liking. She could not recall when she had enjoyed herself so much. Perhaps it was just a guilty pleasure. Part of her did not want to have a good time tonight, almost to prove to herself that she was unable to have fun without Arik. She wondered if she just talking herself into being miserable. She decided that being miserable would not change the reality of her situation. She would will herself to be happy.

Dahlia gave Ze'evi a slip of paper with her phone number on it. "Don't lose this. The number at the residence is unlisted for security reasons."

"I understand. I'll call you later in the week."

"I had a nice time tonight, Ze'evi."

"Me, too."

***

At 6 a.m. on Sunday, Dahlia was already standing in anticipation outside the front gate of the ambassador's residence when Ze'evi's Jaguar XK-E Roadster pulled up. Wearing white chinos, a striped T-shirt, a navy-blue windbreaker, and Docksider shoes, she felt ready for almost anything. She had brought a large wicker basket of lunch goodies that Thelma had prepared, because there were no kosher eateries along Chesapeake Bay. She also had snatched a bottle of Chianti from the bar when no one was looking.

"Good morning, Little Red Riding Hood! I see you packed lunch. You didn't need to do that. The kitchen on board is fully stocked."

When Ze'evi saw Dahlia's face fall, he added quickly, "But I'm sure what you brought will far exceed what my crew stuffs in there! Come on. Hop in!"

They headed toward Route 50 East to Annapolis. The weather was relatively warm for early November, at 55 degrees, and the rising sun was shining through a cloudless blue sky.

"Today will be a great day to sail," Ze'evi said. "Lots of boats out there on the bay today, I'll bet. My information says the wind is blowing at a steady 25 knots from the west and the wave height is no higher than three feet. Perhaps we'll catch a regatta."

Dahlia was impressed by how knowledgeable he sounded. "So, how long have you been sailing?" she asked.

"Oh, I've been around boats since I was a kid. My dad is a sailor, and we'd sail the Long Island Sound and fish on Sundays when the weather was good. When I was in college, I crewed with Bus Mosbacher on the Intrepid during the 1967 America's Cup race out of Newport. It's a 12-meter class racer built of double-planked mahogany on white oak frames. The rudder's separated from the keel, and a trim tab's been added. Above decks, Intrepid's got a very low boom, made possible by locating the winches below decks. Is any of this making sense to you?"

"Of course, it is! Do you think that I don't know about this stuff because I'm a girl? The low boom causes an end-plate effect, which allows a smaller amount of air to circulate around the boom and makes the lower part of the mainsail more efficient. This gives the boat not only less drag in the wind but adds another 10 percent in terms of speed and maneuverability, and that's why you beat the Aussies' Dame Pattie in that race."

"I'm impressed! Not many women even know what the America's Cup is, not to mention Israeli women."

"There you go stereotyping again." Dahlia smiled. "I'm taking notes!"

"I see that! Okay, fair enough. So, when did you get into sailing?"

"I grew up in Herzliya, on the coast. We have a large marina there, where you can take boats out. My friend's dad used to take us out all the time, and he taught us how to sail. We went out pretty far."

"I guess you can't go out too far in any direction or you end up in Egyptian or Lebanese waters!"

"True enough. And if you do you'd better have America's Cup sailing skills to hightail it out of there. Getting shot at helps you build up speed." Dahlia laughed. "When we moved here three years ago, after the Six-Day War, I wasted no time trying to figure out where to sail. I wasn't going to pass on the opportunity that the Chesapeake provided. Nobody in my family sails, but Tomer's family is from Eilat, so he grew up sailing, too. We've spent many Sundays out here."

They pulled up to the front gate of the Annapolis Yacht Club. Ze'evi pulled out a visitor's pass, and in a moment, they had parked and were on their way out to the slip where Ze'evi's boat was moored.

"No need to carry that. I've got it." Ze'evi grabbed the lunch basket from Dahlia's arms.

"Thanks. And a gentleman, too!"

"Wow! Look at this thing!" Dahlia marveled as she walked up the pier to the sleek, shiny, white fiberglass sailing yacht with teak trim. A forest of radar and telecommunications antennae bristled over the bridge. The name on the transom read BIG BAD WOLF.

"It's a Columbia 57," Ze'evi said. "It was designed by Bill Tripp in the early 1960s. There have only been ten built. It was originally designed as a racing skiff, but over the past two years it's been redesigned as an oceangoing sloop, without compromising the basic hull design. It's got a length of 56.5 feet, a beam of 13 feet, and a draft of 8 feet, and can hold a constant 13 knots over a 10-mile course. It sleeps seven comfortably and has a state-of-the-art galley and eating area."

"Is that what you are?" Dahlia asked.

"What?

"A big bad wolf."

"Most people don't know that Ze'ev means wolf, so they don't associate me with it."

"Do you mind having a Hebrew name? Didn't your parents give you an English one?"

"Why should I mind? Ze'evi suits me just fine. It's better than my given name."

"What's that?"

"Like they called me at my circumcision, Ze'ev Yoseph ben Asher Halevi."

Dahlia laughed. "Now that is a mouthful! You're right. Ze'evi is better. So, are you a wolf in sheep's clothing or vice versa?"

"I'll guess you'll just have to find out." Ze'evi laughed. "By the way, you could have an American name, too."

"How can Dahlia be turned into an American name?"

"Why don't I just call you Dolly?"

"Like the Broadway show?"

"Yeah! Have you seen it? It's won ten Tony Awards. I can get us tickets—"

"I don't have the time to go up to New York during the school week, and my parents would take a dim view of my going up to New York for the weekend unless I was going to visit camp friends. They certainly wouldn't let me go off for the weekend with a guy—"

"I have an idea. How about Veterans Day, the eleventh? Do you have school?"

"I don't think so. . . I can check."

And "Well, if you have off, I'll have a limo pick you up in the morning, I'll fly you up to New York on my family's jet. You'll be there in thirty-five minutes. I'll pick you up from Teterboro Airport in my chopper, and from there it's fifteen minutes into the West Side Heliport. We'll spend the day, you'll leave right after the play, and I'll you'll be safely tucked away in bed back here by midnight. What do you say?"

"You have your own private jet? You can pilot a helicopter? No, seriously!"

"It's a Learjet. Doesn't everyone have one? I'm kidding, of course. But yes, I fly a helicopter."

Dahlia looked at him, wide-eyed. "Okay, Ze'ev Yoseph ben Asher Halevi, give me a tour of your dinghy."

"Yes, ma'am! Welcome aboard!" He saluted her.

Ze'evi gazed admiringly at her figure as she ascended the ladder into the boat.

They climbed below decks, and he showed her the essentials, such as how to use the plumbing and the location of the first-aid kits, life jackets, visual distress signals, and explained the operation of the marine radios. Dahlia marveled at the teak bulkheads, brass fittings, and solid copper furnishings in the fully appointed chef's galley and head.

Ze'evi said, "The dining table has a full-motion dental-chair base, which converts the dinette to a double sleeping area if required. I never know when I'll have company on board for the night. I do love to entertain."

He showed her V-berth bedroom at the bow and the salon in the aft cabin.

After the tour, Ze'evi started the engine while Dahlia released the mooring lines. Ze'evi engaged the throttle and slowly maneuvered the boat out of the slip. They motored quietly out of the channel. When they were clear of the marina, Dahlia expertly operated the winch to hoist the mainsail, and Ze'evi cut the engine. Suddenly, all fell silent except for the wind blowing and filling the sails.

Once out in the bay, Dahlia deployed the jib in a wing-to-wing fashion, turning the boat to race downwind. Ze'evi set the course for a straight shot east toward St. Michaels. Dahlia sat in the cockpit, near the wheel, holding a bottle of St. Pauli Girl beer and letting the fresh, chilly salt-tinged wind blow through her hair.

Ze'evi sat down next to her and asked, "So, what are you thinking about?"

"Not much, really. I'm just glad to be out here. It's been so long since I've been anywhere."

"And why's that?"

"I've been cooped up in my room for weeks."

"May I ask why?"

"I knew that this would eventually come up, so it may as well be now."

"You don't have to reveal anything you don't want to."

"I have a serious boyfriend."

"I hope you're kidding, like me saying I'm married."

"No, I'm not!"

"Then why are you out here with me?"

Dahlia folded her arms across her chest. "Maybe I shouldn't be. I feel like I'm leading you on. I'm really sorry."

"Do you want to talk about it? I'm a good listener."

Dahlia nodded. "Okay, it's a long story. . ." She gave him the general outline of her life for the past sixteen months.

When she was finished, Ze'evi asked, "So, why do you think your parents hate him so much?"

"I'm not completely sure. I think that they feel that he's not good enough for me—not refined enough, or something like that."

"Ah, I see. At least I now understand my role in this soap opera." Ze'evi smiled. "I'm the replacement boyfriend. That explains your sad eyes."

"Please, don't say it like that, Ze'evi. It makes me feel very cheap."

"Sorry. So, why do you think he stopped writing to you?"

"Frankly, I have no idea! He's not dead! My father verified that. All I can think is that he holds against me that he gave up the basketball scholarship and that it just exploded in his head when he saw what he'd gotten himself into with the Army. He was raised to hate Israel, and there I went and threw him into the deep end, all alone, with nowhere to go on a day off even—the ultimate lone soldier. I think that perhaps he feels that I betrayed him and he's punishing me."

"I'm sure he's making friends. He could get himself set up there," Ze'evi said.

"He has trouble making lasting friendships with Jews. Like I said, he was brought up to hate Jews. He's also very shy and a bit of a loner."

"Is that the type of guy you want for yourself? You're extremely outgoing and friendly."

"That's not helpful, Ze'evi."

"I'm being serious, Dahlia. I'm with your parents on this one. This guy is your first boyfriend. It's not uncommon for an idealistic young woman like yourself to get carried away, to simply feel what you want to feel. I'm not trying to talk you out of your feelings. I'm just making an observation, that's all, and I'm trying to be helpful. Look, Dahlia, here's my opinion—for whatever it's worth. You're too young to lock up your heart like this. Even based on what you told me, you both realized you were committing to each other way too early in the game. How were you planning on stringing this along until you were old enough to be serious? From where I sit, this was a long shot at best. I hate to have to say this to you. How do you base a long-term relationship on the first two years consisting only of occasional letters? These things only develop when you really get to know each other, and that requires real human contact for an extended period of time. There's no way you could know this guy. Now you've simply opened yourself up getting hurt. Just my two cents, anyway."

Dahlia locked her gaze on him. "I really do appreciate your advice. You're older and wiser than me. My brain is telling me that, too. If only I could convince my heart, though. I was so sure of this relationship. He's meant so much to me. I'm still in a state of shock that he walked away like that. I never would've expected that he would be capable of that. I was convinced that he felt the same way about me. He gave up a basketball scholarship to UCLA, because I asked him to. I'm still in a state of shock that he walked away from me like that. I never expected that from him. "

"He walked away from a Division I basketball scholarship for you? Holy shit! And now he just broke it off with you without so much as a 'Go to hell?' This dude's a bit unstable, if you ask me."

"He never seemed that way, though."

"Again, you didn't know him well enough. Anyway, if I'm to be the replacement boyfriend, how should I make my approach to you? Should I act cool and detached, friendly and funny, serious, thoughtful and considerate, wise? You pick!"

Dahlia laughed. "All of those things put together, of course."

"I have an idea. Why don't we just get to know each other without any preconceived ideas or artificial expectations and see where this goes? It's much healthier that way. I have no intention of ever making demands on you. I'm really just enjoying your company—"

"And I enjoy your company, too—"

"So, if that's all that comes of us, I'm really okay with that. I have lots of friends, and if you just become one of them, it's all good. Okay? We could be sailing buddies!"

"Great." Dahlia smiled with relief. "I'd like that."

"I brought a beautiful blue-and-white-striped spinnaker—the colors of the Israeli flag—in your honor. Let's put it up. We'll pick up a good deal of speed with that."

The Big Bad Wolf glided easily through the waters of the bay, and within three hours they approached St. Michaels, on the eastern shore at the mouth of the Miles River. They put into the marina, and Dahlia retrieved the sumptuous lunch that Thelma had prepared. They walked over to the Inn at Perry Cabin, a sprawling white historic manor house with magnificent, manicured lawns that meandered down to the water's edge. They found a secluded spot, under a canopy of old cypress trees, with a panoramic view of the bay. The bright sunshine peaked through the trees as Ze'evi spread out a blanket for them. Dahlia laid out lunch, and Ze'evi opened the bottle of Chianti.

"It's such a beautiful day for November," Dahlia said as she looked through the trees.

"It's a good omen." Ze'evi smiled.

She stared at him and smirked. "Sailing buddies!"

"Oh, yeah. I almost forgot."

After they finished eating, they sat in companionable silence. Eventually, Ze'evi asked, "What time do you need to get back?"

"Probably before eight. Why?"

"Oh, nothing. It's just that I booked us both massages at the spa at the hotel. Their facility is world class. It's been visited by the likes of Robert Kennedy, Elizabeth Taylor, and Paul Newman."

"You did not book us massages!" Dahlia feigned annoyance.

"Oh, yes. I did. You don't want me to have wasted my money, do you?"

"I suppose not. But you shouldn't have."

"But I wanted to."

By the time they emerged from the spa, it was past 2:00 p.m., and the sky had turned gray.

"Dolly, I think we'd better get back. The weather has turned."

When they emerged from the boathouse, Ze'evi said, "The wind has picked up to 30 knots, and the wave height is about 5 feet. Are you up for a bumpy ride, or should we drive back over the bridge?"

Dahlia smiled and pumped her fist. "Is there any question? I say we gun this bad boy into the wind and do some real sailing!"

They motored out of the cove and into the salty wind gusts of the bay. Dahlia trimmed the jib and aligned the mainsail as Ze'evi steered from the bridge.

They tacked, at top speed, westward toward Annapolis. As the sky grew darker, the wind picked up, and so did the waves. Initially, Ze'evi was concerned that Dahlia would become frightened when the ride grew rough and unpleasant. But he need not have worried. Dahlia was absolutely in her element, aggressive as hell. Ze'evi had never seen a girl handle the lines of a sailboat as skillfully as Dahlia did, to maximize airflow and lift through the sails and bring the boat about with ease. She whooped and hollered like a banshee every time the boat cut headlong into the 5-foot waves. At sunset, with the wind beginning to die down, they finally pulled into the Annapolis Marina. The clouds parted, revealing a dazzling sunset. The tall spires of the bobbing boats stood out dark against the brilliantly colored western sky.

Dahlia and Ze'evi worked in tandem to break down the sails and stow the gear.

"You told me you sailed, but you never told me you sailed like that!" Ze'evi marveled.

"All of us can be full of surprises," Dahlia said with just a hint of a smile. "I think we're a good team. We really anticipated each other's moves today. You're a pretty good sailor yourself."

On their ride back, they lapsed into another warm, comfortable silence. Ze'evi let Dahlia out at the front gate of the ambassador's residence.

"I had a good time today, Ze'evi. I really needed it."

"I was more than happy to oblige. So, are we still on for Hello, Dolly! on the eleventh?" Ze'evi asked as he gently held her wrist.

"Let me check my schedule, but it should probably work out. Thanks for inviting me." Dahlia made no attempt to pull her arm away from Ze'evi's grasp.

"Good. I'll call you later in the week. And I'll gas up the Learjet."

***

"So, what are you going to be doing today?" Leah asked Dahlia when Dahlia passed through the kitchen on her way out the door.

It was 6:00 a.m. Dahlia had not wanted to wake her parents, so she had said her good-byes the night before.

"What are doing up so early, Imma?"

"I couldn't sleep. I was too excited for you."

"What is there to be excited about? It's not really a date. We're just friends. Ze'evi is very sweet, and we really enjoy each other's company."

"Uh-huh. Well, I'm still excited for you. You've become a completely different person since the Ball. By my estimation, Ze'evi's called every day and you've spent more than an hour on the phone with him each time. How is there so much to talk about? You've just met."

"I don't know, Imma. When we start talking, it just flows by itself. I don't notice the time going by. He's so smart and such a good listener."

"I'm so glad, Dahlia. You see, sometimes it pays to listen to your Abba and Imma. You know that we only want the best for you. Ze'evi is such an impressive young man. Your Abba couldn't be more pleased."

"I'm not seeing Ze'evi to please you both."

"We know that, but still."

"Ze'evi has a full day planned. He has a great sense of fun and adventure, but he's being cryptic about what we're going to do. All I know is that I'm going up to New Jersey on his private jet and then by helicopter into the city. The rest he won't say. He's promised that I'll be back before midnight. Got to go! The limo's outside. "

Leah remained sitting at the table, open-mouthed and then smiling.

To be the only one in the cabin of an aircraft was a new experience for Dahlia. To be the sole reason for an aircraft to take off and land was entirely out of her frame of reference. The cabin contained six oversized seats, all covered in beige leather. There were a small galley, a wet bar, and impossibly large picture windows. Sitting in her seat—but they were all her seats—she suddenly felt like a little girl. What am I doing here? After she strapped herself in, she felt the enormous thrust of the jet, which nearly propelled her out of her seat. Before she could get her bearings, the jet had begun its final approach into Teterboro Airport. At the cabin door, she thanked the pilot. When she reached the top of the staircase, she saw a Robinson R22 two-bladed, single-engine light utility helicopter. She donned her aviator sunglasses and descended the stairs.

A side door to the chopper swung open, and Ze'evi popped out.

"Welcome to New Jersey! What a beautiful day to visit. There isn't a cloud in the sky. That seems to be our MO. How was your flight?"

"Did I just take a flight? One minute, I walked in and admired the interior. The next minute, we landed!"

"These bad boys go pretty fast. Hop aboard. I'm flying us into the city."

Dahlia shook her head and laughed. "What don't you do? I'm getting more and more impressed by the minute."

"I'm glad. Here, put these headphones on."

Ze'evi started up the two rotor engines, expertly operated the T-Bar control, and easily lifted the helicopter into the air. Within ten minutes, they were at the West 30th Street Heliport.

"Ze'evi, this is a whole new way to live, for me. I'm looking down at all the bumper-to-bumper traffic down the West Side Highway, and here we are floating over them as if they weren't there. It would be over an hour into the city if we went by car."

"Actually, going by helicopter isn't just a cool thing to do. It's actually quite cost-effective for me. My time is too valuable to waste in traffic. I make up the difference between this and car travel a thousand-fold in terms of efficiency, so this is a necessity really, not fun." He looked at Dahlia, touched the top of her hand, and smiled. "Except today, of course. Today is a really good day for me, too. We do a tremendous amount of work with the federal government, and today everything's shut down, so this works for me, too. . . Are you hungry?"

"Starved!"

"That's not right. I told them to feed you on the way up. No matter, I've got a great brunch waiting for us."

When they pulled up to Chelsea Piers, they were greeted by the captain and crew of the Spirit of New York, all dressed smartly in their white gold-trimmed uniforms. Behind them, the sleek, sparkling 200-foot white motor yacht lay moored.

"Good morning, Mr. Ehrenreich. Everything is ready for you. Are you ready to board?" the captain asked.

Ze'evi looked at Dahlia. "Dolly, are you ready to board?"

"Where's everyone else? We're the only ones here."

"That's because I bought out the entire cruise for the morning, for our little scoot around Manhattan, so we have the boat to ourselves." Ze'evi grinned like a Cheshire cat.

"Not bad, Ze'ev Yoseph ben Asher Halevi." Dahlia giggled.

They wandered through the art deco below decks, where large picture windows featuring the New York skyline framed the banquet rooms. A crew member took them to the top deck as the boat headed south on the Hudson River along Manhattan's West Side.

The crew member explained that although the top deck usually contained rows of comfortable lounge chairs for passengers to sit in while admiring the city during good weather, they had been removed. Instead, there was a raised platform above the bridge. Ze'evi and Dahlia ascended the staircase, and Dahlia gazed around in wonder. She felt as if she had to pinch herself.

At the center of the platform stood a table and two chairs, all set up for breakfast with white linen, china, crystal, and silverware. A large bouquet of freshly cut red roses stood in the center of the table. Two uniformed waiters stood waiting. Another stood behind an omelet station, already buttering the pan.

Waiting for them on the table were two glasses of freshly squeezed orange juice, a basket of bagels, bialys, sourdough breakfast scones, and piping hot croissants, a platter of smoked fish and cheese, and small tubs of fresh butter, cream cheese, and an assortment of fruit preserves. A small bowl of fresh berries topped each place setting. Freshly ground hot coffee and cream were poured as soon as Dahlia had been assisted to her seat.

"You know, Ze'evi, I have breakfast like this every morning."

"I do, too!" Ze'evi laughed.

"But I think that you're not kidding."

Ze'evi smiled cryptically.

They were handed menus.

Dahlia ordered the wild rice and sweet potato pancake, with a roasted egg and green tomatillo and avocado salsa.

Ze'evi ordered a green salad and a large Spanish omelet.

"I had Prime Caterers prepare this feast downstairs. They're the finest kosher caterers in New York. They're the ones who did the Ambassador's Ball. I took the liberty of koshering the kitchen for you. The Rabbi is downstairs, in case you were wondering."

Dahlia noticed a small vein that bulged on the right side of Ze'evi's forehead when he smiled.

"You're so considerate. You don't miss a detail. In this case, you needn't have bothered. I eat fish out."

"Noted!"

As the boat cruised slowly around the southern tip of Manhattan, two large square towers loomed into view and grew larger by the second.

"They're amazing!" Dahlia said.

"These towers are going to be the tallest buildings in the world, 110 stories in all. They've been planned for more than twenty years even though construction just began recently," Ze'evi explained.

"They look nearly complete."

"That's just the skeleton. It will take several more years before they're done. There are more than 10,000 people working on them. Crazy! It's a whole new design. Instead of the traditional stacked glass-and-steel box construction of many New York skyscrapers, it's two hollow tubes supported by closely spaced steel columns encased in aluminum."

"They look like they're swaying in the wind. I wouldn't want an office on the top floor!" Dahlia said.

"In fact, they can sway up to six feet, with significant wind gusts. They're designed that way so there's no danger that they'll ever topple over. In fact, the physics of the design are such that they could withstand a direct hit by a 707 jet without sustaining much damage. These bad boys are built to last forever."

"Still, I wouldn't want to be sitting on the top floor if a plane hit the building. Just me, I suppose."

Ze'evi laughed. "You're so cute."

"You're not too bad yourself. You know that you're a pretty smart guy."

"I read a lot. I have to. That's the only way to stay competitive in my business. There's always someone out there who wants to eat you. You've always got to be on your guard."

The boat passed Ellis Island.

"Ze'evi, when did your family come to the U.S.?"

"If you're asking me, 'Did my family come through Ellis Island?' the answer is no. Eastern and Central European Jews came over here starting in 1880, because of pogroms, and they all came through here. The Ehrenreichs are an old German Jewish family that came to the U.S. in the 1830s. Back in Europe, they amassed their fortune in the banking business, along with the Rothschilds, immediately after the Emancipation at the turn of that century. In fact, an Ehrenreich fought in the American Civil War."

"Wow! For which side?"

"The North, of course! We freed the slaves. The Ehrenreichs and some other wealthy and established families became a sort of Jewish nobility in New York. It was then up to us to help our poor Eastern European cousins when they landed on our shores. My great-great-grandfather Sigmund was one of the founders of the Hebrew Immigrant Aid Society. In 1852, he was also one of the people who helped build Mount Sinai Hospital in New York. Did you know that Jews had difficulty getting admitted and treated at hospitals in New York and Jewish doctors couldn't practice there either? So, they built Mount Sinai. It was originally called the Jews' Hospital. Can you imagine? In New York?"

"We take a lot for granted," Dahlia said.

The boat continued north up the East River. Ze'evi pointed up.

"That's the Brooklyn Bridge. It was the first suspension bridge of its kind, completed in 1883. The same year of Custer's last stand."

"Custard?"

"No, cuteness. General George Armstrong Custer, U.S. cavalry. He was a tool of the U.S. government and big business interests to screw the Indians out of their land. They tore up all of the Indians' sacred grounds and drove the Indians off their land to build railroads and homesteads for farmers. Well, the Indians were tired of being made idiots of by the whites, who reneged on every treaty they made with them. So, finally, the Indians rebelled. They killed an entire regiment of cavalry led by Custer at a place called Little Big Horn. They all united behind the Sioux Nation and their chief, Sitting Bull, and fought the last of the great Indian wars. They were no match for artillery and Gatling machine guns though. The government herded them onto reservations and occupied their land. "

"That's what everyone is accusing us of doing with the Palestinians," Dahlia said.

"Sort of but not exactly."

Cruising further north, they passed the United Nations Secretariat Building.

Dahlia pointed at the building. "Can we go there? Perhaps we can catch a session? They're always in the process of coming up with another anti-Israel resolution. I think that they're up to 150 by now."

Ze'evi smiled and nodded.

For the next two hours, they rounded Manhattan Island and Ze'evi displayed a nearly encyclopedic knowledge of New York City history, art, and architecture.

"Let me show you where the trinkets are sold," he said.

They took a cab to Fifth Avenue and 57th Street.

"This young lady, is Tiffanys, arguably the world's finest collection of overpriced jewelry in the world."

They wandered through the store's isles, Dahlia intently taking in all of the sparkly items.

"I've never seen diamonds this big. This stuff is incredible! I need sunglasses to walk around in here."

"My parents are habitual customers, so if you need anything just let me know and I'll hook you up." Ze'evi smiled.

"Oh! Very good. I've been meaning to come here to get some odds and ends." Dahlia laughed at her own joke.

Next came FAO Schwartz, with its storybook toy villages that one could walk through: Lego cities, mountains of games, models of every conceivable variety, including military, science fiction, and general fantasy, functional cars and motorcycles shrunk down to children's size, and hundreds of bicycles. There was an entire room devoted to stuffed animals, from ones that you could hold in your hand to towering 20-foot giraffes. There was a gallery of just puzzles. Another room held table after table of Lionel electric trains of every size and gauge, rushing through detailed landscapes and urban settings.

"Here's something for every spoiled brat whose parents have too much money to burn," Ze'evi said.

"Were you one of them?" Dahlia teased.

"Absolutely!"

"I should get something here for Doron," Dahlia said.

"Not here. Everything here is twice the price. There are better places in the City to get toys. If there's time, I'll show you."

Even so, Ze'evi bought Dahlia an original genuine Teddy bear.

"This really isn't necessary, Ze'evi."

"Oh, but it is! You don't need to drag it around, though. I'll have it delivered."

"Thank you. This is very sweet."

Next, they went to Temple Emanu-El, where they silently wandered through the glorious Romanesque cavern that was the main sanctuary, with its frescoed walls and ornate stained-glass windows.

"The synagogue was established in 1845 but moved to this location in the mid-1920s," Ze'evi said.

They made their way up Fifth Avenue and went in to see Henry Clay Frick's private art collection at 70th Street. They wandered through gallery after gallery, seeing the finest collection of Renaissance paintings and Rococo furniture anywhere.

Dahlia was amazed by the breadth of Ze'evi's knowledge of art history.

After they had gorged on the Roy Lichtenstein and Andy Warhol exhibitions at the Guggenheim, Ze'evi asked, "How are your feet holding up? Are you hungry?"

"I'm doing fine. It's a good thing I work out. Otherwise, how would I keep up with you? You're like a machine!" Dahlia smiled.

"No matter, I need to feed you."

They took a cab to the bistro at the Pierre Hotel, for a light lunch. Set in a large indoor atrium, the restaurant featured a dramatic enchanted-forest-like setting. The tables were set in between the twisting, undulating trunks of enormous African Acacia trees. Large picture windows looked out on Central Park South and the long line of horse-drawn carriages that plied their way up Fifth Avenue in the bright November sunshine.

Dahlia had the branzino with fennel and grapefruit salad, and Ze'evi had the pan-seared Chatham cod with grilled endive and king oyster mushrooms.

During the meal, Ze'evi said, "You have a large Hollandaise sauce stain on your cheek."

"Where?"

"I'll get it."

He leaned across the table and, with a napkin, wiped the sauce off slowly and deliberately, a bit slower than Dahlia had expected.

"Must be a big stain!" She giggled.

"Can't be too careful." He smiled.

The waiters brought out crème brûlées, fresh English strawberries dipped in rich Belgian chocolate, and cappuccinos for dessert.

Dahlia licked her lips. "Well, that was lunch! Where to next, boss?"

"Why don't we walk over to the Empire State Building? Have you ever been up to the top?"

Dahlia shook her head.

"You never need to go more than once, but you need to go once."

"Okay. I'm game!"

Ze'evi took Dahlia's hand as he hailed a cab to take them to 34th Street.

On the terrace on the 80th floor of the Empire State Building, Dahlia mutely looked all around. The entire city of New York lay like an aerial photograph, in every direction for tens of miles. She shivered in the cold. Ze'evi took off his jacket and wrapped it around her.

"Thanks!"

He put his arm around her shoulders, and she, in turn, moved in closer without a sound.

"I'm having a wonderful day," she said.

"Kitty cat, there's more to come. Let's go buy some Impressionist art. Seeing all those paintings gave me an appetite."

"That's pretty impulsive!"

"I'm just fooling with you. That was our next stop, anyway, before dinner. Have you ever been to an art auction?"

"No."

"I'm registered at Sotheby's for today's Old Masters auction. They're featuring late-19th-century to mid-20th-century masterpieces. There are a few pieces I'm interested in."

They hailed a cab.

"I'm looking at several Pissarros and Sisleys today. When you're in there, whatever you do, don't raise your hand—even to scratch your neck—or you might be out a hundred thousand dollars. When we're in there, you'll understand why. It's pretty interesting, though. Do you like Chagalls?"

"I love Chagalls."

"Good. There are two very nice ones at auction today. I'll get you one."

"Ze'evi! Don't you dare!"

"Why not? I like you."

"I like you, too, but don't you dare!"

He kissed her cheek lightly. Dahlia felt ashamed, thinking that perhaps she enjoyed it far more than she should.

Sotheby's auction house was an ornate temple of affluence with large marble columns and vaulted ceilings. They were led to a room that looked like something out of Versailles, with large velvet seats. There was no point in sitting uncomfortably while parting with obscene amounts of money. At the front of the room stood a solemn auctioneer at an ornate mahogany lectern and easel, several assistants, and several Brink's security guards. Large spotlights illuminated each piece of artwork as it was skillfully brought in and taken out by the staff.

Dahlia sat with her arms fixed at her sides, fascinated by how much money was changing hands so casually. Ze'evi, for his part, had bid on more than a dozen paintings, but so far, he had ended up with only Pissarro's The Hermitage at Pontoise for a mere eighty-five thousand dollars—a bargain!

When Chagall's I and the Village went up on the auction block, Ze'evi raised his arm to bid.

"Oh, no, you don't!" she whispered.

She wrapped both of her arms around him tightly to prevent him from bidding. God, he smells nice! she thought.

Soon, the lot was sold to a Saudi prince wearing sunglasses and sitting on the other side of the room.

Ze'evi turned to Dahlia. "That was very nice. There's another Chagall coming up soon. I think I'll have to put in a bid on that one, too—"

"I'll have to restrain you again, then!" she smiled.

"It's a chance I'll have to take," he teased.

He leaned over and planted a gentle kiss on her nose. She smiled.

When the auction had ended, he said, "I'll have the picture shipped."

"But you only live a few blocks away."

"True, but if we go home my parents are going to engage us in conversation, and we won't have time for our last stop before the theater. They really are fond of you, you know."

"But they don't even know me."

"They met you at the ball. And they've done their homework, just like your parents have, and they like you already. But you'll get to know them better soon enough. How about joining us for Thanksgiving? We take it very seriously."

"It's a little early for that. Don't you think?"

"What's going to happen? We'd be staying at my parents' house, with my whole family. You'll get to meet my two brothers and my sister. We have plenty of room."

"I can well imagine. Let me talk to my parents about it. I have a suspicion, though, that they'll have no problem approving the plan."

"Then it's done. Have you ever had Chinese food?" he asked.

"Where can you get kosher Chinese food? Chinese food doesn't even have a pretense of kosher. Everything is pork this and shrimp that."

"There's a famous restaurant on the Lower East Side, on Essex Street, that's been around for decades, called Schmulka Bernstein's. It's a deli, but it also has a pretty good Chinese menu. The waiters all look like Hop Sing from Bonanza. It's a riot."

After another cab ride, this one down FDR drive, they found themselves in the middle of the old Jewish section, with its ramshackle tenements. They entered the restaurant below a forest of hanging dried salamis and walked to the back, which was ornate with the red and black glossy decor typical of Chinatown.

"I won't bore you with a history of the Jewish settlement of the Lower East Side," Ze'evi said.

"I could listen to you for hours, but my head is about to explode from all of the information that you've given me so far!"

"So, only one last piece of advice for today. Try the hot and sour soup and the sesame chicken. We'll share the steamed beef dumplings and fried rice."

"You could tell me anything and I'd buy it, at this point, including the Brooklyn Bridge. I'm so far out of my frame of reference today. But it's been a wonderful 'far out.'"

"Good, I'm glad!"

After dinner, Ze'evi announced, "One last ride, and we're on Broadway, but we've got to hurry!"

When they walked through the entrance and into the foyer of the glittering St. James Theatre, with its ornate late-19th-century décor, Dahlia felt like Alice in Wonderland. They were shown to their center orchestra seats, which were only ten rows away from the stage. She sat spellbound and overwhelmed, watching Hello, Dolly! performed by Carol Channing and the rest of the original cast. Dahlia had never seen theater like this before, on such a grand scale with a live orchestra. She held Ze'evi's hand the whole time.

When they left the St. James Theatre, they were met by a Lincoln Town Car limousine driven by a chauffeur.

"No more cabs now," Ze'evi said. "We've got to hurry to get Cinderella home before midnight, or her carriage will turn into a pumpkin."

Retracing their steps from that morning, they made their way back to the heliport and Ze'evi flew her to the airport where the Learjet was waiting for her.

At the foot of the jet's staircase, Dahlia saw that the pilot was standing in the doorway, holding her Teddy bear in his arms. She gasped, leaped into Ze'evi's arms, and kissed him for a long while.

"I had such a wonderful day today! It was such a whirlwind!" she gushed.

He smiled. "And so, it begins. Have a safe trip back, and I'll call you tomorrow at the usual time. Let's figure out something for next weekend. Find out what's showing at the National Theatre, and I'll fly down for the day."

"I'm sorry, but I can't leave until I get another kiss." She smiled with a seriousness in her eyes.

"Happy to oblige, but then you have to scram or you'll get home too late!"

They kissed again.

Ze'evi took a long appraising look at her and then said, "Is it my imagination, or are those eyes of yours no longer sad?"

Dahlia smiled. "Thanks for today," she said.

When Dahlia bounced into the ambassador's residence at 12:15 a.m., Teddy bear in hand, both Benny and Leah were sitting in the kitchen, waiting for her in nervous anticipation.

"Well?" they asked in unison.

***

December 3, 1970

My Dearest Dahlia,

Why aren't you writing to me? I can't believe you would hold on to your anger for so long. After all we've been through and the commitments we've made to each other. A big part of that is learning how to forgive. That's what marriage should be all about. It's not always hunky dory every day, but we decided that day with Suzie Chapstick that we'd never go to bed angry with each other. That means learning how to forgive. Please, let this anger go and just WRITE!

I'll make this up to you in spades, I swear! I've already decided one thing, though. I'll keep writing to you every week no matter what. That is, until I get word from you that you don't want to hear from me ever again. I hope you at least read these letters and don't tear them up as soon as you get them.

Just the act of writing to you gives me comfort. I can still feel connected to you, even if just in my mind.

The rainy season has started in earnest. I know that Israel depends on rain for its water, but this rain is something I've never seen before. It comes down in buckets. The rain in California is nothing compared to this.

We've been out in the field for two weeks now, alternating between marching and doing trench and foxhole warfare. It's been raining continuously for three days and nights now and everything has turned into a river of mud. My pants and boots are unrecognizable and sometimes I even like getting soaked to the skin because it washes off some of the mud. When we practice trench warfare, we have to crawl in water up to our knees. The nights are the worst—especially when I have guard duty. We're up in the hills, so the temperature drops to near freezing at midnight. The clothes they've given us aren't nearly warm enough. What makes matters worse is that they're wet all the time. My fingers are so stiff that I can't oil my gun properly. I'm really scared that my gun will rust and jam during the live fire exercises.

A lot of the guys are wheezing and coughing. I think that by the time we get back to base half of them will end up in the infirmary. I hope they won't get weeded out for that. The guys that are left are really good guys. I'm afraid I'm going to catch pneumonia. I feel like an old lady. My joints are so stiff! In fact, my whole body aches.

The other problem with training in the mud is that people are slipping and falling. We've had a few broken arms and legs from people sliding off slippery rocks. Worse yet, last night we had a forced stretcher march. I'm sure you know what that is, but this one was really bad—a 20 km march in the dark in the pouring rain carrying the fattest guy in the unit on a stretcher over our heads. It went on until 6 a.m. It didn't really didn't bother me that much, so I tried to be Mr. Nice Guy and stood in the middle, practically carrying the stretcher myself on my shoulders. When the sergeant saw that my guys didn't seem fatigued at all, he figured it out. Then he made them carry me—WITH my backpack that weighs 50 pounds—for an additional 10 km. We got back just in time to start the next day of field exercises, running our asses off as if we had actually slept the night before.

All I succeeded in doing was getting everyone pissed off at me. Why do I bother? I keep trying to do the right thing and these guys always figure out how to turn it into something bad. Sometimes the guys think I'm showing off. Why would I want to do that? Have you ever known me to be that kind of guy? I'm just trying to fit in and do the right thing. I still feel like the commanders have it in for me. The sergeants cook up some imaginary offense of mine and force me to put my cot out in the pouring rain and sleep there. One night they made me climb up a rocky hill near the camp on my elbows and knees in the rain. By the time I got to the top, my arms and legs were covered with blood. The skin had just shredded off.

I think they're trying to break me, but I don't know why. They have me pulling twice as much guard duty than everybody else. But I won't give in. I won't!

Some days are better than others. But it's always bad, because I miss you so much.

Yours for always,
Arik

At that time, the Knicks and the Lakers had the most famous rivalry in basketball. They had faced each other in the 1970 NBA finals the previous spring, with the Lakers losing the series in a heartbreaker in the last two minutes of game seven. This year's matchups would be intense and fast-paced.

Madison Square Garden, at 34th Street and 8th Avenue in New York City, was filled to capacity. Seats were impossible to come by, except from scalpers who sold tickets at five times face value after carefully scanning for police presence. The spectators were screaming for Laker blood even as they streamed to their seats and anxiously awaited the start of play. It was the evening before Thanksgiving, and everyone knew that Wilt Chamberlain would be hobbled somewhat by knee trouble. Knicks fans were confident that their team was going to beat up on the Lakers.

Ze'evi and Dahlia left his Maserati at the front entrance of the arena, in the hands of their personal valet who was there waiting for them. They walked hand in hand to the VIP section of the arena, pushing their way through the mob of people who was trying to get to the cheaper seats.

"We won't have to deal with the unwashed masses where we're sitting. My family has courtside seats, right behind the visiting team's bench, for the entire season. This is the hottest ticket in town."

He kissed Dahlia on the cheek. She smiled.

Dahlia had never sat courtside at an NBA game. The evening had been perfect up to this point. Ze'evi had seen to that. They had begun at Lou G. Seigel's, the most exclusive, expensive kosher restaurant in New York, feasting on goose liver pate, rack of lamb with mint sauce, and French champagne. After the game, it would be Rumpelmayer's for dessert and then Rockefeller Center for ice skating and a sneak peak of the new Christmas tree.

Ze'evi was so considerate. He had seen to every detail, from sending the Learjet to pick her up in Washington, D.C. to arranging for them to have front-row seats on the dais at the Macy's Thanksgiving Day parade. And he had told her that the following day she would treated to a shopping spree at Saks Fifth Avenue.

Dahlia shivered with delight. Ze'evi called it her happy spasm. She was having one now. He was so good at giving those to her. Since the last time she had visited him in New York, she had spoken to Ze'evi every night and had gone out with him every weekend. She admired his sense of fun, adventure, and humor. He always found new, interesting places for them to go together. She did what she could to block Arik out of her mind, to block out the pain. She had resolved to maintain her sanity by living in the here and now. She had decided that this was Ze'evi's time.

Thanksgiving was not celebrated at the Israeli embassy or the ambassador's residence, despite the festivities being held all around them in Washington, D.C. Because the Mayflower had not landed on the shores of Ottoman Palestine, there was nothing for Israelis to celebrate. Dahlia was excited to be in New York, instead, at the beginning of the Christmas season. The department stores, decked out in their new bright red, green, and gold attire, were teeming with shoppers and people buying "chestnuts roasting on an open fire" from street vendors.

She hugged Ze'evi tight, kissed him, and whispered into his ear, "Thank you for everything!"

"You're most welcome, kitty cat." He kissed her lightly.

The players from both teams went out on the floor to warm up, taking layups and jump shots.

It struck Dahlia suddenly. She asked, "Ze'evi, who are the Knicks playing tonight?"

"The Lakers. This is the first rematch of last year's championship games. The Lakers are scrapping for revenge. Should be a good one. Wait 'til you see Chamberlain and Baylor come onto the floor. Then you'll get a sense of how big these guys really are! If you want, I can make a call and get us locker room press passes for after the game so we can meet these guys in person. I think you'd enjoy that, kitten."

Dahlia looked out at the court, with a sick feeling in the pit of her stomach. Why did it have to be the goddamn Lakers, of all the teams in the NBA? She shook her head involuntarily.

"Everything okay?" Ze'evi asked.

"Oh, sure," Dahlia said.

The game was a furious interchange, a seesaw, between NBA superstars. Willis Reed scored 38 points for the Knicks. For the Lakers, Chamberlain scored 30 points, and Baylor scored 25 points before fouling out. With fifteen seconds left, Jerry West hit a 20-footer to tie the game. On the next play, Dave DeBusschere was fouled and sank two shots from the free throw line to put the Knicks up by two points. Chamberlain, frustrated, grabbed the rebound from the second free throw and threw it the length of the court to West, who threw up a midcourt shot that went in at the buzzer, sending the game into overtime. Unfortunately for the Lakers, they could not capitalize. They lost by three points, to the Knicks fans' deafening shouts that rocked the arena.

When Chamberlain walked back to the bench to retrieve his gear, he looked up, and recognition dawned on his face. "Hey, Dahlia, so good to see you! How've you been? It's been a while. Came all the way up from Washington just to see us lose?" He wiped his sweaty face with his towel.

Ze'evi was astonished. Under his breath, he said, "Dahlia, how in the world do you know Wilt Chamberlain? There's certainly more to you than meets the eye."

Ze'evi extended his hand to Wilt to introduce himself. "Hi! I'm Ze—"

Wilt momentarily glanced down at Ze'evi and gave him a "Who the fuck are you?" look and then turned back to Dahlia. "What do you hear from Arik? How's the army treating him? Last, I heard, he was having a brutal time. But he's a big boy. I'm sure he's giving them better than he's getting."

He turned around and motioned Baylor to come over. "Hey, Elgin! Look who's here—Arik's girlfriend!"

A small crowd of Lakers players formed around them.

Dahlia paled.

"Hey, Dahlia! How in the world are you! So, good to see you!" Elgin said with a broad smile.

"I was just asking her how Arik's doing," Wilt said.

"Oh! I just got a letter from him two weeks ago. He's doing great, busting his ass but loving life. He misses playing ball, though!" Elgin looked at Dahlia. "So, what he telling you, Dahlia? I hope he's not putting on a brave face just for us."

Dahlia was struggling to maintain her composure. Her heart raced as the harpoon pierced it. My father is right! Arik is alive and doing well.

"I-I haven't heard much from him lately, but I'm sure he's doing fine," she said.

"Well, hey, Dahlia, so good to see you. I'll write Arik and tell him we met. Take care!" Elgin waved as he and Wilt walked away to the locker room.

Dahlia felt her heart screaming out of her chest as a wave of nausea washed over her. As she and Ze'evi made their way into the corridor, she felt faint. That piece of shit is writing to the Lakers but not to me? Why? She just couldn't understand it. Why?

"Hey, Dolly! Are you okay?" Ze'evi asked. "That Chamberlain is such a jerk. Who the hell does he think he is, anyway! He has no right to make you feel so bad."

"He's Wilt Chamberlain, that's who! Arik was very close with him and Elgin Baylor. I'm fine, Ze'evi. I just need to use the ladies' room. I'll be all right."

Dahlia ran into the ladies' room. She barely made it into a stall, kneeled down, and put her head above the toilet before she vomited all of the goose pate and mint lamb.

***

Arik was beyond exhaustion. But he did not mind the tiredness that had seeped into his very joints. It was the terrible sense of foreboding that something was amiss with Dahlia that he could not endure. Is she sick? Incapacitated? Still furious at me for not coming to see her or getting in touch? Has she finally caved to her parents' insistence that she break it off with me?

He was sure that she at least would have written to him about that. This simply was not like her. He found it more and more difficult just to get through the day. His nights were filled with the cramping abdominal pain of longing, frustration, and possible rejection. How can this happen after everything I've given up?

He'd been up all night on guard duty for the second night in a row. That morning of Shabbat, an off day, he walked miserably back to his tent after a meager breakfast of stale rye bread, margarine, olives, and feta cheese. He knew that he needed to get some sleep or he would fall on his face. As he approached the tent area, he heard the familiar bounce-bounce-bounce of a basketball. Usually the courts were empty, but today a lively four-on-four full-court game was in progress.

Arik was amused by the Israeli basketball courts. On the one hand, they made sense, because the backboards were hung from long, recessed frames rather than a simple pole, so there was less chance of a player colliding with a pole. But they made less sense, because the playing surface was a mosaic of flat paving stones.

He sat down for a moment on a mound of dirt and watched the game.

"Hey, Americanos! Ata mesacheck kadur sal?" (Do you play basketball?)

Whenever Arik thought of basketball, he had become so traumatized by the possibility that he may have made the wrong decision by turning down UCLA that he couldn't even touch a ball let alone play. And what would be the point? There was no going back.

"No, I don't play basketball. Sorry."

"I thought all Americans played basketball?"

"This one doesn't."

One of the players—Shlomi, from Arik's unit—trotted up to the foul line and let loose an underhanded, two-handed free throw that sailed into the rim.

He looked up at Arik. "Look at me! I'm just like Vilk Chamberlon!"

"Absolutely!" Arik called back, chuckling. Hardly, he thought.

Arik got up, dusted off his pants, turned his back on the game, and headed for his tent. He did not want to interact with anyone. All he wanted to do was sleep and dream about Dahlia. God, I miss her!

***

"Where are we going tonight? You're always so mysterious. Can't you even give me a hint?" Dahlia smiled and kissed Ze'evi on the nose. "All you told me was to dress for Cinderella's ball, Prince Charming."

"Have I ever taken you anywhere where we didn't have fun? Well?"

"No, I guess not. Not even a teeny-weeny hint?"

"Nope, it's your birthday surprise." He handed her a small black box.

She opened it and then held her breath as he put a diamond-studded tennis bracelet on her wrist.

"Happy birthday, sweetheart." He kissed her on the forehead.

The black stretch Lincoln Continental plowed westward from the Ehrenreichs' penthouse at Park Avenue and 69th Street. They were sitting in the back of the cavernous leather interior, Dahlia snuggled up against Ze'evi, her head nestled against his chest while she admired her wrist.

"Have you ever read Erich Segal's book Love Story?" Ze'evi asked.

"I meant to, but I never got around to it. I was too busy screwing up my life with my own failed love story," Dahlia said flatly. "I know that it's been on the New York Times bestseller list for more than a year."

"Well, you'll never have to read it now, because tonight is the New York premiere of the film, starring Ryan O'Neal and Ali MacGraw, at the Loew's Theater on Broadway. They're both going to be there, along with Andy Williams, who sang the movie's theme song, and most of the cast. Word has it the film will be a blockbuster. Most of the executives from Paramount are going to be there, too. We've got business dealings with the studio."

Despite the biting-cold mid-December night, the crowd in front of the cinema spilled out into the wide street in front of the Loew's Theater, illuminated by powerful spotlights that bathed the entrance. Other more powerful spotlights on trucks moved skyward in circular arcs, casting long beams that reached for the heavens. The limo let off the pair on Broadway, and they made their way to the front of the red carpet.

One by one, black limousines stopped at the curb to let out the movie stars and Hollywood executives. Photographers and journalists were everywhere. Richard Meryman from Life magazine sidled over and engaged Ze'evi in polite conversation. Dahlia stood in amazement as an entourage of stars stopped, on their way up the red carpet, to shake Ze'evi's hand and receive his congratulations on their triumph.

"You're unbelievable, Ze'evi. Just when I think I've seen everything with you, you do something else amazing. Who don't you know?" Dahlia said.

"You'll get a chance to meet them, too. We're going to the reception after the film."

After a brief introduction by the director, the lights dimmed and the curtains parted for the opening credits and narration: "What can you say about a twenty-five-year-old girl who died? That she was beautiful and brilliant? That she loved Mozart and Bach, the Beatles, and me?"

In the film, Oliver, an upper-class, blue-blooded, Waspy Harvard jock who is heir to his family's fortune, meets Jenny, a classical music major at Radcliffe who hails from an Italian working-class family. They fall in love quickly, and Oliver proposes marriage. When he takes her to meet his old guard parents, they shun her because of her poor background. Oliver's father warns him that he will cut him off financially, leaving him without a penny, if he marries her. The couple does marry, and Oliver is cut off from the family's fortune. The couple struggle to make ends meet, including paying Oliver's way through Harvard Law School. Jenny gives up her dream of music and becomes a teacher at a private school. No sooner does Oliver graduate and get a job at a prestigious New York law firm but they learn that Jenny has a terminal illness. Mounting expenses force Oliver to crawl back to his father for financial assistance. Jenny dies in Oliver's arms. Oliver reconciles with his father.

As the film's plot unfolded, Dahlia sat transfixed, her heart racing, bile rising into her throat as it tightened, rendering her short of breath. The similarities between art and life were converging too closely for her. She felt an all too familiar migraine creep slowly toward the top of her head. Her eyes glassed over involuntarily.

She and Arik had come from vastly different classes and backgrounds, and her parents had disapproved of him for those same reasons. Like Oliver, she had stood up to her parents, defying their ire. But that was where the similarity ended. Jenny did not leave Oliver until she died in his arms. Oliver stuck by Jenny through thick and thin.

She had been completely devoted to Arik, but he had chosen to turn his back on her in the most coarse, cruel way, to simply disappear without a trace or even so much as a good-bye. What did I do to him? Arik had made his choices about his future, without coercion from her. What could have caused his rage? What could have caused him to so completely humiliate and crush me? The only explanation that she had been able to come up with was that there was another woman. She had decided that Arik must have met someone in the army, someone who had stolen his heart right out from under Dahlia. She fantasized about this other woman in Arik's embrace.

As Dahlia stared at the screen, she balled up her fists in tearful rage and sobbed.

Ze'evi turned to her and offered her a tissue as the lights went on and she sat red faced, covered in tears, and gasping for air.

"Dahlia, sweetheart, are you okay? If I'd known the film would hit you so hard, I wouldn't have brought you. Although I have to admit, that's the saddest ending I've ever seen in a film. Look around. Every woman in the theater is crying. Do you feel well enough to go to the reception?"

She stared at him with an intensity he had never seen before. She clutched his forearm tightly.

"I don't want to go to the reception, Ze'evi. I want you, Ze'evi."

"Are you sure, Dahlia? I don't want to do anything you don't feel comfortable doing."

"Shut up, Ze'evi. I'm eighteen tonight, and I've made my decision. I want you. I want you tonight. Make love to me, Ze'evi. Make love to me all night long."

"Stay here, sweetheart. I'll make a phone call."

When he returned, he said, "I've gotten us the Tower Suite at the Waldorf Astoria. It's magnificent: a 2,500-square-foot penthouse on the top floor of the hotel. It's got a stupendous view of the whole city. It's fit for a princess like you."

The elevator at the Waldorf ascended to the top floor after Ze'evi had inserted a special key into the control panel. When the elevator door opened, they were in the foyer of the suite. Dahlia entered without uttering a sound. She stood gazing at the magnificent gold-trimmed parlor. The wood-burning fireplace emitted a beautiful, warm glow. The suite looked to her like the East Room of the White House.

"It's stunning, Ze'evi."

"Fit for a queen. You'll get used to this."

"I hope so."

He took her in his arms, and she slid her arms around him and kissed him.

"Thank you for making me believe in myself again." She trembled at the thrill of his touch.

He suddenly broke away from her and held her at arm's length.

"Dahlia, sweetheart. I want you very much, but you must make this decision. I don't want you to feel like I've seduced you."

"You haven't. I've made up my mind." She reached up and stroked his face with her fingertips. "I love you, Ze'evi."

"It's a bit early in our relationship for you to say that. Are you sure of this?"

"I'm as sure as I'll ever be about anything. I'm eighteen now, and I've made up my mind. I want you. Make me yours. Love me, Ze'evi! Love me!"

He smiled, took off his dinner jacket, and looked at her, curiously trying to take her measure. He hugged her tightly and kissed her neck.

"Then let's go to bed!" he said.

She walked into the richly appointed Romanesque bathroom. As she slipped behind the double doors, she said, "I'll be out in a moment."

As she undressed, it occurred to her that this would be her transition from adolescence. She realized that her relationship with Arik had been nothing more than a summer camp romance—despite how intense it had seemed to her. She clearly had not known enough about him. All the romantic talk they had shared had been nothing more than talk. They had spoken of marriage because they had both been so naive. Will, I have to go through several relationships before finding an adult romance that will lead to a lifelong partnership? Is Ze'evi the one? She couldn't tell yet, but she was sure of one thing: Ze'evi already had given so much more than Arik ever could and had opened up a whole new world for her. With Arik, she could never grow like that. Arik could not even keep his word.

Perhaps her parents were right. They simply had lived more and understood how the world worked. She trembled with expectation at the thought about what was about to happen. Ze'evi was so expert and experienced at everything. She decided that he would be a fantastic lover, that he would give her pleasure that she had never experienced. She vowed that she would flow through tonight one moment at a time, savoring every second. In this bathroom, she stood in her French lace underwear and looked at herself in the mirror. She decided that she was ready.

"Hey there! It's awfully lonesome out here!" Ze'evi called through the door.

"I'll be out in a second, sweetheart."

Dahlia reached into her bag and put some perfume on the back of her neck.

She walked out. Ze'evi lay in the bed, with a sheet up to his waist.

"Hey there. You're so beautiful! Come here."

Dahlia groped for the light switch.

"Leave it on, Dahlia. I want to look at you every moment. I want to see you in ecstasy."

"Oh, Ze'evi," she whispered.

"Happy birthday, Dahlia."

He drew her down to him.

***

December 15, 1970

Dear Dahlia,

How are you doing, my love? It's like a blackout curtain has descended over us. I can't stand us being apart on your birthday. I can't comprehend why I'm not hearing from you. Are you even getting my letters? I called your father's office at the embassy again and got connected to Tzippy. She said she couldn't give me your new home number, but she promised to get word to you. I wait for a letter from you every day. I find myself reaching out to you in the dark of night when nothing else is visible.

It looks like the worst is behind me. They moved us to a different sector of the base where we're learning the basics of parachuting. The food has improved and for the most part we're able to get at least six hours of sleep at a time. We occasionally have night exercises, but for the most part they leave us alone. During the day, they make us jump on ropes hanging from high towers to simulate jumping out of a plane. It's this giant scary contraption everybody calls Eichmann. They make us practice again and again until the whole thing becomes second nature. We'll probably have our first real jump next week. Some of the guys complain about the repetition, but I don't want to find out the hard way that I folded my parachute wrong. We'll have to learn how to jump with all of our battle gear and eventually have to do it at night. We're grilled in every little detail so that nothing is left to chance—from the moment you get on the plane until you gather up your parachute on the ground. We learn how to sit, how to stand, how to jump and even how to count backward from 30.

I've gotten some math and electronics textbooks and I'm trying to work on solving problems and understanding the equations. It keeps my mind sharp and keeps me from going insane. You won't believe what some of the other guys do around here to pass the time! They read cheap western novels, play cards or just look at girlie magazines. The religious guys brought Talmuds and Bibles with them and they study in pairs. I try to join them whenever I can—It's like studying with Eliezer again. I find them to be the nicest guys of the bunch or at least the most serious.

If the weather clears up, we'll start jumping out of airplanes for real. Wish me luck.

Can you believe it's been a year since Aspen? Where has the time gone?

I bought you a present for your birthday. I know it's not much. On $35 a month there's only so much I can afford, but I spent my whole day off in Tel Aviv looking for something to get you that would be meaningful. I found just the thing. I hope you like it. I won't send it by mail, because I don't know if you'll get it. I'll hold it for you in safekeeping until I see your angelic face.

Love you and miss you like crazy.

Happy birthday, my sweet girl. We'll be together for your next birthday. I live for that day.

Arik

***

"Ze'evi, I'm so excited that you're coming to dinner. I'm a bit nervous, too, though, I have to admit!" Dahlia said.

"What's there to be nervous about? It's not as if I don't know your parents. I've functioned as a go-between for your father and government officials here. My father has spent tens of millions of dollars funding the campaigns of many of the sitting members of Congress. And money buys access. Never forget that, Dahlia! Money buys access . . . and good behavior. Do you actually think that suddenly the House Appropriations Committee, out of the goodness of their hearts or sudden pangs of conscience, decided to send E-2C Hawkeye spy planes to Israel, just because Abba Eban showed up and gave them a nice speech on the floor of the House?"

"I thought that was how it worked."

"No, sweetheart. They sent the planes because my father and several others made some phone calls up to Capitol Hill to remind some of these clowns that their reelections were less than a year away. Most congressmen spend the lion's share of their terms angling for the next election. That's the problem with two-year terms. They don't give a crap about leadership or legislating. All they care about is money, and since my dad and his buddies have lots of it they all suck up to us and do whatever we ask of them."

"That's so sad. How is the country supposed to run?"

"It runs the way it has always run. Lobbying is all about taking care of the people who take care of you. It was like that in ancient Rome, too. That's just the way it is."

They pulled into the driveway of the ambassador's residence and were met by the security crew. Ze'evi pushed a button on his car's console and both of its side doors opened by flying upward.

Tomer and Yoram slowly walked out of the guard booth. They greeted Dahlia and inspected the white Lamborghini Miura P400-S and its owner.

"This is Ze'evi," Dahlia said quietly.

She knew how suspicious the security guards were about the whole affair. They, too, were stymied about Arik's disappearance, but they were professionally forbidden to go on a scavenger hunt of their own. They were not allowed to get involved in the private affairs of the dignitaries that they were supposed to be guarding. Tomer, for his part, had already made up his mind about Dahlia's new "boyfriend," though.

"It's very nice that the embassy provides you with valet service, Dahlia." Ze'evi laughed. He threw his car keys at Yoram, who caught them in midair. "Be a good chap and park the car, but please go easy on the accelerator. This car is custom-made and cost more than a hundred thousand dollars. I can't have you scuffing the bumpers."

Yoram gave Ze'evi a hard look, dropped his cigarette on the ground, and trod on it, twisting his shoe on the ground.

Dahlia gulped and smiled sheepishly at Yoram and Tomer.

Ze'evi already was on his way to the front door.

"Sorry!" she managed to whisper to the guards before scurrying after Ze'evi.

Yoram, fuming, tossed the keys in the air, from one hand to the other, quietly jumped into the driver's seat, and screeched the car into the garage around the back of the residence.

"Ze'evi, Yoram and Tomer aren't valets. They're our security detail. You can't treat them like servants," Dahlia said when she caught up with him.

Ze'evi looked at her. "Those clowns are security guards? I wouldn't feel safe here if I were you. Sitting around the guardhouse, smoking cigarettes and reading the funny pages? They look like Tel Aviv falafel salesmen. You've been to our house. You've seen what a security detail is supposed to look like. All we employ are ex-Marines who've served at least three tours in Vietnam. Those are tough guys. These guys are valets. Trust me."

Dahlia said nothing in reply.

"Ah, Ze'evi! Welcome our home," Leah said. "I hope that you two had a good time today."

"It's good to see you again, Leah," Ze'evi said, smiling. "You look as beautiful as ever. We had a great time today. Didn't we, Dahlia?"

Dahlia nodded and smiled.

"I got us a private tour of the Capitol, and we sat in on a session of Congress, then lunch at the Old Ebbitt Grill. After that, we got a private tour of the FBI building, through my dad's contacts. Then off to the Corcoran Gallery. Quite a full day!"

Benny entered the hallway, smiling broadly and arms outstretched. "Ah! Ze'evi, how are you? Good to see you, young man! How is your father?"

"Good to see you, Benny. Dad's doing great. He just got back from Japan. There's a new electronics company over there, called Sony, that's trying to get a foothold here in the U.S. They mostly make color TVs and radios, but they're having a bit of trouble competing with our giant companies Zenith, Magnavox, and RCA. They're also working on some home videotape player . . . beta something. I frankly don't see Americans wanting cheaply made Japanese imports when domestic companies are making such fine-quality products. Speaking of which, I need to talk to you about our joint venture with Tadiran Electronics."

"Oh, very well. Why don't we do that before dinner? Come into the library. Is that okay, Leah?"

"Sure, but don't take too long. I don't want dinner to get cold."

"We'll only be a little while," Benny said.

"Dahlia, be a good girl, run along and help your mom. Your father and I have some business to discuss." Ze'evi patted Dahlia on the shoulder.

The two men walked off down the hall toward the library.

Ze'evi said, "Benny, I want to go over the terms of the contracts that are at issue. We're going to need some help getting through your Byzantine government's regulatory bureaucracy. They're driving us crazy. I need you to pull some strings. This deal is potentially worth tens of millions of . . ."

***

Benny had decided that dinner would be a formal occasion despite it taking place on a weeknight when nothing in particular was going on. The staff at the residence had gone into dignitary mode to gear up for the important dinner guest. French cuisine topped off with a standing rib roast in wine sauce, cooked to perfection by Thelma, was the order of the day. Through years of public service, Leah had learned to be a masterful household coordinator.

The Israeli government was in the development phase of a new generation of surveillance satellites, and it needed Ehrenreich Technologies International's help to complete the project. Benny was very adept at making nice with those who needed stroking. Perhaps that was the reason that he was chosen as ambassador. He had a gift.

Benny never took joint business ventures for granted, even those entered into with the "donor class" of American Jewry. Although generous with their funds for Israel, many of them had a patronizing attitude toward Israel and Israelis, as if they were kindly parents indulging a child. Sitting at the table with the grown-ups to enter into joint business ventures was a different matter. American Jews, for the most part, saw in Israel as a place for them to bestow their charity but not a place to do business. The Americans' main goal when financing things seemed to be to get plaques with their names on them, on everything from buildings to park benches to ambulances. Israel was awash with plaques.

The fact that Dahlia was seriously dating this donor was so much the better. If anything came of it, Dahlia would have the life of ease and luxury that she seemed to have been born to have. And if the couple's families grew closer as a result, which they had already, so much the better for Israel as well. It was really a win-win situation. All in all, Benny was rather pleased with himself. He saw the relationship as akin to those political marriages that the nation states of old engaged in to keep themselves from killing one another.

As they enjoyed the foie gras and wild mushroom stuffed ravioli, Benny said, "So, Ze'evi, how is the construction of the cancer center coming?"

Ze'evi laughed and shook his head. "The bane of my existence. My family realizes the incredible importance of having a world-class cancer center in Jerusalem, but the cost overruns in terms of money and aggravation for us have been staggering. Over the years, we've been involved in many construction projects all over the world, and dealing with contractors is difficult at best. But dealing with Israeli building contractors is angst brought to a whole new level."

"In what way?" Benny asked.

"Lots of ways. I could write a book. Here in the States, once you close on a project you lock in the price to within a few percentage points, allowing for change requests. In Israel, when you close, all that means is the buyer is committed to the builder but not necessarily vice versa, plus they can change the price at any time, something about an index. All it is, is a license to steal. We order supplies, say, something simple like floor tiles. Everything is measured, and we order about ten percent more to allow for damage and breakage and what have you. We got a call a few months ago that we'd grossly underestimated the number of tiles, by fifty percent. That's impossible! Our staff are pros. They'd never make that type of blunder. Of course, a little investigation revealed that the tiles had been stolen by the contractor for use on another project and they figured, since we have deep pockets anyway, why not help themselves to some of the goodies. Stupid stuff, like electrical fixtures and even furnishings, disappear on a regular basis, sometimes the very day they're put in. These clowns put in the stuff in the morning and then come back at night, load it onto some truck, and off they go. The next morning, we're told we never ordered the stuff in the first place. Documents disappear. What a circus! The quality of the work is atrocious. Walls aren't put in straight, and even window casings aren't put in properly. It takes three weeks to get a phone installed. One day, we found out that the drain pipes weren't working because the Arab workers stuffed them with steel wool to sabotage the project. Talk about being passive-aggressive."

"We much rather that than aggressive-aggressive," Benny said, laughing. "We've made great strides in Israel since we became a state. We've built cities, a modern society, and made the desert bloom—arguably the only one in the entire Middle East. We've had three existential wars in twenty-three years. Our governmental system is still mired in the old Ottoman system, which makes our bureaucracy challenging. We understand that we have a long way to go, but I'm confident that we'll get there."

"We never know when the next shoe will drop," Ze'evi said. "Our local attorney in charge of the project was doing some funny business with the paying of the contractors, funneling the funds through his own bank account first so he could skim the interest. Meanwhile, he spent a lot of time defending the contractor, until we found out he was representing them on another project. Talk about a conflict of interest! If that ever happened in the States, there'd be hell to pay. In Israel, nobody blinks an eye. Well, we've gotten into the game ourselves. 'When in Rome.' We discovered that the health minister himself was in the midst of a home improvement project, so we kindly provided him with some imported Italian marble. He was very thankful for our generosity. Since then, things have gone a lot smoother. At least, the good people of Jerusalem will get their cancer center."

"I'm certainly not going to try to defend the behavior of our contractors," Benny said, "but all of us in Israel suffer from them. To build a house there takes ten years off one's life. I've heard complaints from American immigrants to Israel that the hardest part of living there isn't the Arabs but the Israelis themselves. That's why Aliyah to Israel from Western countries isn't what it should be. Life in the States is much less complicated. Look, Israel isn't an easy place to live, but there are many emotional and spiritual rewards to those who are willing to make the sacrifice."

"Well, I for one won't," Ze'evi said.

His words hung in the air as glances around the table shifted to Dahlia, who looked down at her plate impassively.

Crash! Suddenly there came a shriek from the kitchen.

Leah said, "I'll take care of this. Nobody needs to get up." And off she went.

The others remained at the table, quietly making small talk and trying to ignore the shouts coming from the next room.

"Thelma! How could this happen? My God! Are you okay? Let me help you up."

"I'm so sorry, Miss Leah, but there was some spilled grease on the floor and I didn't see it. Let me try to save the roast! I'll clean it up. It'll be just fine!"

"It won't be just fine, Thelma. You can't expect me to serve food to company after it has fallen on the floor. I hope that's not what you do all the time!"

"No, Miss Leah. I was just trying to . . ."

"Never mind. We won't starve. Oh, Thelma! Just clean up this mess."

Leah returned to the dining room, looking rather pale. "It appears that Thelma has dropped the roast on the floor. It has begun its final long trip to Chesapeake Bay. No matter. Thelma's not hurt. I guess that's the main thing."

Ze'evi looked at Dahlia and said, in an undertone but loudly enough so that Benny and Leah heard him, "We've let go of our domestic help for far more minor offenses."

"It was just an accident, Ze'evi! No big deal. We would never get rid of Thelma. She's part of the family!"

Ze'evi looked at Dahlia. "Seriously, Dahlia? Hardly!"

***

"Benny, are you awake?"

"Hmm . . . now I am. What is it? It's 2 a.m."

"I can't fall asleep."

"Take some pills."

"It's not that! I'm beginning to have misgivings about that boy being right for Dahlia."

"You mean that man. He's no boy."

"That's what I mean, Benny. He's much more experienced and worldly than Dahlia."

"So, what's wrong with that? If he's a sophisticated young man, that's what we wanted for her. He'll teach her the ways of the world. We've discussed this at length."

"I know all of that, but something I saw in him tonight made me feel that we may have been mistaken about him."

"What was it?"

"I don't know. Just the way he speaks. He has an arrogance about him."

"I don't know if you've noticed, but there isn't a Sabra in Israel who doesn't have an 'arrogance about him.' He certainly is very sure of himself, but why shouldn't he be? His family is very wealthy, but rather than being a spoiled brat like many rich children he's extremely accomplished. Look at all the good he's doing in Israel."

"I know all of that. I just felt a bit disrespected. Like what he said about Thelma, for example—"

"I happen to agree with him on that score. We probably should let her go. It will send a message to the others."

"Benny, for goodness sake! There's no need to send any message. It was just an accident. I won't you let you fire her."

"In what other ways did you feel disrespected?"

"Well, for one thing, he keeps calling us by our first names. I can't get used to that. I'm a bit old fashioned when it comes to those things. He's not our friend. He's dating Dahlia. I remember someone else who had a much finer manner about him—"

"Leah, I thought that we were done with all of that. Why does he keep coming up?"

"I was just saying."

"Arik was polite and respectful because he's still just a boy who came here cap in hand. Ze'evi is a man of the world. He really is more of a peer to us."

"Do you want a peer to us to marry Dahlia? I'm worried for her, Benny. That's all. He treated her like a child tonight. I don't want him to be a bad influence on her, to dominate her. And, besides, are you okay with Dahlia staying here in America to live?"

"Dahlia isn't easy to dominate. She has a strong personality. Rich people live wherever they want to and in many places at once. I'm sure they'd buy a house in Savyon. The last that I checked that's in Israel. We've made the right decision. I just know it."

"I hope that you're right."

The ninety-minute flight from Denver and over the mountains had been a bumpy one due to strong northwesterly headwinds that slowed the prop jet's progress. When they flew over Independence Pass, the wind finally began to die down and the clouds parted. The dying rays of the sun over Roaring Fork Valley stretched ahead of them as they made their final approach into Aspen/Pitkin County Airport.

"Sardy, this is ETI-1. Over," Ze'evi said.

"Go, ETI. Good evening," the air traffic controller said.

"Approaching on 118.1."

"Copy that, ETI-1. Level 10,000. Turn left, heading 325, descend, and maintain 9,000.

"Copy that. Left to 325, down to 9,000."

Dahlia fastened her seatbelt, removed her aviator sunglasses, and readjusted her headphones. She smiled at Ze'evi. Looking down, she saw Aspen glittering in the dark valley. The Maroon Bells still glowed orange in the fading Western light.

"ETI-1, turn right, heading 060, descend, and maintain 5,000. Slow to 220 knots."

"Right to 060, down to 5,000, slowing to 220 knots."

"ETI-1, intercept localizer runway 3. Cleared for runway 3."

"Copy that. Runway 3."

"ETI-1, roger. Cleared to land on runway 3."

Ze'evi deployed the Cessna Citation 1's landing gear and landed the jet smoothly, taxiing to the terminal reserved for private aircraft.

"You're really good, Ze'evi." She finally let out her breath and took his hand. "I was a bit nervous at first. I'd never flown with anyone I knew, before meeting you, but you really put me at ease. How long have you been flying?"

"Since I was eighteen."

"Will you teach me how to fly?"

"Sure! Why not?"

When the door opened, Dahlia felt the familiar rush of chilly mountain air hitting her face.

"Aren't we going to pull up to the terminal?" she asked.

"No need. You'll see."

At the foot of the stairs was a red Volvo and a glistening white and black Jeep Commando C101 with four-foot-tall snow tires. Two men dressed immaculately in white and black ski suits were waiting with it.

"Everything at the house is ready and waiting, sir. The fireplaces are on, the pool's been heated, and Marshall has dinner ready for service."

One of the men handed Ze'evi the keys to the Jeep.

"Thanks, Peter. I want you to meet my girlfriend, Dahlia."

Dahlia smiled and shook the man's hand.

As the men loaded up the Jeep with all of the baggage and ski equipment, Ze'evi helped Dahlia into the passenger seat.

"This is much better that going through the terminal and having to push through the unwashed masses, trying to get to the car. I did that years ago. Incredibly annoying!"

'I've never seen a Jeep like this before," Dahlia said.

"It's called a monster truck, and it can go uphill in snow drifts four feet high. We keep it at the house full-time. It's a Jeep Commando, because it's used by U.S. alpine commandos. I think that they have a lot of them stationed in Scandinavia to protect Europe from the Soviets—Cold War stuff."

"Do you feel like a commando when you drive this?" Dahlia teased him gently.

"Absolutely!"

The Jeep was heated just right, not too hot and not too cold. The plush leather seats are heavenly, Dahlia thought. She felt like Goldilocks. As the Jeep made its way into the mountains north of Aspen, Dahlia saw a part of the town that she had never imagined. Walled, gated mansions lined the winding road. She craned her neck to see through the wrought-iron gates as they passed.

"Slow down, Ze'evi. I want to look at these houses. I've never seen anything like this before. I can't believe people live like this!"

"My God, Dolly, you're so adorable." Ze'evi laughed, but he slowed the Jeep.

Overlooking the houses was Ajax Mountain, its trails all lit up and ant-like skiers slowly inching their way down. They turned on to Starwood Drive and passed through a wrought-iron gate. At the end of a long, circular driveway stood a large gray stone mansion. It had the look of a Scottish hunting lodge, from the outside, with numerous gables and smoking chimneys. The front lawn was buried under a foot of snow but still expertly manicured. The paths were completely clear and dry.

"We're staying at this hotel? It's lovely!"

"Hotel? Very funny, Dolly. Welcome to Chateau Ehrenreich!"

"Really? I don't know what to say!"

"What's there to say? It's just a ski house on the Swiss model. They don't just build chalets, you know. It was designed by Robert Stern, one of the world's leading architects, and took three years to build. It's 14,000 square feet and can be yours for a mere ten million dollars. Nonetheless, it has a really cozy feel to it."

The Jeep pulled up to the massive oaken front door, where the valet staff stood waiting for them.

"Before you go in . . . I bought you a little Chanukah present."

Dahlia kissed Ze'evi. "That's not necessary, really," she said.

She opened the small rectangular box and saw a black leather box inside it.

"My God! What is this?" Dahlia's eyes grew large.

"It's just a small trinket."

She opened the box. In it lay a solid gold Swiss watch.

"It's regarded as the finest watch in the world," Ze'evi said. "I don't know how well it keeps time, but who cares. It's a Patek Philippe!"

"It's magnificent, Ze'evi! It must have cost a small fortune. But I can't accept it."

"Don't be ridiculous, Dolly. It's no big deal." Ze'evi chuckled. "There's a lot more where that came from, trust me. Let's go in."

He fastened the watch to Dahlia's wrist.

The butler took the bags into the house, while the valet drove the Jeep, with the ski equipment inside it, to the garage.

"So, how well do you ski, Dolly?"

"I can hold my own. I skied here last year."

"Do you want me to enter you in any of the NASTAR races?"

"I don't think that I'm that good,"

"That's okay. You can cheer me on tomorrow afternoon. I'm competing in a slalom event."

"Is there anything that you can't do?" Dahlia said, smiling.

The pair walked through a beige marble two-story entryway topped by a five-foot layered brass chandelier. Their footfalls clicked on the beige granite floor that lead to the entry parlor. There was a balcony above that opened to the upper floor. At the center of the opposite wall a four-foot-tall fireplace was ablaze. The living area was richly appointed, with parquet floors, Persian rugs, well-stuffed white sofas, and large white and beige throw pillows. The other furniture was solid mahogany.

"Should I take off my shoes?"

"Don't be ridiculous. We have a staff here that runs around all day long cleaning up after us."

They walked through the aromatic, paneled library, which was filled with old leather-bound books, to another lit fireplace, this one flanked by large leather sofas and loveseats. A large picture window that looked out at Roaring Fork Valley completed the scene.

"We have first-edition signed books by Twain, Dickens, Dostoyevsky, and Tolstoy here."

They wandered into the large, bleached-wood gourmet kitchen, which was topped by beige and brown granite countertops. The Viking stovetop, with its twenty burners, was topped with a large burnished-copper hood. The dinette, with seating for ten, was surrounded by large picture windows.

"My God! This is ten times bigger than the kitchen we have at the residence! You could cook for a battalion."

"Our family just loves to eat. We have a world-class chef on retainer to cook for us when we're in town."

The dining room was a formal affair, in the Chippendale mahogany style, with a large chandelier at the center and seating for twenty. Ze'evi escorted Dahlia down castle-like hallways that were lined with thick, glossy white wood trim and endless hallway sconces. The walls were adorned with original paintings by Chagall, Picasso, Matisse, Cézanne, and a whole host of American artists, such as Georgia O'Keeffe and Andrew Wyeth.

"Here's where we're going to sleep," Ze'evi finally said.

They walked into a white and beige room that contained an Egyptian enameled four-poster king bed with beige satin sheets, rows of goose down pillows, and a white mink comforter. A fully ablaze beige marble fireplace, with his and hers white plush easy chairs and ottoman facing it, rounded out the cozy sleeping quarters.

"Is this real fur?"

"Of course! In the unlikely event, you find yourself in bed without me, I have to make sure my little kitten stays warm. Come, let me show you to your bathroom."

"This bathroom is twice the size of my bedroom!" she said. "You could fit five people in the bathtub."

Passing the steam room and sauna, they walked into a dressing area that contained a full walk-in closet and three large mirrors. It reminded Dahlia of the changing room at Bonwit Teller.

"All the clothes you see here, from the skiwear to the negligees, were purchased for you and are in your size."

Dahlia shook her head. "You got all of these for me?"

"Of course, I did! What else do I need to do to show you I love you?"

"Thank you so much!" Dahlia leaped into his arms and kissed him for a long while.

"There's something more I want to show you," Ze'evi said. "Come."

They took the elevator one flight down and emerged at the indoor pool, which was rimmed with beige art deco columns. The oval, Olympic-sized, azure-blue pool was lit from below so that its surface glowed. Surrounding the pool were plush, padded chaise lounge chairs. At the other end of the vast room, large picture windows looked out at the stone patio and the outdoor pool. A smile crept to Dahlia's lips when she realized that all of it might be hers one day.

"We have a fully appointed spa, including a massage area, exercise room, and racquetball court. Do you play racquetball?"

"No, but I'm sure that it's not that much different from tennis."

Ze'evi led her back to their bedroom.

Dahlia stood by the large picture window of the bedroom and looked out at the town of Aspen, which was stretched out below her like a jeweled carpet.

"It's magnificent!" she whispered, leaning her head back on Ze'evi's chest. "I'm happy, Ze'evi, really happy."

He kissed the back of her head. "I'm glad. Let's eat! I'm starved."

When they arrived at the dining room, the butler approached them discreetly.

"Sir, your friends have arrived."

"Who's here?" Dahlia asked.

"I wanted to surprise you," Ze'evi said. "It's high time you met my circle of friends. There will be three couples staying at the house with us for the week. We all went to NYU together, in the same fraternity. They're what you call the crème de la crème. We're a true circle of friends. Our parents socialize, and we go to each other's clubs to play golf and tennis or ride horses. We travel in a wolf pack, around the world, and sail and scuba together in the Caribbean or Hawaii. We've done some really crazy things together. Sometimes we're really out of control, but don't worry. They're a bundle of laughs. You'll really get along with them."

A gaggle of noise and laughter heralded the arrival of the other three couples. Dahlia wondered whether they were Jewish. They all looked as if they had sprung out of Vogue magazine. Apart from being impeccably dressed in understated elegance, they moved and spoke with a grace that unnerved her. She shook her head in amazement. This is such a different world! she thought.

The wait staff flitted around, serving chilled vodka, caviar, and hors d'oeuvres.

"Dolly, come meet my friends. Everyone, this is my new girlfriend, Dolly! Dolly, this is Kate and Philip, Patty and Brad, and Charlotte and Todd."

"Very nice to meet you all." Dahlia smiled at them nervously.

After having drinks, the circle settled down to a sumptuous dinner that featured a large roasted Argentinian chateaubriand with a red wine and mushroom reduction and pomme puree. The conversation was raucous and, at times, somewhat bawdy. There was much talk of old times, old affairs, pranks, and feats of chivalry and silliness.

Charlotte leaned toward Dahlia. "Dolly, don't pay them any mind. When we all get together, it's like we're back in junior high school again. We've just all known each other for so many years. You'll get the hang of things after a while. Best to just go with the flow."

After dinner, they went down to the billiards room, which had a fully appointed bar and entertainment center. The men sat on plush leather couches around the fireplace, enjoying Cuban cigars and aged single malt Scotch, while the women sat by the bar, drinking vodka gimlets and playing billiards.

Todd leaned toward Ze'evi. "So, what's the story with Dolly? Where'd you snag that extraordinary piece of ass? Wasn't she last year's Playboy Playmate of the year? I'm sure I saw her in there."

"Very funny, Todd. I've told you many times that being a Zionist has its perks. You always make fun of me for attending all those Israeli functions with my parents. Israelis are mostly a fairly provincial lot, but my dad has a soft spot for the Jewish people—the Holocaust and all, you know. I go along for the ride, taking part in all that do-gooder shit. This time, it's paid off big-time. She's the daughter of the Israeli ambassador."

"Holy crap! That little minx is a perfect ten, like some kind of Barbie doll."

"That's why I call her Dolly. She's my little toy."

After an hour, Ze'evi stood. "I suggest we all turn in early tonight. They're opening the ski lifts at Ajax an hour early for us, so we can catch the first powder before all the riffraff shows up. We'll be heading out at about 6 a.m. We'll have plenty of time to party tomorrow night, at the big bash on Galena East! Woo hoo!"

As they walked down the hall to the master bedroom, Dahlia put her arm around Ze'evi's waist.

"I can't wait to get into that bed with you," she said, the alcohol having increased her willingness to display affection. I hope you're not planning on getting much sleep tonight."

He pinned her against the wall, pressing himself tightly to her, and kissed her. "I wasn't planning on getting any."

***

When Dahlia entered the Hotel Jerome the following evening, she was filled with either a painful sense of déjà vu or foreboding. She wasn't sure which. All she knew for sure was that she would rather have been somewhere else. It wasn't that she didn't want to see Penny and Richard. It was only that this would be their first-time meeting Ze'evi. What kind of first impression would he make? He came from a different world than they did. What would they talk about? What did they all have in common?

Memories of almost exactly one year ago, when everything had seemed so perfect, flooded into her mind. They had been a real foursome then. Now, Arik loomed large in his absence. She kept telling herself that he was gone and that she was with someone else, someone who had a lot going for him, someone who was everything that Arik was not. What's wrong with that?

If only she and Ze'evi had been on time. They had made reservations for 7:30 p.m., and she knew for certain that Penny and Richard would have been on time, which, of course, meant that they had been waiting for the past hour.

She had been ready, but Ze'evi had been busy on a conference call to his New York office, some crisis, he had said. Even after his call, he had been in no hurry to get ready, despite her prodding. His circle of friends had melted away for the evening, gone to some big bash.

When they finally arrived, Dahlia's apprehensions were calmed by Penny's open embrace and warm smile.

"It has been six months! Can you believe it?" Penny said. "Without your letters . . ." Behind Dahlia's smile, Penny saw what she needed to in her eyes but maintained her composure. She reached out to shake Ze'evi's hand. "I am Penny, and this is Richard."

"Yes, I know."

An awkward silence ensued.

Finally, Dahlia said, "Sorry we're late, but Ze'evi had a very important long-distance phone call to New York. Some big emergency at work."

"That's okay." Richard smiled. "We just got here ourselves."

Looking into Penny's dark eyes, Dahlia knew that wasn't true.

There was another awkward silence.

"Why don't we order?" Dahlia said.

"Good idea," Penny said. She looked at her menu. "It looks like the same as last year. You would think that a place like this would alter the menu."

The waiter appeared.

"I'll have the tuna crudo."

"I'll have roasted salmon."

"I'll have the rainbow trout with hazelnuts."

Ze'evi was studying the menu intently.

"What will you have, Ze'evi?" Dahlia asked.

"Ummm . . . I'll have the crab risotto," he finally said, closing the menu handing it back to the waiter.

"Very well, sir."

"Oh, and why don't you also bring us a bottle of the Taylor Fladgate 40-year-old tawny port? That would go very well with the fish."

"Good choice, sir," the waiter said, smiling. "That's our best bottle."

"I know," Ze'evi said.

Dahlia turned to Ze'evi, surprised, and said in an undertone, "I've never seen you eat nonkosher. Even the wine isn't kosher."

Penny and Richard spoke softly to each other, pretending not to listen.

"Dahlia, please! I eat fish out, just like you do."

"But the fish I ordered is kosher."

"Roasted in the same pots they roast the pork chops in. Besides, seafood is seafood. There's no difference. I learned the rules in day school, just like you did. What's not kosher about wine? It's just made of fermented grapes and aged in very expensive oak barrels."

"I don't know, but there's some rule that wine has to be kosher."

"And do you know why the rabbis made it so? Because everyone knows that kosher wine is so awful it can't possibly compete with real wine, because Jewish winemakers have no clue. So, they made up a rule to prohibit anyone from drinking real wine, to keep their monopoly. Orthodox Jews can't tell the difference between a cabernet and a chardonnay . . . So, Richard, what college do you go to?" Ze'evi asked.

"I'm a senior in high school," Richard said.

"A senior in high school? Do your parents know you're here?" Ze'evi laughed.

"All three of us are seniors in high school, including Dahlia," Penny said testily.

'You're right, Dahlia, ordering the wine was a bad idea. None of you are old enough to drink!" Ze'evi roared at his own joke, even though no one else found it funny. Dahlia tells me you're into computers, Richard."

"That's right. I'm planning on going to Harvard next year. I'm interested in developing microcomputers that could one day be commercially viable, even for home use."

"I think you've been watching too many Star Trek episodes. So, you'll be talking into your computer like Spock. I think there's a reason the show is set two hundred years into the future, because what you're talking about will never happen in our lifetime. Next, you'll tell me we'll be talking to space stations with flip phones. Beam me up, Scotty!" Ze'evi pretended to be Captain Kirk.

Dahlia shot him a look and said, "Stop being so rude!"

"I'm serious, Dahlia. I got a computer science degree at NYU, and now I'm a senior executive at Ehrenreich Technologies International. We made it possible for Neil Armstrong to say, 'It's one small step for man . . .' on the moon. Without us, he'd still be stepping into the Howard Johnson's. We're now developing satellites that will predict the weather, all around the world, with absolute certainty. I can tell you that innovations in computer science will come out of companies like ours and IBM, not from a bunch of computer dorks at Harvard! If they're lucky, they'll get a job working for us when they graduate."

"That's where you're wrong," Richard said calmly. "Companies like yours are too set in their ways. I think that over the next ten years MIT, Caltech, and Harvard are going to produce a generation of dorks, as you call them, that will turn the whole computer field on its head. The revolution is already starting, with the semiconductor technology that came out of the space program."

"It's always nice to dream," Ze'evi said.

"Excuse me," Dahlia said abruptly. "I need to go to the ladies' room."

"I will go with you!" Penny said.

"What is it about you women always needing to go to the john in groups? I'll never understand that." Ze'evi smirked.

"Well, that is the way we girls are." Penny smiled thinly. "You two try not to kill each other while we are gone."

Nobody smiled.

As soon as they were out of earshot of their boyfriends, Penny said, "Dahlia, what are you doing?"

"What do you mean?"

"With this guy! He's absolutely awful. He's been rude to us from the moment we met. Who does he think he is?"

"I don't know what got into him tonight. He's usually very sweet and considerate to me. I guess these super rich have their own ways—"

"Paapi, this is me. Have you forgotten? I constantly hang out with super-rich people in Mexico, and I know a jerk when I see one. He seems to have an abusive personality. Is he abusing you?"

"Absolutely not! Ze'evi has been so good to me. You didn't see me in October. My letters to you didn't do justice to how I was doing. I was having a nervous breakdown from my grief over Arik. Arik abused me, by disappearing into thin air. I was getting carried away in an uncontrollable whirlpool, and Ze'evi saved me. I feel so comfortable with him, and he's so good to me. You can't know him from a thirty-minute meeting."

"I do not know. I just am running on my intuition."

"Penny, we've been friends for so long. I need you to trust me that I'm doing the right thing. I need you to support me and respect the decisions and choices that I make. That's what friends do."

"Friends, Paapi, speak the truth to each other, because they love each other. I love you now and always. I just am trying to protect you. Have you still not heard any word from Arik?"

"No, not a word. In fact, I don't know what I'd say to him if I suddenly got a letter from him. My parents are good judges of character, and they're very fond of Ze'evi. I now realize that they were right about Arik, too."

"I still think that they are wrong on both scores," Penny said.

As soon as the girls returned to the table, Ze'evi stood and announced, "We'd best be going. Sorry. We have to get an early start in the morning."

"But we haven't eaten anything yet!" Dahlia said.

"Put the bill on my tab." Ze'evi looked at his watch. "We really need to go. We're going to be late."

"Where are you guys going to ski tomorrow? We could join you," Richard said.

"I'm afraid that won't be possible. Dahlia and I are flying out, before the crack of dawn, over to Telluride to do some heli-skiing. The powder up at the top is breathtaking."

"Why don't they come with us?" Dahlia asked Ze'evi, wanting to salvage something out of the evening.

"We're going with a full crowd, and there won't be any room in the helicopter," Ze'evi countered.

"Okay," Penny said. "Have a nice time. Perhaps we can get together later in the week."

"Maybe," Ze'evi said, smiling.

Penny looked at Dahlia, wordlessly telling her that she knew such a gathering would not be arranged and that Ze'evi was lying about the full helicopter.

By the time they got outside, Dahlia was furious with Ze'evi. "Why were you so rude?" she asked. "Those are my close friends."

"Look, kitty cat, why'd you drag us away from one of the hottest parties in town to get together with your childhood friends from summer camp? I'm sorry if you felt I was rude. Your friend Richard, who was pretty rude himself, is a typical nerd living in a science fiction world. And by the way? He's a self-possessed little twerp, arrogant as hell. He actually thinks he and his little band of merry men are going to take over the computer world with no capital to back them up. I did him a favor by introducing him to reality. While you two were in the ladies' room, I spoke to him, in detail, about what's waiting for him in the real world. As far as Penny goes, I never said two words directly to her, so how could I have been rude?"

"It's just that—"

"The party should still be going strong. The circle is there already, and they told me they would save us seats in the front. We'll head over there now. Have you heard of The Doors?"

"Of course! 'Light My Fire.'"

"Well, we're headed to the Galena East nightclub. It's by invitation only tonight."

"I've heard of it. I went there last year. It's the hippie joint, right?"

"Not anymore, not really. It's been bought out since last year, greatly expanded, and completely redone. It's now an upscale private club catering to celebrities and invited guests. Over Christmas, it's totally over the top. This weekend, The Doors and the Grateful Dead are performing there. I know Jim Morrison and Jerry Garcia, and if you behave yourself I'll introduce you. My neighbors Kim Novak and Jill St. John, the Hollywood actresses, are in town for the week, and they're sure to be there. If you want to meet rock stars and film celebrities this week, this is the watering hole."

Dahlia shook her head. "You're incredible."

When they entered the club, Dahlia was overcome by the aroma of incense and marijuana. The room was dark, except for red, green, and blue strobe spotlights illuminating the stage. Black lights were directed onto the dark walls, which were adorned with figures and patterns that shone eerily fluorescent, moving and shimmering. She could make out images of Jimi Hendrix and John Lennon. The air appeared to undulate as the colored smoke in the room moved with the music. There was a dance floor in front of the stage.

The opening act featured what looked like Maharishi devotees playing sitars.

"Purple haze!" Dahlia thought as she inhaled the air.

She and Ze'evi sat with his circle in the front of the nightclub, at the edge of the dance floor, on pillows around a small table. Dahlia ordered a vodka tonic.

The room went dark.

A deep disembodied voice rumbled loudly, "The Doors!"

Deep-purple stage lights came on. The haze thickened. A single white light shone on the iconic mane-rimmed face of Jim Morrison.

He sang "Hello, I Love You." Dahlia was awestruck.

After that song, Morrison stood still and stared intensely into the audience while smoking a joint.

"We're a small group here . . . intimate, almost. I want you all to get to know my buddies. You know I was supposed to be a filmmaker. It took me four years at UCLA film school before I realized I didn't want to be no fucking cinematographer. But at least that's where I met my brother Ray Manzarek here, lying on Venice Beach." Morrison put his arm around Ray's shoulder.

Dahlia gulped. Can't I ever get away from goddamn UCLA?

Ze'evi had a stack of marijuana joints in front of him on the table. He picked one up, lit it, and put it to Dahlia's lips. She inhaled deeply and then coughed. This was her first time, but she was desperate that no one notice. She suddenly felt the room swim around her and felt herself becoming giddy. So, that's what this is like. She looked at Ze'evi and giggled. She finished one joint and took another.

Morrison was singing "Light My Fire."

"I have something for you, kitty cat," Ze'evi whispered to Dahlia. He pulled out a plastic baggie of white powder. "Some snow to light your fire."

He leaned toward her, tilted her neck up with his forefinger, and kissed her gently. She closed her eyes.

"Now, kitty cat, fasten your seatbelt."

He poured a small pile of powder on the table and, with a razor blade, expertly formed two lines. He rolled up a hundred-dollar bill.

"Watch me, Dolly."

He leaned over the table, put one end of the rolled-up bill to one of the lines of powder and the other in his nose, and inhaled sharply. His head shot backward for a moment.

"Now, you," he said.

Dahlia shuddered in a moment of panic. What am I doing? What have I gotten myself into? Who is Ze'evi, really? She knew that she was standing at the verge of something new. Is it dangerous or exciting? This is my time, my time to try new things. And why not? What will be the harm be in trying it just once? I can chalk it up to experience.

Dahlia took the rolled-up bill from Ze'evi and put it to the second line. She inhaled sharply and sneezed, which sent Ze'evi into a fit of laughter.

He cut another line of the strange white powder.

"Try again!" he said. "Breathe slower this time."

She tried again, going down the line methodically, and then she fell backward onto the pillow in a euphoria that she had never felt even in the few orgasms she had experienced. The music was suddenly louder and clearer, the lights and colors more intense. She felt as if she were on the top of the world, all-powerful and brilliant. As she breathed in deeply and rapidly, she felt each individual respiratory muscle contract. Her heart raced, and she felt each of its beats as if it were a drum in her brain. She lay flat on the pillow, her arms and legs spread. In the darkness, Ze'evi climbed on top of her and kissed her deeply.

"I'm shooting through space!" she cried out, her voice getting louder and louder, "I'm sailing through the dark universe! I'm flying through darkness!"

***

The entire company, weighted down by their helmets, rucksacks, and full combat gear, was crouched in long, parallel lines along the length of the desert tarmac. To the west, the dying sun's rays colored a shrinking band of daylight that silhouetted the mountains as the night encroached relentlessly from the east. Sharply contrasted against the western horizon stood a row of a half dozen Nord 2501 airborne troop carriers, their wing and tail lights blinking red as their engines warmed up.

The paratroopers in training had spent all afternoon checking and rechecking, folding and unfolding their parachutes. Junior officers offered encouragement and motivation by reminding them that in every jump school class there is always someone that falls to their death during the night jump. Arik needed no verification of the veracity of that account. He quietly did what he was told, despite the mind-numbing repetition.

Now, all was ready. This was their first night jump. At least in the five daylight jumps Arik could see the ground and gauge when to brace himself and what terrain he would land on. Those jumps had gone off without a hitch for him, although many members of his platoon had sustained broken ankles or tibias when they hit the ground. For this jump, however, there would be no sensory cues. They would be flying through the inky blackness.

Their instructors walked up and down the rows, giving instructions to the trainees as parachutes were strapped on and adjusted. When the order was given, on cue, everyone stood, made the final strap and buckle adjustments and checks, and marched, in two sticks, or lines, of eighteen men each, into the lowered back ramp of the troop carrier. Arik was the first in his stick, and he led the trainees behind him into the semidarkness of the plane's interior. He took his place at the front, nearest to the door through which they would jump. Strapped into his jump seat and bathed in an unnatural blue light, Arik stared at the bulb that shone red beside the door. The door closed, and the plane came to life with a deafening roar. The men, cramped together, all stared at the red light.

Although his daylight jumps had gone well, Arik felt genuine fear about this night jump. Will I be able to find the ripcord and pull it in the pitch dark? Any error would result in his becoming a puddle on the ground less than two minutes after the jump light turned green. He felt a shudder go through him.

The Nord 2501 began a steep climb, its engines droning on and on in a nauseating rhythm. The powerful fumes of airplane fuel made a third of the men vomit all over themselves and the floor. The stench reminded Arik of the bus ride to Camp Moshava. What a time to think about Pinkie Mermelstein! He chuckled to himself.

The temperature in the plane dropped sharply as it gained altitude. Suddenly, the two side doors in the front flew open, and the jump master shouted, "Hikon!" (Attention!)

Arik stepped into the doorway, cocked his head straight ahead, and grasped the aluminum sides of the doorway. He looked out at the black abyss. The frozen night air stung his face. He could see the lights of El-Arish twinkling in the distance far below. He went through the final checklist of what he must do, remembering that he would have no visual cues regarding altitude. He would have to do everything by rote. There was no margin for error or inattention. The time for fear had passed. Focus! Focus! Foc—.

The doorway light turned green, and a voice behind him yelled, "Kfotz!" (Jump!)

Arik kicked away from the aircraft, with both legs. A powerful force caused by the slipstream behind the wings thrust him toward the rear of the fuselage. In a moment, he fell away from the aircraft, its blinking tail lights growing smaller and smaller above him. He felt his equipment bag release and drop on a line 25 feet below him. There was nothing but blackness all around him. He felt weightless, without any sensation of falling. He heard only the sound of the wind and felt only it, sharp and freezing, against his face and hands. He focused on the twinkling lights in the distance as he counted backward from thirty while his numb hand fumbled for the ripcord. When he located it, he curled up into a fetal position and pulled it to deploy the parachute. He felt himself yanked sharply upward by the parachute, which slowed his descent. The wind died down as he neared the ground. During the daylight jumps, he had been able to see the other guys coming down with him, which had been a small comfort. In the darkness, he was flying alone.

Preparing to land, he tucked his arms tightly to his chest and pushed his legs and feet tightly together, bending his knees. Both legs hit the ground at the same time with a dull thud. Mercifully, the ground was flat and not rocky. He rolled, got to his feet quickly, and gathered up his chute, which was flapping in the wind. Relief washed over him. It had all taken place in ninety seconds.

All around him, the other paratrooper trainees landed. Nobody was hurt on the jump. They were swarmed by trucks that encircled them to provide light. They heard the whoop-whoop-whoop of three helicopters circling overhead. The helicopters descended to a height of twenty-five feet, hovered above the men, and shone blinding spotlights down at the trainees, who were loaded down with full battle gear. The cold desert wind howled around them.

They gathered around the captain of the company.

"Okay, chevre! Here's how this will go! It's a thirty-kilometer rapid march back to base, but tonight you get a choice. Each helicopter will drop knotted ropes. You can either walk back or take advantage of our taxi service back to the base and get a night's sleep. Take your pick!"

On command, the ropes were thrown out of the doorways of the helicopters. Arik knew the members of his platoon very well by now. He knew who would choose to walk and who would choose to ride. He didn't wait for anyone.

"See you tomorrow morning, girls!" Arik laughed. I'm going to bed tonight. This is a no-brainer.

In an instant, he jumped at a rope and scampered up the knots. He could see several others also climbing, some making it and others falling. Within thirty seconds, Arik was safely aboard the chopper. At least tonight I got the better of the system.

Chapter 31

January 27, 1971

Dahlia, my soul,

 I've just come back from the hardest week of my life. They call it war week, and it's designed to simulate what it feels like to be in a massive battle. They made us live in a stinking trench for seven straight days in the same clothes and get less than three hours of sleep a night. Even that little sleep got broken up, and many of the guys are delirious. We spent our days digging foxholes and running up hills to assault positions. It was nonstop movement all day and all night. We've been shooting dozens of mortar rounds. One night they had us crawl on our stomachs up a hill covered with thorns and cactuses. By the time we reached the top, the skin was completely shredded off our knees and elbows, down to the bone. I'd done that before, so now I'm an expert. My elbows and knees are completely scarred, so I didn't feel a thing. By the fifth day, the lack of sleep made us delusional. I was starting to feel like I was on some kind of hard drug like cocaine or something. Everything around me was swimming and floating about. I'm walking around like a zombie. I understand that in the past soldiers have died during war week, from the lack of sleep and the dehydration. We eat almost no food and when we do eat it's on the run.

 At one point, we were charging up a ridge with a forty-five-degree incline, in full battle gear, with the instructors yelling at us that we're worthless lazy fucks and practically demanding that we quit the unit. Suddenly a guy in my unit, Gili, called out that he'd had enough and was quitting. He refused to move forward. I kept going, but the instructor stopped me and told me that it was my responsibility to see that Gili made it to the top of the rise. He said that if Gili didn't make it, they would throw both of us out of the unit! I tried to grab him, but he punched and kicked me away and told me to get the hell off him. I wasn't going to let that guy ruin my life. If he wanted to do that, he needed to get in line behind all the other folks hell-bent on that mission. I had no choice. I clocked him with a punch to the head and dragged his sorry ass on my back the rest of the way up the ridge, another kilometer straight up. The next day, Gili was thrown out of the unit. I never saw him again or got a chance to apologize.

 I just slept for 12 hours and had my first meal in a week. They're giving us 48 hours off. Everyone bolted out of here like a bat out of hell. I have nowhere to go or anyone to see, so I'm staying put. I'm enjoying the peace and quiet.

The best part is that I finally have the time to stare up at the tent and see your sweet face in the canvas. Is there any chance that you'll be in Israel for Pesach? I swear I'll move heaven and earth to see you. Please, let's do our best to rebuild what we once had. I'm constantly being propositioned by women here on the base, but I only have eyes for you.

Desperately wanting to see you,
Love,
Arik

***

"Kitty cat, you're about to witness sporting history," Ze'evi said over the din of the whirling helicopter blades. "You have absolutely no idea what's about to hit you. They're calling this the fight of the century!"

They were headed to the top of the Pan Am building, on Park Avenue just a short limousine drive to Madison Square Garden.

"There's never been a fight like this before. Two undefeated heavyweight champions, Joe Frazier and Muhammad Ali, are going head to head to see who's the true heavyweight champion of the world. This isn't just about the fight itself. Ali is the champ of the left-wing, antiestablishment, Black Power movement, and Frazier is the chump of the white establishment, so the whole country is divided along those lines. I don't get how they make that whole distinction, both of them being black and all. Anyway, this fight has been so hyped that Madison Square Garden isn't just sold out . . . people are literally killing each other to get a seat. I heard that even Frank Sinatra couldn't get a ringside seat. But my dad is a good friend of Jerry Perenchio, the fight's promoter, so we've got them. We'll be so close we'll be able to smell their sweat!"

"Wow. I've always wanted to smell Ali's sweat. Speaking of smell, I haven't had any for nearly a week. Did you bring anything to sniff?" Dahlia asked.

Ze'evi kissed her hard. "Now, what do you take me for, kitten? Do bears shit in the woods?"

The traffic heading west on 34th Street was a standstill of honking cars, police and fire sirens, and a kaleidoscope of blinding lights. The streets were filled with pushing and shoving throngs of people who all were headed toward 8th Avenue. The noise was so loud that it permeated the darkened stillness of the stretch limousine. Ze'evi and Dahlia sat quietly, enjoying vodka tonics on ice and several lines of cocaine.

"Let's get the fuck out of here and walk, or we'll never get there in this mess," Ze'evi said.

In a moment, they were out in the street, pushing through the crowd and headed for the VIP entrance. The atmosphere outside the Garden was electric. The street had been transformed into a gigantic circus that stretched for blocks in every direction, like Times Square on New Year's Eve but without the bitter cold. Screaming, shouting fans dressed in brightly colored costumes, each more outrageous than the next, jostled for access to the gates. Beer cans, confetti, and whiskey bottles were strewn everywhere. Scores of NYPD officers tried in vain to control the tens of thousands of partygoers.

Dahlia clung to Ze'evi's arm, desperately trying to avoid being separated from him in the mob. Things got a bit more orderly when they approached the VIP gate, which was protected by packs of gigantic men carrying walkie-talkies.

"Yo, Ehrenreich! Don't tell me you got ringside seats?"

"Hey, Frankie! Don't tell me you didn't!" Ze'evi laughed. "You know what they say: 'It's not what you know but who you know.'"

"Can you introduce me?" Dahlia asked. "It's not every day—"

"Sure! Frankie, my little lady here wants to meet you. This is Frank Sinatra, and this is my girlfriend, Dolly."

They shook hands.

"Well, Hello, Dolly!" Sinatra laughed at his own joke, through his cigar. "This your first fight? How old are you? You old enough to drink?"

"And then some." Ze'evi laughed. "She's not as innocent as she looks."

"Good then. Why don't you guys join us after the fight, for a private party up at the Rainbow Room. We'll have a great time. It's by invitation only."

"Definitely. So, how are you going to get close to the ring if you don't have seats?" Ze'evi asked.

Sinatra laughed. "I got a gig taking snapshots for Life magazine. No joke. I'm an employee of theirs for the evening."

"Well then, I'll have to support the cause by buying a copy."

"See you inside," Sinatra said, laughing.

The arena looked completely different from the last time they had been there. The basketball court and the skating rink were completely covered. All eyes were focused on a central square dot surrounded by ropes, which was illuminated by powerful overhead spotlights.

Dahlia thought, what a fool I was the last time I was here, pining after some shithead I'd foolishly given my heart to. I'm done with all that now. I've hit the big time. Could Arik get front-row seats to the fight of the century? Is he on speaking terms with Frank Sinatra? Of course, he isn't. He isn't even on speaking terms with himself. And to think that I was almost drawn into his dark, lonely world. What was I thinking, getting mixed up with him? The thought of Arik made her blood run cold. This is my place now—at the top of the world.

The noise and excitement in the arena rose to a fevered pitch as it gradually filled with screaming fans.

"Hi, Woody!" Ze'evi yelled out to the slightly built, bookish sort, wearing his iconic glasses on his hooked nose, who was entering the front row.

Woody Allen took his seat next to them.

"This row is Jews only." Ze'evi said, laughing. "I didn't know you were a boxing fan."

"Everybody is a boxing fan tonight! I wouldn't miss this one for the world. Everybody's saying that it will be the fight of the century." Allen said. "How is your dad doing? Thank him for bankrolling my next feature film. Oh, by the way, this is Louise, my ex-wife. We just got divorced."

"How nice for you guys. This is Dahlia. She's the daughter of the Israeli ambassador."

"Shalom, Shalom!" Allen smiled. That's pretty much the extent of my Hebrew. I grew up in Flatbush but never even went to Talmud Torah or Temple as a kid. My grandparents spoke Yiddish when they were yelling at each other and didn't want anyone else to understand. Nobody spoke Hebrew."

"Have you ever been to Israel?" Dahlia asked.

"It's funny, but it never even entered my mind to go. Maybe one day."

"My dad told me about your new film. It's based on the Castro thing. You become a Latin American revolutionary or something—"

"Yeah! It's called Bananas. It's about—"

Suddenly the lights in the arena faded to black and spotlights focused on large, spinning, sparkling disco balls, sending showers of colored lights in every direction. Crisscrossing the arena were streamers of bright orange, green, red, and blue laser light that shone through the haze of tobacco and marijuana smoke and into the stands. A huge organ played the theme song from Dracula. The crowd of 30,000 stood and screamed in rapture. The announcer, wearing a black tuxedo and holding a retractable microphone that was suspended from the ceiling, introduced each fighter. He called out: LET"S GET READY TO RUMBLE!!!! In turn, each fighter paraded down the aisle, from opposite sides of the great hall, arms raised and adorned in a brightly colored silk robe that had his name emblazoned on the back. The noise reached an earsplitting pitch when the fighters made their way to their respective corners.

A uniformed waiter brought over a bottle of chilled champagne and poured it for Ze'evi and Dahlia.

"Dolly, I've put 200 grand down on Frazier at five to one. I've got a good feeling about this. Most of my friends have their money on Ali. With my winnings, I'm going to buy us a gated ski chateau in St Moritz. I'll engrave your name in gold on a plaque at the gate. It'll be a ski-in/ski-out affair on the upper slopes at Corviglia, so you can ski to your heart's content."

Dahlia giggled. "You're so silly, Ze'evi. Would you really do that?"

"Of course, munchkin! You know how much I love you." He gave her a light peck on the nose.

"You promised me a pair of albino Dobermans to play with. Why don't we get them in Switzerland and keep them at the chateau? It would be so much fun having them run with us while we ski. They would literally disappear in the snow!"

Ze'evi whispered to her, "Turn around slowly and look at that distinguished-looking guy two rows behind us."

Dahlia looked and gasped. "Paul Newman? He looks even handsomer in person."

"My dad was a major investor in that Exodus movie. He bought the rights to the movie after Leon Uris sold it to Paramount. Why would Uris do that? What a dolt."

Ze'evi caught Newman's eye and waved at him. Newman smiled in recognition and raised his champagne glass.

Dahlia leaned toward Ze'evi and kissed him. "You know absolutely everyone!" She beamed.

The fight began in a fury. This front row was so close that when the punches landed, Dahlia could almost feel the impacts. Ali dominated the first three rounds, his jabs raising bloody welts across Frazier's face. At the end of the third round, though, Frazier countered with a powerful hook to Ali's face, which snapped his head backward.

Dahlia, completely drunk and covered with sweat, jumped out of her seat. "Kill him, Joe! Kill him!" she screamed.

The fourth and fifth rounds were all Frazier. He landed many left hooks and pinned Ali against the ropes so that he could deliver powerful body blows to his abdomen. Ali reeled backward, almost losing his balance.

"I love Switzerland!" Dahlia shrieked.

Ze'evi grabbed a bottle of champagne from the waiter's hand and popped the cork skyward, sending a shower of the bubbly rocketing up and falling down the couple in a spray. They descended into a paroxysm of laughter.

Rounds eight through eleven saw the momentum swinging back and forth between Frazier and Ali, but in the eleventh round Ali stumbled to the canvas after taking a left hook from Frazier. The rest of the fight saw Ali staggering numerous times and Frazier appearing to grow stronger by the minute. By round fifteen, Ali, completely spent, was using all of his remaining energy just to stay on his feet. He stood there, completely dazed, as Frazier landed more and more punches. At the end of the fight, the judges named Frazier the champion by unanimous decision.

"We won! We won!" Dahlia shrieked as she jumped into Ze'evi's arms. They kissed at ringside for a long time. "You're such a winner!"

"Welcome to Chateau Dolly! I can already smell zee mountain air!" Ze'evi said in a phony French accent.

"I'm going to give you the BJ of your life tonight, sweetheart," Dahlia said in his ear.

"I can hardly wait!" Ze'evi said, smiling hugely. "Let's party!" he shouted, bottle in hand, as he pulled her behind him, out of the arena, amid the pushing and shoving and the flashing lights, and to their limousine, which was waiting outside the VIP entrance.

The art deco Rainbow Room, atop Rockefeller Center, with its panoramic view of Midtown Manhattan spread out below them like a bejeweled carpet, was only somewhat quieter than the Garden. Carlos Santana was playing his signature sophisticated Latin style of music on the guitar, to the beat of a dozen bongo and conga drums, while a disco ball glittered over the hundred or so invited VIP guests on the dance floor. Ze'evi moved easily among the New York City politicians and the Hollywood and rock and roll glitterati who had flown in for fight. He introduced a star struck Dahlia, who played his perfect arm candy and drew interested glances from men all around the room.

Ze'evi approached a large, tough-looking man sitting at the bar. He had jet-black hair, which was greased back over his head, and he was wearing an immaculate gray Armani suit. He had an impossibly large diamond signet ring on his pinkie finger, and he smiled at Ze'evi in recognition.

"Dolly, I want you meet our pharmacist: Big Eddie Gravano."

"Hello, Dolly!" Gravano chewed on his Cuban cigar.

"Very nice to meet you," Dahlia said.

"Where's the craps game, Eddie?" Ze'evi asked.

"The room in the back. We've got a good one goin' tonight. We're startin' at fifty grand."

"Lead on!" Ze'evi said, laughing.

"Isn't playing dice illegal?" Dahlia whispered to him.

"You're such a little girl, kitty cat! Come cheer me on. I wouldn't worry about it. The police commissioner is playing with us. We give him special consideration." He winked at her.

***

At the end of February, Arik was called back into Major Gavi Shiloni's office.

"I have a proposition for you, Arik. Something that will considerably raise your profile in the army and may even get you into an elite unit—"

"Sir, with all due respect, not unlike most Israelis, I never wanted to join a commando unit. All I've ever asked for is a chance to contribute. An ordinary paratrooper unit will do just fine."

"It is not up to you. Where you end up is ultimately up to the General Staff, and you may not even know what unit you are in until you have been in it for months! You have put all this effort into basic paratrooper training. Do you not have ambition to progress further? Are you not interested in wearing the coveted red boots of an elite paratrooper?"

"I couldn't care less what color my boots are. Boots are just something to wear on my feet. All these distinctions that you guys so highly prize, being in this unit or that unit, they really don't mean that much to me. I have nobody to impress. I just came here to be a soldier and fight for Israel, and the paratroops have become my home."

"Let me get to the point, Arik. Have you ever heard of Shuki Baum?"

"No, sir. I haven't."

"Shuki is one of the top experts in Krav Maga in the army. He has never lost a bout. I have arranged for you to fight him in an exhibition match to follow the paratroop graduation ceremony on the top of Masada. Consider it a big honor. This entertainment will be a great way for the graduates to unwind and celebrate after the march. General Uziel Tal will be in the audience. He is the commander of the 35th Paratroopers Brigade." Gavi looked extremely satisfied with himself.

"May I speak, sir?"

"Speak!"

"I've come here from the States to fight Arabs, not Jews. I feel like I'm being turned into a gladiator for entertainment. All I want is to be a soldier. How am I serving Israel by doing this? Besides, how is this an exhibition? I practice Jeet Kune Do, and he does Krav Maga. It's apples and oranges. Nobody is going to get anything out of watching this."

Gavi leaned back on his desk and frowned. "Kundo shmundo! It is all the same! In the end, someone remains standing and the other one gets his ass kicked. I have made up my mind. You will fight Shuki. That is an order!"

"Yes, sir." Arik looked down in disgust, but then a thought occurred to him. "Sir . . . could we do it some other time? You're expecting me to fight someone after completing a ninety-kilometer forced march. That's impossible. I've heard that most people can barely walk after the march."

"You have one week to prepare. Your future as a paratrooper will depend on it. I will see to that."

***

Arik spent the ten days resting, eating, and drinking as much as he could, when he was not off the base on field maneuvers or practicing on the base's firing range. He was trying to recover from his ordeal of the previous six months. He had lost fifteen pounds from the hell he had gone through, and he feared that much of the lost weight was muscle. He spent hours going through his poses, katas, and assault and defense tactics. He found an empty assembly room where he could practice his gymnastics floor exercises and kung fu routines and jump rope. He was careful not to let anyone see him train. At 4:30 a.m., as the sun rose, he climbed to the ridge of the Mahktesh Katan box canyon, faced the sun, got into in a lotus position, and meditated, trying to focus his mind like he had used to.

He recalled what he had been taught: The life goals, or three jewels, for a Taoist are compassion, humility, and moderation. Taoism is about living within nature's laws and in harmony with the cycle of nature. It is about recognizing that everything is interconnected, that everything you do affects everything else around you. Taoists seek to live in harmony with the Tao. Kung fu aims to keep us in harmony and balance.

He wondered, Will I be ready? Will I be publicly humiliated? Will I be denied graduation after nearly seven months of suffering?

He had no answers.

***

The seven-month paratrooper training program always ends, climactically, with a ninety-kilometer, nearly twenty-hour forced march in full battle gear. The march ends at Masada, at the eastern verge of the Judean Desert along the Dead Sea. The march is called the masa kumta, or beret march, because at the conclusion of the march a ceremony awards the coveted red beret to each finisher, indicating that its wearer is now a full-fledged Israeli paratrooper. The march itself, a national sensation, is featured on the radio; some of the participants carry radios and listen to the commercial-free programming that is aired in honor of the march.

Hundreds of trainees assembled at the starting point at Kibbutz Ramat Rachel, at the southern approach to Jerusalem. Before the march, Gavi stood on an impromptu stage and gave the trainees a pep talk.

". . . You have all proven yourselves, time and again, over the past several months. You who have survived are the chosen best. I expect nothing less than one-hundred-percent effort from all of you . . ."

The march was fast-paced and spirited. Old Palmach marching songs rippled through the long line of men marching in the sunshine. Arik, carrying the heavy MAG machine gun in addition to his pack, fell in behind Captain Yigal, the platoon commander, who was walking at the front of the column. The line of marchers stretched for miles as the men broke off into small groups. Sergeants ran alongside the marchers, offering encouragement. Arik felt strong and fit. In fact, he felt euphoric at the thought of the physical effort that was to come. At the thirty-kilometer mark, the trainees were allowed to stop, unload their weapons, and hydrate for twenty minutes.

Arik volunteered to carry the twenty-four-liter container of water on his back for the next leg of the journey.

Because at this point most of the men were loaded down with only assault vests, Captain Yigal picked up the pace to nearly a jog. Arik easily kept pace, but he could hear the labored breathing of his fellow trainees around him.

Another two hours passed, and Arik's legs began to feel the burden of carrying the heavy water tank. The platoon passed Herodion, a first-century fortress built by King Herod I and used by Jewish rebels against Rome in an ill-fated revolt in 130 CE. It was lost on no one that after two thousand years a new, powerful Jewish army had taken control of the old fortress. At the forty-kilometer mark, when the trainees filled their canteens for the last time, the water tank was emptied.

The walk began to descend sharply toward the lowest spot on Earth. They had entered Wadi Kareitoun, a deep, steep, boulder-strewn ravine that stretches for kilometers eastward with barely a foothold. The ravine was usually dry and barren, but winter had brought heavy rain to the center of the country, making the floor of Wadi Kareitoun slippery.

Thirty feet behind Arik, four men bore a stretcher carrying a ninety-kilogram man. He could see their red faces sweating profusely. Fatigue had set in, and they looked nearly delirious. Suddenly, one of the front stretcher bearers fainted, sending all four of them and their passenger to the boulders below.

One man lay unconscious. The tibias of two other men had assumed unnatural shapes; one soldier's bone had protruded through the skin, and the man was actively bleeding. Instinctively, Arik ran back to help. A crowd formed.

"We don't have another stretcher in sight," Captain Yigal barked. "We can't wait. Get a radioman to call for an ambulance. Everyone, we can't stop! There's no time for spectating! We have to get out of the ravine, and fast. No help can reach us here. There will be an ambulance waiting at the entrance to Ein Gedi Park."

As they loaded the bleeding man onto the only stretcher, he lost consciousness.

Arik spoke quietly to Yigal. "Sar-el is actively bleeding and acutely dehydrating. I think he's in dire shape. Please let me take him down myself. I'll get him down faster than the stretcher can."

"Can you do this? You look near total exhaustion yourself. It's 38 degrees Celsius!"

A slight smile crept onto Arik's face. "Yes, sir! I still have plenty of fuel in my tank."

"Then go! Run like a tiger!"

In a flash, Arik picked up the wounded man and put him into a fireman's carry. Blood dripped onto Arik's sweat-soaked shirt. He took off in a near sprint, virtually flying over the boulders. "Make way! Make way!" he called out as he ran.

Heads turned, and quick recognition dawned on the other trainees' faces that this was no drill or sergeant's prank. A significant stream of blood had stained Arik's uniform and was fast running down to his toes. Arik ran at a full sprint for the eight remaining kilometers to the waiting ambulance.

Major Gavi Shiloni, standing at the pick-up point, stared at Arik when he arrived. He became somewhat ashamed when he thought about what was to come. Captain Yigal filed his report on the incident. When Arik gave his version of the event, he did not give Gavi as much as a sideways glance.

The remaining forty kilometers of the march were south along the flat banks of the Dead Sea at night. To the trainees' left, light twinkled in the Moab Hills on the eastern bank of the Sea. All the marchers knew that those were the lights of the enemy, the Jordanians. They understood that one day they would have to fight them.

The trainees hardly spoke to one another. Most of them had reached total exhaustion. Some were near madness as they trudged face down, thinking only about putting one foot in front of the other in grim determination to finish. But they knew that the worst was yet to come. Before dawn, they would have to ascend the 1,300-foot rock face of the eastern cliffs of the natural fortress of Masada. The narrow, steeply snaking path that wove back and forth up the mountain was the only way up for the hundreds of men who already were at wit's end. Less than two kilometers to go!

Arik walked with the front group, reaching the summit just as the sun rose over the eastern horizon. He emptied the remaining contents of his canteen over his head, euphoric over what he realized was his greatest physical achievement to date.

***

The massive, flat-topped mountain overlooking the Dead Sea valley, called Masada, is awesome and dramatic at dawn, with the sun coming up in the east, over the mountains of Moab. Masada resonates with tragic Jewish history.

The final stand of the Jewish rebellion against Rome took place at Masada in 73 CE: From the top of the massive monolith, nearly 1,000 Jews held off the full might of the Roman Empire for three years. When the Romans breached the wall of the fortress and stormed the compound, they found that all of the defenders had chosen suicide over captivity, thus depriving the Romans of victory. Through two millennia, this battle had become emblematic of Jewish courage, sacrifice, and determination in the face of overwhelming odds. It had been an inspirational venue for paratrooper graduation ceremonies for decades, and this ceremony was no different.

The tekes siyyum, or graduation ceremony, for paratroopers was a solemn, emotional affair. It represented more than a half year of excruciating—nearly superhuman—physical and psychological exertion. Members of the General Staff were in attendance to present the paratroopers with their wings and red berets, after an inspirational call to arms, a show parade, and the playing of the Israeli Army's anthem. Rapturous family members made the long trip from central Israel and up the cable car to the top of Masada to share the moment. Upon the conclusion of the "Hatikvah," Israel's national anthem, the family members rushed their children and spouses, and the crowd became a sea of tears and embraces. Arik stood alone, picking his nails and sighing. This was like visitors' day at Camp Moshava all over again. He moved along with the crowd.

Eventually, the crowd's attention was turned to a makeshift boxing ring that had been set up in the square in front of the West Palace ruins. Rows of seats stretched in every direction. Arik felt like a sheep going to the slaughter. Despite his best efforts, he had felt distracted and emotionally drained by his chronic, painful yearning for Dahlia. He was unable to comprehend why he had not heard not a word from her in so many months. In addition to that emotional pain was the physical pain of his arms, legs, and sides, which burned from the long march. He felt dizzy and dehydrated.

Shuki Baum was a legendary fighter and a real showman. He attracted crowds wherever he fought. Gavi had pulled off a real coup, with the help of a mutual friend, in getting him to agree to take part in the fight at the ceremony.

The seats around the boxing ring filled rapidly.

Gavi addressed the audience. "In honor of our new paratroopers, we have arranged a martial arts exhibition. On the bill today, we have Shuki Baum—I do not need to tell you who he is—and our own Arik Meir. It should be a good match. The two will fight until one of them gives up."

Shuki marched into the ring, his arms raised, waving to the cheering crowd. Arik walked in afterward to tepid applause and cat calls from the members of the other platoons.

"Go to Vietnam, and get your ass fried with all your buddies!"

"Americans are sissies! They don't know how to fight!"

The heckling was drowned out by the shouts of the men in Arik's platoon, whose admiration and affection he had earned over the past six brutal months. They had had enough of watching Arik getting beaten up by his superiors, for reasons that were largely unclear to them.

The two men stood at opposite ends of the ring, about twenty feet apart. Thinking that if this was to be a martial arts exhibition he should fight barefoot, Arik stooped down to untie his boots. He also had thought that there would be an announcer. When he looked down, he was caught unprepared. Shuki came charging at him and hit him in the nose with a swift front kick. When the boot made contact, the cracking sound was followed by a torrent of blood that issued from Arik's face. Momentarily blinded, Arik saw nothing but white as he reeled backward and fell to the ground. There were cheers and laughter from the crowd.

"Kick his sorry American ass!"

"Finish him off, Shuki!"

"Leave him alone!"

'He's just finished the march with us! Why are you mocking him? You jerks! You don't even know him!"

"He's one of us! Leave him alone!"

"This isn't a fair fight! Shuki is fresh! Put a stop to this! This is slaughter! Why is this happening?"

Arik's comrades sat in horror. They shook their heads as they looked at the commanders, not comprehending why they had let this happen.

"I thought this was supposed to be a friendly exhibition match," Arik said, wiping the blood off his face and pinching his nose to stop the bleeding.

Shuki laughed. "Who told you that? This is about teaching you a lesson you'll never forget. In America, they have those girly exhibitions. Oh! God forbid someone should make contact or get a bruise. In America, they don't know how to fight. I'll show you how it's done in Israel."

Why is everyone in Israel trying to teach me a lesson I'll never forget? I didn't think I was so stupid to begin with, Arik thought. He felt so weak. Why didn't I hydrate more?

The words of his Jeet Kune Do master, Dan Inosanto, flashed through his mind:

Forget about winning and losing. Forget about pride and pain. Let your opponent graze your skin, and you smash into his flesh. Let him smash into your flesh, and you fracture his bones. Let him fracture your bones, and you take his life! Do not be concerned with you escaping safely. Lay your life before him! The great mistake is to anticipate the outcome of the engagement; you ought not to be thinking of whether it will end in victory or in defeat. Let nature take its course, and use your tools to strike at the right moment.

Shuki lunged at Arik to punch him in the mouth. But Arik gauged the distance between them and backed up just enough that Shuki's fist found nothing but air. The same thing happened when Shuki aimed a front kick at Arik's groin. A roundhouse kick aimed at the side of Arik's head flew harmlessly as he ducked just in time. Shuki continued to lunge at Arik, arms and legs flying in all directions, but Arik dodged backward and around the ring for the next two minutes.

The catcalls from the crowd grew louder and louder.

"Arik, you coward, why don't you stand up and fight like man?"

"You're just a frightened American chicken! Cock a doodle doo!"

"My baby sister could do better than you!"

Some of Arik's comrades were furious and wanted to rush the arena, but they were warned off by the MPs.

Arik remained calm and tried to block out the noise. Focus, focus! His head pounded, and his ears rang. He willed his exhausted limbs to obey his commands.

When Shuki had Arik cornered at the edge of the circle, he threw a high front kick at Arik's chin. Arik caught Shuki's right foot in midair and threw it ten inches higher, throwing Shuki off balance just enough for Arik to land a solid front kick to Shuki's groin. There was a loud thud and, with a high-pitched shriek and gasp, Shuki fell toward the ground. Before Shuki could hit the ground, though, Arik grabbed his outstretched left arm and, with lightning speed before Shuki could react, drove his palm and all of his body weight into the back of Shuki's elbow. The elbow gave, hyperextending into such an unnatural position that the fractured end of the humerus ruptured through the skin of Shuki's elbow, carrying with it the median nerve and brachial artery. There was a mass of spurting blood, and Shuki's hand went limp. Shuki let out another shriek but to no avail. As soon as Arik regained his balance, he thrust his left boot into Shuki's temple, rendering him unconscious. When Shuki slumped to the ground, Arik kicked him again, this time in his left lower ribs, eliciting a sickening crunch. Shuki lay supine and unconscious on the ground. Arik put a boot to his throat. Blood gurgled out of Shuki's mouth.

There was a gasp and then stunned silence from the crowd. The takedown had taken less than thirty seconds.

Arik, still bleeding from his nose, vomited, oblivious to the large crowd.

Standing over Shuki, Arik looked at Gavi, who looked back at him open-mouthed. "Gavi!" he yelled hoarsely, "I didn't want this. You made me do this, to humiliate me in public. This was no exhibition. Shuki told me that. You wanted him to finish me off. I never wanted to fight. The difference between you and me is you're in the army because you have to be. I never had to be here. I volunteered to come to Israel to serve, and you've made my life a living hell. You've made me your personal gladiator. Well, great Caesar, shall this man live or die? You decide!" He held his thumb up and then switched it to point down.

Gavi yelled back at him, "The man was already down. There was no reason for you to try to kill him. You are going to spend the rest of your army career in Tel Mond prison."

"Enough! Enough!" General Tal rose to his feet, waving his arms. "I've seen more than enough of this circus! Get a helicopter, and get this soldier to the hospital. He's been seriously injured. Arik, you go with him and get your nose examined. Then return to base immediately, where you'll be confined to your quarters. Gavi, follow me! The rest of you, the show is over. Get back on the buses. Back to the base!"

The crowd rapidly thinned as everyone scattered.

"What kind of circus are you running here, Gavi?" General Tal could not contain his fury. "Rumors have been spreading about the kind of operation you're in command of. We want our basic training to be tough, so that we can turn our citizens into soldiers, but what you're doing here borders on sadism. We've seen recruits come out of your command with serious psychological problems, unable to continue on to more advanced training. You haven't grasped the law of diminishing returns.

"We know what you've put Arik through. It appears that you've singled him out for extreme hazing, to break him. Thank heavens you haven't, in my estimation. We're fully aware of what happened to your cousin Eldad. He was also an abusive creature who had it coming. Eyewitnesses came forward and reported that Arik had acted in self-defense against him. We conducted our investigation without your knowledge, because we didn't want any of your meddling. We let Arik's hazing go on, for reasons that are beyond your pay grade.

"You're supposed to be running a training camp, not a prisoner of war camp. The fact that he's come through in one piece is a testimony to his toughness—not to any quality of your program. We've also uncovered the falsification of the records for some of your recruits, Arik's included. When that was discovered, we stationed undercover evaluators throughout the base, at key points, to rate the recruits' performance. Our evaluations will stand, and yours will be discarded. Arik will be a fine soldier, despite your efforts. Today's performance is just icing on the cake.

"Arik and several others will be removed from this base, and you'll be reassigned to Mifreket forward base at the Suez Canal. It's isolated there, and you'll have plenty of time to contemplate what you've done—when you're not dodging Egyptian artillery shells. Don't even think of trying to appeal this. I've been sent here by order of the defense minister himself. You should feel ashamed for turning what was supposed to be a sacred moment in the lives of Israeli paratroopers into a farce."

General Tal stormed off.

After getting his nose set and bandaged, Arik returned to the base and went to his tent. The other members of his platoon did not know what to say to him, so they mostly just stared at him or told him, as they walked by, how sorry they were about the way things had turned out. None of them had ever experienced that level of violence up close.

Arik considered trying to engage them in conversation, but to what end? Things suddenly felt tentative and unstable. He did not know what was going to happen next. He felt completely alone . . . again. He lay on his cot, with an ice pack over his bandaged but already grossly swollen nose. All his muscles ached from the exertion and emotional strain of the previous thirty-six hours. His head pounded loudly and his eyes seared with pain as they swelled shut. He gave up the battle and closed his eyes.

At midnight, he was jolted out of sleep by two MPs.

"Private Meir, collect your things, and come with us." The men were polite but very firm in their tone.

Arik, unsteady on his feet, quietly did as he was told. He felt as if the tent were spinning. He gathered up his meager possessions, dumped them into his duffel bag and, without saying a word, exited the tent. The chill wind shocked him, and he struggled to stay on his feet. He was escorted to the back of a covered truck. It was pitch-dark. He felt his way to a bench. There was none, just the cold corrugated-steel floor. He sat with his head and upper torso bent over his knees and tried to get some sleep as the truck bumped along the semi paved road.

By his hazy reckoning, they were headed north. Hours passed as he sat alone, nursing his face, the ice having long since melted. The air seemed to become warmer and more humid. He awoke a while later, when the road smoothed out. Must be a highway, he thought. Must be heading out of the Sinai. He slumped over, still clutching the ice pack to his bloody nose, and fell asleep again.

When Arik awoke the next time, it was full daylight. Looking out the plastic windows, he could make out the ocean, green fields, and houses on a flat plain. He spotted the city of Haifa off to his left as the road climbed Mount Carmel. The truck turned right. He guessed that they were headed for Eastern Galilee. But why? Where are they taking me? Passing the Sea of Galilee and Tiberias on the right, the truck began its sudden rise up the plateau of the Golan Heights. The landscape transformed from the green of the Galilee to volcanic scrubland. On both sides of the road were vast areas fenced off with barbed wire that bore small, triangular yellow signs that read, "ATTENTION! DO NOT ENTER! MINES!"

Suddenly, the truck stopped at a guard station. The MPs ordered Arik out of the truck. In front of him stood a base, of sorts, with tents in a row, some buildings, and strange equipment that he had never seen before. The entire area was cordoned off by a tall, razor-wire fence. An Israeli flag fluttered on a makeshift flagpole. Arik was escorted, duffel bag over his shoulder, through a white gate and arch labeled CAMP NACHSHON.

A penal camp for military criminals, he thought.

They stopped in front of a building, and one of the MPs told Arik to "just stand there." After thirty minutes in the hot sun, Arik was escorted into the darkness of the command center by an officer wearing combat fatigues. He was startled to be greeted by General Tal and another General, Manno Shaked.

General Tal smiled broadly. "Arik, you're quite a good fighter. No, a great fighter. Shuki was the Krav Maga champion of the army and had never lost a match until yesterday. You dispatched him in under thirty seconds, and that after a ninety-kilometer forced march. Remarkable! Where did you learn how to fight like that?"

"I studied Jeet Kune Do in Los Angeles with one of Bruce Lee's disciples, sir."

"Ah. Well, I have made two plans for you: one for now and one for later," Tal said. "I want you to meet General Shaked and your new company commander, Major Ehud Barak."

"Arik," Barak said, "We've been told a great deal about you. I've heard all about your basic training." He reached out to shake Arik's hand and smiled broadly.

Arik liked the major immediately. He was shorter than Arik but powerfully built, suntanned, and wiry. He had a no-nonsense but fair quality about him. His eyes shone with canny wisdom and quick wit. He seemed genuinely interested in meeting Arik.

"Many people in the army are talking about you. Did you know that, Arik?" Barak asked.

"No, sir. I didn't."

"You had a perfect score on your psychometric exams and an outstanding performance record during your basic training. What you did on the beret march nearly defies description. And then to defeat Shuki afterward!" Barak did not mention the falsified records. "I think that you would be a great asset to my unit."

General Shaked nodded his agreement.

General Tal took over again. "Arik, your conduct in basic training showed that you think clearly on your feet and under high-stress situations, including war scenarios. You showed significant leadership abilities commensurate with your enormous physical talents. You've been selected to join this commando unit. Have you ever heard of Sayeret Matkal?"

"No, sir."

"Of course not," Tal said. "You're not Israeli, not really. Sayeret Matkal is the IDF's most elite commando unit, with a proud history dating all the way back to the formation of the Palmach shock units before the State was born. Non-Israelis are never recruited to this unit, but since you were born in Israel we've considered you.

"Matkal is the tip of the spear. Commandos from this unit undertake the most dangerous and physically arduous missions imaginable. We have no tolerance for indolence, idiots, or big shots. We've learned that those clowns get themselves and others around them killed in battle. You'll need to begin another basic training, of sorts, to get up to speed. You'll experience great hardships, but you'll be treated fairly. We know what you've been put through and why, but that's all behind you now. Is this all clear?"

"Yes, sir. "You mentioned that there was a second thing, sir."

Tal chuckled. "You're quite right. I almost forgot. I don't know when you'll have an opportunity, but I want you to consider making an instructional film about hand-to-hand combat, highlighting your skills. Remember: It will be a training film for recruits, so you need to be very clear. If it's good enough, it will become part of the basic training module. We'll find a suitable partner for you to demonstrate your techniques."

"That sounds great! I hope I'll have time to do that."

"We'll make time," Tal said. "Good luck to you."

And with that, the generals left.

"My assistant, Lieutenant Ziv, will direct you to your quarters and acquaint you with your squad," Barak said. "Welcome."

One of the more diabolical methods used to toughen up Israeli special forces recruits was called aggressiveness training. It was designed to maximize the recruit's release of inner aggression and cure the recruit of the fear of being struck. These exercises occurred during bus rides to and from field exercises.

Initially, Arik had thought that a bus ride would be a great way to unwind and rest, compared to the marches that he had grown accustomed to. Therefore, he was a bit confused when the trainers numbered the seats on the bus on his first ride.

Soon, an instructor called out, "Whoever is in seat number three, I want him to go to seat twenty-five. It's the task of the rest of you to prevent him from getting there."

It was musical chairs from combat hell. Total mayhem ensued. The bus became a sea of bloodcurdling howls, kicked heads, broken fingers, smashed noses, and broken ribs. If a recruit occasionally got through, the bus stopped and everyone was ordered out to do fifty push-ups and a half-kilometer run through the rocks and trees. Arik's comrades knew that if he got hold of the "traveler," that traveler's trip to the assigned seat would be over. Arik made things short and sweet, pinning the traveler so tightly that he could barely breathe let alone less escape. But if Arik was the traveler, which the instructor made sure of if he was in a particularly sadistic mood, he muscled his way into his newly assigned seat, significant injuries resulted among the others, and there were the inevitable push-ups and frolic through the meadows. The instructors soon saw the wisdom of excluding Arik from the exercise.

As this went on, day after day, the sense of aggressiveness became hardwired into the recruits. They were told that it would serve them in good stead later on.

Another exercise from which Arik was excluded, except for as an advisor, was Krav Maga training. Word of Arik's mastery of martial arts had gotten out, and the instructors had decided early on not to allow him to spar with any of the other recruits except in a defensive role or as a sparring partner. Arik enjoyed assisting and demonstrating techniques—left jabs, roundhouse kicks, right crosses, uppercuts, and left hooks, among others—any way he could. He joined the other recruits in kickboxing with bags. He was fascinated by the difference in philosophy between kung fu and Krav Maga. In Krav Maga, there was less emphasis on perfecting form and more emphasis on pure aggressiveness made a fine art. He also quietly realized what had gotten Shuki Baum into trouble in their bout, but he knew to keep his mouth shut about it.

Another aggressiveness drill was a combat version of Red Rover. One person was assigned to run pell-mell from one end of the gym to the other, and it was everyone else's job to prevent him from reaching that other end. Just to play with the recruits' heads, the instructors brought in a seasoned Sayeret Matkal veteran, a small man no more than five feet eight but built like a steamroller, to break through the mob of recruits while they tried to block his forward progress. He barreled through the crowd of much larger men, with ease, demonstrating the effectiveness of mental strength, that is, until he reached Arik, who had assumed the pose of a linebacker. The senior man pushed as hard as he might against Arik, grunting loudly, but he could not budge him even an inch. Arik awkwardly wondered what to do next. Finally, Arik decided to lift the man up over his head. The poor fellow kicked the air, flailed helplessly, and cursed profusely. Arik carried him across the gym and gently deposited him on a mat near the doorway. The other recruits stood mute and open-mouthed.

The senior man stared at Arik in astonishment. Finally, he said, "Who are you?"

"Arik. Arik Meir."

"I know who you are. Maybe I should have asked, 'What are you?' I've never seen anything like you before!"

Arik smiled and shrugged. "I hope I didn't hurt you, sir. If I did, I'm terribly sorry."

"Just my ego. I'd already heard about you, but I had to experience your strength in person. I'm Colonel Zvi Langer. I'm your field commander. I'm just glad you're on our side." He laughed. "Welcome to the unit."

Arik hadn't noticed that several junior officers had gathered at the side of the gym to witness the event. One of them walked up to him in the aftermath of the confusion, which had interrupted the flow of the training exercise.

"Arik, you're one strong sonofabitch! I'd heard what you did to Shuki Baum, but I had to see you for myself. I've been in the army for six years, and I've never seen anything like you before." The officer spoke in fluent, unaccented American English.

"Are you American?" Arik asked.

"No, but I spent much of my growing-up years there. I was born here but moved to the States when I was a kid. My dad's a professor at Dropsie College, outside Philly. In fact, he's still there."

"So, you're a lone soldier, too."

"Sort of. My parents are still in the States, but I have two brothers here training in the paratroops. I couldn't wait to get back to Israel. I found people in the States to be too superficial and materialistic. When I'm here, I feel like I'm part of something historic, something bigger than me. I like that. So, why are you here? I've seen your file. You're from LA?"

"Yes, I am. My story is crazy complicated, though. You're the first person I've met from the States since I've been here. In fact, I haven't spoken English in months. I've even started to think in Hebrew. Are you stationed here?"

"I am for now. I get reassigned as I'm needed. I spent several months with Sayeret Haruv, on the West Bank, ambushing and chasing terrorists around the block. They have me doing a short stint training recruits here. I heard what crap they loaded on you during your basic training. That's too bad, but things will be a lot better for you here. I'll keep an eye on you and make sure you're treated fairly. Let's talk more later. I've got to run."

"I don't even know your name!"

"Oh, sorry about that. I'm Yoni Netanyahu."

"Nice meeting you, Yoni!"

Finally, someone I can talk to, someone who can understand me, and—
perhaps one day—someone I can trust.

For the next two weeks, Arik was on the firing ranges more than twelve
hours a day, firing hundreds of rounds from the various weapons used by special
forces worldwide—M16, Uzi, AK-47, CAR-15 carbines, and semiautomatic and
automatic machine pistols—each with specific uses in counterterrorist
operations. He learned the strengths, weaknesses, and optimal utility of each
weapon. He learned a new way of shooting, from the hip, something that he had
been told in basic training was done only in the movies. He was taught that most
terrorists resorted to spraying an area with machine gun fire. He learned that by
placing a weapon in semiautomatic mode he could run rapidly past a line of
targets and shoot bursts of three shots per second at them. With practice, he was
able to hit each target within a two-inch radius with the requisite number of hits.
He learned precision shooting, how to make the accurate shot required to pick
off a terrorist in a crowd while minimizing collateral damage. The endless
repetition of shooting thousands of rounds from all distances and firing
positions, including on the run while loaded down with the full complement of
military hardware, made Arik feel that he was joining the ranks of one of the
most elite and feared special forces organizations on the planet.

He quickly felt at home with the other men in the unit. To a man, they
were serious and mature but not to point of being morose. They were kindred
spirits. There was plenty of time between training exercises for Arik to talk with
and get to know his fellow soldiers. The training, although intense and exacting,
left him with enough time to recharge his batteries. He felt that he had arrived at
a place where the object was no longer to harass the soldiers but to seriously
train them and impart to them the critical skills that they would need in carrying
out the extremely dangerous missions that they would be involved in soon.

There were detailed instruction in open-field navigation and map
reading, survival drills that made war week in basic training look like
kindergarten, and endless complex problem-solving exercises that were
designed to force them to think on the run and improvise as battlefield scenarios
shifted, much as they do in war. Arik was learning how to lead and make
complex decisions, something that he knew he would need to know if he
decided to become an officer candidate one day.

That isn't to say that there weren't forced marches. Sixty-kilometer
trots in full battle gear in the blazing hot sun were commonplace. Arik, just off
the beret march, did not find these too difficult, though. Despite the constant
thirst, he jogged in the front most of the time. That put him in the company of
the officers. He never stopped being impressed by the fact that the officers never
demanded anything from the recruits and noncommissioned officers (NCOs)
that they didn't subject themselves to. They were always setting the example.
What a great way to lead! All of the men in Arik's unit were in really good
shape, so there wasn't the bitching and moaning that he had had to bear during
basic training. The speed and intensity of the marching was a whole different
level, too. Arik reveled in the whole experience.

Yoni was Arik's frequent companion during the marches, and Arik felt
himself opening up to this quiet, serious man who always asked piercing

questions and seemed genuinely interested in the answers. In fact, Yoni was the first person Arik could really open up to—except for Dahlia and the reverend, of course. What will Dahlia say? She had wanted him to join the Israeli military as a means of beginning their lives together, but special forces? He had read about the American Green Berets, but for him to imagine that he would be a soldier of the same caliber and a proud Jew at the same time was beyond his expectation. Dahlia will be so pleased! He silently prayed that Dahlia's parents would finally feel that he was worthy of her.

Dani Zohar was somewhat different than the others. Arik had met him on his very first day at Camp Nachson, their cots being next to each other. Although serious and sharp when he had to be, he had a ready smile and always seemed cheerful. His bright-red hair that always appeared to be on fire and his freckled face accentuated his comedic countenance. Physically very fit, he easily kept pace with Arik and kept up everyone's spirits during the longest of marches and particularly difficult technical exercises. He found the humor, irony, or absurdity in any situation and frequently put even the officers in stitches when he relayed a joke or a funny anecdote. Arik found his presence a welcome counterpoint to the darkness that he frequently felt inside himself. He was drawn to him. Dani also was a great listener, and Arik opened up to him as well. He told him all about Dahlia and how fervently he hoped that the blackout curtain that had descended over him would be lifted soon.

Things were finally coming together for Arik. Yet his mind always returned to the same thought: God, I miss Dahlia!

***

"Where are we going, Ze'evi? You always like to be so mysterious. Why can't I ever know where we're going until we get there? You still treat me like a child."

"Kitty cat, have you ever gone anywhere with me where you didn't have a good time?"

"No."

"So, what's the problem? I promise we'll have a great time. We're headed to Exuma, in the Caribbean. The whole circle is coming. My family has an amazing house with its own private beach. There's nobody around for at least mile in every direction. The house is in a jungle clearing that opens up to the water. There's a full range of watersports. We'll have our own powerboat and fifty-foot sailing skiff moored nearby. We have a catering staff that will serve, clean up, and then discreetly disappear. Don't worry so much . . . By the way, what did you tell your parents?"

"The usual, that I was spending the weekend at your parent's house in the Hamptons. Did you bring anything?"

"I did say we'd have a great time this weekend. Didn't I? So—"

"But how are you going to get it through customs? You promised, no trouble."

"Like I said, don't worry so much! It's not about bringing stuff in. They just don't want to catch you selling the stuff. That makes them crazy. As long as you let them know in advance that you're bringing it in—and you know whom to reward for their efforts—they understand it's for personal use only."

The members of the circle met at Miami International Airport and were escorted to Ze'evi's Learjet.

"Kitty cat, there's another couple you haven't met yet," Ze'evi said. "Dolly, I want you to meet June and Michael. Mike and I were roommates in college. I can't believe you haven't met him yet, in fact."

Dahlia smiled and shook hands with them.

After the plane took off, Kate opened her satchel. "Anyone want hors d'oeuvres?" she asked. She passed around her marijuana-filled satchel.

In a few minutes, they were in the midst of heavy, sweet-smelling smoke and giggles. The vacation had begun in earnest.

After landing in Exuma, they traveled through the jungle in a Land Rover. The house was a sprawling, airy four-bedroom tropical teak-and-bamboo house with a glass wall that faced the private beach and the ocean beyond. It was richly decorated in brightly colored fabrics and wicker furniture in the dining room and living room. The cathedral ceilings were dotted with numerous ceiling fans. The large wraparound terrace featured a built-in grilling kitchen and a hot tub with a panoramic view of the secluded bay below. The bedrooms were luxuriantly appointed, reflecting the impeccable taste of Sergio Blanc, a world-famous interior-design house in Barbados that specialized in island and tropical decor.

***

"Who's up for an afternoon swim?" Patty asked.

Dahlia went to the bedroom that she shared with Ze'evi to fetch her bikini. As she was putting it on, Ze'evi smiled and said, "You won't be needing that. It's a private beach."

"Still. I've never been naked in public before."

"You'd be the only one dressed. You'll stand out more if you wear that thing than if you don't. Anyway, you're not in public. We're all good friends here."

He held her close and kissed her.

"It's going to be okay, kitty cat. Lighten up a little. Just go with the flow. I promise nobody will take a bite out of you. I won't let them."

"A quick sniff would help."

"Coming right up!"

Dahlia took one of Ze'evi's rolled-up hundred-dollar bills. In a few minutes, she felt better about the whole thing.

The hardest part was getting off the veranda. Seeing that everyone else was in the same state of undress made it easier for her.

"That's my girl! You see, it wasn't so hard. Now, was it?"

Dahlia tentatively walked down the stairs, spread her towel on the sand, and lay face down.

Mike sidled over to Ze'evi. "Where'd you find that girl scout? And how'd you ever talk her out of her clothes? Talk about fresh meat! She still has her store label on her."

"You're not going to believe it, but she's still in high school."

"You're fucking going to jail for this. What the hell's wrong with you, Ze'evi?"

"Relax, Mikey. She's eighteen, just. But that's what counts." Ze'evi smiled under his aviator glasses.

"That gal's got a killer body. I hope you won't mind if I sample some of the goods."

"I don't see why not. You'll get your chance tonight. Sharing is a virtue, I always say. I've really turned this kitten out. When we first met, she was Little Bo Peep, pining after some high school sweetheart. She's become quite the nympho of late—sex-crazed, insatiable. I have her doing anything I want. But she has no clue what's coming up next."

"It's like being in college all over again. I have to hand it to you, Ze'evi. You haven't lost your touch. Does she have any inkling about you and Charlotte?"

"Are you kidding?"

"You're such a cad, Ze'evi."

"I know what I want, and I get what I want. You know that. But being the man that I am, I'm happy to share the goods. She's never done anything with multiple partners at once. She wasn't ready before, but I think she's coming around. We're going to have potluck tonight."

"Yummy! I love when we do it with newbies. It makes it so much more interesting. Look at her. She's so pale. She's going to get a serious sunburn. We can't have that. You don't mind if I engage in a little preventive medicine?"

Mike lay a towel on the sand next to Dahlia, who still was face down with her eyes closed, and poured suntan lotion on her back. She bolted up, startled.

He nudged her gently back down on her towel.

"Shhh . . . Relax, Dahlia. No need to be so jumpy. I'm just putting some suntan lotion on your back, so you won't get a terrible burn."

Dahlia stared up at Ze'evi, who nodded his approval and smiled. Meanwhile, Mike slowly ran his hands up and down her body. She started to relax.

"That's it," Mike said. "I don't want to miss any spot, or you'll really be uncomfortable later. Now, turn over."

The discomfort that Dahlia felt at the thought of being touched so intimately by Mike was clouded by the cocaine and vodka that was coursing through her veins. She did what she was told and let herself go, with a long sigh.

Her unease about her nudity began to dissipate when they played a spirited game of five-on-five beach volleyball. She found it curious that nobody leered at her. Ze'evi was right. She fit in with them. She wondered what it would have been like to play nude beach volleyball at Camp Moshava. She giggled internally at the prospect. These people obviously were so much worldlier and grown up. They were not perturbed by simple convention. Everything seemed so natural for them. The casual manner in which the other four nude women wandered around was somehow reassuring to Dahlia. She relaxed more deeply. It's been an interesting weekend so far, she thought. Later, when I reenter the real world, I'll chalk this up to experience. Why not sow my wild oats now, while I'm young?

The afternoon was spent sailing on Ze'evi's skiff. He had brought a captain down from Miami. Loud rock music, champagne, and beer on board set the scene while the sleek white sailboat sliced through the azure waters of the Caribbean.

So, this is how the other half lives, Dahlia thought. My school friends would faint if they saw me. She felt completely removed from that world, as if she were living a pleasure-filled dream. A yacht passed close by, going in the opposite direction. The men on board appeared completely bemused by the five naked woman who stood up to wave at them. Ze'evi passed out scuba gear, and everyone jumped off the boat to admire the tropical fish and coral reefs below.

Ze'evi gave Dahlia a crash course in scuba diving and outfitted her.

"Just stick with me," he said. "We won't go down very deep. The reefs are no more than thirty feet below the surface. Keep your eyes on the regulator."

***

Dahlia went downstairs for dinner, barefoot and dressed in a blue-and-white-striped blouse and small white shorts. Charlotte and June eyed her from the veranda, where they sat sipping cocktails.

"That Dahlia is a real cutie, but she seems so young," June said. "She's dressed like a teenager on a first date. Is she even eighteen? I hope Ze'evi knows what he's doing. He has a weakness for cradle robbing. It makes me a bit uneasy that we're corrupting the girl."

"You know she's the daughter of the Israeli ambassador, right?" Charlotte asked.

"Shit! Really? Do her parents even know where she is or what's going on here? If her presence here gets exposed somehow, this could really get ugly."

"I've thought of that. But the fact is she's over eighteen. She's free to make her own decisions. She's out to explore the world, and if we don't corrupt her somebody else will. We're not kidnapping her. She's here to have a good time, and we can help her try out some new things."

"Do you think she has any inkling about you and Ze'evi?"

"No, I don't think so."

"And you're fine with what's going on?"

"Sure. Ze'evi is like a little boy. I have no problem with letting him play, letting him get it out of his system. He'll soon tire of her, like all the others."

Dinner was a lavish affair, at sunset, in an open-air pavilion. Everyone sat on pillows on a large straw mat. They enjoyed large plates of conch ceviche, grilled jerk chicken crostini, blackened grouper, coconut shrimp, and risotto. Key lime pie and rum cakes rounded out the meal. Flaming tiki torches provided all the light that was needed. A warm island breeze blew through the pavilion on the perfect starlit night.

After dinner, Ze'evi stood up and announce the night's activity. "Welcome to Camp Ehrenreich," he said.

The others giggled.

"I hope everyone is having a grand time so far. I think we should celebrate our first night here with a potluck round robin."

"What's that?" Dahlia asked Charlotte, who was sitting next to her.

Charlotte smiled at her slyly. "One of Ze'evi's ideas of fun. He's got a crazy imagination. I don't know how he comes up with the stuff sometimes . . . Don't worry, Dahlia." Charlotte patted Dahlia's knee. "You'll find it different, but you'll have a great time."

Dahlia's intuition kicked in, and she became apprehensive. She excused herself to the bedroom, where she expertly lined up a column of white powder on a mirror and snorted it in a matter of seconds.

She returned downstairs and found that Ze'evi was leading everyone to a "yoga studio," where they sat in a circle, alternating genders, with their legs crossed. Mike sat opposite Dahlia and eyed her intently. She glanced around the room and felt a pang of panic when she saw what she understood to be a variety of sex toys. There were velvet-covered handcuffs, latex clothes and masks, and whips. A movie camera on a tripod was standing in the corner of the room.

"So, here we go. Welcome to the game room," Ze'evi said. "I did this once, believe it or not, in an experiential learning session at college. All of us know one another by our senses of sight and sound. Getting to know one another using our other senses is a whole new way of team building.

"Here's how it goes. When the lights go out, by using our hands and feet, and what have you, we explore the people around us. The only rule is keep it gentle. No roughhousing. Clear? There's no talking or communication of any kind except by the senses of touch and smell."

Dahlia's panic rose. What's going to happen? Anything can happen in the dark! She suddenly wanted to run away. I'm getting in over my head! Ze'evi was not the same guy that she had first met. She knew that much for certain. He had already surprised her in many ways, and not all of them were pleasant. Is my life taking a very strange turn? Or is this part of growing up, striking outside of my comfort zone and exposing myself to new things? There really isn't anywhere I can go now. I'm in too deep already. She decided to see this weekend through and then make some decisions afterward.

Ze'evi turned off the lights, and there was a slow-motion scramble in the dark, toward the center of the circle. Dahlia sat motionless. She suddenly felt a man's hand running up and down her torso. Then another pair of hands. She couldn't tell whether they were male or female. She was being touched—groped—all over. In a flurry of tugging, her clothing was removed. She could feel herself falling down a vortex in the dark as her body was invaded in multiple places simultaneously. She let out a whimper but was shushed by the others. She submitted to her overwhelming sense of helplessness as she was dragged into the abyss. She knew that she had crossed the threshold into a dimension from which it would be almost impossible to return. She went limp and submitted to the physical assault.

After an hour that had seemed like an eternity to Dahlia, the light was came on. She was lying sprawled in a heap of sweaty, naked bodies. The scene was a swirling haze. She blinked and rubbed her eyes. She was seized by shame and guilt. What am I doing here? How did I sink so low? Panic stricken, all she could think about was running home, back to her parents, back to her safe past, back to an innocent time and place. Back to Arik.

How did I get mixed up in this mess? Ze'evi dragged me into it, but really it was Arik's fault. If he hadn't dumped me and shattered my heart, I never would have been here to begin with. How could that jerk, Arik, do this to me, when I gave myself over to him so completely? I was so careful about giving my heart away before, but now it's strewn in the street for anyone to pick up or kick away.

Dahlia ran out of the yoga studio, clutching her clothing against her body and desperately trying to cover herself, like Eve in the Garden of Eden. She felt so foolish. What's the point of covering up when I've just given it all away to everyone and nobody cares, now, whether I'm naked or not? I need to get out of this lunatic asylum before I go completely mad. But where can I go? And how can I get there? I'm trapped. She ran into the bedroom, shut the door, and lay on Ze'evi's bed, under the covers, crying softly into the pillow.

Ze'evi walked into the bedroom. "What's the matter, kitty cat?"

"I was violated just now. This isn't what I want. I'm doing things I never imagined. This is so degrading. I want to go home." Dahlia continued to sob.

"You know I love you. We're just having a little fun. I wouldn't let any harm come to you. You're acting like a child. You want to go home to mommy? I just figured you'd be ready to play with the grown-ups. Perhaps I was wrong. The weekend is only beginning, and there aren't any flights out until Sunday afternoon. I won't ask you to do anything else you don't feel comfortable doing. Okay?"

Dahlia shook her head and tried to wipe away her tears. She sniffed another line of cocaine. She began to feel better about the whole thing. The rest of the weekend was spent water skiing, scuba diving, and trying out Ze'evi's "sugar cubes," which launched Dahlia to another planet. She paid another visit to the yoga studio—or "game room," as Ze'evi called it—with the toys, but that time alone with Ze'evi.

A big part of her still wanted to run away, but an even bigger part of her wanted more cocaine.

***

When Dahlia returned home on Sunday evening, she went straight up to her room and closed the door. Leah was in the kitchen supervising the dinner preparations. When she heard Dahlia go up the stairs, she called up to her.

"How was your weekend, booba? Have you been throwing up?"

"It was fine. I'm fine!"

"Come down for dinner."

"I'm not hungry."

"Is everything okay?"

"Everything is fine."

"Please come down. I want to talk to you."

"Not right now. I'm very tired."

Leah went upstairs and knocked on Dahlia's door.

"I want to talk to you. Open the door, Dahlia."

"I'm just tired. I want to rest."

"Open the door!"

Dahlia opened it. She knew that tone of voice from her mother meant trouble. Leah walked in to find the room bathed in the light of a single night-light.

"Why are you sitting in the dark?"

"I'm tired."

Leah flicked the light switch on and then gasped.

"What's happened to you? You look terrible! My God! What are the streaks on your legs and the backs of your thighs? What are those red marks on your wrists? What happened?"

"Nothing happened, Imma. The Ehrenreichs have this slippery marble floor in their terrace and stairs leading down to the garden, and I missed some stairs and fell onto a thorn bush. No big deal."

"Why didn't you call us to let us know what happened? Did you get seen at the hospital? I should call the Ehrenreichs. They should have called us."

"I said I'm fine. Don't call the Ehrenreichs! Some ice and rest is all I need."

"Are you telling me the truth?"

"Why wouldn't I tell you the truth? I thought we had this trust thing. Now you don't trust me?"

"I do trust you. I'm just concerned. That's all."

"Thanks for being a concerned Imma." Dahlia smiled and kissed Leah. "All I need is some rest. That's all. I'll be fine in the morning."

"Get some rest, then. You have a full day of school tomorrow. Don't you have a midterm examination tomorrow?"

"Yes, yes. I'm ready. I'll do just fine."

"Okay. Good night," Leah shook her head and left the bedroom, closing the door behind her.

Dahlia waited for her mother to get to the bottom of the stairs before she took the small plastic bag out of her handbag and put it in her usual hiding place.

"Good morning, gentlemen! Come in. Sit down."

Benny and his defense attaché, Eitan Raziel, were escorted into the Israeli defense minister's office.

Adjusting his eye patch, which had become a bit of a tick for him, Moshe Dayan asked, "Coffee?"

"No, thanks," Benny said on behalf of both himself and Eitan.

Dayan said, "I've read the whole Mossad report that you submitted to me last week, through the diplomatic pouch. So, it's true, hey? The Americans have perfected an air-to-surface jamming system for the S-200 anti-aircraft missiles that the Egyptians have deployed? We've lost nearly a dozen Mirage and F-4 Phantom jet fighters over the Suez Canal in the past six months!

"The S-200 is such a long-range, medium- to high-altitude system that it can protect a wide area from air attack. The Soviets have supplied the Egyptians with massive numbers of these missiles, and they've moved them right up to the Canal, in violation of the cease-fire agreement of last September. We can't let that continue unanswered. We've become quite concerned about the Egyptians' buildup of advanced weapons systems. To our knowledge, their system will become operational within the next three months. The Soviets are whittling down our strategic edge. That is of grave concern. They have brought as many as 2,000 personnel, including 150 fighter pilots, to back up the Egyptians. The American state department keeps insisting that no countermeasure to the S-200 homing radar exists. Your information contradicts that.

"I've assembled a series of talking points for you to use in your confidential talks with Congressman Edward Hébert, of Louisiana, the chairman of the House armed services committee. We need to get our hands on that system. Benny, you understand the sensitivity of these talks. They must remain entirely confidential. As you know, this Grumman project was approved and funded by this committee over a year ago, so this congressman has intimate knowledge of the system. And he's a great friend of Israel. The state department, as usual, is being obstructionist in this matter. It is of vital importance that this request to Nixon should appear to be coming from Hébert and not us."

"Of course. I understand. My aide, Levi, will contact Hébert's chief of staff this morning and set up a lunch with him for early next week, when I return to Washington."

They spoke for another half hour about the timetable for delivery of the new F-4 Phantom jets and the schedule for sending Israeli Air Force pilots to Edwards Air Force base, in California, for training on the new jets.

As they spoke, Benny's eyes scanned the pile of personnel dossiers labeled TOP SECRET that were scattered on Dayan's desk. The names on many of them were familiar to him: Ehud Barak, Shlomi Bar Oz, Yoni Netanyahu, Dani Zohar, and Arik Meir. Benny shifted in his seat uncomfortably.

As their conversation was ending, Benny casually said, "Moshe, I hope that you don't mind my asking or consider this prying, but I couldn't help noticing the dossiers on your desk."

"Oh, yes," Dayan said. "We're planning a series of missions for a special Sayeret Matkal strike force, to get our hands on the fire control radar system that directs the targeting of the S-200s we've been discussing and to begin the process of eliminating the threat, should you be unable to get your countermeasure system from the Americans in time or if that system doesn't work. The S-200 missions have been deemed extremely dangerous. We have our top commandos training for it, even as we speak. Our plan is to commence operations sometime in the next two weeks. These guys have all been handpicked. They're the best of the best."

"I couldn't help but notice that one of the dossiers has Arik Meir's name on it," Benny said.

"Yes, the American. He's new to this unit. He joined about six weeks ago. He's quite a remarkable fellow. We would never have considered a new recruit for such a sensitive and dangerous mission, but Arik is no ordinary soldier."

"In what way?"

"Just like the others on this list, a soldier like him comes along once in ten years. Arik had a nearly perfect score on his entry psychometric exams. He has the strength of three men, and he's extremely quick thinking on his feet. He was put through a particularly brutal basic training regimen—through a number of factors, some planned and some not—and came out with an outstanding record. During his training, he was able to sprint twenty kilometers through the hot sun with a fifty-kilogram pack on his back. And during the final beret march, he carried an injured comrade on his shoulders for eight kilometers, in addition to his pack, at top speed through a slippery wadi. In all likelihood, he saved the man's life. Arik is a high-level martial artist. He destroyed Shuki Baum in about thirty seconds. You remember Shuki. He was the army's prime Krav Maga expert—until Arik got hold of him, poor fellow.

"Arik is an expert shot with a full range of weapons, and he has demonstrated extreme cool under live-fire training and high-pressure field exercises. He's also modest, unselfish, and unassuming. He's really a perfect Matkal recruit. You know that we almost never take an American lone soldier in that unit, but Arik is an exception. Interesting thing about him, though. He isn't strictly an American."

"How so?"

"He was born in Israel and was taken as a child to the U.S." Dayan opened the folder. "He comes from Los Angeles, from a very sad background. Perhaps he is his family's redemption? His father, Ze'ev, was an Irgun commander. He was responsible for the Deir Yassin massacre and was one of the fighters on the Altalena. Somehow, he ended up at Hadassah Hospital, without a leg. When his identity was discovered, he was released from the hospital prematurely, into the street, and dishonorably discharged from the IDF without any compensation, by direct order from Ben-Gurion himself. That Deir Yassin business was such an ugly affair. So was the Altalena. I guess having his son here will atone for his crimes."

Benny felt the now familiar abdominal ulcer pain that he had been experiencing of late. He had thought that it was due to the extreme stress of his work, but this pain was much worse, far more profound. He felt a rising acidity in his throat and a terrible choking sensation. His heart began to race. There was a painful pounding between his temples. Suddenly, it all had become terribly clear to him. His ill will toward Arik had nothing to do with Arik at all. It had been something visceral that he had been unable to put his finger on. Arik had reminded Benny of Ze'ev, his father. When had Ze'ev changed his name from Myerowitz to Meir? Now that Benny thought about it, he realized that Arik had some subtle mannerisms that took Benny back to a distant time, when Ze'ev and he had been close comrades—more like brothers, really. It had been so many years ago. He wondered why he hadn't noticed it before. Arik, a child of poverty, had shown his true mettle. He obviously was headed for greatness. Benny now fully grasped what Dahlia had seen in Arik.

He had, of course, had a role in Arik's breaking off contact with Dahlia. His misgivings about Arik had led Dahlia to throw herself into the arms of Ze'evi Ehrenreich. He wondered how he could have been so blind and foolish as to push her toward that man. Benny's guilt and shame only worsened his gastric distress. Dahlia's declining health, poor school performance, and increasingly strident, rebellious behavior and irrationality clearly could be traced to her liaison with Ze'evi. Benny even feared that Ze'evi had robbed her innocence. But he knew that he had only himself to blame. He had compounded a former wrong, Dahlia was slipping out of his control, and now this.

Benny wracked his brain, trying to figure out a way to undo what he had done, but he was at a loss. Trying to break up the affair with Ehrenreich would alienate the greatest philanthropist that he had cultivated for Israel. The Ehrenreichs were quite taken with Dahlia. On the other hand, was Benny willing to sacrifice his daughter for money and prestige? Besides, given how poorly she had obeyed him during the good times, he saw little chance that she would listen to him now. He felt that he had to do something, though. Time was of the essence.

"Moshe, do you think there is any possibility that I could see Arik?" Benny asked.

"What is your interest in him, Benny?"

"He was a close friend of my daughter Dahlia when he was in the States."

"It's a small world. I think that it could be arranged. I just have to find out where he is. He had been stationed in the Golan, but he was recently moved. They are training in an undisclosed location in the central Sinai. Give me a day to find him. So, how is Dahlia doing? If memory serves, she has just turned eighteen and will be entering the army in the summer."

"You're quite correct. She is due to appear at the Lishkat Giyus on July 26th." Benny paused and then added more quietly, "And not a moment too soon."

"How so?"

"I think that her time in Washington has turned her into an American."

Dayan slapped Benny on the shoulder good-naturedly. "Don't worry, Benny. We'll fix all of that when she gets into the army. Give me a day, and I'll get back to you about Arik."

"Thanks, Moshe."

"Have a safe trip back to Washington, and keep me apprised daily on your progress. Where are you going to be for Pesach?"

"We're planning to spend it in Washington. We've got some Jewish congressmen and Israeli lobbyists coming for the seder. It's a good mix of people."

"Very good. And chag sameach."

Benny drove down from the Kiriya, in Tel Aviv, to Jerusalem. When he entered the foreign ministry, he was handed a secure teletype message from Washington.

"Call Leah. Dachuf!" It was urgent.

"Leah," Benny said as soon as the connection was complete, "what's the matter? Is everything okay?"

"Come home, Benny, right away! Everything is not okay! It's Dahlia. While you were out saving the world, your daughter has been going down the drain before our eyes. Things have taken a drastic turn for the worse. I'm very frightened for her, and I have no idea where to turn." Leah was crying.

"Calm down, Leah. What's happened now?"

"You recall Dahlia telling us that she was going to spend the weekend with the Ehrenreichs? Well, she came back from the weekend pale and green. She ran up to her room and wouldn't come down. She vomited in the bathroom, on and off for an hour, and wouldn't let me into her room until I practically threatened to break the door down. Her backside and legs are covered with red streaks that look like she's been beaten. Her wrists have similar streaks. When I confronted her, she told me some bubbe-meise about falling off the Ehrenreichs' porch into a thorn bush in their garden."

"Maybe that's what really happened?" Benny said hopefully.

"I called the Ehrenreichs to find out if they had taken her to the hospital to be seen after the fall, and they told me that Ze'evi and Dahlia hadn't been at their house for the weekend at all."

"Where did they say they went?"

"Apparently, they took off in Ze'evi's jet, to some island in the Caribbean for the weekend. Dahlia vehemently denies that and refuses to tell me where they went or what they did. Her eyes are completely bloodshot. I've never seen her like this before. It's like she has a demon inside her. The principal of the academy called today and told me that she's failing every class because she hasn't been showing up for school. At this rate, she won't even graduate. I'm terrified."

"I'm sure that there is a reasonable explanation for this. Do you think that she's sleeping with him?"

"I think that it's a safe bet. Who knows what else they're up to?"

"First of all, calm down. We need to sit down, both of us, and confront her with all of this. Perhaps we'll get some sense out of her. I think that we should spend Pesach in Israel—get Dahlia out of the U.S. and out of that man's reach. Once she's here, perhaps she'll calm down. Send apologies to our guests, and pack our bags. I'll arrange to set up the house here. A change of scenery will do her some good."

"She'll refuse to come. I know it. I'll have to bring her kicking and screaming."

"Well, then do it! Bring her here, even if Tomer and Yoram have to restrain her. I'm serious."

"What have we come to? It's all your fault. You encouraged this liaison. I had misgivings when I saw how rude he was to us when he was here. You were just star struck, because of their money. You sold your daughter for money, Benny!"

"That's not fair, Leah. How was I supposed to know that Ze'evi would turn out to be this way? I think that we're being punished by God for driving Arik away from her."

"Why do you say that all of a sudden? What does he have to do with it?"

"I've had some major revelations about him today. I'm locating him, and I'm considering inviting him to join us for the seder."

"That's a really bad idea, Benny."

"I think that having him here with us may solve several problems at once. I know what I'm doing. Unless you have a better plan . . ."

"What have you found out about him?"

"Not now. We'll talk when you get here. Come as soon as possible."

Chapter 34

Colonel Langer called the whole company to an early morning briefing. They sat cross-legged on the floor of the khaki tent pitched on the rocky earth. Although it was early morning, the air in the tent was stifling hot as the temperature was nearing 40 degrees Celsius. There was a heavy scent of perspiration. The blowing, talcum-powder fine sand and stinging sandflies added to the men's misery.

In the front of the tent hung a large tactical map of the western Sinai Peninsula, both sides of the Suez Canal, and the Gulf of Suez, heavily marked with red, green, and black arrows. At 7 a.m. sharp, Colonel Langer and Lieutenant Colonel Almog entered the tent and took their places. Arik began to stand up, intending to salute the officers, but quickly realized that he was the only one moving. Surprised, he noticed the amused stares that he was receiving from the men around him.

"There is no tactical or strategic benefit in our adhering to stereotyped 'military' discipline here," Noam Handler, the man sitting next to Arik, whispered to him. "We're all big boys in this outfit, and the emphasis is on getting the job done, plain and simple, not doing all the dopey stuff."

Colonel Langer began, saying, "Boker tov, chevre!" (Good morning, guys!)

With the long wooden pointer in his hand, he gestured toward the map.

"Green Island, or Al Khadraa, is a fortress that was built by British forces during World War II to guard the southern approaches to the Suez Canal at the northern mouth of the Gulf of Suez. Situated four kilometers south of the city of Suez, it's a series of concrete bunkers set on an eight-foot-tall seawall topped by razor wire three rolls deep. It's ringed by machine gun nests, anti-aircraft guns. It's also within range of Egyptian artillery.

"Its location in the center of the waterway gives it a commanding view of the southern sector of our Bar-Lev Line. It was the site of ELINT radar installations that gave a wide early-warning sweep of the sector. Heavily garrisoned by the Egyptians after the Six-Day War and deemed impenetrable by them, it was attacked and destroyed in a massive commando raid by our special forces twenty months ago, in July 1969, in an operation known as Bulmus 6.

"After the cease-fire was called for, the Egyptians and the Soviets used the lull in fighting as a golden opportunity to amass material on the front line along the canal—including batteries of the most up-to-date surface-to-air missiles. The S-200 anti-aircraft missile has a homing device that stays on the ground while the missile approaches its target. Not having the weight of the transmitter in its nose dramatically increases the range of the missile and its effectiveness.

"We've only heard of the S-200's capability through our operatives in Eastern Europe. We have no idea how it really works. We need to get our hands on this system so that we can begin to develop countermeasures. It isn't operational yet, but our assets tell us that in tests it is extremely reliable and deadly accurate. Although the outpost was destroyed more than 18 months ago, it has been largely rebuilt with the help of Soviet engineers and construction crews. The objective is to destroy the facility again and retrieve the nose cones and the ground unit. As in the past, this will be a joint operation between us and the Shayetet naval commandos. Lieutenant Colonel Almog will the field commander, as he led the previous assault on the island. The island is heavily garrisoned by more than one hundred Egyptian and Soviet commandos manning fourteen machine-gun positions and anti-aircraft batteries. The sea lanes are guarded by a dozen torpedo boats and destroyers armed with 37mm and 85mm guns. The garrison cannot be directly bombarded, because of the proximity of the missile batteries to the fortress."

Langer spent the next hour outlining the assault in graphic detail.

Finally, he said, "Understand that this mission is a direct violation of the cease-fire agreement, so it must be handled with ultimate discretion. Since the Russians and Egyptians deny that they have any anti-aircraft batteries at the Canal, our mission never happened either. Our code name is Operation Amud Eish, Pillar of Fire. Good luck, gentlemen!"

At 2100 hours, two waves of Shayetet naval commandos set forth westward, from Port Tewfik toward Green Island, in Zodiac boats. The boats discharged the Israeli commandos nine hundred meters offshore. They swam the rest of the way underwater, using rebreather air systems, each man carrying forty kilograms of equipment on his back. The first wave of commandos breached the outer perimeter, and then the second wave provided fire support to neutralize the initial resistance at the perimeter.

At the same time, A-4 Skyhawks and F-4 Phantoms attacked the Egyptian naval force offshore, destroying the vessels moored there. The noise from the jets obscured the approach of the four Aérospatiale Super Frelon helicopters, which were carrying the Sayeret Matkal strike force and were intended to carry back to Israel the radar systems and missiles that were situated five hundred meters north of the fortress. The naval commandos cut through the barbed-wire fence and stormed the seawall, headed to the concrete bunkers from the south. This assault was to be a diversion so that the Matkal, to the north, could get the radar systems and missiles.

Arik's platoon jumped out of the helicopter and into a massive hail of machine-gun and 37mm-gun fire. The defenders inside the fortress suddenly had become aware of the northern assault. The Israeli commandos hit the ground, running toward the missile batteries. The helicopter that they had been in only a minute earlier burst into flames when it sustained a direct hit from an artillery shell.

Arik's group had been assigned the task of perimeter protection and fire support for the technicians, who worked feverishly to dismantle the ground radar system and S-200 missiles' nose cones and load them into the remaining helicopters.

At the same time, the naval commandos broke through the southern defenses of the fortress and engaged in intense close-quarters combat with elite Egyptian and Russian commandos.

Suddenly, the north gate of the fortress opened, and several dozen Soviet and Egyptian commandos poured out, running and firing in the direction of the missile batteries.

Arik's squad was there to meet them. He and his fellow commandos positioned themselves behind a rocky outcropping and fired at the attackers, but they found themselves pinned down by a hail of machine gun fire. Arik bolted up and threw a grenade at a half-track coming toward them. It exploded, killing all aboard.

"Split up! Split up!" Arik called out. "Three groups form an arc around the technicians. We can't let them come any nearer than four hundred meters from the helicopters."

Dani led a squad to surround the attackers from the west. Arik's squad remained on the north end, while Noam's squad scrambled to the east, forming a field of fire that felled the lead Egyptian assault team. Methodically, the radar system and missile parts were loaded into two helicopters that, when fully loaded, could take no personnel aboard. The two choppers took off, heading eastward, and the naval commandos took full control of the fortress, from the south. Half of the Matkal group got into the one remaining helicopter, while Arik's squad remained behind to provide cover fire. The Egyptians, who were being pursued by the naval commandos, overran Noam's foxhole position, wounding or killing each of the ten men.

The fortress exploded in a huge fireball when the satchel charges that had been left behind by the Shayetet naval commandos detonated.

"Go! Go! Go! Follow me!" Arik shouted as he ran headlong into the attackers, dodging showers of bullets that danced around his feet and whizzed by his ears.

Ten others followed behind Arik. They recovered the foxhole and drove off or killed the attackers. Dani's unit converged on the foxhole from the other direction.

"Evacuate the dead and wounded! To the water!" Arik shouted.

"I can't feel my legs! I can't feel my legs!"

Arik looked down at Noam, lying on the ground. He had been shot in the back. Instinctively, Arik grabbed him like a sack of concrete, slung him over his shoulders, and broke into a sprint toward the shore. Arik's and Dani's squads carried the casualties to the Zodiac boats that had been brought in for the extraction of the naval commandos and remaining Matkal. As soon as the casualties had been loaded on board, the Zodiacs headed eastward toward the Sinai. Arik and his squad remained onshore to provide cover fire for the evacuation.

When the Zodiac boats got about 150 meters offshore, they were hit by a barrage of coordinated Egyptian artillery fire that sank two of them and the remaining boats that were moored onshore. Dani's boat remained intact, and his team furiously rowed out to the channel. Arik looked out and saw Noam fifty meters offshore, splashing helplessly, clinging to the side of an overturned raft, and crying for help. Arik shot into the water. He swam furiously. When he reached Noam, just as he was sinking beneath the surface, he grabbed him and pulled him up. The last twenty Shayetet and Matkal commandos, behind Arik, ran down the bank to the shore under a barrage of artillery shells raining down on their heads.

"Jump into the water! Into the water! This Red Sea isn't going to part for you!" Arik called out as he treaded water while holding a flailing Noam by his belt.

They all jumped into the water and began swimming toward the east, across the waterway to the Sinai.

"Wrap both arms around my neck, and don't let go!" Arik said to Noam. He slung him over his shoulders while kicking furiously with his feet to keep both of them afloat.

Noam held on for dear life as Arik did a slow breaststroke propelling them into the open waterway. They soon were joined by the others. After spending several hours in the water, they were plucked out, one by one, at first light by rescue helicopters.

***

"Are you sure this was your first mission?" Colonel Langer slapped Arik on the back. "You have some serious balls for a beginner. You're everything General Tal said that you'd be. You did a very good job today. The radar system was recovered intact, in good part thanks to your men."

"Thank you, sir. How's Noam doing? I'd like to visit him, if possible."

"His spine was shattered by a large-caliber bullet. It's been stabilized by a team of orthopedic surgeons, but I'm afraid that he'll never walk again."

Arik looked down and sighed, shaking his head.

Langer, who understood that this was Arik's first time dealing with such an experience, tried to reassure him. "Arik, if it wasn't for you, he wouldn't even be alive. You should be proud of what you did."

Arik nodded. He wondered quietly if Noam was better off this way than dead.

Arik thought about his first mission a lot. It wasn't at all like the movies. It was human carnage, plain and simple. He was not proud, just sad. He was told that he would get used to this. But he did not want to get used to slaughtering his fellow man, no matter how good the cause. He thought of Dahlia. What will I tell her when I see her, whenever that is? She'll be proud of me, though, and that's what counts. He knew that he was becoming what she wanted him to be, and he finally felt validated in his decision to become a soldier rather than a college basketball player. He missed her so much. Not having heard from her had only intensified his longing for her.

He spent the next two days being debriefed by military intelligence. When he emerged from the mess tent after dinner on the third day, Dani trotted up to him.

"Arik, you have a visitor. He looks like someone important."

"Who would want to visit me? Who even knows I'm here?" Arik looked at Dani quizzically.

Chapter 35

March 29, 1971

My Sweet Dahlia,

I'm sorry I've haven't written for three weeks, but my life has been turned upside down since my last letter. I've finally been able to get out of that hellhole that was my paratrooper basic training program. The hard part wasn't the long marches, sleep deprivation, or physical exertion. You know how much I like to work. So many aspects of the training were great. Jumping out of planes, especially at night. And the weapons training was right up my alley. It's just that I got the sense that the base commander and his deputies were on some campaign to break me—not to make me into a better soldier but to get me to quit and go home. All the crap I told you about only got worse. The low regard they have for Americans is amazing. You know that all I ever want to do is fit in, but it never seems to work out that way. They constantly reminded me that I'm an outsider. Sorry to be so repetitive, but I really have no one else to vent to. The guys in my unit were okay, but I wasn't able to make any real friends as hard as I tried.

Things finally came to a head when my commander set up a "fighting match" for me against some supposed martial arts big shot right after the 90-km beret march. I thought it was a friendly exhibition until he came at me and put a boot into my face, bloodying my nose. I snapped and sent him to the hospital in critical condition. Apparently, there was some guy named General Tal in the audience. While I was being tortured by my superiors, THEY were being observed by Defense Department hacks to see if I had what it takes to be a commando. That's why they let the torture go on for so many months. Next thing I know, two guys come in the middle of the night—like a kidnapping—and throw me into a windowless truck. The next morning, I was dumped at another base in the Golan. I'd been transferred to some elite secret unit. (I can't tell you which unit because that would ruin the secret. Ha ha!) The training here is really rough, but we're all treated fairly and equally for a change. All the officers are on a first name basis with the recruits, and I finally feel like I've joined a brotherhood. The men here are serious, introspective types, which suits me just fine.

I've become friendly with this incredible guy, Yoni Netanyahu, who's Israeli but whose family has spent years in the U.S., in Philly. It's really a thrill finally being able to talk to somebody that understands me and where I come from. I even enjoy talking to him in English. Apart from tremendous physical skill, he's got his head screwed on straight. We spend hours talking during our free time. My long conversations with him are a great source of comfort to me.

Your dad came to visit while he was on some kind of tour of the Sinai. He seemed genuinely happy to see me, which I found rather odd. Anyway, he told me that all of you are coming to Israel for Pesach. I'm way past missing you. My life for the past six months has been such hell that I would have gone mad if I couldn't keep an image of you, of us, locked up inside my head, some place inaccessible to my situation. I've sat up many nights and stared at the photograph of us together. At times, it was the only thing that kept me sane.

I still can't figure out why I haven't heard from you in all this time. No matter. Just writing to you for all these months has been such a source of comfort to me. My mind is racing out of my head in anticipation of finally seeing you at long last. I've also given a great deal of thought to what we discussed in LA. I really don't want to wait until we get out of the army to get married. I want you. I love you so much.

Please let me know ASAP when you're coming and when I'll be able to look at your adorable face. I'll probably be able to swing 48 hours leave.

With undying love,
Arik

Dahlia carefully folded the letter and stuffed it back into the envelope. She slowly looked up at her mother and father.

"What did the letter say?" Benny asked.

"How could you do this to me, Abba? Why did you have to tell him that we were coming to Israel for Pesach? I don't know if I'm more confused or furious. For the year we were together, I fought with you about him constantly. You had this idea in your head that there was something terribly wrong with him, and you did everything in your power to break us up, which I never understood. When he disappeared in the army, you could barely hide your satisfaction—"

Benny opened his mouth to speak, but Dahlia held up a hand to silence him.

"Then you practically threw me at Ze'evi. But when my relationship with him deepened, both of you became increasingly hostile to him, too. Now, all of a sudden, you've discovered that you like Arik, and you're trying to force him back into my life. I resent being manipulated like this, like your little yo-yo. You and Imma need to back off and let me lead my own life. I'm eighteen years old, and I'll make my own decisions."

Benny finally was able to get a word in edgewise. "I know that you believe that you're very grown up, Dahlia, but you don't have enough life experience to make these types of decisions that will have a profound impact on the rest of your life."

"What are you talking about?" Dahlia's temper was rising.

Leah said, "What we're talking about is manipulation. In the beginning, we were quite enamored with Ze'evi. He was charming, bright, and sophisticated. Over time, though, both Abba and I have seen other sides of him that are less desirable."

"Such as?"

"Well, we've seen the effect he has had on you, for one. Over the past few months, you've lost weight, you come home in a temper, you're always irritable. Your senior year was supposed to be your easiest, and you've always been an excellent student. Now, you're failing in your classes and you walk around the house like you're in a daze. You've undergone a personality change, and you're always very secretive. For all we know, you're sleeping with him as well. All we need is for you to get pregnant. Is Ze'evi hurting you in some way?"

Dahlia glared at her parents. "That's why you told Arik to come by? To save me from the big, bad Ze'evi? No! Ze'evi and I love each other. He's very good to me, and I want to marry him. Arik has made his feelings for me very clear, by his behavior. He has moved on, and so have I."

"Is that what he wrote in his letter?" Benny asked. "Is that why his face lit up when he saw me and I told him that you were coming to Israel? Why he nearly jumped out of his skin? Dahlia, motek, I think that Arik has not moved on at all. He is still very much in love with you."

"Then why didn't that jerk get in touch with me for six months? The international phone and mail system still work, to my knowledge. He was always a conscientious letter writer. It's impossible to understand—unless he has another girlfriend. In fact, he wrote me that he had pretty girls hitting on him from the moment he started his training. He just didn't have the common decency to tell me to get lost after I gave myself to him heart and soul. He cut me off just like that." Dahlia snapped her fingers.

"I didn't get that impression," Benny said.

"Well, I know what I'm talking about, and I have no desire to have anything more to do with him." Dahlia sneered as if daring her parents to oppose her will.

"If that's what you want, fine," Benny said. "You at least should speak to him and be civil. You owe him that. He's here in Israel only because of you. He gave up his scholarship to be with you. You don't know why he didn't write. Perhaps you'll discover that. Whatever you do, don't be cruel to him. He doesn't deserve that."

"How do you know what he deserves or not? He broke my heart. I loved him so much. I was in pieces until I met Ze'evi and he helped put me back together. Ze'evi is beautiful and wonderful. You don't know him the way I do. In his letter, Arik said that you came to see him and were actually happy that you did. What in the world is going on? Why did you go? Why the sudden love affair with Arik? All of a sudden, you're concerned about what Arik gave up to come here. You're unbelievable!"

"A person can change his mind about someone. In a very short while, Arik has made a deep impression on his chain of command—all the way up to Dayan. He himself told me that a soldier like Arik comes along once in ten years. He gave me a rundown of his performance. I now see him in a completely different light. He seems amazing!" Benny said.

"So, that's it! Abba wants me to fall in love with the little hero soldier boy. How nice! But the real heroes who change the world are people with money, lots of money. They're the ones who make things happen in the world. Not politicians or soldiers who run around with guns, shooting people. Israelis don't get it. All they do is talk and shoot. They don't get the money part, because they don't have any, except for the funds that they drag out of rich American philanthropists—"

"Not nice, Dahlia!" Leah said. "I can't believe you're speaking this way. Now you sound like Ze'evi. This is exactly what we're talking about! This isn't the Dahlia that we raised. These aren't the values that we brought you up with. Arik gave up his whole future for you. He earned a free college education at UCLA, something that would have lifted him out of the grinding poverty that he grew up in, but he walked away from it for you, because he loved you. The least you could do is talk to him like a grown-up."

"Wow! All of a sudden you care about Arik's poverty. Are you two insane? Okay. Have it your way. Let Arik come, and I'll talk to him—if you think that's a good idea. I don't. I don't want him to stay after that, though. I see no reason for it."

"It's a bit late for that. He's already been invited for the seder," Benny said flatly.

"Why did you do that without asking me?"

"I want to speak to him myself," Benny said.

"About what?"

"That's entirely my affair. I'm not at liberty to discuss it with you."

"What a great, screwed-up family we are. All of us keeping secrets."

"What secrets are you keeping, Dahlia?"

Dahlia threw up her hands. "I'll talk to Arik. Okay?"

***

The day had finally arrived. Arik's mind was a whirlwind of thoughts and emotions when he raced out of Camp Shacham in Bir Gifgafa in the central Sinai. Ehud, his commander, had been kind enough to not only give him forty-eight hours leave, for the first two days of Pesach, but also convince Eran, the base grease monkey, to lend him his BSA Rocket 3 motorcycle. After two months in the field, subsisting on canned rations and sleeping on hard-packed gravel for four hours a night, the thought of returning to civilization was intoxicating to Arik. He would spend two blissful days with Dahlia, catching up on the previous nine months. Arik's isolation from the outside world had been nearly complete, and he was looking forward to solving the mystery of why he had not heard from Dahlia in all that time.

As he gunned the motorcycle's 750cc, 58 horsepower engine into full throttle, he sped along the desert roads at nearly 145 km/hour. On the route he had chosen, Arik would not have to slow down until he hit Beersheba, and then it would be less than two hours to Herzliya. Visions of the love of his life swirled in his head. He ran through what he would say to her, how he would hold her, and how many times he would tell her that he loved her. He was so excited that she would return to Israel in only three months' time, to enter the army and so that they could start their lives together in earnest. Finally! He thought about the time off that they would have together. He thought about making love with her on a secluded beach in Eilat. First things first, they would go for a spin on the motorcycle, up to Caesarea. They could make it up there and back in plenty of time before the holiday. Such was the rocket that roared between his legs.

Arik had no difficulty locating the Gilads' beachfront estate in the new section of Herzliya Pituach. With its rows of large estate homes that looked out over the Mediterranean Sea, the street that Dahlia's family lived on looked more like Malibu beachfront than the Israel that Arik had seen. He rode up to the garage at the side of the house, flipped his army knapsack over his shoulder, and walked to the front door.

He was let into the cool foyer by the Filipino house attendant, who then led him into the library. A cool ocean breeze was blowing in through the large French doors that were open to the terrace. Arik held a single rose in his hand, which he had picked up in the flower market at Shuk Ha'Carmel in Tel Aviv.

His heart pounded harder when he heard familiar footfalls coming down the marble hall. In a moment, she appeared at the door. He was jolted at the first sight of her. She had lost a great deal of weight, so much that she seemed to be falling out of her summer dress. She smiled thinly at him. Her face was drawn and her complexion sallow.

"Hello, Arik."

Something is wrong. His joy at the anticipation of seeing her rapidly turned into worry. Has she been ill all these months? Is that why I haven't heard from her? What didn't anyone let me know? He felt his throat tighten and his palms sweat.

"Dahlia? Are you okay?"

"Where the hell have you been all these months?" Dahlia shouted. "You had me come all the way here on Sukkot just to be with you for as long as I could. Any amount of time would have been fine. I was so desperate just to see your face. I sat here alone, like an idiot, for a full week, waiting for his highness to contact me. I don't want to even hear about 'Oh, I couldn't get word out. I was stuck at the base and blah, blah, blah.' You told me that you were getting seventy-two hours off, for sure, and you didn't have the common decency to let me know what was going on. After that, nothing for six months—until your letter two weeks ago. I sat in my room for a month and cried myself to sleep every night. Over you, you creep!"

"What are you talking about, Dahlia? I wrote to you, in detail, about what happened to me. I was put in isolation for a month, as a punishment for beating up my asshole Krav Maga instructor. After that, I wrote to you every week—even during field exercises. I even wrote to you, instead of sleeping, when I'd been up for thirty-six hours straight and given four hours to sleep. I spent an hour of that time pouring out my heart to you. I tried calling your house numerous times, and I was told your phone number had been disconnected. I've called the embassy in Washington a dozen times over the past six months. I asked them to give me your new house phone number, but they refused. They said the number was unlisted and private. I even called your father's secretary, Tzippy, on several occasions and asked her to give you a message. She promised she would."

"If that's true, why didn't I get anything from you for months? Do you think that I'm so stupid that I'd believe this bullshit? This is a side of you that I never believed that I would see—sitting there and lying to me with a straight face. I never got any message. Where are all these letters that you claim to have written? I never got a single one. I see Tzippy on a regular basis, and she never mentioned anything about your calling—ever. I even bumped into Elgin Baylor at a game in New York, and he told me that you and he had been writing all along. So, stop giving me bullshit about your letters not getting through to me, you fucking liar! You're writing to the goddamn Lakers and not to me! What did I do to you? You shithead! How can you treat me like that?"

Arik felt that he should respond, but he was speechless. He felt as if he had been hit on the head with a baseball bat.

Dahlia continued her rant. "Now, you show up here. For what? To sweep me off my feet? Did you think I'd swoon for you just because you're wearing your little soldier outfit with your pretty red boots? How dare you?"

"Why are you doing this, Dahlia?" Arik finally managed to say, his tone full of alarm. "I've done nothing to you. Where is the beautiful girl I fell in love with? I want her back. What have you done with her? I came here just for you. I gave up everything for you. Why wouldn't I write to you?"

"Look, Arik, I'm seeing someone in the States, someone with more class than you'll ever have! Did you think that I was going to wait for Romeo to suddenly come back from the dead? I'm sure that you've had plenty of opportunity to chase women in the army. Who could say no to a bona fide paratrooper hero with a pretty red beret? Is that what this is about? Have you been shtupping some girl in Tel Aviv and she threw you out, so you figured you'd come here to see me?"

"Is that what you think? Well, that's not what I did. I spent my time dreaming about you. I've missed you so much it physically hurt. So, let me get this straight? You've had me come all the way up from the Sinai just to tell me to go to hell and that you have a boyfriend? How could you be so cruel?"

"It wasn't my idea to have you come. It was my dad's."

"That's nice. I knew your father hated me from the beginning. I didn't realize he hated me so much that he'd drag me up here just to torture me. Why didn't he tell me all this when he visited my base? And meanwhile, this boyfriend of yours doesn't seem to have had such a good effect on you, whoever he is. Are you sick?"

"What does that mean?"

Arik took a long hard look at Dahlia's face and body. He found his feet again as realization slowly dawned on him.

"Well, for one thing, you've lost at least twenty pounds and your complexion is much paler. You look so thin and fragile. I never could've imagined you looking like this. And your eyes are completely bloodshot." He squinted and took a closer look at her face. "You're high, aren't you?"

"What are you talking about?" Dahlia hissed.

"You're high! And not just on marijuana either. You're doing coke. My God! What has this asshole done to you? I'm going to find him and tear him to shreds. Do your parents know? Of course, they don't! For all their sophistication, they have no idea about these things. You have them completely fooled. Well, you don't fool me. I've been around this plenty back in LA. Are you also stealing money from them to support your habit?"

"Shut the hell up, Arik. This is none of your damn business!"

"It's not? Actually, I think it is. If you told me you were seeing someone who was good for you, despite all my grief I'd at least know you were happy. I'd find a way to live with it. But this man is destroying your soul. You need to get some help, detox, or something!"

"You took drugs in high school, too, you hypocrite!"

"I smoked pot, nothing more. What else are you on? Uppers? Downers? Acid? Mescaline? All of the above? This is going to kill you. You've got to get away from this guy before you OD and end up in a box! Please, let me help you. I've got contacts here already. We can even do this quietly, without your parents—" Arik reached out to her.

She recoiled. "Get your goddamn hands off me! Don't touch me! Don't come near me! Get out! Get the hell out of here before I call security! I never want to see you again. Coming here to patronize me and lecture me? Ze'evi is so good to me. One thing he has that you will never have is class. My parents were so right. You're just a lowlife from the streets of LA. You've never had any class, and you never will. You're beneath me! You hear that? Beneath me! What did I ever see in you? You bastard! Don't you think I didn't notice that you never had any close friends? Even from the letter you sent me, it's clear that you have trouble getting along with people. You're just a loser, nothing more."

"I gave up everything for you," Arik pleaded. "I missed you so much! I'm begging you, Dahlia, please don't do this!"

"I cried myself to sleep for a month because the 'love of my life' didn't give a shit enough about me to let me know whether he was alive or dead. How could you? How could you?" Dahlia shrieked. "I let myself get hurt by you. How stupid could I have been? Well, I've moved on, and so should you. I need to get on with my life, and you need to leave." Dahlia, in tears now, pointed at the door.

Arik felt the world cave in on him. He had never felt so alone. He had given up a real chance to get out of poverty for the love of this woman who had just revealed herself to be a snake. He had been completely charmed by her.

Now, all he had in his life was the dust and dirt of the Sinai. Thoughts of Dahlia were the only thing that had kept him going. Now, there was nothing left. Why didn't I see all this before? He had gotten advance warning of what she could be like, by her behavior toward him at Camp Moshava when, thinking that he was a criminal, she had turned on him. Why did I let her back into my life? Shame on me!

"Good-bye, Dahlia. I'm so sorry to have troubled you today," he said stiffly. "I'll just let myself out. No need to see me to the door."

The loud roar of the motorcycle drew Dahlia to a front window. A cloud of dust was all that was left of the man she once had loved. She stood in the window, looking out silently and weeping.

***

Several hours later, Leah was supervising the kitchen staff in preparing the eggs, shank bones, bitter herbs, and charoset date paste—all of the accoutrements of the massive seder meal that she was hosting for twenty-five guests. Dahlia was quietly helping her by setting the table.

When Tomer stopped into the kitchen to get a late lunch, he stared at Dahlia, frowned, and shook his head. He wondered what had become of the sweet, delightful child that he had once doted on. She had confided in him and he knew that she had looked up to him as the older brother she had never had. She had taken his advice and generally things had turned out well. That is, until the past six months or so.

He had watched, horrified, as Dahlia had changed almost overnight into someone unrecognizable who poisoned the home's atmosphere. He had tried to reach out to her, but she had seemed uninterested in what he said or thought. He had always been made to feel a part of the household but during these few months he had increasingly retreated to the role of security guard, spending his time smoking and chatting with his fellow security guards when not on duty.

He had been on perimeter patrol while Leah and Benny had been out of the house, and he had heard Dahlia's shouting coming from inside the house. Thinking that it was an intruder, he ran toward the building, with his handgun drawn, only to see Arik mounting a motorcycle and speeding away.

Tomer could guess all too well what had happened. He was filled with rage. He wanted to run inside and confront Dahlia. But his training kicked in. He was not supposed to interfere with the internal affairs of the people he was guarding.

Nonetheless, Dahlia was melting down before his eyes. He could see clearly that she was under the influence of illicit drugs. Ze'evi had gutted her soul, but she was too immature to realize it. Worse yet, the Gilads were—somehow—too naive to see it. Until recently, Israeli youth had had very little exposure to rock-and-roll culture. Even the Beatles had been denied access into the country, for fear that they would corrupt Israeli youth. Tomer, however, was well traveled and worldly. He understood all of this, but he was duty bound to say nothing.

"Dahlia, have you heard from Arik yet?" Leah asked. "He should be here by now. It's almost sundown. I hope that he'll make it in time."

"No, nothing Imma. Not a thing. He's probably not coming after all. He's probably stuck at the base. He's done that before, not showing up when he says that he will. If he comes, he comes. If he doesn't, he doesn't."

"Remember, Dahlia: When he comes, I want you to be at least civil to him. Okay?"

"If he comes, I will be. I promised Abba, didn't I?" Dahlia glanced at Tomer and quickly averted her gaze.

Tomer stood in the corner, his arms folded, and silently glared at her.

***

Dahlia spent the Gilad family's week in Israel in virtual seclusion, which allowed her to use the small amount of cocaine that she had managed to sneak into her luggage. She showed no interest in connecting with her Israeli friends, whom she had always professed to "miss terribly" while she was in the States. She spent her time either in her room with the door closed or walking alone on Herzliya Beach below the cliffs. When spoken to, she gave monosyllabic answers. When she looked around, she saw very little that interested her. How provincial it all seems! It's so different than I remembered. How quaint and drab it is, with street after street of apartment blocks, terraces, and rooftop solar panels and water tanks, as far as the eye can see. This place is supposed to be the center of Israeli sophistication? What a joke! She longed to return to the United States, to the Hamptons, to the Upper East Side, to Aspen, to Las Vegas, to Ze'evi. She wanted that life. She did not want to return to Israel for a long time, if ever. She was done with it.

Book 2

Arik awoke face down in the sand. He blinked the sand out of his eyes and spit it out of his mouth. There was blood dripping out of his nose. He felt his left eye swelling shut. As he tried to move, he realized that he ached all over—his neck, lower back, and thighs. He felt the hot desert sun burning the back of his neck. At last, he was able to move his hands and feet. Well, that's good. How long have I been lying here? He pulled himself up and looked around. There was nothing around him but mounds of yellow sand and rocky earth and a ribbon of asphalt that stretched off to the horizon in both directions. Where am I? His dress uniform was shredded, and there were broad areas of bloody road rash on his arms and legs. He finally stood.

The motorcycle. Where's the motorcycle? Realization dawned on him that he had been in a wreck. If he had not plowed into a sand dune, he would have been killed for sure. Where's the damn bike? How bad is it? Eran will kill me! Worse, he won't ever trust me to take it out again. Such is betrayal. Arik's consciousness began to clear, and the crushing sense that he had just lost the most important person in his life sent a searing, nauseating pain into his gut. The pain was so intense that he doubled over and vomited into the sand. Sitting on the ground and clutching his knees, he hung his head and sobbed. He felt as if a trap door to hell had opened under his feet and he was falling through it and into an inexorable downward spiral. He began to hyperventilate. His chest ached. Am I having a heart attack? Bile crept up into his throat.

I should have realized something was wrong when I didn't hear anything from Dahlia for months. I've been living in a fool's paradise, thinking she was waiting for me. He had thought that he knew her, and he had been confident in her devotion to him. In fact, he had been so certain of it that he had based his whole existence on her. She was his constant, his anchor. All she had asked of him was that he write to her, which he had done faithfully. He had poured his life force into those letters. It was as if his blood rather than black ink had flowed out of the pen. She said she never received the letters. But how? It's impossible! Is she lying to me—or even herself—to try to justify the fact that some other guy stepped in and swept her off her feet? She already showed she could turn on me. Why did I trust her? Why? Waves of anguish washed over him, each one forcing him to gasp for breath before the next one, just as punishing, arrived.

"Hey, soldier! Are you okay?"

A passing Jeep stopped, and three soldiers jumped out of it.

"I'm not sure yet. Where am I?" Arik said.

"You're ten kilometers east of Bir Gifgafa. How long have you been out here?"

"I don't know."

"Were you thrown out of a car? How did you get here?"

"I was riding a motorcycle, and I must have spun out. I have no idea where it is. . ."

The soldiers scoured the area. They found the motorcycle, its front half buried in another dune, ten meters away from where Arik was sitting.

"You must have been going pretty fast."

"Yeah."

They pulled the motorcycle out of the dune. The front fender and wheel were bent into a bizarre angle.

"Shit! Eran is going to kill me!" Arik said.

"You're in Camp Shacham, then?" one of the soldier's said. When Arik nodded, he said, "You're right, Eran is going to kill you. Can you walk?"

"Yeah."

"Hop in. We'll take you back. You should have a doctor check you out."

"I think I'm okay, just scraped up a bit."

They lashed the bike to the back bumper of the Jeep and drove Arik to the base, dropping him off near the front gate.

"Thanks again, guys," Arik said.

"Sababa!" (No problem) they called out as they drove away.

Arik pushed the mangled remnant of the motorcycle up to the gate.

The guard at the gate looked Arik over. "Weren't you supposed to be on leave for forty-eight hours? What the hell happened to—Shit! Eran is going to kill you!"

When he arrived at the motor pool, Arik deposited the bike in front of the door to the garage. At that moment, Eran wandered out, wiping the grease off his hands. He surveyed the damage to the bike.

"The front fender and wheel are shot, the exhaust manifold is cracked in two, and the gear chain is snapped. I thought that you knew how to ride. You told me that you knew how to ride, Arik."

"I was going a bit too fast, and I spun out on some loose gravel on the road."

"When you ride through the desert here, you have to slow down. This isn't like Arizona in the movies, where the roads are perfect."

"I'll pay you every lira for the damage. I have nothing to spend my salary on anyway. Starting immediately."

Arik pulled out two hundred lira that he had planned to spend on Dahlia over the weekend and handed the money to Eran.

"First installment. That's all I have," Arik smiled sadly.

Eran waved the money away. "Don't worry about it. I'll get this fixed in no time. My family runs a chain of secondhand-bike shops, and they have extensive repair facilities. They'll have this up and running in no time, which is more than I can say about you. You look like crap! You better go get checked out."

"I'll be okay. Please take the money. And let me pay you more in two weeks?"

Eran just shook his head, and Arik had no energy to argue with him further. He turned around to go.

"Hey, Arik?"

Arik turned back around.

"You're a good guy. We all really like you."

Colonel Langer and Lieutenant Colonel Ehud Barak stood in front of the entire Matkal brigade in a packed dining room after an early breakfast at 6 a.m. On the wall behind them was a large map of southern Israel, from the Dead Sea to Eilat, at the tip of the Negev Desert.

Langer said, "The Arava, as many of you know, has been a major point of infiltration for PLO terrorists trying to get into the Negev from Jordan. In addition to trying to isolate Eilat, by raining down mortar shells on civilian traffic on the main road, they've taken to attacking the isolated settlements that dot the border. Recently, there have been attacks on our potash plants and—even more worrisome—the oil pipeline that runs from the tanker facility on the Red Sea to the Ashkelon terminal on the Mediterranean.

"They're doing this with the tacit consent of the Jordanians and active assistance from the Saudis. At night, the Palestinian terror squads come across the border, hiding out during the day near their proposed targets. After sundown, they carry out their raids and then have the rest of the night to retreat back across the border.

"But General Sharon has come up with a solution. We're going to operate beyond the border, with night patrols into the mountains of Moab establishing listening posts and setting up ambushes for the PLO squads. Our goal is to occupy the town of Safi, which is the main base from which they launch these attacks. There's a brigade of Saudi regulars assisting the PLO, so when we launch our attack we'll be confronting both forces."

Barak divided up the brigade for the various missions of the first phase of the operation, which would last four weeks. The training schedule was passed out to the junior officers, and assignments were made. The men stood and filed out of the hall.

Before Arik could leave, Langer called him over and motioned for Barak to join them. Both of the senior officers had grave looks on their faces. Arik was unsure whether to stand at attention. He looked at them nervously. When they were alone in the room, Arik spoke.

"Sir, I checked the assignments and my name doesn't appear on any of the lists."

Langer said, "That's because you won't be taking part in this operation. What's going on with you, Arik? For the past three weeks—ever since your motorcycle accident—you have been a completely different person than before. You're depressed and moody. You haven't spoken much to anyone in the unit. When you're addressed, you give one-word answers. You're not eating. Your squad mates tell me that you're not sleeping. You've lost at least ten pounds, and you're constantly irritable. During briefings, you seem inattentive, like your mind is elsewhere. Your times for completing the ambush and urban-warfare drills are way up from before. Your shooting is off the mark. It's like none of this interests you anymore. What do you have to say?"

Barak was staring at him with an intensity that Arik had never seen from him before. Now, he added his own statement.

"Arik, we're a family here. We watch out for each other and take care of each other. You have the potential to be a great fighter. You've already demonstrated that during your first operation. Your fighting skills are renowned. But there is so much more to what we do than that.

"What we do here is very dangerous work. Even a slight lapse in judgment or attention to detail could very well result in getting yourself and those around you killed. There are so few soldiers at this level that we can't afford to lose a single one. We aren't like the American army. What we do requires split-second timing, and any deviation can be catastrophic. The change in you has been noticed by everyone."

"I'm doing the best I can, sir," Arik said.

"If that's your best, I should throw you out right now," Langer said, "but I know that you can do better. Something is holding you back. What is it?"

"I've been through a personal trauma, three weeks ago, that has torn out my heart." Arik looked down at his feet. "It's why I came to Israel, to begin with."

"So, this is about a woman, then," Barak said.

Langer said, "I can't allow my men to get killed around you just because some skirt told you to get lost. Look, Arik, you're not Israeli, not really. You went to the States as an infant, and your status can easily be changed to Machal, foreign volunteer. You've done your nine months, and you can be discharged honorably . . . go back home to America and continue your life."

"Sir, I no longer have any life in America. My home is here in Israel now."

"The way things stand now, you can't be part of this unit anymore. It's too dangerous," Langer said. "Now, I can place you in a regular infantry unit, if you like. You'll still be serving Israel honorably, and you can continue your life here as you wish. It would be better for all concerned."

Arik was near tears. "Sir, being in this unit and . . . that woman . . . have been my reasons for living. Now, I'm about to lose both. I have what it takes to be in Matkal. I'm certain of it. I just need some time, sir. As you said, I have the potential. I can regain my footing. I know it."

Langer looked at Barak. "We need to talk. Arik, please step outside. We'll call you back in shortly."

Arik did not know how he made it outside. He no longer felt his legs. It was as if he were seeing himself from outside his body. His heart was racing, seemingly out of his chest, and he was gulping for air. He felt an aura of grief engulfing him. How could my life take such a terrible turn, just when I thought I'd made the right choices? When he had entered the army, he would have been satisfied with an ordinary unit, but since then he had tasted the holy grail of accomplishment in the Sayeret Matkal. The thought of a demotion to an ordinary unit sent a shock wave of shame coursing through him. Even in a life that so regularly had beaten him down, this was too much to bear. He sat on his haunches, his face in his hands. He had nothing left.

Barak appeared in the doorway, and cleared his throat. Arik looked up, and Barak motioned him back into the room.

"Okay, Arik," Langer said, "this is what I'll do. If you need time, as you say, I'll give you time: four weeks. Return home, to the States. I'll say that you're going to visit your sick parents. Spend your time wisely, to purge yourself of this devil that has possessed you. Being back in your old environment may help to clear your mind so that you can figure out what you want to do with your life. If you decide to stay in America, I'll file an honorable discharge for you. If you still want to come back here, then we'll decide if there's still a place for you in Sayeret Matkal. That's the best that I can do, Arik. Pack your bags."

Chapter 2

Dahlia lay on her bed, with her princess phone pressed against her head.

"Ze'evi, I'm home. I missed you so much. I wish I could have stayed with you for Pesach. I absolutely hated being in Israel. I don't want to go back there for anything. When can I see you?"

"I missed you too, kitty cat. Pesach here was lonely without you. I had time to think about us. I want you to stay here in the States with me after high school. You can move in with me here in New York. You won't have any problem getting into NYU, even at this late date, even without a high school diploma. My father can make a few phone calls. You don't have to make up your mind right away. Think it over. Okay?"

"I've thought it over already, over the holiday. That's what I want to do, too. I'm done with all this. I feel like I'm a million miles away from my parents. We're living in a different world than them. They still think I'm twelve years old. They're in for a big shock when I break it to them. Did you really miss me?"

"Of course, I did, sweetheart. Let's get everything set up before you tell everyone, so we'll be ready. Fate favors those who plan. Speaking of which, I'm headed to Vegas on business and to have some fun in the casino. Why don't I have John pick you up in the limo? I'll have the plane all ready and warmed up, waiting for you at Dulles Airport. What better place is there to celebrate our new life together than Vegas? If you like, we could elope and have an Elvis impersonator marry us in one of those love chapels on the strip. That would be so cool."

"The Elvis thing would be pretty funny, Ze'evi. I'll make it happen, but it might be a day or two before I can get away."

After the call, she got up from her bed and locked the door. She opened a small, clear plastic baggie. She made a line of snow on a mirror, and the world was once again at peace.

The following night, Dahlia sat in stony silence at dinner with her family. She had lied about having gone to school that day and had returned home at the usual time. The tension at the table was palpable. Nurit and Doron listlessly moved their food around on their plates. Leah surveyed the scene with dread. She was worried about what kind of family they had become. She felt that Dahlia had dragged all of them down. The little ones had no idea what was going on, but they felt that something terrible was going to happen. They didn't know what, but nobody did. They asked to be excused, and Leah gladly gave permission. They walked quietly up the stairs, schoolbags in hand, to do their homework. Dahlia sat alone at the end of the table, not uttering a sound.

Kordy, the blonde labradoodle, sensing catastrophe, made several whining sounds and disappeared into the kitchen with his tail between his legs.

"Aren't you going eat anything?" Leah asked Dahlia.

"I'm not hungry." She slowly got up from the table and walked into the den to watch TV.

In a moment, she was joined by her father. Standing in the doorway, he said, "Dahlia, come into the library. Now." Benny's tone was quiet but very firm. His day already had gone badly. He had been caught in a row between Foreign Minister Eban and Defense Minister Dayan. This impending confrontation with Dahlia was the last thing he needed, but he knew that he could no longer avoid it.

When Dahlia walked into the library, trailing behind her father, her mother was sitting anxiously on the leather sofa, her legs crossed. Benny leaned against his desk.

"What is this about?" Dahlia asked quietly.

"Why have you been lying to us?" Benny asked. "The glue that holds this family together is trust. You have violated that trust. Why did you tell us that Arik had never come to the house in Herzliya? You made up some nonsense. We know that he came and you threw him out. How could you do that to him? I thought that we agreed. And then you lied about the whole thing. Did you think that we wouldn't find out? And, another thing, you told us that you were spending the weekend at the Ehrenreichs' several weeks ago."

"I did go."

"Stop lying to us already, Dahlia! Enough is enough!" Leah shouted. "What were those scratches on your body? The truth! What have the two of you been up to? What has he been doing to you? We know that you went off to the Caribbean alone with him."

"Why did you force me to face that fucking loser, Arik, in our house? What have you been doing to me? Treating me like a puppet! Both of you, leave me alone already!" Dahlia yelled.

"Watch your language, young lady!" Benny tried to control himself, but he was unsuccessful. "Loser? So, you think that Arik is a loser? Do you have even the faintest notion of what you threw out the door? He's anything but a loser. I think that Tzahal and Moshe Dayan are much better judges of character than you are, chutzpanit!" You're the loser! You've lost Arik, the best thing that happened to you in your whole life, you spoiled brat!"

"How dare you talk to me about that, you hypocrite. We sat here eighteen months ago in this very room and you called Arik a roughneck who hangs out with criminal Negroes. You're a hypocrite and a racist! You've told me a thousand times that Arik wasn't good enough for me. You couldn't wait to get rid of him! You nagged me and nagged me to meet Ze'evi, while I was trying to stay faithful to that shithead. You said yourself that Ze'evi was the right man for me, who could treat me like a princess, like I was Israeli royalty or something. Well, I got together with Ze'evi, just like you wanted. Now, you're trying to break us up. Well, it's too late for that. Ze'evi and I are going to be married. I'm moving out of this hellhole and moving in with him, in New York, and going to college up there. Now, how do you like that?"

Benny's face turned bright red. "You will do no such thing!" he said. "You are going back to Israel and enlisting in the army in July. You are an Israeli, and you will serve your country!"

"It's not my goddamn country. Not anymore! I'm done with all that shit. I'm eighteen, and I can choose my own life without any interference from you. I'm done with all the guilt trips you and Imma have laid on me over the past two years. I'm not marching around in the desert like some idiot when I have better, more important things to do with my life. I'm not falling for some soldier boy with a pretty red beret on his head like some kind of Ken doll."

"Those soldier boys, as you call them, are giants among men," Leah said, "who not only protect Israel but all the children of the gas chambers who are living all around the world. And Arik is among the very best of them. That's more than I can say for your arrogant boyfriend."

"The real movers and shakers in the world are people with money, lots of it," Dahlia said. "I want to be part of that, and I will be. Then I'll stand there with Ze'evi while a line of Israeli leaders fall over themselves to get the opportunity to kiss my ass. All they do is worship money anyhow. Do you think that I haven't watched you ingratiate yourself, regularly, with people with money? Did you think that I was blind?"

"This is disgusting talk, and I won't have it in my house! This is not how we raised you," Benny said.

"Your house? This isn't your house! This house belongs to the government of Israel, paid for by people like Ze'evi. Israelis are all schnorrers. For all your fancy titles, you're nothing more than a government functionary." Red-faced, Dahlia scowled.

Benny slapped her hard across the face, sending her to the floor. "You little spoiled slut! Without me, you're nothing! Nobody!"

Dahlia got up slowly, saying, "I'm out of here. Go to hell!"

"Please, Dahlia, don't do this," Leah pleaded tearfully.

"Imma, I can't stay here anymore. I'm sorry."

Dahlia stormed upstairs and slammed her bedroom door so hard that everything in the house shook. She took her suitcase out of her closet and began to pack. She picked up the pink princess phone next to her bed and dialed Ze'evi's number.

In the library, Leah said, "Why did you have to slap her, Benny? Are you crazy? What did you accomplish, Your Excellency? All you did was drive her further away from us." Leah's voice hoarse with anguish.

Twenty minutes later, Dahlia ran downstairs, suitcase in hand. On her way out of the house, she slammed the door. She passed Tomer at the front guard station.

Tomer grabbed her left wrist. "Do not do this, Dahlia! You will live to regret it. You look like a prostitute. What have you come to?"

"Get your hand off me. I thought that we were friends. You betrayed me to my parents. You're nothing more than a security guard. Nothing! Now, go do your job and guard, and stay out our personal business."

Dahlia's words stabbed into the heart of her faithful friend. He silently released his grip and watched as she walked down the street and got into a black stretch limousine that was waiting at the end of the block.

When Benny heard the front door slam, he bolted down the stairs, taking two at a time. He ran out to the front guard station, barefoot and wearing pajamas. By the time he got there, Dahlia was gone.

"Tomer, where did she go?" he asked breathlessly.

"Sir, she got into a black limousine and sped off."

"Do you have any idea where she's going?"

"Yoram heard something about Las Vegas."

"Do we have any assets out there who can be discreet and handle a situation like this?" Benny asked.

"Our closest team is attached to the consulate in Los Angeles."

"Send them out to Las Vegas. Tell them to find her and bring her back here, by force if necessary."

"Yes, sir!"

***

Dahlia sat in the semidarkness of the back of the limousine, staring at the shops of Connecticut Avenue through the tinted glass. She felt a sudden chill. Something about the plush leather interior of the backseat made her feel very alone. Ze'evi had ensured that the mahogany-and-brass bar was stocked with Dahlia's favorites, so she poured herself a vodka and tonic on the rocks, hoping that it would settle her down.

Ze'evi had left a large mirror propped up behind the bar for her use. How thoughtful of him. He never misses a detail. She picked up the mirror and looked at herself. Her red lipstick was smudged. So was her mascara. Did I put on too much, or did the tears mess it up? She wiped her cheeks with a tissue and reapplied her foundation. Then she adjusted her outfit: a bright-red halter top, black velvet hot pants, fishnet pantyhose, and black patent leather high heels. I'll blow him away with my sex appeal. She thought about the hours of bliss that awaited her when the plane touched down in Sin City.

I certainly have grown up during the past year. This trip will be my final good-bye to childhood. She was certain that her parents would come around, that eventually they would realize that she was no longer a child and would come to respect her as an adult. They'll have to. Children can live without their parents, but when it comes right down to it parents can't live without their children. She had seen that in her father's relationship with his own parents. Her grandparents had gone from being in charge of the family to becoming her father's helpless supplicants. Growing up meant saying good-bye to her past life. A wave of apprehension overtook her.

The limousine drove into Virginia and onto the access highway to Dulles Airport. Dahlia flipped the mirror so that it lay flat. She emptied a baggie onto it and used a razor blade to shape the white powder into a line. In a moment, that line was gone, and the world was at peace again.

She watched as the limousine passed all of the passenger terminals where the unwashed masses who were flying commercial were arriving and departing. Of them, maybe 1 percent had seen the inside of a private jet. But this mode of travel had become routine for her, and she liked it. She would never have to waste time crammed in an airplane with total strangers. She shivered with delight when the limousine stopped at the bottom of the stairs of Ze'evi's Learjet. John got her bag. The chilly air on the tarmac smelled of jet fuel. Las Vegas would be warmer.

As she entered the beige leather passenger cabin, with its oversized seats and mahogany appointments, a Haitian chef was preparing dinner in the galley.

"Good evening, Miss Dahlia. I hope you find dinner to your liking. I've prepared a leek soup and duck à l'orange."

"It sounds very nice, Patrice. Thanks."

On the table lay a bouquet of two dozen long-stemmed red roses and an ice bucket containing a bottle of 1932 Barons de Rothschild Reserve champagne. The card read:

To the future Mrs. Ehrenreich. I'm in Room 204 at the MGM Grand Hotel.

Ze'evi

She smiled to herself as she buckled her seatbelt.

Robert, the pilot, came out of the cockpit to greet her. "Dahlia, I hope your ride out here was satisfactory."

"It was fine. Thanks."

"We should be up in the air for about four hours. We're expecting a smooth flight, so you'll have some time to rest. Please let us know if you need anything at all. If you're ready, we'll get clearance from the control tower?"

Dahlia smiled and pointed upward, twirling her right index finger as if to say, "Rev it up!"

Robert smiled. "Yes, ma'am!"

He and the chef disappeared, and moments later Dahlia heard the jet power up.

After dinner, she wanted to get some rest, but she felt completely wired by an overwhelming sense of expectation as well as the lines of cocaine that she had done. Ze'evi had a small compartment, which he called his medicine cabinet, on the plane. She opened it and found a row of drawers all labeled by the type of drug inside. Ze'evi is so organized and efficient. She liked that about him. One drawer was labeled with an up arrow and another with a down arrow. Others were labeled with the universal symbol for cannabis, a snowman for cocaine, and a yellow submarine for psychedelic drugs.

She reached into the drawer that was labeled with the down arrow and pulled out a bottle of Quaaludes. She swallowed three capsules and washed them down with a glass of Stoli vodka on the rocks. She dimmed the lights, leaned her seat back so that she lay almost flat, and fell fast asleep.

"Dahlia, we're beginning our initial approach into Las Vegas McCarran International Airport," the pilot announced on the PA system.

She bolted awake and was immediately felled by a piercing migraine. The room swam in undulating waves. The light was too bright. She covered her face as the airplane began to descend fast. Too fast! Seized by a sense of panic, she managed to unbuckle her seat belt, haul herself out of the seat, and stagger toward the bathroom, where she hung her head over the toilet and vomited out her dinner and probably everything that she had eaten all day. She clutched the rim of the toilet bowl for dear life. She was dry heaving now, because there was nothing left for her to throw up. She looked down and saw that her halter top was stained. She forced herself to get up off the floor. She grabbed a towel and some liquid soap and frantically tried to scrub off the stain. But all she did was leave a bigger, more amorphous stain in its place. She was so fatigued that she could barely lift her head. *Did Ze'evi doctor the Quaaludes? I'll have to ask him.* She looked at herself in the mirror. Her skin was a pale shade of gray. She was determined to make herself look sexy for her lover, her future husband. She carefully walked over to her suitcase and took out some makeup.

She sat down and applied a coat of foundation, blush, mascara, and lipstick. She took slow, deep breaths and brushed her hair.

What's happening to me? Am I making a mistake? What am I doing? My life certainly has taken a turn. Am I selling my soul to the devil? Ze'evi is so good to me, though. He introduced me to a completely new world. So, what if he has a few quirks. Who doesn't? Nobody can love him as well as I can. Everything will be okay. This crazy world that he has created for himself will pass once he settles down. I'm sure of it. Nobody stays this crazy when they have a family to raise. This has all been so much fun, though.

She decided that she would discuss all of this with him during the weekend. They would have plenty of time when they were alone.

"Dahlia, fasten your seat belt, please. We're about to land," the pilot said into the PA system.

She checked herself in the mirror one more time. All was well.

As the plane landed, she reached into the compartment, took three capsules out of the up-arrow drawer, and washed them down with a glass of water. She opened the snowman drawer and snorted two lines of cocaine. *That should give me some energy.* She was dog-tired.

In the limousine on the way to the hotel, Dahlia looked through the window at the bright lights of the Strip. Her field of view became a kaleidoscope. Colors whirled about in a macabre dance before her squinting eyes. Sands, Caesars Palace, Flamingo, Golden Nugget . . . casino after casino shot by her like meteors in the sky. Her face burned as if it were on fire. The sense of panic returned, starting, almost imperceptibly, in the root of her soul. Initially it was drowned out by her sluggishness, but as the seconds ticked by the panic increased, sending her into hyperventilation. She was sweating profusely, her heart racing faster and faster.

"MGM Grand!" the driver announced as he pulled up at the front door, under a huge awning that was lit up by thousands of flashing lights bouncing off the chrome walls and hotel entrance. The bellman took her bags and led her through the casino, where an even greater flurry of bright lights paired with the sounds of cash and music coming out of the hundreds of slot machines that were lined up in garish rows. The lobby stretched in odd directions. People's faces and torsos contorted themselves into impossibly odd shapes. People spoke to one another as if they were in slow motion, with low-pitched voices. Dahlia willed one foot in front of the other, walking along the bright-red and gold carpet. She took the suitcase from the bellman and hobbled up to the front desk. If nothing else, she was glad to get away from the flashing bright lights and the high-pitched jingling noises.

"I'm Mrs. Dahlia Ehrenreich. I'm meeting my husband here—Mr. Ze'evi Ehrenreich," Dahlia slurred, barely able to get the words out her mouth. She felt as if she were hovering in the air five feet above her body.

The clerk's face began to stretch as if made of rubber, assuming the look of a mirror in a fun house. Voices slowed until they were nothing more than a grumble. Dahlia shook her head, trying to regain control. The panic inside her grew like a wild beast struggling to burst out of her chest.

The clerk fumbled with the hotel register. "There must be some mistake. Mrs. Ehrenreich has already checked in."

"What do you mean she's already checked in? I'm Mrs. Ehrenreich!" Dahlia shouted as she pounded her fist on the counter.

Heads turned toward her and then quickly looked away. The hooker at the front desk was obviously out of her mind.

"I'll get the manager," the clerk mumbled.

The manager came over. "What seems to be the prob—"

"What room is that scumbag in? What room? Give me the goddamn key to his fucking room! Now!"

A dozen heads turned to watch the scene.

The manager spoke quietly as he handed her a key. "Suite 204. But please, Miss, you're making a scene. I'll have to call security if you don't stop."

Dahlia staggered to the elevator, dragging her suitcase behind her. More heads turned to watch as she stumbled in her high heels.

The manager drew the clerk close to him and said, "There's been a terrible racket coming out of 204 all evening. We've had numerous complaints about the shrieking and loud music coming from that room. I have a bad feeling about this. Call security to go up there, but tell them not to intervene unless they feel things are really getting out of hand. Put in a call to the Nevada State Police for backup, just in case these people have firearms."

On the second floor, Dahlia walked backward out of the elevator, pulling her suitcase behind her. Loud cries and laughter filled the corridor. They got louder as she approached suite 204. She turned the key and stepped into the room.

She stood in the doorway, completely disoriented. Bright spotlights bathed the room in blinding light. Behind the lights there appeared to be a movie camera on a tripod. Ze'evi was sprawled on the bed, sweaty and naked and locked in a sex act with Charlotte. Spent alcohol bottles, a mirror holding some cocaine, and hashish bongs were strewn around the room. The room reeked of vomit and sweat.

Mike was operating the camera. When he saw Dahlia, he said, "This is such a great scene. The husband is doing the secretary, and the jealous wife walks in. This will look so realistic!"

"Hello, Dolly!" Ze'evi called out. "How was your flight?" Completely stoned, he grinned like a Cheshire cat. "Hey, kitty cat, take off your clothes and join us. We're shooting some home movies."

Dahlia was still standing in the doorway, stunned. Her senses suddenly sharpened as if, undeterred by the haze of the narcotics, a moment of clarity had jolted out of the depths of her soul.

"What the fuck are you doing?" she screamed. "You brought me here for this? This was supposed to be our weekend alone! We were supposed to talk about getting married! You never intended that, did you? Did you? This was all a big setup. You fucking sleazebag. Go to hell!"

"Oh, lighten up, Dahlia! Always so serious! We're just having some fun. Take off your goddamn clothes and get your ass into the bed with us," Ze'ev said.

The camera continued to roll.

"I'm not your porno whore! You asshole!"

"Oh, really? Have you looked at yourself in the mirror lately? You're nothing more! Just a little skank who'll do anything for a blow of coke."

Dahlia lunged at Ze'evi, reaching for his throat. "You bastard! I gave up my family and friends for you! I hate you!"

Ze'evi jumped up and punched her hard in the face, over her left cheek bone, momentarily blinding her. She fell backward, landing on the floor, but catlike sprang to her feet. She jumped at him and scratched at his eyes. She was grabbed from behind by a pair of strong arms around her waist, which picked her up, leaving her legs kicking helplessly in the air.

"Let go of me! Let go of me!" Dahlia shrieked.

Dahlia saw that she had managed to draw blood: There was a trickle of blood under Ze'evi's left eyelid. He wiped at it with his finger.

"This little bitch has been a bad girl, and now she needs to be taught a lesson," Ze'evi said. "Tear off her clothes. You can all have your way with her. Tie her up! She likes that!"

The camera continued to roll. Mike was still behind it, transfixed.

"This is so great! A real, live rape scene!" he said.

Dahlia's world melted into a slow-motion haze as numerous hands tore at her hot pants and halter top. She was left in just her bra and panty hose. She let out a blood-curdling cry but was silenced by Brad's hand on her mouth. With her mouth still open, Brad's index finger found its way inside. She bit down, hard, on his finger, with all the strength she had left in her frail body. Brad yelped and, for a moment, his grip let go.

Dahlia broke free. She ran through the open sliding glass door and on to the balcony, barely noticing the sudden chill. She looked out at the flashing lights of the Strip below and the milling crowds at the entrance of the hotel. She heard shouts from inside the room. They were coming for her. She climbed onto the railing. She felt as if she were frozen in time. Reality had coalesced into a vortex of bright colors and sounds. She jumped. She landed feet first in a stand of shrubbery and then ran into the street, arms flailing, screaming at the top of her lungs. She ran like a frightened gazelle trying to get away from a lion. Traffic in both directions screeched to a halt to avoid the psychotic half-naked woman who spun around and collapsed in a heap in the middle of the street. The state police swarmed her as the crowd in front of the hotel pointed toward the window from which she had jumped. A squad of police officers converged on room 204.

Dahlia would not remember being picked up by paramedics and rushed by ambulance with police escort to Southern Nevada Memorial Hospital. She would not remember being placed in an isolation ward in the ER, in drug-induced florid psychosis, surrounded by Nevada state troopers. Within two hours, agents of the Mossad also were outside the ER. At 2 a.m. Eastern time, the phone at the ambassador's residence rang.

"Don't speak, Benny. Don't even dare to utter a word. Or I'll strangle you, I swear." Leah was deadly serious. "She wouldn't be here if not for you. Now, it's left to me to clean up this catastrophe."

They were met outside the hospital by two Israeli men. The men nodded at Tomer, who had accompanied the Gilads on the flight from Washington, D.C.

One of the men spoke to Benny. "Shalom, Mr. Ambassador. We're the ones who called you. We've tried to get in to see her, but we were rebuffed and told to wait outside. She's quite sick, but apparently, she's also in very serious trouble with the police. They wouldn't tell us anything. They have a tight cordon around her."

The Gilads went inside the hospital. When they asked the ER receptionist about Dahlia, a physician greeted them. Two men in dark suits and ties joined them, flashing IDs. The three escorted Benny and Leah to a private room next to the ER.

"Good morning, Mr. Ambassador. I'm Special Agent Harriman, FBI. This is Assistant District Attorney Hank Bailey, and this is Dr. Tom Edwards, chief of emergency medicine here at Southern Nevada Memorial Hospital." He gestured for them all to sit. "Your daughter was brought in last night in very serious condition. She was found half naked and unconscious in the street outside the MGM Grand hotel. She had apparently jumped out of a second-story window of the hotel. The room that she jumped from was booked to a Ze'evi Ehrenreich."

Dr. Edwards said, "When she arrived in the ER, she was grossly combative and psychotic, screaming unintelligibly, and then she became unresponsive. She needed to be intubated and placed on a respirator. We ran toxicology screens and found high levels of cocaine, amphetamines, barbiturates, and alcohol in her system. She has had numerous seizures, which have been difficult to control. Her liver and kidney enzymes are greatly elevated, and she is in tachycardia, her heart racing at 140 beats per minute. Her blood pressure is unstable. And she is suffering from severe dehydration. She's in very serious condition."

Leah began to cry. "Is she going to die?"

"We're doing everything we can for her, ma'am," Dr. Edwards said. "She's getting the best of care. She's being taken up to the intensive care unit even as we speak. We've had to restrain her. Her thrashing was pulling out the IVs. We have her on high doses of drugs to maintain her blood pressure and fluids to keep her out of shock. We're watching her kidney function closely to determine whether she needs to be placed on hemodialysis. In essence, we have her in a medically induced coma."

Leah sobbed uncontrollably. Benny sat stone-faced, trying desperately to process what was going on.

"What is your connection to Ze'evi Ehrenreich, Mr. Ambassador?" Special Agent Harriman asked.

"He has been dating our daughter for several months, despite our misgivings. We initially approved of the liaison, but over the past few months he has had an ill effect on her. He completely took over her life. Her health and school performance began to falter, she has been losing weight, and she lost interest in all the things that she had always loved. He has this power over her. I don't know how to explain it. He knows how to manipulate her mind. She's still a very impressionable child. Things came to a head last night, when she told us that she was moving out of the house and in with him. She ran off in a huff and got into some black limousine. That's all we know."

"Had either of you seen any evidence at home that she had been using hard drugs? Or have you had money disappear from around the house?" Harrimann asked.

"I had five hundred dollars disappear from my bureau. We never suspected that it could be her." Leah said. "We've always maintained a relationship of honor and trust with our children. It never occurred to us that—"

"Where is Ze'evi now? Benny asked.

"He's been arrested and taken into custody with five others—three men and two women—pending arraignment. During the police raid, a large quantity of cocaine and psychotropic drugs were recovered from the hotel room. The FBI got involved because of an anonymous tip that led to a warrant to search Mr. Ehrenreich's private jet. A large stash of narcotics was found on board that jet, which had crossed state lines. This has now turned into a federal investigation."

Leah said, "Benny, you're ruined! Our lives are ruined! I can see no way out of this. How could you let this happen to our daughter? I told you early on that he was no good."

Hank Bailey, the assistant district attorney, said, "There's more. We've recovered a movie camera from the hotel room. They had been filming pornographic sex scenes when Dahlia entered the room. She seemed genuinely shocked by what was happening. She was ordered to remove her clothing, and when she refused she was set upon by two of the men, who tore off her clothing and attempted to rape her. She managed to free herself. She ran out of the field of the film and, presumably, that's when she jumped from the balcony. Ze'ev and the others are looking at more than ten years in prison for attempted rape, in addition to the narcotics charges. Our local authorities are coordinating with the FBI, because of the rape charges."

Leah and Benny sat stunned and unable to speak as they processed the catastrophe unfolding before their eyes.

"We'll have to search your residence for any signs of drug possession, Harriman said. "You can let us in to do our work and we can do this quietly, or my superiors will have to go through channels to obtain consent from your foreign ministry through our state department. That could prove to be very messy for you, Ambassador. I'd like to stress that Dahlia is not under arrest. We have no reason—at this time—to charge her with a crime. She appears to have been a victim, plain and simple. But we will know more in the coming days and weeks as our investigation progresses."

"Is there any way that this can be kept out of the public spotlight? It would become a major scandal in my country," Benny said. "Dahlia is a very good girl. She was an excellent student and athlete. Yes, as you say, she is a victim. She has never done anything like this in her whole life. Over the past four months, she became a different person. She fell under his influence and he twisted her mind. She never would have come to this if not for him. We've never encountered anything like this before. We had no idea what we were up against."

Harriman seemed to consider for a moment, and then he said, "That all depends on your level of cooperation. This can be kept quiet—but only if there is no evidence that Dahlia has committed a crime. If she is free and clear, she will have to testify in court against Ehrenreich. Is that understood?"

"Of course," Benny said. "You'll have our full cooperation. I'll need to contact my superiors at the foreign ministry, you understand, to have your Washington field agents admitted to the residence."

Harriman produced a business card and handed it to Benny.

"Ambassador Gilad, I'd like you to call us if you learn anything new or if you have anything to tell us. Please leave all of your contact information with my assistants. You have my word that everything you tell us will be held in the strictest confidence. We will not only strive to keep this out of the public spotlight. If you cooperate with us during the investigation and subsequent trial, we'll push for a closed proceeding and to have the trial transcripts sealed."

"When can we see her?" Leah asked Dr. Edwards.

"We'll let you in when her condition stabilizes. She's going through withdrawal, but don't worry. She's being watched around the clock by a team of specialty nurses. We'll let you in tomorrow morning, in all likelihood." Dr. Edwards touched Leah's arm. "Mrs. Gilad, it's better this way. No mother should see her child in this condition. It's an image that would haunt you for the rest of your life. I want to spare you that. Please, trust that we're doing everything humanly possible for her. Let us stabilize her and get her through this phase."

Benny and Leah spent the worst day and night of their lives, sitting in chairs outside the intensive care unit. Morning brought no relief. After a brief meal, mostly from the candy machine in the lounge, they resumed their silent vigil, not speaking even to each other. They tried to sleep with their heads propped against the wall, but they were awakened repeatedly by a large family that had settled into the lounge. The numerous children were playing a raucous game of tag. The Gilads' eyes burned in their sockets, and their heads pounded.

At about 8 p.m., the following day, the hospital's chief of medicine, Dr. Wilfred Scott, emerged through the double doors that Benny and Leah had been staring at for the thirty-six hours, looking for some sign of life, as if peering through the gates of heaven.

"Mr. and Mrs. Gilad?"

They nodded.

"Dahlia has been stabilized. Her breathing tube is out, and she's awake. Her situation is still very tenuous, so I will allow only one visitor at this time."

"You stay here, Benny." Leah's tone was very firm.

Leah entered the room, which was dark except for the lights of the monitors that flashed and beeped above Dahlia's head. Dahlia, eyes closed, was breathing softly. She seems so childlike, so innocent, Leah thought. How could things have come to such a pass? The idea that Dahlia had almost died sent a shiver through Leah's body.

Dahlia, sensing her mother's presence, slowly opened her eyes. Leah caressed her face gently as she stared silently at her.

"Hi, Imma. I'm so glad that you're here," Dahlia said almost in a whisper. "I don't remember anything after getting on Ze'evi's plane. Where am I?"

Leah reached for Dahlia's hand and gently took it in her own. "You're in the hospital in Las Vegas, sweet girl. You're getting the best of care. You've become ill, and Abba and I are here to help you get better."

"I've really screwed up our lives, haven't I?" an exhausted Dahlia said without emotion. "I'm so sorry. I'm so sorry, Imma. I've been out of control for months. I've been so nasty. I've pushed everyone who was important to me away. I let that creature take over my life, and now it's in pieces. I've ruined our family. I've destroyed my health. Everything that I was is gone. There's nothing left of me."

"The main thing right now is for you to get well," Leah said. "Nothing else matters. There are no more secrets. Abba and I won't let any further harm come to you. Please don't think of anything else right now. Concentrate on getting better, nothing more. This will be a new beginning for you."

Leah felt Dahlia's hand tighten over hers, probably with all of the strength that she had in her enfeebled body.

Over the next two weeks, as Dahlia's strength began to return, she was placed in a private room. She spent many hours speaking with her mother. Leah had decided not to let Benny in to see Dahlia until she asked for him—and she had not. When her vital signs stabilized, she was visited by drug rehabilitation counselors and social workers. The FBI decided to wait to question Dahlia when her mental state had improved.

One morning, after the nurses had helped Dahlia to bathe and dress, she was taken to the sun lounge, where Benny, Leah, Dr. Scott, the nursing supervisor, and the chief of the department of social work were waiting for her.

"How do you feel, Dahlia?" Dr. Scott asked.

"I'm feeling better, thank you."

If Dahlia felt any anger or discomfort at seeing her father, she did not show it. All of the feistiness had been knocked out of her, by either the trauma that she had experienced or the medications that she was on. Benny was unnerved by her dull, docile manner. He missed the Dahlia who gave him a mouthful of conflict whenever she felt it appropriate. He felt terribly responsible for this outcome. He sat quietly and continued to allow Leah handle the situation.

Dr. Scott said, "When you came in here, you were in very serious condition. You've been through two weeks of active withdrawal from the drugs you were taking. You've been hooked on some very powerful narcotics. You still have a long road in front of you, to become completely well, and the recommendations that we will make today will help you along that road. Do you understand so far?"

Dahlia nodded.

The social worker said, "Dahlia, there are many things you will need to do to recover, but there are just as many resources available to help you do so. I've been speaking a great deal with your parents about how to proceed from here. Upon your return to Washington, you will get intensive treatment at an excellent private facility just outside Annapolis, called Tranquility Acres. There they have a multidisciplinary approach to drug rehabilitation. Everything is designed not only to get you better but also to make sure you never get hooked again. They have a ninety-day program with an excellent track record—"

"I will never, ever take any of that stuff again," Dahlia said. "I've abused my body in so many terrible ways. I've been so compromised, by someone that I allowed into my heart and soul. I will never, ever let anyone get that close to me again. Nothing is more important to me than getting back to myself and forgetting any of this ever happened."

"At this point, you may not yet be able to shake off your past so easily," the social worker said. "There are people who want to ask you questions about what happened that night, in particular, and what Mr. Ehrenreich did to you and with you over the past several months. Do you understand?"

Dahlia nodded, frowning.

"We understand it will be difficult for you to talk about all this, but it's most important that you cooperate with them. This is a very critical time in your life. What you say and do will have significant consequences for you in the future. You may have broken the law. We wanted to wait a bit longer to discuss all of this with you, but the authorities need to question you soon."

Leah said, "We've hired the best lawyers in Washington to represent us, and they'll always be beside you when you're being questioned."

"Will I go to jail?"

"Dahlia, nobody thinks that you've committed a crime," Leah said. "Right now, you're being treated as a witness. You'll have to testify against Ze'evi in court. Are you prepared to do that?"

"Ze'evi hurt me. Not only hurt in the way that guys usually hurt girls, acting like a jerk or cheating. He physically and mentally hurt me. I feel like a spent rag, like . . . like he sucked all the humanity out of me. I was taken in by a con man, and he needs to be made to pay for his crimes . . . He made me do some terrible things. Things that I could not have imagined possible before. My life has been so twisted and distorted. I don't know who I am anymore—"

The social worker said, "It's very important that you tell us exactly which drugs you've been taking. It will help direct the team that will be taking care of you and also will give us an idea of how long it will take to detox your body. For example, had you ever tried heroin or any other opiates, such as morphine or mescaline?"

Dahlia shook her head. "No, I took marijuana, cocaine, amphetamines, Quaaludes . . . and I tried LSD twice. I drank alcohol but not regularly, just when everyone got together. I never got drunk just for the hell of it. And I never took heroin."

"That's actually a bit of good news," the social worker said. "The drugs you took, although psychologically addictive, don't have significant physical addiction associated with them."

"What does that mean?" Leah asked.

"It means that with an intensive drug detox, along with the type of holistic, multidisciplinary approach they have at Tranquility Acres, Dahlia should do very well and make a full recovery. It will be very important that she undergo continued psychological counseling and be in a supportive, wholesome environment for the foreseeable future after she leaves the facility, though." She reached over and took Dahlia's hands in her own. "You have a wonderful family that loves you very much. They'll be there to help you every step of the way. Ultimately, though, this will be in your hands to repair, Dahlia. Do you understand?"

Dahlia nodded.

"You understand that Ze'evi may be sentenced to many years in prison for what he did to you?" Leah asked. "Your testimony will be critical. Do you know anything about a film that he was making when you went into his room?"

Dahlia shook her head. "Everything is such a blur. All I remember is fighting and screaming."

Benny thought that it might be better that way. The police had showed the film to him and Leah. He had become extremely agitated watching the attempts to violate his daughter. He felt like calling Howard Ehrenreich and giving him a piece of his mind about what Howard's little nachas had done to his daughter. He wanted to sue the bastard for everything he was worth. He wanted to tear Ze'evi's throat out. But he knew that if he did any of those things he would be signing his own professional death warrant. Everything that he had worked for the past two decades would go up in the smoke of a sex-and-drug scandal. He could imagine the headlines in the Yedioth Ahronoth newspaper or, worse, the HaOlam HaZeh, Israel's version of America's National Enquirer. He thought about Leah and the children being hounded by reporters and publicly shamed. Israel was still a conservative country when it came to these things. For Dahlia to have behaved like a red-light-district streetwalker of HaYarkon Street was beyond his ability to grasp. He was seized by a crushing sense of guilt, knowing that he had had a hand in the situation. His mind and heart raced. He thought about Arik.

Dahlia slept most of the flight back to Washington, D.C., curled up in a fetal position in the seat next to her mother.

Leah stared down at her little girl, who had had womanhood so violently thrust upon her. Leah wracked her brains, trying to figure out how could this have happened, how she and Benny could have had such poor judgment, and how they could have been so misled by societal ideas about who is and is not worth being with. They had traveled so much, and they considered themselves so worldly. They knew so many people. They had thought that they were such good judges of character. Yet their blunders nearly had cost them the life of their eldest daughter. Leah sighed. She decided that the past was past and she needed to focus on the future. But she wondered whether it would be possible to repair the emotional damage that Dahlia created for herself and their family. She admitted that there was bound to be residual effects, but she was not sure what kind or to what extent.

Chapter 4

Dahlia woke up alone in a quiet, well-appointed bedroom with wide windows overlooking Chesapeake Bay. Her first impulse was fear. Where is everyone? She looked out the window at the sailboats. Their brightly colored spinnakers blowing in the breeze made her think about her first date with Ze'evi and how handsome and charming he had been on that blustery, sunny day only six months earlier. It had been early November when they had gone out on his sailboat, and he had made her feel both relaxed and excited for his first touch after weeks of anguish not hearing from Arik.

Her reverie was interrupted by a sharp emotional but almost physical pain in her gut. The reality of the events of the previous three weeks set in as her mind cleared. She realized that she had been confined in a facility, an institution. Is this a mental institution? Am an inmate? Will I find my bedroom door locked from the outside when I try to open it? She was seized by panic.

She looked around the room and saw an elegant wooden desk on which a lamp and writing material were arranged neatly. The dresser and four-poster bed were of solid mahogany. In the corner of the room were two brand-new plush sitting chairs with a side table in between them. Behind one of the chairs stood a floor lamp. She switched on the lamp and realized what a comfortable reading nook the sitting area was. The floor was covered with a plush, cream-colored carpet. Well, if this is a cell for cuckoos, at least it's a nice cell. She opened the dresser drawers and the closet door. All of her clothing was in there, neatly folded and arranged. She sat in one of the chairs and glanced at the ticking bedside clock. It was nearly 6 a.m.

The name Tranquility Acres made it sound like a funny farm. How long will I have to stay here? She found her robe in the closet, and she put it on cautiously as she approached the bedroom door. When she turned the handle ever so slowly, she felt the door open slightly, to her relief. She looked out and saw that she was at the top of a large wooden staircase in what appeared to be a mansion. There were about ten dark-mahogany doors on this level, and they looked exactly like hers. She walked silently down the stairs and into a large, wood-trimmed foyer. There was a grandfather clock in the corner of the room that chimed six times, in Westminster style. The air was cool and dry. The early morning sun from over the Chesapeake shone through the large eastern bay windows.

She wandered through the first floor, past a richly appointed, wood-paneled library teaming with books of every sort and several more reading nooks lighted by Tiffany lamps and featuring plush leather chairs.

What she assumed to be a living room, on this first floor, had a large stone fireplace at one end and a vaulted two-story wooden ceiling. There were numerous sofas. The atmosphere was bright and airy but also cozy. The large, immaculate kitchen area was separated from the dining area by a marble countertop.

She ventured down the hallway, entering a large playroom that was equipped with pool tables, table tennis, air hockey, foosball tables, more large sofas, and a large color TV. Along one wall were shelves full of current magazines.

Now this is a game room, she thought ruefully.

Dahlia walked outside, where the early morning mist doused her senses. When she wandered into the large front courtyard, she saw a swimming pool and tennis courts off to her right. Playing some tennis would do me a world of good. She wondered whether she still could lift a racquet after all that she had been through. She saw a large, open-roofed enclosure beside the pool, with swinging hammocks around an open-air stone fireplace. Beside the fireplace stood an outdoor kitchen that she assumed was used for barbecues.

She saw a gravel running path going off into the woods beyond the tennis court. She walked around the main house, which she now saw was a large red-brick Tudor-style mansion, and then walked under an archway that led to a back terrace portico. A long row of rocking chairs faced a downward-sloping lawn that meandered lazily down to a series of docks along the Severn River. She saw Annapolis's U.S. Naval Academy off in the distance.

She breathed in deeply and sighed. Along with the misty gentle breeze that was blowing in from the bay were the strong scents of roses and cut grass.

"So, what do you think, Dahlia?" a kind voice behind her spoke softly.

Dahlia was startled. She turned around and saw a casual but well-dressed middle-aged woman smiling at her.

"It's very nice here," Dahlia said, smiling tentatively. "Tranquility Acres, huh? It seems very tranquil."

"I'm Barbara, the director of services for the center. Welcome. Your parents will be back later in the day. Can I make you a cup of hot cocoa?"

Dahlia nodded and followed her back inside.

***

The program at Tranquility Acres was segregated by gender, which suited Dahlia just fine. She had had a bellyful of guys, so she was happy to be in a safe, comfortable environment away from them.

At breakfast, she met the other nine girls in the program. Most of them were her age. Arrangements had been made for her to have kosher food, and she was surprised that the other girls accepted her dietary restrictions without batting an eye. When they introduced themselves, they did not ask why she was there either. She decided that she liked the facility. She even began to have hope that she would heal there. She knew herself well, however, so she knew that if healing was to occur it would have to be on her own terms and in her own way. She would not be happy with a cookie-cutter method.

She spent the rest of the morning getting a complete medical exam, providing a detailed history of the past six months, and undergoing a detailed psychological evaluation, including numerous written tests. She was intrigued at what someone could learn about her by looking at a bunch of large black inkblots on a page. Before lunch, she was given a tour of the facility and the grounds and introduced to the staff. It was amazing to her that the facility bore no resemblance to the mental hospitals that she had seen in movies. The campus even included a full-service spa facility, a yoga and meditation studio, and a bike shop.

As if guessing Dahlia's thoughts, Barbara approached her at the conclusion of lunch.

"Dahlia, you'll have an opportunity to utilize all of our facilities. We consider each element here to be equally important to promote your recovery. Now, it's time for you to meet with our group therapy counselors."

Barbara was warm and friendly, but Dahlia sensed that underneath that she was all business. Barbara's efficiency caused Dahlia to feel a sudden rush of anxiety wash over herself.

How did my life take this strange detour? I was supposed to be in the army by now. I was supposed to be by Arik's side. But instead, I switched gears, to become Mrs. Ehrenreich. Now, this? Where will this path lead me? She had no idea. She could not make any long-term plans. She was reduced to living day-to-day. She felt some comfort in the idea that everything had been thought of for her, that all that she would have to do was to go with the flow, but she wondered where that flow would lead. She understood one thing for sure, though: If her life was to move forward, she would have to regain control over that life, and that would mean regaining the trust of her family and friends whom she had so carelessly tossed aside. Where is Arik? And what is he doing now?

Dahlia followed Barbara to the wood-paneled conference room. Bright late-spring sunshine was streaming in through the windows. In the center of the room stood a large oval mahogany table. Barbara took a seat at the far end of the table; beside her sat Benny and Leah. Every seat around the gleaming table, except for one in the front that meant for Dahlia, was occupied.

"Come in, Dahlia. Please, sit down," Barbara said. "Let's begin. You've already met Dr. Sheldon Baker, our staff psychiatrist, and Dr. Liz Stevens, our chief psychological counselor. This is Helen. She directs our interdisciplinary programs, including the group counseling sessions. Sheila is our nutritionist. She'll make sure that you receive a fully balanced diet to help to restore your metabolism. She'll work in conjunction with your rabbi to ensure that the food you have here adheres to your religious beliefs. Your parents tell us that you've lost nearly twenty-five pounds in the past six months. Ruth will be your sponsor and your family liaison. She will work with you most directly. How do you like it here so far?"

"It seems very nice," Dahlia said softly.

"Very good. Our staff has done a preliminary walk-through of the results of your medical exams and psychological exams. From what we've seen so far—and I know that it's very early to tell—but apart from a severe reactive depression from exposure to emotional trauma, you appear to have no serious underlying psychiatric or personality disorders. The psychosis you experienced in Las Vegas appears to have been induced by the mixture of the cocaine, amphetamines, and barbiturates you took—and nothing more. I believe that you've already been told that the drugs you took are only psychologically addictive and not physically addictive. Some of the other girls in the program have addictions far more complex, involving opiates, and these girls have a much more guarded prognosis than you do. All things considered, you're a lucky girl. Another important factor is that you haven't been doing this for very long. Less than six months, by all accounts. I think that, with intensive effort on your part, your prognosis is excellent. But that also depends on how you live your life after you leave here. Your parents have already been completely briefed, and we'll work with your whole family to reassemble all the pieces. They will be able to visit you here, as will your friends. We have a very liberal visitation policy, as we believe that your community can help get you back into life. But let me be direct. If at any time you receive illicit drugs from an outsider, you will be immediately discharged from the program. I want to be very clear about this."

Dahlia nodded, staring intently at Barbara.

Dr. Baker, the psychiatrist, said, "In the early stages, you will be given antidepressant medication to help you sleep. I will meet with you on a weekly basis to determine the efficacy of the drug regimen and monitor you for side effects. If you experience anything untoward, you need to alert your sponsor, Ruth, immediately. I will also monitor you closely for any residual effect of the drugs you took before. Some of them do have a long-lasting effect. Your medical detox will take about four weeks in total. You will be meeting with me, one-on-one, daily for individual psychotherapy in the initial period and, depending on your progress, three days a week after that. This will be in tandem with a group therapy session that meets every other day. There will be ongoing psychological testing, as we move through this program with you, to monitor the efficacy of what we are doing. I am available to speak with you at any time, and I want you to feel free to approach me, especially if you feel a crisis coming on."

Barbara added, "And don't worry about free time. There will be plenty of time to avail yourself of our spa and recreational facilities. We have regular yoga and meditation classes, and a massage therapist is available every day, by appointment. As you develop relationships with the other girls, you'll have much more fun. Your parents have told us that you're quite the tennis player."

Dahlia smiled for what seemed like the first time in months.

After a brief silence, Benny said, "I want to thank you all for admitting Dahlia to this wonderful program. This is the first time in many months that my wife and I have had hopeful and positive feelings about her. Dahlia is our first priority, and Leah and I will do whatever we can to assist in this process. Thank you again."

As Benny had spoken, he had fought hard to keep his emotions in check. He knew that as Dahlia immersed herself in this gentle, healing place, Washington FBI field agents were hovering, ready to pounce on her and grill her about what she had done with Ze'evi, what she had known, and when she had known it. The facility directors had been briefed on the criminal and legal aspects of the case, and they had met with the FBI agents. They would protect Dahlia—for now—and would allow the FBI agents to interrogate her only when she was deemed medically and psychologically stable enough to withstand it. Benny had insisted that she be questioned here, in a comfortable space, rather than be dragged downtown. She was still considered a witness rather than an accused, but how the investigation would shake out was uncertain. The staff of the facility were well aware of Dahlia's identity and the overarching need of her and her family for privacy and security.

Barbara said, "Thank you, Mr. Gilad. Dahlia, do you have any questions for us?"

"I know that I've made a mess of my life and my family's life. I can't undo what I've done, but I want to move forward and put our lives back together—more than anything—and try to restore the wonderful family life we had." Dahlia sniffed and then looked at her parents. "Thank you, Abba and Imma, for loving me and doing all this for me. Is there any way that I can make up the schoolwork that I missed, while I'm here, so that I can still get my high school diploma?"

Leah said, "I've already spoken to the school, and they'll work with us. I hope that it doesn't interfere with the program here."

"We'll do everything in our power to facilitate that," Barbara said with her characteristic efficiency. "We'll have tutors work with her, if necessary, so that she'll be able to submit her work and pass all of her exams."

The meeting ended, and Dahlia walked her parents down the long wooded path to the parking lot.

"I think that this will be very good for you," Leah said, smiling. She hugged Dahlia tightly.

Dahlia turned around and silently fell into her father's arms.

"We have one more surprise for you," Benny said, smiling.

Dahlia raised her eyebrows. "What is it?"

"We won't tell you anything more. Good night, my shining star. We'll come and visit you before Shabbat and bring you food and treats."

He kissed her, and he and Leah left.

***

Dinner was served around a long, formally set table in the dining room. Candelabras lighted the table. Everyone shared in the food preparation, serving, and cleanup. Dahlia's food and dishes were kept strictly separate from the rest, but when the food was on the table she noticed two kosher place settings.

"I'm sorry, Sheila, but only one kosher place setting is necessary. I can't mix the dishes," Dahlia said.

Sheila smiled. "I know that, but two people will be eating kosher here tonight."

"I wasn't told that there was another person in the program that kept kosher?"

"There isn't." Sheila smiled cryptically. "You have a visitor. Turn around."

When Dahlia turned around, her feeling of suspense rapidly morphed into explosive joy and tears. She let out a loud cry and jumped into Penny's arms. The other girls around the table stood and applauded. Soon they all were swept up in the emotional rush that filled the candle lighted room.

***

As the early-summer moon rose over the Severn River, the lights of the U.S. Naval Academy twinkled in the water that was pushed about by the cool evening breeze. The two girls sat on wooden Adirondack chairs in front of the boathouse, watching sailboats bob up and down.

"I've so totally screwed things up, Penny. How could I have allowed my life to go off the rails like it has? Everything was supposed to be so smooth. Who could have predicted this? Why didn't I listen to you? I was so taken in by that shithead. He seemed like he was sent from God to bail me out of the dumps when Arik disappeared. He really seemed to understand my feelings. And besides being a shoulder to cry on—and a spectacular lover—he always knew what to do or say to make me feel good about myself. Now, I see it all as a deliberate act on his part. He played me like a violin. I never realized that I was just a plaything for him, like his sports cars, boats, houses, and planes. He was like a beast, a predator, drawing me in until I was in his jaws. I managed to escape just before those jaws permanently shut around me." Dahlia rubbed her eyes. "And who knows what permanent effects will occur as a result of what I did?"

"What do you mean?"

"The FBI is searching the residence for any drugs I may have left. Right now, I'm just considered a witness, but if they find anything I could be charged with possession. If they find something, my father could lose his position and my family would be ruined. If this ever got into the Israeli papers, we'd all be scandalized. I think that I was very careful not to leave anything lying around, but who knows? I've been so strung out that I might have been careless."

Dahlia breathed in the languid night air and sighed deeply, looking out at the long reflection of the moon on the water.

"When did you find out about what happened to me?"

"Your parents called me from Las Vegas. I was going to come to see you then, but your mom said that it would be better if I waited and came here. It worked out perfectly, because my dad made some phone calls and got me an internship for the summer at a big patent law firm, Wabash and Jamison, in downtown D.C. I have arranged my hours to start at 7:00 a.m. every day so that I can get out by 3:00 p.m. and come out here to be with you."

Dahlia embraced Penny.

"Penny, I love you so much. How can I ever repay this? You're working on a lifelong debt of gratitude here."

"Do not worry, Dahlita. I will think of something!" Penny smirked.

"So, you're off to Boston next year?"

"Yes! I heard in April that I got into MIT for electrical engineering and pre-law, so Richard and I will be close to each other. He has gotten into the computer science department at Harvard. We decided not to move in together, though. My dad is rather traditional, as you know, and would take a dim view of that, but I did not even broach that subject, because I figured that it would be better for us to live with roommates. I think that we would get on each other's nerves during this stressful period. We have the rest of our lives to annoy each other. We can always be together when we want to, anyway."

"You're so smart, as usual. . ."

After a long pause and as if she were reaching deeply into her soul, Dahlia said, "Arik came to see me."

"When?"

"When we were in Israel for Pesach."

"I gather that it did not go well. Did he explain his disappearance? Did he give any reason or excuse?"

"Not even. When I walked in, he acted like we'd just seen each other a week before, like he expected me to be overjoyed to see him. It was so bizarre. He wanted to know why I hadn't written to him. He said that he wrote me every week for months. He said that he tried to call me on numerous occasions and left messages with my dad's secretary. Right before he came, he sent me this long letter about how much he missed me, how his life had been hell without me, how he dreamed about me every night. He said all of this again, with a completely straight face. I just stood there, flabbergasted that he could do that. He never once tried to apologize or excuse himself in even the slightest way. I suppose that he thought that I would swoon for him because he was in paratrooper's formal uniform. I don't know. I don't know anything anymore." Dahlia shook her head.

"So, what happened then?"

"He accused me of being a druggie and said that he wanted to get help for me. He said that Ze'evi was going to kill me. He went on and on about how terrible I looked: my weight, bloodshot eyes, yellow skin. Who says that to a girl, especially one that you haven't seen in months?"

"Someone who loves that girl, Dahlita," Penny said evenly. "I feel like we have been here before. Something about Arik revealed itself or appeared to reveal itself to you, you jumped to a conclusion and accused him of being someone he was not or doing something that he did not do—or not in the same way as you thought—and after you jumped down his throat, you found out that you were entirely premature in your assessment. In other words, you ended up finding out so much more about him, which made you fall in love with him even more . . . but only after you wounded him."

"Penny, this is so different than that. This wasn't a sudden revelation. You know that I grieved for him. I barely left my room. I was beside myself with sorrow. Training accidents happen all the time in the army, especially to guys who like to take risks, like Arik does, so at first, I thought that something terrible had happened to him. I begged my dad to find out if he was okay and to get word to him. My dad said that he saw him and that, physically, he was fine and he was doing well in his training. Why didn't he contact me, then? I've wracked my brain, trying to come up with an explanation.

"I wrote to you that my parents practically forced me to meet Ze'evi, to get me out of my funk and because they felt that he was a far more suitable boyfriend for me than Arik was, right? They said that he had much better breeding, like they were mating dogs or something. Well, Ze'evi made advances to me, and I eventually gave in, because I had drawn the only conclusion that I could: that Arik found someone else in the army. What other conclusion could I reach? Arik was always such a wonderful and consistent letter writer."

"I know what you are saying, Dahlia, but it just does not add up. We both got to know Arik well during camp and the year following. Unless he skillfully and maliciously hid a significant part of himself from us and decided to suddenly reveal it to you to cause you maximum hurt, there must be some other reason that you did not hear from him. This will sound crazy, Dahlia, but could his letters have been censored in some way by the army?"

"I thought of that, Penny, but it's not possible. What kind of military secrets would Arik have known in basic training? Besides, when censors go over letters they just black out the classified stuff and then let the letters go out. The army is very careful about getting out soldiers' letters—especially lone soldiers. They understand how important letters are for morale."

"What about your father's secretary? Arik mentioned her, right?"

"I called her when I got back from Israel, but she denied having gotten any calls from him."

Penny shook her head. "I do not know, Dahlia. This is all impossible to explain, but it just does not seem like something that Arik would do."

"What's past is past, Penny. I'm going to start my life all over again here, with a completely clean slate. Those two guys really did a number on me. Now, I have to flush them both out of my head and move forward with my life. I don't think that I should seek any type of relationship with a guy until I've figured out who I am. That seems to have been my biggest loss in this whole fiasco.

"You know, Penny, I envy you. Your life seems to have so much less drama than mine. You pick a goal, decide on the best way to get there, pack your lunch, and off you go. Things seem so much less complicated for you. You're like my counterpoint."

Penny smiled. "You know that opposites attract. Maybe that is why we are so good together. You crave my stability, and I crave your sense of adventure. You are always looking for Superman. I have a plan for the future. I always have had. Richard was the missing piece in that plan. He showed up, and we are off to the races. Another reason that my life is less complicated than yours is that I can go directly to college after high school while you have to delay starting your life for a couple of years, because of the army. That makes planning for the future a lot more complicated."

"I was ready to throw my whole life away for that creep Ze'evi. I'd already told my parents that I didn't want to return to Israel, that I wanted to move in with Ze'evi and go to college in New York. I looked down on Israel and Israelis, thinking myself better than everyone. What a fool I was, trying to pretend that I was something I'm not! I'll have to work hard to get myself back on track. One thing's for damn sure—I'm never going to take any drugs again. Never! I hate myself on them!"

"Once you decide who you are, you will figure out what you want your future to look like, and only then will you decide who you want to spend it with, like I have decided to spend mine with Richard."

"Do you love him?"

"I do love him, very much. I feel alive when I am with him. He makes me feel special. He is completely attuned to my feelings, and vice versa. Instead of fireworks, I went for the slow, steady burn, and that is what I have gotten. I am completely content."

"I wish I was completely content."

"You will be, Paapi. You will be. Give it time. I am going to run back to D.C. I'll be back tomorrow at 4:30 p.m. I'll bring my tennis stuff."

"I haven't played tennis in nearly a year." Dahlia smiled sadly.

"You will still beat me!"

For the next twelve weeks, Dahlia threw herself into the program, determined to make things right for herself and her family. She attended individual therapy sessions five days a week, enabling her to confront in private the transformation that she had undergone during the past year. She began to understand that she had not handled in a constructive manner her grief over losing Arik. She had allowed herself to be drawn into the clutches of a master manipulator, as a quick fix for a deep wound.

She realized that although she was glad to have shed Ze'evi from her life, the pain of having lost Arik had never gone away. Arik had continued to haunt her dreams almost every night. When wakefulness melted into sleep, Arik's face hovered in the darkness, sending a knifelike pain searing into her gut. Now that the protective cover of drugs had been removed, she felt all of this pain. Somehow, I have to find the strength to bear it.

Group therapy took the longest for her to adjust to. Initially, she found those sessions contrived. She felt embarrassed about sharing her feelings and experiences with total strangers. She was told that sharing would improve her communication skills. When did I ever have a problem communicating? She sat quietly in the sessions and listened as the other girls in the group spilled their guts out for everyone to hear. Many had seriously destructive life histories and, as a result, had been addicted to heroin or opiate painkillers. Dahlia felt sorry for these girls. They came from very dysfunctional homes, and many of them had been physically or even sexually abused as children.

Although that was not the case with her, she had been locked in a perennial conflict with her father that predated this crisis. She had bridled against his attempts to control her and generally her resistance had been successful. Her vulnerability about Arik's disappearance had led her to give in to him finally, with catastrophic results. Why does Abba always feel that he knows better than everyone around him? Only Imma has any spine to stand up to him, and her just barely. What will my relationship with him be like now? She wondered whether he would treat her like a helpless invalid now that she was emotionally impaired. The thought of that possibility, along with the inevitable loss of independence, made her sad and angry at the same time. She knew that if she was to truly grow out of adolescence she would have to regain her footing and her unique point of view. But how?

Dahlia also struggled with the twelve-step aspect of the program. She understood the need for her to make amends to those that she had hurt or harmed, but she wondered about the people who had hurt or harmed her. What about Arik? Where's his apology? Without that, she was left alone to try to quiet the waves of grief that washed over her. How can I discern which things I can change from those I can't? And will I have the wisdom to know the difference?

Every day, Dahlia looked forward to 5 p.m., when Penny's bright-red BMW ground up the gravel driveway. Dahlia would then lose herself in the emotional embrace of her luminous friend. The wonderful influence that Penny had on Dahlia was quickly recognized by the therapists. It also became clear to them that her addiction was not deeply rooted. In response, they focused more on Dahlia's grief and anger that had allowed her to be so misled.

Working through her guilt and shame about the swath of destruction that Dahlia had left in her family was perhaps the most difficult for her. She was pleasantly surprised when her parents visited weekly, spending the afternoon with her—including family therapy sessions. Dahlia rediscovered her parents. She even confronted her anger against her father, acknowledging that it was a motivating force in her life.

Benny came to the difficult realization that he had almost lost his eldest daughter. He realized that the work to be done was more than mending fences. It was important to try to reconstruct what Dahlia had been, and he knew that his direct involvement would be key.

Mercifully, a thorough search of the ambassador's residence turned up no drugs. True to their word, the FBI kept the whole affair under wraps. In close consultation with the Israeli foreign minister, Abba Eban, it was decided that Benny could continue at his post if he made very certain that the situation would not interfere with his duties. Benny thought it miraculous that the embassy staff did not act as if anything was amiss, although everyone knew that Dahlia had been ill and hospitalized. The rumor was that she had contracted a severe case of mononucleosis.

Dahlia enjoyed playing tennis with Penny and her new friends at the facility. She felt empowered as she assumed the role of a tennis pro, giving lessons to the others. After an awkward start, she participated in team-building exercises, which she knew would be important when she went into the army. Once she let go, she realized that the seemingly wide gulf between her and the other girls receded when they were in less stressful situations, such as playing sports and going on hikes. Her diet and vitamin supplements were carefully regulated by Sheila, and she steadily gained weight.

She made full use of the spa facilities and yoga studio. She had always wanted to try yoga and meditation but never had gotten around to it. She immersed herself in daily sessions and found great comfort in them. Leah was positively jubilant when Dahlia asked for a Jewish prayer book and Bible with commentaries to study. With assistance, Dahlia completed her required schoolwork. Her high school diploma was sent to the residence.

***

By early August, Dahlia felt ready to confront the inevitable. She was called into the library one afternoon to join her parents and their attorney, Mark Jacobowitz, in preparation for her questioning by the FBI, which was scheduled for the following day.

That night, Dahlia did not sleep a wink. The next morning, she had to put on extra make-up to make herself appear rested and composed.

Special Agent Harriman and Mr. Bailey were accompanied by an assistant and a stenographer who recorded every word that Dahlia said. As part of the arrangement with Mr. Jacobowitz and because Harriman and Bailey felt that they would were able to conduct a more meaningful interview there, due to

Dahlia's continued fragile state, the questioning took place at Tranquility Acres rather than in downtown Washington, D.C. They sat in the open-air pavilion, where cookies and lemonade had been provided for the meeting. Dahlia's parents sat quietly looking down, hands folded in their laps, and waiting nervously.

The whole scene seemed surreal to Dahlia. They were sitting on plush outdoor sofas next to a built-in fireplace, as if they were waiting for a July 4th barbecue to begin. In her mind, she contrasted their surroundings—a green forest, chirping birds, and a cool late-summer breeze blowing in from the bay—with this pivotal event that could alter the entire course of her life. If only Abba hadn't practically forced me to attend the Ambassador's Ball . . .

"Remember what we talked about yesterday, Dahlia," Mr. Jacobowitz said. "If you feel that any question is inappropriate or about something you aren't sure of, you don't have to answer. Don't guess or suppose. Do you understand?"

Dahlia shook her head at the attorney and then looked squarely at the FBI agent. "I'm going to tell you everything that I know, whether or not I incriminate myself. That's the only way that my life will get past this. I can no longer live with what I did and what I became over the past six months. And I take responsibility for that. But I'd like nothing more than to see that justice is done to Ze'evi Ehrenreich for what he led me to and what he did to me."

"Very well. Let's begin," Harriman said.

Dahlia began by recounting her relationship with Ze'evi, from the moment they met to the places they went to the people they met. She discussed his luxurious lifestyle, the homes, boats, planes, and racehorses, and the celebrities that he mingled with. She left no details out. Although painful, she described the expensive jewelry and furs that he had given her and the slow but inexorable seduction.

Leah wept, face in her hands, as Dahlia described, in detail, her spiritual descent in Ze'evi's ski chalet, including his drugging her with cocaine, the anonymous sex with multiple partners and the subsequent sadomasochistic sex sessions. She spoke slowly and evenly, staring directly at the FBI agent, as if she were reciting a cooking recipe.

When Benny heard about how Dahlia had received the bloody streaks on her legs—which she described in detail—he jumped out of his seat, red faced, and shouted, "I'm going to have that bastard killed for what he has done to my daughter!"

Mr. Jacobowitz jumped up, restrained him, and practically threw him back into his chair.

"Mr. Harriman, my client is speaking rashly and emotionally. He would never jeopardize his status by committing murder. I demand that his remarks be stricken from the record!"

Harriman nodded and looked at the stenographer. "Strike that from the record. I would've reacted the same way if I'd just learned what happened to my daughter. This proceeding is all about Dahlia's testimony, and the record will reflect only that."

Dahlia continued by carefully delineating the particular narcotics that she had taken.

Mr. Jacobowitz cringed when Dahlia admitted having hidden drugs at the residence from time to time. "Dahlia, you don't have to admit that right now!" he said.

"I have nothing left to hide, sir," Dahlia said, looking down. "I've torn my soul wide open. There must be no more lies, deception, or cover-ups."

"Are there any drugs hidden at the residence at this time?" Harriman asked.

Leah shook with fright. Here was the moment of truth. She wondered whether Dahlia would be charged.

Dahlia shook her head. "No, there's nothing left on me, in me, or anywhere else to my knowledge. I'm done with all of that," she said quietly.

The FBI assistant said, "We went through the residence yesterday and conducted a final sweep with a trained drug-sniffing dog. All he came up with were faint traces of cocaine on a mirror in your bedroom, but there's nothing visible on it."

"That's all there is anywhere," Dahlia said.

After another half an hour of interrogation, Harriman finally said, "Well, that's all I have. Are you willing to relate everything you said today in front of a jury? I warn you: It will be stressful repeating all of it while facing your tormentor in the courtroom."

Dahlia nodded. "If Ze'evi gets everything he deserves, it'll be worth it," she said flatly.

Harriman began to pack his briefcase.

"I, for one, believe everything you've told us. Your candor should go a long way. I can only imagine what it must've been like for you to tell me everything in such detail, especially in front of your parents. I'm going to hand all of this to the federal and state prosecutors, and they'll make the ultimate determination regarding whether or not you should be charged with any crime." He smiled at her. "I've done this for a long time, young lady, and from where I sit I don't believe that you'll be anything more than a material witness, given your cooperation . . . which is much more than I can say for Mr. Ehrenreich and his friends. They're in big trouble indeed."

Bailey said, "Let me outline how this is going to go, Dahlia. There are two proceedings. The attempted rape charges will be adjudicated through the state courts in Nevada. You'll need to appear there to testify in front of a grand jury, which should return an indictment against Mr. Ehrenreich and the other men for attempted rape. If the indictment is brought, they'll face trial for that offense and one count of aggravated assault. They'll also face charges in federal court, in Washington, on numerous narcotics charges. If you're found to be innocent, then you'll have to have to testify as a state's witness in that proceeding as well. Do you understand?

"Is there any way that these proceedings could be sealed, to be kept out of the public eye?" Benny asked.

"As much as I'd like to assure you of that, I'm not certain how that can be accomplished," Harriman said. "As you know, your foreign ministry is already aware of what's going on. Her behavior in the lobby of the hotel as well as her display outside, in the street, already made the local papers. Though her identity has thus far been concealed from the press, rumors are already circulating. We won't gratuitously brief the papers, but please understand that all such proceedings are a matter of public record. They can readily be discovered by the news media."

Dahlia shook her head and wept softly. "I've ruined our lives, Abba! I'm so sorry!"

Benny held her tight. "It's okay, my sweet girl. You have only been a victim. I have to believe that things will turn out okay. So far, the foreign ministry is standing by me, pending the outcome of this affair. I'll have to work as if nothing were going on." He looked at Leah. "I'll be judged by how I perform my duties during this crisis. The rest we will leave for God."

Chapter 6

It had been about nine months since Arik had walked up the front walkway to the tiny stucco house with the red-tiled roof in Lynwood, California. It seemed so much smaller than he remembered. His mother was startled and alarmed when she saw him walk through the front door. He had not told his parents that he was returning home. To Arik, the stench in the house seemed worse than ever. It was the smell of bedpans and antiseptic, the smell of defeat.

"What are you doing here, Arik?" Miriam asked. "You didn't let us know you were coming home. Is everything okay? Are you on leave from the army?"

"I've been thrown out of the army, Imma. I've been thrown out of my life. I'm back to square one." Arik sighed heavily, shaking his head. "I have nothing left to do or be."

He walked into the tiny living room. The only natural light in there was a small dusty window that was partially obscured by the large fake palm tree. He hunched down on one of the plastic-covered loveseats, which was even more frayed at the edges than it had been when he left to go into the army.

Ze'ev sat silently in his wheelchair, his leg stump jutting straight out in front of him, and appraised his son. Miriam stood at his side.

"So, what are you doing here, Arik?"

"I've been thrown out of the army, Abba."

"You must have done something pretty bad for them to do that. Soldiers are cannon fodder. They like keeping people in. The more boys they can kill or maim, the better. It takes a lot to get thrown out. So, what happened? You have a hard time controlling your temper, eh? That always gets you into trouble—"

"My commander in basic training made my life a living hell. He got it in his head that he hated me."

"Why was that?" Ze'ev asked.

"I beat up his first cousin, because he—"

"I was against your learning karate, from the beginning! I knew that you had a foul temper and that those skills would be your undoing. You just can't control yourself. All your life, you'll suffer because of it. First, there was that Nazi boy, then it was Ethan. Now, this. Don't you see a pattern?" Ze'ev shouted.

"That's not fair, Abba. Each time, I thought I was doing the right thing. I was doing the right thing!"

"But you never think about the consequences of your actions, Arik. While you were out saving the Jewish people, after throwing away your college career, Ethan called us. He said that your Imma and I are nothing more than parasites and that when he takes over the business he'll stop supporting us—all because of you! He said that it was fine with him if we got put into a homeless shelter. I think that you should go over there and apologize. Maybe Itzik will let you go back to work for him if you behave yourself."

"I'll go over there and tear Ethan's head off with my bare hands! How dare he say that to you?"

"There you go again, Arik. You never learn."

"I'd sooner kill myself than go back to work at Uncle Itzik's lumber yard. I'll never go back there, Abba. Never!"

"Then you had better find another job," Ze'ev said. "Perhaps next semester you can go to a community college and take some courses at night and decide what to do with your life. Take some time to assess what type of man you have become and what you want to be. At this rate, you aren't headed for success, I can tell you that. I told you not to go to Israel—that no good would come of it—but you wouldn't listen to me. You threw away UCLA, that golden, once-in-a-lifetime opportunity, to go find your fortune in the sand. Stupid!" Ze'ev picked up an envelope from the coffee table. "This came a few weeks ago."

He handed Arik an envelope from the U.S. Selective Service. Arik opened it.

"It's a draft notice," Arik said. "I have ninety days to appear at the draft board in Burbank and show reason for a deferment, or I'll be classified 1-A and have to go into the U.S. Army."

"So, is that what you want, Arik? To go off to Vietnam and die in a faraway jungle, for no reason? I told you that armies are always looking for cannon fodder."

Ze'ev grabbed the letter out of Arik's hand. "Your draft number is twenty-nine. You are sure to be inducted. You had better register at community college and get a 2-S deferment. So, what happened to that nice girl you brought here? You were supposed to marry her, weren't you? Isn't that the whole reason that you walked away from everything here to chase rainbows?"

"She left me."

"Did you yell at her? You did, didn't you? Were you mean to her? You and your temper again, always getting you into trouble!"

"I didn't yell at her, not really! She left me for some rich guy who's gotten her hooked on drugs. I only yelled at her when I realized she was high. I wanted to get her some help."

"So, maybe it's better this way?" Miriam said. "Why do you need a girl like that, anyway? Sometimes things happen for the best. Enough of this talk, Ze'ev. Sit down, Arik. Have something to eat. You must be jet-lagged. Get some rest. You'll feel better in the morning. I'll make up your bed and straighten out your room for you."

"That won't be necessary, Imma. I can do that myself."

Arik walked into the musty bedroom where he had spent his sad childhood. It was dark and smelled of mildew and mothballs. Angels and Lakers pennants still hung, lopsided, on the wall. A line of dusty youth-league basketball trophies adorned the top of the dresser. He stared at them for a while. He thought about how much they had meant to him when he had gotten them. They had given him a rare feeling of self-respect. Now, he recognized saw them as just worthless chunks of chrome and wood—like everything in his life that he had valued at one time or another only to find out later that it was just an illusion. He inspected himself in the dark mirror above the dresser. He was a low-life loser after all, nothing more. There was a dusty photo of Dahlia on the dresser. He picked it up and turned it face down.

He pulled the duvet off the bed, revealing a bare pillow and quilt. He lay down on the quilt and fell asleep. He did not emerge from his bedroom for forty-eight hours.

***

Arik sat on a park bench along the oceanfront at Venice Beach, near the empty basketball courts that he had loved, and looked out at the ocean while listening to Simon and Garfunkel's Bridge over Troubled Water album on a portable cassette tape player with a pair of headphones. He sighed at the lyrics of "The Boxer":

> I am just a poor boy.
> Though my story's seldom told,
> I have squandered my resistance
> For a pocketful of mumbles,
> Such are promises
> All lies and jest
> Still, a man hears what he wants to hear
> And disregards the rest.
>
> . . .
>
> In the clearing stands a boxer
> And a fighter by his trade
> And he carries the reminders
> Of ev'ry glove that laid him down
> And cut him till he cried out
> In his anger and his shame,
> I am leaving, I am leaving
> But the fighter still remains.

Arik drove up to Malibu and took a day-long walk along the beach under the cliffs. He breathed in the salt air deeply, listening to the sea gulls that squawked as they swooped down to snatch fragments of food that had been left in the sand by careless beach-goers.

He reminded himself of Otis Redding, "sittin' on the dock of the bay . . . wastin' time" with "nothin' to live for." Although he did not consider suicide, he could certainly see that it would be easier than the torment he was going through. He understood why someone might consider it. His heart seemed to be racing out of his chest. He was short of breath, and he had a sick feeling in the pit of his stomach. He was spinning out of control.

He thought about all the guys that he had played basketball with in the Cage—guys with enormous talent who should have been college bound with basketball scholarships but who ended up going nowhere because either their grades were too low or they got involved in the gangs or the drug trade. All they had left was showing off their basketball skills at the playground, to nobody in particular, going nowhere, with no way out of the material and spiritual poverty that was life in the ghetto. Will that be my fate, too?

Arik wandered into a wood-paneled Irish pub on Main Street in Santa Monica toward the end of happy hour. He had forty dollars in his pocket. He had never done this before, but he had seen this scene so often in the movies: the down-and-out guy whose life has just fallen apart, sitting at a bar and drowning his sorrows in alcohol while he tells his troubles to the disinterested bartender.

This was all new to Arik. He had gotten drunk some in high school, but not often. He knew that he had a terrible liver and was completely unable to hold his liquor.

The bar was crowded, and loud music was blaring. Everybody seemed to be chattering away, laughing and kidding around with one another. What can they be talking about? Why do they have so much to say?

He sat alone at the bar and ordered a Jack Daniel's on the rocks. As he nursed the drink slowly, he noticed that some of his pain was going away. Unlike the scene from the movies, where the down-and-out guy meets an old alcoholic sage or a hooker with a heart of gold, though, nobody spoke to him. Even the bartender appeared to have better things to do. Arik's only company was his own reflection in the mirror behind the bar. He struggled not to look at it.

The room began to spin slowly, and his senses began to fog. After a while, he started ordering doubles. The initial sting of the whiskey dissipated. He was filled with a deep warmth. He sat at that bar for several hours, by himself.

At 10 p.m., the bartender finally said, "You've had enough to drink, son. You best get on home."

Arik staggered out of the bar, vomited in the street, and felt his whole world turn upside down. He tried to take a shortcut home, through an alley, but he never emerged. His blurry world went black, and he collapsed into an unconscious heap near some urine-smelling trash cans behind a Chinese restaurant.

It was morning when he awoke. When he opened his eyes, he felt the sting of the bright sunshine. He tried to sit up, but he fell backward. His head was pounding as if an anvil had fallen on it, and his mouth tasted like stale, sour vomit.

He looked and felt like a homeless bum. In the fuzziness of his mind was the thought that perhaps it was good practice for when his family would be homeless. He realized that this was dead end. He managed to sit up. He stared blankly at the trash cans covered with flies that were buzzing about and cats that were jumping to and fro looking for scraps from the previous night's chop suey.

Think! This isn't me. Adversity was all that he had known in his short life, but he had never given in before. Although he knew nothing about what the future might hold, he knew that sitting in the trash was no way to start. Is doing the Jewish "thing" really for me? He realized that even the moments of joy had proved to be transient and illusory. All of his interactions with other Jews over the previous two years had come to grief—causing him sadness and pain—in the end. I have to go somewhere. I have to belong somewhere. But where?

He knew that he was at a crossroads, a new door, in his life, but he did not know where it would lead.

His first act was to go into the army surplus store and buy a pair of jeans and a green U.S. Army T-shirt so that he could shed the soiled clothing that he was wearing.

To give himself time to air out, he bought a map of Los Angeles county and walked up and down the streets of LA. When he wandered into a familiar neighborhood, he decided to get something to eat. He had eaten at Hartman's kosher restaurant, on Fairfax Avenue, before. He entered it and sat at a table in the corner. After checking how much cash he had left from the previous night's bender, he ordered a pastrami club sandwich, garlic pickles, potato salad, and a cream soda. The walls around him were covered with black-and-white photographs of old New York, including immigrants from Europe, wearing woolen caps, jackets, and knickerbockers, posing in front of the Brooklyn Bridge or in the Lower East Side.

"Hey, Arik!" he heard while he was eating his sandwich.

Murray Glickman and Izzy Feinstein from his class at Rambam walked up to Arik's table.

"What's up!" Murray asked. "Where've you been? We haven't seen you since graduation. Mind if we join you?"

"Sure. Sit down," Arik said.

The last thing that Arik felt at that moment was sociable, no less to people whom he was only peripherally acquainted with despite having spent two years together at Rambam Academy. They had had their chance to draw him into their lives, if they had really cared. But no, Arik had drifted out of their lives as easily as he had drifted in, like a ghost whom one can look at but never touch. He certainly saw no point in drawing them into his personal space now. Besides, he was still grimy from the previous night. So, he vowed to keep things superficial.

Murray and Izzy ordered sandwiches.

"So, what have you been up to?" Murray asked. "We heard you walked away from a UCLA basketball scholarship to join the Israeli Army. Holy shit! Who would do that?"

"I did," Arik said.

"What are you doing back here, then?" Izzy asked.

"I got a four-week furlough, so I came back to visit my parents."

"So, are you in tanks, infantry—?" Murray asked.

"Paratroopers. Tzanchanim."

"So, have you done any dangerous missions behind the Suez Canal?" Izzy chuckled. "How many Arabs have you killed? Bang! Bang! Bang!" He made two pistols with his thumbs and forefingers. "How many times have you jumped out of an airplane?"

"Leave him alone, Izzy. Only commandos go behind enemy lines. The rest of the guys mostly hang around the bases and drill or go on long hikes, unless there's a war. Isn't that right, Arik?"

"Yeah, that's right."

"So, what happened to that smoking hot little Playmate you were hanging around with?" Izzy asked. "Probably ran off with some rich guy while you were in the army, huh?" He seemed pleased with his cleverness.

"What are you guys up to?" Arik asked. He was trying to stay civil. There would be no point in murdering Izzy.

"We're both at Columbia University, in New York," Izzy said. "I'm pre-med, and Murray's pre-law. He keeps telling me he's going to sue me for malpractice, and I keep telling him I'll see him in the ER when he gets a heart attack from all the long hours he'll have to put in before he makes partner." Izzy laughed.

"So, what are you guys doing out here, then?" Arik asked.

"You won't believe this, but we came back for Bracha Epstein's wedding. Who would've thought that a dog like that would be the first one in our class to get married? She's hitching up with some guy called Moish Finkel, from Phoenix. Why don't you come crash the wedding? It'd be so cool if you did. The whole chevre would love to see you."

"Thanks, but no thanks. I think I'll pass. Bracha and I have never really gotten along. But wish her all the best from me." Arik stood up. "Great seeing you guys. Good luck in school. Hopefully, I won't be needing any of your services. I'm late for an important appointment." He made a graceful exit.

Once outside the deli, he continued his long walk to nowhere. For a week, day and night, in the sunshine and the rain, he walked the long, wide, palm-lined streets of LA, staring at the shops, the cars, the flashing neon lights, and people's faces. He looked for inspiration, but he found none.

***

Arik wandered south from Santa Monica and found himself in Marina Del Ray. He felt involuntarily drawn to his master, despite having resolved not to visit him or the reverend (such was his shame at what he perceived as his failure). Suddenly, he was on Beach Avenue. He walked into the familiar doors of the Inosanto Academy of Martial Arts.

Breathing in the incense brought his whole life back to him. He thought about the many years that he had worked, sweated, and trained in this Taoist temple. He thought about how he felt so much more comfortable here than among Jews. He had known nothing but pain and loss from being with Jews.

Arik stared at the statue of the Buddha sitting cross-legged, one palm raised, facing him in the red and gold anteroom. He had never believed conclusively in the divinity of the Buddha, but he had relished many of the truths that he had been taught here by Master Lee and Master Dan:

"Empty your cup so that it may be filled; become devoid to gain totality."

"Knowledge is fixed in time, whereas knowing is continual."

"Knowledge comes from a source, from an accumulation, from a conclusion, while knowing is a movement."

"To know oneself is to study oneself in action with another person."

Arik stared at the wall that was adorned with Chinese murals. They depicted the lineage of the grand masters of Wing Chun, the forerunner of Jeet Kune Do, from its founder, a Buddhist nun named Ng Mui, to Yip Man, Bruce

Lee's teacher. He wondered what their lives were like and what challenges they faced.

Arik believed that the years that he had spent at Inosanto's academy, beginning well before the Torah entered his life, had formed his moral compass. He entered the dojo quietly so that he would not disturb Master Inosanto's class. He found a place in the corner, behind the master's back, and sat in a lotus position, hands on his knees. He looked down at the floor and then closed his eyes.

His meditation was interrupted when he sensed the presence of the master in front of him. When he opened his eyes and looked up, he saw the kind face of Master Inosanto looking down at him.

"What are you doing here, Arik?"

When he looked more closely at Arik's face, he understood at once. "You are in trouble. Come into my office. I want to hear what you have to tell me."

He motioned to Richard Bustillo, his most senior student, to carry on with his master class.

Richard wandered over to Arik and gave him a hug. "Hey, good to see you, man."

"You too." Arik smiled thinly and then followed Dan Inosanto into his office.

Arik related the events of his past year to his master, who sat impassively and without uttering a sound for more than an hour. He frowned when Arik recounted his fights. He appeared genuinely sad when he heard of their outcome.

"Arik, was there no other way to settle these scores than unleashing the full power of your sword? Master Lee teaches that wisdom does not consist of trying to wrest the good from the evil but in learning to ride both, as a cork adapts itself to the crests and troughs of the waves. Arik, I have a terrible intuition that your fighting had something to do with not having heard from the girl and the terrible course of events that followed resulted from the fighting. You may never be able to prove that, but seen in its totality that is the only conclusion I can draw. You must sheath your sword and never release it again in anger, except under the extreme circumstance of threat to your life. You must understand this, Arik."

Arik nodded and looked down, ashamed. "What must I do now? I'm completely lost. I have nowhere to go and nothing to do. Everything I struggled for and hoped for lies in pieces on the ground."

Dan sat quietly for a long while. Arik closed his eyes and waited patiently.

Finally, Dan said, "Keep your eyes closed, Arik, and listen to what I have to say. Block out the light, and allow Master Lee's words to penetrate your heart. Master Lee teaches that every situation in fighting and in life is varied. Nothing occurs according to a fixed pattern. Everything is formless and fluid. To obtain victory, it is essential to not be rigid and formulaic but rather to be like water, formless and shapeless. If you put water in a cup, it becomes like a cup; in a bottle, it becomes like a bottle. By being shapeless and ever-changing, you can instantly adapt to every challenge life throws at you. The moment you stop changing, you will stagnate and lose.

"Arik, you have been too rigid with your plans and expectations. You have not left room for change. Set yourself free to be spontaneous, and life will come to you. Your tree of life has broken, because it is too rigid.

"I have taught you how to confront an attack by deflecting the attacker and delivering the knockout blow all in the same sequence. By your description, you have done this in your fighting. You must now do this in your life. Be economical in your actions and reactions. Do not act according to any preconceived ideas.

"You are lost because you have not laid out your options properly. You cannot choose a path when you wallow in self-pity. Clear your mind of every emotion, and let thoughts enter your head and dance around in your consciousness. There will be many thoughts to begin with, but they will coalesce into two or three paths. Once you are there, you will be able to weigh the rights and wrongs of each choice. Calmly, you will gravitate to the correct choice. I cannot offer you guidance regarding your Judaism, which weighs so heavily on which path you choose. You must go to your religious master so that he can add those pieces to fill out your puzzle."

"I will do this, Master Inosanto."

"We have spare gis in the locker room. Dress, and join us. It will help to clear your heart and mind."

For the first time in more than a month, Arik smiled sincerely.

***

Arik was nervous when he walked into Sunday morning services at the Mount Zion Baptist Church. Why did I wait two weeks before coming to visit the reverend? How will I be received? Arik was certain that the reverend would be disappointed in how things had turned out for him, in how his high hopes and expectations had turned into nothing. Arik was ashamed that he had let him down.

He slipped quietly into the back pew and let his spirit be buoyed by the music of the gospel organ and the choir. Reverend Perkins, adorned in purple and gold robes, was sitting in the front of the church, next to a large cross and facing the congregation. The lively, heartfelt service included readings from the Old and New Testaments. Members of the congregation stood up to tell stories of their lives. These testimonials were punctuated by catcalls and interjections, such as "Glory Hallelujah" and "Thank you, Jesus!" all around Arik. How he wished that he could stand up and share his story with the congregation.

When the reverend stood up to speak, he looked out at the pews and was startled to see Arik sitting in the back of the church. He appeared genuinely alarmed—not the reception that Arik had hoped for but definitely the one that he had expected.

After the service, Arik remained seated, staring down at the floor. When he felt the reverend's presence beside him, he looked up.

"Arik, what are you doing back here? By the look of things, it doesn't seem good. You look like a lost sheep."

"I'm lost and beaten." Arik shook his head, looking down again. "I bet on the wrong horse, and my horse lost. Now, I'm cleaned out. I've had a crappy past that I've struggled to forget. I thought I had a future to look forward to, but now that future has vanished before my eyes. Everything I thought has turned out to be wrong. My whole frame of reference has been taken away from me."

"Son, come on back to the rectory with me. We have a lot to talk about."

The reverend boiled water and prepared a pot of tea for them.

"How long have you been back here?" he asked.

"About two weeks."

"Why have you waited so long to come see me?" he asked in surprise.

"I felt so ashamed of myself that I couldn't speak to anyone when I got back. I've spent my time holed up in my room, wandering the streets, and even in bars, drinking. I've never done that before, but I wanted to try it. It seems to work in the movies when folks are down, but all it did was make me sick to my stomach. Then I went down to Dan Inosanto's place to work out and try to refocus my brain, and he spent a good deal of time with me. I feel like I made a start there. At last, I got the courage to come see you."

"Start from the beginning. The last time we spoke was nearly a year ago. I've been getting your letters, though. You seemed to be going through such a hard time, but you always seemed hopeful that everything was going to be okay. What's changed? I hadn't heard from you in two months, and I was starting to worry. You're always such a consistent letter writer. You look awful. Does this have anything to do with Dahlia?"

Arik recounted the year's events, supplementing what he had already told him in letters and finishing with the state that he had found Dahlia in and how she had treated him.

"I don't understand why she didn't get any of your letters," the reverend said. "How can that be? I've been getting letters from you on a regular basis. Have you gotten mine?"

"Every month, and it helped keep me going during the roughest times. I never got anything from Dahlia, though. Now, I find out she was fooling around with some billionaire playboy while I was busting my ass, sucking sand in the desert. I saw her nasty streak when we first met at camp, but she was able to stuff the genie back in the bottle quickly then, before it caused any real damage. This time, there was so much more at stake, and she showed herself in her full glory."

"Do you think your letters to her could have been confiscated by the Israeli Army?"

"Why would they do that? There wasn't anything sensitive or important in them—anything they wouldn't want our Arab enemies to know. Everybody in Israel is so secretive about everything, though. I'm surprised they let us know where the latrines are at the base, though I did become an expert at latrines, spending so much time cleaning and building them. I became the cesspool king."

"Speaking of the army, did you make any headway with your dad's situation?"

"I wouldn't even know how to broach that subject, though my base commanders wasted no time pulling out my father's dossier to show me that he was a terrorist who got what he deserved. They even knew about my experiences here, with prison and all. They called me a criminal, the son of a criminal."

"How did they find out about your legal troubles?"

"Their spy agency, the Mossad, is the best in the world. They have to be. Israel has no safety net. It's always being threatened with destruction. At every opportunity, they called me a convicted criminal who had fled justice in the States. They kept saying they'd mete out the justice I didn't get here."

"Then they didn't know the whole story."

"Either they didn't or they acted like they didn't. They made me feel like I was in some kind of prison camp. It all turned out to be some diabolical test to see if I had what it took to get into the baddest-ass commando unit in the army."

"You passed the test, of course."

"I did, but it nearly did me in."

"So, what happened then?"

"I think I told you about the public fight I had with some big-shot jerk. After that, I was transferred to the elite unit. Those guys are the real deal. That was the first time I developed any real friendships in the army. I participated in a top-secret mission that took us halfway across the Sinai and the Suez, into Egypt, one night, where we made off with an anti-aircraft missile radar right out from under the Egyptians' noses. We were attacked, and we had to fight them off. I dragged a paralyzed buddy over my shoulders into the Red Sea.

"Dahlia's father found me somehow, and he invited me to visit them in Herzliya for the Passover holiday. When I got there, Dahlia confronted me and accused me of things I didn't do. Apparently, this billionaire playboy got her hooked on drugs. She looked absolutely awful. You wouldn't have recognized her. When I reached out to her, she flinched away and threw me out of the house.

"I went into a deep depression after that. I wasn't able to function as a soldier anymore, so they sent me back here to figure out what I want to do with the rest of my life. I've made some really bad decisions, and now I'm nowhere."

He ran his fingers through his hair. "I tried talking to my parents, but they're hopelessly unequipped to deal with this."

The reverend sat quietly and thought for a long while. Finally, he said, "The first thing you're going to need to do is figure out what country you want to spend the next few years in—here or Israel. Once you figure that out, we can have a conversation."

Arik nodded glumly.

"Son, let's break this down. What would you do if you stayed here? Do you think UCLA would consider taking you next year? If they don't, what options do you have? You could probably go to one of the state schools or junior colleges."

"It's funny you should say that. I called Wooden's assistant, Denny Crum, about three or four times and he never returned my calls. So, I called the head of the booster committee, Mr. Gilbert. All he did was remind me I'd made the biggest mistake of my life and he'd told me I'd live to regret it. He almost seemed pleased with himself, that his prophecy had been fulfilled so soon. He even kept calling me Eric, after all this time. I thanked him for taking my call, but I did remind him one last time that my name is Arik, not Eric.

"So, that door's closed. My father has been nagging me to go back to work for my Uncle Itzik and his worthless, racist son. The thought of working there again makes me want to scream, though. The only reason I tolerated it back then was because I knew I was saving up my money so I could be with Dahlia. But now?

"I was filled with so many dreams of doing something great, something special, something that would make Dahlia proud of me, something that would make me feel like I was worthy of a girl like her. And now, look what I turned out to be, what she turned out to be. Everything is up in smoke. I just can't bear the thought of staying here and enrolling in a community college and starting my life all over again from the very beginning. I don't even have the head for books right now. It's so hard to focus on anything. Even my Judaism, apart from Dahlia, was based on my relationship to the school where Rabinovich was my teacher. But I've graduated from there. I can't go backward. What do I do now? Show up at his door? And then what?" Arik shrugged.

The reverend said, "If you can't go backward, you must go forward. You're a much better person than the situation you're in. This isn't your destiny. The good Lord is pointing you in a certain direction. You must open your eyes and see your path. It's already there, waiting for you. Listen to the still, soft voice of God. Hear him whisper in your ear.

"When Elijah the prophet climbed Mount Sinai, he was looking for the Lord. The Bible says that God sent him thunder, lightning, and a windstorm and he asked the Lord if he could find Him there. God told him that He could no longer be heard in the cyclone but rather in a small, thin voice. It's a lot harder to hear Him in that voice. You have to train your ear to hear him. It's hard, but it can be done.

"I know you feel all alone, but when a man starts out on a new journey he's always alone. When we enter the world, we're alone. The same is true when we depart. You were alone when you first entered our lives, as an atheist. I looked on with joy as you slowly began to find your God and let him guide your steps. I was positively thrilled the first time you asked Maimie to prepare kosher food for you when you came to break bread with us.

"No, son, you need to keep going forward. You must map out your own journey and be prepared to go it alone if need be, but be the best traveler you can be. Who you are and what you will become have only to do with what you make of yourself. They're not based on what others think of you or even how they treat you. Know, though, that if you pick the straight and true path you'll find fellow travelers who will want to travel with you. They'll find you. There's no need for you to struggle. Right now, you see no way out of your predicament. Well, if there's no way out, then you must go further in!

"The Bible, in Exodus, tells the story of Moses, who'd sojourned with his father-in-law, tending his sheep in the middle of a desert, making nothing of his life, looking back to a past when he'd been a prince of Egypt. He saw no way out, until he heard the voice of the Lord speaking to him from a burning bush. The Lord told him to go across the Sinai and back to Egypt to save his people. He went back in, and he did great things.

"Son, I believe you're fated to do great things. You've already done great things. Kevin wouldn't be alive and well if it wasn't for you. You'll always be a hero in this community. You're made of stronger stuff than you realize. Like Moses, you slayed the evil taskmasters. And like Moses, you need to go back to the Sinai and, if need be, back to Egypt to safeguard your people. Never stop having faith in God, because he is not a fickle girlfriend but a lifelong best friend, a loving shepherd who will help steer your path. Arik, go back to your people. Go back to the land of Zion."

Arik sat in reflective silence for a long time, staring at the reverend.

Antwan and Tyrone walked into the rectory. When Arik saw them, he jumped into their arms.

"My God, it's so good to see you guys!" he said.

"How long you staying?" Antwan asked.

"I'm not sure . . ." Arik looked over at the reverend and winked. "But I think I'll be going back to Israel as soon as I can get a flight out."

"Not before you go back to the Cage with us, White Lightning!" Tyrone said. "Everybody'll be so excited to see you."

"I haven't touched a ball in over a year. I'm going to look like a fool," Arik said.

"Aw, man, listen to this guy. He's already setting us up to beat our butts. The best things never change, brother!" Antwan said.

The reverend hugged Arik. "I'm going to change what I said before. The Lord can be found in lightning . . . White Lightning!"

***

Arik spent his final week in the States playing basketball and working out in Inosanto's dojo. He resolved to return to Israel with a clean slate and refocused energy. As he packed his bags to return, he knew that if he were allowed to return to his unit he would be subject to extreme danger. When he said his final good-byes to the reverend and his family, over dinner on that final night, he realized that it might be the last time he would ever see them. They understood that, too.

Chapter 7

When Arik changed planes at Dulles Airport, he discovered that somehow, he had been upgraded to a VIP first-class seat aboard one of El Al's gleaming new 747 jumbo jets. Unbeknown to him, Benny had facilitated his return to Israel.

With his UCLA cap pulled down low over his face, Arik sank into his seat. Well . . I'm on my way back to Israel. He had given up his scholarship for this. The last time that he had been on a plane to Israel, his life had been so joyous, so hopeful. When he had made his decision to walk away from Wooden, he had felt deep down that he was making the right decision. He had turned his back on so much, but he had seen Dahlia's radiant face in his mind's eye. He had thought that, no matter what he faced in the military, Dahlia would be there for him to come home to. She was not only the love of his life but also his best friend. She knew everything about him: his fears and his hopes. She knew what made him cry and what made him laugh. He had thought that he, in turn, knew everything about her. But now he saw how wrong he had been.

Maybe my teammate at Camp Moshava was right, he thought. Dahlia is out of my league. I'm just an indigent low-life from the streets of LA. Why did I think I was worthy of such a beautiful creature? She got what she probably wanted all along. After all, she is a jet-setting beauty. Of course, she should have a billionaire playboy boyfriend. She was more suited to ski race with the rich guy in the Alps than dress up a disheveled poor guy at a ski shop in Aspen.

The thought of that creep's naked body wrestling with hers, throughout the night, in bed made Arik nauseous and furious, though. Didn't I go to Israel to join the army—being separated from her—at her insistence? He had been completely faithful to her, writing to her consistently and trying to call her constantly. How could she not have gotten any letters from me for months? He wracked his brain, but he could not come up with an answer. Maybe she's just using that lie as an excuse for walking away from me and into the creep's arms. Maybe I was just a social experiment for her, all along. He supposed that there was nothing left for him to do but give up and walk away from her. He felt an overwhelming, aching sadness envelop him.

Now what do I have to look forward to? Desert rations? Physical and psychological hardship? No sleep? Sucking in desert sand? Trying to act the hero? Getting my ass shot off? For what? He was not even completely certain that this Israel thing was his fight anymore. But he was in the most elite unit in the Israeli Army, which meant dodging death on a regular basis. He had no family in Israel and nowhere to go on his rare weekends off. Should I wander around, by myself, in a country I know so little about? Should I sit and wait for an invitation from one of the other guys in my unit? But I've shown myself unfit to be in the company of such elite individuals. Will they even let me back into the unit? What will they think of me?

A year earlier, so many possibilities had seemed open up to him. Now, there was nothing but darkness at this crossroads. He thought through what that the reverend had told him. He needed to find a way to get further in! He hoped that he was on his way back to his unit, which had become his home, his family.

I'll live and maybe die with them. So be it. I have nothing else to live for. No future to think about, anyway. Death doesn't scare me. He had decided to completely dedicate himself, body and soul, to protecting his comrades, that is, if they would accept him back. He felt as if everyone else had walked away from him. Even the reverend had told him to return to "his people." Arik guessed that meant his unit. The Arabs will feel the full brunt of my rage, my anguish. Heaven help them.

He fell into fitful sleep.

Several hours into the flight, he was awakened by a well-meaning flight attendant who insisted that Arik eat something. Over his protestations, she went back to the galley to fetch him some dinner.

"I was wondering when you were going to wake up, sleeping beauty. I was getting bored sitting here, hour after hour, reading silly magazines. You really aren't very good company."

He hadn't noticed that a woman was sitting next to him.

"Oh! I'm sorry. I didn't realize I was supposed to be good company."

He tried to go back to sleep, his UCLA cap still covering his face.

Mikki Zohar was a beautiful but very tough young woman. For the flight, her shock of bright auburn hair was tied up tightly in a long, full ponytail. Her skintight leather pants and feminine-cut cashmere top belied her powerful, long-legged, athletic body, which had been fostered by years of martial arts training with her brothers and track and field competition.

The daughter of a highly decorated Israeli general, Mikki had been raised in a strict military family. Her brothers all were serving in crack military units and, not to be outdone, she had rapidly worked her way up the echelons of rank. She was now a lieutenant colonel in the Israeli military intelligence's southern command. She was returning home from a joint exercise with the U.S. military in the Mojave Desert.

Mikki looked patronizingly at the slovenly, unshaven American tourist in his wrinkled college T-shirt, baggy worn jeans, and beaten-up shoes.

"So, UCLA? You on spring break?"

"If you say so," Arik said through his hat.

"Must be nice being a rich, pampered American, wandering about without a care, like you own the world."

He pulled his hat up off his face and stared straight at her. "Tell me something. Do Israelis learn how to become assholes in kindergarten, or is it just something in the water?" Arik pulled his hat back down over his face. "Women."

Mikki detected a profound sadness in Arik's voice. She was taken aback.

"I'm sorry. My comment was uncalled for. I apologize. Can we start again? I'm Mikki. Mikki Zohar."

He pushed the hat up off his face again.

"Like the mouse?" he asked. "They named you after a mouse?" He smiled.

"My name is Michal. I guess it's your turn to be an asshole."

He looked evenly at her. "I'm Arik. Interesting . . . I have a good friend with the same last name. In fact, he looks a bit like you. He's also a redhead."

"What's his name?"

"Dani Zohar."

Mikki's eyes went wide. "How do you know him?"

"He's in my unit."

Mikki sat open-mouthed. "My God! I'm so sorry! I certainly misjudged who you might be. Dani's my brother. I never imagined you to be Mat—"

"I hope I still am. I've already told you too much, but there's nothing to apologize for. It doesn't matter."

"Your secret is safe with me. Really. I'm a military intelligence officer—"

"An oxymoron."

Mikki laughed.

"Why do you say, 'I hope'? Have you been tossed out?"

"No. At least, I don't think so. It's complicated."

"I guess you won't tell me. I'll get all that from Dani."

"I suppose so. You certainly are an inquisitive one."

"That's what they pay me for."

***

At Lod Airport, Arik saw that Mikki had a car and driver waiting for her outside the terminal. She dismissed the driver and took the wheel herself.

"Hop in, soldier. Let me give you a tremp."

"That really won't be necessary. Thanks, anyway. I'll find my own way. It won't be hard for me to get a ride down to the Sinai, and I usually walk from the Tzomet on the main road. The location is secret, so our commander takes a dim view of having rides drop us off at the base."

"Listen up, soldier. I know where your camp is. In fact, I chose the location for it. Remember? Military intelligence? I must say, Arik, you're a cutie. I'm going to have a little talk with Dani. I guess that's the only way I'll find out anything about you. I can already tell that you're a closed book."

He laughed. "Dani won't tell you anything. He's sworn to secrecy."

She winked. "Dani is putty in my hands. Always has been. I've always found ways of getting the best of him."

Arik climbed into the car.

The ride to his base at Bir Gifgafa was Zen-like for Arik. He closed his eyes and leaned his head back against the seat. He let the warm, dry, desert air and bright sun wash over his face. He felt as if he was finally home. The desert felt familiar, almost comforting. The sand and rocks had their own smell, their own 'soul.' He felt them reaching out to him and drawing his heart home. He was indeed ready to go "further in," but he had no idea how far in he would go.

"Well, soldier, here's where you get off!"

"Thanks for the ride, Mikki. Nice meeting you." He shook her hand. "Maybe we'll bump into each other in the future."

"Count on it, Arik. I'll kick Dani's ass for not inviting you to come to us for a Shabbat. Where do you usually go?"

"Mostly nowhere. I have no family in Israel. They wanted to match me up with some family on a kibbutz, but I saw no use pretending total strangers were my family."

"You made a big mistake. The whole point of matching you up with a random family is to highlight the fact that all of us are one big family here in Israel."

"I really don't know what that is—family. Never did. People in my life just come and go." Arik looked down.

"Hmm . . . more to find out about the mystery man. Well, I want you to come to us for a Shabbat. Please, send my regards to Dani. I haven't spoken to him in two weeks. I know your unit is going out on 'maneuvers' in a week. You'll have an off Shabbat after that."

"Shalom, Mikki." Arik jumped out of the car, his canvas rucksack in his hand, and trotted up the road to the gate.

Mikki sat in the driver's seat and stared at Arik until he was out of her sight.

The sentries at the front gate of Camp Shacham saw a figure carrying a large rucksack and jogging around the bend toward them. Instinctively, they raised their M16 rifles, but then they lowered them when they recognized him.

They ran up the road to greet him, each giving him a hearty hug.

"You've decided to come back after all. The chevre were taking bets whether you would come back or not," one of the sentries said, laughing. "Welcome back. Welcome home."

Arik smiled. "I am home."

***

Arik sat in the anteroom of the special operations command at the Kiriya military headquarters in Tel Aviv, while others determined his fate. He felt that he nothing left to lose. It was unusual for someone who had been furloughed from an elite unit to find his way back in. Competition was so fierce, and there were so few slots that the commanders of those units had the luxury of picking only the very best. Generally, anything that could be used to disqualify a soldier would be—and quickly. Arik knew that to be true, despite the assurances to the contrary that his superior officers had given him.

Have I shown myself emotionally unstable and unfit for this level of duty? For all practical purposes, I had a nervous breakdown. Does that show a lack of mental toughness? Will it make me a liability in combat, endangering myself and my comrades?

He wondered where he would be placed if he were rejected from the commandos. Would he be put in a secondary combat role? Or would he be removed from combat altogether and given a desk job? He knew that he could not be choosy. The month-long introspection back in the States had shown him that he had nothing left to do, nowhere to go, and nobody to be with. He would have to content himself with whatever he was given by the Israeli Army.

His life had all seemed so clear to him just a few months earlier, but now he was in uncharted waters. He had no family, nobody to lean on, here. He could not fathom, at this point, what he would be doing the next day. He decided that he would let go of the reins and allow himself to drift.

"Be like water. Be fluid. Offer no resistance. Let the current take you. Accept and embrace your powerlessness." He could almost hear Master Inosanto's voice.

"Arik, come in," Colonel Langer said.

Arik was led into the conference room by Ehud Barak and stood in front of the large table. Involuntarily, he saluted the distinguished group of men sitting in front of him. He recognized General Manno Shaked, the head of special operations, General Aharon Yariv, the chief of military intelligence, and Lieutenant General Haim Bar-Lev, the IDF's chief of staff. The others were a mystery to him. He stood there, at attention, while the five men in the room silently appraised him for what seemed an eternity. Arik was frozen.

Bar-Lev was the first to speak. "So, Arik, how are you feeling?"

"I'm fine, sir."

"I trust that you had some time to think about what you want to do in the future, while you were home?"

"This is my home, sir! I'm serious about that. My intention is not to be clever or facetious. My present and future are here. My month in California has shown me that I have nothing left there. My place is here."

"But your parents are there. Don't they mean anything to you?" Shaked asked.

"They mean the world to me, sir, and when I'm able I'll bring them here to be with me. This was their home, too. They should never have left Israel. I'll right that wrong no matter how long it takes me."

"What wrong are you referring to?" Langer asked.

"The fact that they left Israel when I was a baby and the fact that they had to leave, sir."

"Why do you think that they had to leave?" Bar-Lev asked.

"My father was left penniless to wander the streets of Tel Aviv without a leg after sacrificing himself for his comrades, sir."

"Are you quite certain of that account?"

"I am, sir."

"And you want to rehabilitate his name?" General Yariv asked.

"I do."

"Does the fact that you feel that he was wronged make you angry?" Bar-Lev asked.

"No, sir, but as his son I hope one day to discover why he was treated the way he was and make his and my mother's life better. They can't continue to live the way they are. Time is working against them. My uncle's generosity will run out soon, and they could be left penniless again. I'll never let that happen. I want to be able to take care of them."

"Do you think that returning to the army will enable you to accomplish that goal?" Shaked asked.

"I believe that the army is my home now. I must become the best person I can be, to be able to help them, and I believe this is the place I can accomplish that. I want to fight for Israel and try to restore some sense of dignity to my parents. That's my primary purpose at this stage of my life. That's what I decided while I was away."

"Do you believe that you still possess the mental toughness to be a member of an elite unit?" Bar-Lev asked.

"If you're asking me if can I be an emotionless robot, the answer is no. I'm a living, breathing, human being that made the mistake of letting someone get too close to me and letting myself be hurt. I let that hurt interfere with the mission and my judgment. I won't make the same mistake again. I'm now prepared to demonstrate that I have the toughness to not only be in an elite unit but to excel in one. If given the chance again, I'll prove myself worthy of the uniform and dedicate myself completely to the mission and to my comrades."

"Do you miss your comrades?" Langer asked. "You have not known them for very long."

"I do, sir, very much. They are the best people I've ever met."

Shaked smiled. "Well, you should know, Arik, that they miss you too. They think the world of you. For that reason alone, I think that you should be allowed to return to the unit. Nobody is a better judge of a man's worth and character than his comrades. They are the ones who will be putting their lives in your hands, so they had better be right."

"Sir, I'm prepared to lay down my life for my comrades."

"You know something, Arik?" Yariv said. "I, for one, believe that you are. But I hope and pray that you will never be asked to do so."

"We've decided to allow you to return to your unit," Bar-Lev said. "For now, you'll train rigorously with them night and day. You'll be involved in every stage of operations planning and mock execution. At the same time, you'll see a special unit psychologist for counseling to rid yourself of your demons. When he decides that you're ready, you'll be cleared for full active-duty status. How does that sound?"

"It sounds very good, sir. I thank you for allowing me to return." Arik saluted.

"Collect your things, then, soldier, Shaked said. Major Barak will take you back to your unit."

Arik smiled broadly and saluted again before following Ehud out of the room.

***

"How did they let you back in? Dani asked. "I was sure that I'd never see you again."

He gave Arik a bear hug. The other twenty men in the unit crowded around him, smiling broadly and slapping his back.

"It's really good to have you back, Arik!"

"We thought for sure that you were done for!"

"Did you bring us back genuine blue jeans from America?"

"Forget the jeans, Tzuri. How about gold? They say that the streets of America are paved in gold! You should have brought some back to us!"

"Ya chantarish! You're a dope, Alon! My brother went to America on a tiyul and saw no gold anywhere in the streets!" Tzuri laughed.

"There's definitely no gold," Arik said, "but if any of you are interested in dog shit there's plenty of that in the streets. I brought some back for everyone to share!" He smiled.

"My family was in Chicago for two years, and I'll have you know that American dog shit is the finest-quality dog shit in the world," Dani said.

Arik laughed along with the others.

"Hey, Dani!" Arik said. "I met your sister. She gave me a tremp from the airport."

"Really? Which sister?"

"I thought you only had one."

"Oh, yeah. I forgot."

"We even saved your bed for you, shmendrick!" Gadi said. "Look at the sign over it!"

Arik looked up and saw a handwritten sign:

ARIK MEIR

REST IN PEACE

"Nice!" Arik laughed. "Thanks for the vote of confidence! As they say in English, all reports of my death have been greatly exaggerated!"

"We're going out on a field trip tomorrow night, to pay our cousins across the Canal another visit. Will you be going with us?"

"No, not yet. I think they want to break me in slowly. They want me to train with you lot for several weeks before I go balls in."

The guys drifted away to the dining hall, leaving Arik to get settled in.

"I think that's a good plan." Yoni had wandered over to speak to Arik privately. "Are you ready to go back in?"

"Yeah. I think I am."

"You understand that the work we do here is dangerous in the extreme and even a minute's loss of concentration could result in getting yourself and those around you killed? Your comrades are literally putting their lives in your hands. Look, Arik, you have incredible physical and intellectual skills. You're modest, and you have a wonderful heart. You're a loyal friend and a real thinker. After you left, Colonel Langer called a meeting of the whole unit to discuss what to do with you if you came back. The guys' desire to have you back here was unanimous."

"I didn't realize I was so popular," Arik kidded.

"Arik, I'm being serious. We've watched your emotional breakdown since Pesach. And you know we have no problem getting rid of guys. We do that for a living around here. There are many reasons we let guys go: physical incapacity, lack of operational discipline, arrogance, selfishness, laziness, what have you. You're none of those things. From the moment you entered the army, you were pegged for this unit. I bet you didn't know that."

"No, I didn't."

"When you broke down, you took everyone by surprise. The higher-ups don't like to think they're wrong about someone. They were ready to let you go. I specifically intervened on your behalf, because I think you have what it takes. I reiterated to Langer and Barak that your emotional state came from the loss of someone central in your life."

"Well, that's true. Dahlia had become my reason for living. I had no life at home, no financial prospects. I lived under the constant shadow of my parents' shattered life. Everyone in the world thinks my father is a mass murderer who got what he deserved. Dahlia parachuted into my life, like a ray of light, a sweet flower. She filled that void in my soul. When I had the opportunity to reach for greatness, I walked away from it to pursue the dream of spending my life with her. It never even dawned on me that she'd turn out to be an empty temptress, a beautiful flower with poisonous nectar. Have you ever heard of Sirens?"

"Police sirens?"

"No, the Sirens in Greek mythology. They were beautiful women, with angelic voices, who'd sit on rocks along the ocean and sing irresistible songs to ships passing by. The sailors got so distracted by their beauty that they'd sail the ships closer to the shore, where the ships would wreck and the sailors would die. I think the Sirens ate the flesh of the poor slobs and repeated the process again and again."

"What was your shot at greatness, the thing you walked away from?"

"I think you'd understand, having lived in the States. Well, I spent most of high school playing street basketball in the black ghetto. I was discovered there by John Wooden, the basketball coach at UCLA. He offered me a full-ride scholarship to play basketball. I was pressured for months to accept, but in the end, I turned it all down for Dahlia and enlisted in Tzahal," Arik said flatly.

Yoni seemed genuinely surprised. "Hasn't UCLA been the national college basketball champion for many years running?"

"Yeah, and I walked away from them."

"Does anyone here know that?"

"I don't know. I don't know anything anymore."

"The commanders in the Sayeret are very good judges of people, and they picked you without knowing any of this. Do you know what that means?"

"No, but I'm sure I'm about to find out." Arik smiled sadly.

"It means they see greatness in you, the same way Wooden did. The difference is that here greatness isn't measured in the number of baskets you score but in the number of lives you save. I've suffered greatly in my personal life because of my involvement in the army. I've been trying to get back to the States, to Harvard, to get my degree, and each time my soul gets drawn back here, to this little clump of sand. We're the ultimate guardians of the State of Israel. We are what stands between the hundreds of millions of cutthroat Arabs and our fellow Jews. We're here to assure that what your father went through in the camps never happens again.

"Arik, I'm going to tell you something, and I want you to pay close attention. You came here for all the wrong reasons. First, I don't believe for a minute that you'll find a way to clear your father's name. I'm sorry to tell you that, but it's true. You're being naive. You'll never have access to any records that will help you do that. I have to spit blood to get even basic operational reports. Second, you came here out of love for a woman. Guys have done stupider things for women. Speaking of Greek mythology, didn't Troy get destroyed and tens of thousands of men get killed over someone's love of some dopey woman named Helen?

"Finally, you need to live your own life and figure out the real reason why God put you on this earth. Once you figure that out, the rest will follow. You'll even find the type of mature love relationship that will take you through adulthood—not the puppy love of a summer camp romance, as intense as it may have felt. You've been trying to put frosting on a cake that wasn't ready to come out of the oven. All you did was burn the frosting. I know Dahlia will haunt your sleep for many months to come, but time is a great healer. Those emotions will fade, mercifully, and you'll move on. I know it's hard to believe it now, but I speak from experience. I'm very glad you came back. I believe you'll find your true calling here in this dust. The only way you'll heal is if you attach yourself to something much bigger and greater than yourself. You must be part of the mission. And, what's more important, the mission must be part of you. Greatness awaits you here, Arik. I feel it. Starting tomorrow, we're training for a special mission. I want you there. Meanwhile, today we're going on a sixty-kilometer stroll, in full combat gear, down through the Giddi Pass. Walking in the sun will clear your brain. We'll have a chance to talk more then."

"If you can keep up with me!" Arik laughed.

"Ha ha! I will so kick your ass, Arik! I really missed racing you up the rocks. Most of the other guys can't keep up with me. You've always given me a run for my money. Let's do this!"

Over the ensuing weeks, Arik threw himself back into his training regimen. When he was not taking part in mission briefings and training exercises, he worked his body endlessly. He filled his rucksack with rocks and scampered up hills. He worked out in the weight room. He refined his Jeet Kune Do forms. He felt his soul purifying through his exertions. He prayed every day. As the reverend had reminded him, a big part of restoring his mental and emotional well-being was his reconnection with what had begun his quest in the time before Dahlia had entered his life.

One afternoon, Colonel Langer stood in the doorway of the weight room, watching Arik work out.

"Arik, you're looking good again, getting back into your fighting trim!" he said. "I reviewed your file and saw some notes put in there by General Tal, so I called him this morning. He reminded me of what you did to Shuki Baum and that he asked you to make some self-defense films for training new recruits. We want to standardize the Krav Maga training for the whole army, not leave it to the whim of every individual instructor. Your films will be a basis of that training. Since it's going to be about four to six weeks before we let you loose on the Arabs, maybe we can put your skills to good use in the meantime? You can do the filming at the Wingate over a two-week period. We'll even put you up in a hotel in Herzliya. Interested?"

"Sounds great!" He thought about the Herzliya aspect and decided that he was ready to return to the scene of his confrontation with Dahlia. "I had some great instructors in LA. They not only taught me the Jeet Kune Do but also taught me how to teach. I think this will be a great opportunity."

"Oren Shemer will be your partner. He is a third-degree black belt in karate and one of the finest practitioners of Krav Maga in Israel. He isn't currently active duty. Do me a favor? Try not to kill him while sparring?"

"I'll see what I can do!" Arik laughed.

Langer hugged him from behind and ruffled his hair.

***

Arik took an immediate liking to Oren. Oren found Arik to be a genuine kindred spirit as well. They were excellent sparring partners for each other. After several days of getting to know each other, they worked out a detailed self-defense curriculum for beginners, starting with kata forms, emphasizing body balance and presence of mind, and then progressing to full-contact, hand-to-hand combat. They presented the concepts clearly and included demonstrations. They set up drills so that each skill built on the last. They divided the instruction into modules that each could be introduced at the appropriate phase of basic training and beyond, even up to the commando level. They put in fourteen-hour days during the filming, but Arik had more fun than any time he could remember. The camera guys were hysterically funny.

When the films had been edited, Arik and Oren submitted them to General Tal and waited, nervously, to hear what the higher-ups thought of them and whether they would need to do more work on them at the Wingate. As soon as he and the army's general staff had reviewed them, General Tal himself sought out the two stars.

"Arik, Oren, the quality of the instruction in these films is outstanding. Everything is presented in a clear, concise way. I think that these films will save many lives. If our soldiers can fight properly with their hands and feet, many husbands, fathers, and sons will come home via tremp rather than in body bags. Good work, gentlemen!"

"Thank you for letting us do this," Arik managed to get out, despite his blushing. "I've always wanted to do something like this!"

"Arik, you'll return, at once, to your unit in Bir Gifgafa. There are things afoot that will need your attention. Oren, thank you for your service."

***

After breakfast, Colonel Langer assembled the men in the briefing room. Standing in front of a large map of central Israel and the Gaza Strip, pointer in hand and a grave expression on his face, he began speaking.

"Chevre, it looks like two Israeli tourists on a shopping expedition in Khan Yunis were abducted by clandestine PLO operatives. They've demanded the release of two hundred Palestinian prisoners incarcerated in Bet Lied, or they'll kill the hostages in twenty-four hours. Our A'man intelligence operatives in the area have narrowed their location down to the city block—Salah El-Din Street in the Jarara neighborhood—but unfortunately, they've set up an underground tunnel under the houses on that block, and all the houses are booby-trapped, so, essentially, this is going to be a shell game. We can't go in with massive firepower, or the hostages will be killed.

"This is going to be a classic surgical-strike rescue operation, but we'll still need enough men to search all the houses simultaneously, with sufficient bomb-disposal sappers to deactivate the booby traps. We'll blast holes through the walls of adjacent houses to get through the block, thus bypassing many of the hazards, but the walls themselves may be mined as well. Expect terrorists to pop out of tunnels hidden under the floorboards, and be ready for them. This will be a joint maneuver with Sayeret Shaked. Operations has already worked out many of the logistics, and the corps of engineers have already constructed plywood mock-ups of the target city block so you can train. The other unit will be here within the hour. Good luck, guys. Let's get to work."

The crowd quickly emptied out of the room and headed to the training area.

Langer called Arik over. "We're putting you into this one. Are you ready?"

"Absolutely, sir. I was just waiting for you to ask," Arik said evenly.

***

At 1 a.m., the two units, each with twenty men deployed from Ein HaShlosha and headed west five miles into the Gaza Strip and toward Khan

Yunis. They were to enter the Jarara neighborhood from two ends—the north and the south—and then commence the final assault a half hour before sunrise. They stealthily creeped into Jarara, under cover of darkness, in single file, hugging the walls of the narrow medieval streets. They encountered no resistance.

Salah El-Din Street was a major thoroughfare, however. When they reached it, from both sides, they were spotted by four machine gun nests, which opened fire nearly simultaneously. All hell broke loose. Three Israelis on the north side of the street and one on the south side of the street fell.

Arik yelled, "To the walls!"

The Israelis rushed from the center of the street to the sides, hugging the yellow stone-block walls. Their armed adversaries ran out of the buildings and fired toward them. Arik, crouched behind a car, sprayed Galil submachine gun fire toward a doorway where three men were discharging a steady barrage at the Israelis. All three fell dead. Arik led three other Israelis toward another car out of the line of sight of the machine gun nest, and then he ran into the middle of the street and dove behind a park bench as bullets whizzed over his head.

Dani led the second team toward the other nest while he shot at six men who were running toward them and firing wildly. Butzi Klinger, running alongside Dani, was hit in the head and fell dead instantly. Dani silenced the enemy with a sustained burst from his Uzi.

"Cover me!" Arik yelled.

He sprang up and launched a grenade across the road and up into the second-story window. The resulting boom and flash of light silenced the PLO machine gunners in that nest.

Yuval Fischer led five men into the building that housed the other nest. After a violent firefight that the Israelis outside could only hear, that nest was silenced as well. All five Israelis who had entered the building ran out into the street. There were no casualties, and the whole affair had taken less than a minute.

"Get the wounded out of here!" Arik called out. He signaled five men to evacuate the injured and dead. He then divided his unit up into two groups. "Follow Dani on the west side and me on the east."

Each team included a sapper. Slowly but steadily, they entered each building, looking for booby traps. In each apartment that they burst into, however, they found only terrified pajama-clad residents. Then they entered a small grocery store.

"Watch out, Arik!" Nir, the sapper on his team, shrieked. "Don't move! There's a trip wire an inch in front of you, attached to that box."

Arik froze. Nir carefully stepped forward and deactivated the device.

"Whew, that was close! I owe you one, Nir!" Arik gasped.

As they moved up the stairs, the Israelis trained their guns upward. They were surprised by two men at the top of the second landing, but Arik silenced them with a double burst from his weapon.

"We must be getting closer!" Arik said, turning to Avner. "This building is clear."

The groups of Israelis that had entered Jarara from the north and the south were within visual distance of each other as the entire neighborhood began pouring into the streets.

Arik called into his radio, "Surprised by machine gun nests at the corners . . . Have the whole neighborhood coming out into the street . . . Going to need backup for crowd control, or we're going to start harming civilians."

Israeli Jeeps and trucks full of troops poured out of the base just outside Khan Yunis and sped into town as Arik and his men continued the house-to-house search.

Ohad Zeltzer, a Sayeret Shaked lieutenant, led his squad into an auto mechanic's shop a third of the way up the street, opposite from where Arik's team was coming from.

Suddenly, a loud explosion and flames shot out of the shop. Gasoline tanks in the shop had been ignited by a booby trap in the doorway. Three officers were dead, blown apart. Ohad lay on the ground, wounded.

Arik shouted, "The hostages are in that house! I can see one through the window!"

He ran across the street, where the Shaked men had joined up with Arik's Matkal team. The garage was fully ablaze.

Arik called out to Yuval and Avner. "Follow me into the building. We have to try to rescue the hostages if they're still alive, before the flames engulf the whole structure." He turned around to look at the men behind him. "Take the bodies away. I'll lead the way inside, then the two of you follow me!"

Ohad said, "Don't go in there. It's about to blow. The hostages are probably dead by now. I don't want to lose any more men, going up there to retrieve dead bodies."

"Is that a direct order?" Arik asked. "If not, don't waste any more time."

Ohad fell silent. The flames grew higher.

Arik looked at the other men. "Well, are you in or out? No time to discuss. Just say yes or no!"

Yuval said, "Ohad is right. It's suicide to go in there."

"I'll take that as a no." Arik said. "You, Avner?"

Avner shook his head.

"Okay, girls, have a nice day," Arik said calmly. "I'll catch you on the other side."

He disappeared into the inferno. A chanting Arab mob formed at the end of the street. The chanting grew louder and louder as more locals joined in:

Badr, Badr al Yahud
Rais Mohamad sud Yadsud
Allah hu Akhbar
Allah hu Akhbar!

The remaining men from both Israeli teams congregated outside the building. They feared the worst. A blast of flames shot out of the second-story windows.

Suddenly, a dark mass of humanity burst out of the smoky doorway. Arik, his face blackened, wheezing and coughing up soot, staggered out with a hostage in each arm . . . still strapped to their chairs. And Arik's pants were on fire!

A collective gasp emerged from the group of Israelis. "Are you okay, Arik?" many voices asked at once.

"I'm fine. There wasn't time to untie them, so I took them out as is. I don't mean to sound needy, but I'm burning my ass off."

He dropped to the ground and rolled. The other men used canvas sheets to extinguish the fire from him. He jumped up and looked around.

"I'm good. Have we collected all the dead and wounded?" Arik choked and coughed.

Someone nodded.

"Then, let's get the hell out of here!"

The Palestinians began throwing rocks and Molotov cocktails and erecting barricades of anything that they could rapidly drag out of their houses. The chanting picked up in both volume and tempo.

"The Arabs are coming at us from every direction. They're trying to hem us in."

"These idiots are really starting to annoy me," Arik said in disgust. "Where the hell are those reinforcements? We called them fifteen minutes ago, didn't we?" He picked a pair of RPGs and an Uzi. "Enough is enough! Who's coming with me?" He turned around, ready to face down the mob that was coming up the street.

Dani and his squad emerged from a building across the street, having just finished a firefight of his own. Quickly sizing up the situation, he ran over to Arik.

"Where are you going? You lunatic! The back of your pants are burned off. Everyone can see your ass!"

"We can't wait for the cavalry to show up," Arik said. "We're going to have to blast our way through the crowd. And stop staring at my ass!" He looked back at his men and shouted, "We're moving out to the south. The crowd seems thinner there. Follow me!"

He and Dani took the lead. When they were about fifty feet away from the barricade that had been hastily created by the crowd, Arik let loose an RPG round aimed at the center of the barricade. There was a loud boom, and the barricade splintered into shreds. Two gunmen appeared from behind it. Dani dropped them with two bursts from his Uzi. Five men moved up to Arik's position, and the rest fell in ten meters behind him.

"Shoot over their heads if they're civilians," Arik said. "Anyone armed? Shoot to kill."

The Israelis advanced slowly up the street, shooting in short bursts. The crowd dispersed rapidly as men and boys as young as five years old ran away pell-mell into the alleyways.

From farther up the street, on the other side of the mob, a column of trucks and armored personnel carriers approached at high speed. In a moment, the rescue vehicles had arrived. The dead and wounded, as well as the hostages, were loaded first, and then the rest of the Israelis got in.

"You don't suppose I could borrow a pair of pants from someone?" Arik asked good-naturedly. "And does anyone know what they were chanting?"

Amir, a Yemeni Jew who spoke fluent Arabic, said, "Badr was the great last battle in Arabia, in 624, when Mohammad defeated the major warlike Jewish tribes that were resisting Islam. They were basically saying that the armies of Islam are coming back to defeat and drive out the Jews yet again. All the rest was 'God is great, God is great!'"

"Nice guys with long memories," Arik said. "Well, at least there's one thing we can all agree on."

"What do you mean?" Yuval asked.

"Simple, really. They all want to go to Allah, and I want to help them get there!"

***

"So, this is how it's going to be, eh?" Langer said. "Your first mission back?"

Arik felt a searing worry in the pit of his stomach, but he remained silent, staring down at the ground.

"I've never seen someone, in their second time in combat, take charge and show as much raw guts and leadership as you demonstrated today. This mission—as it turned out—was poorly conceived and planned. Our intelligence was flawed. We had no idea that the locals were so heavily armed or that the PLO presence was so entrenched. And we paid for our mistakes in blood today.

"Several men stood out and saved the mission, but no one did as much as you did. What madness possessed you to run into that burning building? You're a strong piece of work, taking the hostages out still strapped to their chairs, but it was still suicide, plain and simple."

"Sir, you told me the mission always comes first. Getting those hostages out was the mission."

"That's it?"

"Yes, sir, that's it! I did my best, sir. How are the hostages and the wounded, sir?"

"We suffered eight killed and ten wounded. One hostage died of his wounds. The other is still alive but fighting for his life."

Arik frowned.

"Arik, why the long face? You saved a whole world!"

"I don't understand, sir."

"The Talmud says, 'He who saves a single life from Israel saves the entire world.' It's likely that the other hostage was already dead before we got there. His body showed signs of severe torture. You did very well today, Arik. I'm glad you came back. Speaking of 'back,' how's your tachat?" Langer smiled.

"It only hurts when I take a crap, sir." Arik smiled slowly. Langer burst out laughing.

Chapter 9

Following the mission, Arik finally got a badly needed three-day leave, this time with an invitation.

"How's your tachat?" Mikki laughed when Dani and Arik hopped into her command car.

"Wow! News travels fast. Is it in the Yedioth Ahronoth?" Arik laughed.

"No! Haaretz. Only the best newspapers would carry such a story. Everyone in the southern command is talking about it. So, let me get this straight. You chased down a whole neighborhood of hostile, rock-throwing Palestinians while you weren't wearing any pants?"

"Well, essentially, yes. What was I supposed to do? I ran out of the building, with my pants on fire, and we were getting trapped by a mob. I couldn't politely ask them to wait for me to change my pants."

"Were you nervous? It was your first mission back, after all."

"Only when I realized Dani was staring at my ass with considerable interest." Arik chuckled.

Mikki laughed so hard that the Jeep swerved. She had to fight to regain control.

"Well, I'm glad that you guys were able to get away for Shabbat. It should be fun. My other brothers, Opher and Etzion, and my father will be home as well. I can't remember the last time that we were all home together. Arik, have you ever been to Beersheba?" Mikki asked.

"Can't say as I have," Arik said. "I really haven't been anywhere."

"You've been here for over a year and never traveled? I'm amazed," Mikki said.

"I've had a pretty rough year. In the beginning, I spent my free time sleeping in some dank apartment in Ramle, that the army provided for us lone soldiers—you know, the ones who aren't invited anywhere. It was so depressing being there that I chose to stay on base, mostly."

"Well, we're just going to have to change that . . . Won't we, Dani?"

"Absolutely!"

"Why don't we show you some of Beersheba? We still have some time before Shabbat."

They spent a lazy afternoon in the warm sunshine, wandering about the stalls in the Bedouin market. They inspected olive wood carvings, rugs, spices, meats, and clothing. Arik looked around in no small measure of amazement at the exotic sights, sounds, and smells that invaded his senses.

They strolled through the narrow streets of the old city, toward the old Turkish town, and found a quaint, shaded cafe where they sat for more than an hour, enjoying strong Turkish coffee and baklava. The warm breeze seemed perfumed, and Arik closed his eyes and breathed in deeply.

"You look tired, Arik," Mikki said.

"No! Not really. I just don't remember the last time I felt so relaxed. I've forgotten what it feels like."

"Good. I'm glad. You've been strung so tightly for so long that it was only a matter of time before you broke down," she said.

"When we first met, I was at that point. But not anymore. I feel like my life is starting to take shape again."

"Dani still hasn't told me much about you. I haven't had a chance to interrogate him properly. There are methods, however. . ." Mikki gave him a fake evil smile.

"Hey, isn't interrogation by torture outlawed by the Geneva Convention?" Dani smiled.

"Not when it comes to brothers and sisters!" Mikki smirked.

Arik looked squarely into Mikki's deep-blue eyes. "You may as well try to get it directly from me—if you can—but you'll never get it out of me, I swear."

"Oh, I have my ways," she teased. "This is what I do for a living."

The sun started to dip into the west, casting long shadows over the ancient domed sandstone buildings.

"I think we need to go," Dani said. "Shabbat is in an hour and a half."

"I lost track of the time. . ." Mikki said.

The Zohars lived in Savyon Street in Omer, an upscale suburb of Beersheba. The high wall that surrounded the house and gardens was covered in bougainvillea. The garden featured ceramic walkways that led to a wrought-iron, vine-covered outdoor pavilion and a gurgling fountain. Dotted throughout the garden were lush fruit trees and stands of fragrant exotic flowers that infused the air with the scent of jasmine. The house itself, a classic two-story Mediterranean home, had beige stucco walls, a red terra-cotta tile roof, wide verandas, and arched porticos. The large windows were wide open to the warm breeze. The rust, light salmon, and forest green of the rooms' interior provided a cooling effect from the intense heat of the Negev. When Arik walked inside, he marveled at the Spanish and Italianate decor and the tapestries that lined the walls.

"This house is like out of a James Bond movie. I've never been in a place like this!" Arik whispered to Dani. "If I knew you lived like this, I'd have hit you up for more money last week."

"I think you'd have to hit my dad up for the money. It's his house. It's good to be a general in Tzahal."

"Your father's a general? You never told me that!" Arik whispered.

"It's not something that you advertise."

When they heard someone enter the room, Arik and Dani looked up.

Aluf Major General Shmulik Zohar was a large, well-built man in his early fifties with a full head of closely cropped gray hair. His deeply bronzed complexion appeared sandblasted from decades spent in the desert. He wore an open-collared khaki shirt, light shorts, and sandals. He had sparkling blue eyes and a broad, generous smile. Arik marveled at how generals in any army on earth looked the same. Zohar could have been Patton or MacArthur.

Shmulik Zohar also was referred to as the Desert Fox, the scourge of the Egyptian Army. Born in 1920, a child of Lithuanian immigrants who had emigrated to Mandatory Palestine, which was under British rule during the Third Aliya, after World War I, he was raised in the predominately Bedouin desert town of Beersheba as part of the tiny but growing Jewish community there. As a youth, Shmulik did countless hikes and trips throughout the Negev. He grew to love the desert. He loved the subtle rhythms of life that existed within the barrenness of the rocks and sand. He could navigate the desert's trackless paths by hearing and smell alone. He felt at one with its simplicity and starkness.

His desert skills were put to good use in the Haganah in the 1930s when, as a local expert, he scouted out the best places for training camps, secret arms caches, and factories that would be out of the reach of the Arabs and the British. As a young officer during Israel's War of Independence, he led the nascent Israel Defense Forces' mad dash down the Negev to the Red Sea to found the city of Eilat and give Israel access to a commercial gateway to the Far East. During the Sinai Campaign of 1956, Major Zohar led the successful assault on Mitla Pass in the central Sinai. He was drawn back into the Sinai eleven years later, during the Six-Day War, as deputy chief of the southern command. Under Ariel Sharon's command, Brigadier General Zohar drove a reeling, demoralized Egyptian Army across the entire Sinai Peninsula, establishing Israel's western frontier at the Suez Canal.

In his personal life, Shmulik was a no-nonsense but fair and loving father. Although very considerate and attentive to his children's needs, he demanded and got excellence from them. He instilled in them a sense of personal discipline, purpose, and leadership that enabled them to excel in all aspects of their lives. And excel they did. He led by example.

"Shalom, Abba!" Dani said, smiling at him.

Arik sprang to his feet, unsure whether he should salute.

"Shalom, Ha Aluf Zohar," he finally said, taking Shmulik's outstretched hand, which felt more like a bear claw.

"Arik, you shouldn't jump up like that. You're liable to hurt something." Shmulik chuckled. "Dani, be'chayecha, why are you letting Arik sit on such a hard chair? Bring him a cushion."

Arik smiled ruefully. "I guess I'll never live this down. I must have the most famous tachat in Tzahal."

"That may be true, but just as many people are talking about how you got burned to begin with. Your valor and bravery borders on the insane, but there's a Jewish family in Rehovot that owes you a lifelong debt of gratitude. One hostage will pull through because of you. I have a notion that his isn't the last life you'll save during your service—provided that you stay alive yourself. Kol hakavod! I understand that you're a lone soldier and your parents are in the U.S.?"

"Yes, sir."

"You're always welcome in this house, then. Dani, see to it that Arik is invited here whenever he wants to come."

"Ken, hamefaked!" Dani said with a smirk and a mock salute. "Yes, sir!"

Mikki and her mother appeared from the kitchen, carrying trays of hot, moist rugelach, fresh fruit, and iced coffee.

"Ah . . . Shalom, Arik! Dani has told us so much about you. Baruch HaBah! Welcome to our home."

"Thank you for having me, Mrs. Zohar." Arik shook her hand.

"Oy, so polite! Definitely not a Sabra! Please, call me Yael. Your Hebrew is very good for an American. Where did you learn it?"

"That's a very long story. I was born here."

Mikki stared at Arik reflectively and smiled.

Opher and Etzion, the other brothers of Dani and Mikki, appeared from the garage. They were still wearing their uniforms.

"Shalom, chevre," Mikki said. "I want to introduce you. This is Arik."

Arik shook each man's hand.

Dani said, "Arik is in my unit. Opher is a Phantom jet pilot, and Etzion is a tank commander."

"It's so rare, nowadays, that all of us can be together for Shabbat, like in the old days," Yael said, smiling.

As the sun set in the west, the entire house was bathed in a cool orange glow. The ceiling fans circulated the cool, dry evening desert air.

The four young men bathed and changed into clean khaki pants, white shirts, and sandals, put crocheted white kippot on their heads, and headed to the synagogue.

"My Father prays at home on Friday night, as he doesn't like to be harassed by all the congregants telling him how he should run the army," Dani explained to Arik. "Everyone in Israel is a general with an opinion. Shabbat morning he goes to a small shtiebel farther away, where he has been praying since he was young, where they leave him alone. Tonight, we're going to a shul close by, for young people. With any luck, they won't know about your peculiar ailment."

As they walked to the shul, the rays of the setting sun gently touched the quiet streets, which were lined with tall eucalyptus trees.

This place looks like Palm Springs, Arik thought as they passed row after row of magnificent private homes behind gated walls and arched entrances.

The heartfelt prayers and singing in the small Moorish-style synagogue harkened back to those idyllic, innocent Friday evenings at Camp Moshava. Arik realized that he knew some of the words and songs of the service. He felt relaxed as he looked down at his prayer book and welcomed in the Shabbat queen.

When they returned to the Zohar home, they had dinner. Ostensibly, it was a formal affair. In reality, however, it was as boisterous and lively as any close-knit family's banter. There were the usual gossip, rumors, political arguments, and good-natured petty rivalries. For Arik, this was a wondrous new experience—an intact, loving, well-adjusted family of mature peers. He sat and listened to the conversation, moving his head back and forth like a spectator at a tennis match. Whenever he looked across the table at Mikki, her eyes were there to meet his. She was smiling at him—shyly, he thought. Yael was a magnificent cook, and Arik could not remember ever having eaten such a fine meal.

After grace, everyone got up to claim the most comfortable chairs and settle down to a few hours of reading the weekend section of the newspaper and plowing through several kilos of roasted garinim (sunflower seeds).

Dani asked Arik, "What would you like to do now? Rest? Go for a walk?"

"Excuse me, Dani!" Mikki said. "You had your walk with Arik before. Now it's my turn. Arik, would you like to get some fresh air?"

"Sure. Sounds good."

The night air of the desert was crisp and clean but comfortable enough for shirtsleeves. There was absolute stillness, except for Mikki's and Arik's footfalls on the sandy pavement. They found a park bench under a eucalyptus tree and sat down.

"So, mystery man, tell me now. Why were you so sad on the plane? Who are you? And what are you doing here in Israel?"

Arik smiled. "You sure don't pull any punches. I'll grant you that!"

"Well, at least you know that I didn't go behind your back and get all the information from Dani."

"True enough. So, how much time do you have? How about this? Just interrupt me when you get bored. Or, even better, maybe I just find out about you instead?"

"I asked you first," Mikki said. "And I have all night, but we'll probably need to pull the plug at midnight. You need your beauty sleep."

Arik decided to start with the summer of 1969, at Camp Moshava, and then work his way backward then forward to the present.

Mikki sat spellbound as he told his story. She did not utter a sound until Arik looked down at his watch.

"Crap, it's 2:30 a.m.!" he said.

"And you won't tell me the name of the girl who did this to you?"

"I can't, Mikki. I can't. Maybe sometime I'll share it with you, but not right now."

"Do you know what, Arik? I'll respect your privacy, and I won't find out behind your back. You should know, though, that I'd break her neck if I met her. Nobody should have treated you like that. I would have assumed that there was a logical explanation for your not getting in touch. You're such a good guy. I saw that on the plane. You didn't deserve to be treated like that."

"Nobody's ever said that to me before," Arik said.

"You've never confided in a woman before."

Shabbat day was long, lazy, warm, and full of good food, rest, and relaxing conversation. Arik and Mikki took a walk after lunch, and Arik got to learn a bit about her past.

Soon it was Saturday night, and the Havdalah service had ended.

"I hope that nobody has made plans for tonight," Mikki announced. "If you have, cancel them, because I have a surprise. Five tickets to the Yehoram Gaon concert. He's performing at the Orot Hanegev theater downtown. He rarely gets to Beersheba. And when are we all going be all together again, like old times?"

There were smiles all around as the other Zohars nodded.

"Who's Yehoram Gaon?" Arik asked.

Mikki laughed. "Your Hebrew is so good that I keep forgetting that you didn't grow up here. You'll pick up all the slang and culture in no time. In the meantime, you'll really enjoy tonight."

When Arik returned to the base, he felt an inner serenity that he could not remember ever having before. The searing sense of loneliness that had plagued him since his confrontation with Dahlia had been doused by the embrace of the remarkable Zohar family, a family whose accomplishments and dignity were more than equaled by their warmth, closeness, humor, decency, and openness. During one short, magical weekend, Arik had been drawn in. The sense of belonging that he had developed with his comrades in the unit came from their readiness to die for one another, but the belonging that he felt with the Zohars was rooted in a readiness to live for one another. It was a feeling that Arik had tried to achieve with Dahlia and possibly her family. But that had proved illusory.

And he wondered whether it was his imagination or Mikki's attentions were more than just friendship? He could not figure it out. He did not know her well enough. He certainly was not going to jeopardize his welcome by the Zohars by indulging in yet another relationship that he assumed would be doomed to fail. I have no need for a romantic relationship. I won't allow myself to get hurt again. He decided that Mikki, wonderful person that she clearly was, had the potential to be a great friend. He was determined to nurture that friendship.

Life at the base fluctuated between boredom and intense training. The latter included honing weapons skills, doing endurance training such as eighty-kilometer hikes in the burning Sinai sun while wearing full fifty-kilogram battle gear, and practicing house-to-house fighting. Arik spent much of his downtime reading books about electronics and computers. As part a barter agreement way back when they were at Camp Moshava, Arik had taught Richard how to play basketball and Richard had kicked off Arik's interest in computers and electronics. Why don't they teach this stuff in high school? Arik wondered. It will be so much more important in the future than most of the other crap they teach. The time that he spent with his books, slide rule, notepads, and pencils was time away from the endless beige dunes and brilliant-blue sky of the hot, bone-dry western Sinai. Why would anyone want to spend forty years in this sandbox? No wonder Moses and the Israelites were pissed off all the time.

He knew that both he and Mikki would be free for the upcoming weekend, and the thought of spending three days with her filled him with warmth. Where does she want to go? On the phone with him the previous day, she had been vague. All she had said was for him to bring Shabbat clothes.

"Arik, you have a phone call in the office," a voice called in to his tent on Thursday evening.

When he answered the phone, he heard Mikki say, "Hey, stranger! I haven't heard from you in almost a week. What have you been up to?"

"Let's see . . . I spent the week at the King Solomon Hotel, in Eilat, chasing Swedish tourists in bikinis."

"As long as you used protection, good for you. You don't know what they've imported into Israel . . . Seriously!"

"I spent the week sleeping all day in a cave, stomping scorpions and lizards, and I was up all night practicing night assaults on model airliners that they dumped in the middle of the desert on stilts. They say one day we'll put those skills to use in some airline hostage rescue. Of course, that assumes some terrorists would be dumb enough to land their plane with hostages into Israel. But I guess we have to train for everything. Anyway, I can now rescue a plane full of stuffed dummies in under ninety seconds. I'll add that to my résumé."

"I think I liked you better with the Swedish sweeties," Mikki said. "So, are you definitely free this weekend? I've made plans for us."

"Oh, I'm afraid not. My social calendar is fully booked for months!" Arik chuckled. "So, why the big secret? Why won't you tell me where we're going?"

"Okay, okay. I want to spend three days in Jerusalem. I imagine you haven't been there yet?"

"You imagine correctly. I was just on the southern outskirts where we began our red beret march to Masada through the Judean Desert. Where will we stay?"

There was a pause at the other end of the line.

"I was thinking about staying with my Aunt Gila, Imma's sister. They have a very large apartment in Rechavia, overlooking the Israel Museum. They have plenty of room."

"Will they be okay with my coming?" Arik asked.

"Of course, silly! Imma has already told her everything about you. She knows that you're part of the family now."

"Sounds great. I've wanted to visit Jerusalem for a while now."

"Can you get off tonight so that I can come get you? That way we can spend the whole day tomorrow in Jerusalem."

"My leave starts at 6 p.m. My reward for killing the most real scorpions and fake terrorists."

Mikki felt as if she were walking a tightrope with Arik. During the two months since his first Shabbat visit, she had seen a great deal of him, and she felt herself drawing closer to him. They had gone together to see Arik Einstein (one of Israel's premier singing sensations) and Chava Alberstein in concert at the Heichal Hatarbut, the Mann Auditorium, in Tel Aviv. They had spent long, lazy afternoons walking along the seacoasts of Tel Aviv and Jaffa. They had even gone to see HaGashash HaHiver, a comedy group, at the Habima Theatre, the national theatre in Tel Aviv.

She had surprised Arik with tickets to watch the Maccabi Tel Aviv Basketball Club play Hapoel Givat Yagur for the national championship at the Yad Eliyahu Stadium. She regretted that date. He had spent the entire evening in a nervous state as if his feet were tied to a hot frying pan. She had realized, later on, that the game had awakened his feelings of regret at having turned down his basketball scholarship. She wondered if he did play a better brand of basketball than the fellows they had gone to see. He had said that the coach of the Los Angeles professional basketball team told him that that he would be good enough to play professionally in the U.S.

Arik was smart, modest, considerate, and engaging. Above all, he maintained eye contact when they spoke, and he appeared genuinely interested in what she said. She was drawn to his kindness and sense of justice. She was unaccustomed to that. The men that she had dated since Elisha's death were either macho military men with egos the size of Mount Hermon or sensitive poets who she found too effeminate. The one thing that they all had in common was how soon they wanted to take her to bed. She always placed herself in a position to cool down the passions of the male beast and fend off wandering hands. She was proud and tough, and she hated to feel used by men.

That was what she found so interesting yet disconcerting about Arik. They had gone out together so many times and had already confided so much in each other, but Arik seemed to show no interest in her as a woman. He had not even made the slightest move to touch her hand. She could not figure out why. She wondered whether he might not find her attractive. If so, he would be the first. Mikki knew what "assets" she brought to the table. She hoped that Arik did not see her simply as a platonic friend. He certainly didn't appear to her to be a homosexual, but she acknowledged that she could not be sure.

Perhaps, she conjectured, it was that he had found a home in her family's house, with her brothers, especially Dani, and was afraid to risk all of that if a relationship with her failed. He clearly had nobody else to rely on. She could understand if that was how he was thinking.

Or maybe, she thought, he was simply terrified of getting hurt again. She knew that the mystery woman had done a number on him and he was just beginning to feel that his life was coming around again. She questioned whether she should risk sabotaging that. Besides, she was four years older than him and a lieutenant colonel, and he had not yet been considered for officers' training school. She wondered whether it was even ethical for a high-ranking officer to become romantically involved with an army private and how such a relationship would be viewed by her peers.

This all bounced around in Mikki's head as she drove to Arik's base in the Sinai. Never before had she been faced with this dilemma. She certainly did not want to be the next in line to hurt Arik, but there was one thing she knew for certain, in her heart: She wanted Arik to put his arms around her and never let go.

***

"How's your sense of adventure tonight, Arik?" Mikki asked when he got into the car.

"What do you have in mind?"

"I was going to take the more direct, southerly route into Jerusalem, passing through Beersheba, Chevron, Gush Etsyon, and Beit Lechem, rather than the more common route from the Tel Aviv area. Are you game? I wanted to show you the Ma'arat HaMachpela, the Patriarch's Tomb, in Chevron, at night, all lit up. There's so much history on those roads, so much tragedy."

"Chevron is crawling with angry Arabs. I don't know if driving through those streets at night is a good idea. I don't want to have to shoot one of them. I've decided they don't like us too much."

"Don't be silly. They're harmless."

"My ass still says otherwise."

"That's Gaza. That place is a shithole. It's different there. The West Bank is much better. They're more afraid of us there."

They started out at sunset and drove through the dusty, winding mountain roads in the pitch darkness that was punctuated by lights coming from settlements, mostly Arab ones. The Patriarch's Tomb was impressive at night, but Arik did not care much for the dark side streets of Chevron that Mikki insisted on driving through to get to it. They got numerous hostile stares from men and boys who were sitting outside their darkened homes, playing backgammon or smoking water pipes in the glare of their orange front lights.

From Chevron, they continued driving north along the narrow, winding two-lane highway that had only recently been cut out of the side of the hills. They drove through Gush Etsyon, a collection of newly built tiny settlements, with sparkling lights that punctuated the darkness, which had been rebuilt on the site of the 1948 massacres and the Haganah's failed attempts to get help to the stricken settlers.

Back then, Gush Etsyon had been an isolated group of settlements nestled in the Judean Hills. When war formally broke out, with Israel's declaration of statehood in May 1948, the settlements sustained a major assault from the Jordanian Army and local Arab militias. All of the settlers were killed. For nineteen years, the site remained empty. Finally, during the Six-Day War, the site was liberated by the Israeli army. Soon afterward, the descendants of the settlers and others returned to rebuild the settlements from scratch out of the rocky earth.

As they drove north toward Beit Lechem, which Arik knew as Bethlehem, they reached the spot where thirty-five Palmach youth who in 1948 had set out from Jerusalem to reinforce the Gush Etsyon settlements had been set upon by local Arabs and slaughtered like sheep, their mutilated bodies dumped into a ditch.

"Didn't we do the same to them?" Arik asked. "At a place called Deir Yassin?"

"The people who perpetrated that crime were disgusting criminals, despised by the entire Jewish community, who were up in arms against them. Worse yet, they were never brought to justice. Most of them scattered like rats and were never found. When Arabs commit atrocities, which they do a thousand times more often than we do, they're hailed as heroes by their people. Their mothers give out cakes and sweets in the street to celebrate the murder of our women and children. That's the difference. We just want to be left alone. They just want to kill us. People say that the Arabs were especially brutal here in Gush Etsyon because of what happened in Deir Yassin. Such is the nature of attacks that seem like a good idea at the time or are ideologically driven but poorly thought out in execution—and the consequences."

"Didn't we take their land? That would make anyone mad."

"We didn't take anyone's land," Mikki said. "We returned to our own land that we were thrown out of nearly two thousand years ago. We're the ones coming home, not people who happened to wander in here while we were away. Let's say that you owned a house in LA and left it for a while to go live in New York. And while you were away, a group of squatters broke into your house and decided to take it over because it was empty. And then you come back to your house and find the squatters refuse to leave. Do you then say to them, 'Oh, please, stay here. I'll sleep in the street'? Or do you get a court order to evict them?"

"You get a court order and produce a deed of ownership," Arik said.

"Precisely! Our court order was the Balfour Declaration, and the deed of ownership is the Bible. Please, motek, let me give you a word of advice. You can confide in me. You can tell me everything that you feel. I'll never betray you. But please, please don't let anyone ever hear you say that we should give land away to the Arabs—especially anyone in your unit. If your higher-ups hear that talk, your loyalty will be suspect, and you can get thrown out on that basis alone. I know these people well. Okay? I hope that you're not angry at me for telling you this."

"No, not at all. I'm glad. I'm just torn between my duty to Israel and the Jewish people and a terrible sense that we took something that belonged to someone else. That's all."

As they passed Rachel's Tomb in Bethlehem, they saw the southern lights of Jerusalem beckoning in the distance. They drove up into the center of the city and around the walls of the Old City, starting at the Jaffa Gate.

"That's called David's Citadel, but in reality, it has nothing to do with David," Mikki said. "It's just a medieval mosque. And that's Mount Zion, where it's believed that King David was buried."

She pulled the car through the Zion Gate, headed east inside the Old City wall, and parked in a lot adjacent to the Dung Gate.

"Arik, do you know where we are?"

"No, not really."

"Come."

They walked up the hill and into a wide promenade.

"Now, do you know where we are?" Mikki smiled.

Arik was spellbound as he stared at the huge wall of tan stone that stood before him. It was brightly lit against the black sky.

"This is the mother lode," he said. "The reason for everything. I've done some studying about it in school and seen some pictures of it, but I could never imagine what it really looked like. . ."

"Arik, this is why we don't have to apologize for being here. Despite the golden mosque on the hill, this place was ours for twenty-one hundred years before any Arab showed up. This was and is our home. This is the last remnant of Herod's Temple that the Romans left standing when they destroyed it during the Great Jewish War in the year 70. There's a custom that small notes—messages to God—are written, folded up, and stuffed in between the cracks in the stones."

"What do you say to God?"

"You write your innermost prayers and desires, your hopes and dreams. When you put them inside the wall, they go—poof—special delivery to the big guy upstairs. Why don't we both write one? I have to go in on the woman's side, and you go to the left."

Arik put on his red beret. "I'll join a minyan for evening prayers. See you in a few!"

When they returned, Mikki asked, "So, what did you write?"

"Isn't it supposed to be a secret?"

"But you can always tell me. I won't tell. I'll tell you mine if you tell me yours."

"I asked for my father's stump to finally heal. I asked to have his name cleared, so he can finally live a dignified life. And I asked for me to be able to give him and my mother financial security."

"Didn't you ask anything for yourself?" Mikki stared at Arik intensely, with a sense of awe on her face. She had never met anyone like him.

"I don't need anything now. I'm finally okay with where I am. I'm trying to heal, and every day gets better. Okay, now your turn. What did you write?"

"I can't tell you right now."

"Hey, you cheat! That's not fair. You promised!"

"I said that I'd tell you, but I didn't say when. I'll tell you at the right time. I promise."

They drove out of the Old City and parked at the King David Hotel. Mikki had suggested that they have some drinks and a light dinner. They walked through the marble entrance hall and into the bar.

"This is such a beautiful place," Arik said as he stared at the marble vaulted ceiling.

"It was built during the time of the British Mandate. It was the center of the British administration in Palestine. It, too, was bombed by those Irgun criminals, killing scores of people. Sometimes we're our own worst enemies. They may have meant well, but in reality, they brought all sorts of hell down on the Yishuv. They were finally taught a lesson when the Haganah sunk their arms ship, the Altalena, off the coast of Tel Aviv."

They sat and talked for an hour before Mikki rose and said, "We should probably be getting over to my aunt's. I don't want her to wait up for us. And this way we can get an early start in the morning."

"Agreed. I'm beat!"

Mikki's Aunt Gila was a carbon copy of Yael, her sister and Mikki's mother. She was fit, smart, warm, and indulgent. She seemed genuinely happy to meet Arik, and she gave Mikki knowing glances when she thought that Arik was not looking. Arik enjoyed seeing Mikki blush. He had thought that high-ranking intelligence operatives might not remember how to blush.

They walked out on the terrace and looked at the huge panorama of twinkling lights that was spread out before them.

"The Talmud says that every place on earth has a measure of beauty while Jerusalem has ten," Mikki said.

"It's like looking out into the heavens in the desert and seeing all the stars," Arik said.

"That's why they say that Jerusalem is the heavenly city."

She placed her hand on his elbow. Arik remained motionless. They gazed out at the darkness for a few more minutes, breathing in the chilly night air.

"I'm a bit cold," Arik finally said. "Let's go inside for a hot tea or something."

"Sure."

Arik went to bed with a terrible sense of foreboding. His heart raced and his palms were sweaty. He suspected that Mikki had engineered this weekend to take their budding relationship out of the shadows, to make an official transition from friends to lovers. But he already knew love is not simply further than like on the emotion spectrum. Love is an entirely different creature than like or even intense like. Love is often destructive of like. Marriages that have just love and not like often fail.

Mikki had become his best friend in a very short time. She meant so much to him. He had poured out his soul, again, to a woman. And he had done that so soon after promising himself that he would never do it again. Am I a fool, a hopeless romantic, or just lonely and in need of intimate company? He wanted to be around Mikki more than anything, but knew that for her it would mean the whole nine yards. He was so desperately afraid of failure. He knew that he would lose her completely if a romantic relationship with her fell apart.

He lay on his back in bed, trying to sleep. He was distracted by the sound of the cars in the street and the yellow glare of the streetlights below, which were streaming through the window. He heard soft footsteps coming up the hallway. His door opened silently. Mikki let herself into the room and stood over his bed. He knew that if he showed her that he was awake they would go through a one-way door that would slam shut behind them, leaving no way for them to return to moments of innocence with each other. He flashed back to the blissful nights that he spent with Dahlia and how the stars in the universe had seemed to move in sync with one another. His soul had been so drawn to her that he had wanted to go farther and farther into her embrace. Now, he lay in terror of being drawn into an embrace almost against his will. Whether out of panic or subterfuge, he elected to lay motionless and keep his eyes closed. He felt Mikki's presence hovering above him, her hair dancing on his chest. He smelled her perfume. Suddenly, he felt her lips touch his.

Don't move! he told himself. She kissed him twice more, obviously hoping to arouse and rouse him. But he stayed completely still. When she pulled away from him, he turned over, turning his back on her. He felt her stand for a moment at the side of the bed and then, just as silently as she had come in, she was gone.

The next morning, after a quick breakfast of hummus, tomatoes, cucumbers, olives, farmer cheese, pita, and coffee, they were off. Mercifully, at least from Arik's perspective, they were back to their friendly, jovial selves. It was as if Mikki's awkward visit to Arik's room the previous night had not happened.

They spent part of the morning at Yad Vashem, Israel's monument and museum dedicated to the victims of the Holocaust. Arik told Mikki about his father's boxing fights for survival in Buchenwald. When he looked at the mannequins in the blue and white striped prison suits, he imagined his father wearing one. He felt sickened by the photos from the concentration camps and crematoria. All of the members of Mikki's entire immediate family either had emigrated from Germany right after World War I or had been born in Palestine, so she knew of no close relatives who had perished in the camps. She was incredibly fortunate. Israel needed to be led by a generation of Jews who had never felt the lash of the taskmaster. Rabbi Rabinowitz had told him that perhaps that was why the generation who had left Egypt had had to die in the desert and only their children entered the promised land.

"Mikki, let's go see some living Jews," Arik finally said.

She completely understood. "I know just the place."

They parked the car near the Central Bus Station and headed into Machane Yehuda, Jerusalem's outdoor market. On a Friday at noon, it was teeming with humanity. The humid air hung heavy with spices heaped up in piles, baked goods, roasted meat, fresh fish, cheeses, fruits, and vegetables—of every imaginable variety—displayed in outdoor kiosks that were sheltered under canvas awnings to protect them from the sun. They pushed through the crowds of shoppers and vendors, who were loudly hawking their wares. They stopped and bought challah from the Angel Bakery, a large bag of rugelach and bourekas from the world-famous Marzipan bakery, two kilograms of roasted, seasoned sunflower seeds, and Elite spreading chocolate.

"There's a fellow down the street who makes the best lamb shawarma lafas in Jerusalem. Want to eat?" Mikki asked.

"That sounds great. I'm starved."

After lunch, they visited the Dead Sea Scrolls exhibit at the Israel Museum.

"Where's Kastel? Is it far?" Arik asked.

"No. It's just outside of town. Come on. I want to show you something first, on the way."

They drove out of the city, down the hill, and then on Highway 1, for about twenty minutes. The road appeared to have been cut out of the hills. Tight cliffs hugged it on both sides. On either side of the road lay rusted hulks of cars, trucks, and buses.

Mikki pointed at them. "So, what do you think, Arik?"

"That's an eyesore. They should cart that junk away," Arik said.

"That junk is a memorial to all the convoys of cars, trucks, and buses that tried to break the Arab siege of Jerusalem in 1948. This is a graveyard of hundreds of young men and women that died coming up to the city. It's called Bab el Wad. The convoys were shelled from the cliffs above us. These vehicles aren't replicas. They're some of the ones that were left here after the war."

Arik looked at the skeleton of an armored bus. He saw how flimsy it seemed. He thought about his father. "That's what passed for an armored personnel carrier in those days? The people inside were sitting ducks from the shelling. My father lost his leg, trying to rescue his comrades from a burning bus like that."

"Let's go to Kastel," Mikki said.

As they drove through the town, Arik told Mikki his father's accounts of the battle, the stories that he had heard a hundred times since he was a child. They stopped in front of a large stone memorial in the center of town, which bore the names of those who had lost their lives in the battle. They stared at the names for a long time.

"Did your father ever mention the names of any of his comrades who died here?" Mikki asked. "Perhaps we could find them here."

"No, never. But he did describe, in detail, how the town looked and how they evacuated it on that second day. They must've gone out down that street. We're standing very close to the spot where my family's life and fortunes changed forever. It's so crazy actually being here."

They wandered around for a few more minutes.

"Come, Arik. There's somewhere else I want to take you."

***

They stood on the barren hilltop that overlooked the Old City of Jerusalem from the north. The sky was bright blue, and the domed stone buildings of shimmered brightly in the late afternoon sunlight. Arik took a long, deep breath of honeysuckle-scented air and then sighed deeply.

Mikki moved closer to him, wrapped her arm around his waist, and rested her head on his shoulder.

"Please, Mikki. I can't. Please don't."

"Why not? I don't understand. I think that we're ready to move forward. Don't you want me? Don't you find me attractive?"

"It's not that. I'm extremely attracted to you and fond of you. You've become my best friend. I want to be with you so much."

"Then, what's the problem?"

"Well . . . there are several. First, I don't want to ruin such a cherished friendship by getting into a relationship that could fail. Second, I've finally been made to feel so at home with your family. That would go up in smoke if we ever broke up. And third, I'm just not ready yet. The mystery woman, as you like to call her, gutted me from the inside. I'm not capable of having those feelings right now. The pain from her is still too raw. Please, don't walk away from me, but I just can't love you that way right now. Maybe sometime in the future."

"Do you know the King Arthur legend?" Mikki asked.

"Which part?"

"Well, do you know how they picked him to be king when he was young? There was a sword stuck in a stone, placed there many years before. Nobody could pull it out, even the strongest of men. Legend was that only the rightful king would be able to pull out the sword. And though Arthur was only a child, he was able to pull out the sword, so he became king."

"What does that have to do with anything?"

"Do you see all the broken concrete and rusted scrap metal scattered about this hilltop? This place is called Ammunition Hill. It was a major strategic outpost of the Jordanian Army, and you can see why. It has a commanding view of the whole city. It was the scene of one of the bloodiest battles for the liberation of Jerusalem during the Six-Day War. Dozens of Israelis were killed trying to capture this piece of dirt.

"My boyfriend, Elisha Bar Ami, was a lieutenant in the 55th Paratroopers Brigade under General Motta Gur. I was nineteen and so in love with him. I was convinced that I'd marry him. He was killed right here on this ridge on the second day of the war. I used to come here all the time to stare out at the city. I felt his spirit here in the blowing wind. After his death, I went out with many guys, each one more awful than the last. I began to feel hopeless. That is, until May . . . when I met you. You've pulled the sword out of my stone again. I know it. I don't say that lightly." Mikki looked directly into Arik's eyes.

"Mikki, my sword is broken. The mystery woman saw to that. I don't know how to mend it. I have no clue. I know this sounds like I'm making something up just to brush you off or something—the old 'It's not you, it's me' routine. Nothing could be further from the truth. I just don't know how to feel love anymore. I'm so sorry. You deserve much better than I can give you." Arik looked down, his shoulders slumped.

She grabbed both of his hands. "You haven't the faintest clue what I deserve or don't deserve. I'm not some silly schoolgirl. I don't know if you've noticed, but I'm a mature woman who knows what she wants and what she's getting. I won't be put off by what you've said. Tell me that you could never love me, and we'll remain friends. You'll always be welcome in my home in any case. That would be true even if we dated and then we realized that we weren't meant for each other. But I know that we are. I will help you heal, Arik Meir. You are my sword. My heart is a flaming forge that can rebuild that sword. And I will. Take your time. I'm in no rush. You're worth waiting for. Now, I'll tell you what I wrote on the note I put into the wall yesterday. I prayed that one day you'll love me as much as I love you."

Arik smiled sadly but did not say anything.

"Can I at least hold your hand?" Mikki asked.

"Of course." He felt a warm rush of blood flow into his face and hands.

***

Shabbat in Jerusalem is magical. At sunset, the flurry of activity melts away into a citywide serenity. There is almost no vehicular traffic. Thousands of Jews of every stripe, age, and background walk, all dressed up and with tallit bags in their arms, in quiet purpose to worship. The air is fragrant with the collective aroma of Shabbat fish, chicken soup, and cholent.

Mikki, too, was radiant in her finery as she and Arik walked hand in hand to shul. She had bought him a brand-new tightly crocheted white kippah with blue and gray rim. For Arik, the rest of the weekend passed as a shimmering dream. Even the color of Mikki's face seemed different now that everything was out in the open. They walked for miles through the Geula and

Meah She'arim neighborhoods, through the Jewish quarter in the Old City, and back through the streets of Katamon to Rechavia. They milled with crowds in the side streets and main roads, enjoying the golden Jerusalem sunshine. Although they were not quite a couple yet, they held hands for the whole weekend.

"This is why we fight, Arik. To protect these people," Mikki said.

***

When Arik returned to his base in the Sinai, he felt great confidence. He felt that something that had been broken in his heart was finally healing. He felt ready for anything. I'll need all the strength, confidence, and courage I can muster for whatever is to come, he thought.

But Mikki had mixed emotions. On the one hand, she felt good about finally having gotten things out into the open. On the other hand, Arik was so broken that she wondered whether she could help him to mend himself. She wished that they had met before the mystery woman had hurt him. He was such an amazing person that Mikki could not imagine what would drive a woman to disrespect him in that way. She was certain that the mystery woman had done it simply because she had believed that she could get away with it. Mikki knew that, for all of his physical strength and wits, Arik was as vulnerable as a child in matters of the heart. She did not know whether she would ever meet that woman, but she vowed that if she did that woman would feel the full power of her wrath.

Chapter 11

In mid-August, Dahlia was discharged from Tranquility Acres. For the first time in months, she walked through the door of the ambassador's residence.

When she passed through the security gate, she asked, "Where are Tomer and Yoram?"

"They asked to be reassigned. They're back in Israel, booba," Leah said.

Dahlia shook her head, and tears welled in her eyes.

***

The limousine left the Golden Nugget hotel en route to the courthouse in downtown Las Vegas. This was a part of Las Vegas that tourists never saw, if they were lucky. From a distance, Dahlia saw the massive beige sandstone building surrounded by palm trees. It stood tall, in stark contrast to the one- and two-story buildings that lined the sandy streets in every direction. Her heart began to race. She tried to focus on the bright-blue sky, which was unencumbered by clouds, and the warm desert breeze that was blowing in through the open window of the limousine.

When they pulled up to the courthouse, the limousine was suddenly mobbed by hundreds of curious onlookers. She could tell by their dress and mannerisms that many of them were Israelis. A group of them were yelling epithets. She heard, "zonah!" (whore) and forced herself not to cringe.

Dahlia stepped out of the limo and immediately was flanked by her parents and a phalanx of Mossad agents. She scarcely noticed the Ehrenreichs, who had pulled up in a limousine behind them and made their way up the stairs without casting even a sideways glance at the Gilads. Camera flashbulbs went off as reporters tried to shove microphones into Dahlia's face.

"Dahlia! Are you a drug addict?"

"Were you involved in sex orgies?"

Dahlia was wearing a dark suit and a white blouse, her hair was knotted in a tight bun, and her eyes were covered in dark sunglasses. She stared down at the ground, trying to ignore the reporters as she entered the courthouse. A large brass sign on the front of the building read: EIGHTH JUDICIAL DISTRICT COURT, CLARK COUNTY, NEVADA.

Dahlia's high heels clicked on the black granite floors of the huge gray entrance hall. The Gilads were met by Mr. Jacobowitz, who put his arm around Dahlia's shoulder.

"Are you ready?" he asked.

Dahlia nodded.

"So, you understand how this is going to go, right? You'll face the district attorney, a Mr. Charles B. Simpson. He's the prosecutor in the case. He'll ask you a series of tough questions to demonstrate to the court that you're a credible witness. So far, you've been able to convince the grand jury you were forced to participate in the all the activities you describe. Based on your grand jury testimony, Simpson is confident you'll be a credible witness. But then you'll be cross-examined by Harold Bronfman, the Ehrenreichs' attorney. He's one of the leading defense counsels in the country. Money does buy the best.

"We have about an hour before court goes into session. I've worked opposite Bronfman on several occasions. He's a very tough, shrewd interrogator. You understand that Ze'evi is fighting for his future, right? He'll try to drag you down with him. The DA is sufficiently impressed with your innocence, but Mr. Bronfman will stop at nothing to prove that everything you did with Ze'evi was consensual, including everything that was caught on film, that the whole thing was play-acted. He'll also claim you were complicit not only in taking the drugs but in the selling and distributing of narcotics. He'll twist and turn everything you say against you, so keep your cool and answer all of his questions truthfully, but don't volunteer any information or try to bolster your arguments. Above all, don't become emotional. He'll try to draw you in, and if you get excited he has you. Do you understand?"

Dahlia gasped. "How can he do that? That's a complete lie! It's all lies! I was completely victimized by that bastard!"

"I'm sorry to say that the truth as you see and know it has nothing to do with how things may turn out at trial. The courtroom is theater, and the one who puts on a better show in front of the jury is the one who will prevail. The good news is that this is Judge Robert Sullivan's court. He's a fair, no-nonsense guy who plays by the rules. Anyway, the narcotics charges stand in federal court, in Washington, and the Ehrenreichs will be able to plea that sentence down to manageable size. But a rape conviction would add many years on to Ze'evi's sentence. And, Dahlia, you're an important state's witness. But remember: you're not on trial today. The prosecution isn't coming after you."

Dahlia suddenly looked at her mother and father with an expression of resolve that they had not seen on her face in nearly a year. For a moment, it seemed that the old Dahlia was returning.

"I'll just tell the court what I told the grand jury," she said, "nothing more and nothing less. I have nothing more to say. When all you have to tell is the truth and the truth is all you tell, you can't be caught in a lie. I learned that at Tranquility Acres. Worse than lying to the court would be lying to myself, and I'll never do that again."

The Gilads walked through the great oak doors and into the massive courtroom. To Dahlia, it appeared so much larger than on the TV shows that she had watched. The massive mahogany judge's bench towered over the rest of the room. Dahlia and her family sat in the back of the courtroom.

Dahlia stared straight ahead, without emotion, as Ze'evi, dressed in one of his thousand-dollar suits, entered the courtroom, flanked by his entourage of similarly high-priced attorneys. He talked and laughed gregariously with his crew as if this were a Sunday outing. When he had his back to her, she stared at him and saw him for what he was. In her therapy sessions, she had been taught about borderline personalities, such people's inability to empathize, and how they dissociate their emotions in the face of stress or threats. Ze'evi appeared to be showing no concern regarding what was about to transpire. Instead, he seemed relaxed and confident. Did his family pull some backroom strings to get him off the hook? Dahlia had heard of such things. She remembered that

Ze'evi's parents had contacts in the FBI. Is this trial just a show? Why do I feel gutted inside while that monster is acting like this is one of his celebrity parties?

The visitors' gallery was filling up with a loud gregarious crowd that had assembled for the spectacle despite every attempt to keep the proceeding under wraps. Why are all these strangers allowed into the courtroom? It's none of their business. What is this "public record" thing, anyway? Why does it allow total strangers to peer inside my private life?

Dahlia shuddered at the thought that the sex film would be aired in court, seemingly for the entertainment of the masses. The grand jury hearing was held in private. Why not this? She flashed back to Camp Moshava, to when she had called Arik a drugged-out sex fiend. She was engulfed by a wave of shame. He clearly wasn't, but she clearly had been. How did I allow myself to get to this point? Where's Arik now?

Dahlia was jolted out of her thoughts by someone sidling up to her and grabbing her arm. She looked up, startled.

"Sorry I'm late. What did I miss?"

"Penny, I'm so happy you're here! I thought that you'd already started school?" Dahlia gave her a tight hug and a kiss.

"Boston is not far, Paapi. It is only a plane ride. Nothing to it, really—especially for my best friend in the whole world. Did you think for a minute that I would let you go through this by yourself?"

Dahlia rested her head on Penny's shoulder.

Leah reached over and grasped Penny's hand. "We're all so grateful to you, Penny. You are Dahlia's guardian angel."

"All rise, all rise! The Honorable Judge Robert E. Sullivan presiding!"

The jury—eight men and four women, wearing name tags and carrying notepads and pens— slowly filed into the courtroom and were seated in the jury box.

Opening arguments by the prosecution and the defense took up the rest of the morning and the early afternoon. Dahlia sat and listened intently, trying to decipher what Ze'evi's attorney was trying to do to get him off the hook. Ze'evi quietly but excitedly scribbled on a writing tablet and occasionally showing his writing to his attorney.

Then, suddenly, the bailiff announced, "The people call Miss Dahlia Gilad to the stand."

Dahlia was stunned. She had thought that she had more time.

"It will be okay, Paapi," Penny whispered to Dahlia when she stood to walk to the witness stand. "You will do great. Send that bastard to hell!"

Just like in the movies, Dahlia thought as she was sworn in.

***

Dahlia's direct examination by the district attorney took about ninety minutes. In that time, she repeated, virtually word for word, what she had said before, first to the FBI agent at Tranquility Acres and then during her testimony in front of the grand jury. She spoke evenly and without emotion. At one point during her testimony, she looked over at Ze'evi, who was staring at her with a broad smile, as if he did not have a care in the world. She felt a crushing pain inside, but she fought to maintain her composure. Best not to look at the devil, she thought.

Instead, she glanced at her parents, who by now had become inured to her sordid tale. They were sitting quietly. They showed no emotion until the film of the rape scene was shown. Leah wept quietly. Cackles came from the visitors' gallery, which prompted the judge to pound his gavel and issue a warning.

When the prosecution had finished its questioning, Mr. Bronfman stood up. Approaching to within a foot of the witness stand, he glowered down at Dahlia. Standing at over six foot three, he towered over her.

"Ms. Gilad, I understand that you've been Mr. Ehrenreich's girlfriend for nearly a year. Is that correct?"

"Yes, I was."

"And your parents had strongly pushed you to enter into this relationship?"

"Yes."

"Why do you think that is?"

"I had just come out a relationship, and I really didn't want to meet anyone, so I spent most of my time at home. My parents insisted that I go out and meet people, so I went to the Ambassador's Ball. The Ehrenreichs were being honored, so their whole family came down to Washington for the occasion. Ze'evi came up to me to introduce himself and was very charming and dashing. He took me out on the dance floor and swept me off my feet. I felt that the only cure for a broken romance was to meet someone new, even though I still had misgivings. I still missed my boyfriend Arik so much. Ze'evi asked me out onto his sailing yacht for the following Sunday. I hesitated, but my parents practically forced me to go, telling me that they'd heard such wonderful things about him. His family were known and respected everywhere for their generosity and good works in Israel and all over the Jewish world. Ze'evi himself had already become active in Jewish causes and was already making a name for himself. My parents were completely star struck by them. My first two months with him were a complete whirlwind."

"Wasn't Ze'evi good to you—generous, kind, and considerate? Didn't he buy you expensive gifts—jewelry, diamonds, and furs—and take you on expensive dates?"

"Yes."

"He doesn't seem like such a monster. Does he?" Bronfman said.

"In the beginning, he was kind, sweet, and considerate. He was sophisticated, and he never lacked for things to do or places to go. He flew us to London just to go to a rock concert. We went to Broadway and movie premieres, fancy nightclubs, and horse races. He always seemed to know all the right people. He always knew how to have a good time. But then everything changed."

"He stopped being generous to you? Isn't it true that he took you to Hollywood movie premieres and the boxing heavyweight 'Fight of the Century'—front-row seats at Madison Square Garden—very shortly before you broke off with him?"

"Yes."

"Didn't he give you free access to his private jet to use whenever you wanted? And didn't he do so the very night you jumped out of a hotel room window?"

"Yes."

"Ze'evi must be such a horrible person then! Isn't it true that you used him because you felt that you could get things from him that you couldn't get anywhere else, your father being a. . ." Bronfman turned around. "What did you call him, Ze'evi? Ah, yes! A government functionary."

A loud murmur arose from the Israelis in the gallery. Dahlia tried to avert her eyes from her father, but she was unsuccessful. He stared directly at her, not revealing the emotions that were swirling inside him. He knew that he had had a major hand in this whole mess. He realized now that he had put Dahlia into this situation and that he would have to reap the whirlwind of having done that. He wished that they could go back to that bright, sunny day in Herzliya when his golden girl had won the tennis championship and had gone up on the stage to accept her trophy.

Howard and Michelle Ehrenreich stared at Dahlia, also seemingly without emotion. Inside, however, they both were being torn to pieces. They had known that Ze'evi's life had been spinning out of control for the past two years. They had hoped that his liaison with Dahlia, a fine, quiet girl from a good upbringing, would settle him down. They were fond of Dahlia, and they felt awful about how the affair had turned out. They were ashamed of their son's behavior, and they knew that the whole sordid business had been Ze'evi's doing. Howard resolved that he would not let this matter change his attitude toward Israel. Supporting Israel was a separate matter.

The judge pounded his gavel. "Order! Order!"

Dahlia fought to maintain her composure. She shook with fear and rage. This was what Mr. Jacobowitz had explained outside the courtroom that morning.

She looked over at Ze'evi, who was sporting his characteristic Cheshire cat smile. She quickly averted her gaze.

"I was his girlfriend, and I never asked him for anything. In fact, I tried to discourage him from giving me anything, but he kept on insisting that I accept gifts from him. Every time we met, he came with something else—diamond tennis bracelets, platinum earrings, Swiss watches, necklaces. I didn't want any of it."

"Poor thing. I'm sure that you never insisted on returning the gifts once you received them."

"I tried, but he would never take them back. I wasn't brought up to value vast quantities of possessions. We were always comfortable but never rich, and I was fine with that."

Leah smiled sadly at Dahlia and caught her eye.

"But then everything changed," Dahlia added.

"Did there ever come a time when Mr. Ehrenreich forced you to take cocaine or any other narcotics?"

"He never physically forced me, but he was very manipulative and he seduced me to take the drugs, just like he used me as a sex toy. He constantly told me that he loved me, and I was stupid enough to believe him. I wanted to believe him. I now realize that I was nothing more than a plaything to him, just like all of the other playthings he had. My innocence was a challenge to him, and he couldn't wait until I was eighteen, so that he could rob me of it on my birthday. He told me that he would turn me into a real woman and show me the ways of amour."

Leah wept loudly. Benny held her tightly.

"Why did you fly to Las Vegas on the night of April 27th?" Bronfman asked.

"Because he promised me that we would elope there, at one of those love chapels. He said something about an Elvis-impersonator justice of the peace marrying us."

Leah and Benny were stunned.

"So, he provided his own private plane to get you there?"

Dahlia nodded.

"I'm sorry. I didn't hear you, Miss Gilad."

"Yes! He sent his private plane to fetch me!" Dahlia said testily.

"At your seat, was there a compartment that you may have opened?"

"I'm sorry. I don't know what you mean."

"Did you open any compartments at your seat?"

"Yes."

"What was in there?"

"Drugs."

"What sort of drugs? Aspirin?"

"Cocaine, amphetamines, Quaaludes, LSD, reefer. All arranged in neat compartments with symbols on each drawer. He was very organized, I'll grant him that."

"So, you knew what was in each compartment?"

"Yes."

"The flight manifest says that there were three other people on that flight—the pilot, the copilot, and the chef. Is that correct?"

"Yes."

"Was there anyone in your part of the plane during the flight?"

"No. After Patrice served the meal, he cleared up and disappeared into the cockpit."

"Where is this going, counselor?" Judge Sullivan asked with a frown.

"I'm trying to establish foundation, Your Honor," Bronfman said.

"I'm only going to let this go on for short while longer, so get to the point," Judge Sullivan said.

Bronfman turned to Dahlia.

"If you were in the cabin by yourself, nobody coerced you or seduced you to take the drugs in the compartment. Isn't that so?"

"Yes."

"You had already turned eighteen? You said as much earlier in your testimony."

"Yes."

"Do you understand why Mr. Ehrenreich waited until you were eighteen to have sexual relations with you?"

"Yes, because I was a minor until then."

"And afterward you were old enough to make decisions for yourself, legally I mean?"

"Yes."

"Do you understand, young lady, that to be old enough means that you have to take responsibility for your actions?"

"Yes."

"So, you made an independent decision to take the drugs, without anyone there to coerce you?"

"I was addicted by then. I couldn't help myself! I needed those drugs!" Dahlia cried out.

"Isn't it true that you repeatedly asked Mr. Ehrenreich, on many occasions, to provide you with narcotics, because you couldn't afford to get them on your own?"

"Yes."

"It doesn't sound like coercion to me. Does it to you?"

"He coerced me in the beginning, and then I became addicted."

Judge Sullivan said, "Counselors, approach the bench!"

Bronfman and Simpson walked up to the bench. The three men's voices were drowned out by a loud hissing sound that was coming from a white noise generator on the floor near the witness box.

There was a long pause. Dahlia stared at the members of the jury, who were quietly scribbling on their notepads.

As soon as the judge was finished with the attorneys, Bronfman approached the witness box. He looked at Dahlia and then said, "Addicts would do anything to feed their habits. Wouldn't you agree?"

"Some do."

"Even sleep with numerous men?"

"Objection, Your Honor! Baiting the Witness!" the district attorney shouted.

"Sustained." Judge Sullivan looked at Bronfman. "What is the purpose of this?" he asked.

"I'm trying to establish the fact that the film taken in Las Vegas portrayed a consensual sexual situation between grown adults, legal in Nevada! All of the apparent struggle portrayed on the film was just an act."

"Make it short!"

"Isn't it true that you had had sexual relations with every man in that room, during the two months prior to the making of the film?"

Leah fainted and had to be removed from the courtroom to receive medical attention. Dahlia began sobbing uncontrollably. She was still sobbing when she answered.

"Ze'evi ruined me! He ruined me. I was in love with another man, my Arik! We were supposed to be married. But he disappeared into thin air, and I was left emotionally destitute and vulnerable. I was easy prey for that, that . . ."

She pointed at Ze'evi, who was still smiling at her. "That sociopathic predator! He organized a sex-orgy weekend without telling me and broke me in by setting me up to have what he called potluck sex with numerous partners, in the dark. I was groped and violated for hours. He coerced me into going into his playroom with him for sadomasochistic sex sessions. I had no idea what I was getting into—none whatsoever!" She bared her upper arms, revealing scars on the back of them.

Loud murmurs rippled throughout the court. Sullivan pounded his gavel.

Bronfman looked gravely at Dahlia. He picked up a folder.

"These are Miss Gilad's medical records from Southern Nevada Memorial Hospital in Las Vegas."

He laid the folder open in front of Dahlia.

"Would you care to read this paragraph from the record from the emergency department, written by a Dr. Edwards, a board-certified doctor in this State of Nevada?" He pointed to the desired paragraph.

Dahlia read, "This eighteen-year-old woman brought in by emergency medical service in florid manic psychosis—"

"Do you know what psychosis means?"

"Crazy?"

"It means completely out of touch with reality. Wouldn't you agree?"

"Yes."

"Are you under psychiatric care now? Are you taking psychiatric medications now?"

"Yes."

"As someone out of touch with reality, requiring psychiatric care and medications, do you consider yourself a reasonable person to act as a material witness in a state criminal proceeding? Your testimony could have unfathomable consequences for Mr. Ehrenreich. He could be sent to prison for many years, based on what you may say. Doesn't that strike you as a bit absurd?"

Ze'evi smiled broadly. Dahlia could well imagine that he was thinking, That Bronfman is worth every penny.

Dahlia looked down, dejected. But something inside her stirred—a rising tide of anger, a flame that shot out from the inner hell that had possessed her soul. What would Arik say or do at a time like this? This is the time to rise or fall. It's now or never. What I say now will determine who I become as a person. I'll slam the door on the past year and charge ahead into the future! Dahlia had had enough. She stared at Penny, who was looking at her teary-eyed but expectantly. Penny's eyes seemed to be screaming, "You can do it, Paapi! Do it now. Do it now!"

Leah, although in a cold sweat, had been helped back into the courtroom. She was sitting in the back of the gallery, trembling and with her arms folded over her chest.

Dahlia spoke slowly, staring directly at the jury. "I was psychotic when I arrived at the hospital, that's true, but that was due to the chemicals that I had ingested, drugs that Ze'evi made available to me, drugs that he introduced me to. My attorney, Mr. Jacobowitz, explained to me that there is a legal term for it.

It's called the Svengali effect. I was under the trance of an extremely shrewd and manipulative predator, who made me do unspeakable acts, things that I never knew people were capable of. I fell into his spider's web and was nearly eaten by him. He tricked me into coming to Las Vegas to star in his porno film. When I refused, he and his friends tried to rape me, on camera—"

Bronfman interrupted her. "Miss Gilad, you aren't answering my question!"

"Bronfman, for God's sake," Judge Sullivan said, "let the girl speak! I want to hear what she has to say." He looked down at Dahlia and smiled. "Dahlia, please continue."

"I-I jumped from the balcony, to get away from those animals. Jumping into the street, frightened out of my mind, half naked doesn't appear to me to be evidence of a consensual sex act. I never had sex with those other men individually—just as part of that sex party that Ze'evi organized and coerced me to take part in. Even assuming that I had wanted at any time to have sex with any of those men, which I did not, that doesn't mean that I wanted to have sex with them that night at the hotel. If I didn't then and was forced to, that's rape, plain and simple, any way you slice it!"

There was loud applause. The jurors were nodding.

"I was psychotic that night, but I'm not now. And I'm happy to submit to any psychological testing you want to put me through. Dr. Baker, my psychiatrist, and Dr. Stevens, my psychologist—from my rehab center—are also board certified, and they've determined that I have no underlying psychosis, that any mental disturbances came from the drugs, which are now out of my body and will never return. I am a credible witness. I'm not here to determine Ze'evi's fate. The criminal justice system will decide that. I'm simply here to tell you my story and let the chips fall where they may."

"No further questions, Your Honor."

Dahlia left the witness box, the jury filed out of the courtroom, and the court adjourned for the day.

Dahlia jumped into her mother's arms. "Imma, I'm back! I'll never disappoint you again."

"You did a wonderful job in there, Dahlia," Jacobowitz said, beaming. "The DA will definitely get his verdict against Mr. Ehrenreich. Then we'll have to see what happens in federal court. You may still have to testify there."

"I'm due to go into the army right after Sukkot. How would that work?"

Dahlia looked at her father, who looked back at her with pride evident in her face.

"Don't worry about that, chamuda," Benny said. "I've already briefed Dayan about the situation, and he'll arrange your time off in such a way that you can fly to the States, testify, and then return to your unit. It will be a grueling schedule for you, but you'll have no choice. Are you ready?"

"I am, Abba. I am." Dahlia felt finally that she was ready for anything.

***

The day after Yom Kippur, Dahlia and her parents met with Mr. Jacobowitz at his office on K Street in downtown Washington, D.C.

Mr. Jacobowitz said, "It's unfortunate that the whole sordid affair made it into the Israeli papers, after the closed grand jury proceedings when the matter made it into open court. But, as I told you, a drug and sex scandal that involves the daughter of the Israeli ambassador and the son of a rich American donor makes sensational news. The newspapers are in the business of selling papers. Of course, that doesn't help us. In fact, the longer this case goes on, the worse it is for everyone concerned. I've been in touch with the Ehrenreichs' attorneys, and apparently they also want this whole thing to go away as soon as possible. Ze'evi has been found guilty of attempted rape and two counts of aggravated assault. They're going to try to plea bargain on the federal charges. They know Ze'evi will be looking at more than fifteen years behind bars if everything goes to trial, even though this is a first offense. His henchmen have been turned by the federal prosecutors. In return for immunity, they've decided to testify against him. His charges are piling up—not only for possession but also for selling and distributing narcotics. This can work for us. I've been in touch with the feds and we have reached a deal. As part of his plea agreement, Ze'evi will have to make a public statement clearing Dahlia of all wrongdoing. He will do that at a press conference that will include the Israeli media, and he'll say that he coerced her to take the drugs and publicly apologize to her for the attempted rape."

"Why would he do all of that?" Benny asked.

"With a plea bargain and a first offense, he could get less than eight years total and then be eligible for parole. The U.S. attorney isn't interested in ruining your lives. The feds see Dahlia as an innocent victim who has suffered enough already, and they want to mitigate the damage against you. Ze'evi making a public statement like that will go a long way in rehabilitating the reputation of not just Dahlia but your whole family. I've been working with the U.S. attorney's office to make sure that Ze'evi's public confession is a precondition to the plea bargain. In addition, Ze'evi's parents, I'm told, are pressuring him to go through with it. They've threatened to cut him off without a penny. Apparently, they believe Dahlia over their own son. In addition, they themselves are being pressured by unnamed sources, rumor has it."

Dahlia and her parents looked one another and breathed a collective sigh of relief. The color in Dahlia's face, which had been gone for so long, began to return.

***

Although it was early October, the hot sun beat down on the raucous crowd at the induction center outside Tel Aviv. A large Quonset hut was serving as a registration area for the new batch of recruits who were standing in the dusty desert wind. Beside the hut was a long line of light-green buses. Surrounding them were ice cream, newspaper, soda, and falafel vendors hawking their wares.

"Haalo, Haalo. Artic, Artic!"

"Kaasata, Kaasata. Lux Kaasata! Belirah, Belirah!"

"Maariv, Yedioth! Haalo! Maariv, Maariv!"

Loud, emotional good-byes punctuated by hugs, tears, and kisses from family members accompanied the recruits as they made their way to the buses. Dahlia stood quietly with her parents and surveyed the scene.

She had been here fifteen months earlier, with Arik, seeing him off. How strong, tall, and confident she had been. Everything had seemed so bright, so full of hope and expectation . . . only to be shattered to pieces so soon thereafter and in so many unexpected ways. Now, her frame was gaunt and she was fearful of what the future might bring. Am I strong enough to withstand the rigors of tironut? She knew that basic training was not a supportive environment. Not much in Israel was touchy-feely, and the army was the very last place that she would find that anyway. She also knew that the sense of superiority that she had felt toward Israel and Israelis only four months earlier was illusory. Now that she had returned to Israel with her tail between her legs, she would have to prove herself worthy of the uniform or at least survive the training.

Am I ready? She had no idea.

Leah looked deeply into Dahlia's eyes. "Are you ready, booba?"

"Yes, Imma. Definitely!" Dahlia smiled at her parents as she boarded the bus.

"Mikki, are you off tomorrow evening?" her father asked.

"No, but I can be. Things are somewhat quiet right now, so I can take off for a few hours. What's up?"

"Do you remember Uri Shalev? He was my staff officer during the Six-Day War."

"Of course. I used to babysit for his kids. I was particularly close with their oldest daughter, Sarit. I haven't seen them in years. It's like they dropped off the face of the earth. Where have they been?"

"They've just returned from three years in the U.S. His wife, Shulamit, is a physician. She did a medical fellowship in New York, at Mount Sinai Hospital, while he was an emissary for Bnei Akiva. They're coming for dinner, with the kids, and they'd love to see you. Can you come?"

"Sounds like fun. You know I always look for an excuse to eat Imma's gourmet meals!"

When she arrived at her family's home the next evening, she noticed that Uri looked the same except that he had put on some weight and his large handlebar mustache had grayed slightly. Sarit, all grown up, had graduated from high school and was just starting the army. She still was as cute as a button, though, and she was delighted to see Mikki.

Yael had chosen French cuisine as the theme for the evening and paired each dish with the appropriate wine. The food was practically inhaled by everyone.

"So, Uri, what did you do in the States?" Yael asked.

"While Shulamit worked in the hospital I worked on the Aliyah Project. It's a tough sell. Jews generally want to go on Aliyah to live in Israel when they're under stress. Jews in the States are mostly very well off, though, so most have little motivation to move to Israel. They like their comfortable lives in the States, and they're not ready for what would await them here. Most things are so much easier there. Life is softer there, but there are things that we can learn from them to make our lives here easier. I think that we overcomplicate things here, with our bureaucracy. So, it can be a hard sell, getting people to want to come here.

"During the school year, I worked with the Board of Jewish Education in New York to maximize Israel and Zionist studies in Jewish school curriculums. During the summer, I taught Ivrit and Zionism at a Bnei Akiva camp in Pennsylvania. It's like an Israel in miniature, and I found that these kids were most likely to make Aliyah, so I felt that I could have the greatest impact there."

Mikki's ears perked up. "What was the name of the camp?"

"Moshava."

"Were you there the summer before last?" Mikki asked.

"Yes. Why do you ask?"

"I know someone who may have been there then."

"Oh, who?"

"Arik Meir."

Shmulik and Yael stared at Mikki intently.

"As a matter of fact, he was. He's an interesting fellow. Most of the American boys are as soft as their parents. They wouldn't last a week in Tzahal. Now, Arik was a beast, tough as nails. He was extremely strong and athletic." Uri laughed. "When he first arrived, I got mad at him for something trivial and tried to embarrass him by making him do push-ups in front of everyone. Most of the other campers couldn't do ten. I gave up after he did fifty. He could have done them for a week. He was the nicest fellow, though—kind and considerate. He was a wonderful basketball coach with the small kids and also helped with construction projects.

"Yes, he has a special gift for basketball! That can certainly be said. In a major basketball game against another camp, he took over the game and beat the other team almost single-handedly. He even played against a guest kushi professional basketball player from Los Angeles and nearly beat him. It was astonishing to watch. I think that he was offered a scholarship to play college basketball for a championship team in California. I never saw him again after that summer, so I suppose that he accepted that offer and is playing for them—"

"He's here in Israel, serving in an elite Sayeret brigade. He's being considered for the officer's training program," Mikki said proudly. "He walked away from that scholarship offer, to come here."

Shmulik added, "In fact, he's a ben bayit. He practically lives here."

Uri smiled. "Arik in Sayeret? I pity the Arabs. Good luck to them."

"He has already distinguished himself and has gotten noticed by some in the general staff," Shmulik said. He proceeded to tell Uri what was now referred to as the tachat story, to everyone's raucous amusement.

"Tell me. Did Arik have a girlfriend while he was at camp?" Mikki asked.

Shmulik and Yael shot her a knowing look.

"It's funny that you should ask," Uri said. "He dated Benny Gilad's daughter, Dahlia. You know that they're still in Washington? I had dealings with Benny. I don't know what ever became of that. Probably nothing. She finished high school and was supposed to return here to begin her tironut in July, but she got herself involved with the whole mess reported in the papers and had to delay her enlistment. She's just starting now, I believe."

"She was the prettiest girl in camp but a bit of a snob. She was in my shevet," Sarit said.

"You know . . . rumor has it that Benny is slated to become foreign minister when he finishes up his stint as ambassador . . ." Shmulik said, apparently trying to take the conversation in a new direction.

Meanwhile, Mikki was sitting quietly, the wheels in her mind turning. She now knew who Arik's mystery girl was. She had never met Dahlia Gilad, but she had heard people say that she was a pampered tennis brat. Like everyone else, Mikki had been following the whole scandal in the Maariv newspaper. She wondered how Arik ever could have fallen in with Dahlia and what he had seen in her. She knew that he had been lonely when he met Dahlia. Mikki decided that she would find out where Dahlia was doing her tironut and make her sorry that she had ever been born. Mikki had an excellent working relationship with every base commander in Tzahal. It would take her only minutes to locate Dahlia.

After the guests left, Shmulik called Mikki in to the library.

"Mikki, I saw your face when Uri talked about Arik. And I saw your face change when he mentioned Dahlia. Nobody on earth knows you better than your Abba, and I know what you're thinking. Please, don't do what I think you're going to do. I know what you're capable of. When you're on a mission, you are a tigress, and heaven help the person that gets inside your jaws."

Mikki smiled. "I have no idea what you're talking about, Abba, but if I did I'd never do anything that you wouldn't want me to do. You know that."

Smiling, Shmulik shook his head. "Speaking of Arik," he said, "I found out something about him that you should know." He pulled out a worn, gray-covered dossier. "I don't know if it makes a difference to you." He handed the folder to her. "Ze'ev Myerowitz is Arik's father."

Mikki thumbed through the folder. "Whoa! He was an Irgun terrorist? He was the senior officer in command of the Irgun and Stern Gang unit that committed the atrocities at Deir Yassin. It says here that he lost his leg on the Altalena when it was shelled. Arik keeps insisting that his father is a Haganah hero who lost his leg saving a busload of his comrades during the battle for Kastel. We visited Kastel together, and Arik gave me a detailed account of the battle and where his father lost his leg. And I kept going on and on about how the Irgun were nothing more than a band of worthless thugs and criminals. Whoops! Well, either Arik knows the truth about his father but is too ashamed to say it or his parents have kept everything from him. Poor thing. This explains why his father never got any invalid compensation after the war! Arik keeps insisting that he'll clear his father's name and get him the recognition and money that he deserves."

"Does this change your feelings for him?" Shmulik asked.

"Absolutely not! Not one bit. I don't believe that children should be punished for the sins of their parents. Arik's life has been a living hell. Now, at least, I know why. He has suffered enough and through no fault of his own. I'm in love with him, Abba, and I believe I have what it takes to help him heal."

Shmulik beamed at her. "Mikki, I'm so glad that you're saying this. I was hoping that you would feel this way. Your Imma and I raised a good girl. We're very fond of him, too. Arik's best trait is his basic humanity and decency. You do know how to pick them! We were unsure of what you'd do after Elisha's death. We have the feeling that you scare men away."

"Why would you say that?"

"You're beautiful, fit, tough-minded, and accomplished. I know that many men are intimidated by you."

"Then, let them be. The right one for me would never be intimidated or anything else."

"So, do you think that Arik is that one?"

"I do."

"He's not intimidated by you?"

"Don't be silly. Of course not! I'm struggling for his affection. He was so wounded by this Dahlia character that he's afraid to jump into something new. But I know that he has serious feelings for me."

"Metuka sheli, give him time. Arik is worth it. He's a wonderful fellow, and I think that he would be very good for you."

"I agree. Laila tov, Abba. Good night!"

Tzrifin was the site of a massive basic training base just outside Rishon LeZion in central Israel. Through it pass thousands of trainees making the transition from civilian life to army life. From the general pool of trainees, individuals are singled out for specialized training as infantry, tank personnel, paratroopers, and even medics and clergy. Those who are not considered fit for advanced combat training, due to physical, intellectual, or attitude deficiencies, are designated for support roles, such as drivers, cooks, and clerical personnel. Those were the lowest beasts on the military totem pole—the jobnickim. The length of a recruit's basic training also varies based on the track to which he or she was assigned.

One bright October morning, a fresh batch of recruits were starting their third week of basic training. Two command cars pulled up in front of the administration office at Tzrifin base. Lieutenant Colonel Mikki Zohar walked into the office, followed by her staff of junior officers. The soldiers in the front office stood, snapped to attention, and saluted.

"At ease, chevre. I'm here to see Major Lior Kramer, bevakasha."

"Major Kramer is expecting you. He asked that you wait for him in his office. Right this way, please, Colonel. May I get you a cup of coffee?"

"Lo todah. No thanks, not for me. Perhaps my staff would like some."

When Kramer entered his office, he said, "Boker tov, Mikki. Ma nishma? How are you? Why are you guys snooping around here for talent so early in the training cycle? It's too early to tell who might be good and who won't. You know that. So, how can I be of service to you?"

"Precisely, Lior. Times are changing, and our enemies are getting more cunning. I don't need to tell you what you can read in the newspapers. Between the War of Attrition on the Canal, Fedayeen infiltrations in the Jordan Valley, and attacks on our assets overseas, we're facing a multifaceted threat matrix, and I need to recruit larger numbers of personnel earlier in the process. I sit on A'man's central committee, and we've come up with criteria so that candidates can be vetted more efficiently. We've come up with means by which even junior officers can detect—even early in basic training—the types of special talent that will be useful to us. I really don't want to disrupt your training schedule, but my staff can impart those criteria to your junior officers—your lieutenants and captains—within three hours, and then they will be able to manage this with less time expenditure and better results than what is currently employed."

"Is your staff ready to go now if I can assemble my officers?" Lior asked. "Do you have all of your materials?"

Mikki smiled. "Lior, how long have you known me? Of course, I do. Give us a meeting room, coffee, and bourekas, and we'll get started."

Mikki gave the members of her staff their orders and assignments, and then they were led away. Mikki stayed on with Lior.

"So, Mikki, ma inyanim? What's up with you? How's Opher doing? I haven't seen him since induction."

"Opher's fine, but what he tells me really worries me. He's been doing reconnaissance fights over the Canal, and he's constantly being locked on by radar from increasingly sophisticated Soviet surface-to-air missile systems. We've lost several planes over the Canal in recent months. I'm really afraid for him, to be frank."

"Sounds like we're going to need more help from the Americans. I hope our diplomats in Washington aren't asleep at their posts." Lior sighed.

"Speaking of which, do you have a recruit named Dahlia Gilad?"

"Yes, the ambassador's daughter. Don't tell me you think that she would be a good intelligence candidate?" Lior shook his head.

"No, of course not, but why do you say it that way?"

"Because I think she's got a few screws loose," Lior said. "You've read about her in the papers, right? She's a real piece of work, that one, getting involved in that whole mess with that billionaire playboy. What a soap opera! She's spent too much time in the States, being a pampered kitten, and completely forgotten how to be an Israeli."

"Anyway . . . can you point her out to me? We have a common acquaintance."

"Sure! They're due to assemble for inspection in ten minutes. I'm going out to review them, and you can tag along."

"Show me who she is, but be discreet about it."

The area where the new recruits were housed consisted of neat rows of green and khaki tents. In front of each unit stood lines of freshly minted soldiers that Mikki thought of as no more than kids. There were dressed in worn, poorly fitting fatigues called dagmachim. The men had shaved heads, and the women had their hair tied up in tight buns. They were standing rigidly at attention.

Major Lior looked out at the assembled rows, which were divided into kitot, or squads. He turned to Mikki and said quietly, "Take a look at Kita Daled, front row, second from the left, the skinny blonde girl. That's her."

"Are you quite certain?"

"Yes."

As Lior and Mikki walked by that particular row during his inspection of the squad, Mikki stopped in front of Dahlia and took an appraising, hard look at her through her sunglasses. Dahlia, thin and pale, was wearing a worn, rumpled uniform two sizes too big for her and staring blankly into space. Mikki struggled to figure out what he had seen in her, to reconcile this pathetic creature with the Miss America that Arik had described. She wondered how such a worthless rag could have locked up his heart to such an extent that she had nearly destroyed his life. Mikki could have lifted her off the ground by clutching her throat with just one hand. She wanted to.

In Mikki's opinion, the emotional price that Arik had paid was too high to go unpunished. She had vowed to see to that. If not for Dahlia, Mikki's relationship with Arik would have been progressed quite nicely rather than being tortured as it had been since they met.

"You're a martial artist, as I recall?" Lior said, bringing Mikki back from her musing. They continued down the ranks.

"You remember correctly. First-degree black belt in karate and Krav Maga."

"Then, you may be interested in what we have to show the recruits this morning." Lior smiled. "There are many new things being introduced into the army. There was a sense among the generals that hand-to-hand combat training in Tzahal was much too haphazard and uneven, so they asked the top two martial artists in the country to come up with a detailed Krav Maga curriculum that will carry recruits through from basic training all the way into the commando program. It's extremely well done. I've seen it in its entirety. It runs for about two hours in total, but we'll only show them module one today."

"Who did this? Shuki Baum?"

"No, Shuki's gone. He was the big shot . . . until he got into the ring with some new paratrooper, who not only thrashed him in under twenty seconds but inflicted such devastating injuries that he's been permanently disabled. Interestingly, the guy who did that to him stars in this film, along with Oren Shemer."

"I know Oren," Mikki said. He's a very nice guy. Who's the paratrooper?"

"That's what's so strange. They won't release his name. It's crazy. Something about security. Nobody knows. So, we just call him Hercules." Lior laughed.

"Now you have my interest. Why do you call him that?"

"No need to explain. Come in and watch the film, and you'll see for yourself."

The assembly hall quickly filled with several hundred new recruits. Mikki stood off to one side. She noticed where Dahlia sat, in the center of the second row from the front.

The sergeant introduced the film. "Okay, everyone settle down. It's movie time here in our resort. Tzahal has now begun to standardize Krav Maga training. Your instructors have already completed and mastered the course. The point is of this course if for you to come back from the front via tremp and not in a body bag. Now, you may be thinking, 'Why would I want to sit through a boring training film.' Right? Well, prepare to be entertained. The instructors are the two top Krav Maga experts in the country. These fellows are real eye candy, too, so girls, enjoy yourselves, and guys, eat your hearts out."

There was general laughter as the lights went out.

Mikki's jaw dropped when the two instructors on the screen began their introduction of the course. Their skin oiled, they both were stripped to the waist, clad in black and red linen pants, and sporting thick black belts around their waists. After the introduction, they engaged in a full-fledged mock bout to demonstrate the full effect of the techniques that they would break down and teach later in the course. They looked like Greek gods locked in mortal combat. They displayed the techniques in real time, which for them was lightning speed.

"These guys look like Bruce Lee!" someone in the audience said. "How are we ever going to be able to do this?"

The sergeant bellowed, "You will learn this bit by bit. They are great instructors. This beginning is just to show you how it looks when it's done correctly."

Mikki felt as if she were crawling out of her skin. Arik had never told her about his fight with Shuki Baum. She also wondered why Arik had not told her that he had produced such a film. And she wondered when he had filmed it. She could not imagine that he would have been capable of doing it before he went to the States, before he had met her and her family. He seemed calm and relaxed in the film, so he must have known her by the time he filmed it. But he had never mentioned it. His modesty still surprised her. She felt an overwhelming rush of affection toward the Hercules, her Hercules, on the screen. But she wondered whether he really was hers. She suddenly remembered Dahlia. She glanced at the gaunt recruit in the second row. Dahlia was looking down, hands on her forehead, eyes averted from the screen.

Mikki thought that any small discomfort that Dahlia was feeling at seeing Arik on screen served her right.

"Dahlia Gilad, is all this boring you?" the sergeant bellowed. "Have you already mastered these techniques? Why aren't you looking at the screen? Even a little jobnickit like you will need to have some knowledge of self-defense."

He paused the film.

The room erupted in laughter as Dahlia sat up. She looked mortified. There were catcalls of "American!" and "Mefuneket!" (Spoiled brat!).

"See what I told you?" Lior said.

"She clearly hasn't made many friends here," Mikki said.

"From the moment she got here, she has been showing off about all the places she had been to and the things she has done—private planes, ski trips to Switzerland, meeting movie stars, and what have you. She brought enough clothing for a battalion. It's not a great way to make friends, especially among the recruits coming from poor Yemenite and Moroccan families who can't put bread on the table. They all recognized her from the papers. Where she comes from isn't her fault, but rule number one in basic training is to keep your mouth shut and your head down, especially with her history. Her corporal told me that during the first week she stuffed her locker with ten pairs of French lace underpants. When she emerged from the shower one morning, they were all gone, and then over next few days she began to notice that her whole plugah was wearing the prettiest knickers in the company. It would really be funny if it wasn't so pathetic. She always seems to be a step behind everyone else, whether in hikes, obstacle courses, or on the shooting range. Working in a team, she holds everyone back. She's never on time. As you know, recruits aren't very tolerant. She has already been the butt of some other nasty pranks."

Mikki nodded. "This is a big problem for you, Lior. A person like this can really hurt team cohesion. I don't need to tell you how destructive someone like this can be for a unit. This girl has to be brought down to earth, hard and in a hurry. I'd show this little princess no mercy. She needs to learn quickly how real life works. It'll do her some good."

"I couldn't agree with you more. My sergeants are experts in attitude adjustment for troublesome new recruits. Let's just say . . . measures are being implemented." Lior smiled.

Mikki fought to keep a smile off her own face. She could not have paid for a better performance both on and off screen. She decided that she would never breathe a word about today's events to Arik.

***

About a week later, Mikki picked up Dani and Arik from their base in the Sinai so that they could spend three days sailing and dancing in Tel Aviv with her friends, many of whom she had known since her Gadna scout days in high school.

Most of Mikki's friends had met or heard of Arik, and he was very well received into the crowd during the visit. The festivities culminated at the José Feliciano concert in Ramat Gan on Thursday night.

They walked out of the concert and into the fresh night air to Dani's car en route to his favorite steakhouse in Tel Aviv.

"So, big shot, why didn't you tell me anything about the film you made?" Mikki asked Arik. "It's quite a hit with the recruits, especially the female ones."

"What's to tell? They asked Oren and me to make an instructional film about hand-to-hand combat, so we did it. No big deal."

"Why didn't you tell me that it was you who thrashed Shuki Baum? He was the best of the best!"

"I didn't pick that fight. It was just thrust on me. I did what I had to do to defend myself. I wasn't trying to prove anything to anyone. I just wanted to forget it ever happened."

"Your modesty can be really annoying sometimes," Mikki said.

"I don't understand boasting. What does it get me?"

"Well, anyway, you're pretty good at fighting. You know that?"

"Thanks."

"I'm pretty good at Krav Maga myself. Perhaps we should spar sometime," Mikki said, grabbing Arik by his elbow.

"Have you lost your mind, Mikki?" Dani said. "Zeh meod mesukan! It's very dangerous. Even if you're just fooling around, accidents can happen. I don't want to see you get hurt."

"I think he's right, Mikki. We shouldn't do that," Arik said, grabbing her hand and kissing it.

"How about . . ." Mikki whispered into Arik's ear, "if we both started out dressed the way you and Oren were in the film? And then we go on from there."

"Now, that's an unfair advantage." Arik smiled. "I'd lose for sure."

Mikki looked at Arik with a curious expression and said, "And I would win."

Chapter 14

"Arik, I hope that you haven't made any plans for Sukkot. You have forty-eight hours off," Mikki said.

"You know me—the social animal. I've been fending off invitations all week."

"Okay. I'll come get you at the usual time, then."

"That won't be necessary. I have a surprise for you. I'll pick you up at Ramon," Arik said.

"What kind of car did you get?"

"Well, it's not exactly a car . . . I got a Harley FX Super Glide, 1200 cc. Eran's brother sells used bikes, and he gave me a great deal. It runs like a dream."

"I hope that you won't try to kill yourself on it again."

"I don't have any reason to anymore. Besides, you'll love it. I feel like Peter Fonda on it."

"I don't like how that movie ended."

"Not this time. Besides, I got us both helmets."

***

Mikki spent every second of the 120-kilometer trip from Ramon to Beersheba in a panic, uncertain whether Arik's skill in handling such a powerful motorcycle was equal to the speed at which they were going. Not that she minded one bit holding on to him for dear life. That was the only good part. She was just glad that they reached her family's house with each of them still in one piece.

"Well, metuka, what do you think? She rides like a dream, huh?" Arik said.

"As long as the dream doesn't turn into a nightmare. I don't get frightened often, but I was today."

"Wow, I finally got the better of you!" Arik smiled.

"You always have the better of me." Mikki kissed him on the cheek. "My brothers have been home for a day already, and they were supposed to put up the Sukkah, so all we have to do is sit and eat."

"I actually like building them. I'm good with my hands, you know."

"I'll be the judge of that." Mikki smirked.

Arik blushed.

"Seriously, Mikki, I built one in Washington when I was with Dahlia's family. I saved their hides at the last minute. Their builders deserted them the morning before the chag, so I put up a Sukkah for twenty-five people in four hours. Fully decorated. They were obviously profuse in their thanks to me," he said sourly.

"Arik, in my house we don't keep score on who did this or that. Stuff just gets done by whoever happens to be around. So, just take a deep breath and relax. We have special guests joining us for the meal. He's your namesake. My father served under his command in the '56 and '67 wars. He's a bona fide

Israeli legend but the sweetest man you could ever meet, so unlike his public persona. My father and he have become close confidants over the years."

When Arik walked into the house, he was taken aback by the powerful aromas emanating from the kitchen. His nose seemed twisted into knots by the mélange of saffron, zaatar, cumin, truffle oil, roast lamb, couscous, and schug.

"What is that smell coming from the kitchen?" he whispered to Mikki.

"Do you mean the tribe of Bedouins that just invaded the house?" Mikki laughed. "It's my mother's specialty. My father grew up in the desert and spent a great deal of time in Bedouin tents, bribing, cajoling, making friends and alliances, and settling scores over the years. It is said that his efforts over thirty years are, in large part, responsible for the Bedouins becoming good, loyal citizens of Israel rather than a potential fifth column like other Arab communities. During his travels, he has had to eat with them, bending the kosher laws when needed. His activities have saved many lives here in the south of the country . . And he developed a real taste for their cuisine, so my mother had to quickly add that to her culinary repertoire. Amazing, isn't she?"

"You're in for a treat. Come, let me show you something." She took his hand and led him out to the back courtyard.

Most of the Spanish courtyard had been transformed into a gigantic Bedouin tent replete with plush Persian rugs and ornate cushions, mahogany standing trays, copper tea service, and incense and oil lamps. The mock tent was cut away at the top, revealing a thatched cover.

"For our Sukkot meals, we sit on the cushions and eat with our hands, off gigantic trays, with lafa breads, like Bedouins do. We have to pick our guests carefully, because this isn't for everyone . . . especially those folks who come here expecting a formal holiday meal. I tell them to come back at Pesach."

"Actually," Arik said, "you're doing it the right way. Isn't this what the Sukkot holiday is all about? Trying to reproduce how our forefathers in the desert ate and lived. They certainly didn't live in rectangular fiberglass boxes topped by bamboo poles that they would have to carry around for forty years—even though they're technically kosher to sit in. Most people can't stand storing that stuff in a garage all year round. I can tell you that 99 percent of the rabbis who made up all these rules never actually set foot in the Sinai."

She leaned over and kissed him on the cheek. "My, my! I'm dating a Yeshivnik! Who would have believed it of me?" She smiled.

Arik, Dani, and his brothers went off to shul. When they returned, they were greeted by their guests, who were enjoying iced tumblers of single malt Scotch.

"Arik," Shmulik said, "I want you to meet Mikki's chaver, also named Arik."

Arik reached over and shook General Sharon's hand.

"Naim meod. I'm honored, sir."

"This is my wife, Lily, and my sons, Gur and Omri."

"Very nice to meet you all," Arik said as he shook hands with them.

Arik wondered how a man so powerfully built, whose lined, smiling face appeared, like Shmulik's, to have been sandblasted by years spent in the field, had such a soft handshake. He saw in General Sharon's eyes great depth and honest wisdom that touched him immediately. Arik was very taken with Sharon. He suddenly thought it strange that Shmulik had so casually called him Mikki's chaver, boyfriend, as if it were a given. Did Mikki tell her parents I'm her boyfriend? Or is it wishful thinking on Shmulik's part? Arik could not guess. What was clear to him, though, was that the acceptance that he had found in this remarkable family was genuine and strong. He felt a sense of warmth that he had never felt from the Gilads.

Yael and Mikki emerged from the kitchen, carrying in their arms what appeared to be bales of brightly colored fabric.

"We can't very well sit in a Bedouin tent in street clothes." Yael said. "I went shopping today in the souk and picked up a few things."

She distributed brightly colored gallabias. She had carefully estimated everyone's size. In short order, the Sukkah looked like a Bedouin family gathering.

"Mikki, this is going to be an amazing Sukkot!" Arik said.

"You should see Yom Kippur around here," she said, laughing.

After Kiddush and hand washing with water from copper kettles, everyone settled down to enjoy a sumptuous feast of spiced lentil soup, lafa, hummus, techina, pickled olives and baby eggplants, roasted stuffed poultry, and lamb kebabs over maqluba rice and vegetables.

"So, Shmulik, how are the earthworks around the Ruafa Dam coming along?" Sharon asked.

"Everything is on schedule. The lake has been deepened, and the banks and walls along the shoreline are nearly complete. We've already secured the necessary pontoon bridges, and we're currently having them mounted on tank treads. The only thing that we don't have is water. On Sukkot, we pray for rain. This year, we'll pray extra hard. The war game is planned to simulate a Suez Canal crossing."

Arik looked at Sharon very intently.

Sharon said, "That is the only real intangible. We must begin training at the lake by mid-November so that our scheduled full-scale exercise can take place in January."

Sharon looked at Arik and Mikki. "We're in a bit of a quandary now. From July of '67 until about a year ago, when the cease-fire took place between us and the Egyptians, we had regular exchanges of artillery fire, aerial bombardments, and commando raids across the Canal, which took many hundreds of lives but kept the Russian surface-to-air missiles at a safe distance, allowing us to maintain air superiority over the Canal. I believe that Opher's squadron is tasked with patrolling that sector?"

Mikki and her father nodded.

"Ah, yes," Sharon continued. "Well, when we signed the cease-fire with the Egyptians, the naive Americans were overjoyed, thinking that it would be a first step to a comprehensive peace. In reality, the Egyptians and their Russian advisors used the truce as a ruse to bring hundreds of SAM batteries—those surface-to-air missiles—right up to the Canal, right in front of our noses, without us being able to do a thing about it."

Shmulik said, "The general staff at southern command met last year to formulate a response to this threat. Our thinking was to make a preemptive strike on the western side of the Canal, near Kantara to the north and Suez from the south, to establish a beachhead and then to destroy all the SAM sites and go back across the Canal. We thought that it was an effective military strategy that would send a message to the Egyptians that we wouldn't tolerate the SAMs so close to our lines. Us doing nothing sent the opposite message—weakness. We could one day regret our decision to do nothing. Who knows? It was a political decision made by Dayan and Golda. If memory serves, Arik, you spent some time on the other side of the Canal."

"Yes, sir. I was on the mission that retrieved the S-200 and 1S-32 rocket-guidance and 1S-12 target-acquisition systems."

"Without the option of crossing the Canal now, en masse," Sharon said, "we need to train for a possible future crossing under realistic conditions, should full-scale war break out. The question has been where." He looked at Mikki and said, "Your Abba discovered that the Ruafa Dam, near the Abu-Ageila junction, which catches the water from the El Arish Wadi, has created a long artificial lake that, when filled with water, will simulate the conditions along the Suez Canal. We plan on staging full-scale Canal-crossing exercises there."

Mikki said, "I have great trepidation about the government's overreliance on the Bar-Lev Line as a defensive perimeter. Conceptually, it's as outdated as the Maginot Line was in '40 in the face of combined air and mechanized assault techniques. I fear, as well, that we'll pay for our complacency. All of our intelligence assessments indicate that the only thing that will head off full conflict with the Egyptians is to reengage in long-term limited conflict—even if it means facing off against the Russians in the air and on the ground. Our Chel Ha'Avir F-4 Phantom jets have done very well—against even the Russian pilots—but while we sit on our hands, the enemy gets stronger day by day."

Opher said, "I downed two brand-new Russian-piloted MiG-21s over the Canal last year, but I've been locked on by those new ELINT radars over the past several months."

Sharon nodded. "I've brought this matter up with Dayan and Golda time and again, and all I get are sympathetic nods. Nothing more. I'm afraid that they just don't perceive the danger the way that we do. We do have problems closer to home that pose a more immediate threat. Gaza. In a sense, it's a more complicated problem. Though we broke the main Palestinian force there during the Six-Day War, scattered terrorist cells remain hidden underground, among the population. They're organized into local command centers that are, in turn, controlled by a central command in Lebanon and Syria. They scatter among the population, terrorizing them into submission in an attempt to undo all our economic, social, and material advancements and try to recruit new fighters to their cause. Even buses ferrying Arabs back and forth to employment in Israel are being bombed to dissuade Arabs from cooperating with us. The cruel methods that their death squads employ against their own people defy description. Mutilated and tortured bodies turn up every day. Dayan is happy to stay out of this fray and let them kill each other off. I disagree. I think that a growing PLO presence is a clear and present danger to us, as Arik saw during his raid. Besides, if we are to govern there, we're ultimately responsible for the well-being of all people under our administration.

"While the War of Attrition was going on, we had our hands full. Now, we have time to focus on this. Part of the reason that this so hard is that the terrorists have become very adept at blending into the population. Conventional warfare is useless here. It would result in an unacceptable civilian loss of life. There has to be a way of flushing out about 700 terrorists from a terrified population of nearly 400,000 and let them go back to normal life. Initially, we couldn't come up with a plan, so we began gathering intelligence about all the minutiae of daily life there, with the idea of detecting subtle alterations in the routine."

Mikki said, "For two months, we've walked around every square inch of the refugee camps, towns, and overgrown orange groves. It was clear to me that the PLO had local command headquarters hidden in the groves and underground bunkers. We realized that communication up and down their command chain was key to their survival. My team identified some of the terrorist chiefs. Instead of arresting them, we began to track their movements to headquarters and the location of individual terrorist cell hideouts. We've divided the entire Gaza Strip into square-kilometer quadrants, and we'll assign each to a squad which will include combat troops and intelligence officers whose sole purpose is to monitor daily life and look for even the slightest deviations. We have to get into their heads. We have to find rendezvous points for supplies and information. We've looked for subtle markers that they might use to signal one another. We'll have the squads vary their pattern of activity so that they're unpredictable. Once we find a terrorist cell, we can eliminate them at will. If at any time a squad needs backup—for example, if they found a headquarters or a heavily armed group—a call would go out to the Matkal and they'd come in for a surgical strike with overwhelming firepower."

She stared at Arik, who shrugged.

Sharon said, "Mikki's staff and my operations group have already laid the groundwork for the campaign, and we're starting to recruit what we're calling antiterrorist guerrilla warriors from the various Commando units. Individual Matkal squads will form liaisons with the intelligence operatives, so the response will be seamless if need be. The terrorists are becoming more organized and are receiving some sophisticated weaponry by sea, so this won't be a cakewalk. We expect significant casualties, at least in the early phases, but we have no choice. The PLO poses a mounting security threat to the center of the country."

Yael walked in with dessert. She served the affogato, a sweet, cold ice cream-like confection, with spiced, sweet herb "whiskey" tea.

"I'm taking my prerogative as hostess to switch gears here," she said. "You all have time for staff meetings next week. It's Sukkot, and we've come together to relax. And relax we will. I think that your discussions will become far more interesting after some of the whiskey tea. I've taken the liberty of adding some of my own ingredients."

Sharon raised both of his hands. "I surrender! When a Yiddishe mama says to stop talking about work and eat, there is no choice but to obey! Your cuisine is legendary for a reason, Yael. It's no secret that many on the general staff vie for an invitation from you. You could give the finest restaurants in Tel Aviv a run for their money." Sharon rubbed his hands together. "From now on, no more shoptalk."

Mikki whispered to Arik, "Now, that's something that you don't see every day—Sharon surrendering. He also knows how to balance work and home life, like just like my Abba. They're real role models."

The conversation shifted to family matters and lighthearted anecdotes. The guests stayed until nearly midnight.

As he and his family were leaving, Sharon approached Arik and smiled at him. "I've heard about you. Your name has gotten around. You're a fine young man and a credit to your unit. Keep up the good work." He patted Arik on the cheek.

"Thank you, sir."

Mikki smiled, pride written on her face.

Everyone retired to bed. Arik and Mikki went out into the courtyard, to the sound of the tinkling water in the fountain. They swung quietly in a hammock. Arik's head was still spinning from the whiskey tea.

"This Gaza project sounds like great fun. I can't wait to get started. We'll kick butt!" Arik said.

"Arik, my love, this is really no joke. I know that this plan will demand an intense and dangerous long-term commitment from your unit. The plan is very complex. You'll be hearing more about it in briefings over the next four weeks."

"You know that I'm just an action junkie, right? Don't worry about me, sweetheart. I'm a big boy."

"The thought that I may have signed your death warrant terrifies me, my precious."

"I'll watch myself. Don't worry so much. I used to have something to die for. Now, I have something to live for. So, this is what home feels like?" He gently kissed her on the cheek.

"Your home. Our home." She turned her head and kissed him on the lips. He felt every shred of residual hurt and inner angst ooze away from him as his heart began to race.

"I want you, Arik. Tonight," Mikki whispered as she placed her hand on his leg.

"Here, in your house? Your father would . . ."

Mikki moved her hand, making it impossible for him to continue speaking. He gasped.

"Arik, go to bed, but don't go to sleep or I'll be forced to wake you," she whispered.

***

Arik lay in bed, staring up into the blackness as his heart raced. He wondered what was about to occur and how. Involuntarily, his mind flashed back to Aspen. He had not experienced intimacy in well over a year. Never much for casual relations, he had felt in his soul that Dahlia would be the one he would spend his life with. But then he had realized that his dreams were just that—dreams.

Now, instead of feeling joy and anticipation, he was becoming clammy and he felt a tight knot developing in his stomach about what would transpire in only a few moments. Part of him loved Mikki deeply, that was certain. But he wondered what lay behind that opaque curtain that is the future.

Again, he felt as if he were swimming against the tide. He was so afraid of losing Mikki. Why does it have to be this way? Why can't my life go along in an orderly fashion, like everyone else's? Why do I have to stand at the gates of paradise and hell simultaneously? Why does ecstasy have to come at such a heavy price? He felt foolish, manipulated, and trapped. He suddenly remembered what the reverend had told him: "If you see no way out from where you are, go further in."

He heard soft footfalls at his door. The door creaked open softly. Mikki slipped inside and locked the door behind her. He saw the faintest outline of her figure, wearing a house robe, by the light of the full moon that was streaming in through the rustling curtains. The robe fell to the floor and, in a moment, he was swept away in a rush of warmth and love.

"This is our time, Arik," she whispered. "Our time."

At 4 a.m., Arik awoke to find Mikki lying next to him and staring straight at him from only three inches away.

He blinked and then said, "I just had the craziest dream. I dreamed that an angel from heaven came down, lifted my soul out of my body, healed all its wounds, and infused it with honey and fragrance. It then kissed me and hovered brightly over me."

"A Yeshivnik and a poet!" Mikki smiled. "I have to go. Someone will be up soon."

She kissed him lightly and then got out of bed.

"One last thing before you go?" he whispered.

"What?" She tied her robe.

"You know that I'm going to marry you," Arik said.

She leaned down and kissed him again, softly, on his lips. "Yes, Arik, I know."

Arik blinked, and the angel was gone.

The army's patrols in Gaza began in earnest. The soldiers were trained not only in close-quarters combat but also in special techniques to find and flush out terrorist cells. Arik's company moved out to a small clandestine camp named Camp Maoz, just west of Sderot and a mile east of the Gaza border. Arik and his squad were there to deal with any serious threats that the intelligence units and scouts might find. Assigned the task of locating terrorist hideouts, the intelligence personnel developed and improvised ingenious techniques and continuously varied them to keep the Arabs off guard. The patrols in the towns and refugee camps intensified.

The assembled commando platoon fell silent as the commanders entered the front of the Quonset hut that was adorned with a large detailed map of the Gaza Strip. As the senior intelligence officer in charge of the antiterrorism campaign in Gaza, Mikki called the meeting to order. Several men smiled and turned around to look at Arik, but he remained impassive, staring straight ahead.

Inside, however, he was bursting with pride at seeing Mikki at work. Here, she was no woman but a seasoned professional, although her tightly fitted khaki uniform screamed otherwise. She was tough and all business, and the elite soldiers responded appropriately, with none of the usual smirking of elite male soldiers when faced with an extremely attractive woman. They knew that what she was telling them could spell the difference between life and death for them. They hung on her every word.

She began by outlining the background of the increased PLO presence in Gaza and the effect that it was having on the local population. She explained General Sharon's plans for eliminating 700 terrorists out a population of 400,000 without harming civilians or even interfering with their way of life— first in general and then in greater detail. During the previous three months, Mikki's teams had divided Gaza into square-kilometer quadrants and developed human intelligence from a network of informers, shtinkerim, and agents posing as Arabs who had infiltrated the population. The structure and hierarchy of the terrorist organization had been discerned, as had a long list of potential targets. Those targets had been prioritized.

Ambushes of security patrols were sporadic but becoming more commonplace. Terrorists that were driven off ran into buildings and, when pursued, simply disappeared into thin air.

Mikki pulled out a measuring tape and asked, "Does anyone know what is for?"

There were no takers, so she answered her own question.

"A common trick is to create false walls in apartments, creating spaces behind them for terrorists to hide. So, when someone threw a grenade or was driven off in an ambush, they might run into a house. A thorough search would turn up nothing . . . until we started using a measuring tape to measure the outside and inside dimensions of the house. A discrepancy usually means a false wall with a secret compartment. We've already caught dozens of terrorists hiding behind these walls.

"Some of our crew also carry collapsible ladders to suddenly appear over a fence of a private home instead of knocking on a locked gate. Our teams are hiding on rooftops and in trees, always watching for irregular movements. Any change in routine activity is suspect. Our teams have become very inventive at rooting out these vermin and are always changing their tactics.

"Yet, despite many successful interceptions, we believe that men and arms are being smuggled in from the sea and rapidly absorbed into the population. The terrorists are divided up into regional networks, each with their own commander. These, in turn, are broken up into cells. We're making considerable headway, though."

Mikki pulled out an intercepted letter. Written from a cell member to a regional commander, it outlined the increasing difficulty that the terrorists were having in maneuvering and finding hiding places. "The Jews are driving us crazy," the letter said.

"We have undercover squads of Sephardic Jews and Druze posing as Arabs," Mikki said. "We've planted phony terrorists that can land ashore, be chased by Israelis, and hide among the populace. They seek out real terrorists to join them, and they're frequently taken to their commanders, who we then taken into custody or eliminate at our leisure.

"The PLO are being driven underground—literally. Their citrus groves are quite different from ours. They allow the trees and underbrush to grow unimpeded, making them perfect hiding places. The groves are surrounded by thick cactus hedges, making it harder for us to get equipment in. General Sharon wants to bulldoze the hedges, but he's meeting stiff resistance from the civilian authorities, who complain to the prime minister's office. Something about ruining the environment."

Peals of laughter rippled through the room.

"The reason that I'm here is that open, armed clashes with our troops have become more frequent as the terrorists have grown more desperate. We're going to form you up, by platoon, into rapid-response teams that will be ferried by helicopter into each hot zone. Each of our patrols will have direct radio contact with you and, in turn, until this operation is concluded, you'll stay in a continuous state of konnenut, ready to move within seconds when called. We will convey further instructions as circumstances warrant. Meeting adjourned. "

The meeting broke up, and the men filed out of the building. Mikki remained behind with Shaked and Barak, to go over more specifics. Arik took his time getting up and averted his gaze from Mikki until the last moment before he walked out the door. The expressionless, mutual eye contact, which lasted only a fraction of a second, said everything that needed to be said. Arik's eyes said, "I'm crazy in love with you and so proud to serve under your command. I'm in awe of your professionalism and newly amazed by you as a person and officer with every passing minute. You bring out the best in me, and I'll do whatever it takes to make you proud. I'd lay down my life to obey your orders. You're also sexy as hell, and I can't wait to make love to you again!" Mikki's eyes said, "Thank you for being able to separate work from personal life. Anything else would jeopardize the mission and result in one of us needing to be recused. This is a matter of life and death. It's so good to see you here as a soldier, in your professional capacity. Your skills are ideal in this type of campaign so will prove invaluable in the weeks ahead." Her eyes also said, "Oh! I did glance at your butt as you walked in, and I can't wait to jump your bones again. I love you, bachurchik!"

***

Within seventy-two hours, the alarm in Camp Maoz sounded.

A combined infantry and intelligence patrol convoy riding through outskirts of the Jabalia refugee camp had come under fire. It was suffering casualties. Time was of the essence. Thirty men poured out of their tents, in a practiced maneuver, and in less than two minutes loaded into three Huey helicopters. The men were laden with weapons and ammunition for the ten-minute hop into the heart of the firefight. The choppers hovered three meters above an open schoolyard about two hundred meters from where three Israeli patrol cars had come under fire. From their vantage point, they could see that the attack was coming from a building and the ten Israelis were pinned behind their vehicles. The Israelis could not get inside their vehicles to escape. Such was the intensity of the fire raining onto their heads. There were dead and dying on the ground behind the cars and inside the cars. The commandos jumped out of the choppers and hit the ground running. They divided into two assault teams, converging on the stricken convoy from opposite directions.

Arik's team approached within ten meters of the convoy. Five soldiers were crouched in a firing position behind the engine blocks, their guns trained on the windows of the buildings where the gunfire was coming from. They were motionless, as if frozen in time.

They aren't shooting back, Arik thought. Why?

As he approached the nearest vehicle, he saw that one of the soldiers was Mikki. Wearing a green field cap, she was standing as if plastered to the side of the command car. He noticed a ten-centimeter spot of blood spreading on her trousers. She had been hit in the side of the hip.

He wanted to shout, "Mikki, get down!" or "Why aren't you shooting back?" but he dared not distract her.

In a moment, the reason that nobody was shooting back became clear. He saw that the Arab gunmen were standing in the third-floor windows of the building across the street. They were firing automatic weapons down at the Israelis while holding young children in front of them as human shields. They assumed—correctly—that the presence of the children would make the Israelis hesitant to shoot back.

Arik swore in disgust. At the captain's command and in the blink of an eye, the squad leaped into the line of fire and, as if on cue, fired three rocket-propelled grenades at three windows simultaneously. The instant fireball silenced all life on that third floor. Arik and Mikki locked eyes for an instant. He winked at her and quickly followed the other members of his squad into the building. A symphony of staccato explosions, like fireworks, followed from inside the building. Then there was total silence. The dead and wounded soldiers were evacuated from the street.

When Arik finally emerged from the building, Mikki was still leaning against the command car.

"I'm not going to question why you didn't shoot at those children if you don't question why I did," Arik said flatly. "I'm not much for moral ambiguity when lives are at stake. Arabs love to paint us as the bad guys to the whole world but use our ethical sensibilities against us. They put those children in danger, and they're responsible for what happened to them. My conscience is clear."

"Thanks for not questioning my judgment, Arik. That was a real tough call. I'm sure that there will be questions asked when we get back, though," she said.

"I'm sure the higher-ups won't have any better answers either," he said. "You okay? You've been hit. Go back with the others. A whole bunch of those guys escaped out the back door and ran into the orange grove while we were clearing the building. We're going in there after them."

"I'm fine. The medic checked me out. It's just a flesh wound. You can't go into that grove half-cocked until we've had a chance to plan our response. I've already told your captain. The Arabs want you to go in there after them. They're drawing you in. You don't know your way through there. You'd be a sitting duck. We're developing a whole contingency plan for how to deal with this kind of thing."

Arik lowered the waistband of her slacks on the left side and looked at the bloody bandage. "Doesn't look too bad, but you'll definitely need to get bathing suits with wider bikini straps over your hips." He chuckled.

Mikki punched his arm but could not help smiling.

They called for the extraction team, and within thirty minutes everyone was back at the base.

***

The following week, Sharon himself led a small squad of commandos and intelligence officers into the grove where the ambush had taken place. A hands-on commander, he often insisted on taking personal command of critical operations, despite the personal risk. Flanked by Mikki and the Arab owner, he walked the length and breadth of the huge overgrown orange grove. Arik's squad of ten men stood ready and watching a short distance away.

When he stumbled on a metal fence post that was sticking up out of the ground, Sharon asked, "What's this?"

"It marks the boundary between my property and my brother's," the Arab said.

Mikki stared at him silently, her face emotionless.

They walked another kilometer and saw nothing. After that, Sharon dismissed the grove owner. Sharon led the group back to the so-called boundary marker. He looked at Mikki.

"Don't you think it odd that the Arab farmer needs a boundary marker here?" he asked. "This man was born here and has lived here all his life. He knows every tree and stone. Why would he need a marker?"

Mikki put her index finger to her lips. "Over there!" she whispered. "There's a small trail through the trees. You see how the branches are pushed aside down below? People must be going through there."

Before anyone could say anything, Mikki had crawled away on her hands and knees and disappeared into the underbrush.

Arik rushed up to Sharon and whispered, "What's she doing? I don't like this. I'm going in after her!"

Sharon smiled indulgently. "Don't let your feelings for her cloud your judgment. Mikki's a big girl. She knows exactly what she's doing. She's one of the best intelligence operatives in the army. She'll come back with the goods."

For what felt an eternity to Arik, there was total silence. After a half hour, Mikki slithered out of the underbrush, covered in dust.

"At the end of the trail, I found a dozen more fence posts," she said. "One of them had a can bent into a point at one end—a pointer. The pointer led to a clump of cactus hedges. In the midst of the hedge and the sharp needles poking out in every direction, I found a ventilation pipe. I searched the other hedges and saw other pipes in a tight, semicircular arc of about twenty meters. It can only mean one thing. We're standing on top of a vast underground bunker. It could be their central command hideout."

"Did you see anything that resembled an entrance?" Sharon asked.

"I spent some time looking, but I couldn't find anything. These guys are good."

"If we can't go to them, why don't we make them come out to us?" Arik said.

All eyes turned to Arik, and the other members of his squad walked up to where he was standing.

"I say we drop tear gas canisters, lots of them, down the ventilation pipes and have our men saturate the area to locate the secret entrance to the bunker. We'll smoke them out. When they come out, we'll be ready for them," Arik said.

Mikki smiled at him. "You're not as dumb as you look."

He smiled back and stuck up his middle finger at her.

Sharon chuckled.

The reinforced Matkal squad located the bunker entrance minutes after the canisters had found their underground targets. Twenty senior terrorists, including the regional commander, the feared Abu Iyaad, were captured as they streamed out from underground, blinded, coughing, and wheezing. Not a shot was fired. Each terrorist was held at gunpoint and duly thrown to the ground, hog-tied, blindfolded, and gagged. One by one, they were led out and put into a waiting van.

Arik's team, wearing gas masks, entered the bunker and recovered a treasure trove of documents, including maps, orders, communiques, and lists of operatives active throughout the Gaza Strip.

This raid proved the undoing of the whole terrorist network. The individual cells were mopped up systematically during the ensuing weeks. Sharon hoped that Gaza and the Gazans could enjoy a few years of peace and quiet before the next challenges mounted.

Chapter 16

"Dahlia, did we put you into the army too soon?" Benny had called her long distance from Washington, D.C. "Perhaps we should have waited several more months, until your condition was more stable. This may be too stressful for you. Imma is sick with worry. It's hard enough managing this long-distance. I sit here in Washington and think about you all day. Remember: Doda Ruti is just a phone call away if you need her. I thought that this would be a way for you to resume a meaningful life. Please, let me know the minute you feel that this is too much for you. I'll arrange some form of Sheirut Leumi, nonmilitary national service, for you. After all, you can qualify, as a religious girl."

"No, Abba. I wanted to go in now. A delay of three months was all I could get away with before too many questions would be asked. I'll get through this. I made the social-suicide mistake of talking too much about myself to the girls in my unit, never thinking for a second that they'd turn on me like jackals. All I can do now is keep my head down and do what I'm told. The quieter that I am now, the better off I'll be. Perhaps I'll slip under the radar and get through this peacefully and move on. If I don't do this now, I'll never feel like I'm getting control over my life. No matter how bad things may get, I have to persevere."

Dahlia hung up the phone.

Those were very brave words that she had said to her Dad. The problem was that she did not believe them. She felt like a hollow, fragile eggshell. The last thing that she had needed was to see Arik's face again full on. Watching that film had brought everything back in a torrent. She had flashed back to when she had seen him work out for the first time, in the Camp Moshava gym. The pain, regret, sense of betrayal, and guilt gnawed at her like cancer.

She understood that so much of this situation had been her fault. Her pain at losing Arik had driven her into the clutches of Ze'evi. If only she had forgiven Arik when he had visited at Pesach. Maybe I should have accepted his version of events, whether it was true or not. Did he ever lie to me? Why would he start? Perhaps there was a good reason that he didn't get in touch with me. He seemed so happy to see me when I walked into the room at Pesach. He seemed genuinely concerned about what I'd become. In return for that, she had turned on him and thrown him out into the street. She had been so cruel to him and had hit him where she knew that she could wound him—his poverty, lack of social connections, and pervasive sense of aloneness. What kind of person have I become? Arik, by his own devices, was now known throughout the army. Everyone was wondering what his name was. She knew it. She knew it only too well. Wasn't it me who said that one day Arik would do great things? I tried to convince Abba and Imma that coming from nothing wasn't the same as going to nothing.

These thoughts invaded Dahlia's mind almost constantly, even keeping her awake at night. She was crying into her pillow about Arik, again. The previous year, she had cried because she did not know where he was. Now she was crying because she knew where he was but he was unattainable.

Dahlia resolved to find Arik and beg for his forgiveness. She missed him terribly. Thoughts of Arik were a lifeline to her past, a time when she had felt loved and respected, a time before exploitation and violence, a time before degradation. Her thoughts of him kept her going. They gave her a glimmer of hope and self-respect.

***

Mikki's aide called, interrupting her staff meeting. "Colonel Zohar, I'm sorry to disturb you, but you have a phone call from Major Kramer."

Mikki excused herself.

"Shalom, Lior," she said into the phone. "I didn't expect to hear from you so soon. Is everything okay with the program that we implemented?"

"The program is fine. Everything is going well with that. We do have a strange situation here, though, and I'm not sure what to do. Does your unit do internal investigations?"

"It depends. What's going on?"

"Over the past several weeks, we've seen a disappearance of a significant amount of inventory from our storerooms. We've tried to investigate the matter internally, but our MPs are at a complete loss. We can't catch any unauthorized personnel coming, in and we don't see anything going out. We've searched the base up and down, and the stuff is nowhere to be found. I think we may have a black-market ring operating here, but they're very slick."

"What sort of inventory? Guns, ordnance, or explosives? I'll have to get the Shin Bet involved. We could be having a major security breach." Mikki's voice was rising.

"That's what's odd. It's nothing like that. We're talking about work uniforms, food, medicine, blankets and Jerri cans of diesel fuel and cooking oil. They just vanish into thin air. We have guards posted around the storage facilities twenty-four hours a day, seven days a week, but it does no good. I know that this sounds trivial to you, but it's driving our supply people nuts. We've even tried to investigate whether there are any black-market buyers for the contraband, but we have no leads."

Mikki laughed. "I think that I know what's going on. You're being played a fool by some of the Sayeret guys. Sometimes, for the sheer sport of it, they break into bases to pilfer supplies. It serves three purposes: One, when these guys have downtime, they get bored. This gives them something to do just for the fun of it. Two, they hone their skills at breaking and entering without detection. If they can do it to us, they can do it to the enemy. It's a rite of passage for new members. Three, they're chronically undersupplied, and they supplement their own inventory by stealing."

"Are you telling me that our most elite soldiers are thieves?"

"If you don't know that already, you're a sitting duck." Mikki laughed. "I'll help you find your thieves. You know that this isn't the job of military intelligence, but I'll do it as a favor for you. On one condition: no reports, no paperwork. I'll take care of this quietly."

He readily agreed.

***

Mikki went with her small squad of MPs to Tzrifin base to set up ambushes around the storerooms. They waited. Nothing happened.

During afternoon assembly, all of the platoons in the battalion lined up on the parade ground. After a perfunctory march, they were divided up into squads and told to stand by their tents.

Lior ascended a small podium and then announced, "The numbers have been tallied. The platoon with the highest composite score for navigation, obstacle course, running, and shooting will spend tomorrow on a trip to Jerusalem, which will include a tour of all the battlefields around the Old City, culminating in a visit to the Kotel, the Western Wall." He removed a small note from his pocket. "The winner is Kita Daled. You leave after morning inspection tomorrow."

A cheer erupted from the winning unit.

For Dahlia, the trip would mean a blessed day of rest from the painful drudgery of not only the mind-numbing running, hiking, and shooting but also the seemingly endless punishment details that she had had to endure. She had been forced to spend all of her downtime cleaning latrines or washing pots in the kitchen. As a result, she smelled so bad that nobody would sit next to her during meals. Nobody wanted to sleep next to her either. She often found her bed dragged outside the tent and into the rain. Her fingers and knees were raw and bleeding from all the work that she had been forced to do for the past five weeks.

She was certain that she was doing penance. She had had barely a day off, not that she had felt like going anywhere that day. All she wanted to do was sleep. It was amazing how something as simple as sleep could assume such paramount importance. Her world had narrowed to her bed and the four panels of her tent. This world was populated by hostile creatures ready to pounce on her at the slightest provocation. The confrontations had not come to blows, because she always backed down. She withdrew into herself, looking for that inner strength that everyone talks about, but she found none. She had always been surrounded by friends, family, or people who admired her. Even with Ze'evi, she had been in a circle of friends, however malignant they had turned out to be. Even then, at least she had not been alone. Now, she had become Arik. Where does he find the strength to spend his whole life alone? she wondered. She had not been able to bear it for a month. God, I miss him . . . still love him . . . still ache about how things turned out. She hoped that the next day, on the trip, would be a better day.

The next morning, Dahlia celebrated by waking up early, taking a quick shower, and putting on her dress uniform for the first time in five weeks. She grabbed her Uzi and went outside. The entire platoon assembled by unit for inspection in front of their tents. They stood at rigid attention. The excitement in the air was palpable.

"Present arms!"

The lieutenant, surrounded by the platoon sergeants, made his rounds.

"Private Gilad, what in the world is on your weapon?" he asked.

"Nothing, sir."

"Give me your weapon."

She handed it to him.

"Do you call this nothing?" he bellowed.

He pointed at the tip of the Uzi's nozzle, where there was a rim of dirt that she had not noticed. He ran his little finger down the end of the barrel. It came away with grains of sand.

"What is the meaning of this? Do you think that this some sort of joke?"

He turned the weapon upside down, and a stream of sand poured out of the nozzle.

"Sir, I cleaned the weapon this morning. I have no idea how this happened."

"You obviously left your weapon unguarded," the sergeant of Dahlia's platoon said.

"Was I supposed to take the gun into the shower with me?"

"You're supposed to have a friend watch it for you. Oh, I forgot. You have no friends."

The rest of the members of Dahlia's unit chuckled. Ruchama, Osnat, and Edna snickered especially hard. Dahlia understood. They had sabotaged her weapon so that she would be excluded from the outing. She had had enough.

"You bitches!" she whispered.

"It's quite clear to me that this squad is highly dysfunctional," the lieutenant said loudly. "You're all supposed to be looking out for each other, taking care of each other. How will you fight an enemy when you fight amongst yourselves? Your trip to Jerusalem is canceled. I'm going to arrange a team-building exercise for you pathetic lot. Kita Daled will stay here, on base, until you learn how to get along and function as a unit. You see that road leading out of the base? You'll collect rocks from that pile, line the road with them, and paint every stone white—even if it takes you all night. This is a twenty-four-hour job, and you'll work until the work is done. Be back out here in work clothes in twenty minutes. Go!"

Back in the tent, Edna pushed Dahlia to the floor.

"You little shit! Because you couldn't get your crap together, we all got screwed. I'll kick your ass! I was looking forward to that trip."

Dahlia jumped up and lunged at Edna, grabbing at her neck. Osnat grabbed Dahlia, by her neck, from behind. Dahlia bit Osnat's wrist, and Osnat let out a shriek. The three recruits rolled around in the dirt.

"What the hell is going on here?" Corporal Rona said when she burst into the tent. "Gilad, is this all your doing, as usual? Do you want to spend a week in the brig?"

"None of this was my doing! One of these bitches sabotaged my gun, trying to keep me from going on the trip, not thinking that it would mean everyone would be grounded!" Dahlia said.

"Are you going to believe that lying snake?" Edna said.

"It was Ruchama," a quiet voice in the corner said.

All heads turned toward Riva. She was low-key, serious, and mature, a rare combination in that platoon.

"When Dahlia was in the shower, Ruchama picked up some sand and poured it into the weapon," Riva said. "This trio of terror has been bullying everyone else for long enough. I'm fed up. While it's true that Princess Dahlia has been a royal pain in the ass, these three are the main reason this kita is so screwed up."

The other girls in the tent nodded.

"Ruchama, you'll spend three days in the brig. The rest of you, get going!"

Half of the kita was assigned to gathering rocks and loading them onto a tender. The rest brought a dozen buckets of white paint from storage. When the tender was full, the recruits took it out to the road, where they laid the stones out in a long double line that led to the entrance to the compound.

"Riva, thanks for standing up for me," Dahlia said.

"What's fair is fair," Riva said, smiling at Dahlia. She looked out at the road. "We have our work cut out for us. It's over a kilometer out to the entrance. We'd better get going."

The girls worked throughout the day in the hot sun, tears of sweat rolling down their faces. They took the occasional water and bathroom break every few hours. Their meals of canned sardines, pita, and olives were delivered to the work site. As the day turned to night, spotlights were brought out on a trolley and attached to a generator, enabling their work to continue. Slowly, the recruits painted their way toward the entrance.

Four shadowy figures wearing black fatigues and carrying large empty backpacks cut a small hole in the perimeter fence no more than thirty meters away. They were not spotted by the recruits. They had come from a waiting command car parked just outside the entrance. They made their way silently into the supply warehouse and loaded Jerri cans of motor oil into their backpacks. When they emerged from the warehouse, all hell broke loose.

Spotlights flashed on, and the four figures were swamped by a cordon of MPs with weapons drawn. A voice from a bullhorn instructed them to raise their hands, which they did.

"You're all under arrest. Put your hands up!"

On their hands and knees, Dahlia and Riva watched the ruckus in numb amusement. Any entertainment was better than the mindless crap that they had put up with all day and into the night. They ached all over, and their vision was blurry.

The four figures remained standing with their hands up, and the commandant was called.

"Colonel Zohar, we have our perpetrators."

Mikki marched out of the command center. The rest of her retinue followed her, matching her brisk pace. "Good work!" she said into the radio as she went.

With arms folded over her chest, Mikki approached the perpetrators.

"What the hell? What do we have here?"

She shook her head in mock disgust as she tried to hide her own amusement. "What are you four doing here, causing all this trouble? I have a good mind to throw you crooks into the brig for a month."

"Colonel Zohar, we're in the middle of a top-secret training exercise." Arik smirked. "Aren't we, Dani?"

Dani nodded.

"We'd rather die than reveal the true nature of our mission!" Gadi said.

"Who are these guys, Colonel Zohar?" Captain Skolnick asked Mikki.

"I'm about to find out. Leave these men to me. The rest of you, go back to the motor pool, collect your gear, and wait for me there. Our work here is nearly done. I'll join you as soon as I interrogate them personally and hand them over to the local authorities."

They left Mikki alone with the perpetrators.

"I should have known that it was you! You knuckleheads! Don't you think that I have better things to do than waste my time playing cat and mouse with you children? You idiots need to find a better way to amuse yourselves. You're Sayeret Matkal, for God's sake. You're just lucky that it's me. If they'd called the Shin Bet, it would have gotten really ugly."

Arik laughed. "I can think of a much better way of amusing myself." He grabbed Mikki by her belt buckle and pulled her toward him. "We were just having a little fun."

"Stop, Arik! Not now! There are people around here who can see us!" Mikki whispered.

"There's nobody around but those dopey recruits over there."

He grabbed her and, before she could pull away, laid a smooch on her lips, much to the amusement of Dani and the other two commandos. She giggled and wrapped her arms around his neck. She knew well who was watching from the rock work detail.

"Motek, I've made reservations for us in a suite at the King Solomon Hotel in Eilat for the weekend. Will you be ready at six?" Mikki asked.

"No, seven thirty, and don't forget to bring that cute black bikini you bought, with the wider straps."

"What are you going to wear?"

"Guess you'll just have to find out. Maybe nothing!" Arik laughed.

"Okay," she said in a voice just loud enough for the four commandos to hear. "Take your contraband, and get the hell out of here. And please don't come back, or Kramer will start an official investigation. The last thing that you need is to get hauled in front of Shaked to explain your actions."

"You said 'please' with such sincerity that we'll have to oblige," Alon laughed.

"Good night, Colonel!" Arik saluted her as he and his fellow commandos backed out through the hole in the perimeter fence. They threw their stolen goods into the waiting command car, jumped aboard, and howled as the vehicle drove off.

Mikki standing there with her arms folded, shook her head in mock disgust.

Dahlia, on her hands and knees, stared at the scene. She was transfixed, unable to move. She was beyond tears. Her worst fears had been realized. He's permanently beyond my reach! How did this happen? Arik is mine! Arik is mine!

Her catatonic state was interrupted by Rona, the fat, nasty corporal of Dahlia's unit, who kicked a pile of dirt into Dahlia's face, momentarily blinding her. She coughed and spit out sand while looking down at the dirt, in a helpless rage.

"What were you looking at, Princess? Are you looking for a husband over there? Those elite commandos are the pillars of Israel. It's because of them that you dim sluts can shake your little asses in your discos in Tel Aviv. Without their bravery and sacrifice, there'd be no state. You haven't earned the right to even look in their direction, no less stare at them. Do you think that any of those men would even pay you the courtesy of farting in your direction? Now, get back to work, you worthless piece of crap! It's bad enough that I'm stuck out here all night with you losers."

Dahlia stared blankly at the cold, dark sand and thought of suicide.

***

"Mikki, great job! You caught the cattle rustlers! Who were they?" Lior asked over the phone.

"I told you that we weren't dealing with a criminal element. They were a squad from Sayeret Matkal just having a bit of fun during downtime."

"Well, if you have to be stolen from, it may as well be by the best. So, what did you do with them? Did you hand them over?"

"No need. I know who they are. They're not going to escape anywhere. These guys play by their own rules, but I've already filed a report with their commanding officer, and they'll be receiving a reprimand. You won't have any further trouble from them."

"Thanks, Mikki."

When Mikki hung up the phone, she received a kiss from Arik, who rolled on top of her. She embraced him.

"I love you so much, Arik."

"I love you, too, Mikki. You've given me my life back."

Arik began to climb out of bed.

"Stay in bed with me just a minute more, booba?" she said. "I need a few more hugs."

"You've asked so nicely, how can I refuse?" He kissed her again.

"I'm very nice. Don't you know that by now?"

"Well, actually . . . I just got a taste of the business side of Lieutenant Colonel Zohar. I don't think I ever want to cross you again." Arik smiled.

"I'm very good at leaving the Lieutenant Colonel at the front steps of my home. My father was a very good teacher in that regard. My mother was an officer, too. I'm not sure you knew that. My parents met in the Haganah. At home, though, they were just Abba and Imma."

"I see that every time I go to your family's house. All of you seem so well adjusted. It's the exact opposite of the way I grew up. There's no anger and strife in your home. You're all so supportive of each other. It's one thing to be welcoming to me, but you also always welcome each other."

"What do you mean?"

"You all always seem genuinely happy to see each other."

"Because we are."

"I hope you don't mind if I feel a bit jealous. That's all."

"What's there to be jealous about? You're part of the family now. Really!"

She drew him close. "The home that we will build will be the same. You fit right in with us. It's like you're just one of my brothers. But I'm so glad you aren't." She said pinching his butt.

He chuckled, kissed her one more time, and then got out of bed and put on gym shorts, a T-shirt, and sandals. Smiling, she watched him.

On his way out the door, he said, "I'm going to make us a cup of coffee and some toast and eggs before we go out for our run. And I still have to pray Shacharit. Cream and sugar?"

"No, I like it black. Thanks."

They had gotten into Eilat the previous night and the thought of spending three blissful days alone with Arik sent a spasm of joy through Mikki. They had planned a whole schedule of activities, including long runs on the beach, horseback riding, scuba diving, dirt bike riding in the desert, candlelight dinners, and long nights of lovemaking. With him she finally felt like a woman, a lover, a wife and, hopefully, a mother to his children, all while remaining exactly herself. She felt that her heart was home.

She put on some running clothes and tidied up the bedroom. Arik's paratrooper's uniform had been carelessly tossed across a chair, his bright red beret still attached to the shoulder strap of his shirt. She was certain that he would have a lieutenant's bar on there soon. She marveled at how much this strange, marvelous lone soldier had accomplished so quickly, having come from nowhere. She thought about what he would become.

She folded his slacks and hung them up in the closet, over his red boots, which were leaning against the Galil rifle in the corner. She hung his shirt and then picked up his beret.

"Coffee's ready, booba," he called from the kitchen. "I'll put the toast on and make us some eggs when I'm done with Tefillah. Okay?"

"I'm just getting ready, matok. I'll be out in a minute."

When she placed his beret on the side table, she noticed a small photograph inside. She carefully removed it. Arik and Dahlia were smiling, standing arm in arm in what looked like a country setting, perhaps summer camp. Mikki felt a searing pain in her gut. She wondered why Arik still was carrying the photo in his beret. She felt like a jealous wife who has discovered that her husband is having an affair. She wondered whether Arik still had feelings for Dahlia, whether he hoped, one day, to get back with her. She wondered whether she should tear up the photo. But she knew that would do no good if she could not tear up the photo of Dahlia that still lay in Arik's heart.

She looked at the picture long and hard. She admitted that Dahlia had been beautiful before the ravages of physical abuse, drugs, alcohol, and madness had taken their toll. Of course, she knew that Arik had good taste. Dahlia had been so much more than the wizened army private that she was now. And Dahlia was in Israel now. If Arik wanted to seek her out, or vice versa, there was nothing that Mikki could do to prevent it. She fought back tears and sighed. She wondered whether she should confront him. He obviously did not try to hide the photo. She hoped that he had kept it in his beret by accident, having forgotten to remove it when things went bad with Dahlia. He rarely wore dress uniforms. She carefully returned the photo and finished dressing.

She was no quitter. She never had been. She resolved to fight for Arik's love and affection. Their relationship was still in its early stages. It still needed to be developed and nurtured. She decided that she would fill his heart with love, because if their love would not bind them nothing else would. She decided that Arik simply needed more time.

"Everything is ready here, motek," Arik called from the kitchen. "Come. I don't want it to get cold."

She walked out and smiled at him.

"Is everything okay?" he asked.

"Everything is wonderful when I'm with you." She looked deeply into his eyes and kissed him.

"Mikki, I love you more than my life." He held her tight, resting his head on her shoulder and kissing her neck.

Officers' training school at Bahad 1 was like a resort compared to what Arik had been through. There comes a time in the career of a soldier, even one in special forces, when he or she gets pulled out of the unit and put in school with men and woman from all of the branches the military to determine who will be the next generation of officers. The Israeli military boasts no officers' training academy like the United States' West Point or France's École Militaire. Instead, all officer candidates begin as recruits and are selected for advancement purely on merit. The components of the selection process are many and varied: exemplary performance in training, the initial psychometric exams, and the soldier's social and emotional intelligence as estimated by his or her commanding officer. They also are picked by their peers. Only the best soldiers in each unit, platoon, company, and battalion are chosen for advancement.

At the one large training officer center, Bahad 1, the emphasis is not on physical hazing but rather on real-time training in leadership skills. Officer candidates are taught real-time decision making with the use of maps of enemy territory and scenarios for joint attacks that utilize infantry, armor, and close-air support. They spend three months in the field, navigating and participating in live-fire exercises. Unlike Arik's previous live-fire experiences, this time he was acting in a formal leadership role, leading an entire company in a simulated battle. He was evaluated, in real time, on his ability to improvise, adapt to new, unexpected battlefield conditions, and adhere to the primary dictum that guides every officer in the IDF, namely, to lead from the front—the follow-me principle. The exercises included role playing, case analysis, and group discussions, all to simulate how the candidates would react to complex problems.

After those three months in the field, the candidates attended a week of lectures and seminars in the relative comfort at the IDF Commander Training Institute. For Arik, that meant finally sleeping in a real bed in a room with a roof over his head, electricity, and running water.

All of his trainers, seasoned combat veterans, used bloody real-life experience to teach rather than relying on training manuals. They had learned the lessons of the '48, '56, and '67 wars. During Arik's entire officers' training, he was closely and carefully observed by the trainers and behavioral psychologists, who were assessing the candidates' emotional stability and leadership qualities.

Even at that late stage, many officer candidates are weeded out and moved into noncommissioned officer training. Only the best of the best are allowed to advance to second lieutenant. There is such a slim margin for error in the IDF that instructors cannot afford to be wrong about an officer candidate. Too many lives are at stake. It was, therefore, no surprise to anyone when Arik, as the top candidate in his class, was chosen to lead the march in the graduation parade.

The graduation ceremony, or tekes, was held at the Western Wall square, in Jerusalem, in the bright sunshine. It was attended by members of the Knesset, Israel's legislature, government ministers, and members of the general staff. The officer candidates' family members were in attendance behind velvet ropes.

Arik's "family" were standing in the front of the VIP section. Shmulik, Yael, and Mikki nearly burst with pride when the IDF Chief of Staff General David (Dado) Elazar approached Arik to pin second-lieutenant bars onto his shoulders. Arik stood at attention and saluted sharply.

Shmulik turned to Mikki and whispered, "Mark my words, Mikki, Arik himself will be here one day, as a general pinning bars on new officers."

Mikki wrapped her arm around her father and leaned her head on his shoulder.

Arik returned to his unit in the paratroops but this time as a platoon commander. He would be called back to his Sayeret Matkal unit only during times of need or for special missions.

***

After completing her basic training, Dahlia was assigned to the medical corps, to be trained as a nurse at Tel HaShomer Hospital. It was not glamorous work, but at least she was able to spend many nights at home in Herzliya. Because her father was slated to be the next foreign minister, the family was making preparations for moving back to Israel. She was there to help with the move and make sure that the house was set up for her family. She was happy that at least she would not be alone anymore. She was determined to keep her head down at work and not repeat the interpersonal mistakes that she had made during basic training. Her social life ground to a halt.

April 19, 1972, Independence Day in Israel, was a glorious spring day. In Tel Aviv, the day was marked by citywide celebrations, parades, performances on outdoor stages, picnics, patriotic music blaring from speakers on car roofs, and thousands of happy people milling around and eating falafel and shawarma pita hawked by vendors on every street corner.

The highlight of the celebration was an air show and paratrooper demonstration, along the Tel Aviv beachfront, which drew thousands of spectators armed with binoculars and cameras with telephoto lenses. There were Mirage and Phantom jet flybys in tight arrowhead formations, helicopter demonstrations featuring mock airborne assaults, and a mass skydive by paratroopers. At the center of the beachfront gathering stood a dais draped in Israeli flags, which served as seating for the military and political dignitaries. The aerial displays were narrated by a military spokesman who described each maneuver over the loudspeaker.

With Golda Meir and Moshe Dayan was the new foreign minister, Benny Gilad. He was glad to be home again after having spent three stressful years in Washington, D.C. He was so proud to be looking up at the sky, above the surf, at all of the aircraft that he had helped to procure from the United States. He had been instrumental in securing Israel's future. He looked over at Leah. She smiled at him, understanding what he was thinking.

The Nord 2501 military transport aircraft flew slowly up the beach, from the south, at about 2,000 meters altitude and discharged its paratroopers.

Dozens of men dropped out of the belly of the aircraft, releasing their blue and white patterned parachutes as they exited the plane to the oohs and ahs of the throngs of people lining the beach. The chutes fluttered down to the shallow waters as the men came ashore, simulating an amphibious assault. Cheers and applause resounded as successive waves of men hit the beach.

Benny looked through his binoculars at the fifth airplane, with unease. Something obviously had gone wrong. People continued cheering until reality hit. One paratrooper's chute had gotten tangled with the static line, which was hanging out of the door of the plane, leaving him dangling twenty-five feet below the aircraft. Benny could tell that the paratrooper was unconscious, his arms and legs flailing randomly after having been buffeted into the side of the aircraft and then dropping to where he now dangled. Gasps rolled through the crowd when it became clear that there was no way to rescue the paratrooper and that landing the airplane would mean certain death for him. The airplane circled around and around while the frantic flight crew tried to work out a way of saving him.

Benny watched the unfolding tragedy as if he were in a trance. The crowd grew silent, punctuated by occasional cries. Suddenly, a figure appeared in the door of the airplane. It was there for only a split second and then, like a spider attacking prey in its web, the figure jumped from the airplane. It caught hold of the parachute lines that held the unconscious paratrooper and then climbed down them. The two figures merged as the spider appeared to latch himself to the unconscious paratrooper. The airplane circled again, out to sea and in a steep climb.

"What the devil is he doing?" asked one of the dignitaries on the dais.

The spider drew a knife and cut the parachute lines that were holding the two of them to the airplane. Both men began to free fall. Shouts and cries rose from the crowd.

"My God! They're both going to die!"

A reserve parachute deployed when the men were 500 meters from the surface, and they both fell hard into the shallow water, in a heap. Incredibly, they were alive. A loud roar erupted from the crowd, many of whom thought that it was the best stunt that they had ever seen. The dignitaries on the dais, many of whom were seasoned paratroopers themselves, knew different. They knew that they had just witnessed a miracle. Rescuing an unconscious "towed jumper" was considered nearly impossible. In fact, no one had ever seen it done.

No sooner did the two men hit the water than they were swarmed by paramedics and MPs in Zodiac boats. Still peering through his binoculars, Benny strained hard to see the faces of the paratroopers. He could not believe his eyes when he saw that Arik was the spider.

Dayan, looking through a telescope, nudged him from the side. "I told you, Benny! Once in ten years."

Arik was indeed his father's son. Benny's pride in Arik was tinged with a terrible sense of guilt that came rushing back at him. He had tried so hard to forget Arik and the whole nasty affair between him and Dahlia. After all, Dahlia finally had settled down, all things considered, and was trying to move forward constructively with her life. But now, the whole thing came rushing back to him.

He wondered how he could have driven Dahlia away from such an exceptional man. Dahlia had come within inches of irrevocably ruining her life, all because her own father had failed at his chief task in life: protecting his children. Arik clearly was destined for greatness. Dahlia had told him as much, years earlier. She had said that Arik would go to Israel to finish what his father had been unable to. Dahlia had been more correct than she possibly could have imagined. Benny turned to Leah, who was looking through her binoculars.

She asked, "Is it possible? Is that Arik?"

He nodded. As always, Leah understood everything that he was thinking.

At the other end of the dais stood the Zohars, who also had been watching the whole event through binoculars. Mikki had told them that Arik would be jumping and they would not have missed it for the world. What they saw vastly exceeded their wildest imagination. Yael's heart almost burst with pride and joy as she hugged Mikki tightly.

"Mikki," Yael gushed. "You really know how to pick your men. First Elisha, now Arik! This is so wonderful! We're so fortunate. Arik always outshines even his own past achievements."

Arik was none the worse for wear. The other paratrooper, who suffered a concussion, broken ankle, broken collarbone, and three broken ribs, was rushed to Tel HaShomer Hospital. Arik became front page news in the Maariv, Yedioth Ahronoth, and Haaretz, much to the consternation of his commanders, who would have preferred that their commandos' faces and names be shrouded in secrecy. Recriminations flew around General Shaked's office that such a valuable security asset had accidentally been made public. Some said that Arik should not have been allowed to take part in the exhibition. He had been volunteered for the exercise in a careless moment by his immediate superiors. Arik was given strict orders not to speak to the press.

***

The next morning, Benny and Dahlia shared breakfast with each other. For Benny, that was one of the best things about being back in Israel. Although he had been glad when Dahlia went into the army, he had missed her terribly and had been so worried about her—even after the months of hell that she had put him and Leah through. Now back home, Dahlia had emerged from her basic training a changed person. She had put back on most of the weight that she had lost under the terrible influence of cocaine. The glow was back in her eyes, and her complexion was improving. She was nearly back to her sunny, enthusiastic, confident self. As a nurse, she had regular hours, so she and Benny could spend quality time with each other over a serene breakfast. Doing so had become a ritual for them. It also gave them the opportunity to mend their relationship, which had been so strained for most of the last year that she had spent in the United States.

"What happened on the beach yesterday, Abba? It made the evening news. Everybody is talking about it." Dahlia took a sip of her coffee.

"It was even more dramatic being there. The newspapers can't convey the full sense of it, the shock and anguish among the thousands there."

Dahlia quietly reached for the Haaretz newspaper that lay on the other side of the table. When she saw the front page, she said, "My God! That's Arik! I can't believe it. I always knew that he was an amazing athlete with lightning reflexes, but this looks like a miracle—"

"We were standing there on the dais, watching the drama unfold," Benny said. "General Hofi, an old paratrooper himself, stood next to me, transfixed on the scene. He said that he had never witnessed such a thing before. No one had ever even heard of someone being able to climb down parachute cords in the buffeting winds. It's considered physically impossible. Not to mention the sheer guts it took to pull it off. Dayan has been tracking Arik's progress, as has much of the top brass."

"Why is that?" Dahlia asked. She did not remember anything that her father had told her months earlier, at Pesach, about Arik's military success.

"His superior soldiering skills were noted very early on in basic training, and he was put through a vicious trial by fire to see if he had what it takes to be one of the few that the IDF can depend on to carry out their most difficult missions. His performance continues to astound the general staff. Dayan said that a soldier like Arik comes along once every ten years."

"Is he Matkal?" Dahlia asked.

"You know that, strictly speaking, the unit doesn't officially exist."

"He is, isn't he?"

"The extraordinarily dangerous missions that Arik has already undertaken behind enemy lines are shrouded in legend and mystery. He has Shin Bet agents keeping tabs on him. His knowledge is that sensitive. No joke!"

Dahlia shook her head ruefully. "This is what I threw away. And for what? For some worthless, manipulative playboy who nearly ruined my life and our family. Arik was practically on his hands and knees, begging me." She raised her voice, saying, "You and Imma called him 'a hoodlum from the streets of LA.' Huh!" She lowered her voice again. "Abba, you thought that he was a criminal when he visited us for Sukkot in Washington. You hated him, from the beginning, for reasons that I will never understand. I tried so hard to convince you."

"Frankly, Dahlia, I didn't fully understand it myself then. There was something about him that deeply disturbed me, but I couldn't put my finger on it . . . until that meeting that I had with Dayan about a year ago. I stumbled on Arik's dossier, laying on his desk, and learned about Arik's success in the army."

Benny was pleased that Dahlia had become sensible again. He credited the army with having matured her, and he was grateful to it. The main thing was that he and she finally were able to sit quietly and talk with each other, even about at topic as contentious as Arik had been. He decided that she was growing up after all. That made him proud but apprehensive. He knew that it was time.

"There's something else that I need to tell you, Dahlia."

He told her the family's secret. She sat still as he revealed his private guilt, the true identity of Arik's father, and why Arik had grown up the way that he had.

Dahlia stared at her father in mute shock, her rage and shame growing darker by the second. This was about so much more than her failed relationship with Arik. She understood everything. It was all so clear. Every time that she thought she knew Arik and what made him tick, something new came up. More pain. More hurt. This time her whole family was involved. They were responsible.

"Abba, why haven't you said anything until now? Does Imma know? How could you let such a thing happen? How could you let this go on for so long? My God! We're such frauds. Here we are rising to the top of Israeli society, harboring such a terrible secret." She covered her face with her hands and shook her head.

"I tried to fix this early on," Benny said, "but I was shot down and threatened if I didn't keep quiet. When I finally could have done something about it, I'm embarrassed to say that I lost my nerve. And we just went on with our lives—"

"But what about their lives, Abba?"

"I really didn't know how to fix it—as ambassador and now as foreign minister—without implicating myself and our family for letting this go on for so many years. My position is too sensitive. It would ruin us. Can you imagine the public scandal—especially now that Arik is a household name—not to mention our dirty laundry that has already been aired in public, over you?"

"But how can we sit here and do nothing, Abba? What does that say about us?"

On the spot, Dahlia resolved to repair what had been broken and to make everything right. *I don't know how I can do it without destroying Abba and our family, but I'll figure that out.* She had to find Arik. She had not spoken to him in over a year, and that time had been the disaster at Pesach. She had no idea how to even reach him. After the parachute episode, the security cordon around him had tightened. His unit, by definition, was separate from the rest of the army. It was unsheathed, like a royal bejeweled sword, only when absolutely vital for national security. Now that he had been thrust into the public eye, purely by accident, he would be pushed even farther into the shadows.

Even if I can find him, will he even look at me? Why should he, considering the way that I treated him? She did not dare hope that they could ever be friends again, no less try to reconstruct what they once had. Besides, she knew that he was with another woman. *That tough bitch who I saw at Tzrifin base.* She was that intelligence officer, Mikki Zohar, General Zohar's daughter. *Arik certainly landed a big fish.*

What will I tell him when I see him? Will he listen to me long enough for me to tell him the truth?

She did not have to wait long to find out.

Dahlia had been assigned to Ward Daled, a guarded hospital ward at Tel HaShomer Hospital that housed high-priority patients.

Shimon Ben Azai was lying in bed with his broken leg in traction and his aching head, broken collarbone, and ribs wrapped in bandages. His father had told him that he was lucky to be alive. His parents, of Yemeni descent, had come to Israel about twenty years earlier, during Operation Magic Carpet, a major emergency airlift that transported the majority of Yemen's Jews to Israel within a space of several weeks, settling them in development towns that really were no more than ghettos. Theirs was Kiryat Malachi, the city of angels, named after Los Angeles, California.

Since their arrival in Israel, Yemeni Jews had formed a persistently disadvantaged social and economic underclass, struggling for jobs, education, and acceptance by the Ashkenazi elite. They felt that they were living under a glass ceiling that prevented their advancement in Israel. The Ben Azais were immeasurably proud of Shimon's appointment to an elite military unit. He was the first commando in the family, perhaps the first in their whole community. For them, his appointment meant that he would get a chance at economic and social success, something that veterans of the special forces enjoyed after discharge from the army. But now this tragedy had occurred. They wondered whether Shimon would be allowed to continue in his unit when his tibia and collarbone had mended. They knew that he had not died on that day only thanks to the American Superman.

Arik was in high spirits when he entered Ward Daled. He flashed his black ID card to the guards at the front entrance to the ward and then walked over to the nurse's station. Sporting a wide, toothy grin, he asked the nurses at the counter where he might find Ben Azai.

The two nurses gaped like schoolgirls at the figure who was standing before them. Arik was deeply suntanned, muscular, and chiseled like a classical statue. His powerful arms were bursting out of his commando dress uniform, which was adorned with black paratrooper wings, officer's bars, and discreet miniature campaign ribbons.

His face appeared sandblasted from the months that he had spent in the field, but his features softened when he flashed his generous, kind smile.

The head nurse, a heavyset middle-aged woman in a tight white uniform, burst out of her office, waving her hands.

"Bevakasha, adoni chayal. Excuse me, but this is a secure ward. Orders are that nobody but immediate family are allowed—Oy! Selicha, lo yadati mi ze. Sorry, I didn't see who it was. Please, Lieutenant Meir, right this way."

He followed her like a puppy dog, flashing a smile and a wink back at the two younger nurses.

The two girls giggled.

One of them said, "Oh, my God! He's so gorgeous! He looks like a Greek idol. His pictures in the papers don't do him justice."

The other said, "I can't believe that we just saw him in person. I can't wait to tell my friends. Can you imagine what it must be like making love to him?"

Dahlia stood silently listening in the anteroom as she arranged her patients' medications on a cart. She stared at Arik through the doorway. He's bigger and taller. Perhaps he grew some more since I last saw him. Perhaps he's just larger than life. His features were far starker, his jaw more powerful, and his very presence more commanding. His eyes, though, still betrayed a soft kindness when he spoke. Perhaps even a hint of sadness. Is it still about me or about his family?

Either way, she felt responsible for everything that had gone wrong in his life. This was her chance to see him again, to speak to him. And what? To apologize? To tell him that I've changed? That I'm here in the army after all and not in the States? Most importantly, she needed to speak to him, to tell him why everything was the way that it was—not just now and not just with her but with his family. She knew Arik's essence, why he had grown up and suffered the way that he had. She needed to share that story with him. She dared to hope that they would be friends again. She had realized that she still loved him. Perhaps . . .

Dahlia finished loading the medication cart. Miri, a sweet, chatty nurse with curly black hair, grabbed the cart from her.

"Sorry, Dahlia. It's my turn to give out the meds to Ben Azai." She winked.

"I know, but I need to do it now. Please!" Dahlia whispered.

"Look, Dahlia, I want to have another look at Mr. Gorgeous, just like you do—"

Dahlia grabbed the handle of the cart and ran pell-mell down the hallway, stopping abruptly at Ben Azai's door.

She conjured up her best professional manner and casually walked into the room. She saw Arik with his back to the door, chatting amiably with Shimon's parents.

Shimon's mother, a dark-complexioned Yemeni woman who was wearing a black kerchief, had placed her hands on Arik's head to bless him for having saved her son. "You should enjoy success and happiness all the days of your life. And may God bless you with a beautiful wife and strong and healthy children." She kissed him on the forehead.

Arik blushed and thanked her.

Dahlia stood silently behind Arik.

"Do you think that Shimon will be thrown out of the unit because of his injuries?" Saadia, Shimon's father, asked Arik sternly.

"I don't see why he should be," Arik said. "After all, none of this was his fault. It was just a freak accident. How could he possibly know that there'd be a malfunction in the door's release mechanism?"

"Boker tov, Shimon. It's time for your pain medication," Dahlia said, fighting to keep her tone even and professional.

Arik turned around slowly, recognizing the voice. Given the presence of the Ben Azais, he kept his tone warm and friendly. "Well, look who's here!" he said in English. And then, in Hebrew, he said, "I won't disturb you, Shimon, if you need to take your meds. I should be going anyway. I'll come back some other time. Don't worry about the unit. I'll see to it your position with us is secure."

Dahlia struggled to maintain her composure. She said, "No need to go. This will just take a minute."

Dahlia administered the medications and then slowly walked out of the room.

When she was gone, Shimon whispered to Arik, "That nurse—her name is Dahlia—is an angel of mercy. She's as beautiful on the inside as she is on the outside. She's kind, wise, and has a real instinct about always doing the right thing. I know it sounds crazy, but when I get out of here I want to ask her out. Patients do fall in love with their nurses, you know."

"Yes, I know, Shimon," Arik said. He was thinking about his own mother and father, but he could not get away from the vague sense of disgust and hurt that he felt at having bumped into Dahlia. "Maybe you should ask her out."

After another half hour of pleasant conversation, Arik left Shimon's room. On his way out of the ward, he saw Dahlia waiting for him at the security desk.

"Shalom, Arik."

"Hello, Dahlia!" Arik said in English. "Fancy meeting you here! Well, if it isn't my favorite junkie! How's your billionaire boyfriend, Ze'evi Ehrenreich, doing? I hear he has friends in high places! How's prison treating him? I know you must miss him terribly, but I'm sure he'll be out in eight to twelve years if he behaves himself. Then the two of you can reconsummate your love for each other."

"I deserve this. I know, Arik. And you don't owe me anything. But I must ask you for a favor. May I speak to you for a few minutes?"

Arik sensed the apprehension in her voice. He also could not help but notice that the gleam and life had come back into her eyes and skin. She had put some weight back on. He admitted to himself that he found her beautiful again.

"I suppose you can. I'm not due back to the base for several hours, but I have other errands to run and have to sneak around snoopy reporters constantly trying to harass me."

"You're the same hero that you were on the basketball court, saving Shimon's life. How did you do such a thing? My father told me that it had never been done before."

"Apparently, my hanging around on the ropes course at camp paid off."

"Your name is everywhere in the news."

"Lucky me. Publicity isn't a good thing in my line of work. The stakes are very high, and we're playing for keeps. There are many folks in the defense ministry that are pretty upset about the publicity, actually. Some of us have had to grow up fast. Getting shot at all the time gets old after a while. Playing against Black September terrorists isn't like playing basketball against Morasha."

"I saw you in the Krav Maga training film when I was in tironut."

"So did the rest of the country. So, how's your family doing? I hear your dad is foreign minister. Very nice. I trust your Mom, Nurit, and Doron are doing fine."

"Yes, thanks."

They walked to the small outdoor café adjacent to the hospital lobby. They ordered two chocolate croissants and café hafooches and then claimed a small round table shielded by an awning from the bright April sunshine.

"What can I do for you, Dahlia?" Arik stared at her intently.

"Well, firstly, I want to apologize for the way that I treated you last year, when you came for Pesach. I was so angry with you for not having heard anything from you for six months. I thought that you had simply lost interest in me, that you had met someone else in the army. I imagined women here throwing themselves at you in droves. You are and have always been a highly desirable man.

"I cried for weeks when I went back to Washington after that Sukkot that you were supposed to spend with me here. I lost weight. I had no desire to do anything but sleep. I locked myself in my room whenever I wasn't in school. My parents felt that they needed to intervene to get me out of the terrible depression that I was in. Abba started taking me to his events to get me out of the house. I still don't understand why you didn't write to me. What did I do to you? I gave myself over to you completely. There was no way for me to get in touch with you. You completely disappeared from my life."

Dahlia looked down at the table and played with her napkin. Arik sat and stared stone-faced at her without moving a muscle.

"I met Ze'evi at the Ambassador's Ball," Dahlia said, "and he seemed extremely charming, at first. My parents strongly encouraged me to go out with him. I resisted the idea at first, but I was beyond grief over you. I gave in and went out with him.

"He was funny, well connected, smart, rich, and never lacked for fun things to do. He had lots of friends who always knew how to have a good time. He took me sailing on his racing yacht, out of Annapolis, and drove me around in his Maserati convertible sports car. He took me out to the ballet and rock concerts. He pilots a private plane and helicopter, and he flew me out to New York for an evening at a Broadway show or a movie premiere. We met Hollywood actors, like Michael Douglas and Warren Beatty, and had courtside seats to the New York Knicks and championship boxing. He seemed to know everyone. I was taken in by his sophistication. He had a key to the Playboy Club in New York, and we even met Hugh Hefner and Frank Sinatra. He seemed to know something about everything. We flew to the Caribbean for sailboat races, and he taught me how to scuba dive. To an eighteen-year-old girl at the Jewish Academy, he was irresistible. The whole thing descended on me like a hurricane. He was twenty-three and had just graduated from NYU."

Dahlia wiped her eyes but managed to continue.

"I didn't realize at the time that I was being manipulated, that for him I was simply arm candy, a plaything. My naïveté was a challenge to him. He teased me that when I turned eighteen he was going to give me the gift of womanhood. He took me back to Aspen, over Christmas, where we stayed at his slope side mansion, with his close circle of friends. He hosted a big party at a fancy club, for all of his rock star friends. The Doors were performing, but the place was crawling with celebrities like Steven Stills, Mick Jagger, John Entwistle from The Who, and band members from Three Dog Night. People were snorting this strange white powder in a line on a mirror with rolled-up dollar bills. I had never seen that before. Ze'evi convinced me to try it. He called it snow. I had never seen snow before."

"Sort of like me the year before," Arik said. That's sort of ironic."

"I inhaled it, and suddenly I felt as if I had been shot into space. It was the most intense exhilaration I had ever felt in my life. The whole world appeared to swirl in the most brilliant colors."

"More than our first kiss?" Arik asked testily, his arms folded over his chest.

Dahlia blushed and looked down. She sighed before continuing her story.

"I began asking him for more snow, and he gave me more and more. I took it home and hid it in my closet. I was taking pills, uppers and downers, anything I could get my hands on. He introduced me to LSD, which I tried three or four times. I didn't realize how hooked I was. My parents had never come in contact with anything like that before, so they suspected nothing, but Imma began to notice that I was losing weight and losing interest in school and my friends. She would constantly ask me if everything was okay. I lied. 'Of course, I am,' I would tell her.

"I even stole money from my parents to get pills and coke when I couldn't get them from Ze'evi. Once, I took five hundred dollars from my mother's bureau, and when she saw that the money was missing, she went ballistic and accused the staff of stealing. I'm ashamed to tell you that the kitchen staff were the prime suspects because of their skin color. It was so sickening."

"I suppose you stood up for them and took responsibility."

Dahlia stared down and pursed her lips.

Arik sighed and shook his head.

"Ze'evi breezed into the residence as if he owned the place and called my parents by their first names, something that really irritated them. They're a bit old fashioned like that, you know." Dahlia smiled. "Imma reminded Abba how you called her ma'am and him Mr. Ambassador. Ze'evi called the black people at the house 'the servants.'

"He even threw the keys to his car at Tomer when he arrived, as if he were the valet, telling him to 'be a good chap and park the car, but be careful not to scuff the bumper.' He told him that the car was custom-made and cost over one hundred thousand dollars. Tomer was ready to snap his neck and would have. He called him 'a spoiled punk.' The whole security detail hated him from the start. I don't know why I didn't listen to them. My father was afraid to confront him, because his dad is one of the richest Jews in the States and the largest contributor to Israel Bonds.

"Abba went to Israel in March that year. That's when he saw you, and that's when I got your letter. Abba found out what was going on with you and all that you had accomplished in such a short time, and he invited you to come visit us for Pesach, without asking me first."

"I'm sure that made you furious," Arik said. "He invited me in the hope that I'd remind you of your past and somehow turn you around, because you were going down the crapper. He never thought for a moment about me as a person, my feelings, and what was likely to happen when I showed up. Very nice man he is! A bit manipulative."

"Anyway, after you left that day, you can imagine the blowup at the residence when Tomer finally told my parents that you showed up and how I treated you. Abba slapped me repeatedly, called me a cheap slut who was throwing her life away. That's when they began to suspect that I was addicted to drugs, I think, but they didn't know what to do. They were at their wits' end. Abba tried to ground me, but I threatened to stay in the States, leave them, become emancipated, and move in with Ze'evi in New York and go to NYU. I was certain that I was in love with him and that he felt the same way about me. I thought that I was all grown up, that I could make my own decisions."

"All bad ones," Arik said. "I heard about your trip to Las Vegas. I never imagined my girlfriend would achieve such fame and notoriety."

"I heard that it was pretty bad in the papers here."

"You have no idea! They went into sordid detail. You put on quite a performance. Perfect for Las Vegas. Your little episode could have threatened your father's whole career. How could you let yourself be compromised like that by such a criminal? Just when I thought I knew you. Tomer filled me in on all the details that never made it into the papers. Believe me, I got no joy watching your downfall. When I saw a picture of you in the papers, leaving the courthouse, I felt sorry for you. Newspaper clippings are funny things."

"When did you speak to Tomer?"

"When he came back here, he asked me to meet him. In fact, he told me most of what you've just told me."

"I didn't know that you even cared to ask," Dahlia said, smiling slightly.

"Actually, I didn't. But Tomer and I have become friends. He told me a lot of things. Who do you think tipped off the FBI to break into Ze'evi's private jet and find his stash of hard drugs? Who do you think had a friendly chat with Ze'evi's father to inform him of the consequences of Ze'evi not apologizing to you in public?"

"Tomer?"

"Tomer and his buddies considered killing Ze'evi and making it look like an accident. They eventually thought better of that and waited for an opportunity to screw him, which they did! I heard your boyfriend got twelve years in his plea bargain. He could get out in eight if he behaves himself. You see, Tomer told me plenty!"

"Did he tell you about your father?"

"What do you mean?"

"Arik, there's more. So much more. I found out why your father was denied compensation after the war and why you grew up nearly penniless."

"Go on!"

"Your father was a great war hero."

"Tell me something I don't know. This simple fact has somehow escaped the notice of those idiots in the defense ministry. That was one of the reasons I decided to come here and give up the chance to play for UCLA. It wasn't just about you, sweetheart," Arik said sardonically. "Keep talking!"

"Well, apparently there was a mix-up, a case of mistaken identity. There was another person, another Ze'ev Myerowitz, who was a commander in the Irgun, that Jewish terrorist org—"

"I know who they were. Keep going!"

"Well, that other Ze'ev commanded the force that broke into Deir Yassin in the middle of the night and murdered more than three hundred innocent, unarmed Arab men, women, and children. It set off a firestorm among the Arabs and was likely the reason why the entire population of the Etsyon Bloc were murdered and their bodies mutilated, as well as the attack on the medical convoy in Jerusalem, going up to Mount Scopus, resulting in the murder of more than thirty doctors and nurses. Ben-Gurion was furious and demanded justice for the Irgun perpetrators. Ze'ev Myerowitz escaped to Marseilles and ended up on the Irgun weapons ship Altalena and most likely died on that ship when it was blown up in Tel Aviv harbor under Rabin's orders. Rabin knew that Myerowitz was on board the ship, and he was out to get him. But Myerowitz's body was never clearly identified. Ben-Gurion needed a body and a perpetrator, and he thought your father was him, that he somehow got smuggled into the hospital. So, they filed a report that he had lost his leg on the Altalena."

"So, let me get this straight. My dad rescues five guys out of a burning bus during the battle for Kastel, getting his left leg blown off in the process, and then get blackballed because that knucklehead Ben-Gurion thinks he's an Irgun guy with the same name? That's ridiculous! Didn't they have personnel records? His medical records? Even back then, they couldn't have been so disorganized!"

"There may have been records, but all of the central command's records were stored in the basement of the Jewish Agency building, in Jerusalem, and were destroyed when it was bombed by the Arabs."

"But there were eyewitnesses from that day in Kastel. Why didn't they vouch for my dad? What about the guys he saved in that bus?"

"That whole unit was decimated over the following year, during the war, including their commanding officer. As far as the bus goes, all the guys died of their wounds within weeks of the event . . . except for one, my dad!"

Arik just sat there and stared at Dahlia for a moment. "Why didn't your father do something about this all along?"

"He says that he tried many times but Ben-Gurion needed a scapegoat and there was nobody else to blame, nobody who was in command on that day. Everyone else involved in the atrocity had fled the country and disappeared. He wouldn't listen to Abba. He even tried to get hold of his hospital records, thinking that they would show that he had been hospitalized before the Altalena affair. But Rabin told him to keep his mouth shut and never bring it up again, especially since Rabin gave the order to fire on other Jews, killing so many on the Altalena. Everybody wanted both the Deir Yassin and Altalena affairs to fade away into the mist."

"That explains Ben Hecht's motivation for writing his book Perfidy. What about now? He's the foreign minister, for God's sake!"

"He tried to bring it up with Dayan last year but was still shot down," she lied.

"Now, of course, he can't go public, because the scandal would jeopardize his career. So, when did he figure out I was the scapegoat's son? That's probably the reason he disliked me from the beginning. I was a ghost come back to haunt him."

"Actually, he found out only two weeks before you showed up for Pesach. Dayan told him."

"Which is one of the reasons he invited me. Now I get it. Guilt is a powerful thing. Isn't it?"

"He was going to tell you then, but the whole thing blew up with me, and he never got the chance."

"Like it would have made a difference, if he wasn't going to do anything about it anyway? Wow! This is something! Oh, by the way, for the record, I wrote to you every other week, from the beginning of my tironut until I came to see you on Pesach. I called the embassy and your house many times, and I could never get through. I was told that number was disconnected and for security reasons was unlisted. I never made it to you on Sukkot because I was incarcerated and placed under guard in a punishment detail day and night for nearly two weeks and then given no leave for nearly two months. Not that I had anywhere to go, anyhow. When did you stop writing to me?"

"What? November, after I met Ze'evi."

"Nice touch, screwing a guy with the same name as my father. I stayed faithful to you. You accused me of—What did you call it?—shtupping some girl in Tel Aviv. There were many women who presented themselves to me in the army, from the moment I arrived at tironut—firing range instructors, secretaries, and what have you—but I turned them all down, telling them I was in a committed relationship. Believe me, with all the hell I went through, I certainly could've used the stress relief! But I didn't, and there you were strutting around like a hooker."

"That's not fair! I didn't!"

"Didn't you? That's not what Tomer told me. Walking around in a sleeveless bright-red halter top, black velvet hot pants, fishnet stockings, high heels, and a mountain of makeup. As a high school senior! What do you call that? Snorting cocaine on Ehrenreich's private jet when you weren't giving him blow jobs.

"You know what, Dahlia? You're your father's daughter. He's a scumbag, and so are you! If it wasn't for my dad, yours would have been toast and you would never have been born. In retrospect, that might not have been a bad thing. And all he got for his bravery was a miserable, poverty-stricken life, with one leg blown off, in and out of the hospital for the past twenty-three years, while your father went off to glory and celebrity. Your father never came clean and stuck up for my dad, just like you never stuck up for Thelma and the rest of the black staff at the residence when they were being shaken down just because of their race. What a piece of work you all are!

"You just love your privileged little lives, and damn everyone else. You never believed enough in me—in us—to think there might have been a legitimate reason you didn't hear from me. The fact is I have no idea why you never got my letters. I wrote them, and I never got anything in return after Sukkot. Quite frankly, at this point, I don't give a crap if you believe me or not. You and Ehrenreich deserve each other."

Arik pulled his beret off his shoulder, took a faded photograph from it, and put it down on the table in front of Dahlia.

"I just remembered I still have this on me. Our picture from camp. Do you remember it? I've kept it all this time, in my beret, even after the disgraceful way you treated me. It reminded me of the happiest time of my life, when I was convinced I'd met the love of my life. I used to look at it all the time. I took it on missions. It gave me strength during basic training when I was going through living hell. Early on, after you threw me out of your house, threatening to call your security detail on me, I still kept this in my beret. I nurtured the vain hope that you'd come to your senses and come back to me some day. I was in such denial. The fact is, until just now, I completely forgot it was still in here.

"You can have it. I have no further use for it or for you. Until you experience some real adversity in your life, you'll never grow up. You'll always think you can get anything you want in life just because of your looks. I have a newsflash for you: Those looks won't last forever. Then, all you'll have left is what you are on the inside. And, from where I sit, that isn't very attractive at all."

"I did experience adversity—during rehab, the court case, and tironut," Dahlia said.

"Please! Don't make me laugh. You haven't experienced anything. Don't kid yourself. I don't even know how they ever let you be a nurse, working around narcotics, with your history."

"I've been clean for over a year, and I intend to stay that way. I've been working very hard to turn my life around. That's plenty of adversity. We've kept the whole drug thing very quiet, and I've lived like a nun since that episode. My father pulled strings for me to get this job, that's true. They have very tight medication inventory control here, and I was closely observed by my supervisors for several months."

"That's self-inflicted adversity. I tried to help you, because I cared so deeply for you, but you threw me out like a dog. You said I had no class. You said I was a loser. Boy, you picked a classy way to break it off between us. What a princess you are."

"So, how's your fancy, high-powered girlfriend? I hear that she's one of the top—"

"You walked away from the privilege of discussing my private life. Mikki is none of your business," Arik said evenly.

"I suppose that you're going to run off now and publicize the whole thing about your father just to ruin me and my family and get your revenge."

Arik pounded the picture on the table so hard that the dishes jumped.

"I'm not like you, Dahlia. I never was. I've never knowingly hurt anyone just for kicks. I'm not wired that way. I'll keep your secret, not because I care a bit about you or your nasty family but because I'm a man of honor. A loser without class, perhaps, a bit rough, like your father called me, but a man of honor nevertheless. Which is more than I can say about you 'classy' types with your charmed lives. I'll find a way to clear my father's name without destroying anybody else and without any help from you or your two-faced father, thank you very much. Frankly, I'm afraid to publicly confront him, for fear of what he'd do to me. I can't have him ruin everything I've worked so hard for during the past two years. You and your family have ruined me and my father once, and I won't take a chance on a second time.

"In retrospect, thinking about it, it's amazing that who your family was never came up when you came to my house in LA for Pesach."

"What do you mean?"

"My father might have known who you were and who your father was. I would have known then what sort of traitor he was to my dad and my whole family. Come to think of it, that must be why my dad seemed to recognize you when we went to visit him in the hospital. Remember? My father is a miserable cripple, but he's nobody's fool. He always taught me an apple doesn't fall far from the tree, and for all your charms I probably would've let you go then if he'd said something. Yours isn't the kind of family I want to be a part of. I would've taken the scholarship, and that would've been the end of it."

"Then, you wouldn't have become who you became here in Israel."

"You think I give a shit about that? I just did what I did to make the best of my life after what you did to me. I'm no great Zionist, but once I make a commitment I stick to it, unlike you. I gave you everything I had, everything I was. I know it wasn't much by Gilad standards, your royal highness. Certainly not by Ehrenreich standards. But it was everything. And look what you did with it. You turned out to be such a sleazebag! Meeting you was the biggest mistake of my life.

"Hey, why do you have an Olympic symbol on your lapel? Huh? So, now you're a member of the Olympic team, too? You really are a big shot," Arik said.

"No."

"So, why are you wearing it?"

"I'm going to Munich as a nurse for the team. I've known many of the members of the team since I was a kid."

"Oh, how nice for you! What are the odds you'd be going to the Olympics if your mom wasn't on the board of Wingate? Slim to none, as an ordinary staff nurse in Tel HaShomer! Always living off your father or mother pulling strings for you. You lot! You'd get nowhere in life without it. You all make me sick!

"And I also found out you paid my way in Aspen without even telling me, like I was some kind of charity case. Penny hadn't paid for everyone at all. Richard paid for himself. I wanted to pay. I'd worked my fingers to the bone for that money so I could pay my own way and even have enough left over to buy something nice for you and have a sense of self-respect. You took even that from me, and you paid for me with money you didn't even earn. You treated me like an inferior even during the good times. You're a disgraceful human being.

"Have a nice life, Dahlia, and don't ever contact me again. Have fun in Munich, and send my regards to Himmler!"

Arik stood up and walked away. Dahlia sat alone, clutching the photograph.

Arik decided that he would not tell Mikki about the encounter. There would be no point.

Chapter 19

There was a lot on Leah's mind. She knew that transitions are always hard, but she thought that this felt like something more. Even though this was a big promotion for Benny, moving the family, yet again, had proved a major challenge. She needed to be back in Israel, at Benny's side, for the many events that he attended. Benny had been back home, in Herzliya, for six weeks already and was shuttling daily to the foreign ministry office in Jerusalem. But Leah had needed to close up the house in Washington, D.C. and prepare for the cargo lift that would take everything to Herzliya by boat. There were so many details to see to, and ensuring that everything went off without a hitch was on her. In addition, their successors, the Rabins, would be arriving in a month and would need to be oriented to the social scene and their responsibilities in Washington. There also was the problem of taking the children out of school before the end of the school year in Washington. Everywhere she turned, she felt the same sense of disruption, which was extremely stressful; she was accustomed to having everything buttoned up at all times. At least now she had the opportunity to take a few blessed days off from the chaos and spend some time in Antwerp with Omah Liesel, her mother's sister and her only living relative, who somehow had survived the concentration camps.

Omah Liesel and Opah Alfred had decided to move to Belgium after the war, because of Opah Alfred's diamond business. Leah had not seen her aunt in so long and, given Benny's new position, did not know when she would have a chance to again. Omah Liesel had become quite elderly and frail, and Leah was very attached to her.

With the rash of terrorist incidents that had been directed at air carriers all over Europe, Benny was nervous about Leah stopping in Europe. He had wanted her to travel by El Al from Washington to Tel Aviv directly, but she insisted on seeing Omah Liesel . . . for what could be the last time. She had assured him that all of the European airports had stepped up their security measures and that everything would be fine. This was just a short flight. The Belgians were quite meticulous, and they was confident that they would not let anything go wrong on their precious Sabena Airlines on a short afternoon hop from Brussels to Tel Aviv.

"Flight 751 ready for boarding. Gate 8A!" a voice from the loudspeaker announced in English and then in French.

As Leah was standing at the gate, she felt a slight chill when she saw several Arabic-looking men and women in line. Her first impulse was to alert security, but she felt a bit foolish. In her new high-profile role, she should not create a scene, especially one based on such obvious stereotyping. Her creating an international incident so early in Benny's tenure as foreign minister would be disastrous.

She reassured herself that many Palestinians flew back and forth between Europe and Israel and preferred to use a European carrier rather than El Al.

She found her seat in the first-class cabin, next to a gregarious diamond dealer who told her that his name was Yitzchak Mizrachi, and then shut her eyes to avoid conversation. She was dog-tired. The Boeing 707 took off smoothly and then settled into a smooth, calm flight. Leah fell asleep, for the first time in a long while able to put her cares behind her.

She was jolted awake by a loud crash. A man dressed in black had kicked open the cockpit door in front of her. She heard shouts in English and French.

"You will do as I say and fly where I tell you, and in return I will not blow your brains out and crash this aircraft! We are not afraid to die."

Leah heard shouts and screams coming from the back of the plane. Suddenly, a loud gunshot rang out, and amid agonizing screams she heard someone fall to the floor.

"They've hijacked the plane!"

"That man's been shot!"

"They're going to kill us all!"

From his aisle seat, Yitzchak had a better view of what was transpiring. He leaned toward Leah and said, "There are two women and a man holding grenades and what appear to be machine guns. What do you think they want? What are they going to do with us?" He was pale, and his hands were shaking.

After the initial shock had set in, Leah lowered her head into her hands.

She wondered what she had been thinking, putting herself at such risk and trusting the security skills of an arrogant European country. She second-guessed why she had not flown El Al? She wished that she had trusted her instincts at the gate. If she had alerted security, maybe she could have averted this whole thing. She had no idea how these terrorists had managed to get weaponry on the plane. On the other hand, she was well aware that even El Al planes had been hijacked during the previous few years. She wondered when the craziness was going to end and what Israel—and Benny—could do about it.

These thoughts swirled in her mind, but she remained silent in her seat. She had been taught in foreign service orientation classes that, in the event of a hostage situation, the best course of action was to remain calm and quiet and not call attention to oneself—and, above all, not to try to do anything heroic. This was not a Hollywood movie. Already, someone on the plane had violated that rule and had paid the price.

A tall, muscular Arabic-looking man emerged from the cockpit. Holding the intercom microphone in his hand, he addressed the passengers.

"Good afternoon, ladies and gentlemen. My name is Captain Ismael Rifat. This plane is now under the command of the Popular Front for the Liberation of Palestine and, in the name of Allah and the Palestinian people, I welcome you to Air Palestine. Our flight has been renamed the Victorious Jeddah. I urge each and every one of you to remain in your seats and obey the commands of my staff, and no harm will come to you. You have already seen the result of insubordination. The first thing I will need is everyone's passport. Reach into your bags, and pass your passports to the person in the aisle seat. Abdel will collect them. Remain in your seats!"

One of the female terrorists emerged from the galley, carrying what appeared to be white putty wrapped in clear plastic. She opened a gym bag and pulled out wires that were attached to small plastic boxes, one of which had an antenna. She gave Rifat a thumbs-up.

He nodded at her and then announced, "In case any of you still have any ideas about overpowering us, Samira has placed plastic explosives at strategic points around the fuselage. At my command, a radio-detonated signal will blow this plane into a thousand pieces. Remember: The difference between us and you is that we are not afraid to die. You Jews and Christians are all cowards."

A collective gasp rippled through the passenger compartment.

The plane continued over the Adriatic Sea, now en route to Cyprus.

At 6:10 p.m., the phone in the office of Golda Meir, the Israeli prime minister, in Jerusalem rang. It was Moshe Dayan.

"Golda, we've just received word from flight control in Nicosia, Cyprus," head said. "A Sabena Airlines flight from Brussels to Tel Aviv has been hijacked by terrorists. They've threatened to blow up the plane with a hundred passengers and crew on board if their demands aren't met."

"Summon all of the Cabinet ministers for an emergency meeting in thirty minutes," she said. "Do we know yet where they are flying or what their demands are?"

"Not yet, but we should find out soon enough."

In less than thirty minutes, the prime minister was presiding over the Cabinet meeting.

"As you know, we have an ongoing hijacking situation," she said. "The terrorists have spoken to no one yet, except the control tower in Nicosia, Cyprus. They have not made any demands, and we do not know where they're going. All that we do know is that the plane is still heading on a course due southeast and is currently over Cyprus. There are three possible scenarios, since we do not believe that the terrorists plan on blowing up the plane in midair or they would have done it by now: Damascus, Beirut, or here."

Shimon Peres, the transportation minister, said, "If they fly to Syria or Lebanon, we'd be unable to rescue the hostages at all. That would mean acceding to their demands. It has been the standing policy of our government never to negotiate with terrorists, the idea being that it would only encourage more outrageous acts."

Pinchas Sapir, the trade and industry minister, said, "What choice do we have if they fly out of our grasp? They would kill every one of them."

Golda looked at Moshe. "What if they fly here, to Israel?" she asked. "What then?"

Looking impassively at her, Moshe said, "Worst case scenario is that they crash land the aircraft into the middle of Tel Aviv, hitting—for example—the Shalom Tower. That would cause maximum damage on the ground. They could literally ignite the whole of downtown Tel Aviv. Or they crash the plane into the airport, killing everyone there. Or they could land the plane at the airport and begin a whole diplomatic and psychological merry-go-round with us."

Golda said, "We need to be ready for all eventualities. We could certainly try to negotiate with them, but my gut feeling tells me that we will end up employing the military option. What is the state of readiness of our commandos, to stage a rescue operation on an aircraft?"

"Sayeret Matkal has been training for about a year or so on a retired El Al 707 out in the desert, trying to perfect their techniques for antiterrorist operations inside aircraft," Moshe said. "They've worked on lightning-fast over-wing approaches to emergency exits, breaking in the doors from the outside, disabling hydraulics and electrical systems from inside and outside the aircraft . . . all while dealing with screaming, frightened passengers. Their firearms have been chosen with great care so as to ensure the neutralization of the terrorists while minimizing risk to innocent civilians."

"Has this ever been attempted before, anywhere in the world?"

"Not to my knowledge. We're in uncharted waters. But if anyone can do it, our boys can."

"Let's hope that it does not come to that."

An aide discreetly walked into the room and handed a note to the prime minster.

"It appears that the aircraft is headed straight for Tel Aviv," Golda said. She looked up from the note and said to Moshe, "I want all of our top military commanders in the control tower at Lod within the hour. Who knows what will transpire over the next twenty-four hours? This will be kept from the press until I give the direct order. Meeting adjourned."

***

As the ministers filed out of the room, Golda motioned for Benny to stay behind.

"We have just gotten word from the Belgian embassy. They have shared the passenger manifest with us. It appears that your wife is on the plane."

When Golda's words sunk in, Benny said, "Oh, my God!"

"What possessed her to go on a European carrier?" Golda asked. "Didn't she attend the security briefings?"

"She did, but she's so headstrong. I couldn't talk sense into her. She was visiting family in Antwerp, and she was in a rush to get home. She's been shuttling back and forth between Washington and Tel Aviv for the past six weeks. In this transition, she needed to be in both places at once."

Golda grabbed his forearm.

"You can be sure that we will do everything in our power to assure her safe return home. We are going to explore every avenue at our disposal."

"I know that for sure. I appreciate your speaking to me about this."

"Go with Moshe to the control tower. I want you there on the spot, to see everything in real time."

"Thank you, Golda."

From Dayan's car phone, Benny put in a call to Tel HaShomer Hospital. Dahlia rushed to the main passenger terminal at Lod Airport.

The call went out to the senior commanders of every branch of the IDF, the central command, air force, paratroops, the Shin Bet, the Mossad, and the

A'man, as well as Dado Elazar, the IDF chief of staff. Within the hour, all of them were assembled in the control tower at Lod Airport.

Dayan was appointed chief negotiator. At his side was General Aharon Yariv, the commander of military intelligence, who was a highly seasoned hostage negotiator, had spent a great deal of time in Arab countries during the past decade, and was highly familiar with the psychology of the Arab mind.

A squadron of Chel Ha'Avir (Israel Air Force) F-4 Phantom fighter jets shot into the air over the ocean, just west of the coastline, to escort the plane. On direct order from the prime minister, they were to shoot the plane out of the sky if it was determined that the hijackers were planning to crash land into the heart of Tel Aviv.

On the plane, one of the male hijackers walked down the aisle, collecting passports. He was followed by the woman who had previously indicated to the new captain that the explosive rigging had been completed. The female hijacker trained her AK-47 on the passengers, while the man, scanned each name and photo and pulled yellow cloths out of a satchel at his side.

"All Jews will wear yellow headbands!" he announced.

"What are they doing?" Leah asked Yitzchak. "I can't see."

Yitzchak turned white. "They're separating Jews from non-Jews! Jews are being required to wear yellow headbands. It's like in the ghetto. Who would have thought such a thing possible in 1972? Why? What are they going to do with us?"

Leah flashed back to her childhood, when she had been chased down a Vienna street by brown-shirted Nazis during the Kristallnacht pogrom in 1938. She tried hard to control her breathing. She squeezed Yitzchak's arm to reassure him or perhaps to reassure herself.

"At least now we know that they aren't planning on blowing up the whole plane," she said. "We need to live from minute to minute now." She forced a smile.

Goldman . . . Fischel . . . Silverberg . . . Yaniv . . . Schloss . . . Steinman . . . Feinstein . . . Harel . . . Slowly, but surely, passports were collected and yellow headbands were put on.

Leah's dread was mounting. She knew that there was no way that she could remain anonymous. She had a diplomatic passport. Moments from now, she would be discovered, and then what?

Father O'Malley and his small flock of pilgrims on the plane insisted on wearing yellow headbands as well, but they were rebuffed by the terrorists.

"If you love your Jews so much, we will find something else to do to you. But for now, Jews first!"

A fresh wave of horror swept through the cabin.

Williams . . . Smith . . . Salame . . . Ben Sasson . . . Thompson . . . Isaacs . . . O'Reilly . . . Hamdi . . . Yusuf . . .

"I swear, I'm not Jewish! I swear!"

The hijacker looked at the man's passport and then back at the man's face. He smiled.

"With a name like Jonah Hillman and a hook nose like yours, I beg to differ."

"I'm not Jewish! Only my father is Jewish, but my mother isn't. I never converted and—"

The stock of the assault rifle crashed down on the man's nose, breaking it and spraying blood in all directions.

"Now you will not look Jewish, you stupid fuck! Now, put on the goddamn headband!"

Leah had turned in her seat to watch the whole nauseating episode.

"How ironic," she whispered to Yitzchak. "For the past twenty-five years, Jews in Israel and abroad have been arguing with one another about mi hu Yehudi, who is a Jew. Nobody can come up with a definition, with so many people coming to Israel from all over the world, all claiming to be Jewish. Many aren't, according to the rabbinate. Our enemies, on the other hand, seem to have absolutely no problem making such a distinction. Perhaps we Jews need to realize that we're still in one boat and not spend so much energy fighting amongst ourselves."

As he approached the front of the coach compartment, the male hijacker called out, "Rifat, here is someone who will not need a headband. Hey, fatty! Give me your fucking passport."

Rabbi Chanoch Bornsztain was the Grand Rebbe of the Radomsk Chassidic sect. Before World War II, that sect had been one of the great rabbinic dynasties of Poland, going back more than two hundred years. But it had been decimated in the ovens of the Chelmno extermination camp. A heavyset man, Rabbi Bornsztain was wearing a long, black silk kaftan, woolen Tzitzit fringes, a white shirt, and a large black velvet skullcap. He looked charismatic, with his long, gray beard and sparkling blue eyes.

On their way home, Bnei Brak, after having visited family in Antwerp, he and his wife now were quietly reciting Psalms and the Shema Yisrael prayer.

"Passport! Passport! Are you deaf? Or don't you speak English?"

The rabbi did not budge but continued praying.

The hijacker put a handgun to the rabbi's forehead.

"I am going to blow your fucking Jew brains out if you do not give me your passport."

Rifat walked over to his man. "Easy, Abdel! No need to do that. I know how to get his passport."

Rifat pulled out a shiny, razor-sharp commando knife and put it to the rabbi's throat. He almost lifted the rabbi out of his seat by pulling his beard skyward. The rabbi showed no emotion. The passengers nearby rose in their seats as if to assist him, but they were warned off at gunpoint.

In a flash, the blade went down, slicing the rabbi's beard in one motion, leaving a large clump of hair in Rifat's hand. A gasp rippled all around the rabbi's seat. The rabbi let out an almost silent groan and then resumed his prayer.

"You live your sheltered life, locked away in your little ghetto. Welcome to the real world, fat rabbi!"

"So, is that what you think?" the Rabbi said suddenly, in accented American English. "Is that what you think?" His eyes were ablaze. "I'll give you my passport." He stood up as if to open the overhead bin but instead pulled up his sleeve. "Do you want my passport? Here is my passport!" Waving his right forearm like a banner, he revealed the tattooed numbers for everyone to see. "This is my passport, given to me at the gates of hell when they shaved off my beard. So, you're not the first." His face was red with rage. "So, you think I'm sheltered? I was a sonderkommando in the Chelmno concentration camp for two years. For two years, I pulled thousands of Jewish corpses out of the gas chambers, tore the gold teeth out of their mouths, and dumped their bodies into the crematorium. So, you think I'm afraid of death? I outlived the SS, and I will outlive you!"

The rabbi stared unflinchingly at Rifat.

"I will blow his fucking brains out!" Abdel yelled, pointing his AK-47 at the rabbi.

"Leave him alone," Rifat said quietly. "This is a holy man of Allah. Something about him gives me the creeps, like we better not harm him. I am told that these people hate the Zionists as much as we do."

Seeing the rabbi standing and staring down the terrorists, in dignity and defiance, undeterred, and with the ragged remnant of his beard now stained with a trickle of blood from a gash on his upper cheek caused rows and rows of passengers around him to weep. Jews wept. Secular Israelis and non-Jews wept. Even Father O'Malley wept. Many wept in grief and anguish. Some wept in pride.

"Please, sit down, Rabbi," Rifat said finally.

The rabbi did. His wife began to care for his wound.

"Okay! Show's over! The rest of you, give me your passports," Rifat said.

"I'll tell you what, Leah," Yitzchack whispered, "This rabbi has serious guts. Who would have thought?"

Leah nodded.

"Give me your passport, Miss."

Leah calmly reached into her purse and gave her passport to Rifat.

"Well, what have we here? A diplomatic passport. Who are you?"

Leah remained silent, looking down at her lap.

"I asked you a question! Tell me who you are."

"Leah. Leah Gilad."

"I am not stupid. I can read. Now, who are you? Are you a diplomat for the Zionist regime?"

"For Israel? No."

"So, who are you? My patience is wearing thin." Rifat touched the holster of his 9mm Beretta.

"I'm the wife of Benny Gilad."

"The new foreign minister, I believe? Very good. Very good indeed. It looks like we have netted a nice big fish." Rifat broke into a big smile as he continued to look at Leah. "I think that you will prove quite useful to us. Quite useful."

Leah felt the oxygen go out of her lungs. Panic enveloped her as she realized that she might not survive the ordeal.

From the control tower at Lod Airport, the IDF chief of staff, Dado Elazar, ordered General Manno Shaked, the commander of all IDF special forces, to summon the Matkal.

After a brutal day that they had spent marching through the Judean Desert, in full combat gear, the members of Arik's unit finally settled down to dinner in the base mess hall. They felt much better after their well-deserved shower and shave and had put on T-shirts, gym shorts, and sandals.

Ehud Barak walked into the mess hall. From the look on his face, his men knew immediately that something was up.

"Chevre, we have a situation."

The mess hall emptied in less than ten seconds.

***

An hour outside Cyprus airspace, Rifat made an announcement to the passengers.

"I hope that you all had a good rest. We have been cleared for landing in Beirut. The Lebanese Army and the PLO have planned a welcome reception for you." He laughed.

The passengers stared blankly ahead in resignation. Long past tears and physical exhaustion, they appeared more like zombies than the living. No one needed to speak, because everyone was thinking the same thoughts. How would they be treated when they had landed? They expected no mercy or even pity. They had heard enough accounts of how Israeli captives were treated—very few emerged alive. Would their death be quick, or would they have to endure torture and depravity? The young women among them were especially concerned about whether they would be raped. The terrorists were accountable to no one, much less to the Geneva Conventions. Raw fear tore through the hearts of those captive souls as the plane slowly inched closer and closer to the Mediterranean coast.

Leah was shaking with fright, thinking of what would be done to her when the plane had landed. She stared blankly out the window and prayed.

And then, she saw it. At 7 p.m., the coastline became visible, lighted by the setting sun behind them. She did not know whether to feel elated or terrified, so at first, she was simply confused. She recognized the Shalom Meir Tower below! They were not over Beirut, after all. They were over Tel Aviv!

She wondered why the terrorists had flown the plane to Tel Aviv and what they hoped to gain. She could not begin to imagine. It would have been so much more logical for them to go to Beirut, unless they intended to crash the plane into the middle of downtown Tel Aviv! She had read plots like that in spy thrillers and she feared that she was about to become part of one. The realization that she was going to die within the next five minutes caused her entire consciousness to move into slow motion. She saw herself as a child in Vienna, a teenager in Germany, a fighter in the Palmach underground, and a wife and mother. She thought of Nurit and Doron and what would become of them without a mother. She was grateful that at least Dahlia was grown up. She imagined that Benny was beside himself with worry about her, likely having heard by now that she was on board. She wondered whether his worry would be converted to grief as he and all of Tel Aviv witnessed the conflagration that would become her tomb. Finally, she wondered how she could have been so stupid.

The airplane swung around, going into a steep turn over the Judean Hills as it descended toward the setting sun. At almost exactly 7 p.m., it touched down gently on the main runway at Lod Airport. It was escorted to a remote airstrip far from the passenger terminal.

Lod Airport went into lockdown. Passengers from other flights and awaiting family members were evacuated to a safe zone. Other aircraft were removed from main runway positions. Border guards ringed the perimeter with armored vehicles armed with 7.62mm MAG machine guns. Admission to the airport was restricted to ambulances, firefighting equipment, and military vehicles with written orders, so when the men of Arik's unit showed up at the main entrance to the airport in a commandeered civilian Plymouth Valiant and dressed in T-shirts, gym shorts, and sandals, they were brusquely turned away by Uzi-toting border guards wearing green berets.

"The airport is closed. You clowns are going to have to turn around and go back to the beach."

The guard stuck his Uzi into the driver's side window of the car.

The driver was not amused.

"May I suggest that you get on the phone and call up to the control tower, to General Shaked? He's expecting us. I'd do that right now, if I were you."

"Who are you guys, and what is your business here?"

"We can't tell you that, and our business is none of your business."

"I have my orders, and my orders are not to let anyone in who is not on my list, so either you tell me who you are or you just turn around like good little boys."

Dani, who was sitting in the passenger seat, got out of the car. "I have a better idea. Why don't I come over there and kick the crap out of you?"

Seeing the commotion, several other border guards approached the car.

"I have an even better idea," the first guard said. "Why don't I shoot you in the head and be done with it?"

Dani was losing his temper. "You're going to be very sorry for delaying us."

Arik jumped out of the backseat. "Now, now, boys, play nice," he said. "So sorry to have troubled you, gentlemen. We must have taken a wrong turn. We were headed for the beach, and we're late for our volleyball game."

Arik shot Dani a look. They casually got back into the car. They knew that creating a scene would serve no purpose.

The driver made a U-turn and headed back the way they had come for about a half mile, before making a sharp left turn onto a dirt service road that led to an abandoned warehouse. Behind the building lay the twenty-foot-tall perimeter fence topped by two feet of coiled razor wire. The commandos timed the patrol vehicles.

"Last one over is a rotten egg!" Arik called out cheerfully.

In less than thirty seconds, all five men were over the fence and running to an empty El Al cargo hangar. It was Ehud Barak's designated meeting point for their "volleyball" tournament.

***

Rifat and Samira were standing in the cockpit, holding the pilot and copilot at gunpoint. Rifat ordered the pilot, Reginald Levy, to establish contact with the control tower.

"This is Mr. Goldberg," Moshe Dayan said, "I've been appointed as your contact person, by the Israeli government. You've hijacked a commercial airliner and entered our airspace illegally. You're in violation of international law."

Rifat spoke calmly. "Stealing someone else's country is a violation of international law. I will speak to someone who has the authority to carry out my demands."

"I have that authority."

"I am going to make this very simple. I am going to read out all the names of our 317 freedom fighters that are languishing in your prisons. You are to release them, or I will begin to execute the hostages one by one. I will begin with the foreign minister's wife. You have eight hours."

Thus, began the duel of wits between Rifat and Dayan.

For Barak's men, the situation was uncharted territory. When the assault group met at the hangar, none of them knew what to expect. Working in conjunction with the brass in the control tower, Barak began formulating a plan. He split up his men into three squads. Arik's group, the primary assault squad, donned dark camouflage and headed for the thorny underbrush that surrounded the runway, out of sight of the terrorists. They were laden down with a full battle load of ammunition and grenades. Arik scanned the aircraft for a target. He found none, but he had been briefed that the initial strategy was to make the plane unflyable without triggering the onboard warning lights. His squad's task was to cover the personnel—El Al mechanics and Matkal commandos—who were converging on the aircraft.

Earlier, the entire team had met with El Al technicians, who had determined that the best way to disable the aircraft was to drain the oil lines to the hydraulic fuel systems, which could be done by approaching the aircraft from the rear and then opening the hydraulic valves.

All the while, Dayan methodically explained to Rifat that Israel was prepared to accede to the terrorists' demands but that unraveling the red tape to accomplish the release of so many prisoners would take time. After all, those prisoners were scattered in many different detention facilities. Rifat became annoyed and restless. He expressed second thoughts about having landed in Israel and threatened to leave the country. He demanded that the plane be refueled.

Arik's squad was summoned back to the hangar, which now held an identical Boeing 707. Throughout the night, they practiced sprinting up the wings, along the fuselage, and into the emergency exits. They repeated the maneuvers more than a dozen times, each time refining and recalibrating the choreography, like a fine ballet. This was Arik's favorite part of the process. For him, practicing commando maneuvers was the same as perfecting a turnaround backward dunk or a flying side kick. Repetition was the key to success. After several hours, Barak was satisfied that they had perfected the method of the assault. All the while, Dayan tried to bore Rifat with a minute-by-minute account of the bureaucratic measures to free the prisoners and the diplomatic maneuvering through third parties to schedule a flight from Tel Aviv to Cairo, the capital of Egypt, a hostile country.

Arik and his fellow commandos donned white coveralls. After a false start when Manno Shaked realized that the so-called mechanics were wearing combat boots rather than awkward work boots, the squad was called back to change. After changing their boots, they repeated and perfected the attack maneuvers. The commandos finally made their way to the plane, under the watchful eye of the terrorists. Ostensibly, they were there to refuel the plane and make final preflight preparations. Arik stationed himself discreetly under the front emergency exit.

Under the watchful eyes of the terrorists, the so-called mechanics made a big show of refueling the plane. All the while, they actually were disabling the plane's navigation and steering systems.

Rifat noticed some of the warning lights flashing. He instructed the Belgian flight engineer to leave the aircraft to check on the cause of the warning lights. When the flight engineer saw the so-called mechanics, he understood. He gestured to the cockpit that everything was fine, just as the wires to the warning lights were cut, shutting them off.

Very slowly, the air was let out of the tires. The plane's pilot, Captain Reginald Levy, a World War II RAF fighter jet veteran, realized that the plane was being disabled slowly and systematically. He silently signaled to his copilot, and he understood that the ordeal would end soon and in Israel.

By 3 a.m., the air inside the plane's cabin had become hot, humid, and thick with body odor and vomit. Nobody on board was able to sleep. No one had had anything to eat or drink in twelve hours. The lights had been kept on, but the ventilation system had been turned off. Several of the passengers had fainted, and water was becoming in short supply. The men had stripped down to their undershirts, but they still were bathed in sweat. Without ventilation, a strong smell—a mixture of human waste and disinfectant—came from the bathrooms.

Leah shifted uncomfortably in her seat. She was clearly distraught.

"What's the matter?" Yitzchak asked.

"I've got to use the toilet," Leah said. She raised her hand reluctantly.

Rifat turned around, his ever present 9mm pistol held in front of him. "What is it?" he asked.

"I have to use the toilet, please."

Rifat laughed over the loudspeaker. "The wife of the Foreign Minister, Mrs. Gilad, needs to take a piss. Let me see a show of hands. How many people think that I should let her go? . . . I'm sorry, Mrs. Foreign Minister. Nobody raised their hands. I am afraid you cannot go." He sneered.

"I've been sitting here for nine hours already. You can't expect me to pee in my seat, but that's what I'll have to do."

Rifat laughed. "That would be quite funny."

"Until we all have to live with the already worsening smell," Leah said.

Rifat thought for a moment. "Okay, but make it fast."

She slowly walked to the malodorous lavatory. When she reached for the door, Rifat stuck his foot in front of her.

"No closing doors," he said flatly.

"You can't expect me to do it with you watching me."

"You can do it in your seat. Take your pick." He pointed his gun at her head. "It would make quite a headline in Tel Aviv: 'Wife of the Foreign Minister Shot in the Head While Taking a Piss on the Toilet.'" He proudly laughed at his own joke. "Now, piss!"

She was mortified but relieved herself anyway. She prayed silently that the hell that she and the other passengers were in would end soon. Part of her preferred death to this humiliation. Her mounting desperation suddenly prevailed over good sense. She looked up at the leering Rifat and said, "Have you no sense of shame or dignity?"

Rifat's grin exploded in rage. "What about the dignity of the Palestinian people? Have you Zionists no shame about that? Twenty-four years of refugee camps, poverty, misery, and persecution while you Zionists have your little party in the sun. Not for long! The Arab world will not abide this injustice forever. We are rising up all over the world, and we will hunt you Jews down like the dogs you are and give you what you deserve! All this pretty talk about 'the ingathering of the exiles' and 'making the desert bloom' and all that crap. Our little exercise today is an alarm clock to the world to wake up to the terrible injustice that you Jews have done to us."

"The land is ours just as much as it's yours," Leah said. "We lived here for thousands of years before the first Arab showed up, and we were thrown out of our land by the Romans and left to wander for two thousand years. We're simply coming back home."

"Is that so? So, Mrs. Foreign Minister, can you give me your ancestors' address? Where exactly did they live? Where were they buried? Where did they work? Where did they play? Can you tell me that? Of course, you can't! And do you know why? Because they were never there."

Leah, feeling empowered, forgot that she was still sitting on the toilet, half naked. She said, "If you dig six inches below the surface anywhere in this country, you'll find evidence of our forefathers. The temple in Jerusalem has been uncovered, the Dead Sea Scrolls—"

"Those Jews are long gone," Rifat said. "You have been descended from Gypsies and Khazars, adopted the Jew faith, and now, after you have been slaughtered and thrown out by the Europeans, you have come here to steal our homes. The Europeans helped you to drive us out of our homes and gave you our land to relieve their guilt about your history. Why did they not give you Switzerland? There is no people on earth that would have put up with this treatment. The Palestinians have been very patient. We are a patient people. But no longer. It is time to take back what is ours!"

"And there's no possibility that we could live in peace and share this land or divide it up?" Leah asked cautiously. Many progressive Israelis are in favor of that."

"I do not give a shit what they are in favor of. I would burn Tel Aviv to the ground if I could. My father was a baker in Jaffa, and so was his father before him, and his father before him, for three hundred years. That all came to an end in July of 1948, when the Zionists gave him twenty-four hours to pack up and get out or risk getting himself and his family killed. I grew up in a refugee camp in Jordan. I knew nothing but living in a tent—winter and summer, in the rain and frost. I have nothing to lose. I will fight to the death to get my father's bakery back, if you Zionists have not bulldozed it already to make way for some apartment complex. Why should we give you half our land? You are willing to split it up, because you all know in your heart of hearts that it really does not belong to you. Remember Solomon? I studied your Bible at Oxford." For the first time in the entire hijacking, Rifat sounded emotional.

"So, you're prepared to die today?" Leah asked.

"Who knows how this is all going to end. If we have to die, so be it. I am not afraid to die. I am going to Paradise with Allah, where there will be no Zionists. You see, all of you are going to hell with the pigs and the dogs. I may die today, but so will you! Now, get your pretty little ass off the toilet and get back to your seat!"

Leah pulled up her slacks and quietly walked back toward her window seat. In the aisle, Rifat suddenly grabbed her by her ponytail and dragged her backward and screaming into the front galley.

"Please, don't! Please! Please!"

"Let me show you what I do to Zionist bitches!"

"No! Please, let me go!" Her cries reverberated throughout the cabin.

Rifat slammed her face down onto the floor, making her nose bleed, and pinned her there so that Samira could cut off her ponytail with her razor-sharp commando knife.

"You know, Samira, I should start a collection of Jewish hair. I feel like Geronimo cutting off the scalps of the white men who occupied their territory."

"Maybe we should scalp her?" Samira giggled.

"Perhaps we will. There is still time." Rifat laughed.

The passengers would long be haunted by Leah's sobs contrasting with Samira's laughter as she kicked Leah's ribs with her boots.

***

The next morning, two delegations—one Belgian and one from the International Red Cross—attempted to approach the aircraft. They were rudely rebuffed by the terrorists. Rifat had decided that he needed to let the Israelis know that he meant business and that time was running out.

Later that morning, the front emergency door swung open. In the doorway, Leah stood wide-eyed and terrified. There was a hushed silence in the control tower as the Israeli military and government personnel saw, through binoculars, Leah with a hangman's noose around her neck and two bricks of plastic explosive strapped to her waist. Samira was holding a gun to the back of her head. Her hair appeared to have been cut off.

"Mr. Goldberg," Rifat said into the radio, "let me tell you how things are going to go now. You have exactly two hours to deliver my men to the tarmac and have the TWA airplane ready to fly them to Cairo, or I will push Mrs. Gilad from the plane with that noose around her neck. Before she has a chance to die by hanging, I will detonate her and, with her, the gas tank under the wing, blowing up the plane."

Leah was suddenly pulled back inside by the noose.

Benny fainted. He had to be taken from the control tower to the VIP lounge, where Dahlia was waiting, shaking with fright.

Captain Levy was sent out to discuss the details of the new plan. He let the Israelis know that the terrorists meant business. He also coolly gave them intelligence on the terrorists' state of mind, their weapons, how many they were, and where they were stationed in the plane. With that new, detailed information in mind, the assault team returned to the hangar to refine the plan further.

Meanwhile, the Israelis assembled 317 Arabic-speaking Sephardic Israeli soldiers, put them in track suits, and even allowed them to speak to the terrorists over the intercom, thanking them for having secured their release.

The assault teams returned to the plane. This time, they were armed with Beretta .22-caliber handguns, more than adequate for close-quarters combat. The fear was that 9mm weapons were too powerful and might ignite a fuel tank.

The new weapons also were easier to conceal when they were instructed by Rifat to unzip their coveralls to the waist, to show that they were unarmed, as they approached the aircraft. They also were searched by Red Cross personnel, who found the weapons further down in their coveralls but reassured Rifat that the technicians were unarmed.

At Barak's signal, one squad stood by each of the two exits and one squad managed to enter the aircraft from below.

Leah was filled with dread and a sense of foreboding. She knew that the terrorists were negotiating for the release of their comrades. She was uncertain whether they would let them the passengers live even if the Israelis acceded to their demands. The female terrorist who had removed the explosives from Leah had placed them in the cockpit and wired them into place. Leah wondered whether they were going to blow up the plane like they had done in Jordan in 1970 but this time with everyone still on board.

She stared out the window, trying to figure out was going on.

Rifat announced on the intercom, "It appears that the cowards in your Zionist regime have decided to release our freedom fighters from their unlawful imprisonment. Your ground crews are making ready for our departure. We will be flying to a friendly Arab capital—Damascus."

There were collective gasps and cries from the passengers.

"My God! They're going to kill us all!"

"Shemah Yisrael!"

Some started singing "Ani Maamin," the song sung by Jews in the cattle cars on their way to the Nazi death camps.

Leah stared blankly out the window at the airline mechanics and maintenance men, who all were wearing grimy white El Al work uniforms, milling around on the tarmac near the airplane. She was beyond fear, pain, or shame. She was entirely resigned to her fate. She had decided that this was not going to end well for her. Her scalp, face, and ribs ached terribly, and she dared not look in a mirror. Her gaze was unfocused, blurred. She watched the technicians crawl around the tarmac. They looked like white lizards swirling in an abstract pattern that you might see in a kaleidoscope.

Suddenly, something caught her eye. Despite her blurry vision, she recognized some of the mechanics: Ehud, Dani, Marko, Bibi, Arik . . . Arik!

She knew that the plane would not be going anywhere tonight or any other night, but she wondered who would have to die in the process.

The constant squawk of the radio fell silent. She wondered whether the negotiations had failed, when the shooting of the passengers might start, and whether she would be the first. She saw a line of buses approaching the plane. The buses stopped about thirty feet away, and then Arabs in identical blue and white track suits slowly walked toward the plane. They marched in a procession, as if on parade, in front of the terrorists that were milling around in the cockpit and at the rear doors of the aircraft. She refused to accept the possibility that Israel had capitulated to the terrorists' demands by releasing mass murderers from prison so that they could kill again. Rifat was standing in the cockpit, looking out the window, smiling broadly.

Suddenly, there was a deafening crash. Sergeant Uri Laskov kicked open the front door of the plane and burst through it. Rifat jumped out of the cockpit and emptied a half magazine of bullets at him. Uri, wounded in the chest, fell to the floor of the first-class galley. Arik jumped in behind him and shot the gun out of Rifat's hand. Rifat, in a panic, darted into the lavatory and slammed the door behind him.

Arik smiled and then shrugged. "You've got to be kidding me!" he said out loud in English as he pumped a magazine of bullets from his Beretta into the unarmored lavatory door. He then kicked in the door and found Rifat's bullet-riddled body draped over the toilet.

Behind Arik, Samira jumped out of the cockpit, aiming her commando knife at his neck. She was tackled and disarmed by Marko. She somehow managed though to get hold of Marko's Beretta, though, with her right arm and fire a round into Bibi's shoulder.

Arik tore the handgun out of her grip and flipped it back to Marko.

"Nice girls don't play with knives and guns," Arik said to her in English as he grasped her right forearm between his fists and snapped her radius and ulna in two as if they were matchsticks.

She let out a blood-curdling shriek.

"You won't be causing any trouble with that arm anytime soon," he said.

Arik pushed her up against the wall, ten inches off the floor, using his forearm as a bar under her jaw to cut off her flow of oxygen. Her blouse rode up, revealing an electronic transmitter around her waist, under her slacks. Based on the information from the pilot, Arik immediately understood that the transmitter was for detonating the bomb in the cockpit.

"Pull her pants down, Marko!" Arik cried.

Marko carefully removed the detonator, disarmed it, and then pulled her slacks back up.

"Now, where are the rest of your friends hiding?" Arik asked Samira. "Where are the timer explosives?"

"I will not tell you anything, Zionist pig! You can kill me. I do not care!" She resisted his grip and spit into his face.

"Who said anything about killing you? I'm not going to kill you. I'm just going to cause you the worst pain you've ever experienced in your whole life. Now, where are the others? And where are the explosives?"

He dug his fingernail hard into the xyphoid process, at the bottom of her sternum. She howled and began hyperventilating.

"Amos! Hail the control tower," Arik said. "We have to get the passenger staircases here on the double. I think there are timers set to blow up the plane any minute. We have to get the passengers off the plane now! Hurry!"

Over the din, Arik heard Itzik call out from the rear of the plane, "All clear! Four terrorists in total, all secure. We're starting to unload the passengers, in case they prepared any other surprises."

"Sorry to eat and run, but I've got to go! It's been real!" Arik silenced Samira with a punch under her eye. She was carried off the plane, bleeding and unconscious.

In numb shock, Leah had witnessed the fury of the assault that had unfolded ten feet in front of her. She found herself curled up in a fetal position, partly out of fear but also so that Arik would not see her. A moment's distraction could have been fatal for him. After the humiliating hell that she had been put through by the terrorists, Arik and his men had swooped in like avenging angels. Through her delirium, she realized that her life had come full circle. This young man who she and Benny had had little regard for—who they had snubbed and driven out of Dahlia's life—had become a legendary giant in Israel. And he had done it all through his own devices and talent. He was indeed his father's son. Now that the immediate threat had passed, she wanted to let him know that she was there and perhaps establish eye contact to express her gratitude. He was no more than ten feet away from her, in the front of the coach compartment, but his back was turned as he directed the evacuation.

She tried calling out his name, several times, but no sound came out of her throat. Her throat had seized up. In a moment, she was lost in the crowd of people who were frantically pushing and shoving in front of her as they tried desperately to get out of the aircraft.

"Arik, there's a young girl in row ten who appears to be seriously injured, with multiple gunshot wounds," Itzik called from the back of the plane.

Arik bounded across the top of the seats like a cheetah and grabbed the girl in his arms.

"Make way! Make way! Wounded first!" Arik said as he pushed passengers aside in the aisle.

Arik carried her out the rear door. Together, they slid down the wing and landed on a pile of army mattresses. He handed her into the waiting arms of the paramedics, who took off in a Magen David Adom ambulance.

He repeatedly climbed back up the wing and into the rear of the cabin, helping to calm the crowd and assist older passengers and children in jumping from the wing to the mattresses below, until rolling staircases could be brought and attached to the doors. Sappers entered the aircraft and disarmed the explosive devices.

As soon as the bombs had been disarmed, buses pulled up to the aircraft. Within a few minutes, the rest of the passengers had evacuated down the staircases.

Still in shock, Leah was standing at the foot of the stairs, trying to find Arik in the crowd. But she was having no success. He had simply vanished.

When she walked up to the nearest bus, she was met by Ehud Barak.

"Mrs. Gilad, there's a car waiting for you on the other side of the plane. Please, come with me."

"Thank you for everything that you did today. You are true heroes of Israel."

Barak smiled. "Are you okay? Do you need an ambulance? Let's take you to the hospital. Your face is all swollen, and both of your eyes are blackened."

"Please don't. Physically, I think I'm okay,"—she clutched her ribs—"but I'm emotionally traumatized. Can you get me something to put on my head? It's going to take a while for me to recover from this. All I want to do is see my husband and children again."

"Of course. I understand. Your husband and daughter have been here from the beginning. They're in the VIP lounge with the other family members of the hostages. I'll take you to them." He took a red beret out of his pocket and fastened it onto her head.

"Thank you."

Barak held her arm as he led her into the gaily-lighted room full of dignitaries and well-wishers mingling with the freed hostages. She became dizzy and disoriented by the bright lights and photographers' flashbulbs. In only thirty minutes, she had gone from the gates of hell to this happy chaos. Her knees felt like rubber. She felt nauseated and faint.

Suddenly, she was swept off her feet by Benny and Dahlia, who both were weeping tears of joy and relief. They held on to her tightly, all too aware of how close they had come to losing her. Dahlia grabbed a moist napkin and wiped her mother's stunned, bleeding face. Leah took a long drink of ice-cold Tempo cola.

Members of the general staff lined up to greet Leah and wish her well. She thanked every one them for their courage and professionalism. They all drank a L'Chaim, a toast to life, for the great deliverance. Leah continued looking for Arik in the crowd. She thought that this would be a wonderful opportunity for her and her family to publicly thank him, but he was nowhere to be seen.

Leah discreetly walked over to Manno Shaked. "The boys were so brave and professional on the plane," she said. "I would love to thank them in person. They swooped in like guardian angels, and then they were gone. Just like that. I thought that they would be here."

Manno said quietly, "Those men are the best that we have. They are our guardian angels. We have to keep them close to the vest and unsheathe them very carefully and sparingly. They were flown out by helicopter within fifteen minutes of the rescue, and they're probably back at their base by now. Ehud is here as their spokesman. I'm sure that he'll be happy to convey your good wishes. If you put something in writing, I'll be sure to have it read to them at the base. It will be greatly appreciated. I'm just glad that you got out in one piece. You came very close—"

"Thanks again." She nodded and shook his hand.

"You're quite welcome." He smiled.

The Gilads drove home in silence.

When they pulled up to the house, Leah finally spoke. "I was long past hope of ever seeing this place again. I was singled out by those animals and physically degraded. I think that they may have broken my nose. Look at what they did to my hair!" She began to cry.

"Are you sure that we shouldn't take you to the hospital?"

"No, I don't want to go. I'll go to Ichilov Hospital. Tomorrow. There's something that I need to tell you both before I drop off to sleep."

"Imma, please let me help you to bed," Dahlia said. "I'll bring you some hot soup."

"Get some rest, motek," Benny said. "We'll have ample opportunity to talk tomorrow."

"No, Benny, this can't wait. Dahlia, please don't go."

She told them about the toilet and hair incident and about her angel who had seen to it that justice was done to her tormentor, how she had seen Rifat's bloody corpse draped over that same toilet.

"Did Arik say anything to you?" Dahlia asked.

"He didn't recognize me during the rescue, and I couldn't get his attention afterward. Manno told me that the men were whisked away within minutes after they stabilized the scene. I would like to contact him to convey my gratitude. Is there anything that you can do, Benny?"

"Please, don't do that, Imma," Dahlia said. "Arik did what he had to do, what he was trained to do. Being a hero comes naturally to him, but I don't think that he wants to hear from us personally. We need to let this go. No, let him go." It's only right. Let's concentrate on getting you better."

"Dahlia's right," Benny said. "Get some rest."

***

One hour before Shabbat, Arik roared his Harley Davidson up Savyon street in Omer and into the Zohars' driveway. As he pulled in, he revved the engine loudly twice. Mikki, who was waiting for him, bolted out the door, at full speed, followed by Shmulik and Yael. She leaped into his arms, wrapped her legs around his waist and her arms around his neck, and kissed him hard. Not to be outdone, both of her parents hugged Arik tightly.

"We read the mission summaries and saw the photos taken by the passengers during the operation," Shmulik said, beaming. "You burst in like John Wayne and killed their ringleader. You Americans have such a love affair with your cowboys. We're so proud of what you did. It was simply a great piece of commando work."

Arik smiled back and put an arm around Shmulik's shoulder. "I have only one love affair in my life, and that's with your daughter. Thanks to Mikki, I know what I'm fighting for and I never let myself forget it."

"You're our fourth son, Arik. Welcome home!" Shmulik kissed Arik on the cheek.

"I don't think I've eaten in two days," Arik said. "The sheep in the shuk that I passed driving down here started to look good—uncooked!" He laughed.

Yael smiled broadly. "I'm so glad that you're starving. I've prepared a feast in your honor."

In his usual bedroom, Arik shed his uniform and jumped into the shower. Mikki laid out clean clothes for him to wear now, as well as the clothes that he would need later for Shabbat. When she picked up his soiled uniform to put it in the laundry, she noticed that the photo was no longer in his beret.

She smiled.

Lufthansa flight 681 from Tel Aviv gently touched down at Munich's Franz Josef Strauss Airport. Dahlia stared out the window beside her seat. She had traveled throughout Europe a great deal, but she never had gotten used to the gray, gloomy skies of late August. Israel was always bathed in bright sunshine at that time of the year. But she simply had needed to get out of the house. The past few months with her mother had been very difficult. Leah was irritable, and her sleepless nights were punctuated with nightmares and screaming. Thankfully, Dahlia had been able to get her into Professor Shaul Melchior's private psychiatry clinic. Leah was now going there for counseling during the day and taking strong sedatives at night.

Back in March, Dahlia had been presented with the opportunity to accompany Israel's team to the Summer Olympics in Munich. She had always had an interest in sports medicine, and traveling with the team would allow her to gain some experience in it. Arik was right. She did always get the plum assignment because of her parent's connections. But protectsia was simply part of life in Israel. If she had not accepted the opportunity, someone else would have.

For Dahlia, the best part about the trip was that she would be representing Israel to the world. This particular Olympics was especially poignant, because it would be the first one held in Germany since the Holocaust, which had ended only twenty-seven years earlier. And here she was, proudly representing a sovereign Jewish state, one of the nations of the world. Even if Israel did not win a single medal, just being here was victory enough. Dahlia also was looking forward to assisting Gita Weitzman, the nursing director of surgical intensive care at Rambam Hospital in Haifa, whose trauma unit saw countless civilian and military casualties each year. Rambam was the go-to facility for serious sports injuries in Israel. Gita had represented Israel in the 1960 Olympics, in Rome, as a high jumper. The Israeli sports medicine staff had brought a fair amount of medical supplies with them, but Gita had reassured Dahlia that the quantity was overkill. She had said that the most that would be required of the staff would be administering first aid until the injured athlete was transferred to one of the world-class medical facilities in Munich.

After collecting their luggage, the members of the Israeli delegation gathered in front of the buses that were to take them to their quarters. Shmuel Lalkin, the head of the delegation, read out the room assignments. Esther and Shlomit were assigned to a women's dormitory but, due to insufficient space in that facility, Gita and Dahlia were to go stay at the same dormitory as the men, at Connollystrasse 31, albeit one floor above them.

The following day's opening ceremony would be an all-day affair despite its official afternoon start, so after dinner and few drinks everyone settled into their rooms.

By noon on opening day, the excitement outside Olympic Stadium was at a fevered pitch. Impossible as it seemed, the energy continued to rise as tens of thousands of fans and dignitaries crowded into the venue. Athletes crowded into the staging area, milling about and socializing. Each team had its own custom outfit of blazer, slacks, and fedora. Dahlia felt very stylish in Israel's blue blazer, light khaki pants, and white fedora. The Israeli flag and seal were displayed on her left breast pocket. As the music started, Dahlia proudly looked around herself at the team. She had known most of them through her mother's involvement with Wingate, but she had a special place in her heart for the lovable "big galoots" on the wrestling team. Many of them had known her since childhood, and they treated her like a younger sister.

The procession began, and the countries' teams marched slowly into the stadium. After Ireland, Israel filed into the stadium. When the Israelis entered the parade track, the stadium erupted into thunderous applause. Dahlia and the other Israelis broke into broad smiles and waved to the onlookers and fans. Dahlia experienced intense exhilaration about the sheer size of the venue and the throng that was cheering for Israel. The delegations paraded around the field and then assembled in their assigned places. After the ceremonial speeches, including one from the German president, the Olympic torch was lit and the chairman of the International Olympic Committee declared the Games of the XX Olympiad—the 1972 Summer Olympics—open.

After the ceremony, Dahlia wandered around the Olympic village, taking in the sights and sounds, with members of the Israeli team. She thought that it was so amazing to see so many people from all over the world, and she took the time to approach people and introduce herself. Before the trip, she had memorized the flags of the Arab countries and resolved to be careful of introducing herself to anyone from them. According to its motto, this was supposed to be "the "cheerful Games," but why tempt fate? In her wandering, she could not help but notice the sheer number of fit, cute guys that she saw.

That evening, most of the athletes attended a massive opening reception on the floor of the Sporthalle, the Olympic Sports Hall, where the gymnastics and handball events would take place. The entire venue had been turned into a giant disco, with techno bands—music that had recently become popular—playing music at a deafening level. Dahlia saw mountains of shrimp, mussels, and German pork wieners on the long buffet. They looked so good to her, and she was famished. In all of the excitement, she had forgotten to eat. What harm will it do to compromise on my kosher restrictions . . . just a little? She found the shrimp a bit fishy but decided that it was better dipped in the reddish-brown sauce next to it. She thought the sausage was amazing. Gallons of tap beer were being served. A beer drinker herself, she enjoyed the evening more and more.

Dahlia had no trouble finding dance partners, because she was more worldly and sophisticated than the other women in the Israeli delegation, who congregated shyly at the side of the hall. Why not take advantage of this occasion? She had not gone out socially for so long that she had almost forgotten what it felt like. Soon, she was dancing up a storm with a succession of eligible bachelors from a dozen countries.

A tall, blond athlete with a kind face approached her. "I'm Werner. Would you care to dance?"

"I'm Dahlia. Yes, nice to meet you."

Dahlia enjoyed the dancing tremendously, although she could not hear anything that her partner was saying over the deafening techno. They soon retreated to the side of the hall.

"So, what is your event, Werner?"

"I'm with the West German swim team. I'm doing the 4 x 200-meter freestyle relay as well the individual 200-meter freestyle. You?"

"I'm not competing. I'm a sports medicine specialist with the Israeli delegation. I'm getting the athletes ready for competition, with a view toward injury prevention, conditioning stretches, and what have you and providing initial treatment for sports injuries."

"Auch, how nice. My sister was in Israel last year. She spent the summer on a kibbutz in the Galilee. Is that where you are from?"

"No, I'm from a small town on the seaside, near Tel Aviv: Herzliya.

"Is this your first time in Germany?"

"Yes. Do you live here, Werner?"

"I'm from Hanover, but I went to university in Bavaria, and I trained here for the Games."

"So, you're a local expert."

"There are so many nice things to do in Munich, and they've really dressed the place up for the Games. There are some great clubs in town: jazz, disco, techno. We also have fairytale castles like Neuschwanstein. Do you want to take a spin around town? It's quite noisy in here. I'll give you a nighttime tour."

"Sure, I'd like that."

Dahlia excused herself from the rest of the Israeli delegation, told Gita not to wait up late for her, and went off with Werner.

She waited at the curb while Werner went to get his motorcycle. When he pulled up on a BMW motorcycle, he handed her a helmet. She put it on, hopped on, and off they went. He showed her all of the sights—the Old Town Hall, the Marienplatz, or central square, and the Nymphenburg Palace—which were all brilliantly lighted. They ended up in Schwabing, an area known to locals for its nightclubs and bars, and sat there talking until midnight.

Afterward, Werner took her back to Connollystrasse 31.

"I had a great time tonight," he said. "My week is packed until the 31st, with the relay finals. I really can't see you much until then, but I'll get you seats to the swimming events, if you like. It should be very exciting. There's an American swimming sensation, a Jewish fellow, Mark Spitz. Have you heard of him? They say that he's going to walk away with all the singles gold medals."

"I've heard of him but never met him. I'll come to watch you. It should be fun."

Werner kissed her on the cheek.

***

The first week of the Games, Dahlia dutifully watched the Israelis compete in wrestling and weightlifting. They competed their hearts out but did not qualify for the medal round. She was quite busy in the locker room, applying icepacks, assisting with aquatic therapy, dressing wounds, and taping sore wrists and ankles.

One evening, Dahlia went out with Werner for a night on the town with some of his teammates. He suggested the Hofbräuhaus am Platzl, a famous four-hundred-year-old beer hall famous for its huge selection of beer, traditional Bavarian food, and music. She had read in her guidebook that it was a favorite of Adolf Hitler, who frequented it with party officials whenever he visited Munich. She felt a bit creeped out by that but agreed to go, deciding that since Hitler would not be in attendance on that night she would feed her curiosity. For several hours, they laughed, rollicked to the music, ate Bavarian pork chops, fried onions, and potatoes au gratin, a specialty of the house, and drank large steins of frothy beer. Werner and his buddies were amazed at how much beer his little Israeli fräulein could consume.

Dahlia excused herself from the table for a moment.

Klaus, one of Werner's teammates, leaned toward him. "Werner, that's quite a cute little leibshoen you've picked up. She doesn't even look Jewish," he joked.

"What's a Jew supposed to look like?"

"You know. Short, chubby. Swarthy. Curly, black hair. Big nose. You know that most of them really do look like that," Klaus ribbed him.

Another teammate, Rudolf, said, smirking, "So, Romeo, have you sampled any of the kosher meat yet? It looks rather tasty!"

"You're both schweinhunds. That hasn't been on my mind, and I have no intention—"

"Well, you should!" Klaus said. "Any man would! It's raining gold, and you're standing under an umbrella."

"I don't know . . . I sense something about her, something in her past that would make her unavailable for casual sex. I don't know why, but I feel it. I won't push it unless she lets me know that she's ready."

***

The women's gymnastics events were riveting. The big star was Olga Korbut, a Soviet gymnast who wowed the audience with her effortless technical skill. After helping her team to win a gold medal, she fell short in the individual vault final but finally won gold on the balance beam and floor exercise events. Thus, continued the Soviet domination of indoor Summer Olympic events.

As she watched the rings, pommel horse, and floor exercises of the men's team gymnastics competition, Dahlia's thoughts drifted to the past, to Arik. What happened to us? We were so sure that we'd be together forever. How did we screw it up so badly? Why didn't he write to me when I missed him so much? And then, how cruel she had been to him when he had come to Herzliya for Pesach, how stupid she had been to follow a cruel pied piper and be suckered in. She thought back to her catastrophic meeting with Arik at Tel HaShomer Hospital. It was there that she had seen a side of Arik that she had not known existed: hatred. God, I miss him! I still love him! She felt a sharp pang, knowing how far away he was, both physically and emotionally.

The swimming competitions were the most exciting of all. Mark Spitz won seven gold medals in individual and team swimming events. It irritated Dahlia that he always was referred to as "the Jewish American" swimmer rather than simply "an American" swimmer. What difference should him being Jewish make? But some things don't change with the passage of time, even here in Munich.

Werner picked her out in the audience and smiled at her prior to his 4x200 meter relay. He and the other members of the team won the silver medal in that event, and later he won the bronze in the 200-meter freestyle. When he emerged from the locker room, she jumped into his arms to congratulate him.

***

September 1st was an off day for the Israeli weightlifting and wrestling teams, so Dahlia was able to take a break. Gita chided her about not spending more time with the Israeli team, but she understood that Dahlia was a free spirit. On yet another overcast, dreary day, Werner picked Dahlia up at Connollystrasse 31 on his motorcycle.

"What do you want to do today? I'm feeling adventurous," Dahlia said.

"I think that today we should do something different. Have you been to Dachau?"

"As a tourist or a prisoner?"

"Not funny, Dahlia."

"Sorry . . . Where were your parents during the war?"

"My father was a foot soldier in the Wehrmacht. He wasn't Nazi SS, in case you're wondering. He fought in North Africa and Italy, under Rommel, and ended up in the Battle of the Bulge in December of 1944. He surrendered eventually to the Americans, in March of 1945 outside of Hamburg. My mother worked on the Enigma Project, doing secret codes. Do you think that all Germans were Nazis?"

Dahlia shrugged.

"The fact is that most ordinary Germans feel that we too were occupied by the Nazis during the war. Many feared for their lives if they spoke out."

"Werner, I've seen those newsreels from before the War. Those Nuremberg rallies . . . There were millions of ordinary Germans there that just adored the Führer. They threw flowers at the marching soldiers."

"We didn't know then what Hitler would become. We were so destitute after the First World War and the Depression. He offered us hope for prosperity. That's what we were cheering about."

"Then he led Germany to commit the most terrible crimes in human history."

Werner looked down and frowned.

***

They drove out of town, along the Autobahn for several miles, and then took an exit that led to the site of Dachau concentration camp, which was no more than a large clearing in the lush woods. The gray day had given way to a fine, misty drizzle. Werner gave Dahlia a light poncho to wear. They left the motorcycle and their helmets in the parking lot and walked down the gravel path. Suddenly, the massive gate to the compound loomed in front of them. He held her hand tightly.

Dahlia stared quietly at the words on the gate: ARBEIT MACHT FREI (WORK BRINGS FREEDOM). How many times was I told about those terrible words that adorned the entrances to the hell on earth that the Nazis created for the races that they disapproved of? And this is one of them.

They walked along, slowly, entering the barbed-wire enclosure. They were alone. They passed rows of wooden barracks, many of which had been reconstructed to look like they had looked during the War.

"Were your parents in the camps?" Werner asked.

"My father was born in what was then Palestine, and my mother grew up in Vienna. She was sent to Theresienstadt camp, which was less brutal than the others. Eventually, she was placed with a German family in Munich as part of the Lebensborn project, which presupposed that Jews with Aryan racial features could be rehabilitated." As Dahlia said that last word, she grimaced.

"I've heard of it. I guess that explains your pure blonde hair."

"Racially pure, that's me!"

"I'm sorry, Dahlia. I didn't mean it like that."

After seeing the barracks, they walked up a long path to a large brick building with a tall smokestack. They walked inside and then stood still, looking at rows of open double doors. These were the openings to the crematoria ovens.

Dahlia thought about Arik's father having been in Buchenwald. How many people passed through this opening in their last moments on earth? She sniffed quietly, tears welling up in her eyes. She could not speak.

Werner held her close. "I'm sorry. I'm so sorry. Perhaps coming here wasn't such a great idea."

"No, Werner, I'm glad that we did. I needed to see this, especially on a trip like this . . . and with you." She embraced him, holding on tightly. After another hour of looking through the museum and the small bookstore, Dahlia and Werner walked hand in hand through the camp gate.

Dahlia felt the irony of that moment. She felt herself drawing closer to Werner, a German, a non-Jew as they walked hand in hand out of Dachau concentration camp. I'm very fond of him, but where can this relationship lead? How will it end? Is it just a brief dalliance or something more? She did not know, but she decided to let it play out. All of my best-laid plans turned to disaster. Why not just let events carry me for a while and see where they lead?

On the drive back to Munich, they stopped for a late lunch at a small cafe along the road.

"Do you know the address of the family that took your mother in? You said that they lived in Munich."

"My mother stays in touch with them. She gave me their address."

"Would you like to visit them? I can take you there."

"I have no more days off until after the Games, but I plan on staying here for a few more days after the closing ceremonies, just to travel about. I might go then. I'd also like to visit the Black Forest. I hear that it's beautiful in mid-September, with the changing colors."

"Why don't we go together? There are some very charming guesthouses along the way where we could spend the night."

Dahlia smiled slightly and nodded. "I'd like that." She leaned over and kissed him.

***

Sunday, September 3rd was a big day for track and field event finals. Werner got tickets for Dahlia and him to see the women's pentathlon 800 meter and men's 10,000 meter races. They also went to the last of the swimming finals.

That night was the big disco bash at the P1 club. The largest and one of the oldest nightclubs in southern Germany, it had room for nearly 1,000 partygoers to revel on it massive dance floor. The pounding techno-disco music was accompanied by glittering laser lights and streaming psychedelic wall displays. The nightclub was filled with athletes from all over the world who were happy to see and be seen at the hottest event in town. Dahlia had brought from Israel a sequined blouse, skintight white silk pants, and high heels, just in case. She was so glad that she had. When Werner picked her up, he gazed admiringly at her.

As soon as they walked into the nightclub, the beat of the music hit them viscerally and they were immersed in the sound. They danced for an hour. Werner went to the bar to get them drinks. They continued to dance, champagne glasses in hand.

Suddenly, Dahlia was shoved from the side, spilling her champagne all over her face and chest.

"What the hell?"

She turned around and saw the hate-filled face of Leila Marwani, a sprinter from the Syrian team, who had a male teammate by her side.

"Look at the famous German medal winner Werner Lampe with his little Jewish bitch. Why don't you take her back to Auschwitz, where she belongs? I think that she would make a fine lampshade."

Dahlia lunged at her, punching her nose hard enough to draw blood. Werner tried to separate them, but the Syrian man jumped at him. Werner dropped him with a kick to the groin. Dahlia grabbed a bunch of Leila's hair and slammed her head to the floor.

The dancing stopped. The dancers looked around, startled and confused.

Leila stared up at Werner as she wiped her bloody nose with a napkin. She yelled, "You started the process with these fucking Jews, and we will finish them off!"

Dahlia's clothes were torn and dirty. She grabbed Werner's elbow and said, "Please, take me home, Werner. I don't want to be here anymore."

Outside the nightclub, he held her tightly and said, "I'm so sorry for that."

"It wasn't your fault, Werner, but don't you see? This shit never ends. I think that tomorrow night I'll spend the evening with my delegation. They're going to see Fiddler on the Roof. I need to clear my head. Perhaps an evening of 'doing Jewish' will help. I've barely spent any social time with them since I've been here."

"Auch. But promise me that we'll see each other later in the week." He kissed her gently.

"I promise."

It was a cloudless September morning. Throngs of athletes were leaving the Olympic Village and heading toward the venues. Dahlia was particularly excited about the men's basketball final. She somehow had missed the earlier games, but she would be at the final. Israel was playing the Soviet Union for the gold medal. In the Basketball Hall were at least 7,200 people. Israeli flags were fluttering everywhere. Basketball fans from all over the world had come to witness the great miracle that was unfolding. Nobody would have expected this matchup. The Soviet team was warming up at one end of the court. Suddenly, to thunderous cheers from the crowd, the Israeli team, in its blue and white uniforms, ran onto the court from a corner of the arena. She watched, astonished, as the players ran in, bounced basketballs, jumped toward the basket, and casually laid the balls up and in.

She strained her eyes to see the players. She got out her binoculars and looked through them. She saw Arik—Arik!—running toward the basket and taking layups and jump shots. Also on the Israeli team were Elgin Baylor, Mark Spitz—who was wearing a bathing suit instead of shorts—and Larry Pollack and
• Stuie Fishman, the phenomes from Camp Morasha. What are they doing here, on the Israeli national basketball team?

Play commenced at a furious pace, the Soviets matching the Israeli team point for point, but Arik seemed to be playing flat footed. At halftime, the score was tied at 42.

Dahlia rushed down to courtside and screamed at Arik to stop fooling around and let loose like he had at camp. He looked in her direction, expressionless, and then walked away. She yelled louder, "What are you waiting for, Arik? Arik!"

The second half seemed to drag on, like the first. But suddenly, with seven minutes left in the game, Elgin and Arik opened up and let loose a thundering barrage that sent the Soviets reeling. There were midair twists and turns, hook dunks, spinning dunks, no-look crosscourt passes, and ball handling at such speed that their hands were almost invisible. Arik jumped from the top of the key and executed an unbelievable dunk. The Soviets, bewildered and confused, allowed their game to falter. The Israelis won, 84-64.

Dahlia had a front seat at the medal ceremony. Her heart almost burst with pride when the Israeli flag was raised, amid a loud roar of shouts, whistles, and cheers. Standing on the middle podium with the rest of the Israeli team, Arik leaned forward as a gold medal was placed around his neck. "Hatikva" began to play.

Loud shouts, screams, gunshots, and the sound of crashing furniture jolted Dahlia wide awake.

The alarm clock beside her bed read 4:35 a.m. Hell seemed to have broken loose one floor below her.

Gita was up and out of her bed, reaching for her sneakers. "Dahlia, put your shoes on. Now!"

"What's going on?"

Dahlia looked genuinely puzzled, but she put her shoes on.

There were more gunshots and then a sudden triumphant cry of "Allah hu Akhbar! Allah hu Akhbar!"

"We're under terrorist attack," Gita said. "We have to get out of here right now. It's only a matter of time before—"

"We can't go down the stairs," Dahlia said.

They heard footsteps coming up the staircase and shouts getting closer to their room.

"We have to jump from the balcony. There's no other way out," Gita said.

They heard machine gun fire again, followed by cries of anguish. The terrorists were nearly at their door. Suddenly, there was loud pounding at the door and shouts in Arabic.

They're trying to break the door down!

Dahlia and Gita ran out to the balcony.

"Jump now, Dahlia. Jump!" Like a cat, Gita vaulted over the railing and landed on the pavement below.

As Dahlia climbed onto the railing to jump, she flashed back to the bright shining lights and sounds of that night in Ze'evi's hotel room in Las Vegas. She hesitated. Suddenly, gunshots tore through the bedroom door. As Dahlia let go of the railing, she felt a sharp thud against her shoulder, as if she had been hit by a baseball bat. She became disoriented. She hit the pavement, facedown, with a sickening crunch. Lying on her left forearm and the side of her face, she felt searing, nauseating pain shoot from her left arm, shoulder, and cheek. Still disoriented, she looked down and saw her forearm dangling at an unnatural angle, blood spurting out of her wrist. Her nose was bleeding, and a spot of blood on the upper left corner of her shirt was spreading at an alarming rate.

Gita was there, trying to drag her by her right arm and screaming down at her, "Get up! Run, Dahlia, run! Run! There's no time! Run!"

The terrorists had reached the balcony. They began to spray the area with gunfire. Gita finally succeeded in dragging Dahlia to safety under a concrete awning ten feet away. As soon as the shooting subsided, they ran flat out for fifty yards. They bumped into Shaul Ladany, an Israeli race walker, who had jumped as well. He explained that he had run over to the American dormitory to alert the staff of the attack.

"We're under attack!" Shaul told Gita. "They've killed Weinberg and Romano and have corralled everyone else into apartment one. Run down the street. There's a police station at the end of the street. Get help!" He suddenly got a good look at Dahlia. "Wait, Gita, Dahlia's been shot in the chest!"

For Dahlia, the world seemed to be in slow motion. Voices were muffled. Sounds were distorted. Her T-shirt was soaked in blood. Her eyes had glassed over, and her speech had become slurred She could not feel her arms or legs. The world began to spin, and then everything went black. She collapsed in a heap on the grass.

"Gita, if we don't get her to a hospital fast, she's going to die!"

Gita needed no further prompting. She was a trained battlefield nurse. She scooped Dahlia up into her arms and began running toward the police station. A passing police car summoned an ambulance. Suddenly, the whole area was alight with sirens and police heading toward Connollystrasse 31 from every direction.

***

When Dahlia awoke, she was lying on a gurney, on clean sheets and a pillow, and wearing a hospital gown. There was an IV in her right arm. Gita was at her side, stroking her forehead.

"Where am I? What happened?" Dahlia said. Clarity was coming back but slowly.

"We've been attacked by Arab terrorists. They've killed Romano and Weinberg and taken nine of the team hostage. We narrowly escaped with our lives. You've been shot through your shoulder and broken your left arm. You've also got quite a black eye and a bloody nose, but there are no major facial injuries. We're in the Technical University Rechts der Isar Hospital's trauma unit—the best in Munich. They'll take very good care of you. We've already contacted your parents. They wanted to come, but in view of the situation here the Shin Bet has instructed them to stay in Israel for now. We told them that you're safe and that we'll take good care of you."

Dahlia tried to sit up but fell back in reaction to the searing pain in her chest and arm. She groaned and then asked, "What do you think will happen to the others?"

"Who knows? The terrorists are demanding the release of over two hundred fifty jailed terrorists in Israeli prisons, or they'll kill all the hostages. The problem is that Golda has already said that Israel will never negotiate with terrorists."

Dahlia narrowed her eyes. "Bastards! Do they actually think that they'll get away with this? Are we going to send Matkal in to rescue them?"

"Nobody knows yet. Even if we wanted to, who says that the German government would allow us to come in and shoot up the place?"

"This is so great! Here we are in Munich only twenty-seven years after the Shoah, thinking that we could simply pretend that it never happened and come here, have a big party, dance with Germans, eat their wiener schnitzel, and forget that we're simply Jews in Germany after all. You know, Gita, that hurts me more than my arm does. How foolish we were coming here . . . just to watch Jews being killed in Germany because they're Jews . . . again."

The curtains parted, and in walked a tall, muscular man with Mediterranean features and a thick mustache. He appeared to have a large weapon holstered under his blazer. "Shalom, ladies. I'm Udi. I'm here from the Israeli consulate to make sure that you're okay."

"Mossad?"

"Like I said, I'm here to make sure that you're okay. Once you're feeling better, we'll need to ask you some questions about what happened this morning. Gita, we'll talk to you while Dahlia is—"

"Dahlia is what? What are you talking about?"

The curtain parted again.

A tall, blond, balding man in a long white coat suddenly appeared. He was speaking to someone behind the curtain. "Ich spreche kein Hebraeisch."

"That's okay, Heinreich. I speak English. Some of us do, you know!" Dahlia called out.

"Dahlia, manners! We're guests here!" Gita said.

The man turned toward Dahlia. "Gut mornink, Fräulein. My name ist Professor Karl Gradinger. I am chief of traumatology in zis clinic. You have had quite a shock zis mornink. I vill take a look at you."

He pulled down Dahlia's gown, exposing her left shoulder. She winced when he pulled off the temporary dressing to expose the bullet hole. From that entry wound, a trickle of blood ran down her arm. At his direction, she leaned forward, exposing her back. He inspected the larger bullet hole, the exit wound. He moved her shoulder through a full range of motion and tested her motor strength. She winced in pain. He checked her brachial pulse, inside the elbow, and then gently removed the temporary splint from her forearm so that he could check her radial pulse, at the wrist, as well as finger motion and sensation. Dahlia sickened when she saw her mid-forearm, which was bent backward sixty degrees, giving the appearance of another elbow. On the palm side of the arm, one end of the ulna was protruding through the skin. Blood was dripping from that wound, too. Dr. Gradinger replaced the dressings.

"Well, Fräulein, I have looked at your X-rays, and it appears zat you have sustained a compound midshaft fracture of your radius and ulna zat will require immediate surgery. You were very fortunate. Ze gunshot vound zat you have sustained to your left shoulder area ist superficial. It ist a through-and-through injury, which means zat ze bullet came in your front and came out your back, over here, so you do not have a bullet inside you. It broke ze tip of your acromion bone, but zat will heal without consequence. Had ze bullet come down four centimeters lower, it vould have hit your subclavian artery and you vould have been dead in under five minutes."

"Isn't there any way that the surgery can wait until I get home? With all due respect, I have had more than enough of Munich. I want to go home."

"I'm afraid, Fräulein, zat vould be very inadvisable."

He looked at Gita and Udi. "Her vounds and ze bones need immediate attention. Delay vill dramatically raise ze risk of infection and possible gangrene." He looked at Dahlia again. "Besides, if I vere you, I vould get my care here. In Germany, our orthopedic techniques are far more advanced zan in Israel and you vill get much better care."

Dahlia glared at him. You sanctimonious, arrogant Nazi prick.

"You zee," he said, "here in Germany, ve use ze latest bone plate fixation technique to repair the fractures. It is called AO: Arbeitsgemeinschaft für Osteosynthesefragen. Zey vill not have zis in Israel for years."

He gave Dahlia a self-satisfied grin before continuing. "Zit also appears zat you may have broken your nose. While you are in ze operating theatre, ve vill have our facial surgeon set your nose as vell. Ve vill make ready for surgery soon. Ja?"

After the doctor walked away, Dahlia looked at Udi and asked, "Did he just say he's going to do an arbeit macht frei operation on me? Why doesn't he just pin a yellow star on my gown and send me off to the soap factory?"

She was livid. She glanced down at the chair, at her T-shirt which had been placed there. The left sleeve was torn, and the Israeli flag in the upper left corner, under the Olympics symbol, was soaked in blood.

Gita said, "Look, Dahlia, just let him do what he needs to do, and then we'll go home. They're very good here. I had a chance to wander about the trauma ward and speak to some of the nurses here while you were resting. It's really quite impressive. We can learn something from them." Gita opened the curtains. "The spotless cleanliness here is unheard of in our hospitals. Just take a look. Everything here runs so quietly and efficiently that you would never believe that we're in a trauma hospital. I have seen several road accidents come in and be treated with a quiet speed and efficiency that I have never seen before. They have a completely holistic approach to care here. Everything is done as a team. The patient is rapidly triaged, and preset specialty teams, depending on the nature of the injuries, converge on the patient and do everything at once in a team approach. Nothing is left out, and patients are treated very efficiently. It runs like a symphony orchestra. I'm quite impressed."

Dahlia listened intently and eventually relented. Within minutes, she was being wheeled into surgery. Udi, who had arranged to change into scrubs and mask, accompanied her into the operating room, his concealed weapon at the ready.

When Dahlia awoke, she was in the recovery room. Gita, her face ashen, was at her side, holding her hand. Udi was standing at the door, his face drawn and sullen.

"Is it done?" Dahlia asked.

"Yes," Gita said quietly.

"What's going on? Did they rescue the boys?"

"No, Dahlia," Gita said, looking downward. "They're all dead." She gave a long, heavy, bitter sigh. "The details are still fuzzy, but it appears that the terrorists and hostages were driven to the airport after midnight, giving the appearance that they were leaving. The athletes were placed into a helicopter and chained to their seats, to be transferred to a waiting airliner. As the terrorists were making their way to the helicopters, a shot rang out from the police. The terrorists fired back with machine guns at the police, and one of them threw a grenade into the helicopter. It blew up with all the boys inside. They died instantly. Rumor has it that the heads of the Mossad and Shin Bet were here in the command center, trying to convince the Germans to let us rescue them ourselves. They refused, thinking that they could do it themselves. Simple arrogance on their part. They have no experience with this, and they botched the operation."

"And, as usual, we paid the price," Dahlia said tearfully.

"Yes. There will be a large memorial service later today in Olympic Stadium. Your father is flying in with some other government officials."

"I-I just want to get out of here," Dahlia said.

"You need to rest."

"Crap! I'll be at the memorial service if it kills me. I'm serious. I want out of here today! Tell Dr. Mengele that I'm fine, and sign me out today!"

"Let's see how you do. If you're strong enough to travel, we'll sign you out. You've lost a lot of blood. But now you have a visitor." Gita turned, pulled open the curtain around Dahlia's bed, and left the room.

Dahlia looked up. Werner, pale and distraught, was looking down at her. He was wearing a blue and white skullcap. She stared at him but said nothing for a long while.

"How are you feeling?" he asked. "Are you in much pain?"

"Some. The medical staff here is very good. I think that they patched me up as best as could be expected."

"I was so worried about you when I heard, but I waited until you were out of the recovery room to see you."

"Thanks," she said weakly.

"What are your plans?"

"I'm going to stay just until the memorial service. My father is coming in as part of the government delegation. Afterward, I'll go home, where I belong. I think that I overreached again . . ."

"What do you mean?"

"I've been trying to live someone else's life, and I've forgotten how to live my own. Every time I do it, my world somehow comes crashing down. This time in a most terrible way." Dahlia began to weep. "Those men were like brothers to me. I've known them almost my whole life. When we came here, I paid little attention to them. I took them completely for granted. I went off on my own, with you. I never even got to say good-bye to them. I'm absolutely shattered. I'm going home, where I belong, Werner. I'm so sorry."

"Dahlia, I understand. You should know that I think that you're an incredibly beautiful person inside and out. The time that we spent together will always live in my heart as a fond memory. I'm a better man for having known you."

"Even with my black eyes?" She had noticed that effect of her broken nose.

"Even with your black eyes. I won't forget you. I love you, but I know that I must let you go. Please, don't think that everyone hates Jews. I know that today it's hard to believe that, but Israel will know no better friend in Europe than Germany. Perhaps one day I'll travel to Israel, and when I do I'd like to call on you."

Dahlia stared up at him and blinked.

Werner leaned down and kissed her.

***

The Olympic Stadium was packed for the memorial service. The Olympic flag and the flags of most of the participating countries had been lowered to half-mast. The crowd was a sea of blue and white skullcaps. Even the German president was wearing one. Everyone stood quietly at attention as the remnant of the Israeli delegation entered the stadium. What a contrast to the last time, less than two weeks ago, when we walked in to music and loud cheers. Dahlia walked in just behind the Israel flag bearer, wearing her blue blazer and white fedora, with her arm in a sling and her head held high, and took her place on the podium, next to her father, who was gravely staring into space. He hugged her tightly around the waist but taking care with her injuries.

There was a long program of speeches by German and Israeli dignitaries. Dahlia wept openly, holding a tissue to her lips, when the Kaddish and "Hatikvah" were chanted.

After the ceremony, Gita and Dahlia went back to Gita's hotel room. Gita changed into scrubs.

"Where are you going?"

"We've been asked by the German authorities to help identify the bodies . . . before placement of the shrouds for their transfer to Israel."

"I'm coming with you," Dahlia said flatly.

"No. I don't want you to. Stay here and rest."

"I won't! I'm a still a member of the medical team and a soldier in Tzahal, and I will function as such!"

"Are you sure that you're up to it?"

Dahlia nodded. "I'll dress quickly. Please, help me with my scrub shirt."

They entered the Bayerisches Landeskriminalamt forensic morgue in downtown Munich and then were ushered into the examination room. There, on exam tables, lay the charred bodies of the men whom, only a week earlier, Dahlia had laughed with, eaten with, drunk with, and cared for. Gita, Dahlia, and Dr. Amnon Galili, the forensic pathologist who had just arrived from Israel, walked from man to man and took copious notes and photographs. After an hour, Dr. Galili began comparing the dental records that had been shipped from Israel and to the current X-rays to identify the bodies for burial back in Israel. Dahlia did her best to maintain a flat countenance as she and Gita went about the painstaking work. With her good arm, she helped with the shrouds.

Before the departure of the flight home, Dahlia went down to the quiet, dimly lighted cargo hold of the El Al Boeing 707 and walked among the bodies, which were in plain pine coffins arranged in rows and draped in Israeli flags. She was returning to Israel a changed person filled with powerful resolve. This is what Arik meant by 'significant adversity.' He was right. Things will be different from now on.

She suddenly felt a new purpose in her life. She made up her mind that she would no longer be simply a floor nurse. She would no longer wander. She would no longer allow events to overtake her. She would no longer be led astray by people she would later judge marginal to her primary priorities in life.

Instead, she would proactively steer her course, command, and play a pivotal role in the outcome of events around her. She wanted to be in a position such that the decisions that she made would have a profound positive impact on people's lives. She decided that she would get into a trauma nurse training program. She was determined to be indispensable and powerful. She felt that she had always had that ability in her but somehow had let it slide during the previous few years. She had become lazy and superficial and allowed herself to be victimized. But no longer. Her epiphany hit home with the force of a freight train. It's time for me to grow up and be counted! I will no longer succumb to despair and temptation. I will grow. I will lead.

***

The ordeal in Munich had played itself out on Israeli television. The image of one of the terrorists, wearing a white ski mask, taunting the police and the media from the balcony of Connollystrasse 31 would haunt a generation of Israelis. The fact that Jews had been murdered in Germany, again, simply because they were Jews hit home for Israelis, and they were shaken to the core. Clearly, the Black September group's attack, which had been designed to rattle the Israeli people and the Western world, had had its effect. What Black September had not counted on was the ferocity of Israel's response to the atrocity, which would transpire during the next decade. Jewish blood was no longer cheap. For the men of Sayeret Matkal and the Mossad, the attack was a clarion call to arms, unprecedented in Israel's war on terror and injustice. Israel's response would be called Operation Wrath of God.

***

Arik and the other men of his unit left their forward base in the Golan along the Syrian border and walked into the nearby Moshav Ramat Magshimim, where they stood by helplessly watching the horrific events unfolding on TV. Why weren't we called in to handle the situation in Munich? Arik wondered. They had the expertise and the firepower to end it quickly and efficiently. They had waited for the phone to ring with a call from the office of the IDF's chief of staff sending them on their way. But the call had never come. The German police had thought that they could handle the situation on their own. They had tried, with tragic results. They would have eleven more Jews on their consciences, in addition to the other six million.

The news anchor reported that, in addition to the eleven deaths, one member of the Israeli delegation had been seriously wounded. Apparently, that person was a nurse who was accompanying the team. Arik was dumbfounded as he watched the remnant of the Israeli delegation enter the Olympic Stadium for the memorial service. Behind the Israeli flag bearer walked Dahlia in her blue blazer and with her arm in a large white sling. She held her head high, and her swollen, blackened face was solemn. Arik watched as she walked up to the dais and took her place alongside her father, a crumpled tissue covering her lips. He thought about his admonition to her about growing up through adversity.

A powerful rage seized him and the other highly trained killers in his unit. We'll make those bastards pay for what they did to those eleven athletes. I'll make them pay in spades for what they did to Dahlia.

***

Pan Am flight 972 from New York landed in Rome at 2 p.m. and discharged its passengers. Although it was late September, long past the summer high season, Rome was still a popular destination for American tourists and graduate students who loved climbing over ancient Roman ruins for pleasure or study. With its wealth of Renaissance art, restaurants, architecture, and Catholic worship, the eternal city was a paradise for the mind, heart, and palate, continuously showering its visitors with a warm welcome.

The passengers lined up quietly at customs. Among the passengers who had just arrived from Kennedy Airport was a tall American with a light-brown beard and a short, blonde ponytail tied tightly in the back, under a worn baseball cap, who was wearing rumpled jeans and a torn T-shirt. He handed his passport to the officer in the booth, who looked up at him appraisingly. The photo displayed the smiling face of a hippie who had had one too many experiences with marijuana.

"Kurt Simmons?"

"Yes."

"Good afternoon, Mr. Simmons. What is the purpose of your trip to Rome? Business or pleasure?"

"Actually, neither. I'm a graduate student at UCLA, in classical studies. My area of specialization is the late Roman Empire, specifically Marcus Aurelius and the early barbarian invasions."

"Are you native to LA?"

"Yes, I grew up there."

"Are you a Dodgers fan?"

"No, Angels."

"Who's your favorite pitcher on the team?"

"Nolan Ryan. He had an ERA of 2.28 this year with 19 wins and 16 losses. It's a shame they didn't win the pennant. With Bob Oliver and Sandy Alomar power hitting, they should've gone much further than they did."

"My brother also lives in LA. We go to visit him. His name is Leonardo Sciotino. Do you know him?"

Kurt smiled. "No, I'm afraid I don't."

"He's a big Dodgers fan. It's a shame that the Dodgers can't play the Angels. That would be interesting."

"I know, but teams in the American League don't play the National League unless it's the All-Star game or the World Series."

"Yes, I know about how your bazbol works." He stamped Kurt's passport. "Welcome to Rome."

"Thanks."

Kurt collected his small duffle bag and rucksack from the luggage claim and walked out of the terminal. A cab stopped at the curb in front of him.

"Mr. Simmons?" the driver asked.

"Yes."

"I'm Adler. Welcome to Rome."

***

By all accounts, Wael Zwaiter was a refined, cultured man. Born in Nablus in the mid-1930s, he studied Arabic literature and philosophy at the University of Baghdad. After completing his studies, he moved to Libya and then to Rome, where he worked as a translator for the Libyan embassy. Gifted in languages, he spoke French, Italian, and English, in addition to his native Arabic. His home was a mecca for intellectuals and students alike. The big project of his life was the translation of One Thousand and One Arabian Nights from Arabic into Italian. He was also the PLO's representative in Rome. It was rumored that he had developed ties to the Black September terrorist organization and had a reputation as someone who knew the "lay of the land" in Europe, having traveled freely and extensively throughout it, which made him useful as a facilitator.

He was held for questioning by the Italian police several times: in August 1972 in connection with the bombing of an oil refinery by Black September, a booby-trapped tape recorder placed on an El Al plane earlier that month, and the 1968 hijacking of an El Al plane headed to Algeria. Each time, he was released for lack of evidence. It was rumored that he had handled all of the logistics for the Black September operatives who carried out the Munich massacre.

Zwaiter, who had a weakness for fine Italian wine and cuisine, frequented the most expensive restaurants in Rome. He was known for his generosity and entertained lavishly. The night of October 16, 1972, having hosted a large dinner party at an exclusive hotel, he walked home with two friends. They chatted amiably, continuing the stimulating conversation from the long, relaxing dinner. He planned to turn in early that night, because he had a very busy schedule the following day. He dropped his friends off at their apartment and walked the rest of the way home on his own.

As he walked the final block to his apartment, he paid no attention to two men dressed in jeans, leather jackets, and dark-visored helmets, who were sitting on a BMW motorcycle at the corner. When Zwaiter was twenty feet away from his front door, the motorcycle went up the street, slowed down, and stopped behind him. Curious, he turned around. The man sitting on the back of the motorcycle reached into his jacket, withdrew a 9mm Beretta machine pistol with silencer, and then slammed twelve shots into Zwaiter's head and chest. Zwaiter was dead before his body hit the ground.

The assailants drove away in no particular hurry. Despite an intense citywide manhunt by the Carabinieri, Italy's national police, the assailants were never apprehended.

The PLO blamed Israel for the assassination, claiming that it was revenge for the Munich "incident." PLO Deputy Chief Abu Iyad stated to the media that Zwaiter had been a man of peace and had had no relation to Black September or any other terrorists. He even said that Zwaiter had been "energetically against political violence."

The Israelis, for their part, denied any involvement in the affair, claiming that the assassination must have been carried out by warring factions within the PLO.

Arik and Mikki's relationship had progressed to the point of ease. There were no pretenses, stress, or personal friction between them. That is not to say that they did not have disagreements, especially regarding politics. Mikki was a right-wing firebrand who believed that not one inch of land that had been "liberated" during the Six-Day war should be given away to the Arabs. She bridled when Arik referred to the land as "captured" and scoffed at the concept of giving the land "back" to the Arabs in exchange for peace. Eventually, the pair realized that neither would be swayed, and they added politics to the list of things that they would leave at the front door of their marital home. Mikki had penetrated Arik completely and had a strong, instinctive feel for what he needed and when. She was always ready to meet that need. Arik finally felt complete inside and confident in his abilities and his future. The world seemed to present limitless possibilities to him when Mikki was at his side. From Mikki's viewpoint, Arik enabled her to express her femininity, her inner emotions, and the full force of her intellect. She never could have believed that she would be in a relationship with a man in which intense love and passion were so thoroughly interlaced with respect and consideration. She had found a man who would enable her to have the same home life as her parents did. That thought alone made her shiver with delight every time that she and Arik spent time together.

By some miracle, they both engineered a week off and flew off to Italy. They explored the ancient ruins of Rome. They spent a blissful two days in Positano, exploring the Amalfi Coast and the island of Capri, where they wandered all day among the grottos and ruins after spending a blissful night in an ancient pension. They ate breakfast on a terrace atop the cliffs of Sorrento that overlook the Bay of Naples, with the city of Naples in the distance, and then explored the city of Pompeii and climbed Mount Vesuvius.

"This city was destroyed in 79 A.D., because of what they did to Jerusalem nine years earlier," Mikki said.

"I didn't realize being in intelligence means you know the mind of God," Arik said.

When they passed under the Arch of Titus, in Rome, they spied the mural of the victorious soldiers that marched through the city, bearing the menorah from the Jerusalem Temple on their shoulders. That mural was above another mural, which read "JUDEAE CAPTA."

"This is what we fight for, Arik! Notice that it doesn't say, 'Palestina Capta!' There were Jews in Israel two thousand years before the first Arab showed up and 2,500 years before the first Muslim showed up. When we won in '67, we got the land back! I do feel for the Palestinians, but they're unfortunately in the way of our historic return to our homeland. Jews didn't leave of their own accord. We were thrown out. And all we want is what belongs to us. As they say here, Capiche? There's a lot that you don't know yet." She kissed him on the cheek.

***

They both had at least three days off each month, usually after the completion of a mission. For Arik's birthday, Mikki surprised him with two tickets to see the singer-songwriter sensation Svika Pik at the Hamaara nightclub in Jaffa. Mikki wanted to drive into Jaffa and park at the police station, but Arik insisted on them taking public transportation. They left Mikki's car at Dani's girlfriend's house in Ramat Aviv and took a bus into Jaffa.

At that time in the late afternoon, the bus was jam-packed with a humid sea of humanity: workers returning home after the day's work. Arik reached into his pocket, pulled out three liras for their fares, and put them into the coin machine beside the bus driver. The driver pulled two miniature receipts bearing unintelligible numbers from a receipt board that contained hundreds of such receipts and handed them to Arik. As they walked down the aisle of the bus, the bus lurched forward. They held on to the overhead pole for dear life as the bus rounded a street corner at thirty kilometers per hour.

"I still don't understand why you want to take the bus when we can drive," Mikki said.

"I almost never get to ride a bus and mingle with the masses, as you like to call them, but I have another reason this time. You'll see when the time comes."

"I smell another mystery, mystery man. Every time that I think I know you, I don't. It's been a while since I've had one of these moments. I'm hopelessly spoiled, I suppose." She caressed his hand.

The bus wove its way through the broad, tree-lined streets of northern Tel Aviv, with their busy, colorful shops and Israel's lone skyscraper—the gleaming white Shalom Meir Tower—and then past Dizengoff Circus, Israel's version of Piccadilly Circus, with its outdoor cafes, steakhouses, and brightly flashing lights. Finally, the bus headed southeast, past Allenby Street. The houses began to look older and the streets narrower and less well kept.

Mikki and Arik exited the bus. They trod streets that were grimy and strewn with garbage and rotting food. The trash cans were overflowing, and hundreds of cats darted about, collecting the trash on their own schedule. Competing with the cats was a throng of ragged homeless people who were going from trash can to trash can, looking for scraps of food. The air was filled with the odor of human perspiration and stale urine but peppered with the better aromas of fried falafel and roasting kabobs hawked by dozens of vendors in grimy kiosks who were shouting about their wares. News vendors featured the full range of written media, from the highbrow Haaretz to the Maariv and Yedioth Ahronoth populist newspapers and all the way down to the HaOlam HaZeh tabloid. Buses tore in and out the Central Bus Station, the Tachana Mercazit, at high speed, belching out clouds of diesel fuel exhaust and sending pedestrians darting away for dear life. Off to the side stood a long line of Mercedes sheruts, shared taxis for those who wanted a more intimate form of public transportation than buses. Screams of "Yerushalayim! Yerushalayim! Yerushalayim!" in rapid staccato, as if fired from a machine gun, filled the air as a line of patrons pushed and shoved, trying to claim one of the seven seats in the sherut. As soon as each sherut was filled with its load of human sardines, it sped off down the street, past the stores that were selling mountains of old shoes.

Off to the side of the main thoroughfare sat small pockets of homeless men and women who were seeking refuge from the mingling crowds but getting as close to passersby as they dared. Deeply tanned, unwashed, and smelling of human waste, they all appeared to be wearing the universal uniform of urban wretches: dirty, gray, torn rags. Many were missing an arm or leg. With hands outstretched, they begged for agorot, aluminum coins widely regarded as worthless. The men were unshaven, with ragged beards. Their eyes looked up blankly, begging for a kindhearted soul to stop and show some sign of humanity toward them.

Arik walked slowly up to one of the homeless men who was sitting in filth. He crouched down in front of him.

The man stared up at him. One of the man's legs was stretched out to one side at an impossible angle. His other pant leg was tucked under his torso. In front of him was a small battered, grimy aluminum pan that contained a half dozen agorot.

"How are you?" Ari asked him quietly.

The man's dark-brown eyes radiated deep sadness borne of years of deprivation and want. "I'm very hungry. Do you have some money for a hungry man? I'm so hungry and tired. I need to eat."

Arik noticed that the man had lost most of his teeth. He kneeled down in front of him.

Mikki wanted to pull Arik away. She was put off by the smell and the filth. Besides, they had reservations for 7:30 p.m. to celebrate Arik's twenty-first birthday at the exclusive Pundak Shaul restaurant in the Yemenite Quarter. She did not want to be late. But she stopped herself when she realized that something profound was occurring. She stood quietly a foot behind Arik as passersby slowed down to look but then rapidly walked away.

Mikki stared as Arik engaged the man in conversation for several minutes and even put his hand on the man's shoulder. She could not hear what he was saying, given the noise in the street.

Arik reached into his pocket, pulled out a 100 lira note, and put it into the man's hand. "Please, get some food for yourself, maybe a clean place to sleep tonight." He smiled.

The man stared down at the money in disbelief.

"May the Almighty bless you with a lifetime of happiness and success," he said as tears of joy filled his eyes and began to run down his face.

"Thank you very much," Arik said.

Arik slowly stood up and turned to Mikki. They resumed their walk toward the Yemenite Quarter.

Arik said, "That man is my father. For three years, my father sat here with these Jews, hungry, cold, wet, dirty, and tired. I wanted to see this for myself. I wanted to see how my father was rewarded for his heroism. I wanted to see where I came from. My life won't have meaning until I can figure out how I got where I did. That's the reason I came to Israel. I have to figure it out."

"I didn't want to tell you this," Mikki said, "so I've kept it to myself for months. Every chance I could, I've scoured the military archives in the Kiriya, in Jerusalem, and in Holon. For months, I've devoted hours and hours to looking for evidence that your father was in the Palmach. Nothing's come up. All I've seen is that Ze'ev Myerowitz was a commander in the Irgun. There's no record of your father having served in the Palmach. I'm so sorry, Arik! I've tried and tried. I know how much this means to you. There just isn't anything."

"And your parents are okay with you marrying the son of a mass murderer? I'm surprised your parents have me in their house at all. The Gilads thought I was too rough and low class for their taste. I'm just the son of a homeless criminal who got what he deserved."

"I can't believe that you're saying this after all this time, Arik. Has that been on your mind for the past two years? Don't you know that my parents feel nothing but love and affection for you? You're part of our family. We don't give a damn what the Gilads thought of you, and neither should you. You're your own person—regardless of who your father was or wasn't. You've proven yourself to the whole country. You need to stop dwelling on the past and look toward the future. Our future! I love you with all my heart and soul. My whole family does. That should be enough!"

"It's not about that. I don't dwell on Dahlia and her family at all. It's just that all along I've thought that I'd find some way to discover my father's innocence, his heroism. Today I came face-to-face with what I was born into. With you telling me about your search, all hope is lost. I just need to accept what I am. There's something I never told you, though. About a year ago, I bumped into Dahlia, when I was visiting Ben Azai after the parachute accident. She was a nurse at Tel HaShomer, on his ward."

"You never told me. Why not?"

"There was no point in upsetting you. I just wanted the incident to go away and never come up again. The meeting was purely accidental. She saw me and approached me. If I'd seen her first, I would've avoided her like the plague. I know you're wondering if I still have feelings for her. Let me assure you I don't. And I mean that from the bottom of my heart. Our conversation ended with me telling her and her nasty family to go to hell. I just didn't want her name to come up in our conversations ever again. I'm yours, Mikki. Body, heart, and soul."

"So, why are you bringing it up now?"

"It's something she told me back then. She said her father admitted that my father saved his life and he felt terribly guilty about he'd treated me . . . and that his original animosity toward me was because I reminded him of my father. He last saw my father when he was about my age, and I guess I look a little like him. She was trying to apologize for the way she and her family treated me. But I've been haunted by what she said. It seemed like proof that my father had been screwed—"

"Why didn't you tell me this before? Perhaps I could have helped."

"You have been trying to help, but without objective proof I couldn't do anything about my father. I just wanted to block her out of my mind. She sickens me."

"Then, I say that we put that bastard's head in the ringer. It would cause a major scandal."

"He's the foreign minister, Mikki. I don't want to cross him."

"I'm not afraid of him. My father is certainly not afraid of him. He could eat Benny for breakfast."

"What if Dahlia just lied to me about all that to ingratiate herself to me in some way? I don't trust her. She knows me inside and out, like you do, and she knows my deepest wants and desires. I couldn't try to challenge her father. I've never crossed him, but I've heard he can be ruthless. I'd end up destroying myself, everything I've worked for the past three years. If your father stuck his head out and it turned out to be a hoax, it would shame your whole family and ruin your father's credibility, too. I'd rather just live with the reality I already have than drag everyone down with me. I have to believe Benny would have come clean by now about my father's heroism if it was true. I can't believe he could live with himself harboring such a terrible secret. There has to be another way to find out. If we could just find something, I'd confront him, but I can't do it before then."

"Arik, my sweet boy. I'll keep looking. I'll turn over heaven and earth if I have to . . . Now, you have to promise to make love to me all night long. I've found a charming little place for us to stay in Jaffa. You won't be getting much sleep tonight, I'm afraid."

He smiled and raised his eyebrows. "I'm going to have to eat, or I won't be able to perform. I'm starved."

"Pundak Shaul is a wonderful place. Prepare for a treat. Happy birthday, my love!"

Chapter 23

They slipped off the INS Eilat at 21:00 in almost complete silence. The only sound was the howling of the wind, and the lapping of the salt water waves against the hulls of the sleek black Zodiac Mark 7 rubber boats. Behind them, the sailors on board the ship manned the cannons and machine guns. They were on full battle alert. The entire armada was cloaked in the black shroud of a moonless night. All lights and radar were off, and strict radio silence was observed. Up ahead twinkled the lights of the famous Sands Hotel on Dove Beach in southern Beirut.

The Matkal commandos were sitting with their naval counterparts. They were neither scared nor excited. Arik, in fact, looked down at himself in some amusement. He had always expected to be wearing a ski cap, black stretch T-shirt and slacks, and combat boots on a mission like this one. At least, that was what he had seen in the James Bond movies. But here he sat in the darkness, wearing a blond ponytailed wig, an oversized leather jacket, a loose tie-dyed T-shirt, bell-bottom blue jeans, and sneakers. He had hidden four grenades, a MAC-10 submachine gun, a 9mm Beretta with silencer, and eight magazines with thirty bullets each under the T-shirt and stuffed into pockets that had been specially sewn inside the jacket.

This mission—the most audacious mission that Israel's commandos had ever undertaken—had been two months in the planning. It was to be Israel's definitive response to the horror of Munich. It had begun one morning two months earlier, when Barak walked into the morning briefing room at the base and asked, "Who's interested in a nice suicide mission?" All hands went up. He spread a detailed street map of Beirut out on a large table and gave the men a brief outline.

Thus, began eight weeks of intense tactical training that strained the members of Arik's unit to the limit both physically and psychologically. The mission was deemed dangerous in the extreme. And there would be no safety net, no backup. One slipup, and they would all be dead—or worse, captured. The mission was to be a combined operation involving the air force, navy, communications corps, A'Man, Mossad, and commando units from every branch of the military. Arik's unit, Sayeret Matkal, would work in close cooperation with Shayetet 13, the naval commandos. Usually friendly rivals, both units knew that teamwork between them in this mission would mean the difference between life and death.

The complexity of the operation was unparalleled. There were numerous simultaneous targets and objectives. Arik's unit was assigned the most delicate objective of all: the assassination of three key figures in the Black September terrorist movement who were considered primarily responsible for the Munich massacre. The image of Dahlia, wounded, flashed through Arik's mind.

The three men were Abu Youssef, nicknamed Muhammed Najer, a leader of Black September, one of the principal planners of both the Munich and the al-Fatah terrorist operations, and the intelligence chief for the group's worldwide operations against Israeli installations; Kamal Adwan, the man responsible for running terrorist operations inside Israel; and Kamal Nasser, the official spokesman for Black September.

Arik knew that these men had a lot of Jewish blood on their hands, but the thought that they had woken up the previous morning without the slightest notion that he was coming to kill them sent a chill up his spine nonetheless.

The lead-up to this mission had been filled with intense, grueling training. Mock-ups of the targets, made of plywood and cinder blocks, had been constructed in the desert. The commandoes had spent long hours listening to lengthy intelligence briefings, and memorizing gigantic wall maps that showed the key avenues, streets, and landmarks of Beirut so that they were as familiar with Beirut's streets as they were with Tel Aviv's. Every day, the commanders had quizzed the men on every aspect of the mission.

They had practiced the landing from the sea and the assault techniques off the coast of Tel Aviv and in abandoned high-rise apartment buildings on the shore until they perfected them with split-second accuracy.

The weapons training had taken place at a secluded training ground on the West Bank. The choice of weapons and explosives that they would use was meticulously planned. Everyone understood that they could not expect backup or a plan B extraction. If they were discovered or became involved in a major fire fight, they would be on their own. To ensure deniability by the Israeli government, the commandoes would carry no Israeli weapons and would speak only English. They used American MAC-10 (.45 ACP) submachine guns, because they were lightweight, included silencers, and were very effective in close-quarters combat. The only drawback of them was that they had limited range.

It had been IDF Chief of Staff Dado Elazar's idea for the commandoes to wear costumes, including the shorter men dressing as women. Too many men running around, even dressed in civilian clothing, would arouse too much suspicion. Therefore, Ehud Barak became a buxom brunette, and Lonny Rafael and Amiram Levine became blonde bombshells. Those three hid their weapons in their bras, under their clothes, and in their purses. The others wore blue jeans, tie-dyed shirts, and leather and denim jackets, all in extra-large sizes to accommodate their weapons.

This night was no drill.

The Matkal were wearing plastic ponchos over their wigs and jackets. Several hundred yards from the shore, the Zodiacs' engines were cut, and the naval commandos silently paddled them toward shore. As they approached the Sands Hotel, the naval crews jumped out and lifted their Matkal brethren up out of the rafts so that their shoes remained dry. Mossad agents who had taken their places in advance patrolled the secluded beach.

The agents had rented three Buick Skylark cars and a Plymouth station wagon to ferry the sixteen men who squeezed into them for the five-mile ride to Rue Verdun, their objective. At 1:30 a.m., the commandoes in the first car piled out of their car around the corner from Rue Verdun and just out of sight of the machine gun emplacement that guarded the Iraqi embassy. The other cars slowly inched up Rue Verdun to number seven.

Barak, dressed like a female prostitute, was standing outside the building. Her "lover," Betzer, who had been walking up and down the street, arm in arm in an intimate embrace with her, was surveying the scene.

It was time to go.

Betzer and Yoni led the first team to Abu Youssef's apartment on the sixth floor, while Arik and his team remained in a car in the front of the apartment building to provide cover. Suddenly, from up the street, came two cars filled with Force 17 al-Fatah gunmen. Arik and the other members of his team were out of their car in a flash. They had seen the terrorists before the terrorists had seen them. When the two cars slowed down to inspect the ruckus in front of the building, the Israelis were upon them. Before they could react, Arik pumped a full magazine of 9mm bullets from his silenced automatic Beretta into one of the cars, killing all of the occupants.

The lead car slowed down, and its occupants spilled out. But Barak, Ami, and Arik were ready for them. When the terrorists turned to fire, they were mowed down by a hail of nearly silent MAC-10 rounds. Unfortunately, one bullet penetrated their car's engine compartment, activating the horn, which wailed loudly.

Shit! Arik thought.

Much of the sound was drowned out by a nearby disco's blaring music, but the doorman of an adjacent building heard enough. He ran inside the building, rousing the residents with shouts of "Al Yahud!" (The Jews are here!)

There was no time to lose.

Barak motioned to Arik.

Arik led his team, Yishai, and Ami in bounding up the stairs to the second-floor apartment. Yishai reached into his rucksack for plastic explosive to blast the door open.

"No time!" Arik whispered. With one swift motion, he kicked the door off its hinges. The inside of the apartment looked like something out of Arabian Nights. The living room was adorned with exotic tropical plants, Oriental rugs, and expensive Persian curtains. On the wall was a large painting that featured Jerusalem and the Dome of the Rock.

There was movement behind the curtains.

Kamal Nasser jumped out from behind the curtains, brandishing an AK-47, and began firing wildly at the Israelis. Yishai, hit in the thigh, dropped to the floor. Arik and Ami dropped to one knee and, in expert firing position, fired a burst of six 9mm slugs into Kamal's forehead, blowing it apart. He slumped to the floor in a pool of blood and brains.

Arik heard a rustle behind the curtain near the front door.

He swung around and fired a burst at it. A small figure fell to the floor, leaving a large bloodstain on the curtain. Arik and Ami wasted no time in piling the contents of a file cabinet into their waterproof rucksacks. As soon as they had finished doing that, Arik ran to Yishai, ready to carry him out the door. He suddenly looked down and, in a sickening moment, saw the lifeless body of a young child of no more than nine years old lying on the floor in a pool of blood.

"You murdered my baby, you Jewish pig!"

Kamal's wife, Maha, ran out of the bedroom, in her nightgown, screaming hysterically in Arabic.

Arik looked down, frozen in shock. "I'm sorry! I'm so sorry!" he said in English.

"That's all that you filthy Zionists know how to do—slaughter Palestinian children. You should be ashamed!" she shouted in fluent American English.

Arik stood there speechless. Time seemed to stand still.

In the distance, sirens were growing louder by the second.

"In a minute, we're going to have the entire Lebanese army up our asses, Arik!" Ami yelled. "We have to get out of here now. You're going to get us all killed!"

A Land Rover full of Lebanese Army troops screeched up the street.

Arik slung Yishai over his shoulders and he and Ami raced out of the apartment, down the stairs, and into the street. Betzer, who was standing in the middle of the road waiting for them, tossed a grenade on the canvas roof of the Land Rover. With a loud bang, it exploded, killing everyone inside. Arik laid Yishai by the fender of the Buick.

Two armed men sprang out of the apartment building next door. They ran toward the Israelis, firing at them. Arik turned around and fired three shots into each of them, killing them both.

More sirens were growing louder.

"Everyone, back into the cars!" Barak shouted. The commandos threw their wounded into the cars and got in after them. They raced down the street and turned onto the coastal road, blending into the nighttime traffic, just as they saw a mass of cars with sirens converging on Rue Verdun. The last car out sprayed ninja spikes on the pavement behind them to impede pursuit. They reached the deserted beach at the Sands Hotel in twenty minutes flat. On the way, they had passed several Lebanese Army trucks that were screaming off in the other direction. Barak signaled the naval commando teams in the Zodiac rafts to return to the beach. They were there in less than three minutes. Everyone ran toward the rafts.

In the melee, Arik realized that he had left the two rucksacks full of papers in the Buick. How could I have been so careless? Those papers were important intel! He had let his emotions get away from him. He knew that he could have gotten himself and his comrades killed. I shot and killed a child! He felt a mixture of shame and guilt as he began to run back to the Buick to retrieve the rucksacks.

"What are you doing, Arik? There's no time!" Barak said. "We need to get out of here. Now! We're already on borrowed time."

Arik ran back and flung himself into the raft as it pulled away from shore, the naval commandos paddling furiously toward the darkness. The Israelis saw the first flashing lights and sirens entering the hotel's parking lot.

When the INS Eilat pulled out of Lebanese territorial waters, the crew turned the ship's lights back on and Barak popped the cork of a bottle of champagne to celebrate the almost perfectly executed mission. They had accomplished their goals and struck a decisive blow against the Black

September terrorist group's leadership right in their headquarters, and they had gotten away without any Israeli fatalities. They had found and taken a treasure trove of documents. The paratrooper units, which had burst into the Democratic Front for the Liberation of Palestine (DFLP) headquarters, had killed scores of highly ranked terrorists and blown up their building. They themselves had suffered only two dead and several wounded. They had been evacuated by a helicopter bearing the familiar Blue Star of David—right in the middle of Beirut!

A victory feast of lamb kabobs, hummus, salad, pita, and falafel was served to the joyous commandos who whooped, hollered, and hugged one another.

Arik stood alone outside, against the ship's railing, staring out quietly into the cold saltwater spray and howling wind.

Barak spotted him and joined him.

"I heard what happened in the apartment, Arik. War is a tough and dirty business. We try so hard not to injure the innocent, but sometimes that's impossible. We do better in this regard than any army on earth. You did what you had to do, and you did it damn well. I'm proud of you. It could've been another terrorist behind that curtain, and he would have killed all of you.

"These people murdered our athletes in Munich, Arik. Don't beat yourself up about this. You'll have many more missions in the future. There will be many more times that you'll be faced with moral ambiguity, but the citizens of Israel are depending on you. What we did tonight may save countless Jewish lives. Your reaction simply demonstrates that you're just human after all, not a mindless killing machine. The minute you become one, I don't want you under my command. Come inside. Have something to eat." Barak put a fatherly arm around Arik's shoulders and escorted him inside.

The INS Eilat sailed back out into the inky blackness that was the Mediterranean, a sea shared by Jews and Muslims.

Jake Marcus had never been so nauseated in his whole life. By the time the Piper Cub aircraft landed at the Israeli Air Force base at Sharm el-Sheikh, he was ready to kiss the tarmac. The flight from Sde Dov Airport, just north of Tel Aviv, had taken nearly four hours.

His journey had begun when he had seen a notice on the bulletin board at his yeshiva. It was a call for rabbinic interns who would be willing to officiate at a military seder. He had been given the choice of the Golan Heights, the Suez Canal, the Mitla pass, or Sharm el-Sheikh. Jake had chosen Sharm, for no other reason than that he liked the song about Sharm el-Sheikh that had been composed after its conquest by the Israelis in the Six-Day War.

When he had visited the Kiriya, Israel's military headquarters, he had been promised that he would fly to Sharm on an Arkia commercial flight. But when he had arrived at Sde Dov Airport, just north of Tel Aviv, there had been nothing but Quonset huts and a row of aging Piper Cubs waiting for him. Jake had been directed into one of the Quonset huts. In it, he found a hairy beast in a green jumpsuit who was chomping on the largest cold cut hero sandwich that he had ever seen held by a human being.

The beast mumbled, "You must be the rabbi. When I'm done with my sandwich, I'll fly you down to Sharm."

"No Arkia Airlines?"

"No Arkia! Just me and you!" He handed a stack of vomit bags to Jake, saying, "You'll need these."

"I've been on many airplanes before. I shouldn't need these."

The pilot laughed. "I don't know if you've noticed, but we're not going on a 747. You'll need the bags."

They walked out onto the tarmac.

The aging two-seater plane reeked of airplane fuel. Jake was nauseated even before the door closed.

"Make sure your seatbelt is fastened."

The plane climbed into the air at what felt to Jake like a nearly vertical angle. Within ten minutes, he had thrown up his breakfast. By the time the Piper Cub stopped at a small landing strip in the Sinai to refuel, Jake had thrown up three more times and had reached the point that vomiting had no effect on the nausea. He lay stretched out on the hot, sticky tarmac baking in the desert sun as if it were a luxurious featherbed. His respite was too short, however. After only fifteen minutes on the ground, he had to re-board the flying vomit machine. It took another two gut-wrenching hours to reach the Israeli Air Force base at the southern tip of the Sinai. Being in the Piper Cub when it landed between rows of F-4 Phantom fighter jets in the light of the late afternoon could have given Jake a thrill, but instead it left Jake with an odd sense of unease that he could not put his finger on.

Excitement and anticipation replaced nausea as he pulled his rucksack and guitar from the cargo hold and was led into the administration office.

"Welcome to Sharm, Rabbi," the duty officer said. "I hope you have a pleasant stay. As we already have a rabbinical staff here at the main airbase, you'll be assigned to a small outpost up in those mountains. It's called Tzhabel Tzafra." He pointed southwest, at the mountains that separated the base from the famous Straits of Tiran, the narrow waterway whose blockade had led to the Six-Day War. "It's a small base but very compact. You'll find the staff up there to be engaging and helpful. My assistant, Erez, will drive you up there."

Jake climbed into a waiting Jeep.

"Ever see Phantoms up close?" Erez said.

"No."

"I have some time. Let me give you a tour."

Erez drove onto the tarmac and threaded his way between the rows of fighter jets that were sitting out in the open. He pointed out the aging Mirage and Mystère jets and the new acquisitions from the United States, the vaunted F-4 Phantom jets.

"Climb up the ladder, and have a look inside," Erez said. He whispered to a patrolling security guard, who nodded his assent.

"Are you sure it's okay?"

"No problem." Erez smiled.

Jake was amazed how small the Phantom was and how cramped the cockpit felt. He quickly climbed back out of it.

"I find it odd that these planes are sitting out here in the open like this, unprotected," he said.

"Where else should they be?"

"I don't know. In a bunker, perhaps?"

"Why?"

"Well, for one thing, just over that ridge and across the Gulf of Suez, not more than twenty kilometers from here, is the entire Egyptian army. And from my recollection, they don't like us very much."

Erez laughed. "This isn't Vietnam. This is Israel! It really doesn't matter where the planes are. They're quite safe. The Egyptians are scared to death of us, after the thrashing we gave them in '67. They wouldn't dare try anything. Did you see the security guard that we passed? He's a reservist, and his gun is a manual single-lever-action Czech rifle of World War II lineage. In fact, he has no bullets in it."

"Why not? What's the point of him being here?"

"Do you think that we'd trust a reservist around these twenty-five million dollar babies with a loaded gun? He might discharge his weapon. And then, poof! Let's just say that the guards here for show." Erez winked at Jake. "Meanwhile, let's take you up to Tzafra while it's still light. The mountain roads can be treacherous after dark."

In the fading sunlight, the Jeep climbed the dirt road that hugged the edge of the yellowish-pink sandstone rock face that led up to Tzafra.

Tzafra was a small intelligence base nestled atop a mountain that slopes down to the Red Sea at the southern tip of the Sinai desert. From there, to the right lay Egypt, and to the left was the Arabian Peninsula. Tzafra had a commanding, unobstructed view of the entire waterway and surrounding land masses, making it an ideal location for an observation and electronic listening post. The base itself consisted of about a dozen prefabricated buildings surrounded by thirty-foot-tall walls of khaki sandbags. At its center stood a small nondescript khaki building bristling with antennae. Among the prefabricated buildings were dormitories and a small dining hall for the several dozen men and women whose mission was to serve as Israel's eyes and ears to the south, twenty-four hours a day, seven days a week. Life there was divided into stressful eight-hour shifts in the OPS electronic surveillance shack and sixteen-hour blocks of boredom. The base was isolated. There was nowhere for the personnel to go.

Jake was met by a junior officer, who escorted him to his sleeping quarters.

"Shalom, Rabbi," the officer said. "Welcome to Tzafra. I'm Amir, your 'host committee.' I see that you have a guitar. I think that you will be busy here. In addition to preparing for the seder, koshering the kitchen for Pesach, and supervising the cook, you'll be expected to provide entertainment to the soldiers. I think that a sing-along under the stars would be a welcome thing. A campfire is impossible, but a bunch of candles on a tray can be arranged." He smiled and winked at Jake. "You know that this is a highly restricted zone—for personnel under special orders only—but your kipah is your passport here. You're definitely considered a low security risk."

"Unless my guitar playing stinks." Jake laughed. "I'm no Jimi Hendrix."

"To these kids, you are, no matter how bad you are. They don't get out much."

Word of the sing-along traveled fast. By the time dinner was over, there was a crowd sitting in a circle, candles already lit.

"I'm Rabbi Jake, and I have a bunch of songs in my repertoire—both English, Hebrew, religious, and secular. I'll also take some requests from the Song Festival and the hit parade."

Within a short time, everyone—even the shyest and inhibited—had joined in. Some were convinced to sing solos. Jake was amazed at how in Israel even the most secular soldiers had a good grasp of religious Hebrew songs. The artists requested ranged from Shlomo Carlebach and The Rabbis' Sons to Arik Einstein, Yehoram Gaon, and Shlomo Artzi. English favorites by The Beatles, Simon and Garfunkel, Bob Dylan, and The Doors rounded out the list. Everyone, at least for a short time, was transported away from the mountaintop, away from boredom and the dreary, endless sand and sky.

***

Arik was grateful for his time off for the Pesach holiday that had been granted to the whole unit as a token of thanks for a job well done in Beirut. He was still reeling from images of that Arab boy lying on the floor in a pool of blood. He had been a child, not a terrorist. Who was to judge what he might have become? He may have been the person destined to broker lasting peace between Israel and the Arabs. Now, that possibility had been shattered in a hail of gunfire that had come from him, Arik. He was filled with a sense of sadness.

Children aren't supposed to be part of this conflict. Their job is to enjoy their childhood.

Thank God, I have a few days with Mikki. I'll feel better just being with her. Mikki was so hardheaded and practical that she always seemed able to get him out of his funk. And she did so with great cheer. Their mutual neck rubs also helped considerably. He loved the way that she lit up the moment that she saw him no how busy she was.

Mikki was stuck at the base for the holiday. The Egyptians loved to provoke anxiety around Jewish holidays, so they tended to plan artillery bombardments and commando raids across the Canal to coincide with them. There was word of some troop buildups on the Egyptian side of the Canal, and as commander of the base she had to be present just in case the Egyptians made a move.

That didn't mean that she could not entertain guests when she was not supervising the men and women under her command at the OPS radar consoles. If anything happened, she would be less than two hundred feet away. Having Arik with her for the holiday was all that she needed. She felt no urge to be anywhere else. Arik understood her role at the base, and he could be extremely discreet when he had to be.

Mikki was busy at the OPS at 7 p.m. that evening, having received signals that the Egyptians were test-firing their surface-to-air missiles. Her absence left Arik free to jog along the mountain paths, read, nap, and just generally relax.

After dinner, Arik drifted toward the sound of singing that he heard coming from one of the sandbag enclosures. He recognized the Israeli songs right away and began humming along as he approached. But he was intrigued by the English songs and even more so by the Hebrew religious songs. He had heard all of them while at Camp Moshava nearly four years earlier. That summer seemed like a lifetime ago. It had been a time of innocence and hope. A time with Dahlia.

Problems that had loomed so large back then seemed so far away, but yet other problems had not been resolved even after all that time. The songs reminded him of his parents. He had not been a good son. He had not kept in contact with them as much as he should have. When he had returned to Israel, he had jumped headlong into his new life, a life with Mikki.

Arik noticed that the rabbi was singing with an American accent. I vaguely recognize him, come to think of it, but from where? He had not participated in a sing-along since that fateful summer that undoubtedly had changed his life—for good or the bad he did not know. For all the years that had gone by, his life still was in a state of flux. He approached the circle and continued to listen to the singing.

"I have to get to the kitchen to kasher the utensils," Jake said finally. The crowd thinned.

The chevre thanked him for the chance to "get away" from where they were and told him that they were looking forward to the next evening's seder.

Arik walked up to Jake.

"Where do I know you from? It's driving me mad," Arik said.

When Jake looked up at him, recognition dawned. He smiled. "You're Arik Meir! You're the basketball phenom that kicked Morasha's ass and played one-on-one against Elgin Baylor. You were the camp celebrity. Everybody knew you. I was in Eidah Bet, I wasn't part of the cool jock crowd, so you would never have noticed me. You guys built the tennis bleachers, as I recall. I see you're a chayal. Are you stationed here?"

"No, I'm just visiting. I'm a guest just like you. I'm sorry, but I don't remember your name."

"Jake Marcus."

"That's right! I remember now. You used to play the accordion, if memory serves." Arik smiled.

"Don't remind me. I'm still trying to live that down. The guitar is so much better."

Arik nodded and smiled.

"Didn't you date the daughter of the Israeli ambassador? She was in the shevet above me. I haven't seen her in years."

"Frankly, neither have I. So, what are you doing here?"

"Well, the following summer I was in Mach Hach. . . and in the middle of the summer, my parents came from Israel and surprised me by telling me I'd been enrolled in a Bnei Akiva yeshiva high school in Israel. They were desperate to get me out of the U.S."

"Vietnam?"

"No, but I was involved in the antiwar movement and started to look and act like a hippie, so my parents panicked and shipped me off here."

"You certainly don't look like a hippie now. Are you becoming a rabbi?"

"No. After I completed my Bagrut high school matriculation exams I went off to study in a yeshiva."

"Very nice. So, you're going to be staying here, then?" Arik asked.

"Not sure yet. My parents are pressuring me to return to the States to go to college there."

"Why in the world would you do that? You've already been here for three years and are completely adjusted to the life here. That's usually the hardest part of being a new immigrant. To leave now seems foolish, in my view."

"I want to go to medical school. Being a doctor here is my dream."

"You can study here in Israel."

"But I'd have to go in the army then, unless I could get an educational deferment and go later as a doctor—"

"So, what's the problem with that? Sounds good to me! The Israeli Army is a great experience for an American guy. It doesn't only toughen you up. It also give you a real sense of why Jews came back to this sliver of dirt on the eastern shore of the Mediterranean after two thousand years. The problem I see with many Americans is that they're in too much of a hurry to run off to college to pursue their careers. They forget about trying to pursue their own identities."

"Do you think the army would give me that sense?" Jake asked.

Arik smiled. "As a matter of fact, I do. I know you're probably thinking, 'I'll go back to school in the States, get my doctor's degree, and then I'll go back to Israel fully trained.' Many people do just that, but it's very seductive to stay in the States after you're done. You start thinking, 'Maybe I'll stay a few years and make some money, and then I'll go.' The next thing you know, you have a wife, kids, and a mortgage. By then, you're planning your retirement in Israel but you're too old to make a contribution. You'll become yet another American Zionist wannabe who loves Israel from a distance and thinks writing checks is enough."

"That's a depressing thought," Jake said.

"Seriously, though, you're in a unique position to make huge decisions that'll have a profound effect on the course of your life. I did. I gave up a basketball scholarship to UCLA to come here to protect my country and the Jewish people."

"The national champions? You would've played with Bill Walton!" Jake said, amazement written on his face.

"Yeah, I probably would have," Arik said, looking wistful.

"Do you regret your decision to come here instead?"

"I used to, but not anymore. I've thrown my lot here, with Israel, come what may. This is my home now."

Amir walked up to them. "Do you guys want a tour of the facilities?"

"I thought we'd seen everything," Arik said.

"Not quite!" Amir said. "Why don't the two of you come with me? We'll hop into my Jeep."

They drove down a long, dark, winding dirt road and stopped at what appeared to be a cutout in the cliffs. Several hundred feet below lay the large expanse of the Red Sea. As the three men stared into the dark cavern, floodlights flashed, revealing a gleaming array of black and white Hawk missiles pointed out toward the sea. The glowing missiles contrasted sharply with the blackness of the night.

"This is our protection! Nobody would dare come near us!" Amir beamed.

Arik gave Jake a worried look. He said quietly in English, "The one thing that worries me is how much the Israelis underestimate the Arabs' ability to fight. Just because they got the crap kicked out of them in '67 doesn't mean they'll let us do it to them again. I can't shake the feeling that we may one day pay the price for that arrogance."

Jake spent the next morning, the morning before the seder, in the kitchen with the staff, frantically trying to keep the kitchen kosher while the food preparations took place. He managed some measure of success. He spent the afternoon pouring over the Hagaddah for commentaries to read aloud during the festivities.

By evening, everything was ready. Inside one of the sandbag-wall recesses, the tables had been set up in a U-shaped configuration under strings of colored lights hanging from one wall of sandbags to another. Above all was the dark canopy of a cloudless night adorned with twinkling stars. A white tablecloth was draped over the entire table, which was covered with piles of matzo, Haggadahs, and rows of wine glasses. At the center of the table was a large seder plate.

Jake was standing at the head of the table. Next to him was Arik.

Mikki came over to thank the rabbi \for coming to the base and conducting the service. "Shalom, Rabbi Jake, and welcome to Tzafra. I'm Mikki Zohar, the base commander. I trust that you've been treated well here?"

"So far," Jake said, smiling.

"I'm sorry that I missed your kumsitz last night. It was quite a hit with the chevre. Arik told me all about it. I hope that you'll give us a repeat performance tonight."

The seder proceeded under Jake's skilled leadership. The singing was spirited, and the sermons and the Haggadah explanations were inspiring.

Mikki marveled at her unit. She saw a side of her charges she had never seen before. For months, she had seen them as skilled intelligence professionals with military discipline. But Mikki could have seen that in the soldiers of any Western army. She now saw them as Jews, links in the long chain of generations that dated back to the time when the children of Israel went out of Egypt as free men and woman after centuries of slavery. These young men and women who were sitting along the length of the bright seder tables in their dress military uniforms, with their heads covered, were only one or two generations separated from the devout Orthodox Jews who had been persecuted in the ghettos of Eastern Europe, North Africa, and Yemen. They were young, strong, proud Jews singing age-old Jewish songs of freedom.

Mikki was particularly taken with a passage from the Haggadah that she had never noticed despite having celebrated many Seders since her childhood: "In every generation, Jews should see themselves as if they had gone out of Egypt. In every generation, there are forces bent on the destruction of the Jewish people." She thought about what lay just over the mountains to the west: modern-day Egypt. The descendants of the enslavers again were bent on destroying Israel, destroying the Jews. She thought about the Russian-supplied massive military buildup near the Suez Canal and shuddered. She wondered whether she would be ready. She wondered whether Israel would be ready when the eventual onslaught came.

The seder lasted well into the night. There was even spirited dancing.

Afterward, Mikki approached Jake. "Thank you very much, Rabbi Jake, for a most inspiring seder. Tonight, I saw in the Haggadah insights that I'd never seen before, and I'm sure that I'm not alone in feeling this way. Arik tells me that you're planning to return to New York after your term of study ends in June. You should consider staying here in Israel and throwing your lot in with us. You'll never regret it . . . but you might regret it if you return to the U.S. Just know that Israel is your home, not the U.S. Safe travels, Rabbi Jake."

"Thank you, Commander, for letting me come and see all this."

When Jake returned to Tel Aviv after the holiday, he made very certain that he traveled by Arkia, Israel's domestic airline.

***

The recruits were dog-tired and bleary-eyed. Having just returned from two weeks in the field, drilling in assault and ambush techniques punctuated by thirty-kilometer forced stretcher marches in the mountainous desert, they had not slept in thirty-six hours. Their fatigue was accentuated by profoundly sore muscles and tendons and stress fractures in their feet. Finally, back at the base at 9:30 p.m., they were promised a night's sleep, a glorious gift.

At 1:30 a.m., the entire company, nearly one hundred men, were awakened by shouts to be dressed and outfitted in full battle gear in ten minutes. A mad dash commenced. The resourceful among them were always ready for this contingency and slept in their shoes, some not having removed them in two weeks except to take quick showers. They grabbed their weapons, assault vests, thirty-kilogram backpacks and magazines full of bullets and rushed into formation at the center of the quad.

A sergeant shouted, "Ready for attention!"

The entire company shouted back, "Attention!"

A first lieutenant bellowed, "After me, at a run!"

Thus, began a ten-kilometer run back into the hills. Several of the recruits vomited out the meager meal that they had been allowed before drifting off into their three-hour nap. The recruits followed the lieutenant into the hills and thorny shrubs at a brisk pace. The night was moonless, and their way forward was illuminated only by the twinkling stars above their heads. At the ten-kilometer mark, they stopped, breathless, at a clearing in the rocky terrain at the top of a hill. The area was illuminated by flaming torches that flickered around them. Each sergeant stood in front of his platoon. All were standing silent and immobile, waiting to see what would happen next.

Someone shouted, "Present arms for the company commander!"

Since their induction, they had had only glimpses of him. This man or, more correctly, this godlike figure was the stuff of legend. He was one of the most respected field commanders in the paratroops, and they felt honored for having the privilege of serving under him. His combat experience and leadership skills were regarded throughout the army as second to none. He appeared to have been born for this moment. A tall, muscular man with chiseled features bathed in firelight, accompanied by his adjutant, appeared from behind a rocky outcropping. He walked to the top of the outcropping and faced the recruits, who were standing in mute awe. He was flanked by large Israeli flags that were fluttering in the firelight.

Arik had been in a place such as this only three years earlier, when he had been a new recruit. Time had passed so quickly, yet so much had happened to him. So many changes and tribulations had molded him into what he had become. *I wish Abba could see me now.*

He said, "Company August '73! You've been given the privilege to join the most elite airborne company in the army. Your officers and NCOs have been carefully selected from the finest units, for their tactical and leadership skills. You've all volunteered to be Israeli paratroopers, but you'll all have to earn that distinction. You're going to work harder than you ever thought possible. Your commanders will demand nothing less than 110 percent effort from you. Failure to do so will result in immediate reassignment. Let me be very clear about this.

"Yitzhak Sedeh, the founder of the Palmach, once wrote and I quote, 'Heroism is a form of sacrifice, is not aggressive in its nature. Neither is it degrading; rather it is a positive form of service. In its essence, it is altruism. Heroism is a positive human trait. There is no heroism without a human goal and without humanity, since its objective is preserving human life. It is, therefore, why it is so difficult for the genuine hero to kill. He will commit this act only when there is no alternative, when there is absolutely no doubt regarding the justification for the killing, when this act is absolutely necessary to save a life. Neither can the ignorant be a hero, since ignorance is lack of involvement in what is surrounding you. Lack of involvement is lack of love and sacrifice and no heroism.'

"This is our motto: Purity of Arms!

"Acharai, Tzanchanim!" (Follow me, paratroopers!)

Arik paused and looked at his charges as if he were looking through them.

"Burn my words into your souls, and never forget for a moment who you are and what you are!"

A voice called out, "Attention, Arik Company! The commander departs!"

One hundred men stood sharply at attention and shouted out in unison, "Attention!"

Arik vanished as if into thin air.

***

The air was heavy with expectation. It was September 1973, the dawn of a new year: 5733. It was a year of nervous optimism. The Israeli economy had seen a major upswing, and the average standard of living had improved considerably during the past few years. Israelis were on the move, many striking out outside Israel for the first time. Instead of opting to go to nearby Europe, hordes of Israelis flocked to India, Thailand, Nepal, and South America.

Israelis consummated their passion for European fashion and football and American jeans and rock and roll. More and more BMWs, Volvos, Plymouths, and Buicks adorned the streets and highways of Israel.

Above all, there was a sense of peace and security that came from the fact that all of the front lines opposing Israel's main foes, the Egyptians and Syrians, were far from population centers, a situation that would have been unthinkable before 1967. There was even talk about shortening the period of military service for Israeli men from three years to thirty months. True, there had been war jitters back in the spring, but they had turned out to be false alarms. The millions of lira that they had cost the Israeli taxpayers in troop mobilization costs had been for naught. The Israeli military command, under criticism from the government, would have to think long and hard before ordering another mobilization. Most military and Mossad analysts had concluded that the quantitative and qualitative combined military strength of the

Egyptian and Syrian militaries was grossly below par and that it would be at least three years before any attack on Israel would be possible.

Arik and Mikki were standing side by side holding hands at the all-white splendor that was the table set for the night of Rosh Hashanah at the Zohar family's home. For the first time in months, everyone had made it home. Dani was standing with his now fiancée, Efrat, across the table from Arik and Mikki. Etzion and Opher were at the other end of the table, facing Shmulik and Yael. The table was immaculately appointed with bone china, silverware, and the finest Waterford crystal. A large white velvet cloth covered the holiday challahs, which were surrounded by silver honey dishes, apples, and exotic fruit with which to bless the coming year. It was to be a year of one, and possibly two, weddings. The lights were dimmed, allowing the room to be bathed in the flickering candlelight emanating from two large, multitier silver candelabras that stood in the center of the large dining room table.

There was absolute silence from the others around the table as Shmulik recited the holiday Kiddush, the inaugural benediction with the wine.

"May this year bring forth all of its blessings on our home."

Shmulik dipped the challah into honey and proclaimed, "May it be the will of the Almighty that this new year be as sweet as this honey."

He looked around the table at the two couples and said, "May you all be blessed to build beautiful and faithful homes in Israel."

Arik raised his silver cup of wine and put it to Mikki's lips. She sipped the wine and then grasped the cup and put it to Arik's lips for him to take a sip.

They looked deeply into each other's eyes and whispered, "Amen."

Yael was teary-eyed as she watched the four lovers.

The two days of Rosh Hashanah were filled with penitent and celebratory prayer, ram's horn sounds, sumptuous meals, long walks in the desert park near the house and, for Arik and Mikki, late-night lovemaking.

These were days of respite from the unease that hung over the Zohars' home. Yael, insisting that nothing disturb the peace of the holiday, had forbidden any talk of work or other outside concerns.

"That will all wait until after the holiday," she had insisted.

After the Havdalah service, which signaled the close of Rosh Hashanah, the phones rang, twice each time, summoning Opher and then Etzion. Within ten minutes, they each were in uniform, packed, and on their way out the door.

"What's going on?" Yael asked them. "Why the rush to leave? You were supposed to stay until tomorrow morning. Let me make some food for you to take with you. Who knows when you'll have a chance to eat?"

"Imma, something is going on at the Canal," Opher said. "Our spotters have detected large-scale troop movements along the Egyptian side. I have got to get back to base immediately."

"I've gotten the same word," Etzion said. "I'm heading back to the Mitla Pass. The ordnance teams are frantically arming the tanks."

Mikki already was on the phone with her commander, General Zeira, the chief of military intelligence. Shmulik went up to his room and packed his uniforms in preparation to return to the southern command center. Yael rushed into the kitchen to prepare several days' worth of food for each of her charges.

"Arik, I just spoke to Zeira," Mikki said, "and he told me that things are still pretty quiet at both fronts. The likelihood of an attack is low, so I don't need to run out tonight. I'll be heading out to Tzafra at noon tomorrow."

Arik wasted no time before contacting General Shaked's office on the secure line. He remained on the phone for ten minutes, nodding and saying, "Yes, sir . . . Yes, sir . . . Yes, sir . . . Okay, sir."

When he hung up the phone, Mikki asked him, "Nu? Ma inyanim? What's up?"

"I've been relieved of my company command and reassigned to command a small Matkal unit. We've been ordered to the listening post at the top of the Hermon, to fortify the Golani garrison up there. There's something very odd going on at the border with the Syrians, but nobody really knows what's happening. If the generals know, they're not saying. My orders are to be up there by tomorrow night, so I'll leave here when you do, at noon tomorrow."

"I have got a really bad feeling about this, Arik. If they've ordered you up there, it can't be good. I smell a cataclysm brewing, despite Zeira's assurances. I've been arguing vigorously with him at staff meetings over the past month. I'm looking at the same recon images and intelligence reports that he is, and it's as clear as day to me that we'll be at war within several weeks—with both Egypt and Syria. I can't comprehend his blindness. I'm worried that he has Golda's and Dayan's ears and they're basing their defense policy on his recommendations alone, like the fate of the whole country is hanging on one man's opinion. That scares me, really scares me."

"Mikki, let's go to bed early," he whispered. "There's one other thing we need to do, and I want to do it at sunrise. I thought it could wait, but it can't, apparently, if your assessments are correct. Let's have one last night together. If you're right, who knows when we'll see each other next? It could be quite a while. If there's a war, I have a feeling that it'll last more than six days."

She looked hard at him. "You're right, of course. Let's go to bed."

The two lovers made no pretense of sleeping in different bedrooms that night. Shmulik and Yael smiled slightly at each other, nodded, and wished the couple a good night.

Hours of restless lovemaking ensued, followed by an hour or two of fitful sleep. At 4 a.m., the pair slipped out the door, each holding a satchel.

On Arik's Harley, it took them only an hour to reach the edge of the Ramon Crater in the desert. They arrived just as the sun was beginning to peep over the eastern horizon, painting the canyon red and beige. They sat at the edge at the empty observation post and quietly shared a thermos of hot coffee. At first, they did not say much, although they both had a lot to say. Then it all came out in a torrent.

Arik reached into his satchel and pulled out a small box.

"I know it's not very much, but someday I'll buy you something much larger. I hope you like it."

Mikki gasped when she opened the box and saw the diamond ring inside.

"It's so beautiful, Arik! Just like your eyes."

"My eyes are beautiful because they're only for you. You're my other half. You're the reason I was put on this earth. Be my life. Be my wife, Mikki."

She said through a veil of tears, "We've spoken about this so many times in so many ways over the past two years, and now that it's here, for real, it's overwhelming. My soul is completely swept up into yours." She kissed the ring. "This is our bond forever, in pure faith and trust and justice, in mercy and loving kindness."

He took her hands in his and kissed them. "It's my most fervent wish that the Almighty bless our union and that we may be privileged to build a home like your parents have."

They held hands as they watched the sun rise up over the desert.

"I have something for you," she said. She pulled a black folder out of her satchel.

"What is it?"

"Something I found just this past week. I was looking for an opportunity to show it to you, and this is perfect. I found it in the Palmach archives annex in a warehouse just outside Tel Aviv. It's the manifest of new recruits to the Palmach coming off the blockade-running ships. This folder is from 1946. Take a look at the entry from April 12th."

Arik ran his fingers down the entries in the long table, which included names, birth dates, places of birth, and DP (displaced persons) camp of origin. His fingers stopped at the fifteenth entry from the top of the page:

Wolf Myerowitz

Born: August 4, 1910

Place of birth: Lwów, Poland

DP Camp: Bergen-Belsen, British zone of occupation, West Germany

Assignment: Palmach Central Command

Arik's hand trembled. He turned pale.

"This is my father! You've found him! At long last! Here is proof, finally, that my father was in the Palmach underground! My God, Mikki. You did it. You did it! No one else could have done it but you. You're my angel sent by God. My life is finally coming full circle. We need to bring this to the attention of the proper authorities. My father will finally be vindicated. I've been waiting for this my whole life. We need to do this right away! Oh, Mikki!"

"We will, booba. Hopefully, this scare at the borders that we're going through will prove to be another false alarm. When the dust settles, I'll bring this to Zeira's attention and he can pass it on to Golda. You know that nothing happens in Israel during Sukkot. The whole country comes to a standstill. Let's leave this until after the holidays, and by the time your parents come here for our engagement party we'll have some wonderful news for them. My Abba and Sharon will get personally involved in this, if need be, and heaven help Benny Gilad if he gets in our way. We'll hang him out to dry in the open air like a fish. Meanwhile, I won't let this file out of my sight for a minute. I'll carry it with me wherever I go." She smiled.

"I love you so much, Mikki! I'm the luckiest man in the world. I'm redeemed through you," he said tearfully.

Her face suddenly turned ashen.

"I'm seized by a terrible fear—a premonition—that this is going to be an awful war. Your being on top of Mount Hermon right in the jaws of the Syrian Army scares me to death, like I might not see you again. I know that outpost well. It isn't well equipped for combat, and it's a prime strategic target. My colleagues in the northern command have told me that there are millions of dollars of state-of-the-art American-made electronics up there and they're poorly protected. You're going to be a sitting duck up there. They're sending you up there to beef up the garrison, but I fear that it may already be too little too late. I can't bear the thought that the love of my life will be cannon fodder. Again. I lost Elisha. If I lose you, too, I won't want to live." She began to cry softly.

"Mikki, my soul, this is what I've trained for all these years. This is what I'm good at. I'm a survival machine. I'm a war machine. I'm going to make the Syrians sorry they ever disliked us in the first place. Please, have faith in the Almighty and me. Please! It's you I'm worried about. You'll also be at a listening post. You're also in danger. What if I lose you? How could I live?"

"I'm at a very isolated spot at the tip of Sharm el-Sheik, far from the front. I'm not concerned for my own safety. I'll just be holed up with my quiet crew, up there in my little perch, directing traffic for the duration of the war. Just think about our future and the bright future that awaits your parents. Arik, take care of yourself! Please! You're no good to me in a box. I'm completely consumed with affection for you, Arik Meir. I've whispered my new name to myself so many times during private moments: Mikki Meir . . . Mikki Meir . . . Mikki Meir . . . Godspeed, Arik. Come back to me, and make me the mother of your children."

Chapter 25

The sun was setting on Monday, October 8th, when Yoni's convoy of armored personnel carriers rolled into what was left of the northern command center at Nafach after the Syrian 9th Division had broken through the perimeter and sent General Raful Eitan and his staff reeling backward, beating a hasty retreat three miles to the west. They had been forced to direct the battle from a circle of armored personnel carriers parked at the side of a road, vulnerable to attack from air and artillery.

The thinly manned Barak Brigade, defending the central Golan and Nafach, in particular, and facing 900 Syrian tanks supported by 140 batteries of artillery, itself had only 177 tanks and 11 batteries of artillery. In the first thirty-six hours of the fighting, the Barak Brigade had been nearly crushed, with 90 percent of its tank commanders killed or wounded as tens of thousands of Syrian, Iraqi, and Moroccan troops poured across the border, encircling or overrunning all of the Israeli border forts up and down the Golan Heights.

Despite sustaining great losses, the Golani Infantry Brigade had driven the Syrians back out of the Nafach camp. The road leading up to the camp was littered with destroyed hulks of Syrian and Israeli tanks and with Syrian and Israeli dead. Only several hours earlier, it had been a raging battleground that was the last line of Israeli defense between the Syrians and the Sea of Galilee. From their forward positions, the Syrian tank crews could see the Israeli city of Tiberias and sense that Israeli defenses were collapsing. Although driven back temporarily, the Syrian 9th Division regrouped and retooled that night in preparation for a final push to regain the central Golan Heights.

In northern Golan, the situation was no better. The Syrian 3rd and 7th Armored Divisions faced a single Israeli brigade, the crack 7th, commanded by Colonel Yanush Ben-Gal, who would be acknowledged after the war as one of the field commanders who had stopped the Syrian onslaught and saved northern Israel. On the Booster and Hermonite ridges, Ben-Gal's brigade fought the Syrians to the last man and the last tank. Tank squadrons that had been reduced to one or two tanks faced off with and destroyed Syrian tank columns of twenty or thirty tanks by superior gunnery, raw bravery, and sheer grit and determination. By the evening of Monday, October 8th, surviving tank crews on all three Golan fronts were at the brink of exhaustion and even madness. Many of the soldiers had not eaten or slept in forty-eight hours. They were dangerously low on fuel and ammunition, and every tank had been hit and sustained some damage. Most of the tanks, which had sustained direct hits from armor-piercing rockets and shells, reeked of burning flesh and blood from their crews having been roasted alive. The responsibility of refitting and cleaning the tanks, replenishing fuel, and assembling tank crews from the ragtag shell-shocked survivors fell to the ordnance crews, which were working around the clock under an endless barrage of Syrian artillery fire. There seemed no stopping the Syrian onslaught.

The underground northern command center at Nafach was reoccupied by Colonel Uri Orr's 79th Brigade, which had pushed back the Syrian 9th Armored Division. The Syrians halted just east of Nafach and regrouped for the next day's counteroffensive. The northern command center was filled with panic-stricken, exhausted, sweating Israelis. Generals and other senior officers huddled over maps. Chaos and disorder hung heavily in the stale, smoke-filled air. Outside in the sharp, cold evening, Yoni's men were ordered to guard the perimeter of the compound. Syrian tanks continued shelling the area, reminding the battered Israelis that the Syrians were only minutes away. Yoni went from man to man, offering encouragement and hope amid the shells that were landing in the exposed foxholes where they lay.

Yoni's sentries at the western gate of the compound, adjacent to Tapline Road, were the first to spot a Syrian armored personnel carrier (APC) barreling at breakneck speed up the dirt path from the main road and through the eucalyptus trees. As it approached the gate, they began firing their submachine guns at it. Continuing at full speed, the APC burst through the perimeter. The Israelis scrambled for their rocket-propelled grenades. The APC's headlights began flashing rapidly on and off as it slowed to a stop twenty feet inside the gate. The door swung open, and a lone man emerged. Twenty muzzles were pointed at him. He waved his arms wildly in the glare of the headlamps.

Yoni was in full sprint toward the ruckus at the gate. "Hold your fire! Hold your fire," Yoni yelled when the identity of the disheveled man dawned on him.

Five more men piled out of the back of the APC.

"Arik! What in the world are you doing here in a Syrian APC?" Yoni asked. "Where are you coming from? My God! Look at you! You look like you've walked through the gates of hell and back!"

They hugged.

"Yoni, I'm trying to think of something clever to say, like 'I just went out for a relaxing afternoon stroll and happened to bump into the entire fucking Syrian Army!' Do you guys down here have any clue what's going on up north? Yanush's 7th Brigade is holding back two Syrian armored divisions with just knuckles and knives. They've been almost completely destroyed. There's nothing standing between the Syrians and the Dan River and Rosh Pina. It's like the end of the world! The roads and fields are littered with hundreds of burned-out Israeli and Syrian tanks, and dead bodies from both armies are strewn around like rotten cabbages as far as the eye can see. I'll tell you what, though: Our tank crews are giving back better than they're getting. These guys are scoring twenty to twenty-five tank kills each. I don't know how they're doing it. I'm in absolute awe. They're nearly out of ammo, though. I've never even imagined anything like this!"

"You still haven't told me what you're doing wandering around all by yourself, all over the Golan Heights in a Syrian APC. What the hell are you up to? What unit are you with?"

"Like there was a unit I could hook up to. Like there's any semblance of military order. It's every man for himself up there. Units are forming spontaneously and randomly, by anyone who can carry a gun or drive a tank and isn't completely out of his mind with shock. Complete chaos! This is nothing like the Six-Day War. What ever happened to Arabs running away? They're kicking the living shit out of us. You really want to know where I've been since Yom Kippur?"

"Well, it's been pretty quiet here this evening, so far, but the Syrians are just over the ridge. They've been lobbing shells at us, but otherwise there's been no frontal assault. The men are eating and trying to rest, so, yeah, I'm all ears."

"Holiday camp!" Arik said. "So, this APC is on loan to me, courtesy of the nice people of the Syrian 7th Armored Division just up the road at Booster ridge. The crew was initially reluctant to part with it, so we had to kill them all, and man, is this thing stuffed with goodies, but I'll get to that later. I'm getting ahead of myself."

"You're such a lunatic, Arik, but you're my lunatic. That's why I love you so much!" Yoni laughed. "Continue, please."

"A week before Rosh Hashanah, Colonel Yanush Ben-Gal, the commander of the 7th Armored Brigade, got a strong sense that the Syrians were up to something, because of credible intelligence reports of Syrian troop buildups all along the Purple Line, and he got authorization from General Hofi to move large elements of the brigade from the center of the country to the Golan Heights to reinforce the Barak Brigade that was stretched pretty thin along the southern sector. Lucky, he did that.

"Anyway, the observation post on top of Mount Hermon reported a significant buildup of infantry and artillery elements on the Syrian side, to the northeast. Ten men from my unit were ordered up to the post, to beef up the Golani unit stationed up there. In all, we were fifty-five men, including air force and military intelligence personnel. The northern command never thought for a minute that the post would be the target of a Syrian assault. The only reason we were sent up there was a nod to Yanush, because of his concerns. I brought detailed maps of the compound and the whole area with me to maximize the defense of the perimeter. Lucky, I did.

"When I got up there, two days after Rosh Hashanah, I was shocked to see that the post's fortifications had never been completed. Like they didn't have seven years to do it! The main gate of the position was half off, swinging on its hinges. The bunkers and forward communication trenches were only partially complete. All this crap to defend priceless, world-class American and Israeli electronic surveillance and radar systems. I radioed back to Hofi's headquarters that there were daily increases in the concentration of armor and artillery in the valley below us. All I got was deaf ears. I don't know what those guys were thinking.

"On Friday morning, the entire valley below us was jam-packed with Syrians. And I still couldn't get anyone's attention at headquarters. There were no defensive preparations I could engineer either. We had nothing but a few machine guns, bazookas, and mortars. We're completely isolated up there. That night, everyone went to say Kol Nidre, like they didn't have a care in the world. My unit took up recon along the approach roads.

"At about 1:45 p.m. Shabbat afternoon, en masse, the Syrians took the camouflage nets off their guns and began raining hundreds of shells down on our heads. Most of the staff and technicians ran into the central hall of the bunker. We went up to the observation point, looking for any sign of a commando assault, but we had to withdraw. The shelling was so intense. At 3 p.m., four Mil Mi-8 helicopters full of commandos approached the upper ski lift. I managed to hit one of them with my bazooka, and it burst into flames, but the other three managed to land. There were only ten of us up there, and they had nearly ten times as many. Two of my guys were hit and killed. We had only three MAG machine guns in all, and two had been damaged in the artillery bombardment. About a hundred commandos came running up at us in all directions. I kept firing at them, and I dropped a bunch of them until I ran out of ammo. All we had at that point were a few grenades and our Uzis. This craziness went on for about an hour, until we ran out of ammo. There were only six of us left. The technicians were cowering in the bunker, sucking their thumbs. We ended up withdrawing into the great hall of the bunker, where we destroyed as much of the electronic equipment as we could and locked the steel main doors. We didn't get to finish the job, because the Syrians found the ventilation ducts and began dropping smoke grenades into the room. It was getting ridiculous. We were sitting ducks in there. The building was completely surrounded by hundreds of Syrian commandos.

"Nachum, my assistant, and I pored over the maps and found a secret underground passageway coming off the main room, and twenty of us, including the technicians, crawled out from the hall through that passageway. It went along a communication trench right under the Syrians' noses. We got out of there under cover of darkness. Behind us, we could see the compound getting blown to bits. We got out in the nick of time.

"We thought we were home free, but as we passed the upper ski lift the Syrians opened fire on us, with automatic weapons from a range of about two hundred yards. By then, each of us had an Uzi with one magazine left. Nachum and I ran toward the fire and managed to silence the position, only to run into another ambush. These next guys showered us with machine gun fire and grenades. Nine of our group were hit and killed. We had no bullets left, so we decided to roll down the hill on our stomachs, including the wounded. When we were out of range, we ran down the road like madmen, each of us carrying a man on his shoulders. Up ahead of us were three of our tanks. We thought we were out of the woods, when one of our own tanks began firing at us. Luckily, none of us was hurt by that. In all, out of the fifty-five guys at the post, only eleven of us managed to escape back to our lines at Majdal Shams.

"You're not going to believe this, but when we got there we were called cowards because we didn't stay and fight. Fight with what? We had nothing left. All we could do was get the hell out of there so we could live to fight another day. Those Syrians weren't in the mood to take prisoners.

"The Golanis down there were fixated on the observation post. They started making plans to recapture it. At that point, I felt the whole exercise was pointless while the whole Golan was going up in flames. The five remaining guys in my unit were free agents—unassigned to a unit—so when I heard that the Kuneitra seam between the Barak and the 7th Brigade was breached and Nafach was under attack, I decided we needed to get down here to see how we could help. We walked to El Rom and got the tremp of our lives, crowded into an open command car. We had four near misses from Syrian tank fire. At Booster, I saw the oddest thing. Facing Yanush's tanks were rows and rows of Syrian infantry walking around with these green briefcases. On cue, they opened them up and produced wire-guided missile controls. They fired at our tanks and, one by one, our tanks went up in smoke. It seemed too dangerous to be in a vehicle. They were sitting ducks. I figured we'd be less of a target on foot.

"Lucky, too, because a minute after they dropped us off, the command car we were in sustained a direct hit by an artillery shell. It was vaporized."

Yoni and several others who had gathered around Arik and his men were listening in mute horror to what Arik was saying.

"We watched as Colonel Yanush's tanks fired on the Syrians," Arik said, "from Booster, as they tried to cross the ditches. At first, they succeeded in stopping them, but the Syrians brought up bridging tanks and the tanks started pouring across. After dark, I stood on the ridge under a rock face and watched as the Syrians came across the border. The entire valley below was illuminated by what looked like hundreds of cat's-eyes. The tanks maneuvered like it was daylight. I think that may have some infrared night-vision equipment. How can we beat these guys if we're flying blind at night?"

"It was a set-piece battle pattern like I read about in Soviet military histories. They attacked in layers—infantry first, followed by armored infantry, followed by main battle tanks. They're as disciplined as anything. So much for our qualitative edge! What a pile of bullshit we've been fed by our high command. We don't have any coordination between our infantry and armor. Nobody ever saw the need for that. What's the purpose of infantry in a set-piece tank battle? They taught us that. Now, I've seen us pay the price.

"Coming down Booster ridge, into the valley, we managed to sneak up on a row of rocket men, and I mowed them down with my MAG, but it was a useless effort. There were so many of them, and they just kept coming. There were at least two battalions of tank-killing infantry in our area alone. Behind them rolled columns of tanks working in tandem with the infantry, in total discipline. We joined up with twenty Golani guys and fanned out in the pitch dark, hitting one squad after another.

"The scariest part of the whole thing was seeing our fighter planes, our vaunted, invincible Chel Ha'Avir, swooping down to stem the hemorrhage, themselves getting shot down by surface-to-air missiles, one by one. I don't know if any of them made it back to base alive. These Syrians have done their homework. We're in serious deep shit. I had box seats to Armageddon."

"That's quite a story," Yoni said. "Now, how'd you get the APC? And what kind of goodies did Santa bring?"

"I thought you'd never ask. I noticed that when the infantry with the briefcases advanced, they advanced in lines and after dispensing their missiles they fell back to APCs that had accompanied them, to pick up more of those briefcases. The unit behind them fired while they did that. One unit's APC strayed too close to our line of fire. After we ambushed that unit, we jumped into it, said, 'Bye, bye,' to the crew, and took off with a truckload of these briefcases, back up the hill, all the while trying to avoid our own guys, who were starting to shoot at us, too. It was crazy! It was too dangerous for us to stay on the road so we veered into the open fields and took our chances. I also have a small surprise gift especially for you."

"I hate when you have a surprise for me. What is it?"

"It's not what. It's who!"

"What are you taking about?"

Arik walked Yoni around to the back of the APC. When he looked inside, Yoni saw a man lying on the floor, hog-tied, with his arms and legs behind him. Behind him were rows and rows of green briefcases and wooden crates that were embossed with Arabic and Cyrillic letters.

"Who is this? A Syrian officer?" Yoni asked. "He's wearing a Syrian uniform without insignia."

"This is where it gets interesting. His name is Ivan."

"Ivan?"

"Ivan Petrovski. When we killed the Syrian crew, he threw his hands up and surrendered without a fight. It seems like we bagged ourselves a Soviet advisor! Undoubtedly, he was just a technician whose job was to instruct and supervise the use of these rockets. He called them Saggers. So much for the Soviets' denials of direct involvement in this mess."

"The whole inside of this APC is filled with these briefcases and crates," Yoni said.

"Yeah. Enough to destroy a whole tank battalion. Apparently, these puppies are manufactured in Eastern Europe. As we've seen, they're deadly accurate. The crates contain dozens of the newest generation of armor-piercing rocket-propelled grenades, the RPG-7s."

"So, how'd you get here, in the end?"

"I couldn't very well drive around here, in a Syrian APC, like it was the San Diego Freeway. It was sunrise when we got the hell out of there. If the Syrians weren't going to get us, our guys would have, so I drove into a thick eucalyptus grove and laid low most of today. Then, when it started to get dark, we made a run for it. I was going to come down the direct road through Ein Zivan, but the fighting was too intense there, so I headed north to Wasset, then came down the Tapline Road with the Syrians on my tail. All the way down the road, we were dodging Syrian tank and artillery shells falling all around us. One blew up about twenty feet from the truck, lifting us into the air. That scared the crap out of me. Here we are with a truckload of missiles and RPG-7s, with my men and this guy crowded inside. It was like driving a stick of dynamite. I said, 'Well, what the hell. At least if we go, it'll be fast!' I didn't need to have a ringside seat for the rest of this catastrophe. I floored it and pealed up the road. Well, here I am. Captain Arik Meir, reporting for duty, at your service! I want to put me and my squad under your command, sir!"

"Well, let me think about that." Yoni scratched his head.

Arik grinned his best foolish, toothy grin and gave Yoni a mock salute.

"Well, meshuganah, you've got some serious guts," Yoni said. "You're lucky Zvika Force didn't get a piece of you."

"What's Zvika Force?"

"Haven't you heard about Zvika Greengold? This guy's the only one left alive from his tank company, and he's running around theTapline Road like a one-man army knocking the crap out of the Syrians. People say he has about fifty tank kills so far. His gunnery is dead accurate, and he's been shooting at any Syrian vehicle that moves in his direction. If he'd seen you, you would've gotten your balls shot off."

Arik breathed a sigh of relief. "Maybe that was the guy who was shooting at me. Geez!"

"What would I tell Mikki?" Yoni asked. "She needs you with them still attached." Yoni chuckled. "Oh! By the way, Dani is here someplace, patrolling the perimeter with Starlight night-vision goggles."

"Speaking of which, what's going on in the Sinai?" Arik asked.

"We don't know much out here, but they say the Egyptians broke through the Bar-Lev Line and are advancing into the desert."

"That's just great! We've really been caught with our pants down. How the hell is this going to end?"

"Arik, buddy, we don't have the luxury of that kind of speculation. You know we were overrun here yesterday. All the fences and perimeter structures were flattened by the Syrians. They had this place surrounded. General Eitan and the other commanders barely got out of here by the seat of their pants yesterday morning, from the northern gate you just came in, and they ran the war from their APCs out in the open by a roadside. This place was just reoccupied about twelve hours ago by Colonel Orr's 79th Armored Brigade. We've got a country to save. Things are hanging on a knife edge. Come with me. You need to share everything you've told me and the contents of this APC with General Eitan. He's in the command center."

Turning to his men, Yoni said, "Take this Russian into custody. I'm sure intelligence will want to have a chat with him."

"I always loved show and tell," Arik said. "Meanwhile, let's get my guys something to eat. They haven't eaten or slept in forty-eight hours."

When Arik walked into the dusty gloom of the command bunker, he was dumbstruck. Huddled around the table and maps was the entire northern command. In the center sat Generals Hofi and Bar-Lev, and standing over them were Generals Motta Hod and Raful Eitan. They all were haggard, exhausted, dirty, and unshaven. The smell of perspiration and tobacco smoke was nearly overwhelming.

"Ah, look what the wind blew in," General Hofi said. "Arik, you look like you spent the last two days inside a cement mixer."

The reply tumbled out of Arik.

"Almost. I was in a borrowed Syrian APC full of missiles and antitank RPGs with a captured Russian advisor in tow. My men and I barely escaped with our lives, off the top of Mount Hermon, and in the process of trying to get down here we stumbled on to the most devastating tank firefight imaginable, in the pass between the Hermonite and Booster ridges.

"I watched in a daze as the 7th Brigade held back a force of Syrian tanks and armored infantry that outnumbered them ten to one. It looked and felt like the whole world was on fire. What was most disturbing was the Syrians' effective use of infantry. I must tell you that a significant percentage of Yanush's tanks are being destroyed by individual infantrymen shouldering wire-guided antitank missiles called Saggers. They're either vehicle-mountable or man-portable. I estimated that they had a range of three thousand meters and armor penetration of two hundred millimeters at sixty-degree impact, and they weigh at most ten kilograms. They're deadly accurate. I've personally seen fifty of our tanks go up in smoke from these things. And then the Syrians' tanks follow along behind their armored infantry.

"I sat and watched these for a while, and I noticed that the two most serious defects of the original weapon system are its minimum range of between five hundred and eight hundred meters—targets closer than that can't be effectively engaged—and how long it takes the slow-moving missile to reach maximum range, which is about thirty seconds. That gives the intended target time to take appropriate action, either by retreating behind an obstacle or a dune, laying down a smoke screen, or returning fire. I think these things can be beaten, but we need to develop countermeasures in a hurry. In my humble opinion, we need infantry support out there to attack these missile operators. The tanks can't do this on their own. The minute a tank commander sticks his head out of the turret to work the machine gun, he gets cut down."

The generals stood and watched Arik gravely as he spoke.

"Anyway, I brought a whole APC load of these missiles, with a Russian advisor in tow, who will spill his guts to stay alive. Maybe if we develop countermeasures—"

"Are you a tank operator or an expert in tank warfare?" shouted General Hod.

"No, sir!"

"Then, why are you standing here giving us a lecture on tank warfare, Captain? I think that you're out of your depth and pay grade. We have bigger problems to solve here. Go back out on patrol, soldier!"

Yoni said, "Sir, with all due respect, he doesn't claim to be an expert at anything. He's just telling us what he saw and heard. I believe that we ignore what he's saying at our peril. We're hemorrhaging tanks, and we can't afford to lose many more. Arik has possibly provided us with an opportunity. We should take a look at what he's brought and not dismiss him outright."

"How do you know all of this, Arik?" General Hofi asked.

"While we were in hiding, I learned much of this from the Russian."

"Do you speak Russian?"

"No, sir. He speaks fluent English."

General Raful Eitan, the supreme commander of the northern front, a usually quiet, taciturn man who, when he spoke, caught everyone's attention, finally made his thoughts known. "I believe that Yoni is right. Arik may have unknowingly provided us with a significant key to unlocking part of the quandary that we find ourselves in. Have these missiles inspected by our operations center, and turn the Russian over to the A'man for interrogation. Good work, Captain Meir." Raful smiled. "Don't go far. There are intelligence officers who will want to debrief you on what you went through on Mount Hermon and what you saw at Booster ridge."

Once outside the room, Yoni pulled Arik by the sleeve. "Let's go out to the perimeter and talk to some of the guys. Most of them are young kids and reservists who only forty-eight hours ago were sitting in synagogue, safe and warm. Now they're outside, cold, dirty, exhausted, and scared out of their wits. I think talking and kidding around with them would raise their morale. They all know who you are, and knowing that you're here with them will go a long way."

"Absolutely! What are we waiting for?" Arik said.

They walked from each soldier to the next, saying encouraging words to them:

"Yehiyeh beseder! It will be okay."

"We're at the tip of the spear!"

"We're playing a small but vital part in a major event in Jewish history."

"The whole country is watching us. They will long remember what we're doing."

"We're fighting for our parents, wives, friends, and neighbors."

"Chazak ve'ematz. No fear, just guts now. Fear can come later, when you're home safe with your girlfriends."

"There's nothing you'll do in your lives that's more important than what we do here tonight and the next few days."

"Fight like hell! We're so much better than them!"

"We're going to make them feel sorry they ever crossed our border!"

One of the guys asked, "Arik, do you think that we're going to die out here?"

"We're going to keep each other alive," Arik said. "I'll happily sacrifice my own life to keep you alive. I mean that."

Yoni and Arik walked out to the southeastern quadrant, expected to be the most likely point of attack, where Yoni had stationed the most seasoned, elite troops. Most were from Arik's own Matkal unit. Knowing that his buddies were here gave Arik a warm feeling. He approached the senior officer of the unit, from behind, and gave him a bear hug that lifted him off the ground.

Dani knew that could be only one person.

"Hey, Arik! You lazy bum! Where have you been? Yuck. You smell like dog vomit!"

"Oh, you know . . . The Golan is so pretty this time of year—with the wildflowers and all—I thought I'd take a little look around. How are you guys doing?"

"As good as can be expected," Dani said. "We're armed to the teeth, but we don't have any heavy weapons. These guys are pros, but I hope that the tank crews can hold the line, or we'll have a bloodbath here. Who knew that the Syrians had so many goddamn tanks? Our guys are destroying them as fast as they can see them, but they keep on coming, more and more. We've been watching Ben Hanan's brigade get whittled down to almost nothing. Each one of our tanks are irreplaceable. The ordnance guys are rebuilding the smashed tanks right here in the field, literally assembling tanks from working parts of destroyed ones. We don't have a single tank that hasn't sustained at least some damage."

"Have you heard anything from Mikki, Opher, or Etzion?"

"Not a thing! There's a blackout on communications."

"Well, let me know when the Syrians show up."

Arik crawled into the foxhole, shut his eyes, and immediately fell asleep. He got three hours of badly needed rest. At 5 a.m., he was jolted awake by a whoop-whoop-whoop sound. He knew that sound from Mount Hermon. Soviet helicopters! There were three, and they were skimming the ground, landing just out of sight, below the ridge to the northwest.

"Commando raid! Commando raid! Everybody up!" he shouted.

Yoni was already on his feet and running for his APC. His men were close behind him, heading for their three vehicles.

Arik jumped into the passenger side of a fourth vehicle, while the other members of his squad threw themselves into the back and began adjusting their ammunition harnesses. Dani was already at the wheel. The engine was racing.

"Where did you come from? I didn't see you!" Arik said.

"You didn't want me to miss all the fun, did you?" Dani smiled.

"Check your rifles, ammo cartridges, and grenades!" Arik called out.

Yoni hailed them over the radio and then said, "Okay, girls. By my estimation, there are about forty or fifty of them half a kilometer out, in that patch of tall grass. Everybody look sharp, and move on my signal. We need to catch them in under ten minutes after they land. They're at their most vulnerable before they can deploy."

The line of vehicles stopped just short of the ridge, and then the commandos poured out and ran up the path. At the ridgeline, they watched Golani infantry soldiers shooting a vehicle-mounted MAG wildly into the high grass, where they presumed the Syrian intruders to be. The soldiers were felled by the Syrians' return fire. The Israeli commandos crouched low and cautiously approached the tall grass, before suddenly springing up and charging into the thicket in a classic close-quarters combat pattern. Yoni signaled for Arik and his group to outflank the Syrians from the side. The Syrians were still in process of deploying. Thus, in two directions simultaneously, the Israeli commandos charged into the grass, firing their assault rifles in almost a continuous stream of fire. Most of the Syrians were cut down in the first few seconds. The rest tried to escape back toward their lines, away from the Israelis, but were mowed down by a tank that rumbled up the road from the other direction. A single Syrian popped up and discharged his weapon, killing one soldier and wounding another. Arik ran toward him and silenced him with a burst of fire.

When the men gently lifted the body of the dead soldier, his helmet came off and fell to the ground. With it came a large, knit skullcap. Behind his ears small side curls were discreetly tucked away. When Arik stared at the young man's innocent-looking face, he saw a child of no more than eighteen. He had to fight to catch his breath, as if he had been sucker punched.

"His name was Yochai Neriya. He was a new recruit just out of the Yeshivat Har Etzion," Amnon, a sergeant in Yoni's squad, said. "He was a hesdernick who had just completed his basic paratrooper training. You know what hesder is?"

"Yes, it's a combined program that incorporates rabbinical studies and military service," Arik said.

"Yochai's father was evacuated, as a young boy, from the isolated religious settlement of Kfar Etzion, just south of Jerusalem, in 1948, just before it was overrun by local Arab militias and all of its defenders were killed. He lost both parents—Yochai's grandparents—in that hopeless battle. The Neriyas were among the first families to resettle Kfar Etzion after it was liberated in 1967—real pioneers. The old site, abandoned for nineteen years, had to be rebuilt from scratch in the middle of nowhere. I know the family. They're devoutly religious, followers of Rabbi Kook, a great mystic who believed that the return here to Israel was the beginning of the coming of the Messiah. These people are willing to sacrifice everything to fulfill that dream."

"They just did," Arik said flatly. He looked down, heartsick. "What sort of God would let such an innocent, defenseless child be killed in such a brutal way? It's so unfair."

From his early association with Rav Rabinovich, back in high school, Arik was familiar with the world of devoutly religious Zionists. This young man was cloistered in a loving, spiritual home, only to be thrust into this living hell. Who allowed him to be sent to the front so early in his training? He had his whole life ahead of him.

An odd thought crept into Arik's mind. This boy will never know the touch of a woman. He was certain that the boy had practiced neghia, like the kids in camp, with the expectation of experiencing intimacy after marriage. But for him that would never be. A great sadness washed over Arik. He had seen so much death, but this one really moved him.

"This is so unfair, Amnon," Arik said as he lay Yochai's body on a blanket on the metal floor of the command car and placed his kippah back on his head.

"It gets worse. He was an only child."

"What? Who allowed this?" Arik almost shouted. "There's an express rule in the army never to put an only child into a combat unit!"

"That's true, but he volunteered and asked to fight as a paratrooper. He managed to get parental consent to join. The army allows that."

"Someone should have had a lick of sense. Somebody should've put their foot down. In my view, that was a selfish thing for him to do, all the idealism notwithstanding. What are his parents going to do now? Even idealism wears thin in the face of overwhelming tragedy." He sighed deeply. "Okay, let's get the hell out of here."

In all, there were forty Syrian dead. Their commander was wounded and taken prisoner. The Syrians' weapons, brand-new Kalashnikov rifles, were taken as booty.

Dani ran toward Arik. He was in fine spirits. "We kicked some serious ass, Arik. Look at these bayonets. They can be used as can openers."

"Dani, I'm not in the mood." Arik frowned.

Arik's men collected the new Syrian weapons and ammo, loaded the rest the dead and wounded Israelis into their APC, and drove back to Nafach in a hurry, just as the Syrian 9th Armored Division launched their attack. When the squad arrived at Nafach and the personnel there saw more than one hundred Syrian tanks heading up the hill and directly toward them, pandemonium broke out at the northern command center. All that stood between the infantrymen, commanders, and a Syrian armored division was Yossi Ben Hanan's remnant of the 7th Brigade: ten refurbished battle-scarred tanks. The officers wondered how long they could hold out. Behind them lay the undefended approaches to the Galilee. Reports from the southern Golan were even worse. The Syrian Army had broken through the Israelis' last line of defense. They were swarming at will. They were headed toward the Sea of Galilee. This was it.

From Jerusalem, Moshe Dayan considered evacuating the Golan entirely and establishing a line of defense at the Jordan Valley. He exclaimed to his staff that they were looking at the "ruination of the Third Temple."

From less than two kilometers to the east, the officers at the northern command center heard the constant boom of Ben Hanan's few remaining tanks locked in a death struggle with the Syrians. They watched the macabre fireworks display in the sky over their heads: Squadron after squadron of Israeli Air Force Mirage and Phantom jets that had come to join in the battle vaporized in balls of flame as each in turn was hit by surface-to-air missiles.

Those Syrians must be laughing their asses off. Arik gritted his teeth.

Yoni got off his radio and walked up to Arik, Dani, and Gidon, who were standing together.

"Colonel Orr's brigade made it up to the Golan from the Jordan Valley, to reinforce Ben Hanan, but they're getting hammered," Yoni said. "They've taken heavy losses. Ben Hanan's company exists in name only, at this point. It could be just hours before the Syrians get here. Our chances are getting slimmer by the minute."

"We're going to have to tell the men," Dani said. "It's only fair. They need to know what's coming. Let's split up and inform the guys on the perimeter."

The three men went from foxhole to foxhole, passing on the message. They had been surrounded by the Syrian 1st Armored Division, which had bypassed the position on its way to within four kilometers of the Jordan River and the Bnot Yaakov Bridge. All around them, Orr's brigade was fighting an ongoing battle with the Syrians, trying to cut off the advancing Syrians from the flank around Sindania to their south. All around the southern reaches of Nafach, the men saw Israeli and Syrian tanks and APCs in a death struggle. If the Syrians destroyed Orr's last few battle-worn tanks, they would come for them.

Arik had no illusions about their chances of survival. The small band of infantry that had been assigned to perimeter defense was lightly armed with rifles, grenades, and a few RPGs in hastily dug foxholes. If the Syrian tanks broke through, the fight would be over in a few minutes. Even the Syrian Sagger antitank missiles that Arik had captured had been spirited away during the night, not that anyone would have known how to use them. Arik was prepared for death but felt surprisingly at peace.

Arik and Yoni locked eyes. They were thinking the same thing.

Arik smiled and shrugged. "It is what it is," he said quietly.

Yoni looked down and whispered, "Maybe it's better this way."

***

Most of the men were sitting and staring out with grim determination. Some were weeping.

"Why do we have to sit here and die for no reason?" one soldier asked.

Arik said firmly, "Where is there to run to? When Yoni came up here yesterday, he saw droves of shell-shocked men running off the Golan in a panic. Where were they going? If the Syrians pass the Jordan River, they'll be in Tel Aviv in under a week. Is that what you want to be witness to? It's far better to fight and die, if necessary, like men, right here, right now! I don't know about you, but under the circumstances there's nowhere else in the world I'd rather be than right here, fighting to preserve a two-thousand-year-old dream. It's on our shoulders now. We need to support the tank crews any way we can."

Yoni smiling, walked over and patted Arik on the back. "Aren't you glad you came back from LA?" he said.

The Syrian tanks never broke through the perimeter. Colonel Peled's large reserve armored division finally pushed up the Golan escarpment from the Jordan Valley just in time, reinforced Orr's and Ben Hanan's brigades, and counterattacked. In a massive firefight that lasted twenty-four hours, they sent the Syrians hurtling in a panic eastward past Sindania and Ramtania and back toward the Purple Line, the prewar border.

The following day, Raful met with Yoni and the other senior infantry and armored division officers to plan the impending Israeli counterattack across the Purple Line and into Syria itself. Additional reinforcements from Israel proper had finally arrived. Many of the tanks had worn out their treads by driving across the whole country on them in a mad dash north to get to the Golan. Such was the organizational chaos and the lack of tank carriers. However, by late Tuesday, October 9th, the ordnance teams had completed all of the necessary repairs to the armored vehicles, the tank crews, now rested and fed, were ready to move, and the infantry was poised to assist them and protect them.

"Hey, Arik!" Yoni said. "Raful has assigned infantry units to support each of his tank battalions across the northeast frontier and head off the rocket men. We're going into Syria to kick some ass. He mentioned you by name and told me to convey his thanks. You did good, boychick!"

On Thursday, October 11th, under a barrage of Syrian shells, Ben Hanan and his reconstituted armored brigade was ordered to move rapidly forward to capture the Maatz crossroads, cutting off the Syrian retreat on the main Kuneitra–Damascus road. Although he initially had hesitated to go farther without infantry support, Ben Hanan ended up going ahead. Fearing the worst, Yanush, the brigade commander, sent Yoni's company to catch up to Ben Hanan. There was no way to navigate the roads in the pitch darkness, and the maps were incomplete. No one wanted to wander about and get lost in Syria proper with roving bands of enemy infantry all around.

As soon as Yoni was able to establish radio contact, he and Ben Hanan decided to meet halfway. Ben Hanan ignited a destroyed Jeep and, using the plume of flame as a signal, directed Yoni's battalion toward him. The infantry followed behind Ben Hanan's tank column, heading into the darkness.

After only a few hundred yards, the column was hit by a barrage of RPG rounds coming in from the right side. Ben Hanan's Centurion was hit by an RPG-7, setting fire to the canvas cover on the gun breach. Machine gun rounds ignited and popped off the gun breach like firecrackers. Ben Hanan's clothing caught fire, and his screams were heard over the open radio frequency, which was broadcasting to the whole sector. Yoni jumped up on the tank and put out the fire with an extinguisher. He motioned to Arik to take a squad of men to outflank the Syrian position. The sounds of incoming RPG rounds soon were drowned by continuous bursts of machine gun fire. Then, all was quiet.

Arik returned to Yoni's position.

"Arik, what did you find out there?" Yoni asked.

"About twenty of them shooting RPGs. Piece of cake."

"Now you're just being an arrogant schvitzer, Arik," Captain Boaz Davidi said.

Boaz was Yoni's subordinate. He was a consummate capable professional but quite full of himself. Arik and Boaz did not much care for each other, and exchanges between them were sometimes heated. Yoni let the banter go on, because he trusted the two men and was confident that, despite their differences, they would rely on each other if placed in a life or death situation. It took a long time for Yoni to trust his subordinates. He had been disappointed so many times. These two men were different, though. They were special.

"Not at all," Arik said. "What I was trying to say is that it was easy because the Syrians have overspecialized their infantry. The rocket guys have no protection from a sustained infantry assault. Their focus is just tanks. This makes them easy pickings for an infantry assault. We need to work this into our attack plans. Now, if you let me finish . . ." Arik glanced over at Ben Hanan. "All the more reason for us to stick more closely together and not run off half-cocked."

The tank crews were at their wits' end. They had no equipment for night fighting, and they were getting hammered continuously by Syrian missiles. The tank battalion withdrew to an abandoned Syrian camp for the night. While the tank crews slept, Yoni's men watched the perimeter and supervised the refueling and rearming of the tanks.

At 5:30 a.m. the next morning, Ben Hanan took the remnants of his brigade to the village of Sasa and the commanding heights of Tel Shams, which overlooked the main road, again without infantry support. At the Maatz crossroads, they again came under heavy missile fire. Ben Hanan volunteered to go on a flanking movement to take Tel Shams from the rear. His and ten other tanks roared off, once again without infantry support, without waiting for the others to refuel and rearm.

Within fifteen hundred meters of Tel Shams, Ben Hanan's group met ten Syrian tanks and destroyed them all. But as they climbed toward the Syrian position, they were met by a barrage of antitank missiles from the high ground. Four of the Israeli tanks were blown to smithereens. The screams of the injured reverberated through the air, and they were caught on the brigade's frequency for everyone on the Golan front to hear.

Ben Hanan himself was severely injured. He screamed, over the radio, "My leg, my leg! I've lost my leg!"

The rest of the crew of his tank were incinerated. The six remaining tanks were completely exposed to the Syrian fire from above on the ridge. Syrian intercepts got the message, and their infantry units were sent out to attack the stricken tank column.

Yanush ordered a relief tank column to go get Ben Hanan out, but it faltered under another hail of missiles, adding to the casualty toll.

Through his binoculars, Yoni saw the pillar of black smoke from a burning Syrian vehicle that marked the spot where Ben Hanan lay. He turned to Arik and Boaz and said, "We have to go in and get them out. They're sitting ducks. I know what you're thinking, Arik, that they shouldn't have gone out without infantry support—"

"I didn't say a word."

"But you thought it!"

"As it happens, I was thinking about Mikki just now." Arik smiled.

Yoni chuckled. "Thanks. I needed that. Let me go talk to Yanush."

"I'm sorry, Yoni," Yanush said when Yoni presented his plan. "I can't let you go. It's suicide! Ben Hanan has gotten himself into a Gordian knot, and we'll probably lose him. Even if you guys got through, to do an evacuation like that with the Syrian battery dropping bombs on your heads, in lightly armored APCs, is a fool's errand—not to mention the high probability that you'd be ambushed along the way. You can hear the Arabic groans of the wounded Syrian soldiers nearby over Ben Hanan's radio. They're that close. The Syrians are undoubtedly trying to pinpoint their location, just like we are. I can't risk your lives. If you guys collide with them, this could turn into a bloodbath. I don't have the resources to give you any backup."

"But I think it's a calculated risk. I have some of the best infantry fighters in the army in my unit now. I'd easily put my life in their hands. They're skilled, experienced professionals, many of them Matkal. If anyone can do this, they can."

"Then, I'll let you go. But, you may not order any of them to join you. This is strictly a volunteer mission, and they need to know their chances of returning alive."

Yoni took fifteen of his best men, Arik and Boaz among them.

"Now, the two of you, it's time to start getting along," Yoni said. "Our lives may depend on it."

They drove up the road toward Damascus, into the twilight, in Yanush's fastest APCs. On the way, they saw the tank crews, the survivors of the attack, their tanks having been blown up around them. Blackened and dazed, they were dragging themselves back to the Israeli lines. When they declined Yoni's offer of an escort, he gave them detailed directions.

"These guys are tough as nails," Arik said, shaking his head.

When they approached Ben Hanan, he screamed at them, "Get out of here! They've been shelling us continuously for over an hour. They stopped just now, undoubtedly because they were waiting for you to approach and get in range. Don't come any closer. It's your death warrant."

Yoni called back, "Don't move, and shut up! I'm in command now."

The APCs sped up along the road, dodging artillery shells. When they finally reached Ben Hanan's tank column, Shmuel, Yoni's driver, pulled Ben Hanan into a ditch, poured water on his wound, and applied a tourniquet while in consultation with a doctor on the radio. Arik and Boaz climbed into the wrecked tanks, one after another. They were looking for survivors, but they found only burned, blackened corpses.

The price of folly, Arik thought.

Boaz, for his part, thought that Ben Hanan was a showman with a penchant for exaggeration. When he looked down at Ben Hanan in the ditch, he saw that the leg that he had claimed he lost was still very much attached although he did have a compound fracture of the femur. Both dirty ends of the bone were protruding from the skin and the open wound was bleeding.

"Hey, Yossi," Boaz said. "Where is that lost leg of yours that you told the entire Golan about over the radio? Oops! It's here, still attached to you. Here it is! I found it!"

Arik's thoughts went immediately to his own father's injury. He snapped, "Why don't you shut your mouth, Boaz? You think you're so damn smart, making fun of somebody who's seriously wounded."

"Arik, what's wrong with you? I was just kidding. You're such a goody two-shoes," Boaz said.

"Is that so? Then why doesn't this little goody two-shoes break both your legs and sit around and make fun of you?"

Yoni ran over to them. "What did I tell you two women about cackling? This isn't the time and place."

At that moment, artillery shells and Katyusha rockets began raining down on top of the site. Everyone jumped into the ditch for cover.

"If they hit the APCs, we're screwed," Arik said. "We'd have to carry these men all the way back on our shoulders."

The shelling went on for twenty long minutes.

Arik crept over to Yoni just as Boaz approached from Yoni's other side.

Looking at Boaz, Arik smiled. "Hey, asshole, you thinking what I'm thinking?"

Boaz smiled back. "It takes one to know one."

Arik looked at Yoni and said, "Hey, chief, those jerks up there are making way too much of a racket. Someone needs to go up there and tell them to shut up. They're disturbing my beauty sleep."

Boaz nodded.

Yoni looked at the two of them. "When I volunteered us to do this, Yanush told me it was a suicide mission. I weighed our chances and options and decided it could be done. But what you two idiots are proposing is suicide. We have no idea of their strength. There could be a whole company up there, for all we know. I couldn't bear to lose both of you, as much as you drive me crazy.

The fact that the two of you don't get along adds a further element of risk that makes your plan entirely unacceptable."

"Hey, Yoni," Arik said. "I don't know if you've noticed, but we're up to our asses in alligators here anyway. Unless you have a better idea of how to get these wounded out of the trenches under fire, no less take them home, let us go! I promise, Boaz and I will behave." He looked at Boaz. "Won't we?"

Boaz nodded.

"Take another five guys with you," Yoni said. "You'll need the firepower. Arik, take the MAG. The rest of you, take the Kalashnikovs and as many cartridges as you can pack into your harnesses. The two of you, play nice, for God's sake!"

Dani jumped into the ditch. "I'm going with you!"

"No, you're not, Dani. I don't need Mikki losing a brother and fiancé at the same time," Arik said.

"I don't give a shit what you say, Arik. If you go, I go, unless you shoot me in the head right now!" Dani pointed at his temple.

"Hmm, that's a tough call." Arik smiled. "At least that would be quicker."

Arik recruited four more volunteers from his unit.

"We'll organize the wounded and pack everything into the APCs when you give the all clear sound—three bursts of three shots," Yoni said.

"Got it!" Boaz said.

The seven volunteers trotted up the road.

Yoni and the others continued to tend to the wounded in the ditch while on the radio with the trauma specialists. Within thirty minutes, they heard and saw a cacophony of sound and light coming from the upper ridge. Punctuating the roar of explosives were the staccato of automatic gunfire and the agonizing screams of wounded and dying men. Twenty minutes later, it was over. An eerie quiet washed over Yoni's men. They stayed in the ditch, waiting in blind apprehension.

Three bursts of three shots.

"Go! Go! Go!"

Yoni and the others wasted no time loading the wounded into the APCs and packing up every piece of valuable equipment that they could haul.

"Those guys better get down here fast. Syrian patrols are going to be on us like hornets," Yoni said to Ben Hanan.

Fifteen minutes after they had given the all clear signal, the small band of seven men made their appearance, running down the road at breakneck speed. There were no casualties. Yoni sighed in relief.

"That'll teach them." Arik was laughing.

"What happened up there?" Yoni asked.

"What'd I tell you? There were two platoons, but those guys are so specialized they were full of antitank munitions, rockets, and artillery but not much small arms. They had practically no means to defend themselves. The last thing they thought was that we'd come up after them! They won't be causing us any further trouble."

"You guys made quite a racket, though. You woke up the whole neighborhood. We'd better get out of here before the whole Syrian Army comes looking for us. They're not going to be happy when they find out what you did to them."

They finished loading the APCs and made a mad dash back to the Israeli lines.

As soon as they were back at the base, Ben Hanan and the other wounded men were evacuated all the way to Haifa's Rambam Hospital trauma unit.

When Yoni, Arik, and the other officers entered the command center, they were startled to see Moshe Dayan standing next to Yanush, leaning over a map. Dayan looked up, smiling, to greet them.

"Do you guys have any idea what you accomplished? Take a look at this map," Dayan said.

Yoni spoke for the group. "We rescued Ben Hanan, sir."

"Let me show you what you really did . . . Do you see Tel Shams here? It was the Syrians' last line of defense. The rest of their forces have scattered northeast, toward Damascus, in total disarray. The enemy up in Tel Shams was well dug in, with a clear line of fire on us and able to block the forward progress of an entire division. Ben Hanan's brigade wasn't the only one to suffer from them. Now, having taken Tel Shams, our forces have pulled to within thirty miles of Damascus. The whole city sits within our artillery range. There's talk of a cease-fire, but what you did will have not only tactical but strategic significance. Good work, gentlemen!"

Dayan shook Yoni's hand.

"Yoni, you'll be reassigned for possible duty in the Sinai," Yanush said. "Arik, have your little band of lunatics pack their bags, too. You're all shipping out. Our work up here in the north is nearly done. You're needed in the Sinai."

"With all due respect, sir, we'd like to stay up here, if it's all the same," Arik said.

"Can't you guys just follow orders? Why do you guys always have to be a pain in my side? You're always playing by your own rules!"

"Wait, Yanush," Dayan said. He looked at Arik. "Why do you want to stay up here, meshuganah?"

"I was thrown off Mount Hermon on the first day of this thing, and I swore I'd be back to help liberate it again. So, it's personal. I lost many friends up there. And now, it's payback time!"

"Look, Arik," Dayan said. "I just got out of a heated meeting with senior commanders Hofi, Eitan, Drori, and Peled. We're going back up to liberate Mount Hermon. But the operation is going to be a Golani affair. Every paratrooper in the northern command is itching to do precisely what you want to do, but it's a matter of pride for the Golanis after they lost the post to begin with."

"Sir, my unit rescued five Golanis off the mountain and carried them on our backs for kilometers. That makes us honorary Golanis. I really want to stay and take part, sir. Please! There are enough guys down in the Sinai to do what has to be done there."

Part of Arik wanted to return to the Sinai so that he somehow could hook up with Mikki, but he thought that there would be time for that later. There was still some serious fighting left to do up here before he could think of himself. He had decided this was his place for the time being.

"What am I going to do with you? You maniac! You can be so exasperating!" Sometimes I don't know whether to hit you over your head or kiss you." Dayan sighed. "Okay, I'll tell you what. I can't get you to the Israeli peak, but we're going to liberate the Syrian one, too. You'll be assigned to Colonel Nadel's 317th Paratroopers Brigade. Please, follow his orders. Good enough?"

"Good enough! Thank you, sir!" Arik saluted him sharply.

"Dani, you started out in Golani, so take your men and join the attack on the observation post on the Israeli Mount Hermon."

Outside the command center, Yoni whispered to Arik and Dani, "They're sending my unit to a base outside Tel Aviv. We won't be there long. I know how to pull strings. I'll catch up with one of you two on Mount Hermon by the end of the week."

Arik put his arms around both of them. "Listen guys," he said, "I'm going to start on the Syrian side and then go back up to the Israeli peak. I won't be denied. It'll take a while before the Golanis get going anyway. At the first chance I get, I'll sneak over and join your party. All I ask is that you guys stay alive, or I'll kill you myself!"

"What you just said made absolutely no sense, but I got the idea," Dani said, smiling. "I'll do my best."

It was October 20th, and the war clearly was winding down. The Israelis were now across the Suez Canal, a mere hundred kilometers from Cairo, and within artillery shot of downtown Damascus. Dayan emerged from a Security Cabinet emergency meeting that had been convened to discuss U.S. Secretary of State Henry Kissinger's latest cease-fire proposals. Golda Meir and her Cabinet had decided that Israel would stall for at least thirty-six hours so that its final military objective could be realized.

The twin peaks of Mount Hermon had been split before the war, with one under Israeli control and the other under Syrian control. They were of vital importance to Israel. From them, the Israeli military could monitor Syrian Army deployments and communications all the way to Damascus. Strategically, leaving the Syrians with both summits would give Syria a towering vantage point from which to observe the Golan Heights and most of northern Israel. Politically, the Israeli government wanted to deny the Syrians any victory in terms of territorial gain. Most importantly, though, the Israelis wanted to undo the shame associated with the loss of its Mount Herman post during the first day of the war. Time was short; in a day, the cease-fire would be forced on the Israelis by the Americans and the Soviets.

Dayan ordered General Yitzhak Hofi to retake Mount Hermon at all costs. It was decided that Colonel Amir Drori's Golani Brigade would recapture the Israeli peak and Colonel Haim Nadel's 317th Paratroopers Brigade would capture the Syrian peak.

The only way to reach the Syrian peak was by helicopter. The danger to the airborne force was extreme. Most of the one-hour flight time was over Lebanese territory, so the helicopters would be susceptible to attack from Syrian aircraft as well as anti-aircraft missiles. In addition, at that time of year there were uncertain wind updrafts on Mount Hermon, making helicopter flying particularly dangerous.

The risks were deemed so high that General Hofi visited the paratrooper veterans, just before their departure on the mission, to offer anyone who did not want to go an opportunity to bow out. But this was Israel's premier fighting brigade. The opportunity to do their job was all that they wanted in return for their years of grueling, high-risk training. Nobody stepped aside.

"We'll get the job done, sir, perhaps even without losses!" the company commander bellowed.

Arik was standing next to the helicopter, in full battle gear, with the rest of the men. He felt a cold shiver run down his spine at that remark. He had been on enough missions to know that the only way to stay alive is to be brutally honest about the risks and to stay hypervigilant throughout in order to mitigate those risks in real time. Shooting one's mouth off like that struck Arik as not only unprofessional but a bad omen.

At noon on October 21st, the helicopters took off under cover of fog and Israeli suppressive artillery fire. The element of surprise was complete, but no sooner had they landed on a narrow ridge that overlooked the Jordan Valley than their position was discovered and pounded by Syrian artillery shells. Arik motioned for the company to take cover on the west side of the ridge, against a flat rock face. Syrian shells sailed harmlessly overhead. From that high vantage point, they saw Chel Ha'Avir Phantom fighters engaging in dogfights with Syrian MiGs right in front of their noses. They watched in fascination as seven MiGs were shot down. Five Syrian troop helicopters flew overhead to reinforce the garrison above. Three were shot out of the sky by the Phantom jets. The other two escaped back to Syria.

Arik's orders were to lead the men 550 meters down a narrow boulder-strewn path that led to a long, narrow mountain road called the Serpentine. That would take them straight to the Syrian enclave. They were almost on top of the fortification when the shooting began. The vanguard company leader who was heading the charge in front of Arik was torn apart by a burst of machine gun fire. The rest of the company hit the ground hard.

It took two hours of furious suppressive fire and a grenade assault led by Arik to silence the Syrian position. The Israelis' audacity was rewarded by the sudden arrival of a large Syrian resupply truck convoy that discovered too late that they were surrounded. Arik's men showered the trucks with submachine gun fire. The inhabitants of all but one truck bolted out of their vehicles and disappeared down the path. The last truck managed to turn around and flee. When the Israelis looked inside the captured trucks, they found that they were filled with heavy mortars and ammunition.

Having secured the position, Arik's company went another 550 meters along the Serpentine road, following Captain Shai Lyn's company. Their progress was accelerated by a closely coordinated rolling artillery barrage that had preceded them. Resistance was light, and by midnight on October 22nd they had secured the Syrian peak. When the Israeli flag was raised atop the fortifications, Arik breathed a sigh of relief. The Israelis had suffered only one death and a handful of wounded in the capture of the Syrian peak.

Arik wondered how the Golanis were doing on the Israeli peak. Specifically, he silently prayed that his future brother-in-law Dani would emerge in one piece from that slaughterhouse. Advance intelligence had told them that the Syrian garrison that was manning the hilltop bunkers was filled with many well-armed elite commandos. Arik looked to the south and saw the flashes of light. When he heard the distant sounds of man-made thunder, he knew that the bloody battle for the Israeli peak of Mount Hermon had begun. He realized that his battle was over. Knowing that he did not want to be stuck on the formerly Syrian peak for the remainder of the war, he led his fifteen-man Matkal unit into Colonel Nadel's field headquarters.

"Shalom, Arik," Nadel said. "Good job up there. You made it look easy. There were almost no casualties. Your men were a great help to us."

"May I speak freely, sir?"

"Of course."

"My men and I want to join the Golani assault on the other peak. Those guys are up to their asses in trouble if the sounds of the battle are any indication. Matkal is here to fight, not to babysit a bunch of rocks up here. We request permission to leave at once."

"Listen, soldier, all of us are here to fight and not babysit, not just you. Before the campaign, Hofi met with Drori and me. I suggested that when we were done here we could head southwest and trek up the eastern slope of the Israeli peak and attack on both sides—Golani from the west and us from the east. Hofi shot me down and told me that it was Golani's show. Even Drori couldn't sway him. He gave me specific orders to sit tight up here unless we're needed in reserve. Yoni feels the same way that you do, but his orders are to stay put on the embankments below the cliffs, to pick off any Syrian stragglers running down from the summit. And he is staying put, so—"

"With all due respect, Colonel, your orders were to have the 317th up here in reserve until called to the other peak. My unit isn't technically part of the 317th. We're just attached to you temporarily. Besides, the other half of my platoon is with the Golani anyway. And finally, as you know, Matkal doesn't officially exist. So, who would miss us? I have maps of the area, and I could get up there in two hours."

"Arik, you're talking about a fifteen-hundred meter climb with forty kilo backpacks, guns, ammo, and grenades, along boulders, tight cliff paths, and switchbacks in the pitch dark. That's insanity! Why don't you wait until sunrise?"

"I don't want to wait until sunrise. I sense real trouble over there, and maybe we can help."

"Oy, Arik! You and your band of meshuganahs. What am I going to do with you?" Nadel scratched his head.

"Thanks, boss. Let's share a beer in Tel Aviv next week."

Nadel waved Arik and his men off, shaking his head and saying sternly, "Arik, this conversation never happened!"

The concrete bunker complex at the top of the Israeli Hermon peak was bristling with dozens of snipers armed with infrared night-vision spotting scopes, heavy machine guns, mortars, and antitank missiles. A hundred meters in front of the concrete fortress was a long row of foxholes and trenches. Behind the foxholes, along the bunker walls, were rows of captured Israeli machine guns that other Syrians had trained on the slope. They had a clear field of fire over the foxholes. When the Golanis had charged within range at the beginning of the assault, the Syrians opened up a barrage from both positions, mowing down the first wave.

There had been mass confusion among the Golani when they had realized that the red tracer fire that they saw coming at them was not friendly fire from confused advance units but the Syrians firing at them with Israeli guns. The Syrian Army's Soviet guns had green tracers. The number of Israeli casualties had piled up. Among them were the commanding officers who had led the assaults. Ironclad IDF tradition called for commanders to lead from the front so, with mounting casualties in the officer corps, the attack had begun to falter. Even Colonels Amir Drori and Yudke Peled had been seriously injured. They both had to be evacuated downhill. After a while, there had not been enough men available to carry the seriously wounded down, and they lay sprawled up and down the hill like rotting cabbages.

Another column of tanks, under the command of Yosef Nissem, had been sent up the mountain to assist in the attack. But those tanks became bogged down in an antitank ambush for several hours.

By the time that Arik and his intrepid band of Matkal had showed up at the base of the western slope, it was 5 a.m. The sun was just coming up, leaving the concrete bunker complex in shadow. The field below the system of bunkers was strewn with dozens of bodies, some wounded and some dead.

Arik walked up to a lieutenant and said, "Let me speak to someone in charge."

Lieutenant Shachar Amitzur looked at Arik. His face was gray and blank. "I'm in command, Captain. There's nobody else in this sector. All the senior officers in the initial assault were either wounded or killed. There are two other lieutenants to the north and south of us, several hundred meters away. We're in complete disarray. The men are exhausted. Many are shell-shocked. Some are just frustrated. And morale is dropping fast. There's talk of withdrawal again."

"What the hell happened here?" Arik asked. "It's October 8th all over again! You guys are reenacting the Charge of the Light Brigade! Okay. We're going to have to reorganize if we're going to have a successful final assault. The first thing you're going to do is stop running up the hill like idiots, into the sunrise, before you all get yourselves killed. My men and I are going to take a stroll around this little amusement park for about forty-five minutes to assess the Syrians' defenses, and we'll meet you back here. I want you to collect every lieutenant and sergeant you can find and bring them to this command post. Understood?"

"Yes, sir!"

Arik and his men walked off into the rising sun.

Word got around that Arik Meir and his unit had come in to join the fight. Morale improved immediately. The men now had confidence that, somehow, the day would end well. Arik's valor, fighting skills, leadership, and tactical experience had become legendary in the army. The men retired from the slope and returned to camp to await further orders. By the time that Arik returned to the command tent, the officers and NCOs were there waiting for him. When he entered the tent, all conversation ended.

Arik spread out his map of the compound and surrounding terrain on a large crate. Luckily, he had taken the map with him when he was driven off the mountain on October 6th.

He said, "Okay, listen up. The compound is surrounded by pillboxes and foxholes manned by snipers and machine gunners. They're spread out in a wide one-kilometer arc around the compound. The positions are fifty meters apart. That's about twenty in all. Interestingly, the foxholes are far enough in front of the compound so that if we knock those out we'll still be out of effective range of their guns on the bunker roofs. You may ask how I know this. Well, you may have wondered why their tracer fire is red and not green. I hope you figured out it wasn't friendly fire. It was the Syrians using our own weapons against us, the ones they captured when they took over the complex. I guess it's some stupid sense of irony for them. But that will be their undoing. They don't realize the full limitation of our guns, which have a much shorter range than theirs.

"So, before the final assault on the bunkers, we'll first neutralize the foxholes, get the wounded down—leave the dead for now—and then begin the final assault under suppressive fire from our mortar barrage and MAG machine gunners. My unit will perform phase one: taking out the foxholes. The rest of you, get stretchers and teams ready to transport the wounded down the mountain. How many men do we have?"

Amitzur said, "Sir, we started out with two hundred in our initial assault force. We've taken 50 percent casualties."

"Okay. Twenty-five men will evacuate the wounded. Seventy-five will stay here for the final assault. Amitzur, you stay here and direct traffic. Two men per stretcher, not four. There are too many wounded. They can all rest later and get massages from their girlfriends, for their sore muscles—and then some—when they get home."

There was general laughter.

"Okay! Matkal?" Arik said.

Fifteen men gathered around him.

"We go in with blades and grenades," he said.

He had been training his immediate subordinates for a long time in some of the finer points of Chinese martial arts, including sword combat. He had taught them that there is much more to martial arts than punching, kicking, and grunting.

Now, he reached into his backpack and pulled out what appeared to be two large black knives.

"What are those?" Amitzur asked.

"These puppies are Chinese fighting swords specially modified for me. Careful! The blades are double edged and razor sharp. I'm going to be paying a polite visit to the nice gentlemen in the foxholes. This should take about two hours. Get your men fed, rearmed, and organized. You're going to be very busy soon."

Arik slung both blades into the harness over his shoulder and loaded up the front of his harness with ten grenades and his trusty Beretta 93R, a selective-fire machine pistol, just in case. When he headed out, he looked like a ninja warrior, his similarly equipped men following.

***

Arik and his men slowly began the climb on their stomachs.

When Arik and Dudi, a junior officer in his squad, approached within fifteen meters of the first foxhole, they were met by a shower of machine gun bullets. They used rocks and boulders for cover. Arik picked up baseball-sized rocks and threw them against the boulders ten meters on each side of his position, drawing the fire to those fake positions. He jumped out of cover, like a jack rabbit, and lobbed a grenade into the foxhole. The foxhole erupted in flames and then fell silent.

Arik turned to Dudi and chuckled. "That'll teach 'em to mess with Sandy Koufax."

"Who's Sandy Koufax?"

Arik signaled behind him to the rest of his squad. "Fan out! I'll empty out the central foxholes, and you guys split up and work your way from the outside in."

The men crawled off on their knees and elbows.

Arik continued his advance, dispatching another foxhole with grenades. Deciding to avoid more explosions, he got out the Chinese fighting swords. He continued to crawl on the ground. He looked like a lizard on amphetamines. He crept up to a foxhole and jumped in. By the time the gunners could react, it was already too late. The twin blades flashed and slashed with lightning speed and deadly accuracy. There was barely a cry. Not a great profession for a nice Jewish boy, Arik thought, covered in Syrian blood. He went from one foxhole to the next, doing the same thing.

His men enjoyed similar success. Within ninety minutes, the foxholes were clear. The Matkal ran back toward the command post, ahead of the inaccurate machine gun fire that fell harmlessly behind them.

Setting an example, Arik carried two wounded men at a time, one on each shoulder, out of the line of fire so that the Golani could take them the rest of the way down the hill. In an hour, two dozen wounded men were taken to the rear, all while trying to avoid Syrian mortar shells that accurately targeted them in the early morning sun.

When Arik walked back into the command tent, he was met with startled stares. Completely covered in blood, from head to toe, he was barely recognizable.

"Don't worry, none of this is my blood. I think. I just created a few dozen more Syrian widows," he said flatly, looking down at himself.

He gathered the junior officers around a makeshift table that was covered in maps.

He outlined a general plan of attack for the compound and divided the men into assault squads. He gave each a mission and a sector. He pointed out the secret escape passages at the north and south sides of the compound, one of which he had used to get the men out on that first day of the war.

"You'll set up two flanking squads and go in through here and here. They shouldn't expect you coming in from there. We're going to do to these bastards what they did to us on October 6th. Is everyone ready? The men from Golani will lead the assault."

The Golani officers nodded.

Arik told them to muster the men. He was going to give them one final "pre-game locker room pep talk."

Suddenly, it dawned on Arik he had not seen Dani or any of his company since he had gotten to the Israeli peak.

"Amitzur! Where are the men from Plugah Gimel?"

"You mean Dani Zohar's boys? They've been gone for hours, sir. They were trying to stage an assault from the eastern side. Drori warned them about going that way, when he discovered the nature of the terrain, but Lieutenant

Zohar felt that it would increase the element of surprise if they came from that way. They had a sapper but no metal detectors in their plugah. There had been rumors of mines on that side. We haven't heard a word from them for hours."

Arik stared intensely into Amitzur's eyes. "Do you understand the battle plan? Can you lead these men up into the compound? Just do what the Syrians did to us three weeks ago, when they drove us out, only in reverse. Remember: Crawl in through the northern side of the compound, where that emergency escape exit is, where the communication trenches are. Understand? Do you understand?"

Amitzur nodded.

"I have to go find Dani's group," Arik said. "I have a very bad feeling about this. If any of them are left alive, they're in serious trouble. I was stationed up here just before the war, and I know the terrain well. It was foolish of them to attempt the eastern approach, especially in the dark. Gather the men!"

Amitzur nodded again and ran off.

In moments, one hundred broken and tattered remnants of the advance assault Golani team gathered around Arik, who was standing on an ammunition crate.

"Men, this hasn't been the best night of our lives, but by all accounts, it has probably been the most important. We've lost countless friends and neighbors up here in this hell, but don't think for a moment that this was all for nothing. This small fortress is the eyes and ears of northern Israel, and it will remain so for generations. Whoever has this fortress controls the Golan and the Galil. Never forget that! I was up here on the first day of the war. I know what this place means. The battle we fight here today will be spoken of by the Israeli people for a hundred years. We're almost there. The Syrian garrison up there is depleted. This place is ours to take. Not tomorrow, not next week, but by noon today! We must gather the rest of our energy and make the final push to the top. Victory will be ours! Today!"

The soldiers let out a cheer and then chanted, "Golani! Golani! Golani!" They formed up in attack squads of five to ten men. They were rearmed for the final assault.

Arik picked five men from his own Matkal plugah. You guys come with me. The rest of you, stay here and help Amitzur. He's a fine soldier, but he lacks experience. See to it he doesn't let things fall apart here."

Motti Landau, a stocky bear of a man who had been an Egged bus driver in Petah Tikva, grabbed Arik's arm. "Leave it to me, boss. I'll help Amitzur lead the attack."

"I know you will, Motts. Frankly, I'm scared of you."

They shared a badly needed laugh.

Arik trusted Motti implicitly. He had been Arik's NCO when he joined Matkal. After doing his nine years, he had become a reservist. Now in his mid-thirties, Motti was physically slightly off his game, but Arik knew that his experience and leadership skills would be invaluable up on the ramparts.

Arik and his five men suited up with FN MAG machine guns and vests with hooks for ten grenades and pockets for cartridges of hundreds of rounds of ammunition. They set off to find Dani and his men.

The terrain was extremely jagged, with tiny crevices, high rock walls, and steep drops. At times, they had to navigate by walking sideways. Arik passed the top of the Mount Hermon ski lift, its tower and chairlift heavily damaged during the initial Syrian assault on the summit on the first day of the war. *How many men did I lose in the ambush here just weeks ago?* The thought of them, his buddies, brought tears to his eyes.

He suddenly flashed back to three years earlier, to a very different ski lift, the one at the top of Snowmass in Aspen. *Life seemed so innocent, so bright and hopeful, back then. Snowmass's ski slopes are soaked in beer and wine. These slopes are soaked in Jewish blood.* He thought about the ski trail at the top of Snowmass, the one called Big Burn. The irony of that name hit him as he crunched across the blasted, blackened volcanic earth. *What do they know about a mountain on fire?*

It took nearly an hour for Arik and his men to reach the other side of the compound.

On an inclined knoll fifty meters below the steep ridge that supported the concrete walls of the eastern side of the bunker, they came upon a grisly site. Bloody body parts were strewn everywhere. Some men were still alive but missing arms and legs. Some had gaping abdominal wounds. All were writhing in agony. In the distance, Arik saw a lone figure standing. *Dani!* Arik ran toward him.

"What the hell happened, Dani? And why the hell are you standing there like that?"

"Arik, don't come any closer," Dani cried out. "Stay away! I fucked up. We're standing in the middle of a minefield."

Arik halted in his tracks. "Okay, how'd this happen?"

"I had the brilliant idea of bringing my men around for an eastern assault. Drori and Peled discussed it at headquarters when they were planning the campaign. With the slaughter on the western side, I wanted to try to surprise the Syrians from the rear and get directly into the compound, with the sun behind us as it was coming up. I led the men into the mines in the dark. You see what happened. I've been standing on this mine for about an hour now. I've run out of ideas for how to get off it without getting blown up. But there's no way out of this. I'm just going to lift my leg and—"

"Don't you dare, you stupid son of a bitch. What am I going to tell your sister? That I let my future brother-in-law blow his ass off just because I was too cowardly to do anything about it? Mikki and I could never live with that. Efrat would go to pieces. Just let me think for a minute. Don't move a muscle!"

Arik stood there above Dani for fifteen minutes, his arms folded over his chest. He stared intently at the downward slope.

Finally, he said, "Dani, just don't do anything until I tell you to. Okay?"

"Okay! What crazy scheme are you cooking up in your twisted mind? Please, don't do anything stupid. Let me die here. I deserve it. How can I live with myself after what I did here? Mikki needs you! She loves you!"

"You didn't do anything wrong. I would've done the same in your position. How could you know that this area was so heavily mined? We had no clear intelligence on that score. I couldn't bear to see the look on Abba's and Imma's faces if anything happened to you."

Arik handed his MAG to Nachum, his aide, and slowly unbuckled his grenade harness, letting it drop to the ground. He crouched and tied his combat boots tight.

"What are you doing, Arik?" Dani asked.

"Dani, when your father was assigned to the Israeli consulate in Chicago, as military attaché, did you ever play tackle football in school?"

"I did. But what does that have to do with my current predicament?"

"Well," Arik spoke as calmly as if he were ordering a falafel lafa. "Suppose you were a quarterback about to throw a forward pass and a linebacker came charging at you—"

In a flash, Arik raced downhill toward Dani at full speed. From about four feet away, Arik launched himself at him with all of his might and hit him full force at pelvis level. They both went flying away downhill from the mine as it went off, flinging them further away. The last thing that Arik felt was the concussive force of the mine and a sudden searing white-hot light on his face. Everything went dark.

By 9 a.m., the commander of the Syrian garrison had left the front gate of the post, brandishing a white flag. The Israelis gave him a loudspeaker, and he ordered all of his men to lay down their arms. The Syrians' battle was lost, and he knew that there was no point in continuing to fight. An aide of the Syrian commander disagreed with him, however, and shot him in the stomach. By 11 a.m., Israeli flags were flying over both of the Mount Hermon peaks. The remaining members of the Golani team cheered. The final assault had succeeded with minimal casualties. The Israelis had blanketed the compound with mortar and artillery fire. The Golani squads had gone in from the sides of the compound, as Arik had instructed, and surprised the Syrians from within.

Word came over the radio. A cease-fire had been declared. The war was over.

The area around the compound on the Israeli peak was finally quiet in the late October sunshine. A quiet, chill wind was blowing though the volcanic hills and crevices of the northern Mount Hermon. Many dead and wounded soldiers were still scattered around the bloody ground as far as the eye could see. They gave silent testimony to the gruesome hell and extreme sacrifice that had been the Golani's toughest fight in its history.

Among the dead and wounded lay Arik's burned, motionless body.

Chapter 27

The scene in the triage bay of Tel HaShomer Hospital looked like a scene out of Dante's Inferno. During peacetime, the trauma unit had a capacity of twenty-five beds, which was more than enough for the usual daily toll of vehicle crashes, military training accidents, and wounded soldiers coming in from the front during the Wars of Attrition. But not today.

It was October 24th. A cease-fire on the Golan and the Suez Canal had just been announced, but from the scene at the hospital no one would have known that. The emergency room was overflowing with nearly a hundred men, and the open clearing outside held hundreds more on makeshift cots. Agonizing screams and cries of grown men filled the air. They lay covered in blood and gore, and many of them had been burned beyond recognition. Dozens were missing arms, legs, or eyes. Their battlefield dressings were growing increasingly saturated with blood. Some had open head wounds or chest and abdominal wounds with entrails dangling grotesquely from them. This living hell was sorely testing the limits of strength and sanity of the trauma crews, doctors, nurses, and paramedics, many of whom had not slept in forty-eight hours. They were working around the clock in a desperate attempt to salvage as many lives as humanly possible.

The injured, dying, and dead were the flower of Israel's youth, strong and confident, having been brought up in the shadow of the glorious victory of the Six-Day War. Those days were long gone now. The Israelis had been overconfident. They had become complacent. The Egyptians and the Syrians had not cut and run. Instead, they had trained, armed themselves, and scrapped back for revenge. The price that Israel had paid in blood for its hubris was staggering. For many, it was already too late: Dozens of men lay silent, no longer in agony, finally at peace.

Over the din of the cries went the shouts of the medical staff working in organized pandemonium, running to and fro with bags of blood for transfusions, defibrillators, blood plasma, IVs, antibiotics, morphine, dressings, airways, and tourniquets to stanch the hemorrhages of countless arms and legs. As quickly as the men could be triaged and sent to the operating rooms, more helicopters landed in turn, spraying dust and the odor of diesel fuel, their crews bringing more mangled human remnants to the emergency room. The whole area reeked of burning flesh, human waste, vomit, and cordite. They were tank operators, infantrymen, pilots, and sailors who, with their very bodies, had stopped the onslaught of the combined military might of the Arab world and, in all likelihood, saved the Jewish State from extinction.

In the almost three weeks since the war had begun, Dahlia had not left the trauma area. She worked twenty-hour days, ate on the run, and slept sitting up in a plastic waiting-room chair whenever sheer physical exhaustion overcame her. Although she usually dressed immaculately, in a smartly pressed military nurse's uniform, with scarcely a hair out of place, she was now wearing blood-spattered green scrubs that she changed every three days or so. Her disheveled hair was tied up into a bun to accommodate a surgical nurse's hat when necessary. Surviving on adrenaline alone, she threw herself into the horrific bloody scene that was unfolding before her, going about her work with cold, professional, tireless efficiency.

She was assistant director of the trauma team. Those who worked under her looked to her for the strength and guidance that they needed to keep these broken men alive. After managing the initial triage, Dahlia organized small teams to care for specific injuries and saw to it that they had all of the necessary supplies. She headed up an elite specialized team that worked with the surgeons to rapidly stabilize and transfer poly-trauma patients to the operating room. She had learned something from the Germans, after all.

On this particular afternoon, everything seemed to happen in slow motion. The helicopter settled gently onto the landing pad. A team of paramedics ran under the whirling blades. They brought out a litter bearing a soldier who had extensive burns all over his body. He had a gaping chest wound, and blood was gurgling from his mouth. His abdomen was distended, and his left leg was rotated into a grotesque angle, with blood spurting out of a large lateral wound in his thigh. His femur had been snapped in two, and the ends of the bone protruded from the skin.

Dahlia and her team ran out to assist the paramedics in unloading the litter from the helicopter.

"Dahlia, this one's bad. Apparent blast injury. He's got multiple rib fractures, a pneumothorax, ruptured spleen, and compound femur fracture, along with extensive burns. We had to pull him off the top of Mount Hermon. What a nightmare it's been! But he's apparently some elite commando, and we had orders to expedite his transfer. We were trying to take him to Tzfat or Rambam Hospital in Haifa, but they were operating at double capacity, so we were diverted to here."

The soldier's face was burned, swollen, and covered with dust. Working in tandem with the trauma physician, Dahlia saw that he was in hypovolemic shock, with labored breathing and a thready pulse.

Dahlia called out, "Get me an airway tube! Stat!"

The others on her team scrambled to find one in the trauma kit that they had brought, but someone must have taken it for another patient.

"Go get one! I don't know how long he'll be able to breathe on his own!"

Two peripheral IVs were immediately inserted into his arms, and he was infused with plasma and lactated Ringer's solution. His blood was typed for transfusion and then two units of packed cells were hung simultaneously. Dahlia's team worked at lightning speed. Within seconds of spotting the wound in the left side of his chest, she had put in a chest tube. Cardiac monitors were placed on his chest. Sinus tachycardia. His heart rate was 130. Dahlia put a central IV line into his neck and a large pressure dressing around his bleeding thigh wound.

"He's stopped breathing!" she yelled. "Dammit! Where's that airway tube? Hurry!"

She jumped over to his head, pinched his nose, and placed her lips to his to blow life back into his lungs. An electric shock surged through her. *I know these lips!* As recognition dawned on her, she stifled the impulse to vomit and faint. Her brain exploded with emotion. Her heart began to race, and she mustered all of the control that she could to keep herself from hyperventilating. She looked down at the man's chest and spotted that old transverse scar across the top of his left pectoralis muscle. Don't let your emotions carry you away! She was a highly trained trauma specialist now, not that sunny teenager who had first spied that scar. He was the love of her life—once and for always—and she was all that stood between his life and his death. Involuntarily, tears streamed down her cheeks, but she continued breathing into him, her face smeared with the blood that was oozing out of his mouth and into hers and mingling with her tears. This is the most important—and hopefully not the last—kiss of his life.

The endotracheal tube finally arrived. She intubated him and attached the tube to an Ambu bag so that she could to assist him with breathing.

"Are you okay, Dahlia?" Dr. Amnon Chazoni, the trauma physician, asked her. "Do you know this man?"

"I'm fine," she said, still squeezing the Ambu bag, pumping air into the man's lungs. Her face and scrub shirt were covered with the man's blood.

The doctor understood.

"We're a small country," he said. "When something like this happens, we will invariably care for our own friends, neighbors, or even family."

Dahlia screamed inside her head.

"Really, I'm fine!" She wiped her face and mouth with an alcohol-soaked towel, still pumping the Ambu bag with her other hand.

"He needs to go up to the OR, stat, and get his chest and abdomen opened. If he doesn't get that femur put back into place and the artery repaired, he's a goner," Chazoni said.

Within five minutes, the trauma and orthopedic surgical team, headed by Professor Reuven Schteinberg, came down. They undid the dressings and performed a rapid assessment.

The orthopedic surgeon in charge looked gravely at Dahlia and her team. "The left thigh wound is contaminated and has caused a devascularizing injury to the lower leg," he said. "The vascular team is getting hammered, so we may need to take the left leg off at mid-thigh. If he gets secondarily infected, even if we can hook up the arteries again, he'll end up with anaerobic osteomyelitis and the gangrene will kill him—"

Dahlia felt herself getting overcome by nausea and lightheadedness again. My God! Arik is going to become like his father, fighting a lifelong battle with a crippling disability. Even if he survives! She flashed back to that moment in the gym when she had watched him, for the first time, doing his gymnastics and kung fu. How magnificent he was! She suddenly felt wracked by guilt. This is all my fault! He gave up the UCLA basketball scholarship and came here primarily because of me. And I ended up destroying him. He never would have come to Israel and fought in this war if it hadn't been for me. She wanted to scream in anguish. Get control of yourself! Think clearly!

She grabbed hold of Professor Schteinberg's forearm and, with a primal fire in her eyes, stared intensely into his eyes.

"Under no circumstances are you to amputate the leg! None! Do you hear me?"

"Dahlia, you know I wouldn't do it unless it was absolutely necessary, but the vascular—"

"I don't think you're understanding what I'm telling you. No circumstance! You and I both know that they can do the femoral artery repair on that other soldier with just one vascular surgeon. Get Avi out of there, and have him join you for this one. I know this soldier better than anyone in the world. If you take off the leg, you'll have a suicide on your conscience. It will also kill his parents. Under no circumstance are you to take the leg! Do you understand me?"

Schteinberg felt Dahlia's nails digging into his forearm and her hand shaking.

"Okay, Dahlia, I'll do whatever is humanly possible to save the leg. But if he starts to develop Clostridia gangrene, like we've seen with many of the men, and he goes into septic shock, I'll have no choice. I'll have to save his life. Fair?"

"Okay, fair." She gulped for air, fighting tears. "As soon as you're done, find me and let me know what happened."

"I will."

Arik was wheeled away, surrounded by an eight-person surgical team.

Dahlia was left standing alone, covered in Arik's blood, with him leaving her again, perhaps for the last time. Impulse told her to run screaming out of the trauma unit and follow him upstairs to wait outside the operating room. But she had too many other patients to try to help, and her team was depending on her. She decided that she would stay where she was and throw herself into her work. Besides, she knew from experience that time would pass more quickly if she did.

Arik's surgery lasted eight hours, with two teams working on him. Afterward, Schteinberg found Dahlia still at work in the trauma unit.

"Dahlia, surgery went as well as could be expected. He's neurologically intact. His chest is stable, with the tube showing good suction now. He had a liver contusion and a ruptured spleen. We removed the spleen and washed out the abdomen. We were able to close the abdomen over a suction drain to drain out any potential infection. We cleaned the thigh wound, and we were able to do a direct repair of the femoral artery. We cleaned the femur and left the wound open. His burns have been extensively cleaned, and he'll require many dressing changes until the wounds and burns begin to heal. The femur has been stabilized by a Wagner external steel frame. Let's pray that the pins don't get infected. If you can tear yourself away from here, he's up in the surgical ICU, in a medically induced coma on a ventilator. Remember: no guarantees on the leg."

"I understand." Dahlia shook the doctor's hand. "And thanks." She smiled with relief for the first time in weeks as she felt the blood drain back into her face.

She made sure that her team had everything that they needed to continue. And then she asked Dr. Chazoni for leave.

He looked at her and smiled. "I was wondering when you were going to take some time off. You haven't stepped outside this unit for nearly three weeks. Go to him. He's a lucky man."

She bolted up the stairs, taking them two at a time, as her heart raced almost out of her chest.

***

Arik lay unconscious in the quiet gloom of his room in the ICU. The ventilator was rhythmically pumping oxygenated air into his lungs. He had numerous IVs of antibiotics attached to both arms, two units of blood running in simultaneously, a Foley catheter, a chest tube, a nasogastric suction tube, and an abdominal drain. His face was still swollen and burned, but the nurses in the ICU had cleaned him sufficiently that his facial features were almost recognizable. Dahlia leaned over and kissed him on the cheek. His heart rate was 85 beats per minute. She sat next to him silently and stared at him. She held his clammy, swollen hand and resolved never to leave his side again.

"Well, buddy boy, it looks like you just got yourself a private duty nurse," she whispered.

She nursed her own doubts, though. What will happen if he wakes up and rejects me? Or if he gets upset, thinking that I'm taking advantage of the situation to push myself on him? After all, he was alone in the world, for all practical purposes, this lone soldier. He had muscled himself through life, invincibly, by dint of his intelligence, wits, strength, bravery, and skills. She remembered his father, how he had paid a terrible price by becoming a broken shell of a man. Is it Arik's turn?

No! I'll never let that happen to him! If he'll have me back, I'll devote myself to him for the rest of our lives. I'll work hard to make him happy. I'll erase the toxicity that polluted our relationship. Perhaps now he'll think that I'm worthy of him.

What am I saying? I'm just kidding myself. Arik belongs to someone else. He has moved on. Although Dahlia knew that Mikki had been the one responsible for making her life a living hell during basic training, she also knew that Mikki was really quite suited to Arik—perhaps even more so than Dahlia was. Through the grapevine, she had heard that they were quite happy together and were going to be married.

Dahlia began to feel very foolish, even to the point of considering herself a fraud. Am I motivated by guilt about the shameful way that I treated him? I still love him deeply. I know that for certain. Thinking long and hard about it, she resolved to do her utmost to assist in his recovery and rehabilitation so that he would have the best possible chance at a normal life. Where he went after that would be his choice and his decision. I can say good-bye to him and hand him off to Mikki. When Mikki came, she would not be happy to see Dahlia, but Dahlia would explain to her that she had no intention of getting in her way. That would be Dahlia's final gift to them, to Arik.

She watched his face and respirator-generated rhythmic breathing throughout the night. One night, she had to stand at a respectable distance from the foot of the bed when his heart had stopped beating and the code blue team had worked on him. She sobbed silently as electric paddles were applied to his chest, causing his upper torso to jump off the bed. She breathed a sigh of relief when his heart returned to normal sinus rhythm. Whenever she was not on duty, she sat at his bedside, day and night, staring intently at the heart monitor and listening for every life-sustaining heartbeat while reciting psalms.

Over the next four weeks, while still in the medically induced coma, Arik underwent five more surgical wound washouts. Dahlia never left his side when she was off duty, despite entreaties by her superiors that she go home for a while. She was cautioned that she would burn out, but she was undeterred. She bathed him, cleaned his wounds, changed his extensive burn dressings, and assisted the nurses in monitoring his vital signs and fluid balance. She was brought clothes from home, and she showered in the staff locker room. She wondered where Mikki was.

Dahlia winced when she changed Arik's burn dressings, watching helplessly as chunks of flesh tore off his body every time she pulled off a piece of dressing. He underwent numerous procedures to remove his layers of burned skin and replace them with skin grafts. As his vital status began to improve he was slowly brought out of the coma. He shook in agony during every treatment as he slowly moved toward consciousness. Finally, he began to open his eyes— briefly at first and then for longer periods of time over the next few days. Initially, he had a vague blank stare, his eyeballs still swollen, but he seemed to try to focus on Dahlia whenever she positioned her face directly in front of his.

At the six-week mark, the endotracheal and chest tubes were removed, and Arik finally was able to breathe on his own. He turned his head and blinked at Dahlia, who smiled tentatively back at him.

"Where am I?" he rasped. "Am I in heaven or hell? What are you doing here? You're the last person I expected . . ."

"You're in Tel HaShomer Hospital. You've been here for six weeks," Dahlia said, smiling at him.

"Has Mikki been in to see me?"

Dahlia shook her head. "I'm sorry. She hasn't been here yet, Arik."

"Please, get in touch with her. Tell her where I am and that I'm awake and miss her terribly."

"I will, Arik. How are you feeling? Are you in pain?"

"Not much. The last thing I remember is running toward Dani in that minefield to knock him off the mine. The rest is a blur. How's he doing? Any word from him?"

"He's been here several times, looking in on you. He's okay, thanks to you. He told me that you literally tackled him off the land mine like a football linebacker and when it went off your body took the brunt of the blast. You had a bunch of shrapnel in your thigh, abdomen, and chest, but most of it has been removed. You've had a great team of surgeons taking care of you nonstop. You must be a VIP or something." She winked at him.

"Maybe it's my boyish good looks." Arik chuckled and then winced. "It only hurts when I laugh, so whatever you do don't be funny."

"I wouldn't dream of it."

***

The following day, when Arik woke up from his afternoon nap, Dahlia told him that he had visitors and propped him up in bed.

Shmulik and Yael Zohar walked into the room. Having just come from work so still wearing his major general's dress uniform, Shmulik cut an impressive figure to Dahlia's eyes.

In a quiet, dignified manner, he asked her, "Will you excuse us for a few minutes?"

Without a sound, Dahlia nodded and then slipped out of the room.

"How are you, Arik?" Shmulik asked. "We've been waiting day after day for you to wake up, praying for you to wake up."

"I'm fine, sir."

"Arik, you must never again call me 'sir.' In a country where privates commonly call their officers by their first name, I've never stopped being impressed by your great humility and sense of respect. You're truly a rare person here in Israel. You've earned the right for me to call you, 'sir.' I know what you did for Dani on Mount Hermon and, for that matter, during the whole conflict. Your name has become a topic of conversation among the entire leadership of the army."

"Where's Mikki? Why hasn't she come to see me? Is everything okay? . . . I'm worried."

"Arik, Mikki's gone."

"I don't understand."

"Tzafra sustained a massive air assault by the Egyptian Air Force during the first hours of the war, on Yom Kippur afternoon. They were in the middle of Yom Kippur services, leaving a skeleton crew to man the OPS. The Egyptians flattened the outpost into dust. Everyone up there was killed. It took nearly a week to identify the bodies and get them all off the mountain. Mikki was buried at Har HaMenuchot military cemetery, in Jerusalem, a month ago."

Arik lay in numb shock, hyperventilating, as the words sank in. He pulled the blanket up over his face and began to weep softly.

"No! No! Mikki was my life. We made so many plans about the future. We were going to get married after Chanukah. Things were finally going well for both of us, and now I'm ground into the dust again. Again! I've lost everything. This is so unfair! How can my life go on?" Arik's voice broke. "It's all my fault! I encouraged her to take field command of the base rather than become a staff officer at headquarters. If she hadn't listened to me, she'd still be alive! I want to die! Please, let me die! I want to be with her!" Arik wailed in anguish, tightly clenching his fists around the blanket.

Shmulik tearfully embraced him and held him as he sobbed.

"Arik, we spend our lives always feeling like we're in control of our destinies. When I was young and brash, I was convinced of it. As the years have passed and I have seen so much loss and sacrifice here in Israel, I have learned—through bitter experience—how little influence we have over the course of events and how our lives are governed by a higher power.

"Like you, our lives are shattered over this. We had so looked forward to your marriage and all of the joy that would follow. None of that will ever be. War is so senseless and pointless. All it does is leave a trail of sorrow and pain.

But don't you dare blame yourself for a minute. Command of that base would have fast tracked her rise to the general staff. You both knew what you were doing. How could anyone have predicted that such a thing would happen? That posting was considered low risk by everyone.

"Mikki was so in love with you. When you came into her life, she became like a flower that had experienced rain again. We saw her grow and blossom as a human being, as a woman. You were the missing link in her soul, and we will always be so grateful to you for making her last years as happy as they were.

"If it weren't for you, we would have lost two children in this terrible war. Imma and I will always be there for you, for whatever you need. I'll make certain that you never want for anything for the rest of your life. You have earned that and so much more. Be strong, Arik. Chazak ve'ematz."

Arik sobbed uncontrollably.

Yael leaned over and gave Arik a tearful hug. She kissed him, still gently clutching his frail body. "We'll always love you, Arik. Our home will always be your home. Abba and I will be here for you. If you need anything, you need only ask."

The Zohars sat quietly with him for about an hour.

When they stepped outside, into the hallway, they found Dahlia standing there alone.

"Shalom, Dahlia," Shmulik said. "We've never met, but Mikki told us a great deal about you."

Yael stared at her so intensely that Dahlia shuddered.

Shmulik said, "Nobody should pay for their father's sins. Yet the Torah tells us that occasionally sons have to. Arik has paid a terrible price for his whole life. I have never met anyone quite like him. He is such a unique and special human being, such a gentle and dedicated soul. Very few people will ever know the full extent of Arik's deeds and sacrifices for this country. He has become another son to my wife and me."

Dahlia's facial expression indicated that she did not understand why she was the recipient of this particular lecture.

"Mikki's gone," Shmulik said. "She was killed on the first day of the war."

Dahlia gasped. "Oh, my God! I didn't know! I'm so sorry. I'm so sorry."

"Mikki told us all about your relationship with Arik in the past and how you mistreated him more than once. I don't know why or how fate has now brought you back into his life, and I don't know what your intentions are with him. But I do know that he's extremely frail and vulnerable right now. The last time that you hurt him, you left him an emotional cripple. It took Mikki years to teach him how to love again and be happy. But God has seen fit to hurt him terribly once again."

Shmulik looked at Dahlia long and hard. He shook his index finger at her and then said, "Tread lightly, Dahlia. That's all that I will tell you. I'm watching you. Take good care of him. He's all yours now, if you'll have him and if he'll have you. But if you hurt him or mistreat him in any way ever again, he won't recover and you will—in all likelihood—kill him. Then you'll have to deal with me! Arik has become an invalid. He's looking at a lifetime of disability. You had better know what you're getting yourself into long-term. If you're not prepared to see this through completely, walk away now, before he becomes emotionally attached to you again. You have very large shoes to fill, young lady. Do I make myself perfectly clear?"

Dahlia was pale as a ghost. "Yes, sir. You do," she whispered, wide-eyed.

Shmulik and Yael turned around and slowly walked away.

***

Dahlia went back into Arik's room. She sat quietly next to his bed for hours, staring into his blank face.

The next morning, Dani and Yoni came to visit Arik. Dani was still on crutches. When Arik saw the two men, he burst into tears.

Dani stumbled toward his bed. "My God! You saved my life, Arik. I owe you everything!"

He locked Arik in a tight bear hug.

"Easy, Tonto! They say I can still break in half." Arik winced.

Yoni motioned to Dahlia.

"I'll leave you three alone," she said, leaving the room.

"Dani . . . Abba and Imma came to see me yesterday and told me . . ."

Dani's eyes welled up with tears. He stared at Arik and grasped his hand.

"Dani, what I wouldn't have given for me to die and have Mikki grieve for me. The gates of hell have opened up and swallowed me whole. I have no reason for living. Mikki was the single, solitary reason for me to go on with my life. All I've thought about for the past twenty-four hours is killing myself as soon as I'm able. Why didn't I die that day on Mount Hermon? If only—"

"Please, don't talk like that, Arik," Dani said. "No amount of crying will bring Mikki back. It's for God to decide who lives and who dies, not us. You must grieve. That's natural. But you'll survive and move forward with your life. There must be a good reason why the Lord kept you alive."

"Like what?" Arik practically yelled.

Dani's voice dropped to a whisper. "Like a beautiful, kind, strong, smart, dedicated, wonderful woman who has not left your side for the past six weeks. The woman who, on October 24th, saved your life—and your left leg, may I add."

"Dahlia?"

"Dahlia! I have never in my life seen such dedication and love like she has for you. She has not gone home once in the past six weeks. I know that your relationship with her has been a roller coaster ride and she definitely had her problems, but you haven't seen her in over a year. Have you? She has matured and come into her own. Dahlia the brat never could have done what she has done for you now. She's the leader of the trauma team here. And she did it on her own steam. She's brilliant, tough, fair, kind when she needs to be, and a natural leader. She's highly respected all over the hospital. Most importantly, she loves you very much. She's mortified about how she treated you. I've spoken to her about this at length, in case you're wondering how I know all of this—"

"Mikki hated Dahlia," Arik said. "She would sometimes go on and on about what a terrible person Dahlia was."

"That was only because of how she treated you, and that was only in the beginning. After a while, Dahlia's name didn't come up, except in passing. Mikki told me as much. She was only upset about the effect Dahlia had on you. She never knew her personally. I know that this is a strange thing to say under the circumstances but if she saw Dahlia today, especially in view of what she has done for you and how dedicated and loving she has been to you in the hospital, Mikki would be okay with her. She only wanted you to be happy. Nothing gave her more pleasure."

"Dahlia tore my heart out. I felt from the first month I met her, back at camp in the States, that she was the one for me for the rest of my life, but then she revealed a side of her that was so breathtakingly awful. She left a gaping crater in my soul. How can I forgive that? After the whole blowup, I was a mess. For the longest time, I was unable to give away my heart again, for fear of getting hurt again.

Mikki showed me how to love again. The truth is that the relationship Mikki and I had was an adult romance between two mature people, without the childish drama I had with Dahlia. It's not just that I moved on from Dahlia, per se, but that I grew out of that type of relationship. Mikki filled my heart with love and joy. Mikki was my rock and anchor. I was everything with her. Now, I'm nothing without her.

I watched my father live a tortured life, now here I am. I've become like him. Dahlia is so immature that I don't believe she could even begin to handle what lies ahead for me. I don't even understand what she's doing here now. Why has she attached herself to me all these weeks? I don't want to be with her. I don't forgive her for what she did to me. Dahlia isn't worthy to shine Mikki's shoes. I want Mikki!" Arik cried, shaking his head.

"Look, Arik, if it wasn't for Dahlia, you wouldn't be here on this earth to forgive her or not forgive her," Yoni said. "I didn't know Dahlia before this, but I knew a lot about her. People talk. I never told you this, but I wasn't all that surprised when you came back from seeing her before Pesach that first year in the army. She was known as fickle and prone to prejudging people. That was her immaturity. But she's a completely different person now. I believe she has that maturity now."

"There was a time when Dahlia and you gave your hearts to each other, before circumstances tore you apart," Dani said. "There was something real between you two. You can recapture it. I know it'll take time. My heart is shattered, too, over losing Mikki, but I can't watch you end your life like this after everything you've been through. Mikki would never want you to be alone, not for a minute. Nobody knew Mikki better than me. I've thought about this for weeks, after I found out what Dahlia did and continues to do for you. I feel that Dahlia coming back into your life is no coincidence. There is a hand guiding you, Arik. Give her a chance. I think that she might be worth it. Arik, we'll never be brothers-in-law, but we'll always be brothers. Our bond is forged in blood and fire. You nearly gave your life to save mine. That's a bond even stronger than family. That bond is forever."

Arik looked down at Dani's ankle, now in a walking boot. He lifted his chin and asked, "How are you doing?"

"I'm just getting over a broken tibia. You see, there I was, just standing around on a land mine, minding my own business, and this crazy lunatic comes flying through the air like a missile, knocks me off of my feet, and I break my leg. Can you imagine the chutzpah?"

Arik smiled weakly. "You've got to watch out for those missiles . . . Hey, did we kick those damn Syrians off the mountain? I'm sorry I had to check out before the final act."

"Didn't you hear?" Yoni said. "We chased those idiots nearly back to Damascus. We probably would've occupied it and Cairo, too, if the Russians and our dear Jewish friend Kissinger hadn't stepped in to spoil all the fun."

"It's always the Jews!" Arik said. "Dani, how are Opher and Etzion doing? Nobody's said anything about them."

"Etzion is fine. He's in a tank somewhere in Africa, outside of Cairo. He crossed over the Suez Canal just behind Arik Sharon, over a pontoon bridge. Opher was shot out the sky over Ismailia by one of those new Soviet-made SAM-6s, but he managed to bail out and was immediately rescued. Thank God. He's okay, too."

Arik smiled sadly, tears still in his eyes, and sighed. "Thank God they're all right."

After the two men left, Dahlia slipped back into Arik's room.

The two of them stared quietly at each other for a long while.

Day after day, a team of physiotherapists struggled to get Arik out of bed but found that a sitting position was all that he could manage. His legs simply had stopped working and would not obey his commands. Arik's frustration and fear that he would end up like his father grew each day. Dahlia adjusted her work schedule so that she could be there for him, catering to his every physical need, as the volume of new wounded arriving at the hospital abated. She brought a small folding cot into his room, next to his bed, and slept there so that was available to get him food, drink, or pain medication should he require it at night. Even as the weeks passed, though, all she could get out of him was small talk about the here and now. There were so many things that she wanted to say to him and so many things that she wanted to hear from him. He bore so little resemblance to what he had been, and she acutely felt the dissonance between her memories of him and what the saw in front of her. Arik barely showed any emotion, except when he was in extreme pain. Dahlia was frightened, but she quietly persevered.

Suddenly, one afternoon, Arik spoke.

"Do you remember, Dahlia, you once called me a loser? You were so right. My entire life has been nothing but a long string of loss. Every time I think my life is going somewhere, I end up back at square one. Again, I'm lost and alone. No one ever gets used to pain and loss, but this time it's so much worse. I've lost who I am, what I am. I've lost Mikki. This whole thing about being selfless and putting others before yourself is for the birds."

"You aren't a loser, Arik, not by a long shot." Dahlia shook her head. "You're such a spectacular human being. I've been haunted for years by what I said to you that day. I even contemplated suicide at one point. It didn't take me long to realize that I was the real loser—not you, Arik, not you. You're a real live hero. People are talking about you everywhere."

"I'm supposed to feel heroic, huh? Instead, I feel like crap. I'm so tired of being heroic. Heroes just get their asses shot off. Heroes are the ones people visit in cemeteries, fondly remembered for a second and then left to lie in the dark earth for all eternity while the living carry on with their lives. Heroes are black and white photographs on a coffee table. Heroes end up being silenced while the whole world chatters away all around them." Arik broke down into tears again. "My dad ended up alone, in the street. All the people he helped and saved turned their backs on him. I never fully realized, until now, what he went through. I never fully understood who he really was. In the end, at least he had my mother. I have nobody. I can't even freakin' walk! Goddamn it!" He pounded his fist on the bed, crying out in helpless rage. "My life is over! Over! I want you to get me some cyanide, please. I want to kill myself."

Dahlia sat quietly, not uttering a sound. For months, she had touched every part of his body while caring for him, cleaning his bedsores and emptying his bedpans, but she dared not even touch his hand now. They sat for an hour without saying a word. Finally, she dared to speak.

"Arik, I only found out about Mikki when her parents came to visit you after you woke up."

"Why are you telling me this?"

"I'm telling you because I don't want you to think that I've been with you all this time to somehow take advantage of your condition or atone for my past sins. I don't want you to think that I've been manipulating you while knowing that she was gone."

"You know, it's funny how that thought never crossed my mind once, all this time, until you said it, but now that you have, why are you doing this? You've practically moved into this room. So, it's not out of guilt?"

"Honestly . . . I know that what I'm about to say will make you mad, but I have to say it anyway."

"No way," Arik said, shaking his head. "I'm done with anger over you. I thought about you long and hard after you threw me out of your house. I had a lot of time to think during my furlough from the army."

"What are you talking about? You were furloughed? When?"

"After that Pesach. When I left your house, I crashed the motorcycle on my way back to the base. I was nearly killed that day. I went into a deep funk but did my best to hide it. Again, I was Mr. Tough Guy. My commanders noticed it immediately, though. My performance and focus wavered. We were slated to go out on a particularly dangerous mission in Jordan, but I was held back. I thought they were going to throw me out or put me back into an ordinary unit. Instead, they told me to go back home, to LA, for a month to think about what I wanted to do with the rest of my life.

"When I got home, I spent a long time walking along the beach in Malibu, alone. I got drunk one night and woke up covered in vomit in a back alley, like the bum you once called me. After two weeks of wandering around, I started to work out at Inosanto's dojo again, and I got some insights from. I eventually went to speak to the reverend. We sat and talked for hours. That helped me make up my mind. I also saw my dad in a completely new light. Having spent time in the army here, I finally understood his basic mentality. I got infused with a new sense of purpose. I decided to return to Israel. When I returned here, I was readmitted into my unit with open arms, on the condition that I get psychological counseling. You did a lot of damage, girlie. Now look at me. I ended up becoming my dad."

"Not quite," she said. "Your life will be very different from his."

"Is it true you saved my life and leg when I was brought in?"

She nodded. "You were dying. At first, I didn't recognize you. It was only when you stopped breathing and I gave you mouth-to-mouth resuscitation that I recognized your lips. I thought I was having a heart attack."

"I always knew I was a good kisser." He smiled slightly.

"Your leg, chest, and abdomen sustained terrible injuries from the blast. They were going to amputate your leg and be done with it. I went crazy on the chief surgeon and forced him to try to save it. It took them eight hours to do that."

"I guess I owe you one."

"You don't owe me anything. After we met at Tel HaShomer two years ago, I knew for certain that I was still in love with you, but I had no clue how to make anything happen between us. I knew that you were in a serious relationship. I've dated some since then, but I haven't been as lucky as you. What you said about 'experiencing adversity' really resonated with me, and then came Munich—"

"I saw you there."

"What do you mean?"

"Our unit was in the Golan at the time, and we all went to Ramat Magshimim and watched the whole horror on TV. I thought about you and wondered what happened to you. I knew none of the women were killed, but then I heard you were injured. When I saw you walk into the stadium with your head bandaged and your arm in a sling . . . it really hit me hard. I swore I'd get the bastards that did that to you. The whole country cried, but for me it was personal, visceral. I won't deny it now. I still had feelings for you. It gave me special pleasure to exact revenge on your behalf. Within a month, my unit burst into Fatah land in Lebanon and shot up a dozen terrorist training camps. We killed hundreds of those animals. I was in such a murderous rage."

"Were you involved in the mission to Beirut?"

"Can't give you specifics, but many of us were."

"Hmm . . . So, after Munich I decided to change the trajectory of my life and make something of myself, by myself, without anyone's help," she said. "I signed up for a trauma nurse training program and put some of my experiences in Munich to good use. Because of my involvement at the Olympics, I returned to Munich five months later, believe it or not, to the same trauma hospital that I was treated in, for a twelve-week training fellowship. And I came back with a whole new way to organize the Tel HaShomer trauma unit based on the German model. In March, I was appointed assistant leader of the trauma team, and here I am."

He smiled at her. "You've become quite a gal."

She flashed her left forearm at him and pointed to her upper chest, smiling sadly. "I have my 'adversity' scars to prove it. But this is what I'm trying to say, Arik. When you came in wounded, I did all that I could to express my love, even if it would mean getting you ready to have a normal life again and passing you off to Mikki. I was ready to do that. I had decided that it would be my parting act of love for you both. My motives for doing what I have been doing for you have been entirely unselfish. I hope that you believe that. I was crestfallen when I heard that Mikki had been killed, because I knew what she meant to you. After I heard, though, I was determined to stay with you."

"And you haven't left my side for nearly ten weeks? Not even to go home?"

"That's true. And if you'll allow me the honor, I never want to leave your side ever again for the rest of my life. I know that I may have lost you forever, but I want to try. I want to take a chance on us again."

She reached into her bag and pulled out a yellowed, creased, black and white photograph.

"Do you remember this? Our picture from camp? You left this on the table that day we met here. You told me to take it, and I did. I've looked at this picture so many times since then. I want us to be those people in the photograph again. I want that more than anything in the world. I want us again, Arik. I want us!"

"Because you feel sorry for me? Because I'm just a crippled crazy person who cries in his sleep?"

"I don't feel sorry for you, and I won't let you feel sorry for yourself. And for your information, your mother didn't marry your father because she felt sorry for him—despite what you believe. Your Imma told me as much when I was at your house in LA for Pesach. She saw him for what he was and is, and she still wanted to spend her life with him no matter what. And lastly, your life isn't finished, not by a long shot. Great things lay ahead of you. I'm certain of it. And I want to be part of the adventure that's going to be your life. You'll never be alone if I have anything to do with it, Arik. I know that you will grieve for Mikki. You must, and you will. I just want to be at your side and help you to work through the things that you need to do to get back to a normal life. And I'm prepared to kick your ass to motivate you to get back to the best shape that you can get into. And then . . . the sky's the limit. There, I've said it. Now, you can throw me out." She sighed.

"Don't be ridiculous, Dahlia, nobody's throwing anyone out. But I need to work through my loss in my own way and my own time. You and I have both changed a lot and grown up. We can never again be those people in the photograph. Too much has happened. I've lived an entire life here. I've just lost the great love of my life. Let's take this one day at a time and get to know each other again. Okay? You're talking about a long-term commitment. Let's see if we're ready for that. We're not going anywhere anytime soon, so we have time to explore each other as people. That's all I can give you right now. Fair?

"I promise you one thing, though. I'll grieve for Mikki every day of my life. She wasn't the tough bitch I've heard people say she was. She was a sweet and wonderful person. She was my soulmate. I'll visit her gravesite every year on her yahrzeit and say Kaddish for her."

Dahlia realized, despite her great affection for him, that he was right. He had been through so much that there was no point in her throwing herself at him. He no longer considered her the love of his life. He needed time to heal, and she could play a pivotal role in helping him to do that. If she was to be his mate, she would have to not only heal what had been shattered but step into somebody else's shoes.

"I accept that, Arik."

"Can I ask you a favor? Can you please get in touch with my parents and tell them I've been slightly injured during the war but I'm recovering well and will be in touch when I'm able? I've been a bad son, not getting in touch, but I can't just lie to them and tell them everything's okay. It's better to let them think I'm an inconsiderate son than know the truth."

"Arik, I've been in touch with them already. They were informed of your injury early on, by the embassy in Washington, and they wanted to come here right away. I contacted them personally to reassure them that your injuries weren't too serious and to explain that it wasn't the right time for them to come. I couldn't bear for them to see you now. It would kill them. I'm in contact with them all the time, and they trust that I'm taking good care of you and will tell them when to come."

***

Sleeping in that cot next to Arik's bed, Dahlia endured his nightly terrors in which he moaned in his sleep and woke up hyperventilating, shaking, in a cold sweat. He cried out Mikki's name in his sleep while Dahlia lay wide awake, listening.

"Dahlia, I'm afraid to fall asleep. It's always the same. Every night. I can't bear it!"

"I've gotten used to your nightly screaming, and I ask you all the time what it's about, but you refuse to talk about it. Please, tell me what the dream is. Perhaps talking it out will help."

"Okay. I'll tell you. I'm in a foxhole in Nafach with Dani, Mikki, and Boaz. We're trying to repel a Syrian infantry battalion that's charging up the hill at us. I keep shooting and shooting at them with my MAG, but it does no good. My bullets just bounce off them. Then they're suddenly upon us. Leading the charge are Derrick Smyth and his gang dressed in Syrian Army uniforms. They jump into our foxhole and stab Mikki and me repeatedly with their bayonets, laughing hysterically. I look over and Dani and Boaz are sitting there without legs. I'm screaming, 'Help us! Help us!' but nobody comes to rescue us. It's so terrible! Every night, it's the same!"

Dahlia sat next to him. She took his head into her arms and stroked his neck as he wept. "It's going to be okay, Arik. It's going to be okay."

She sat next to him for a long while, quietly, and held him.

"I want to get you some help, Arik. I've been through all this before, with my mother after the Sabena hijacking. Dr. Melchior is one of the top psychiatrists in the country. He did a world of good for her."

"I don't need a psychiatrist. I'm not crazy. I just have bad dreams. That's all."

"I know that you're not crazy, but you've been through such terrible things. They're calling it battle fatigue. It's a new name for what they called shell shock in the Second World War. It's a real condition. Many of the men have come back with it. You're not alone. There are medications and counseling that Dr. Melchior can give you that will help. He doesn't usually come to the hospital to see patients, but I'm sure that he'll make an exception for you."

"Okay, I guess. I just can't live like this anymore. All I want is for the dreams to go away."

Arik spent hours every day staring out the window and saying very little. Dahlia sat quietly next to him. His nights continued to be punctuated with screams and sweats. She breathed a sigh of relief when Dr. Melchior finally appeared at his bedside and Arik opened up to him. She was greatly comforted when Arik asked her to remain in the room for the counseling sessions. Gradually, she learned things about Arik that she either had never known before or had been too immature to appreciate. She learned about Mikki as a person and how fortunate Arik had been to be in a relationship with her. Most importantly, she finally understood the type of adult relationship that Arik had been looking for all along, something that she had never provided him with even during their best times together. She wondered whether he would have achieved what he had over the past three years if she, rather than Mikki, had been by his side.

But her feeling of inadequacy gave way to a grim determination to fill Mikki's shoes no matter the cost to her or how long it would take to achieve it. She knew that she could never be Mikki, but she decided that she would be the best Dahlia that she could be. She would become the catalyst that Arik would need to achieve his maximum potential.

After having spent more than twelve weeks in bed, Arik was wheeled into the physiotherapy gym for the first time. It was a completely different world. The first thing to hit him was the intensely bright light from the open picture windows and sliding doors that led out to the grassy courtyard. Despite it being early February, the day was warm and the sun was shining brightly. Arik squinted and held a hand over his face. The past few weeks of his life had been darkness punctuated with low-level gray light. Now the world flashed into full color in front of him.

That morning, he had looked at himself in the mirror for the first time since the war. It had been an out-of-body experience, almost as if he were looking at someone else. Who is this atrophied scarecrow? he had thought. Never one to back down from a challenge, he had realized that this challenge would be his greatest. He knew that he would never be physically what he had been before, but he decided that neither would he sit around and feel sorry for himself, even though the temptation to do so was overwhelming at times.

The pain in his left thigh was still considerable, but he had gotten used to it. Besides, there was work to be done. What the hell! I have nowhere else to go and nothing else to do. As it had for so many Israelis in October 1973, his old world had ended forever and a new chapter had begun.

I'm lucky. For 2,700 Israeli boys and men, there would be no new chapter at all. He looked around the large room, with its multiple treatment mats, parallel bars, and staircases. He saw men who four months earlier had been at the peak of their manhood but now were fragments of their former selves. Men without arms, legs, or eyes, men with terribly scarred faces, and men with distorted torsos were everywhere. Some men were paralyzed from the waist down or—even worse—from the neck down.

Arik had been lucky. He had come into the hospital with extensive burns, large wounds in his leg and chest, and internal abdominal bleeding, which been stanched just in time by removing his spleen, but aside from scars that he would have for the rest of his life his injuries seemed fixable. At least, he hoped so.

He stared long and hard at the parallel bars at the side of the gym.

"Do you remember what I used to be able to do on parallel bars, Dahlia? Now I can't even walk between them."

He thought about the life that awaited the family members of these men. He thought about his dad and how his life had been. He began to tremble.

Dahlia hugged him and kissed him behind an ear.

"It's going to be okay, Arik," she whispered. "You're the center of my world, and I'll be there with you every step of the way."

"My dad had to rehabilitate on a street corner. These men will all be helped by the government for the rest of their lives. I'll bet if my dad had gotten the proper care for his leg from the beginning he wouldn't have had to battle those recurrent infections in his stump for the past twenty-five years . . . I hope one day to get back to nearly the way I was, but there's only so much you can do without an arm or a leg. Nobody was more determined than my dad, but it was all too much for him, so he simply gave up."

It took two physiotherapists to help Arik get up into a standing position. He was astonished that his body had completely forgotten what to do. His knees shook, and he felt extremely lightheaded. He was unable to will one leg to go in front of the other. The physiotherapists helped him to get down on a mat.

"The first thing that we're going to have to do is work out all the stiffness in your joints. You haven't moved in months," Dorit, one of the physiotherapists, said.

"I feel like the tin man in The Wizard of Oz," Arik said. "I just need some engine oil, and I'll be as right as rain."

The initial joint mobilization sessions were intensely painful. Whenever Arik reached the end of his range of motion, he cried out in agony. After each session, he lay in a cold sweat, breathing heavily. When his wounds had healed sufficiently, the physiotherapists were able to immerse his legs in a hot whirlpool bath before the stretching exercises, which made his progress quicker. His weight bearing was hampered by the slow healing of his femur. Each step he took caused him to wince. He developed a leg length discrepancy, his femur having shortened at the site of the fracture.

The doctors decided that it would be best to do further surgery. They removed the external steel frame that held the femur together and put an intramedullary (Küntscher) steel rod into his femoral shaft to align the femur, pull it out to full length, and hope that doing so would enable him to bear weight more evenly. It was another month before Arik had regained a reasonable range of motion in his legs.

At that point, Arik began a course of four hours of physiotherapy and two hours of occupational therapy each day. After two weeks, he could walk unassisted in between the parallel bars while holding on to them. On the exercise mat, he worked out first with exercise balls and then with dumbbells. The pain that he experienced from the abdominal wounds when lifting progressively heavier weights gradually dissipated. Dahlia rearranged her work schedule so that she could attend all of Arik's physical therapy sessions. She rapidly became a favorite among the soldiers in the gym.

Arik marveled at Dahlia's luminous presence. This was the Dahlia that he remembered from the tennis court, the Dahlia that he had fallen in love with years earlier. The difference was that now she was mature. More than just her physical beauty boosted morale on the ward. Her forceful, ebullient spirit pushed the soldiers forward, motivating them and giving them hope. As Arik became increasingly independent, Dahlia worked tirelessly with many of the other men. She still refused to leave the hospital, instead insisting that her mother bring clean clothes and uniforms to her.

"One rarely sees such rapid progress in these cases. Most of my patients can't tolerate more than two hours of therapy a day. I can barely get Arik out of the gym. He's driven in the extreme," Dorit said to Dahlia.

"You should have seen him before the war," Dahlia said. "He looked like a Greek god, and he was an incredible athlete. He has the soul of a champion. He's determined to get back to his previous form, if it takes him the rest of his life."

"He should do very well, with such a dedicated partner helping him at every step. You have a rare combination of talents, with your nursing and sports background. All the men so appreciate your work here. You've become like a mother to them."

Arik's spirits gradually improved as his body responded more readily to his commands. At about the six-month mark, he began his own exercise regimen, going to the recreational gym to shoot baskets. He even insisted that Dahlia leave the hospital during her time off when he was sleeping, which she agreed to grudgingly.

Shmulik and Yael were frequent visitors to Arik. Initially, they resented Dahlia's presence, thinking of her as an interloper who was taking advantage of Arik's weakened condition. After all, he had been Mikki's fiancé and Dahlia had been an evil presence in his life. They doubted that she was worthy of such a prince. However, the sad reality that Mikki would never return to reclaim him began to sink in. As the weeks wore on, the Zohars began to appreciate Dahlia's dedication to Arik.

One afternoon, they walked into Arik's room to find Dahlia down on her knees, putting slippers on Arik's feet in preparation for him to take an assisted walk down the corridor. When Dahlia heard their footsteps, she turned and looked up.

"I'll leave you all alone," she said quietly, standing up.

"No need to go, Dahlia. Please, stay," Yael said.

"Arik, we've gone through Mikki's personal effects, looking for the black folder that you asked for," Shmulik said. "We can't find it anywhere. What was in it? She never mentioned anything about it to us."

Arik sighed. "Just before the war, when I gave Mikki her engagement ring, she gave me the folder. She had discovered it in the Palmach archives near Tel Aviv. Dahlia, do you remember the conversation we had when you revealed that my dad saved your father's life? I never confronted your father about it, because I knew he never cared much for me. I was in no position to force the truth out of him. I feared for my own status. I thought your father would have the decency to come clean on his own, especially after he knew who I was."

"Forgive me for saying this, Dahlia, but your father is a fool and a coward for not clearing up this mess. Look at all the suffering that he caused!" Shmulik shook his head.

Yael said, "Shmulik, there's no need to upset the girl at this point. What's done is done."

"I know my father's faults very well," Dahlia said. "I'm no longer a child. My father disliked Arik from the moment he met him. Yes, Arik, even at Camp Moshava. He made up some excuse for hating him, something about his being a street hoodlum. It was only later that he realized what it was about Arik that made him so uncomfortable. We had a major shouting match when I told him that you were coming to our house in Washington for Sukkot."

"Why did you let me come, then?"

"Because if forced into a choice between my father and Arik, I knew then—already—that I'd pick Arik. I spent the year we were together fighting with my parents about our relationship. I was young and easily lead astray. The last thing I would have believed was that I'd be led astray by my own parents. I'd always been at odds with my parents, especially my father. There was always an underlying tension in the atmosphere at home. I've heard a great deal about what type of home you have, Mrs. Zohar. My home was never like that, but I swear by all things sacred that if I'm privileged enough to build a home with Arik it will be like yours."

Dahlia looked at Arik. "Arik, what was in the folder?"

"After searching for some clue about my father's identity for over eighteen months, Mikki discovered a folder that contained Palmach enlistment records. She found an entry dated April 1946 clearly showing my father's name. He joined the Palmach immediately upon disembarking here in 1946. He was never in the Irgun at all. It was a case of mistaken identity. There was another Ze'ev Myerowitz who was a member of the Irgun. My father was never the terrorist he was accused of being. We were going to make it public to the family at our engagement party after Sukkot. I was worried that the folder would get lost, so Mikki assured me that she'd keep it with her at all times until she could present it to General Zeira, who she said would pass it on to the defense ministry. She must have had it with her in Tzafra."

"That place was reduced to dust," Shmulik said. "There was nothing left. Unfortunately, without proof, even if Benny came clean, I'm not sure that it would help. It didn't help before. I'll keep looking, Arik, and I'll turn over heaven and earth to find another clue. I'm a firm believer that an apple doesn't fall far from the tree. I know the apple. Now I have to find the tree."

***

A week later, Arik was in the gym, helping a paraplegic member of his unit to improve his basketball shooting skills, when Dahlia appeared at the door.

"Back to your old tricks, eh, Arik?" Dahlia smiled at him.

"Just like a lifetime ago at camp!" he said.

"There are some people here to see you," she said.

"Who can be here to see me? I don't know anybody."

"Oh! Poor you! Seriously, there are."

She wheeled him to the visitors' lounge, where two infantry officers in dress uniform were waiting for him.

"Now I must be in trouble," Arik whispered playfully to Dahlia. "It's probably something about the fuel Jerri cans our little band of merry men repeatedly stole from a Golani base last year."

But they both turned serious when the officers requested that all other visitors and patients be escorted out of the room and the door closed.

"What's this about?" Arik asked.

Solemnly, one of the officers produced a sealed envelope and handed it to him. It bore the seal of the defense ministry.

He shrugged and then opened it. Inside was a letter:

April 28, 1974

Captain Arik Meir,

You displayed great heroism and valor during our most recent great conflict. May it be our last. Your selfless devotion to your comrades as well as your superb fighting skills without regard for your own personal safety during the fiercest combat of the war has earned you the grateful admiration of all of the people of the State of Israel. It is quite clear that the extreme bravery, sacrifice, and valor of yourself and those like you turned the tide of the war that literally threatened our existence.

It is my honor and privilege to recommend you for the Ott Hagvurah, the Medal of Valor, Israel's highest military award. The awards ceremony will take place at a ceremony in the front courtyard of the Knesset on July 21, 1974, at precisely 9:30 a.m.

Future generations of Israelis will long remember those who served this nation during its darkest hours.

Your family should be extremely proud.

Best Wishes,
Moshe Dayan
Ministry of Defense
State of Israel

Arik was motionless and silent.

"Arik, what does it say? Is everything okay?" Dahlia asked.

He quietly handed the letter to her.

"My God, Arik! What is this? Since you've come back from the Golan, we've never once spoken in any detail about what you've been through. I never wanted to bring up your experiences for fear of traumatizing you further. What did you do to deserve this?"

"I'm not interested in this," he said softly.

"I'm sorry, Arik, what did you say?"

"I said . . . I'm not interested in this in the least." He turned to the officers and said, "Sirs, would you please kindly tell Mr. Dayan to stick this letter up his ass? I'm not interested in his 'honors.' Sacrifice, indeed! I'm going to walk out of here one day, which is more than I can say about most of these guys. If they want to award sacrifice, let them lay medals on the bodies that were strewn on the fields of the Golan during the war and on the body fragments and blood that decorated the interior of the Centurion tanks in the Valley of Tears. Why'd you ask these other men to leave the room? They deserve medals more than I do. If they gave a medal to everyone who deserved one, I think they'd run out of medals! It's disgusting that these clowns are looking for poster children to parade around! Please, take this back. I'm not interested. I want to be left alone. I just want my life back."

The officers stood there, stunned. They quietly took back the letter and left.

"Dahlia, please don't say anything to me right now. This isn't about any sense of modesty, as you call it. I'm genuinely nauseated by this."

Dahlia needed no prompting. She sat next to him quietly, held his hand, and stared at him.

The days passed, and Arik's condition steadily improved.

One morning, as Arik was eating breakfast with Dahlia in the cafeteria, a slim woman with Sephardic features and her black hair in a ponytail approached them.

"May I help you, ma'am?" Arik asked curiously.

"Are you Arik Meir?"

"Yes."

"I have been looking for you for months. I have inquired about you at the defense ministry. Apparently, your whereabouts are a closely guarded military secret. No one would tell me anything. It was only by chance that I found you through one of the doctors who work here."

"Dahlia, did you know I'm now a military secret? I must have really pissed off somebody high up by my response to the medal thing last week."

Dahlia shrugged.

"I am Orah Shiloni. My husband, Gavi, was your commanding officer during your tironut. I was going through his personal effects, and I found this box of letters all neatly arranged with your name and a Dahlia's name on them. When I discovered them, I began a several months' long search for you."

The letters appeared to have been carefully opened.

"I'm Dahlia!"

Dahlia took the box from the woman. She sifted through the letters quickly. They were the letters that she had written to Arik each week from September to November 1970 as well as Arik's weekly letters, which he had written faithfully to her until March 1971. Her letters still smelled of lavender. Her face turned ashen gray. Stunned, she began to hyperventilate.

"Oh, my God! Oh, my God! Arik! Arik!"

She lowered her head, dropped to her knees, and clutched the box to her stomach, shaking back and forth. Tears streamed out of her eyes and onto the envelopes. She let out a loud agonized cry and covered her face. The letters dropped to the floor.

"Here are all your letters to me, Arik! You did tell me the truth all along. I can't live with myself! You were loyal and faithful to me, and I was too young, stupid, and reckless to realize what I had in my hands. You were so right. I never gave you the benefit of the doubt. I did the most terrible things. I don't deserve to be in your presence, let alone to have your love. My corporal in tironut was so right when she said that I don't deserve to even look at you. I'm so ashamed. Oh, my God! I'm so ashamed! I was so cruel to you when you came for Pesach. I sat in judgment of your pure heart. You gave up so much for me, and I was too stupid and strung out to understand or appreciate you. I'm responsible for everything. I shattered the crystal vase of our love with my own two hands." She gulped air and dropped to her knees on the floor.

Arik touched her face and then slowly leaned over, picked up the letters, and smelled the lavender. He sat frozen, his hands shaking. He clutched her head to his chest and kissed the top of it. He lifted himself out of the wheelchair, his legs trembling and his arms on the arm rests barely supporting his weight.

"Orah, your husband has done me more harm than the entire Syrian Army ever could. You have no clue what damage he did to our lives. It's a miracle that Dahlia is sitting here next to me. How dare he not come here and face me like a man, sending his wife, like the coward he is, after what he did to us. You tell that disgusting son of a bitch to come here and face me directly or I'll hunt him down like a dog if it takes the rest of my life." Arik roared that last bit, red-faced and shaking his fist at her.

Heads turned to look at him.

Orah looked down and said, "I wish that he could. You deserve for him to come here and apologize on his hands and knees for what he did. He was an abusive, inconsiderate man, even to me, and I considered leaving him. After he was relieved of his command by General Tal, he was sent to the Suez Canal to command a forward base on the Bar-Lev Line. He was killed on the first day of the war, in the initial Egyptian assault. All that I can do is offer my profoundest sorrow for what he did to you. Please, accept my apology."

It was Dahlia's turn to speak.

"Orah, you could have destroyed the letters, and no one would have known. I thank you from the bottom of my heart for searching for us. You have restored an important part of who we are, something that had been hanging over our heads for years. Now we may be able to mend our lives and move forward. May you find the peace that you so richly deserve."

"Dahlia, I'm so sorry," Orah said, before turning around and leaving.

Dahlia and Arik looked at each other silently for a long time, Dahlia weeping softly.

"Where do we go from here?" Dahlia asked. "What do we do now? We're in uncharted waters. We've been living under the veil of monstrous lies and deceptions that nearly destroyed us both. How can we fix us and get back to the us that we had during our first year together? Is it still possible to recapture that love?"

He wiped the tears from her face and said hoarsely, "We're done crying. It's time to start living. Our first act of rebirth will be to read all the letters." He smiled and held her in his arms. "Do you remember when you used to call me booba sheli?"

She laughed through her tears and nodded. "When you almost ran off with Suzie Chapstick!"

They both laughed. She rested her head on his shoulder, and he dried the rest of her tears with a napkin from the table.

They spent the rest of the day lying next to each other on Arik's bed, arranging the letters according to date and reading them to each other. They reveled in the bittersweet mirth of a better time gone by. Dahlia finally understood the full nature of Arik's suffering during his first year in Israel. She stared at him in awe and hugged him tightly. They fell asleep in each other's arms.

***

The following day, Arik began his morning workout. Dahlia was back on duty. Arik was told that a special guest was waiting for him in the visitors' lounge. His leg hurt considerably, so he stayed in his wheelchair.

When he opened the door, he saw a stern, distinguished middle-aged man in uniform standing there. Arik pulled himself out of his wheelchair and stiffened to attention.

"At ease, Captain Meir . . . Arik. Please, sit back down."

It is not every day that General Raful Eitan, the commander of the northern forces of the Israeli Army, comes to visit! Arik relaxed somewhat but remained standing.

"I spoke with your doctors, and they told me that among all of your injuries you did not sustain any brain damage. So, I want to know, what's going on in your head, Arik? From the moment you entered the army, we all knew that you were a very special soldier. How do you say in the United States? A cut above the rest. Not only in the war but throughout your service, you consistently showed yourself to be absolutely outstanding. Very few Israelis ever have even a chance to be in Sayeret Matkal. Almost never does someone who grew up in the States get such an honor. But you're the best of the best. You have always been intelligent and sensible. So, when the defense minister recommends you for an Ott Hagvurah, you throw it back in his face? How can you dare to do this, Arik? This doesn't make any sense! Atah lo beseder, Arik? Bechayecha?"

Arik stared down at the ground impassively. "I meant no disrespect, sir, but I just don't want it. I don't deserve it. I only followed orders and did my job as a soldier," he said quietly.

"It is for us to decide who gets such a high honor, not you, Arik. Your whole unit—I think that they called you all Sayeret Hameshugaim—will be honored. If you don't want it, very well. I won't force you. But you will be the only one, and one day perhaps you'll regret your decision. Such an award will open up many possibilities for you in Israel, that is, if you plan on staying here and not returning to the States. This award is not like the Congressional Medal of Honor that they give away in the United States. They give that out much too easily. This award has been given out to no more than thirty men since 1948, and most of them received them after their deaths. We take this very, very seriously, and to my knowledge nobody has ever refused this, Arik, in the whole history of Israel. Your attitude is astounding and, frankly, impossible to comprehend."

"I understand, sir. I mean no disrespect, sir."

"Look, Arik, your unit saved my life and the lives of all the others in my command post in Nafach on the third day of the war. Your suggestions about infantry support to defeat the terrible missiles were taken very seriously and saved many other lives on both the Golan and the Sinai. I will be forever grateful to you for that. You, Yoni, and the others marched into a wall of machine gun and artillery fire in Tel Shams and Mount Hermon, without any fear. The Golani owe you a great debt of gratitude for what you did for them on the day that you were wounded, not to mention that you almost gave your life to save the life of Shmulik Zohar's son. I can't order you to accept this award, but I ask you personally to reconsider. Please, think it over."

"I'm very flattered by the commendation, sir, but I've already made up my mind. I'm very sorry."

Arik saluted the general.

"Shalom, Arik," the general said. And then he was gone.

***

Arik related the morning's events to Dahlia when she arrived at the gym after her shift.

"I never broached the subject with you, Arik, for fear of upsetting you, but I must ask you why won't you accept this award. Look, everyone in Israel feels as you do about this crappy war. You're definitely not alone. How do you think all the mothers and wives of those who were lost feel? They feel the loss as much as you do, if not more! The government has set up a commission headed up by Chief Justice Agranat to look into what happened. In all likelihood, the people in charge will pay for what they did. Perhaps the government will fall and the Likud Party and Begin will come into power."

"Great. Just what we need—an Irgun terrorist as prime minister! Anyway, I just can't accept it. I'm sick of all this and of them, all of them. Will a stupid ribbon on my chest help me walk right again? What a pathetic gesture! Maybe I should go back to the LA and live with my parents. Two cripples in the same house. I'm sorry you can't have your fancy war hero, Dahlia. I hope you can still accept me as I am and not walk off again, like you did before. I'll never be able to dunk a basketball again. I've become just like my father—"

"Stop it, Arik! Stop it!" Dahlia shouted. "I will not hear this kind of talk ever again! I will never leave your side. Never! Ever! Shortly after that Pesach episode, I knew that I'd made the worst mistake of my life. I was desperate to get back to you, but I knew that I'd lost you forever when I saw you with Mikki one night during my tironut. Tragedy has brought us back together. I can never replace Mikki, but you're the great love of my life and I'm committed to being your helpmate for the rest of that life. I'm sorry, soldier boy, but you're stuck with me. Get used to it. You are my life!"

Arik stared blankly down at the mat.

***

The following day, Arik looked up from the therapy mat, where Dahlia was helping him until her shift that was scheduled to start at noon, to see his two favorite people in the world—other than her—staring down at him.

Arik smiled broadly. "How did you two monkeys find me? I thought my whereabouts were top secret."

"They are!" Yoni laughed. "But you know Dani and I have our ways!"

Dani said, "You look good, Arik. When are you coming back to the unit?"

"Unless we organize a jail break, I'll never get out of here. I think they keep Dahlia around to keep an eye on me because they know what I'm capable of," Arik said, smirking at Dahlia. Smiling back, she shook a fist at him.

"Listen, Arik," Yoni said, his voice turning serious, "I'm your commanding officer and a brother to you, so don't bullshit me. Tell me why you won't accept the Ott Hagvurah. Don't tell me stories about righteous indignation about the cause of the war. All that is well above our pay grade. You're right. We had a job to do, and we did it. Quite well, I think. The rest we'll leave to the Israeli voters and God. Dani and I feel the same way you do, but the people in this country are very, very depressed. You haven't been outside for months. You don't know how depressed they are. The government needs real live war heroes, and I have no idea why they picked us but they did. We're all going to accept our commendations together. We need you with us."

"I just can't do it," Arik said tearfully.

"Why, Arik, why?" Dani asked.

Yoni, not a man of many words, looked at Arik intensely before finally saying, "I know what this is about. This isn't about this war at all. Is it? This is about your father! You won't accept the award because of him. He never got the recognition he deserved after the '48 war, so you won't accept this."

Arik looked down and nodded. "Yoni, I didn't come to Israel because of Jewish pride or any sense of Zionism. We've talked about that, you and me. You're the big Zionist. You and your brothers were brought up in a loving, Jewish, Zionist home so, in a sense, it was much easier for you. My reasons were far more complex. I came here for two reasons: out of love for this woman and to finish the work my father never got to. I wanted to beat these bastards at their own game. I did that, and now I'm satisfied."

"So, that's it? You're finished?" Dani asked.

"That's it! Plain and simple. I won't accept any award until my father's name is cleared and he gets the recognition and the compensation he earned so long ago but was denied. He can never reclaim his lost years, but I have to see to it that he spends the rest of his life in some measure of comfort, even if I have to get an attorney and take it to Israel's Supreme Court. It'll make the Kastner Affair look like small potatoes. At this point, don't put it past me to go the Yedioth Ahronoth. They'd eat this story up. I have nothing to lose. I'll take this and smear it in Golda's, Rabin's, and Dayan's faces. Let the Israeli voters decide if my father is innocent or not. Those three have dirty hands in this affair, following in Ben-Gurion's footsteps. No, my brothers, I can't accept this medal. Go in peace and accept your awards. You guys so deserve it."

Dahlia had never hated her father more in her entire life.

***

"What do you mean that all of the Ott Hagvurah recipients refuse to accept them!" Dayan thundered, pounding his fist on the table.

Raful handed a piece of paper to him.

"Here's a petition signed by all of them and their families," Raful said. "It's about Captain Meir. They won't accept it if he doesn't."

"Did they say why? They better have a very good reason. This is ridiculous!" Dayan scowled.

"They did. I spoke to his comrades at length."

Raful relayed the whole story about Ze'ev Myerowitz.

"Are you quite certain about this?" Dayan asked. "I've seen Ze'ev Myerowitz's records . . . I've always assumed that he was an Irgun terrorist responsible for the Deir Yassin massacre. How can a mistake like this have gone on for so long? Where are this Ze'ev's dossier and service records, that is, if there is a second Ze'ev?"

"They were supposedly blown up when the Jewish Agency building in Jerusalem was bombed, and we're apparently left with just the terrorist's records."

"This all seems a bit too contrived, a bit too convenient. Where is Arik's father now?"

"He lives in the States, in Los Angeles, supported by his brother."

"Again, a bit too convenient. Perhaps Arik's father really is the terrorist and he lives in the States so that he won't have to show his face here. We're going to have to corroborate this story somehow. Who else was there on that day in '48? There must have been witnesses."

"I've had my assistant go through the military campaign archives in Tel Aviv. According to the accounts, in the confusion of the massive final assault on Kastel, following the assassination of Abd al-Qadir, the commander, Gazit, called for a tactical retreat from the village. They filled an armored bus with all the excess ammo and guns so that they wouldn't fall into the hands of the enemy. Somehow, they became separated from their unit during the chaos of the retreat. They came under heavy small arms and mortar fire from the Arabs. There were two men in the Jeep behind the bus. The bus driver was killed when the bus sustained a direct hit in its gas tank and caught fire. The Jeep driver was also killed, by flying shrapnel. There were six men in the bus, including the driver. The second man in the Jeep apparently was able to pry open the door of the burning bus, and they pulled out all five of the men inside, but when he went back for the bus driver the bus blew up."

"What happened then?"

"That's where it gets confusing. One man was found severely burned, missing his left leg at the mid-thigh, unconscious. Another, grossly disoriented, had burns over about 50 percent of his body and was suffering from smoke inhalation. Seven men were taken to the hospital. Three were dead on arrival, and the other two died of their injuries a short time later."

"You're telling me that the man without the leg was Ze'ev Myerowitz, Arik Meir's father? So, who was the other one who survived?"

"Benny Gilad."

Dayan stared at Raful for a moment. Now he understood Benny's interest in Arik several years earlier. Finally, he said, "It should have been easy enough to check the identity of that man in the Jeep who did the heroic act. These men had written orders. We should know who's who."

"Apparently, somebody else was supposed to be in that Jeep, manning the machine gun," Raful said, "but for some unknown reason, another person— who we now believe to be Ze'ev Myerowitz—took his place that day."

"Why didn't Benny say anything when he was released from the hospital?"

"He did, but it was precisely at that time that the whole extent of the Deir Yassin horror became known. Ben-Gurion went absolutely ballistic. He took the names of the perpetrators and swore that he'd somehow destroy the lives of the people who had taken part in it. When Benny came forth with his report, it was suppressed by Ben-Gurion, because he was convinced that Ze'ev Myerowitz was the terrorist. There was nothing that Benny could do. When the Altalena sank, Ben-Gurion became convinced that Myerowitz had lost his leg while on board. Nobody could talk sense to him. Benny was threatened with be charged with complicity with Ze'ev if he kept pursuing the matter, so eventually he dropped the issue.

"Where is Benny now?" Dayan asked.

"He's in the U.S., in meetings with Nixon and Kissinger."

"Call the embassy in Washington and send word to Benny that he must return to Israel at once. I'm going to speak to Golda this afternoon and discuss this matter with her before it gets out of control. I smell a major screw-up. Get hold of Begin and ask him to join us if he can. He should know who was on the Altalena when it went down and in Deir Yassin on the day of the massacre."

"One more thing, sir. Arik is ready to go to the newspapers and blow this wide open to the public."

"Well then, post a Shin Bet security detail around him. Let's solve this in a quiet way so that it doesn't become a public scandal. That's the last thing that we need in the middle of the Agranat Commission's investigation. The public is furious enough with us as it is. The entire top echelon of the government is in danger of being thrown into the street over this crisis of confidence that the war has caused and our inability to anticipate a surprise attack of such magnitude, that cost the lives of so many of our young people. The media are circling around us like sharks, just itching to create a new scandal. This isolated incident from twenty-six years ago may be enough to topple the whole house of cards, especially if Arik goes public with it along with his refusal to accept the Ott Hagvurah. Regardless of who this one-legged man in the States is, this has to be straightened out with maximum speed and efficiency . . . and quietly."

Chapter 31

Arik's condition continued to improve, and Dahlia began to make inquiries about getting him discharged from the hospital. She was met with sympathetic but unsatisfying answers.

"I'm sorry, Dahlia. He must remain in the rehab unit. His condition is still unstable, and he must be under supervision," the rehab unit's medical director, Dr. Yishai Cohen, said.

"That's total bullshit, and you know it," Dahlia said. "He's doing much better. He's ready for discharge. He's been here for more than six months. He needs to get out into the world. He's going stir-crazy in here. This is starting to become his prison."

"He's a lone soldier. He has no family here, no one to receive him," Dr. Cohen said.

Like his father, Dahlia thought.

"We can't send him out into the street. What would he do? Who would take care of him?"

"I'm his family! I'll take responsibility for him, and I'll take care of him. He'll stay at my home," Dahlia said, emphasizing her words by pointing her index finger toward her chest.

"I'm sorry, Dahlia, but I have my instructions. Arik must remain where he is for now."

"But why, Yishai?"

"I'm very sorry, Dahlia, but that's all that I know."

When Dahlia left the administration building, she spied two old friends of hers. She ran to them and practically jumped into their arms as she hugged each of them tightly.

"My God! How long has it been? How are you?" Dahlia asked them excitedly. "I haven't seen you guys in at three years, I think, since Washington—"

"Look at you, Dahlia," Tomer said. "You have not only grown into a beautiful woman but the light that I saw in your eyes as a teenager, that went out the last year that I was in Washington, has returned. The last that I saw you, you were fighting with your parents about not returning here at all, about not going into the army. And then there was that night in Las Vegas . . . when I tried to stop you . . . And now, you look like a totally different person. What are you doing here at Tel HaShomer? I see that you are still in the army."

"Better question: What are you guys doing here? I practically live here. Are you visiting family or a friend?"

'No," Tomer said, "Work! I've got some guard duty here, on a patient. Some VIP, I think. We were just heading into the commander's office to get our orders."

"Hmm, sounds secret," Dahlia said.

"After we left the embassy, we came back here with the Shin Bet," Yoram said. "We have been doing personal guard duty for high-ranking officers with strategic clearance, keeping them out of trouble." He laughed.

"Well, I'm the assistant team lead of the trauma unit," Dahlia said, "but my main job really is taking care of Arik. He was severely injured on Mount Hermon just a few hours before the cease-fire went into effect. He nearly died here several times, but he's finally on the mend. I'm trying to get him out of here, but I'm hitting a brick wall."

"So, the two of you are back together? I never for a moment thought that that would happen. You are a special girl. How did you do it?" Tomer laughed. "Seriously, you have come such a long way in only a few years, from that girl who ran off one night to assistant nursing director. I am in complete awe of you, Dahlia."

Dahlia nodded and smiled. "I came into the army a nasty, spoiled brat, but by the time I completed my basic training and then went through what I did in Munich I had all the silliness knocked out of me the hard way. I knew that I had made terrible mistakes in my life, and I was determined to make something of myself and, if I could, claw my way back into Arik's heart."

"I am glad that you succeeded," Tomer said. "From the moment I met Arik that Sukkot of '69, I liked him. I thought that he was honest, loyal, and powerful but very kind and considerate. Those are not common attributes in a man. Take it from me. And one thing that I always knew about you is that if you really want something you will stop at nothing to get it."

Dahlia looked hard at him. "I know what you did to Ze'evi. You were the anonymous tip that led the FBI to his Learjet. Arik told me."

"I would have killed him for you. He deserved it."

"I'm so glad that you didn't—not for his sake but for yours . . . but thanks all the same."

Yoram winked at her. "We've got to go. We'll look you up soon. We can get together and talk some more!"

"Count on it." Dahlia gave each man a bear hug again and a kiss on the cheek.

Tomer and Yoram walked inside the administration building. They were ushered into the Shin Bet commander's office.

They stood at attention.

"Relax, gentlemen," Colonel Alon said. "Coffee?"

They both declined.

"We have a very delicate situation here. General Hofi recommended you. I understand that you were his personal bodyguards during the war on the Golan?"

They nodded.

"Do you recall on the third day of war when the forward headquarters at Nafach was in imminent danger of being overrun? There was a group of paratroopers that saved the command center post at Nafach from a major Syrian commando incursion. They also saved a complete armored battalion from annihilation while taking out a key position that was blocking the forward movement of an entire brigade of ours into Syria.

"These cowboys wiped out a whole infantry platoon that were shooting missiles at Yanush's tanks in the Valley of Tears. They then commandeered an APC full of Sagger missiles, overcame its crew, captured a Russian advisor, ran through and around Syrian tanks, and brought a treasure trove of missiles and the new RPG-7s with them back to Nafach, while being fired on by both our guys—unintentionally, of course—and theirs.

"Their escapade helped us to unlock the problem of missile assaults on our tank positions. We were able to formulate countermeasures that saved many lives. I joined Hofi a week later, when he returned from Tel Aviv to the front. He was flabbergasted by their performance. An officer in that unit was severely injured on Hermon at the end of the war. He's in the rehab at Tel HaShomer. He will need to be watched and have his movements restricted for the time being. He's a wily sort, as you can imagine, and could easily escape, even while in a wheelchair."

"But why does he need to be watched?" Yoram asked. "He should go out and get a well-deserved hero's welcome. Shouldn't he?"

"I'm not sure," Alon said. "But apparently the orders come straight from the top. Do you have your team assembled?"

"Yes, sir!" Tomer said.

"Remember, Tomer, you're not guarding a criminal. This man is a national war hero, a treasure. Be discreet and low-key. Your job is to keep outsiders, especially the media and other curious people, away from him."

"Who is this man?" Tomer asked.

Alon handed him a white envelope with the logo of the ministry of defense on it.

Tomer opened it. Inside was a letter. It said only the following:

Captain Arik Meir

Tel HaShomer Hospital

Rehab Center Agaf Bet

Third Floor

Room 35

Tomer and Yoram showed no emotion as they read the note. They were not surprised.

"My team is ready. We will deploy immediately. We will watch this man twenty-four hours a day. Access by written permission only," Tomer assured the colonel.

As they walked out of the building, Tomer smiled slightly. He was so glad Dahlia had won Arik's heart back. And he was happy that it was his team and not another that had been chosen to watch Arik. He knew that some other guys might try to be rough with him, not realizing that was the last thing that Arik needed. Besides, he thought that it would be better to keep this in the family, so to speak.

"What are you doing here, Tomer?" Dahlia asked when she saw him back at the hospital.

"I am not sure, but my orders are to watch Arik twenty-four hours a day."

"Can somebody please tell me what's going on? Is Arik in trouble? Has he done something wrong? No matter what his good intentions are, trouble always seems to find him."

"To be honest, Dahlia, I am not sure myself. But quite the contrary. It looks like you have hooked yourself a national war hero."

"There were so many heroes during that war, living and dead."

"Not like this one. He has accomplished extremely significant things, and he has shaken the chain of command all the way up."

"He won't talk in detail about his experiences during the war, and I don't push him. I guess that explains the letter from Dayan about him getting the Ott Hagvurah."

"Wow! You should be very proud of him!"

"He told Dayan to stick it up his ass." Dahlia shook her head ruefully.

Tomer sighed. "Typical American cowboy. I guess that could be why I am here. Whatever his reasons for doing that, it has rattled the top military and political echelons . . . Where is he?"

"He's in the gym, shooting baskets with some of the guys."

"Wonderful. I am glad that he is doing so well. I heard how badly he was injured. I remember how good he was when he came to Washington for Sukkot—"

"Tomer, he's playing from a wheelchair. He can stand and walk for short distances, nothing more. He's working fourteen hours a day on getting back into some physical shape. His determination borders on the extreme, but it's very slow going. Please, don't be shocked when you see him. Act as natural as you can."

Tomer followed Dahlia toward the sound of bouncing balls and catcalls. He was amazed when he saw ten men strapped tightly into strange wheelchairs without armrests and with wheels tilted at an odd angle. Many of the men were amputees. Some were paraplegic. Tomer saw the joy on their faces and realized immediately that this gym was a sacred place to them. It was a respite from the terrible reality of their present life and their trepidation of what the future would hold. In the gym, all was peace and joy. The men wheeled around at lightning speed, helter-skelter, chasing a basketball and crashing into one another as they tried to get to the basket. Wheelchairs tipped over and then instantly were righted by their occupants. In the middle of the melee, Arik directed traffic. When Arik got the ball at the top of the key, he sent the basketball sailing with the lightness of a feather into the hoop.

When Arik spotted Tomer, he waved at him wildly. Tomer stood at the side of the court, watching the play. He was visibly moved by what he was seeing. He had not seen Arik in more than a year. He barely recognized him. Arik was about half the size that he had been. A wave of sadness washed over Tomer as he thought about what Arik had given up. Tomer had been a spectator in the epic that had been Arik's life, and he now fully understood why Arik had no interest in the high honor that they were trying to bestow on him. For all the time that Arik had spent in Israel, he had never really absorbed the societal norms of what was important and what was not. He obviously had no idea of the medal's significance. Tomer did, however, see Arik's persistent spirit and leadership ability spilling out on the court.

Looking at Dahlia, Tomer also saw her in a new light. Clearly, she was going headlong into a new relationship with Arik. But this time her eyes were wide open. Tomer understood what lay ahead of them. He looked at Dahlia with intense pride in what she had become. He had told her years earlier that she was a very special girl that just needed to grow up a bit. She finally had. Tomer used all of his professional self-control to force a broad smile that concealed his broken heart.

At the end of the basketball game, Arik wheeled himself over to Tomer. He hauled himself up out of the wheelchair and hugged Tomer as tightly as he could.

"Tomer! So good to see you! I was wondering when you'd come visit!"

"It took me a while to find you. You have gone into hiding. But you know you cannot hide from me forever!" Tomer smiled. "How do you feel?"

"Every day it gets a bit better. I'm getting stronger. I'm working on a sequel to my Krav Maga film!" Arik smiled. "Dahlia will set me up with a sparring partner!" Arik sat back down in his wheelchair.

"Heaven help the guy that you spar with!"

"How long can you stay?" Arik asked.

"I have some time off, so I want to spend some time here with you guys." Tomer looked at both Arik and Dahlia and smiled. "I clearly have a great deal of catching up to do!"

Arik took Dahlia's hand in his and kissed it. Dahlia leaned over and kissed him on the forehead.

Arik began passing the time between therapy sessions by reading computer textbooks. He was glad that his mind was clearing. The first few months after the war had been such a fog that he barely remembered them. If it wasn't for Dahlia's loving but firm hand, I might have died—or worse, become a replica of Abba.

A week later, he was lifting weights in the gym when Dahlia walked in. She was smiling, but she seemed nervous.

"Boker tov, booba. You have company."

Before Arik could reply, he heard the familiar clop-clop-clop of crutches on the tile floor. He knew. His heart raced.

Abba! Imma!

He saw his father's familiar tired face, his hulking but stooped over posture, and his left pant leg safety-pinned up to his thigh. But unlike the man that Arik was accustomed to, this man's eyes were shining brightly.

"Arik, my boy, Dahlia has told us everything. Thank God you look okay. I'm so proud of you. Apparently, you're quite the hero! Imma and I were heartsick with worry, not having heard from you since before the war. The consulate in LA informed us that you'd been injured, and we wanted to come right away, but Dahlia, who had been writing to us all along, said that it wasn't the right time to see you, so we waited. And waited. Suddenly, late last week, we received a call from the Israeli embassy in Washington that we must come to Israel at once. We thought that something terrible had happened to you. Then, the day before yesterday, two round-trip first-class tickets to Israel on an El Al jumbo jet came by special delivery. So, here we are!"

Arik stood up and rushed into his father's arms.

"I did it all for you, Abba, all for you and nobody else. I came to finish the work you started here. I've grown up, all my life, under a terrible shadow. I couldn't continue my life that way. I've been prepared to give my life to give yours meaning."

Miriam said, "Ze'evi, we did a good job of raising him. We only had one, but we had a good one. How do you feel, Arik? Dahlia told us how badly you were wounded and under what circumstances. You look well, all things considered."

Arik kissed and hugged his mother.

"You always told me I was built like a horse," Arik said. "I knew one day it would come in handy."

He was careful not expose his abdominal and thigh wounds to his parent's eyes.

Ze'ev asked, "Where did you serve, son? Were you in the Golan, Suez . . .?"

"I was up in the Golan, Paratroop Brigade. I went up there about two weeks before it all started and stayed almost to the end of the last Mount Hermon campaign, when I was wounded."

"The weapons today are so much more powerful than in my day. It's a miracle that you survived."

"Many of my friends didn't. It was so awful! Standing next to your friend one minute, the next he's in a hundred pieces in front of your eyes. The thing is, though, in the end it doesn't matter whether you're big or small or weak or strong. Those who survived did so out of plain dumb luck—or Providence, if that's what you believe in. This wasn't like the Six-Day War. So, Abba, who sent you the tickets?"

"You know, Arik, I really have no idea. The envelope simply said, "Israel Embassy, Washington, D.C." There was a small note that said, 'Please come to Israel ASAP. Your son is in Tel HaShomer Hospital recovering from his wounds.'"

"And that's it?"

"That's it! And first-class tickets, no less."

"I wonder who sent that to you . . . It's the strangest thing."

Looking at Dahlia, Miriam said, "I can't begin to thank you for what you've done for Arik. He probably wouldn't have survived if it wasn't for you. And then we'd have nothing left. Nobody should know what it's like to lose an only child. It would be the end of my life if he died."

"Dahlia picked us up from the airport and brought us to our hotel, the Tel Aviv Hilton, right on the beach," Ze'ev said. "Who would have thought that Tel Aviv would change so much in twenty-five years, since I've been here. It's such a beautiful and modern city. They even have a skyscraper." He looked at Dahlia and said, "I have no words for you, my dear. You're a true woman of valor. Arik is so fortunate to have you. Your dedication to him can only be matched by my Miriam's to me."

Dahlia took Arik's hand in her own, kissed it, and smiled. Miriam kissed her on the cheek.

Ze'ev suddenly turned serious. He sat down on a chair next to Arik and spoke in a low voice.

"Dahlia told me that you got a letter from Moshe Dayan, recommending you for an Ott Hagvurah, and you turned it down. Is that true?"

"Yes, Abba. It's true."

"Why in heaven's name would you do such a thing? Very few soldiers ever get picked for such a high honor! You're probably the only person in Israel's history to turn down such a thing. They would never have considered you for this unless you did something extraordinary during the war. It's a big slap in the face to them. I think that it's a very foolish thing to do."

Arik said, "How about those thousands of heroes during the war—wounded or dead—who saved the country from destruction but won't ever get recognized for their sacrifice? Why am I being singled out? It just doesn't make any sense to me."

"It doesn't matter, Arik. The important thing is that they did and you must accept it."

"I can't, Abba. I just can't do it." Arik said softly.

"Why, Arik? Please, tell me why. I want to understand."

Arik took a long, deep breath before speaking.

"It's because of you, Abba. You did something so heroic many years ago, and not only were you not recognized but these same people cast you away like a spent rag, turning your life into a living hell—a hell that was our home and my life for so many years. I came here to beat these people at their own game. The Ott Hagvurah was a perfect opportunity for me to tell them all to go to hell, that I don't value who they are and their stupid awards. These people nearly lost the country six months ago. They would have if it wasn't for the incredible bravery of young men who sacrificed everything to preserve the Jewish State. I hate that ruling clique. I want no part of them. If it wasn't for Dahlia, I'd go back to the USA and never come back here."

"My life is forfeit," Ze'ev said. "I have no idea why I was singled out, why I was treated that way in reward for what I did. But there's no way back from that. This is the hand that I've been dealt, and I've long since run out of tears. I've made peace with my lot in life. If it hadn't been for Miriam, I would have been in the next world many years ago. Look, Arik, whether you accept the award or not will have no bearing on me. I'll still be the same. But for you, it can mean everything. You haven't been to college yet, and you have such a long way to go before you settle down. If you're going to stay here in Israel, and it seems that you are, having this award will open up many doors for you. It will elevate you out of the life that you grew up with. There are no more scholarships waiting for you back home. Please, Arik, accept this award. Do it for me! Let me have the pleasure of seeing you receive it from these people, as you call them. That will be my revenge and redemption."

"Okay, Abba. I will. But just for you. And when I do, I'll give it to you to keep and never even ask to look at it."

"Okay, chaboob sheli!" Ze'ev hugged his son.

***

Dahlia was the first to see them standing in the doorway to the gym. When she did, she felt her blood boil.

"May we come in?" Benny asked quietly. "Shalom, Dahlia. We thought that you would be here. You've scarcely been anywhere else for months."

Benny turned around and gestured for his security entourage to wait outside the door as he and Leah slowly walked into the gym.

Leah gasped when she saw Arik. She had not seen him since the Sabena hijacking, and she barely recognized him now.

"What are you doing here?" Dahlia whispered her father. She was fuming. "I asked you not to come. You haven't been here once since Arik was hurt, and you picked today to show up? The Zohars are here at least once a week."

Ze'ev turned around slowly to look at his old friend. It had been so many years since he had seen him, and Benny had changed a great deal, but Ze'ev recognized his eyes. Everyone in the room froze.

"Shalom, Benny. If I may call you that. Or, if you wish, I can call you, 'Your Excellency, Mr. Foreign Minister.' You've done very well for yourself over the years, I must say. How may we be of service to you?"

Benny, for once in his life, was at complete loss for words. He was always in control, in every situation in his life. He usually was the one giving orders. He was a man with few peers. He generally was the one who was praised and fawned over. But now he was standing in front of a hunched over, broken man who was quietly, with an emotionless serenity that unnerved Benny, looking straight through him and into his soul.

Ze'ev raised his index finger to make a point. "If you're here to nudge Arik to receive the Ott Hagvurah, you don't have to bother. He has changed his mind. He will accept the award. You can go tell Dayan and the rest of your ruling clique."

Ze'ev swung his crutches around in preparation to walk away. "Now, if you'll excuse us? I have nothing more to say to you. I saved your miserable life, Benny. We were friends for years, in the Palmach. You watched me go down in flames, and you never lifted a finger to help me. All these years! You're a very treacherous friend indeed. Please, go. Leave me and my family in peace."

"May I have your permission to say one thing before I go?"

"Speak."

"I have a letter here from Prime Minister Golda Meir, requesting your presence at her office in Jerusalem at 10 a.m. tomorrow morning."

"Why? What does she need from me? So, this explains the El Al tickets and the hotel. Just tell her that I'm a broken old man who just wants to be left alone. Now, leave me alone!"

"Please, Ze'ev, please. I know that you have every right to hate me, but things can be set right."

"What things? What can you possibly say to me now that would make anything right?"

"Now isn't the time and place. Not in front of the children."

"What are you talking about, in front of the children?"

"In front of Arik and my daughter, Dahlia."

Time stood still.

"Dahlia is your daughter?" Ze'ev turned and stared at her in complete surprise. He looked at Arik. "Arik, you knew this all this time and never mentioned a word to me or Imma. Not for years! Why didn't you say anything? I just don't know what to say!" He turned very pale. "Miriam, please get me a glass of water. I feel like I've been betrayed all over again! Benny, of course you knew all along about who Arik was. It must have been very difficult for you to interact with him. You were probably glad to get rid of me when I left Israel for the States. I undoubtedly gave you a guilty conscience. Then, bad luck for you, my son showed up. The good Lord certainly has a sense of humor." Ze'ev laughed sardonically.

"Arik has been like a son to me, too!" Benny said.

Dahlia wanted to wring her father's neck. She took a deep breath and shook her head in disgust. Arik stared down at the floor.

Finally, Arik said, "Abba, I didn't want to hurt you. When Dahlia and I began to see each other, I had no idea her father was connected to you. I didn't find that out until eighteen months ago and, by then, Dahlia and I weren't together anymore. I thought the matter was over and there was no point in bringing it up just to hurt you. Dahlia didn't come back into my life until I was wounded in the war. So, you see, there was no way Dahlia and I could've helped solve your problem, because we were no longer in touch. Then the war came, and there was no—"

Dahlia was hiding her face in her hands, afraid of what she was witnessing. She knew that Arik was right. If they were to get back together, truly, this day of reckoning had to come. She too had hoped that between the two of them they would have solved Ze'ev's problem by now.

"What problem, Arik? Have you figured out how to grow me a new leg?"

"Please Ze'ev," Benny said, "don't involve the children. They're entirely innocent here. They can only be accused of loving each other. This is between us. Everything will become clear tomorrow."

"Who will be there?" Ze'ev asked.

"Golda, Yitzhak, Moshe, Raful, Shimon, you, and me."

"Am I being put on trial? What have I done to deserve this? What is this all about? Tell me!"

"Please, Ze'ev, not now. You've waited for twenty-five years. Please, wait one more night. I swear to you that everything will become clear tomorrow. The prime minister has arranged for her personal limousine to pick you up from the hotel at 8 a.m."

***

Dahlia followed her parents out the door and then pulled her father into a corner, asking her mother to leave them for a few minutes.

She whispered, "Part of this whole reconciliation is your coming clean with Arik. The time has finally come. You'll get no better shot at this."

"What are you talking about, Dahlia?"

"There's one more secret that you haven't shared with Arik—or me, for that matter. I discovered it while working on a hunch."

"I'm sorry, Dahlia, but I really don't know what you're talking about."

"Don't you? After I found out about our correspondence being intercepted by his base commander, I decided to check whether his phone calls to me at that time were diverted as well. It took a great deal of prodding, but I was able to get the truth out of Efraim, your chargé d'affaires at the embassy. I then got confirmation from Tzippy, who I tracked down in Kfar Saba."

"Please, Dahlia."

"Did Arik try to call the embassy on numerous occasions during the period between Sukkot of 1970 and Pesach of 1971? Answer me truthfully. Yes or no? Is that why you changed the phone number at the residence?"

"What difference does it make now?"

"It makes a great deal of difference to me, Abba. It makes a great deal of difference to Arik and me. I'm fully committed to him, and I won't have this hanging over our heads. Now, did he or did he not try to contact me?"

"It's true. He did, on several occasions. I never passed on his messages to you, because I felt that he wasn't good enough for you. But I have lived to regret my decision so many times, Dahlia. I saw what that criminal Ehrenreich did to you, to our family. I almost lost you when you overdosed. I also did everything I could to keep our family from being publicly shamed during your time in the rehab center. When you were going through hell during your tironut, I knew all about it as it was occurring—through channels—but I kept my silence, because I felt that it was good for you, that it would turn you back into a mensch. As painful as that experience was for you, I felt that it was my responsibility to you. I think that they call it tough love in the States. In reality, it was I who needed to be turned into a mensch! I was too embarrassed to admit all this to you—what I had done.

"I saw how Arik became a national hero in Israel. As you well know, Imma unfortunately had to see up close what heroism Arik was capable of, during the Sabena affair. Very few people will ever know the full extent of the service and sacrifice that Arik has given to our country, before and during the war, and how many Israelis are alive today because of him. I felt so guilty about what happened to you to during the Olympics. I thought that somehow your brush with death was divine retribution for my misdeeds. When I saw you in that hospital bed in Munich, I felt my world caving in, especially after what had just happened to Imma.

"Don't think for one second that all of this with Arik and his father hasn't been eating me up alive, from the inside, for years. I have been living on ulcer pills after a terrible episode of vomiting blood that landed me at Beilinson Hospital one night. I created a terrible mess in our lives, and I just haven't been able to figure out a way to make things right. I haven't come here to see Arik sooner, because I couldn't face him. You already had told me that he knew everything. What could I have said to him? I had no way of making things right without destroying our family—"

"When Arik didn't turn up at Aunt Ruti's that Sukkot, I looked high and low for him," Dahlia said. "I came home only because Imma told me that you'd help find him and let me know what had happened to him. I kept asking you if Arik was okay. I was in the depths of despair. I was so worried about him. I thought that something terrible had happened to him. You told me that you'd checked on him and he was okay. Was that a lie, too? It was, wasn't it? You never checked on him, did you? Did you? And I'll venture a guess that the reason why you changed the phone number at the residence was because Arik had tried to call several times and, lucky for you, I happened to be out at the time. But you weren't going to take a chance that he'd catch me at home. Were you? It had nothing to do with security or any phone threats."

Benny looked down to the ground, ashen-faced, and nodded.

"Does Imma know about all this? What you did?"

"No. To this day, she doesn't."

"Oh, Abba! How could you do this? How? You have much to atone for, Abba. Tomorrow, you'll try to correct an old injustice that you perpetrated on Arik's father. But you need to resolve matters with Arik, too. Don't you see why he doesn't want the medal? So many people have caused him and his family so much pain that he finds even an Ott Hagvurah to be a pitiful attempt to right a wrong. He feels that it doesn't even come close to addressing the main issues in his life. He's lost the most important person in his life. He loved Mikki, and she loved him. A medal will never restore Arik to what he once was or give back to him what he once had, and he knows that well. He couldn't care less about a medal. I've struggled so hard over the last six months to repair our relationship, a relationship that never should have been broken. Our letters were intercepted by his base commander, driving us apart needlessly, and your terrible actions completed the process.

"Abba, you'll have your chance tomorrow. The only way forward is for you to tell everyone the truth. No more lies, no more deception. This business with Arik's father will, hopefully, be finished at long last. Sit down with Arik and, for the first time, open up to him, man to man. He's earned that. He wants that so much more than a silly ribbon on his chest. Tell him the truth about everything. Bare your soul to him. He deserves it. What's more important, for God's sake, is to ask him for his forgiveness. Do the right thing, Abba.

"You have no idea of the deep affection and respect that Shmulik and Yael Zohar have for Arik. He became another son to them after we threw him into the street. They immediately saw Arik for the person he is, which is far more than I can say for us. Only a miracle brought Arik and me back together again, and it at such a terrible cost to the Zohars. Erase this mark of shame from our family. Do it tomorrow."

"I will, my sweet and wise daughter. Tomorrow." Benny sighed and walked away to rejoin Leah.

Dahlia turned around and walked back into the gym, where Arik and his parents were waiting.

Ze'ev gestured to Miriam. "I'm very tired, Miriam. I need to go back to the hotel to rest. All this has been too much for me. My own son . . ." He got up to walk out, straining against his forearm crutches.

"I'll take you back to the hotel," Dahlia said.

"Stay here, Dahlia," Tomer said. "I've already arranged for my security detail to escort them."

She whispered to Tomer, "Please, see to it that when that limo picks them up in the morning, I'm in it."

"I will," he promised.

In a moment, Arik and Dahlia were alone.

Arik yawned and stretched out his arms. "I thought it all went rather well. Don't you?"

They locked eyes and then, relieved that the inevitable confrontation was over, burst into raucous laughter.

Chapter 33

The next morning, a black Mercedes limousine pulled up to the curb in front of the Tel Aviv Hilton. Two tall, muscular men with shaven heads, wearing dark sunglasses and earpieces, leaped from the front seats. A frail, middle-aged couple were waiting at the curb. Ze'ev Meir, completely spent from his emotional ordeal of the previous day, had been unable to sleep. Because he lacked the strength to propel himself with his forearm crutches, he was sitting in a wheelchair. Miriam, equally upset and pale, wheeled him to the limousine.

"Ze'ev Meir?" one of the men asked.

"Ken. Yes," Ze'ev said quietly.

The man gently lifted Ze'ev and settled him into the backseat. To Ze'ev's astonishment, Dahlia was sitting there, waiting for them and smiling.

"What are you doing here, Dahlia?" Miriam asked.

"I've decided to come along to make sure that both of you have a very good day."

Ze'ev took her hand and smiled. "I'm feeling much better, just seeing you."

She gave him a big hug.

"Do you know why I'm being called to Jerusalem?" Ze'ev asked. "I feel like I'm going to be put on trial, like I've done something wrong. But I'm the one who has been wronged."

"You have been wronged. Perhaps they're calling you in to apologize for what they did to you."

"From your mouth to God's ears." He laughed, before turning serious again. "But I'm not certain that I'm ready to forgive them."

As they traveled eastward along Highway 1, Ze'ev looked at the green road signs that said "Jerusalem" in Hebrew, English, and Arabic. The green coastal plain gradually gave way to barren, rolling foothills dotted with shrubs and large boulders. The cloudless sky was bright blue and the air was crisp on that spring morning. After they passed the Latrun Junction, the road narrowed and was flanked by high, cut-out stone cliffs. Ze'ev looked in wonderment at the ordinary civilian traffic that lazily snaked its way up the winding four-lane highway. They entered the tight Sha'ar HaGai Pass through the Judean Hills, and he spied the rusted hulks of the armored vehicles that littered the side of the road as a memorial to the '48 war. When he saw an armored bus, he felt a sharp pang in his gut and his heart skipped a beat.

"Look, Dahlia! Look at those buses! Those are the vehicles that we used to break the blockade, to bring desperately needed food and arms into the city. Oy! How many of my friends were lost right here in Bab el Wad as the Arabs shelled death onto our heads right in this spot. Do you see that bus with the slits as windows? It was in such a bus that your father was riding when he was hit with that mortar shell. It's a miracle that any of us made it through. We eventually broke the blockade, during Operation Nachshon at the end of March 1948, but at such a heavy cost. I saw my best friends blown up into bits right in front of my eyes. I fought in Deir Muheisin, along with your father. Driving the Arabs out of their positions there was the first step in opening the road to the city. It's so strange for me now to be here and see a beautiful road clogged with ordinary Israeli traffic going to Jerusalem without a care in the world. I might as well be looking at traffic on the San Diego Freeway, in La Jolla."

"None of this would have been possible without your sacrifice," Dahlia said. "Nobody can restore you back to health, but never think that what you did was for nothing. Look around. You should be enormously proud of what you did."

As they approached the city, the road sign for the Kastel exit appeared ahead on the right.

"This is where I lost my leg, trying to save your father."

"I know. I know," Dahlia whispered.

As they entered the city, Ze'ev and Miriam gazed at the sheer expanse and size of the city. They saw the under=construction new Jewish neighborhood called Ramot, off to the left on the distant hills.

"Is all this in our hands?" Miriam asked Dahlia.

"Yes, as far as the eye can see," Dahlia said, looking north toward Nebi Samuel, the Tomb of Samuel, in the distance, "and many miles more, since the Six-Day War."

"The last time that we were here, we could access the city only through a tiny corridor flanked by barbed wire and Jordanian snipers," Miriam said.

"They're all gone now. Now our big worry is the traffic that chokes the road. It would be lovely if we could have a big underground highway that would go north–south so that we could rapidly access all parts of the city. Or even a trolley system that could easily get someone from here to the Old City in minutes. Perhaps someday," Dahlia mused aloud.

The limousine went up Ruppin Road, turned right, and then pulled up in front of a large complex constructed of familiar Jerusalem stone. They had arrived at the Knesset building.

Waved in by knowing nods from the gate sentries, the limousine entered the walled complex, which was surrounded by barbed wire and heavily armed troops. A small sign in front of a nondescript building said, "OFFICE OF THE PRIME MINISTER."

One of the men in the front of the limousine gently assisted Ze'ev out of the car and wheeled him down a long corridor. Dahlia and Miriam followed behind. They were met by the prime minister's aide, Freuka Porat, who led them past a glass-enclosed office space called the aquarium and into the prime minister's conference room, a large, wood-paneled room adorned with multiple maps of the Middle East and a large portrait of Theodor Herzl.

Freuka offered them refreshments, but no one was in the mood to eat or drink.

"I can't bear what's about to happen," Miriam said.

"I'll stay here with him and make sure that no harm comes to him. Don't worry," Dahlia said.

"You're an angel, Dahlia." Miriam kissed her and went outside to wait in the anteroom, as she had been directed.

In a few minutes, the door opposite them opened. In walked a very distinguished entourage. Benny came first, followed a bald man with a familiar black eye patch. Ze'ev recognized his old commander Rabin behind them. He was followed by Raful Eitan and a lean, gray-haired gentleman whom Ze'evi recognized as Shimon Peres. Ze'ev had met Peres several times during his Palmach days, but the years had changed them all. Finally, a grandmotherly woman with familiar wavy hair set in a bun entered the room. Ze'ev tried to rise from his wheelchair, as a show of respect.

Golda Meir smiled brightly at him. "Please sit, Ze'ev. There is no need to get up."

The room was quickly filling with smoke from Golda's and Yitzhak's chain smoking.

Benny discreetly walked up to Dahlia.

"What are you doing here?" he whispered to her.

"I'm here to make damn sure that you behave yourself." Dahlia gave him a hard, unflinching look.

Benny stared at her and smiled slightly, proud of what she had become. For a brief moment, the path that she almost had taken flashed through his mind.

"I'm afraid to say, Dahlia, that you've become like your father," he said.

Dahlia smiled slightly.

"Come, Benny," Golda said. "Let us begin. Shalom, Dahlia. How is the army treating you?"

"Very well, Madame Prime Minister. Unfortunately, Tel HaShomer Hospital is still too busy."

"You are quite right," Golda said, smiling sadly.

Having taken a seat, Benny said to Golda, "I've brought something to show you."

"We'll look at it after we've had a chance to speak to Ze'ev Myerowitz," Golda said evenly.

Moshe Dayan turned to Ze'ev and said, "You're probably wondering why we asked you to join us here."

Ze'ev nodded.

"So, I'd like to review, if you don't mind, the events of the days and weeks leading up to the day that you were injured. What was the date of your injury?"

"I joined the Palmach upon my arrival in Israel in 1946, with the Aliyah Bet. At the end of March 1948, I was deployed from Camp Jonah and, on April 1st, we moved up to Kibbutz Hulda, which became the staging operation for the attack on Na'ana. Most of us fell back to Hulda after we occupied Na'ana, and the following day we assaulted Deir Muheisin as part of what became known as Operation Nachshon."

Yitzhak was taking careful notes of Ze'ev's story.

"On April 7th, I and a few dozen Palmachnikim were detached from the main group and told to load armored trucks and buses with brand-new rifles, machine guns, and mortars, along with about fifty thousand rounds of ammunition. The munitions had just come into Tel Aviv by way of the USS Nora that had run the British blockade. I was placed under the command of General Rabin here, in the Harel Brigade. We were to take back roads up to

Kastel, to reinforce the brigade there, under Mordechai Gazit, that was hanging on to Kastel by their teeth, having repulsed four Arab assaults. They were dangerously low on ammunition and were down to about seventy men. We managed to make it through by the morning of the 8th, and we took up positions with them. When the Arabs discovered that we had killed their leader, Abd al-Qadir, the night before, they went crazy and began an all-out assault on our position in the village. The Arabs had nearly one thousand troops under Abu Dayieh. They were partially made up of the regular Jordanian Army and British deserters, but most were irregulars from surrounding villages. They came at us all at once, and we were nearly overrun. Gazit ordered a tactical retreat out of the village, trying to save our new weapons and ammunition. Those who couldn't leave were taken prisoner. They were all killed, and their bodies were mutilated."

Ze'ev paused to wipe away a few tears.

"We had loaded up an armored bus with all the ammunition and the spare guns. There were five boys and a driver on that bus. I was following behind in an open Jeep, manning the machine gun. We were at the outskirts of Kastel when mass confusion set in. We got separated from the others, and we fell under a heavy mortar barrage. The bus in front of me took a direct hit and burst into flames. My Jeep driver was killed instantly, by flying shrapnel."

The room was silent. Everyone was listening raptly to Ze'ev's retelling of what had happened on that fateful day.

"I heard screams coming from the bus. I ran over and couldn't open the door. The heat had jammed the mechanism and the door handle was burning hot."

Ze'ev held out his hands, which were still scarred from the third-degree burns that he had sustained. "I was eventually able to tear the door open. I pulled Benny Gilad out first, then the other four, and carried them over to the side of the road, all the while trying to avoid the mortar shells that were still coming down on our heads. I was running back to the bus, to pull the driver out, when the ammunition inside ignited and the bus exploded. The last thing that I remember is a white-hot flash and being thrown into the air. I woke up in the hospital, without a leg."

"Ze'ev, do you recognize the foreign minister?" Raful asked.

"Will all due respect, General Eitan, please don't treat me like a child or a senile old man," Ze'ev said testily. "Benny and I were comrades for two years. We trained day and night together, got burned in the hot sun together, got soaked in the mud together, froze at night on guard duty together, marched together, shared secrets together, went on leave and chased girls in Tel Aviv together. We were like brothers. When I was nearly killed saving his life, though, he broke off all contact with me. I was cut off, without a lira from the government. I was homeless, literally begging in the street. Benny was raised up after the war, celebrated as a hero. He has made quite a career for himself. And he never raised even a finger to help me or contact me." Ze'ev pointed his finger at Benny and shouted, red-faced now, "Is this how friends behave? Shame on you!"

Dahlia felt a wave of nausea hit her.

Yitzhak asked, "From the time you came to Israel, did you ever make contact with the Irgun or Lechi? When you were in Poland, you attended rallies held by Jabotinsky before the war, and you were a bit of a follower."

"That's true, but when I got to Israel, though I had considered joining the Irgun I saw that they were mainly fighting the British. I was liberated by the British in Bergen-Belsen, and I couldn't bring myself to fight them. I was grateful to them. When I passed the physical fitness test, I was seen as a good fighting prospect, so I was accepted to the Palmach, where I could fight Arabs, who I felt were the real enemy."

Shimon asked, "What do you know about Deir Yassin, Ze'evi?"

"It was a terrible business. I believe that it occurred at the same time as our battle at Kastel and only three or four kilometers away. I read about it in that awful book Perfidy by Ben Hecht. Frankly, what was even more despicable about the affair was the cover-up. The incident has been practically erased from popular history. Is this even taught in schools?"

Golda shifted uncomfortably in her chair.

"Ze'ev, would you please leave us for a few moments?" Moshe asked.

Dahlia wheeled him out, leaving him with Miriam, and returned to stand quietly in the corner of the conference room.

Golda motioned to Freuka and whispered, "Please have Menachem join us."

Soon, a thin, bald, bespectacled man with an intense expression on his face entered the conference room through the side door.

The deep enmity between Menachem Begin and the Labor Party elite was very well known. In Knesset debates, Ben-Gurion did not even dignify Begin's presence, instead referring to him as "the man sitting next to Dr. Bader." However, after Ben-Gurion retired to Sde Boker in the Negev and then Begin joined the national emergency government on the eve of the Six-Day War in 1967, the deep hostility began to thaw, at least somewhat. Labor Party leaders at least spoke to Begin then. Although it would have been inconceivable for Ben-Gurion to invite Begin to a meeting like this one, Golda could do so. Indeed, since Menachem was head of the opposition party, Golda saw briefing him about national emergencies and other private matters as part of her job.

"Shalom, Menachem," Golda said. "Good of you to come. We are trying to right a great wrong."

"How can I help?" he asked.

"Who was Ze'ev Myerowitz?" Golda asked.

"Ze'ev was one of my best lieutenants. He led the raid on Acre Prison, to free our prisoners, and he was one of the men who infiltrated the King David Hotel and placed the bombs. He and I parted ways when he went out on his own with a group of Irgun and Lechi fighters to carry out the massacre at Deir Yassin. I completely disapproved of the mission at the time, but in retrospect it had the desired effect."

Dahlia felt a burning pain in the pit of her stomach but maintained her outward composure.

The same could not be said of Yitzhak Rabin, who said loudly, "Which was?"

"Frightening the Arabs out of their homes, thus depriving the Mufti of the irregular fighters that he needed to slaughter our convoys, including the Haganah forces protecting them." Menachem's voice rose steadily as he explained. "Deir Yassin saved countless Jewish lives. No more Jews to the slaughter like sheep!"

"They were murderers who slaughtered innocent women and children and brought the wrath of the Arabs down on us," Yitzhak said.

"If it wasn't for the Irgun, everyone in this room would still be answering to the British Lord High Commissioner!"

"You give yourself too much credit, Menachem," Moshe said. "Our blood was as red as yours. The Haganah died by the thousands so that we could all be sitting here. You can tell your fairy tales to the people of Gush Etsyon and the medical staff of Hadassah who were killed in revenge for Deir Yassin!"

"Until you turned your guns on your fellow Jews on the Altalena. You, Yitzhak, gave the order!" Menachem pointed a finger at him accusingly. "If it wasn't for me and my unwillingness to point a gun against a fellow Jew, despite what you did to us, we would have had a civil war! I urged my fighters to become members of the new Israel Defense Force rather than fight on alone. Don't kid yourselves. Most did so because they were following my direct orders and not for any love of the Haganah."

"Enough!" Golda shouted. "We've been through this a thousand times. We did not come here today to debate Israeli history. We are here for a very special reason . . . Menachem, what happened to Ze'ev Myerowitz after Deir Yassin?"

"I was furious with him about the incident, and I wanted him out of Palestine, so I assigned him the task of organizing the arms shipment from France aboard the Altalena. When the ship was shelled by Rabin's assassins, off the coast of Tel Aviv, Ze'ev refused to leave his post. He was a good soldier. He died on board, but his body was never found."

"Are you certain that Ze'ev died?" Moshe asked. "Perhaps he was injured and survived? Could he have survived and just sustained a leg amputation?"

"Not to my knowledge," Menachem said.

Golda motioned to Dahlia that she should bring Ze'ev back into the room.

When Ze'ev returned, he and Menachem locked eyes.

Golda asked Menachem, "Do you know this man?"

He looked long and hard at Ze'ev. Suddenly a look of recognition dawned on his face. "My God. I never thought you survived!"

Everyone in the room held their breath. Dahlia felt as if the room were beginning to swim. *Was I wrong all along? Was Arik wrong about his father all along? Has Ze'ev been living a lie? Or worse, did Arik know all along and lie to me? But even if Ze'ev was part of the Irgun, so what! Menachem Begin himself, the master terrorist who was ultimately responsible for all of the terrorism back then, including Deir Yassin, is allowed to lead the right-wing Revisionist Party. Begin could even become prime minister one day if the current government* falters. Why should Ze'ev be the fall guy for the whole debacle, when nobody else ever got prosecuted for it?

Dahlia felt a silent scream fill her lungs.

Menachem stared intensely at Ze'ev, and then he asked, "Czy mówisz po polsku?" (Do you speak Polish?)

"Ja robię," (I do,) Ze'ev said tentatively.

"Czy ty się ze Lwów?" (Are you from Lwów?)

"Tak jestem. Skąd wiesz, kim jestem? Czy kiedykolwiek spotkał?" (Yes, I am. How do you know who I am? Have we ever met?)

"Nie. Ale wiem o was. Każdy w Polsce wie o tobie. Byliście wielkim bohaterem dla nas wszystkich. Byłem tam w Warszawie, przy drodze krajowej bokserskim meczu mistrzostw, kiedy zniszczył Stanisław Kowalski uchwycić tytuł. Byliśmy wszyscy bardzo dumni z was dumny z bycia Żydem. Bóg jeden wie, mieliśmy trochę do dumy zaledwie rok później." (No. But I know about you. Everyone in Poland knew about you. You were a great hero to all of us. I was there in Warsaw, at the national boxing championship match when you destroyed Stanisław Kowalski to capture the title. We were all so proud of you, proud to be Jewish. Heaven knows, we had little to be proud of just a year later.)

"Zgadzam się." (I agree.)

"Ostatnim, że słyszałem, że zostali uwięzieni w łódzkim getcie. Byłem pewien że nie przeżyje." (The last that I heard you were trapped in the Lodz Ghetto. I was certain that you didn't survive.)

"Przetrwanie obozów było mi łatwiej niż to, co stało się później, kiedy tu przyjechałem." (Surviving the camps was easier for me than what happened later, when I came here.)

Moshe said, "What's going on now?"

Yitzhak said, "Why are you speaking in Polish? What are you hiding?"

Menachem smiled. "I'm not hiding anything! Do you know who this man was?"

"No!" Golda said. "But we are all dying to find out! That is why we are all here, for God's sake! So, you know him? Wait." She turned to Dahlia and whispered, "Please, take Mr. Myerowitz outside again for a few minutes."

Dahlia did as she was told, but she felt heartsick. Was Arik's father an Irgun terrorist, after all?

Dahlia returned to the room quietly, scared of what she was about to find out.

Menachem said, "I didn't know him. I knew of him. This man is Wolf Myerowitz! I was fascinated by his career when I lived in Poland before the war. He was the middleweight boxing champion of Poland in 1938. Imagine a Jew being able to do that. He was undefeated in thirty bouts with goyim! He made his way up through the Maccabi sports system and eventually became a professional boxer. He was the pride and joy of the Jewish community, even the Hassidim, who were so used to getting beaten up by the Poles. The called him Wilk, the Wolf! Here was a Jew who could give it back to the Poles in spades! Wolf was my hero!

"I was at the title fight against the reigning Polish boxing champion, Stanisław Kowalski. They fought to a packed arena in Warsaw. When Wolf knocked out Kowalski in ten rounds, the place erupted. Fights broke out between the Jews and the Poles. The fighting spread, and by week's end there were pogroms all over Poland. It was after that incident that I left Poland for good. The last that I heard of him was that he was trapped in the Lodz Ghetto. I assumed that he was killed in the camps. I never dreamed that I would see him again!"

Yitzhak put his cigarette in the ashtray next to him, flicked his wrist, and asked, point blank in a dry, emotionless voice, "Menachem, did this man serve under your command in the Irgun? Yes or no."

"What? Absolutely not! This is the first—Oh, my God. Is this man being accused of being involved in the Deir Yassin affair? It has just occurred to me that they have the same name. I never associated the two men. He was Wolf, the other one Ze'ev. Wolf means Ze'ev in Hebrew. Has there been a mix-up because of the similarity in their names?

Golda asked Dahlia to bring Ze'ev back into the room.

When they Dahlia wheeled Ze'ev in again, Golda said, "Menachem, look at this man. How can you be sure that this is not the man who served under you in the Irgun?"

"It's just not possible!" Menachem said. "The Ze'ev who served under me was a small, wiry, dark man with the darkest brown eyes you ever saw and jet-black curly hair. I always said that he looked like the devil. He had a bit of the devil in him, which suited us just fine. The gentleman in front of me has graying blond hair and blue eyes. The man in front of me never served under my command. I knew all my men very well. They were like family to me." He pointed an accusing finger at Yitzhak and shouted, "My Ze'evaleh was murdered by you on the Altalena!"

"How dare you, Menachem! Your criminal gang would have brought down all the Yishuv! I did the right thing!" Yitzhak shouted back at him.

"Only God will decide if you did the right thing! One day you will be judged Yitzhak!"

"Enough! Enough!" Golda yelled. "We have a man's life at stake! Stop bickering like a pair of hens!"

Menachem looked at Ze'ev and said, "Wolf, I hope that whatever this terrible confusion has caused gets resolved soon." He turned to the prime minister. "Golda, I must go. I'm late for this morning's Knesset debate."

"Thank you very much for coming, Menachem," she said.

He got up and was escorted out of the room.

Benny looked at Rabin. "Yitzhak, do you recall my pleading with you, on numerous occasions, to validate my report of the battle, how I said all along that this Ze'ev saved my life and the lives of four other men and that he was no terrorist? You told me to keep my mouth shut if I knew what was good for me. You suppressed my report. You put a gag order on me to prevent me from discussing this with anyone, including Ze'ev. Why, Yitzhak? Why?"

Rabin shifted uncomfortably in his seat. "I passed the report to the old man, who tore it up and threatened me with the consequences of filing a false report. This Ze'ev's file was nowhere to be found. All we had to go by was a dossier on the other Ze'ev." He picked up a worn brown folder. "Ben-Gurion swore that he'd bring that Butcher of Deir Yassin to justice. When he heard that Ze'ev was severely wounded, he assumed that it occurred during the shelling of the Altalena."

Ze'ev slowly stood up, trembling and struggling to hold his body weight on his forearm crutches. "Do you mean to tell me that my whole life has been wrecked because of a mix-up of names? That I was sent into the street like a dog and made to live a life of poverty and misery, begging for grushim, homeless, sitting in the filth of the Old Bus Station in Tel Aviv, and for years living on my brother's charity, all because of Ben-Gurion's close-mindedness? Benny, you knew all along? Why didn't you do anything after he left power?"

"I brought it up again and again afterward," Benny said, "but at that point nobody wanted to hear anything more about Deir Yassin or the Altalena. It fell on deaf ears. I'm so sorry, Ze'ev. I'm so sorry for not persisting even longer, for as long as it took . . ."

Golda looked intently at Benny and said, "You said before that you had something to show us."

"Ze'ev, there wasn't a day that this didn't eat me up inside, but I felt powerless to help you. I prayed that something would come along that would finally bring this to light. Yesterday, after we met, I recalled that our Palmach battalion commander kept a diary. I went to his widow in Kiryat Shmuel, on the off chance that she might have kept it and that it might have something helpful in it."

Benny produced an old, handwritten journal. He handed it to Golda, pointing out the entries from those fateful days in early April 1948.

In silence, Golda slowly thumbed through the brittle, yellowed pages. She suddenly stopped.

"Ze'ev Myerowitz's heroism on the second day of the battle and his injury are clearly described here. Ze'ev is mentioned by name and so are the names of those who he saved . . . including yours, Benny," Golda said.

With tears in his eyes, Benny looked at Ze'ev and said, in a faltering voice, "We were brothers then, and I want to be your brother again more than anything . . . this time for the rest of our lives."

Moshe smiled at Ze'ev. "Ze'ev, your son, Arik, is an extraordinary young man. His actions, along with those of other men like him, saved this country. He, too, is a hero of Israel. I guess the apple doesn't fall far from the tree. He so deserves the honor that we want to bestow on him. It is the least that we can do. But he refuses it."

"Because of the injustice that was done to me. He was born into a bitter and angry home, and he swore when he came here that he would finish what I had started. He didn't come here out of any love for Zion. He was raised to hate everything that I came from. He saw the world through my eyes. He wanted nothing to do with Judaism even. It was just a quirk of fate that drew him back to Jewish life and Israel."

Recognition was dawning on the others around the table. Dahlia blushed.

Raful said, "We all know Arik's dossier. He was quite the hero before he set foot on our shores for the first time. He was clearly destined for greatness."

Ze'ev said, "When that happened, that incident in LA, he decided to go to Israel despite the tremendous opportunity that he had to go to college. He turned down a full basketball scholarship to UCLA, the national basketball champions, to come here to fight in the army. He did it, as Dahlia told me today, to possibly clear my disgraced name . . . and he was nearly killed for it."

Golda said, "We cannot undo what was done to you over the past twenty-five years, but you have my word that I will sign an executive order to give you every lira in compensation that you should have received since April 1948, with all applicable interest. And you will receive all benefits afforded to Nechei Tzahal, our wounded warriors. You also have never received any commendations for your valor and bravery under fire." She looked at Moshe. "We will make sure that all is set to rights." She walked over to Ze'ev and kissed him on the cheek. "Thank you for all that you have done for the State of Israel and the Jewish people. And thank you for sending Arik to us."

Everyone rose from the table and saluted Ze'ev.

Ze'ev said, "I just don't know what to say."

Golda said, "There is nothing that you need to say. Your actions and those of your son have said everything that ever needs to be said. Thank you again, from the bottom of our hearts. I hope that you can find it in your heart to forgive us."

Dahlia wheeled Ze'ev out of the conference room, Benny following behind. Miriam and Leah were waiting in the anteroom.

Ze'ev turned to Benny and sighed. "We're going to have to find a way to get past all of this and move on, Benny. Regardless of what has occurred between us, we are now tightly bound because of our children's love for each other. We have our children to cherish, and they have their whole lives in front of them. Please, let's not dwell in the past anymore. We aren't getting any younger, and holding grudges is more corrosive to those who hold them. I don't want to be bitter anymore. I have been angry for so many years. All that I ask for is some peace of mind."

"You're quite correct, Ze'ev. I have made such a mess of everything. And I know that it will take a long time to forgive a lifetime of betrayal, but I hope and pray that we can resume our friendship so that we can truly become one family. We're brothers. My home is your home for always." He handed his house keys to Ze'ev. "These are yours to keep and use anytime you please." He hugged Ze'ev tightly.

***

"What happened in Jerusalem? You guys were gone almost the whole day!" Arik asked when Dahlia walked into his room at the rehab unit.

She jumped into his arms, smothering his face in kisses. Behind her followed an entourage: Benny, wheeling Ze'ev, followed by Miriam and Leah.

"Arik! We did it! We did it!" Dahlia said. The words could barely tumble out of her mouth quickly enough. She breathlessly gave Arik an account of all that had happened at the prime minister's office.

Benny nodded at Tomer who, on cue, reached into a cabinet and pulled out a bottle of champagne and glasses for everyone.

"This calls for a L'Chaim!" Benny said.

Holding his glass, Arik said, "Hmm . . . I guess I'll have to accept the medal now, after all!"

Everyone laughed.

"We'll have something to tell our children and grandchildren," Dahlia whispered into Arik's ear, hugging his neck from behind.

Arik held her arms and smiled.

Arik and Dahlia had been looking forward to the trip to Washington, D.C. This was the first time opportunity that they had had to get away since the two children had been born. Now that the children were school-aged, Savta Leah and Savta Miriam felt comfortable taking care of them. Doing so even gave Savta Miriam a sense of purpose and comfort after Ze'ev's passing. Saba Benny was constantly shuttling to the Knesset, so he generally was unavailable.

Arik had not been back to Washington, D.C. since Sukkot nearly thirteen years earlier. During the flight, memories of that time flooded into his consciousness. As the El Al 747 circled above the U.S. Capitol in preparation for landing at Dulles Airport, Arik looked out the window at the Washington Monument and the Lincoln Memorial. He was transported back those golden days in the fall of 1969, so early in his and Dahlia's relationship, when they had spent a blissful ten days together, walking hand in hand on the National Mall at the end of a perfect day of sightseeing. Those memories were followed by darker ones, of Pesach the following year and events that still, on occasion, triggered terrible, nauseating waves of grief for him. Arik shifted uncomfortably in his seat.

"What are you thinking about, motek?" Dahlia asked. "You seem nervous and distracted. Are you okay? Is your leg bothering you? It always seems to on long flights, especially when you're under stress."

"I'm fine," Arik said as he turned to her and smiled. "I'm just a bit nervous about tonight. Alexei and I have been working on this project for about three years now and, despite all our research, I really have no firm idea whether any of the Silicon Valley companies have come this far with display technologies and microprocessor memory platforms. There's so much that these new start-up companies hold back that you don't know if you're innovating on their work or just copying them. Everyone is so afraid of tipping their hand too soon. They're afraid that someone else will come in and render their work obsolete before they can bring their product to market. Things are moving so fast now. The whole thing is such a shell game."

She held his hand. "You've been through this a hundred times with Alexei over the past few months. All the due diligence has been done. There is nothing more that you could have done. All that you need to do is meet the right people, smile a lot, shake the right hands, and it will flow from there. You'll do fine, Arik." She kissed him.

"I hope that the economic attaché at the embassy did his job corralling the right people for us to meet and show our products to. The America–Israel Chamber of Commerce and Israel Bond receptions don't quite seem like the right forums for this. I feel like I'll be competing with Jaffa orange growers and hummus salesmen for attention. I can't believe there aren't specific technology-based trade groups we can hook up with."

"Abba has already assured us that there will be plenty of technology nerds for you to interact with. Don't worry so much," she said.

He tickled her side. "So, that's what I am to you, my little kitten? A nerd? Eh?"

She giggled. "Only when you're so nervous. You're being silly, booba. You can walk right into a wall of tank fire directed straight at your chest without flinching, but you're afraid of a room full of fat, well-meaning American Jews sipping champagne in thousand-dollar Armani suits? I have a very good feeling about this. Besides, if this meeting turns out to be for naught, you'll just have to find a different forum to present your devices to.

"Just don't tip your hand until you know that you have someone serious to talk to. There are going to be some big-money players there who already have significant interests in computers and telecom, like IBM. Venture capital is what this meeting is all about. The Israeli government has a great stake in your mission here. They want a foothold in the high-technology sector, because they believe that Israel is ideally suited to become a world leader in it. It's also important for national security. They want you to make a good first impression with the Americans.

"Alexei's English is only fair, but you still have that cool California surfer look. You're not a typical Israeli. The foreign ministry chose well. Begin has gone for the polished, classy man to represent Israel now, not the open-collared kibbutznik."

"Wow! I've finally become classy? Have I ever told you that I love you very much?"

"No, never." Dahlia teased. She squeezed his arm tightly and kissed his neck. "And yes, you're all the class that I ever want or need."

On the way to the Sheraton Washington Hotel on Connecticut Avenue, the cab rushed past an endless whirl of trees and shrubs in riotous autumn splendor.

"I'd forgotten how lush everything is here," Arik said as he gazed out the window. "In Israel, it seems like we have to spit blood every time we plant a tree, to make it grow. Here, millions of them just grow effortlessly on their own. It's funny how that never dawned on me when I lived here."

"I, too, am seeing Washington with a completely new set of eyes, as if I'd never been here before except in a past lifetime," Dahlia said.

The grand hotel entrance was a portal into a new world for Arik. He wondered what would drive a grown man to wear a long red and gold striped coat with matching cap and snap to attention like a soldier as each cab pulls up.

"Your bags, please, sir."

"That's okay," Arik said. "I can carry our bags."

"Let him take our bags," Dahlia whispered to Arik.

"Ah, yes." Arik handed the bags to the doorman. "Please, take it easy with those briefcases."

"I will, sir," the doorman smiled at him politely.

Arik kept the bags in his sight as they traveled on the tall brass and burgundy trolley through the ornate marble and mahogany lobby. He was amazed by the gigantic crystal chandeliers and thick plush burgundy and gold carpeting. There was marble of every color on the walls and floor. The lobby was lined with shop windows featuring diamond-encrusted jewelry and mannequins in long, flowing silk gowns.

There were many fine hotels in Israel but none that looked like this. The front desk and bell staff were a model of efficiency and discretion. In a moment, Arik and Dahlia were upstairs, in their suite.

Their suite contained a foyer that was decorated in burgundy and gold silk with velvet and mahogany trim. There was a large color etching of the U.S. Capitol hanging on a wall. A large canopy bed dominated the bedroom, and double doors opened to a large bathroom and dressing room. At its center stood a large oval marble Jacuzzi bathtub with three steps leading up to it.

Arik looked at Dahlia. "Holy cow! Look at this place! I can't believe the embassy got us this. Why?"

"Don't you get it?" She laughed. "You're the Israeli government's golden boy. This isn't only about your company's agenda. You're on display. You're expected to mingle with the hoi polloi and make nice with all the fat-cat Jewish donors. This is about parading around their Yom Kippur War hero, who's tall, blond, tanned, and handsome." She gave him an affectionate hug. "People want to meet you, motek. You're a bit of a celebrity, like it or not."

"I don't feel like a celebrity," Arik said uncomfortably.

Dahlia opened the closet and pulled out a black garment bag that was hanging there. "The dinner tonight is black tie," she said over her shoulder.

"Black what?"

"Black tie. Tuxedos. And here's yours." She turned around and handed the garment bag to him. "Do you recall a month ago when I took your measurements? I sent those to Sergio's, the tailor who used to make Abba's tuxedos when we were in Washington. And presto, they made your tux and had it delivered here, to the hotel. You'll be wearing a black bow tie and this ruffled shirt."

"Ruffled shirts are for girls. Do you even know how to tie this thing?" Arik asked, pulling out the bow tie.

"Leave it to me, bubbele." Dahlia said. She kissed him on the nose. "Let's take a long bubble bath. It will help us get refreshed from the flight. You seem very stressed. I think that some downtime will help with that . . ."

***

Arik stood in front of the mirror and looked at himself in the cummerbund, tuxedo pants, and white ruffled shirt with the sparkly black buttons and cufflinks. He laughed at himself.

"I look like such a dandy in this! Are you almost ready, motek?"

The bathroom door opened behind him.

"What do you think, lover boy?" Dahlia asked playfully. "How do I look?"

He spun around and gasped.

She stood silhouetted against the bathroom light, in a long black silk gown with one shoulder strap covering her scar. The black dress shone in stark contrast to her long blonde hair that ran down both shoulders. She was wearing a jeweled necklace, white gloves, and patent leather shoes and clutching an evening bag.

"You look so amazing, my sweet girl—like a vision."

"Do you still think that I'm beautiful?

"You look like an angel," he said.

Dahlia whispered softly, "Let me help you with the bow tie."

When she was done, she admired him and said, "Now, you look like James Bond!"

"I like my martinis shaken and not stirred," Arik said in his most debonair voice as he leaned against the wall.

They both laughed.

***

The Israel Bond dinner was in the grand ballroom of the Mayflower Hotel, farther down Connecticut Avenue. When the cab pulled up to the curb, Dahlia realized that she had been there once before, at the Ambassador's Ball all those years ago. She fought off an inner panic as they entered the very same room that the ball had been in. She took Arik's arm as they walked into the glittering roomful of extremely well-dressed, well-heeled guests. Small groups were clustered, chatting amiably, in the light of the enormous chandeliers. An orchestra was playing contemporary music softly in the background while uniformed, white-gloved waiters flitted discreetly among the patrons, offering champagne and crudités. Arik and Dahlia wandered around, looking for anyone that they knew. She knew how uncomfortable he felt. He had never been in this type of setting before. But she also knew that he would have to get used to it.

"Ah! Shalom, Arik! Shalom, Dahlia! I hope that you had a good trip and your accommodations are to your liking. I'm Yaron Fleisher, the chargé d'affaires at the embassy. It's so good to finally meet you, Arik. It's not every day that one gets to meet such a—"

The Israeli ambassador, Yehuda Gold, walked up to them. "Shalom, Arik. How are you these days? It's been a long time since we had a chance to speak. I'm told that you've been extremely busy lately but that the projects you've been working are veiled in some secrecy . . . although I've heard some rumors. Sharon told me that you've been extensively briefed by the defense ministry on how to present your materials. Ah, Dahlia! So good to see you. You look as beautiful as ever. How are your Imma and Abba? Please, send them my best!"

"I certainly will. They're babysitting the grandchildren." Dahlia smiled.

"There are a many important people here tonight who would like to meet you," Gold said. "The economic attaché has already laid much of the groundwork for your visit. This is the first of several meetings that we've arranged for you, with both representatives of large technology corporations and newcomers to the field with great potential. This is a real opportunity for you to establish business connections between us and American technology giants."

"This all sounds very exciting," Arik said. "We've been working toward making these connections for quite some time. I'm confident the Americans will be impressed with what we've accomplished in the high-tech field.

Arik turned his head when an old family friend, the defense minister, wandered over, champagne in hand, and put his other hand on Arik's shoulder.

Ariel Sharon smiled. "Ah! Arik, good to see you again! I just bumped into your father-in-law in Jerusalem last week. Shalom, Dahlia!"

Dahlia nodded and smiled.

"We've arranged for you to meet with some very important and influential people. Well, here are a few of them now. Dahlia, I hope you don't mind, but I must steal your husband away for a few minutes. These are people I want to introduce him to."

"Only if you promise to bring him back."

"I promise!"

Leaving Dahlia alone at the bar, Arik followed Sharon, who casually walked up to a group of men who were standing at the side of the dance floor and chatting amiably among themselves.

In an undertone, Sharon said to Arik, "These men are among the captains of American industry. They control the computer field by supplying the major hardware for companies like General Electric, ETI, Bell Telephone, and IBM. Some of them are top executives at major defense contractors, like Lockheed, that are spearheading President Reagan's Star Wars program. They're extremely well-connected politically, and they're helping Israel to get the advanced weaponry that we need pushed through Congress."

"Ah, Ariel! How the hell are you! When did you get in? How long are you and Lily staying in town?"

Howard Ehrenreich was a portly balding man with a double chin, he was wearing a tuxedo that appeared a bit too tight. He had a broad smile and permanently sported a lit Cuban cigar in his mouth.

"Very well, Howard," Sharon said, smiling. "We just got in yesterday and can only stay a few days. I have some meetings up on the Hill in the morning, and I'll stop by to see Baker and Reagan tomorrow afternoon, at the White House, before heading out on a fundraising trip to LA for Israel Bonds. Arik, this is Howard Ehrenreich—"

"That's a real shame. I was hoping that the two of you could join us for dinner tomorrow night at the club."

"Howard, I'd like you to meet Arik Meir, an up-and-coming computer entrepreneur who has developed—"

Arik stepped forward to shake the man's hand.

"Well, well, well, what have we here?" Howard said, "A bona fide Israeli war hero? Gentlemen, this little soldier boy got the Israeli equivalent of the Medal of Honor for bravery in the Yom Kippur War. Did all sorts of craziness and saved a lot of lives, they say. Isn't that right, Arik?"

Arik looked at Sharon nervously and smiled thinly. "My mom thinks I'm a big hero."

Everyone laughed.

"Well played, Arik, well played! They say you were also in on that Entebbe raid. I mean, rumor has it. You guys pulled off quite a heist over there, better than the movies! Folks say you silenced the guns that cut down

Netanyahu and carried his body to the plane." Howard chuckled, quite pleased with himself.

Arik felt his blood run cold. He looked over at Sharon, who was frowning. The names of the Sayeret Matkal members who had gone to Entebbe were supposed to be a closely guarded secret. Only Yoni Netanyahu's name had been released, because he had been the field commander of the mission and his heroic leadership had put him in harm's way. When he had paid the ultimate price, the mission had been renamed after him: Operation Yoni!

Even Arik, Dahlia, and her parents never spoke about the whole affair after his return. Who the hell is running around shooting his mouth off to a bunch of rich American donors? The operational details were still highly classified. They were a matter of state security. How dare Howard Ehrenreich say Yoni's name and chuckle in the same sentence!

"I've heard those rumors, too," Arik said evenly. "You know how rumors get started. Most are simply conspiracy theory. I think the general account of that night was covered very well in the media. And of course, Charles Bronson did a great job in the movie. But that's pretty much most of the information. I know as much as you know. If I may, I'd like to talk to you about some of the really exciting technology we've been—"

"Oh, come on, Colonel Arik! Tell us the inside scoop of what really happened there. We're dying to hear every detail straight from the horse's mouth. You know a lot more that you're letting on. They say you were Yoni's second in command, drove Idi Amin's black Mercedes, and took over the assault on the old terminal to free the hostages after he was shot, despite being wounded yourself."

Howard also appeared unwilling to take no for an answer. Sharon stared at him and Arik apprehensively.

Arik spoke slowly. "Okay, I'll tell you a closely guarded secret. Although I was born an only child, I lost my brother and best friend in the world that night. We did what we were sent to do. We did our job that night. We rescued more than one hundred innocent Jews that night. We stood up to terrorism. We made the world just a little safer for the Jewish people around the world that night, so we can all enjoy parties like these, in tuxedos, as proud Jews. The little-known fact is that while all the celebrations were taking place at Lod Airport that day, when the hostages got off the plane to meet their families at the passenger terminal, to the tune of 'Hevenu Shalom Aleichem,' there was another plane that landed at a remote air force base in the Negev. Nobody saw that plane but our weeping families. I helped carry Yoni's body off the plane. Jews around the world got to celebrate and boast, while we got to spill our blood. Now, if you'll excuse me?"

Arik looked over at Sharon, who smiled quietly back at him with no small measure of pride. Arik slowly turned around, shook his head, and left the group. He quickly scanned the ballroom, looking for Dahlia, but she was nowhere to be found.

***

"Hey, stranger! Can I buy you a vodka tonic? Now, what's the prettiest girl in the room doing, standing all alone, with the saddest eyes I've ever seen on a human?"

Dahlia turned around. "I've heard that pickup line before, but I don't remember where. You can meet anyone at an Israeli Bond dinner." She smiled thinly at Ze'evi.

"Do you remember, Dahlia, when we met in this very room fourteen years ago?" he said.

"I spent most of those years trying to forget," she said.

He stared at her figure. "How have you been? Looks like you've recovered very well since Vegas. I tried to get hold of you, to see how you were doing, but you never answered any of my calls or letters. I was so concerned about you. I even wrote to you from prison."

She stared at Ze'evi's face, feeling rather uncomfortable. She wished that he would stop looking at her breasts. *He was a swine even back then, only I was too immature to see it, and he certainly hasn't changed.*

"Really, Ze'evi, I'm sure that you were deathly worried about me, after all the coke and speed that you pumped into me. You were the last person in the world that I ever wanted to see again after the trial. I had some explaining to do to myself—how I let myself be compromised and manipulated by you for months. You somehow thought that you could buy me with all your gifts and your pseudo-sophisticated sweet talk, like you buy everything else that your heart desires. Looking back, I was young and stupid and I let myself be pulled in by your phony charms. Speaking of which, how is Charlotte? Has she seen through you yet? Oh! I almost forgot to ask! How was prison? I hear that Yves Saint Laurent has a new line of prison outfits: 'For the convict who has everything—"

"Oh, Dahlia! You're being so harsh. I'd almost forgotten how emotional you get. I see that not much has changed over the years. But you never failed to turn me on. So, how long are you in town?" He smiled his broad, million-dollar smile, the one that had won her heart many years earlier. "What do you say, kitty cat? Why don't we get together for dinner tomorrow night, for old times' sake? You can make something up for soldier boy over there." Ze'evi jerked his head in the direction of the ballroom, where Arik had gone.

"You're something else! What the hell is wrong with you? You're nothing more than an overgrown teenager."

Dahlia held up her left hand, on which she was wearing her engagement and wedding ring, and said, "I see that you have one, too. Mine actually means something to me."

"Sorry, I hadn't noticed the ring. That rock isn't even a carat. That's all your hero husband could come up with? You could've had everything, Dahlia, and for some inexplicable reason you jumped off of a second-story balcony, like a lunatic. Who does that? Look at all the trouble you caused."

Dahlia had to marshal all of her self-control to prevent herself from landing a Krav Maga punch to Ze'evi's nose.

"Are you still high on cocaine? You know, Ze'evi, every girl with a brain in her head grows up dreaming of marrying a man, a real man. I never realized that, as one grows up from a teenager into an adult, you walk through many doorways that are one-way only. Once you're through, the door slams shut behind you. I almost threw away the most important person in my life and ended up with a shitty weasel like you, somebody I would've divorced in short order. Thank God, I came to my senses in the nick of time, before you killed me. I had to fight my way back tooth and nail, for years, to repair the damage that I caused—because of you—to myself and everyone around me. In the end, I got my man, a real man, someone to spend my life with. You haven't the faintest clue of what Arik's accomplished in his life, what an amazing husband and father he is. You do nothing but find new, clever ways of pleasuring yourself and hiding behind your family's money.

"Arik doesn't know the full extent of what you did and nearly did to me, the real reason that I jumped from the balcony that night. He never even asked to see the film. You think that you have a circle of friends? Arik's circle are all Shin Bet and Mossad. You forget that Arik is a trained killer. If you don't want to find yourself face down in a dumpster, inside a trash bag, with your throat slit, I suggest that you walk away now and pray that he never finds out about your game room, you worthless piece of crap!"

Dahlia walked away from the bar and back into the ballroom. She spotted Arik and went to him.

"What are we doing here?" Arik asked her. "This is a den full of vipers."

"I'll say!" she said.

"Those Ehrenreichs are everything you said they were. I met Howard. Wow! What an asshole." He told her about his encounter with Howard.

"The apple doesn't fall far from the tree," she said.

She told him that she had bumped into Ze'evi at the bar. "This evening has turned into a disaster. I don't want to be here anymore. Let's get out of here. We can go to the embassy tomorrow and set up some meetings with the other people on your list."

"Okay. Let's go."

As they turned to leave, they both heard a familiar voice call out, "Dahlia! Dahlia!"

Dahlia spun around and saw Penny running toward her in her gown and high heels. Penny jumped into Dahlia's arms.

"My God, Penny! What are you doing here? I'm so happy to see you! What a wonderful surprise. Are you here alone?"

"Richard is sitting at our table in the corner over there. He noticed you first. It is so good to see you both. We have not seen you since the wedding. What has it been? Ten years? Come."

Dahlia and Arik followed Penny to the table.

"Richard," Arik said, "you look terrific! How've you been?"

Richard smiled broadly. "Doing great, Arik, but busy as hell. I must be putting in hundred-hour weeks, but Penny keeps me sane. Ever since the company went public, it's been nothing but run, run, run. These days, it seems like I'm in the air more than I'm on the ground. We're rolling out our new operating system for a new generation of microcomputers. We're going to give Apple a run for their money."

Arik's eyes went wide. "I've been reading all about you in Digital magazine. You're turning the whole computer world upside down. This is exactly why I'm here. Have you heard of Professor Alexei Lazaroff? He and I started a small computer hardware company subcontracting to Elran and the Israeli army. We've been pretty busy ourselves. We've turned the basic music CD into a mega storage medium—"

Richard's eyes grew just as wide. "Are you serious? What have you naughty boys in Israel been playing with?"

"Oh, you know, this and that."

"Okay! You've caught my interest." Richard laughed. "You show me yours, and I'll show you mine."

"You first!"

"Okay, okay! Years ago, back at camp, you and I talked about shrinking computers down and making them powerful enough that they'd be useful to—no, revolutionize—the way we live. Remember? My idea was to put a computer into every home in America and then somehow network them together so that thousands of them would be talking to each other through a central server. The U.S. military has been doing this for quite a while. Well, I worked through the bugs at MIT and, with a few buddies, I came up with some prototypes."

"I read something about this in the journals and magazines, but you were very short on the details," Arik said.

"And for good reason. Competition is so fierce that unless you have all your regulatory and patent ducks in a row and know what not to publicize, you'll be robbed blind and others will take the credit and make all the money from your discoveries. You always have to be a step ahead. We're in a major war with Apple now.

"We went to all the usual suspects in the computer field—IBM, Digital, Bell, and that fat slob Ehrenreich at ETI—with our proposals for venture capital, and we were met with nothing but snickers and condescension. That idiot Ehrenreich actually told me that the computer would never be a home device. The man is totally stuck in the mainframe, key punch, and reel-to-reel computer mind-set. He said there's no role for interactive screens in computing and computers will only be necessary for governments and large corporations and everything else is science fiction. He even told me that building an operating system for a microcomputer is twenty-five years into the future. Well, this guy is living in a dream world. He's in for a major surprise.

"So, anyway, I met these two guys, Bill Gates and Paul Allen, at the computer center at Harvard back when I was at school. They were developing a version of the BASIC computer language for the first-generation Altair microcomputer for some company in Albuquerque. They were under extreme time pressure, so I joined them and we got a working version of BASIC running in under three weeks. Bill and Paul eventually moved down there and developed countless versions of BASIC for every version of microcomputer that was coming on the market all over the country. I stayed on at MIT and—not sure if you knew this—wrote the code for DOS as my doctoral thesis. Meanwhile, Bill and Paul moved their company out to the Seattle area, where Bill is from, and set up shop in a small suburb called Redmond.

"When I finished my degree, Penny and I packed up and moved out to Seattle to work with them. We were lucky." Richard reached for Penny's hand. "Penny's a partner in a big patent-law firm in Seattle, and her dad was so enamored with our ideas that he footed all my start-up costs for going into business with Bill and Paul. We called our new company Microsoft. Things have gotten so crazy so fast. We went public about two years ago. The rest, as they say, is history. So, that's my story. You?"

Arik smiled. "Well, after we got married in '74, I continued in the army until '79. I was honorably discharged, but I still have to do miluim, reserve duty, even today. After I got wounded again in '76, at Entebbe, Dahlia put her foot down with Defense Minister Shimon Peres and convinced him I'd be more valuable to the country in military intelligence than in a pine box. So, he promoted me to lieutenant colonel, and the defense ministry sent me to the Technion, in Haifa, to get a degree in computer engineering. People at the Technion get it. They see a time when portable microcomputers will be a fixture on the battlefield, to increase real-time situational awareness and calculate trajectories for mortars, artillery, and tactical air support, as well as advanced communications. We've made significant breakthroughs in that area. We put microcomputers to good use during the Lebanon War. After I finished my Master's in computer engineering, and my commitment to the army, I started a small company just outside Rehovot, near the Weitzman Institute, with one of my professors, Alexei Lazaroff, who emigrated from the Soviet Union to Israel in the early '70s.

"Alexei is one of the geniuses who developed the Soyuz space program in the '60s and wrote all the code for their control systems. He was arrested by the KGB and jailed as a subversive enemy of the state, because he was Jewish and applied for a visa to Israel. He was Sakharov's bunkmate in the Gulag. The U.S. government secured his release for a few thousand tons of wheat, and he moved to Israel in '75. His special area of expertise is semiconductors and RAM. How big are your displays? How much memory do your operating systems have?"

Richard beamed. "Our displays are desktop styles that look like TV sets, with a black screen background. They're about fourteen-inch diagonal and about twenty-four inches deep, and the console weighs about thirty-five pounds. We have a separate CPU and keyboard. We have about five hundred kilobytes of hard drive memory and about thirty kilobytes of RAM. We use these soft data discs we call floppy disks—state of the art! They're five and a quarter inches and can store 360 kilobytes. And I've adapted DOS to run our machines."

Dahlia and Penny stared at the two men in fascination as if the rest of the dinner and the endless parade of boring speakers had melted away. They moved their heads back and forth as if they were watching a tennis match.

"I'm very familiar with DOS," Arik said. "What if I told you, Richard, that I could dramatically increase your hard drive memory and allow you to dispense with all those floppy disks you guys are selling? And what if I told you that you could shrink your display to thirteen inches, attach it to your keyboard, and throw the CPU under that keyboard so the whole thing folds up and fits neatly on your lap? If I told you that you could use CDs to store data just as easily as music and that we have a drive to run that data and hook it up to the CPU? That it'd have the memory of twenty floppy disks at five megabytes? Would you be interested?"

Richard nodded vigorously.

"The portable unit I brought here is a quarter the size of Compaq's portables, and it runs on DOS 1.13. It has a ten-megabyte hard drive and 544 kilobytes of RAM. I can plug the CD drive into my unit for additional storage. The whole unit weighs less than ten pounds.

Richard was open-mouthed. "Now, you're talking science fiction. That's not possible yet. We've been dreaming about stuff like that, but that's at least five years away. I'll believe it when I see proof."

"I brought some prototypes with me, but somehow I can't seem to get anyone's attention tonight."

"Well, you got mine, that's for sure. Can I see them?"

"Sure. I'd be happy to play show and tell."

"Hey, guys? What are we? Chopped liver? Are you guys going to talk shop all night?" Penny grinned. "How long are you two staying in town? Which hotel are you at?"

Dahlia said, "We'll be here for about a week, at the Sheraton Washington, but we're flexible, depending on how Arik's presentations go."

"Wonderful," Penny said, "It is settled. We can celebrate our reunion tonight, and you two can talk shop at breakfast. When Dahlia and I get bored, we will go shopping in Chevy Chase."

Dahlia looked at Arik and then said, "Sounds like fun!"

"Sounds good to me!" Arik smiled.

"Then, it is done," Penny said. "Waiter!"

***

At breakfast, in the hotel's dining room, after the wives had left, Arik opened his briefcase and produced the CD-ROM drive and the laptop prototypes. After a short tutorial from Arik, Richard was able to navigate the devices and test their capabilities.

"I'm floored, Arik! These screens are in color! We've been working on this, but it's been very slow going." He manipulated the multiple squares on the screen with the mouse. Each time that he clicked the mouse on one, it opened a new view. "This is a real game changer! And I thought you were just some dumb jock!"

"Watch this," Arik said. "Try this. It's called a stylus. You can use it to manipulate the squares on the screen without the mouse. We've equipped this with touch-screen technology adapted from the Magnavox Plato IV system. We call these small squares windows, because each is a window into a small world of its own. Take a look. You can minimize or maximize each window, as needed, with those thingamajigs in the corner. We started out by placing tactical battlefield maps in each window, to view different maps, assets, and scenarios simultaneously. Our ultraportable computers have proven invaluable on the battlefield. Necessity is the mother of invention. And believe me, we have plenty of necessity in Israel. The main thing the Yom Kippur and Lebanon Wars taught us was that the Arabs are becoming better soldiers. They're smart, well-trained, determined fighters. Most importantly, there are many more of them than us. Our qualitative edge that everyone likes to talk about is shrinking. If we're going to survive and thrive, we need to be way ahead of them technologically. You can be sure that I only brought the toys the government has released for civilian use. We're keeping far more goodies close to the vest. Our company has a significant relationship with the defense ministry, but we're actively working on civilian uses for our technology."

"Does the Israeli government know you're talking to me?" Richard suddenly became serious. Please, know that everything you tell me will be held in the strictest confidence."

"The ministry of defense is completely in the loop. I was thoroughly briefed before I left. I'm permitted to interact with anyone who was at the Bond dinner last night. I know well what I can share and what I can't. Didn't you notice that it was rather exclusive, without all the usual yentas? The guests were vetted carefully. The ministry thought the return would be higher with a targeted audience. The Israel Bond thing was just a pretext. They're trying to keep the contacts low-key for now. You saw that Defense Minister Sharon was there, right?"

"Yeah, I did notice."

"I was even instructed to interact with Ehrenreich. You can imagine how much I looked forward to that, knowing the whole story with Dahlia."

Richard nodded.

"When that blew up—the guy's an asshole—I wasn't sure where this was all going to go," Arik said. "Dahlia and I were on our way out the door. But then you popped up!"

"I know the whole story with Ehrenreich better than you realize," Richard said. "I had the pleasure of his son's company for drinks one evening in Aspen, the year after we all went there together. What a jerk! He called me a nerd and a dork. He's a real sweetheart, that one. I can tell you there are parts of ETI, notably their satellite telecommunications network, that I'd like to get my hands on. The rest of that company is worthless. It should be broken up and sold off in a fire sale. Don't say a word, but Microsoft is planning a hostile takeover. We'll see who's the dork and who ends up out on his ass."

"I didn't know you met that guy. I never did—"

"You didn't miss anything."

The two men smiled wryly at each other.

"Hey, what about U.S. patents?" Richard asked. "This stuff is a game changer, really explosive. Is it protected?"

"My father-in-law developed a lot of contacts during his time in Washington, and he hooked us up with a big patent law firm downtown, Wabash and Jamison, who have handled all the paperwork. We have eleven patents in total. Three are still pending."

"Very good. Penny would be happy to take a look at those for you, if you like. You know, she worked at that law firm as an intern the summer between high school and college. Small world." Richard gave Arik a long, thoughtful look and took a sip of his espresso. "You know, Arik, for the past sixteen years I've always felt a debt of gratitude to you that was never repaid."

"What are you talking about? You don't owe me anything. I never—"

"Please, let me finish. That summer of 1969 was a major turning point in my life. I know it for sure. I began that summer as an insecure kid. I walked around my whole life until then with a major inferiority complex, a real chip on my shoulder. I was always in bunk Bet, never Aleph. I always felt like a loser. You saw I was bullied. I never stuck up for myself. Even with all my computer smarts, I probably would never have had the guts, the self-confidence, to move forward if it hadn't been for you. You were Mr. Popular Jock at camp. And, through our close friendship, I became more confident and popular, too. You even showed me I could play basketball. I never would've had the guts to ask Penny out. I know it sounds crazy, because our lives have both moved on so much since then, but those years were very important ones, emotionally, for me. That trip we took to Aspen was the defining moment in my relationship with Penny, and I know full well that none of that would have happened without you.

"Penny is my life's partner. And I've always been looking for a way to repay what you did for me. Now, thank God, I've been given an opportunity. I know only too well what you and Dahlia have been through. It was always so much simpler for Penny and me. I also realize that it's only because of all yours and Dahlia's sacrifices and those who fought and continue to fight side by side with you that I can feel proud to be a Jew.

"So, for me, this is a golden opportunity, too. I've been looking for a while for ways to help the Israeli economy in a more meaningful way than just planting trees and fund-raising. Building a partnership between my company—which I can tell you will one day be one of the largest in the world, if we play our cards right—and Israel is a marriage made in heaven. And what better way to do that than buddying up with my old friend. I want you to fly out to Seattle with me tomorrow and meet my partners. I've already briefed them on our conversation from last night, and they're excited to meet you."

The men shook hands warmly.

Richard looked up. "Oh! Our ride is here," he said.

A chauffeur-driven black Bentley limousine had pulled up to the curb. A uniformed man emerged and sprang out to open the door for the two men.

"Where to, Mr. Green?"

"John, where are the ladies?"

"They're at Bloomingdale's, off Wisconsin Avenue in Chevy Chase, sir."

"Please, call Mary, the store manager, and tell her to let them know we're on our way."

The chauffeur picked up the car phone.

"I can't believe you have a phone in your car, like the President," Arik said.

"If I have anything to do with it, within twenty years everybody will be carrying one in their pocket. Mark my words, Arik, your devices are a great leap forward in that direction."

In a short while, all four friends were in the limousine.

"Richard, honey, since we are all flying out in the morning, why don't we have them over tonight, at the house?" Penny said. "It will be so much easier than driving back into town to pick him up in morning traffic and then have to drive back out to the airport."

"That's a fabulous idea. Are you guys game?"

"We're really in uncharted territory, so sure," Arik said. I'll reschedule my other meetings."

The excitement in the car was palpable.

***

Arik and Dahlia checked out of the hotel and the foursome got back into the limousine. They followed I-66 over the Potomac River.

"We got this place about eighteen months ago," Richard said. "I needed to be in Washington constantly, with all the legislative, regulatory, and Sherman antitrust hoops we need to go through, so we decided to buy this small horse farm in Middleburg. It's a lot more comfortable than a hotel room. I'm not sure I remember . . . you guys ride?"

"We enjoy riding on the beach in Caesarea from time to time," Dahlia said. "We don't have any riding clothes, though."

"That's no problem," Penny said. "We have plenty of riding gear, and our staff has every size hunt cap in the tack room. This is going to be so much fun!"

The "small" horse farm was a 500-acre gated estate nestled in the rolling hills of northern Virginia. At its center stood a stately fieldstone farmhouse that the Greens had expanded to a 12,000-square-foot country manor, with formal boxwood ornamental gardens that led to a pool. There were gated grass tennis courts nearby. At the other end of the property was a sprawling, immaculate barn complex, including twenty stalls that housed thoroughbred and European warmblood horses, and even more immaculate outdoor riding arena and paddocks. The members of the staff were hard at work, grooming and training the horses for dressage, jumping, and fox hunting.

Penny called over the barn manager.

"Francis, can you get four horses tacked up for us? We'll take them out for a hack before lunch."

The four went into the changing rooms. Penny and Dahlia walked out of the ladies' changing room, dressed in tan stretch breeches, polo shirts with the stable insignia on it, knee-high black riding boots, and black velvet helmets. Richard walked out of the men's changing room, dressed similarly.

When Arik emerged from the changing room, wearing a formal English riding habit, everyone burst into hysterical laughter.

Dahlia said, "Now you really look like a commando, Arik. Go look in the mirror!"

When he did, he joined in the laughter.

"Dahlia, you have to take a picture of me and send it to Dani and Efrat. They'll die laughing!"

Dahlia giggled and snapped a picture of him, and then all four friends posed for a shot using the delayed-reaction feature on the Nikon SLR camera that was mounted on a tripod in the barn.

"That photo will go over the mantelpiece," Richard said.

"Do me a favor, Richard," Arik said. "Snap another picture of Dahlia and me like this. I want to send it to my children's godparents, Saba Shmulik and Savta Yael."

After spending the morning riding in the woods and rolling fields, the foursome settled into a set of doubles tennis. When they finished, a lunch buffet was waiting for them on tables under green umbrellas at courtside.

"I remember when Dahlia played against Billie Jean King and the two of you would go at each other to the death every morning at 4 a.m. at the tennis center," Richard said.

Arik smiled. "I still play okay, but I can't move nearly as well as I used to."

"How's the leg?" Richard's face looked serious.

"Good, mostly. After we got married, Dahlia worked me over relentlessly—no mercy from that woman!—at the Wingate Sports Rehab Center in Netanya. When she left the army, she got her Master's degree in physiotherapy and rehabilitation, specializing in sports medicine, and put her skills to good use on me. After months of intense rehab, I was able to return to my unit. I was an instructor in the beginning, but then I was called back to fight in '76—"

"Few people know that you almost died then," Richard whispered.

"And I hope to keep it that way," Arik said. "The leg makes its presence known every time it rains, which luckily isn't often in Israel. Long plane rides are also hard. You know, the sitting. Speaking of which, I need to make my reservation for tomorrow's flight to Seattle. Do you have a good travel agent? The embassy won't pay for this trip, because it's unscripted."

"You won't need any of that tomorrow," Richard said.

The rest of day in Middleburg was dreamlike. Discreet staff catered to their every need. After an afternoon swim and rest, they were served a formal dinner in the dining room. The chef came out at the end of the meal, at Richard's request, and was congratulated on a great meal and wine selection.

"I stole him from one of the best French restaurants in New York," Richard whispered to Arik. "It took him a while to learn to cook kosher, but I had a Chabad rabbi work with him for a few months."

Arik laughed. "I could really get used to living like this. Couldn't you, Dahlia?"

Dahlia smiled and nodded.

Richard smiled slightly and whispered, "You will, Arik."

***

They got an early start in the morning. By 9 a.m., the limousine was heading down Route 50 and into the back entrance off Ariane Way, past the commercial terminals at Dulles Airport.

"Where are we going?" Arik asked. "We've passed all the terminals—"

"Not all," Richard said. "We're headed to the private terminal."

When the limousine pulled up to the entrance of the terminal, they were directed around the back of the building and onto the tarmac. The driver stopped the car at the bottom of a staircase that was attached to a gleaming white Gulfstream III corporate jet emblazed with the Microsoft logo.

"Dahlia, we have to get ourselves one of these," Arik said. "This is the only way to travel."

Richard smiled. "You will, Arik. You will."

Dahlia felt a painful twinge in her gut as she climbed the stairs to the plane, but she smiled back at Arik with a twinkle in her eye.

The mourners were sitting in a row of low chairs facing the seemingly endless line of visitors who had filed past them. Some were talking in hushed tones to the family. Others just passed by and said, "May the Lord comfort you among all the mourners of Zion and Jerusalem." Since early that morning, they had come from every direction. Long lines of cars and minivans filled the tree-lined side streets of Kfar Shmaryahu, a normally very quiet, exclusive suburb of Tel Aviv that was nestled on the cliffs overlooking the beach. The mourners waited patiently in long queues that stretched several blocks to get through the security gate, where the customary body scanners and bomb-sniffing dogs awaited them.

From the gate, there was another line to enter the large mansion that for years had been tucked discreetly away behind high walls and lush vegetation. People stood in complete silence, whether in respect to the gravity of the moment or simply in reaction to the oppressive July heat and humidity. In the house, the uniformed staff quietly ushered the mourners through the large marble foyer and into a vast cathedral-ceilinged sitting room that opened to a veranda overlooking the Herzliya beach and the blue Mediterranean Sea beyond. A cool ocean breeze was blowing in through the array of French doors that were open to offer some relief from the sweltering heat.

There were so many faces, so many people from every stage of his life, people whom he had touched in some way, people whom he had loved, hated, worked with, fought with, or barely knew. There were people of every stripe, facet, and stratum of Israeli life, from government ministers and industry leaders to shopkeepers and bus drivers. There were Hassidic rabbis, university professors, and Ashkenazi, Sephardic, and Ethiopian Jews. And there were soldiers, so many soldiers of every rank and branch of the military.

Those who sat with the family told endless stories of how Arik had touched their lives and made them better. Representatives of organizations and institutions that Arik had generously supported over the years had come to pay their respects. It was not uncommon for their serious conversations to be punctuated by moments of laughter when they related some practical joke that Arik had pulled on one of his friends or business associates. A common theme was how Arik had loved to live and how he had always lived with an intensity that defied description. He had seen the good in everyone around him and never prejudged a person's potential to grow. And grow they had.

At the center of the mourner's row, Dahlia was surrounded by her three grown children, Roni, Mikki, and Galit, and their spouses and her many teenaged grandchildren, who were Tweeting on their smartphones. On a side table was a large photo, framed in black, of Eyal, her fourth child. He was in his Golani dress uniform, and there was an Israeli flag in the background. A night out with his friends at the Dolphinarium nightclub on the Tel Aviv seafront in 2001 had turned to tragedy when a suicide bomber had killed him and many others.

Dahlia, the family matriarch and now past seventy, still retained her elegant, regal air. Graceful from decades of tennis, yoga, and Pilates, she moved easily. She had a quiet confidence and control about her, which came from a lifetime of privilege in Israel's intellectual, political, and socioeconomic elite. The wife of Israel's wealthiest man, daughter of an Israeli ambassador and later foreign minister, she had dedicated her life to building Israel's national sports teams, notably the Paralympic team, and she had done so with great passion and integrity. Her years of philanthropy to institutions dedicated to the care of injured war veterans and children with birth defects had earned her the title Mother of the Disabled.

The visitors came and went well into the evening. Roni, her elder son, led the men clustered in a corner in their evening prayer and then recited the Kaddish.

Dahlia looked over at Roni and smiled slightly. Arik had been so proud of Roni, watching him grow from a brash young Givati commander into a mature, caring, deeply spiritual man. In his later years, Arik had spent long hours with Roni, walking, talking, playing tennis, and trying to solve all of the world's problems. As Arik's condition had worsened, Roni had taken to sitting by his bedside and studying the Talmud with him. Arik had drawn strength from that and, for a time, had appeared more like he had been before his pancreatic cancer diagnosis.

From the corner of the room, where the prayers were being held, the chief rabbi of Israel walked up to Dahlia and the women of the family. He had officiated at the funeral and at the burial in Har HaMenuchot military cemetery in Jerusalem.

"Thank you, Rabbi, for your service. It was very uplifting," Dahlia said.

"He was a very great man. His passing is a tremendous loss for the people of Israel. There wasn't a segment of society that he didn't touch with love and compassion, and we are better because of his life's work. We are all going to miss him. May you find comfort in seeing so very many people here whom he touched in one way or another. He was a true hero of the Jewish people. May your family find comfort with all of the mourners of Zion and Jerusalem."

"Rabbi, you're very kind," Dahlia said quietly.

She looked up and, to her surprise, saw a group of three tall, distinguished-looking African-American men walking toward her. All heads in the room turned to look at the new arrivals. Dahlia stood to embrace the older, gray-haired gentleman in the middle.

"How are you, Dahlia?"

"As good as can be expected. So good to see you, Antwan. Thank you for coming all this way. How did you find out about Arik?"

"News travels fast over the Internet. We first saw it on the CNN website. It was the banner headline. It's trending on Twitter and Facebook, and the Congressional Record recorded it as well. We packed up and flew right out as soon we heard."

"Please, let me introduce you to my children," Dahlia said. "This is Congressman Antwan Perkins, from California's 44th district. He's the son of the late Reverend Perkins. Remember? Abba spoke so much about the reverend and the profound effect that he had on his life. He was another father to him. If it wasn't for the reverend, Abba's life would have turned out very differently. He was a very great man."

Arik and Dahlia's three surviving children stood to shake the congressman's hand.

"We heard about Eyal. We're so sorry for your loss," the congressman said.

Dahlia picked up Eyal's photo from the end table. She said, "Arik once told me, in the hospital after he was injured in the Yom Kippur War, that heroes end up as pictures on a coffee table. Eyal was my hero. Arik was my hero. Now, they're both gone."

She looked down and sighed. She picked up a second picture frame, from the same table. It bore an old, creased, yellowed black and white photograph of a smiling young couple. She showed it to Antwan.

"This was us, during our first summer together. Do you remember when I met you in LA in the spring of 1970? That wasn't even a year after this was taken."

"Of course, I do." He smiled. "How could I forget? You made quite a splash when you visited the Cage."

"Arik was a great warrior in his youth," she said. "As time went on, he became a man of peace. He suffered greatly through his life, as a result of his experiences in the army, and he wanted to see a day when Israeli young people wouldn't have to go through what he did. He was a great supporter of the Oslo Accords. He even went to the talks, as a technical advisor for our delegation. He was devastated when Rabin was assassinated."

"Yes. We saw you both on TV during his funeral," Antwan said.

"He continued to work for peace afterward, with his friend Bibi, the prime minister. Arik and Bibi's brother Yoni were close comrades in the army. When Eyal was killed, Arik became very conflicted about our chances of making peace with the Arabs. He became obsessed about Israeli cybersecurity on a national level. You may have heard that in 2010 he became technology minister. He had to leave the private sector to do that, but he did it readily. He wanted to serve the people again. Like I once told you, it just never ends. Unfortunately, this is life in Israel. Our neighbors don't wish us well. Now, with Iran going nuclear and ISIS, Hamas, Hezbollah . . . Who knows?"

"Did Arik suffer much at the end?"

"He did, but he never complained. You knew him."

The congressman shook his head.

"Ah, I'm sorry, Dahlia. I want to introduce you to my sons: Clarence and Harrison. Clarence is studying political science at Howard University in Washington, D.C., and Harrison is premed at Ohio State."

"Very nice to meet you. Welcome to Israel," Dahlia said. "Your grandfather would have been very proud of your accomplishments. He meant a great deal to us."

They nodded.

"I have something for you, something from us," Antwan said.

He pulled out a large picture frame and handed it to Dahlia. At the top of the frame was a color photo, and at the bottom was what appeared to be a letter. The picture was of a large group of neighborhood activists standing in front of a large building. Beside the entrance to the building was a bronze plaque: DAHLIA AND ARIK MEIR COMMUNITY CENTER. In the center of the crowd stood Arik and Dahlia, both smiling broadly.

"Children, this picture is from the dedication ceremony for the community center that Abba and I donated to the people of Los Angeles about ten years ago," Dahlia said.

"To be exact," Antwan said, "to the people of Watts. You all should come and see it when you're next in the U.S. It's a 500,000-square-foot, state-of-the-art sports center, housing facilities of every type. There are basketball and squash courts, indoor tennis courts, a soccer field, an ice hockey rink, a full-scale Olympic aquatic center for recreational and competitive swimming and diving, a weight training facility, and a gymnastics and martial arts arena. Your parents' charitable foundation has seen to it that the center will be fully staffed for every sport for the next twenty years. Because of your mom and dad, there is no membership fee for the kids. The facility is kept in immaculate condition, and it's open eighteen hours a day. It's had a profound effect on underprivileged kids from Watts, one of the roughest neighborhoods in LA. It's opened up all kinds of possibilities for young people, which will have long-term ramifications. Since the center opened, the youth crime rate in the city has dropped considerably. Arik also set up incubator enterprise zones in Watts, where high school dropouts are literally pulled off the streets and put into job training programs and then offered decent-paying jobs. Other cities are looking at that project as a pilot program. Charitable foundations are planning to fund similar programs in other cities around the U.S. You father did good, real good."

"Isn't that the same trip when Abba got the honorary doctorate of humanities from UCLA?" Roni asked Dahlia.

"Life is full of ironies," Dahlia said. "Arik took his foundation staff to the poorest neighborhoods in Israeli cities and development towns where immigrants from Ethiopia, Eritrea, and Sudan had settled, met with their civic leaders, did detailed needs assessments, and charted their potential for growth. He set up a dozen enterprise job creation zones all around the country to get these people on their feet. He also set up the same type of enterprise zones near ultra-Orthodox areas to help deal with the high poverty and unemployment rates in their society too. It's had a profound effect."

"Abba was awarded the Israel prize in 2011 for this work," Roni said.

"Take a look at the letter under the photograph," Antwan said.

In loving memory of Arik Meir

Dear Dahlia,
  Please allow us to add our voices to those of the men and women across the United States and Israel who mourn the loss of your husband. He was a truly remarkable man, one who, throughout his life, worked tirelessly for the rights and

welfare of the downtrodden and disadvantaged all around the world. He was someone who always knew right from wrong and always fought the good fight. Arik will be sorely missed by the great multitude of people whose lives he made immeasurably better through his generous philanthropy and the profound loving touch that he infused into every one of his projects.

We have always counted Arik and you among our good friends. During this week, the week of Jewish mourning, the flag at the Rayburn House Office Building will fly at half-mast. May you and your family find comfort in the memories of this great man.

Most sincerely,
Congressional Black Caucus
United States House of Representatives

"It's signed by everyone in the Caucus," Antwan said.

"Thank you so much for this, Antwan. You have no idea how much this means to me. Are you going back right away?"

"No. I want to take the boys to Mount Zion, Bethlehem, Nazareth, and Capernaum, by the Sea of Galilee, to show them where Jesus walked and was baptized. I think it will leave a lasting impression. Are you planning to come to Washington any time soon?"

"Everything is up in the air right now. When things settle down, I'll get back to work. I've committed myself to continuing the activities of the Meir Foundation and keeping Arik's memory alive."

"When you come to Washington, please give Monique a call and we'll get together," Antwan said.

"I will. Thank you again so much for coming."

"The family now wishes private time for dinner and reflection," Marco, the chief steward, announced through the PA system. "We will be receiving visitors again tomorrow morning at 9 a.m."

Slowly, the visitors paid their respects and filed out as the sun disappeared over the western horizon and out to sea.

In the street, the crowds thinned and the neighborhood quieted again. A strange stillness fell over the darkening small side street. Armed security agents—tall, muscular men with closely cropped hair, wearing dark suits and ever-present ear phones—patrolled the grounds with dogs and search lights.

When the last of the visitors had been discreetly ushered out, the room grew very quiet.

"What a day!" Galit said. "Who knew that Abba knew so many people? He so rarely spoke about what he did. At home, he was always just Abba!"

"He always had so much on his mind, with the weight of the world on his shoulders, but he always insisted on leaving all of that behind when he walked through our front door," Dahlia said. "He called it work-life balance. He was such an attentive father and grandfather."

"That is, when he wasn't being called away in the middle of the night, into some dark limousine, and reappearing two or three days later," Roni said.

"We never knew where he went," Galit said, "and he'd just dismiss our questions by saying, 'I went to the shuk to buy you a gift, metuka,' and he always brought a gift back with him."

"Yes," Mikki said. "And Imma, you and Abba always mysteriously disappeared, every year, on the day before Yom Kippur. You would never speak of it."

"That's true, Mikki," Dahlia said. "And it was Abba's wish that I never will."

"I think that we all should eat something and then get some rest," Dahlia said. "Shiva isn't a sprint. It's a marathon. We're going to have long days like this all week."

The extended family retired to the kitchen to dive into elaborate platters of pita, hummus, techina, baba ghanoush, olives, smoked fish, cheese, leben, tomatoes, and cucumbers.

Marco walked into the kitchen and whispered into Dahlia's ear.

Dahlia said, "It looks like we're having some more company. If anyone wants to go upstairs to rest, that's fine. I'll remain down here. I'd like Roni, Mikki, and Galit to stay down here with me."

"Who's coming, Imma?" Roni asked.

"You'll find out in few moments. Let's go back to the sitting room."

The computer screen in the guard station at the gate blinked familiar red letters: "Rosh Memshalla bederech" (The prime minister is on his way).

One of the portable handheld radios crackled out, "Megia Megia! He's here!"

Three black limousines pulled up. One by one, each the car approached the guardhouse, the tinted driver's window opened, and the security staff discreetly nodded and motioned the car through. At the front entrance of the house, the first and third cars swung open, and ten heavily armed black-suited bodyguards jumped out. The middle car's back doors swung open, and three impeccably dressed, distinguished-looking men, emerged.

The three men were escorted inside by one of the security agents and led into the sitting room, where Dahlia and her family were waiting for them.

"Shalom, Bibi. So good of you to come."

"Shalom, Dahlia," Prime Minister Benjamin ("Bibi") Netanyahu said, giving her a hug. "How are you managing?"

"Arik had been sick for two months, so it wasn't unexpected, but when it finally happened the shock was no easier to bear," Dahlia said.

The prime minister said, "Arik had dodged death so many times in his life. He always seemed so healthy, active, and strong when we served together. He appeared to be invincible, especially after how he rehabilitated back in '74. He regularly attended Cabinet meetings up until eight weeks ago, and he had just returned from Beijing, wrapping up the administrative loose ends on our trade deals with China."

"I know," Dahlia said. "It was very fast. Perhaps it was better that way, not having to suffer for a long time. He was in a great deal of pain near the end, though. He and your brother were such close comrades and friends. Arik never got over losing him so long ago."

"Yes, I know," he said quietly.

Dahlia showed him the picture and the letter from the American Congressional Black Congress.

"Yafeh meod! Wonderful! Arik was Arik. He never changed or wavered, from his early days in the army to now," Bibi said. Turning to the defense minister, he said, "Gidon, weren't you in the same unit as him in '73?"

"We were all together during those fateful, terrible, early days of the Yom Kippur War. Arik and I were assigned to the observation post on the top of Mount Hermon when we were overrun by Syrian commandos on the first day of the War. We were completely outmanned and outgunned. We fought hand to hand with knives when we ran out of ammunition. We were all nearly captured, but Arik devised a crazy escape plan that got eleven of us safely back to our lines. We started with nineteen, but we lost eight along the way when we were ambushed on the way down the ski slope. Arik helped the rest of us get to safety, and then he went off on his own to fight in Nafach, the regional command center for the entire Golan that nearly fell to the Syrians."

"He was such a lunatic, but he saved so many lives," Bibi said, shaking his head.

The third man, the foreign minister, looked at Dahlia and asked, "So how did the two of you meet? How did a poor, disadvantaged Jewish boy from Los Angeles end up in an elite commando unit in Tzahal, to begin with, and then end up with such a brilliant career at Microsoft that made him one of world's richest men and one of its greatest social activists and philanthropists? There are many Israeli tech start-ups that owe their success to him. He opened many doors in the States to these young entrepreneurs. He was a truly unique individual, though quite mysterious at times."

Dahlia smiled sadly. "It all started a very long time ago, when we met back in the summer of 1969 . . ."

Made in the USA
Columbia, SC
08 October 2018